space helmet for a cow

The Mad, True Story of Doctor Who

Volume 2: 1990-2013

Paul Kirkley

Also available from Mad Norwegian Press...

AHistory: An Unauthorized History of the Doctor Who Universe [3rd Edition]
(print and ebook now available) by Lance Parkin and Lars Pearson

AHistory: An Unauthorized History of the Doctor Who Universe [2012-2013 Update]
(ebook now available) by Lance Parkin and Lars Pearson

*Running Through Corridors: Rob and Toby's Marathon Watch
of Doctor Who* (Vol. 1: The 60s) and (Vol. 2: The 70s)
by Robert Shearman and Toby Hadoke

Wanting to Believe: A Critical Guide to The X-Files, Millennium and the Lone Gunmen
by Robert Shearman

The About Time Series by Tat Wood and Lawrence Miles
About Time 1: The Unauthorized Guide to Doctor Who (Seasons 1 to 3)
About Time 2: The Unauthorized Guide to Doctor Who (Seasons 4 to 6)
About Time 3: The Unauthorized Guide to Doctor Who (Seasons 7 to 11) [2nd Ed]
About Time 4: The Unauthorized Guide to Doctor Who (Seasons 12 to 17)
About Time 5: The Unauthorized Guide to Doctor Who (Seasons 18 to 21)
About Time 6: The Unauthorized Guide to Doctor Who (Seasons 22 to 26)
About Time 7: The Unauthorized Guide to Doctor Who (Series 1 to 2)
About Time 8: The Unauthorized Guide to Doctor Who (Series 3, forthcoming)

Essay Collections
Chicks Dig Comics: A Celebration of Comic Books by the Women Who Love Them

Chicks Dig Gaming: A Celebration of All Things Gaming by the Women Who Love It

Chicks Dig Time Lords: A Celebration of Doctor Who by the Women Who Love It,
2011 Hugo Award Winner, Best Related Work

Chicks Unravel Time: Women Journey Through Every Season of Doctor Who

Companion Piece: Women Celebrate the Humans, Aliens and Tin Dogs of Doctor Who

Queers Dig Time Lords: A Celebration of Doctor Who by the LGBTQ Fans Who Love It

Whedonistas: A Celebration of the Worlds of Joss Whedon by the Women Who Love Them

Guidebooks
I, Who: The Unauthorized Guide to the Doctor Who Novels and Audios
by Lars Pearson (vols. 1-3, ebooks only)

Dusted: The Unauthorized Guide to Buffy the Vampire Slayer
by Lawrence Miles, Pearson and Christa Dickson (ebook only)

Redeemed: The Unauthorized Guide to Angel by Pearson and Christa Dickson (ebook only)

Introduction

So... *surprise!* It came back. Like Pam Ewing, we woke up one morning and there was Doctor Who, doing his ablutions in the shower like nothing had ever happened.

Okay, it wasn't quite like that. We didn't dream those 16 years the show was off the air, like Pammy dreamed an entire season of *Dallas*. Though it's possible we did collectively hallucinate some parts of the Wilderness Years: like the time the Rani took over the Queen Vic in *EastEnders* – in 3D – or when the words "the semen taste" appeared, in that order, in an officially licensed *Doctor Who* product.

Meanwhile, David Hasselhoff, Denzel Washington and David Burton – a popular pantomime performer in the Redhill area – were just some of the people who didn't play Doctor Who during this period. Paul McGann *did* play Doctor Who – but only for an hour so, and the story of how that came about (then went away again) is a saga in itself.

If you're not following any of this, don't worry: all will become clear. Probably.

Doctor Who was all over the shop in the nineties and the early part of what people are still stubbornly refusing to stop calling the noughties. It was in books, comics and computer games; on DVD and CD and the internet; and in numerous fan-made straight-to-video films that included *Doctor Who* actors and *Doctor Who* companions and *Doctor Who* monsters and even some characters who seemed a bit like Doctor Who (but definitely weren't Doctor Who, Your Honour).

The only place it wasn't was the one place it truly belonged: in the corner of your living room. Until one Saturday evening in March 2005, when the Doctor finally landed back on actual telly, in an actual series, which people actually liked. Loved, in fact.

Naturally, this was only the beginning of a whole other cycle of insanity, as a new generation of talented writers, actors, technicians and execs found out for themselves that making *Doctor Who* is a wonderful, ridiculous, exhilarating, surreal and generally batshit crazy experience that would have driven lesser men and women to madness. Or at least back to *Holby City*.

To that extent, this is the same behind-the-scenes story we started telling in the first volume of *Space Helmet for a Cow* – albeit considerably more Welsh.

But it's also a quite different story, in many ways. Firstly, because *Doctor Who* itself is more... I hesitate to use the word "professional," because that would be a huge disservice to all those brilliant people who got the original series made, often against seemingly insuperable odds. But with advances in technology, and more emphatic support from BBC management, New *Who* has never quite had to resort to making giant maggots out of condoms or staging a dinosaur invasion of central London using plasticine. What I'm saying, basically, is it's a lot harder to take the piss out of these days.

Also, the thing about the original series is... we know where the bodies are buried. We know that she rowed with him, he slept with her and he had a nervous breakdown in the car-park of Television Centre. We know this because time has healed, bridges have been rebuilt and people on all sides have been happy to give their less-than brilliantly white laundry an airing.

That's not the case with New *Who*. I don't want to give the impression that making *Doctor Who* in the twenty-first century has been a boiling cauldron of septic rows and recriminations, as the production team lurched from one crisis to the next. Far from it: it appears, on the whole, to have been one of the happiest ships in television.

But it's inevitable there have been bumps in the road, creative disagreements and professional disappointments. Some of these events are still raw. And, crucially, the people involved haven't yet felt ready to go on the record about them. Why would they, when reputations are at stake, and when Brand Who still needs protecting from the circling wolves of the BBC's many enemies?

In those instances, then, what we're left with is speculation, rumour and innuendo – which isn't really in the genial, inclusive and affectionate spirit in which *Space Helmet* is intended. So until those stories can be verified, we'll leave them to the likes of *Private Eye*. (That scurrilous old thorn in the Establishment's side has been particularly candid in its coverage of New *Who*'s noises off. It's all out there if you want to look for it, and some of it will almost certainly be true. It's just that, at this stage, we're not sure which bits.)

Which is not to suggest what you're holding in your hand is some sort of limp hagiography – a whitewashed, vanilla version of events. It's full (I hope) of the same pomposity-popping irreverence as the first book – what newspaper columnists back in the day might have called "a sideways look" at the business of *Who*. Our mission here is as much to celebrate everything that's daft and absurd and wonderfully *wrong* about *Doctor Who* as everything that's brilliant, inspiring and wonderfully *right* about it. But it always, *always* comes from a place of love for the show, and those people crazy enough to sacrifice such things as sleep, social lives and their sanity to bring it to us. The mood lighting here is set to warm and fuzzy, not cold and ugly (yes, even when writing about *Torchwood*).

Another thing that's different about twenty-first-century *Doctor Who* is that its entire life has been lived in the glare of the media spotlight, with all the hysteria that implies. That whole tabloid circus – the endless "Doctor Who Quits!" stories, the plucked-from-the-air (or somewhere worse) casting speculation, and reporters using all their powers of investigative journalism to copy stuff off Twitter: that's a big part of the story of modern *Doctor Who*. And so, without wishing to get too media faculty about it, this is also, to an extent, an in-depth analysis of *Doctor Who*: The Phenomenon – of our little show, created to fill the gap between *Grandstand* and *Juke Box Jury*, punching its weight in the era of Posh and Becks, Kim and Kanye and One Direction (who will eventually enter our story, with car crash results).

The book is also intended to serve as a critical analysis, if that's not too deadening a term, of new *Doctor Who* – hopefully in a fresh and engaging way that's more Gogglebox than Gadamer. (Don't worry, I had to Google him too.) Why? Because you can't talk about the glory of *Doctor Who* without talking about *why* it's glorious (and why, sometimes, it isn't). But, unlike Twitter, not all opinions are my own: I've also included a spread of other critics' verdicts in order to provide a snapshot of how *Doctor Who* has been received more widely. Even if, in some cases, those critics were just plain wrong.

Last year, after a press screening of the new *Doctor Who* series opener, I thrust a copy of *Space Helmet* Volume I into the hands of a slightly startled Steven Moffat. (He didn't say, "Thanks, I've heard this is brilliant," but I'm fairly sure he must have been thinking it.) I don't know if the Moff ever read it, but if he – or any of the hundreds of other people who have helped guide the Doctor on his travels over the past 25 years or so – should happen to read *this* volume, I hope they will find it a fair, honest and affectionate (and occasionally just a little cheeky) appraisal of their efforts. Because this book is dedicated to all of them, whether they like it or not.

Paul Kirkley
Cambridge, August 2016

Previously on Space Helmet for a Cow...

If you haven't read Volume I of *Space Helmet for a Cow* (and I'm not judging you, really I'm not), you missed a compelling story of triumph and tragedy, tears and tantrums, and an awful lot of men called Donald. (I copied that bit from the back cover blurb of the first book, but you won't know that because, let's not forget, *you didn't buy it*. Still not judging. Smiley face.)

What you're holding in your hands is designed to follow on from that first book. (For those not au fait with the secrets of the publishing industry, that's what the whole Volume I, Volume II thing refers to.) So certain necessary assumptions have been made in the text that follows that when I, for example, refer to Adric, you'll know a) who he is and b) why he's funny.

At the same time, I'm conscious that twenty-first-century *Doctor Who* also has a dedicated following among people who aren't that bothered about the old stuff they used to make in BBC Television Centre and its local gravel pits in the days before YouTube and fashion sense. For those people, my aim has been to write the story of New *Who* (yeah, I went there), without *too* much distraction from old ghosts. (There were, for the record, a total of seven Adric jokes, which my editor insisted we cut back to three. So there are now five.)

That said, for anyone who *would* find it useful to take an amusing (it says here) tour through the first 26 years of *Doctor Who*, we have made a bullet point, scale model version of some of Volume I's most pertinent facts and least irritating jokes available to download as a PDF from the *Space Helmet for a Cow* 2 product page on madnorwegian.com. And if, after reading *that*, you find yourself thinking, "You know, this so-called 'classic *Who*' sounds quite the party, I think I'll buy the ebook of the first volume, or order it from any good online retailer and specialist bookstore after all" – well, who are we to stand in your way?

In the meantime, let's flick straight to the back of that book and, in the tried and tested style of all classic *Doctor Who* episodes (especially the ones which were badly under-running) take a moment to reprise the cliffhanger ending to *Space Helmet Volume I*...

# # # # #

As the 1990s dawned, fans and programme makers alike were left to ponder the fate of their beloved show.

"They killed us through scheduling," was script editor Andrew Cartmel's conclusion. "At that time *Coronation Street* was the biggest hit on British television. It was the mountain. It was a monster. Moving us from Saturdays and putting us up against *Coronation Street* was like putting an infant on the M1 and leaving them to walk across. We were doomed. We were sent out on a suicide mission."[1]

"The BBC at the time was entirely run by people who hated science fiction," added [*Remembrance of the Daleks* and *Battlefield* writer] Ben Aaronovitch. "That's why there was no science fiction on the BBC for, like, ten years afterwards. They didn't like it. They were mostly public school, Oxbridge educated people who fear more than anything else the embarrassment of their peers."

In 2007, Peter Cregeen finally broke his silence on the events of the late 1980s. "The reason *Doctor Who* finished in 1989," he said, "was that we had really decided this wasn't the programme it had been and that if it was to have any life again in the future, it needed a long rest.

"Michael Grade had actually tried to cancel the programme a few years beforehand when he'd been the controller of BBC1, so when Jonathan Powell and I talked about not renewing it the following year, I think initially he was probably quite cautious about it, and sort of said to me, 'Well Michael Grade couldn't do it...'

"However, I felt very strongly this was a

programme that had been a great programme, a programme that could still be invaluable to the BBC. Had there been somebody around who was absolutely passionate about the programme – a producer, a writer who had got a vision for that programme that would bring it into a new life and a new world, it could have been an option to push that forward at that stage. But we couldn't see anybody around – I think most people at that stage regarded it as a programme that had seen better days.[1]

For the then-cast and crew, it proved a messy, unsatisfactory end to three years in which they had worked hard to restore the series' credibility in the face of public indifference and management hostility.

And so it was that, in 1989, *Doctor Who* – the television institution that had kept generations of children and adults pinned behind the sofa as it pushed restlessly at the limits of human imagination and potential (while straining the BBC's budgets to breaking point) – was sentenced to die a quiet, unheralded death, sliding from the schedules with barely a whimper, let alone a bang. From its first baby steps as a runtish upstart battling against institutional indifference and snobbery, the show had faced down numerous threats of cancellation and, thanks to the heroic efforts of a succession of indefatigable stewards – who refused to buckle even when the odds were so stacked against them they were in danger of being crushed – had doggedly earned its place at the heart of the British cultural landscape.

From Dalekmania to *The Daemons* to Tom Baker bestriding Saturday nights like a pop-eyed colossus in 13 feet of Begonia Pope's best yarn, *Doctor Who* had transcended its origins as 405 lines of flickering monochrome to turn its lead character into one of the most iconic heroes of the twentieth century. And now, it seemed, the time traveller had come full circle, seeing out his days as he'd begun them: unloved, unwanted, a ghost at the feast.

But, according to the man with his prints all over the smoking gun, Peter Cregeen, it was never really meant to end like this.

"I said, 'Let's give it a rest'. A lot of people saw that as a smokescreen to cancellation, but it really wasn't. I thought probably it would come back on the air again in three or four years' time. As it was, it took considerably longer than that."[1]

But that's a whole other story.
This is that story...

8 Doctor No

Day of Protest: "We want a new series of *Doctor Who*, a hundred grand in cash and safe passage to the state border"

So far, *Doctor Who* had embraced each new decade with a radical makeover – and the 1990s were no exception. But whereas 1970 had seen the programme reinvented as an earthbound action adventure, and in 1980 it had entered the age of the BBC Micro with a glossy(ish) new aesthetic, in 1990 the BBC wanted to try something even more radical: not making *Doctor Who* at all. ("I'm confident this will be the best season in years," said Jonathan Powell as he looked admiringly at the gaping hole in the schedules.)

But the more Powell, Peter Cregeen and company played hard to get, the keener producer Philip Segal's overtures from the USA became. In mid-January, Segal met with BBC Enterprises representatives (including a certain Verity Lambert, acting as a consultant for the Corporation) with a view to launching a joint BBC/CBS venture the following year. A month later, he met with Cregeen and Head of Television Drama Mark Shivas – on the very day he resigned from CBS to join rival network ABC, which must have led to some hasty photocopying for whoever was in charge of the agenda.

In April, British Satellite Broadcasting (BSB), more famous for its "squarial" receiver than any of its programmes (apart from the infamous sitcom *Heil Honey, I'm Home*, in which Adolf Hitler and Eva Braun moved in next door to a Jewish couple – with inevitably hilarious consequences), kicked off a planned re-run of all existing *Doctor Who* stories with *An Unearthly Child*. So if you wanted to know where your local *Who* nut lived, all you had to do was look for the house with the stupid square dish stuck to it. That and the Dalek curtains.

Meanwhile, movie production company (it says here) Coast to Coast had re-named themselves Green Light, thus demonstrating a finely-tuned sense of irony if nothing else; the producers were apparently planning a big announcement at that year's Cannes Film Festival. They'd booked the room, invited the press and ordered lots of bottled water – all they needed now was something to announce. In the end, no news was forthcoming and, having failed to excite any interest from American backers, the company started looking closer to home for funding, eventually reaching an agreement with the French-owned production company Lumière Pictures. Meanwhile, Johnny Byrne, a regular writer on the TV series, drafted a new movie script, now trading under the title *Doctor Who: Last of the Time Lords* (the rest of them presumably having died of old age while waiting for this film to happen).

On May 14th, Sylvester McCoy turned up at Television Centre and went to his dressing room to change into his Doctor Who costume. Don't worry – he hadn't got confused and forgotten the show had been cancelled: he and Sophie Aldred were there to record a schools science programme, *Search Out Space*, in character as the Doctor and Ace. All they needed to do now was to explain to school kids who the hell the Doctor and Ace were.

By the end of the summer, John Nathan-Turner had finally run out of things to staple and, after 26 years, the lights were turned out at the Doctor Who office for the last time. (They thought about inviting Michael Grade back to do the honours – "I have pleasure in declaring this office officially... closed!" – but it might have looked like gloating.)

By now, Virgin editor Peter Darvill-Evans (by which I mean he worked for Virgin Publishing, the successor to WH Allen, who had published the classic range of Target

Doctor Who novels, but it's a joke that never gets old) had devised a rough arc for what would be the first four original *Doctor Who* novels, in which the seventh Doctor and Ace would battle a space-time virus called the Timewyrm; American author John Peel was commissioned to write the first book, *Genesys*, set in ancient Mesopotamia, while Terrance Dicks, former Target editor Nigel Robinson and fan writer Paul Cornell were later pencilled in for the remaining three instalments, *Exodus*, *Apocalypse* and *Revelation*. Basically, it was going to be just like the Bible, except with far-fetched stories about magical beings instead of... well, anyway, it was going to be great.

"If anyone offers me a job, I take it," explained Dicks. "It's the freelance mentality. If someone asked me to write on the sex life of the Eskimo, I'd say 'That's always been a particular interest of mine'."[1] Hence his bestselling sizzler, *Fifty Shades of Tungoyortok*.

In late September, BSB dedicated a whole weekend to *Doctor Who* which, as well as vintage Hartnell, Troughton and Pertwee episodes, included interviews, convention reports and other specially recorded items. The weekend opened with the TARDIS materialising in the studio and presenters Debbie Flint and Syama Perera excitedly speculating who might be inside it: "A Time Lord maybe?" "Maybe Doctor Who even?" Oh no, it's just their new co-host, John Nathan-Turner. Try not to look too disappointed, kids. And there was yet more excitement with the release of *The Corridor of Eternity*, a limited edition cassette featuring extracts from Paddy Kingsland's scores for the fifth Doctor adventures *Castrovalva* and *Mawdryn Undead*. In the face of such competition, Sire Records held their nerve and went ahead with the release of Madonna's *Immaculate Collection* as planned.

In November, it was announced that BSB was to merge with satellite rival Sky – in much the same way a shark might "merge" with plankton – and the broadcaster's run of *Doctor Who* repeats was abandoned, leaving furious fans saddled with a stupid square they didn't know what to do with. (This is where, in *Space Helmet* Volume I, there would have been a guaranteed Adric joke.) On the 21st of that month, thousands of fans bunked off work in order to catch the Time Lord's latest adventure

in *Search Out Space* – in which the Doctor appears as the host of a slightly manic game-show pitting Ace against K-9 and a posh alien called Cedric. As an informative cosmology lesson, it's only slightly more useful than *The Three Doctors*.

But the real action was scheduled for the last day of the month, when fans were encouraged to take part in a Day of Protest co-ordinated by *DWB* magazine. The organisers reasoned that, if enough people bombarded the BBC with phone calls demanding the return of *Doctor Who*, the Corporation would have no choice but to capitulate and restore the show to screens immediately. The BBC did go to the effort of recording a slightly snarky recorded message stating: "We apologise, but within our limited space/time continuum, lines to the duty/information office are busy at the moment, but rest assured an automatic record is being kept of all telephone calls on this subject. Certainly a short break for the Doctor should not be seen as a one-way ticket to Gallifrey. Thank you for your interest." Which must have been very confusing for anyone phoning up to ask when *The Antiques Roadshow* was coming back.

In the end, a total of 996 calls were logged, a number of them from people with such suspiciously familiar names as "Alistair Gordon" and "John Turner", and the BBC conspicuously failed to crumble under the pressure. Peter Cregeen did issue another statement, in which he manfully resisted the temptation to use the phrase "total mentalists", while Jonathan Powell agreed to discuss the subject on Channel 4's *Right to Reply*, but then was strangely unable to find a window in his busy schedule. James Arnold-Baker from BBC Enterprises did put in an appearance, during which he claimed "the property is an old one, it's had its day and is no longer commercially viable". Which must have been news to the members of his staff who were busy churning out videos and other products like Santa's elves – even Cregeen admitted that combined merchandise and overseas sales continued to contribute more than £2 million a year to the Corporation's coffers. But hey, that's only money – the BBC was founded on more rarefied principles of quality programming and a commitment to public service broadcasting. Its big launches of that year, incidentally? *MasterChef, Keeping Up Appearances* and a revival of Bruce Forsyth's *Generation Game*. Just sayin'.

The David Burton Years: a new golden age?

With the Day of Protest having bafflingly failed to bring about the return of *Doctor Who*, in early 1991 fans took a different tack: sending £5 cheques to the BBC instead. In total, the Corporation is thought to have received around £7,500 worth of cheques made payable to "Doctor Who". All of which were duly returned before Sylvester McCoy tried to cash them.

There was *some* new *Who* in February – sort of – when an extended cut of *The Curse of Fenric* (the seventh Doctor story famously hacked down to length in the edit, losing hefty chunks of vital exposition in the process) became the best-selling *Doctor Who* video ever, presumably thanks to people buying it to find out what the hell it was actually about. John Nathan-Turner, who helped oversee the project, was encouraged enough to push ahead with other special VHS projects, including compilations of episodes from incomplete Hartnell and Troughton stories, and a compilation of episodes from Pertwee stories that *were* complete – just not on that particular tape. I'm sure it made sense at the time.

In April, recording began on a new straight-to-video drama starring Colin Baker as "the Stranger" and Nicola Bryant as "Miss Brown". *Summoned by Shadows* was the brainchild of *Doctor Who* fan Bill Baggs, a VT editor at BBC Nottingham with aspirations to direct drama. "I'd seen what Keith Barnfather had done with *Wartime* [the very first semi-professional video drama, from 1987, starring John Levene as Sergeant Benton], and arrogantly thought I could do a lot better," explained Baggs. "*Summoned by Shadows* came about because I had the nerve and the gumption to phone Colin Baker's agent and Tom Baker's agent, and we all know which one came through. And I was really grateful."[2]

The story, which also stars Michael Wisher, is set on a distant planet where the Stranger arrives with designs on becoming a hermit.

("You know, when you think about it, Bill, the Stranger and Miss Brown are a bit like the Doctor and Peri, in a way." "So they are! I hadn't thought of that. What a coincidence.") The BBC's lawyers may well have had something to say on the matter – fortunately, the chances of anyone at the BBC watching anything *Doctor Who*-related were less than zero, and Baker went on to star in a further five Stranger films over the next few years – including one in which he gets naked in a cave with Sophie Aldred, complete with gratuitous topless shot (though only of Baker, before you rush out and buy the DVD).

In America, the lack of new episodes had prompted many PBS stations to drop *Doctor Who* – but Philip Segal was still keeping the faith. In mid-1991, he took a job with Amblin Television, and discussions with the BBC were renewed – no doubt helped by Segal namedropping his new boss, a certain Steven Allan Spielberg. "I had the finest calling card I was ever going to have," admitted Segal, "and if I was ever going to have a shot at getting *Doctor Who*, it was then."[3]

Not that the world's most successful film director was exactly a fully paid-up *Who* anorak. "He was aware of it," said Segal. "He liked the notion. He was intrigued. He liked to hear of these wonderful, iconic characters. So it was based on his blessing that I went after *Doctor Who*."[3]

Summer saw the launch of a major *Doctor Who* exhibition at the Museum of the Moving Image on London's South Bank. Featuring props and costumes from the series, the exhibition proved so popular it was subsequently extended several times, eventually running for more than six months before heading out on a tour of the regions. Not bad for an old property that was no longer commercially viable.

In late July, the Doctor entered a new dimension with the publication of *Timewyrm: Genesis*. The cover blurb for The New Adventures novels promised "stories too broad and deep for the small screen" – and they were a bit too racy as well, as it turned out. John Peel's tale of an apocalyptic superbeing crash-landing in the cradle of civilisation attracted the attention of the moral guardians at the *News of the World* with its fruity language and – shock horror – sex. Ace spends her first scene completely starkers, and later has to fend off the lusty advances of Gilgamesh, the hero king of Uruk, who also has a bit of a thing for the local teenage prostitutes. Try to imagine a version of *Caligula* starring children's telly star Sylvester McCoy, and... actually, don't try that. It just gets weird.

And then came the announcement everyone had been waiting for: a new Doctor had been cast, and filming on a new series had already started. Its star? None other than David Burton.

Yes, *the* David Burton. A well-known face around the Redhill area (apparently), Burton has, according to his resume, appeared in "28 professional pantomime productions", and specialises in "eccentric professors and mad scientists". In 1991, he was the subject of numerous press reports that he had been cast as the Doctor, which turned out to derive from the fact that, three years earlier, he had recorded a pilot episode, *Doctor Who and the Monsters of Ness*, for an independent production company interested in pitching for the series. Quite why this had suddenly made the papers is a mystery – but it may have had something to do with the fact Burton was driving about town in a car with The New Doctor Who emblazoned down the side. Yes, really.

Meanwhile, progress had been made on the *Doctor Who* movie, as Green Light announced it had finally completed... a new tagline. From now on, publicity would boast the legend: The Man – The Myth – The Movie. Well two out of three ain't bad.

On August Bank Holiday Monday, almost 28 years after it had been recorded, the unbroadcast pilot episode of *An Unearthly Child* finally made it to air as part of BBC2's *The Lime Grove Story*. ("Twenty-eight years?" said the producers at Green Light. "You guys move fast.") That same month, Peter Cregeen made one of his regular statements on the future of the series, telling *Doctor Who Magazine*: "There's no question of *Doctor Who* being abandoned. It is still an important programme and when the time is right it should return. A decision was taken to rest the programme for an extended period so that when it returns it will be seen as a fresh, inventive and vibrant addition to the schedule, rather than a battle-weary Time Lord languishing in the backwa-

ters of audience popularity." ("Alright, no need to rub it in," thought Sylvester McCoy.)

The fans, though, were having none of it, and in September they unveiled their latest plan to force the show back on the air: they were going to sue the BBC. The consortium – a sort of continuity wing of the Doctor Who Appreciation Society (DWAS) which included Andrew Beech, *Who* historian Jeremy Bentham and *DWB* editor Gary Leigh (nee Levy) – planned to raise £30,000 to take the BBC to court for "blatant apathy and insensitivity in the face of strong demand from their customers". In the end, the action was dropped after they failed to raise enough money – which was a shame, because it would definitely, *definitely* have worked. (Incidentally, do you know what the maximum court sentence for blatant apathy is? Me neither – and I couldn't be bothered to look it up.)

Besides, what the fans didn't know was the BBC was genuinely exploring the idea of a new *Doctor Who* series. Anna Home, head of children's programmes, got very close to commissioning an animated version of the show, but dropped the idea after discussions with – oh hello you – Jonathan Powell. The project never got as far as the casting stage, but SuperTed, Dogtanian and Count Duckula all told their agents they'd do it if the money was right.

Anorak outraged at being branded a *Doctor Who* fan

After the positive response to the previous summer's broadcast of the pilot episode, in 1992 the team at *The Late Show* – BBC2's self-consciously hip arts magazine programme – decided to take a punt on a full series of *Doctor Who* repeats, kicking off on January 2nd with episode one of *The Time Meddler*. The run was launched with a half-hour documentary, *Resistance is Useless*, which told the story of the series through a series of clips and specially-recorded to-camera links by an empty anorak with a Brummie accent. The message seemed to be: "Welcome, *Doctor Who* fans, to BBC2 – the new home of cult TV for all you sad losers who can't get a girlfriend."

The week after the repeats began, there was an even bigger treat for fans of 60s *Who*, when a complete set of film recordings of lost classic

The Tomb of the Cybermen turned up in a vault in Hong Kong. Amidst scenes of wild jubilation in the streets, BBC Video announced plans to rush release the story on VHS, an event covered in surprising depth on Simon Bates' Radio 1 show – though not, sadly, in the legendary *Our Tune* sob story slot. ("Eric was 45, and a member of The Brotherhood of Logicians. He wanted to revive the lost Cybermen of Telos in order to create a society based on pure reason. Sadly, Eric was betrayed by his new allies, who throttled him to death. His mum Valerie says she misses him very much, and will never forget his devotion to cold, hard, inhuman logic – or his love of this classic track from Crosby, Stills and Nash.")

Of course, once people had the chance to watch it for themselves, they realised *The Tomb of the Cybermen* wasn't *quite* the masterpiece they'd been led to believe – but it was still a hell of a lot better than *Silver Nemesis*.

In February, Tom Baker – who was slowly rehabilitating himself into *Who* circles ("My name is Tom Baker and I've been clean of *Doctor Who* for 12 years now") – recorded linking narration for a video release of *Shada* at the MOMI Behind the Sofa exhibition. (The tape, released later in the year, starts out well, with the early instalments dominated by the Cambridge location filming; by episode six, however, it's basically *Jackanory* with the occasional clip.)

By now it was obvious Virgin's New Adventures series was a hit. Marc Platt's *Time's Crucible* kicked off a new trilogy of linked stories under the Cat's Cradle banner – and if you thought *Ghost Light* was complicated, it was nothing compared to this baffling tale of a giant, data-eating lamprey called the Process, which recreates the egg from which it hatched in order to supervise its own birth (don't ask) – while Andrew Cartmel finally got his own writing credit with the follow-up, *Warhead*, which managed to be both the middle part of the Cat's Cradle trilogy and the start of an entirely *different* trilogy. It was all very confusing.

In April, Philip Segal once again received the brush-off from Peter Cregeen, who told him he still thought *Doctor Who* needed a longer rest. ("Okay," said Segal. "I'll tell my boss, Steven Spielberg, what you said, and if Steven Spielberg has a problem with that, I'll tell Steven Spielberg to let you know. Anyway, I'd better go, I've got Steven Spielberg on the line.")

It was only later that Segal realised how resistant the-then current BBC regime were to even talking about *Doctor Who*. "The very idea of them putting any of their resources behind the resurrection of something that was, at the time, hated... I mean, they *hated* it," he said. "It wasn't like 'Oh no, it's yesterday's news' – it was *rubbish* to them. It was just something that wasn't really worth discussing. So at that point all I got was, 'We're putting the show on the shelf – come and give us a call in ten years'."[3]

That summer, however, Segal happened to meet Peter Wagg, another British ex-pat who had found some success Stateside with a drama based on Max Headroom, "the world's first computer-generated TV host". Wagg was impressed by Segal's enthusiasm for *Doctor Who*, and agreed to partner him on the project. By the autumn, Segal was banging on Mark Shivas' door again, with Wagg acting as his agent during discussions in London. Around this time, the duo also found an ally in Tony Greenwood, director of home entertainment at BBC Enterprises.

"You needed a friend in the BBC," said Segal. "The only way to navigate within the BBC is to have a friend who's willing to actually walk down the corridor – because that's what it takes. Without [Tony's] tireless, tireless offers of help, we wouldn't have gotten where we got."[3] Which, for now, was nowhere fast – but Segal was a patient man. And there was more interest from Tinseltown – after a fashion – when Sylvester Stallone paid £12,500 for a TARDIS prop to display at the London branch of Planet Hollywood, the *Rocky* star's joint restaurant venture with Bruce Willis, Demi Moore and Arnold Schwarzenegger. (Whether his superstar friends appreciated the police box's iconic status isn't known, but at least it was somewhere to hang the coats.)

In October, the seventh Doctor acquired a new companion in the shape of Professor Bernice "Benny" Summerfield, a twenty-sixth-century archaeologist described by Peter Darvill-Evans as "Indiana Jones in space". Benny made her debut in Paul Cornell's novel *Love and War*, and would go on to have an extraordinary afterlife in audio dramas, comic strips, animations and countless more novels that continues to this day.

Meanwhile, having had word that BBC1 had no plans to mark *Doctor Who*'s upcoming 30th anniversary – Jonathan Powell probably wouldn't even send a card – BBC Enterprises began floating the idea of making a straight-to-video story themselves. That's actual, brand new *Doctor Who*, made by the actual BBC, featuring actual Doctors from the actual series. All that was different about it was that it wouldn't be shown on actual telly. Enterprises' David Jackson was assigned as producer, and Adrian Rigelsford – a fan who had written a couple of non-fiction *Doctor Who* books – was commissioned to write the script. BBC2's repeats *were* continuing on actual TV – after *The Time Meddler*, fans had been treated to *The Mind Robber*, *The Sea Devils* and *The Daemons*, the latter in a specially recolourised version to restore episodes previously only available in black and white – while new satellite station UK Gold also started airing classic stories, promising fans everything in existence except Terry Nation's stories, which were unavailable owing to a rights dispute. To add to the sudden flurry of activity, in November, the BBC and Amblin were thought to be close to a deal on a brand new 22-episode series. No, really. At this rate, fans would have more *Doctor Who* in 1993 than they knew what to do with.

But if the year was ending on a high, Ben Aaronovitch's New Adventures novel *Transit* managed to leave a nasty taste in the mouth – so to speak – by coming under fire for its X-rated sexual content and frequent effin' and jeffin'. "People *do* have sex," argued Aaronovitch. "The book had to go in the first draft. If I'd had the chance to revise it, which I didn't because I was so late, I would have taken out some of the swearing...

"The reasoning behind the notorious 'taste of semen' scene," he added, "is that I had two characters who were prostitutes, and I didn't want to glamorise that."[4] (That's fair enough – but Peter Darvill-Evans was probably right to reject the book's original title, *Doctor Who and the Taste of Semen*.)

The Dark Dimension: so bad, it didn't even go straight to video

In January 1993, there was another reason for *Doctor Who* fans to get excited: Jon Pertwee was set to return to the role (again) for a new radio serial to be broadcast on BBC Radio 5. "I went to the BBC with the idea myself," said Pertwee. "I'd worked with a marvellous radio producer, Dirk Maggs, on his Radio 4 production of *Superman* some years back.... I said 'Why don't we do *Doctor Who*?' Nearly two years after that, the BBC agreed to do it."[5]

By then, Maggs had handed the project over to producer Phil Clarke, who commissioned a script from Barry Letts, while Elisabeth Sladen and Nicholas Courtney were sounded out about reprising Sarah Jane and the Brigadier.

There were further developments on the movie front, too: Johnny Byrne's script was abandoned and Denny Martin Flinn – who had penned *Star Trek VI* – agreed to take a pass at it. ("Instead of the Doctor just wandering aimlessly about the universe, how about some kind of – I don't know – five year mission? To explore strange new worlds, to seek out new life and new civilizations – that sort of thing? And this ship that's bigger on the inside? What if we also made it really big on the *outside* as well? Like a big, giant starship. Just an idea.")

There was good news for *Who* fans in February when Jonathan Powell left the BBC for Carlton Television, and was replaced as BBC1 Controller by Alan Yentob – an unabashed sci-fi sympathiser who, as head of BBC2, had created a successful early evening "cult TV" slot made up mostly of US imports like *Star Trek: The Next Generation* and re-runs of vintage ITC fare. "I definitely saw the appeal of sci-fi – to younger audiences and even older audiences,"[3] admitted Yentob, as his fellow execs slowly backed away with a look of horror on their faces. Appearing on magazine show *Good Morning with Anne and Nick* shortly after his appointment, Yentob told viewers: "I would not rule out the possibility of *Doctor Who* returning. But I don't want to be attacked in three or four years if I haven't brought it back." Three or four years? He'd be lucky if they left him alone for three or four *hours*.

Unfortunately, negotiations with Amblin

had run into the sand again, with Philip Segal's team apparently unable to offer a deal the BBC was happy with. But there were still plenty of reasons to be cheerful: at a BBC Enterprises press launch to publicise the show's upcoming 30th anniversary – attended by Jon Pertwee, Peter Davison, Colin Baker, Sylvester McCoy and Nicholas Courtney – Tony Greenwood confirmed a script had been written for a direct-to-video special, but said funding was still being sought. He promised "the door [on the show] is not closing any time soon", prompting Jon Pertwee to respond: "The door's closing on *me* any time soon."

In fact, the third Doctor was in fine fettle during the recording of the new radio serial, *The Paradise of Death* – though his co-stars admitted to a few first-night nerves. "I think the main thought in our minds was: my God, is this going to work?" said Lis Sladen. "Can this gel? Can it be done? I think Barry was like that, too. But it was incredible – it really just came together."[6]

Which is more than can be said for the TARDIS. At a photo shoot to publicise the serial, Pertwee, Sladen and Courtney were astonished when the Doctor's iconic police box prop arrived from BBC storage on the back of a lorry – completely flat-packed. Having delivered the immortal line "there's your TARDIS, mate", the driver insisted it wasn't his job to assemble the dusty, cobwebbed blue panels – so Sladen, Courtney and the photographer had to put it together themselves, as Pertwee looked on, claiming his original *Doctor Who* cloak was too valuable to get dirty. "Which was odd, because I could have sworn I'd seen it at auctions half a dozen times," said Sladen. "It was almost as if he'd had a whole bunch of them run up just to sell."[7] The very idea.

In America, meanwhile, Green Light were determined to ensure Denny Martin Flinn's script maintained clear blue water between *Doctor Who* and *Star Trek* by approaching a potential director by the name of... Leonard Nimoy. Nimoy was interested, and apparently had Pierce Brosnan in mind as a potential Doctor; he had even agreed to start shooting – but, with the clock ticking down to the moment the film company's rights to the property expired, Philip Segal smelled a rat.

"Green Light's contract said they had to be in physical production [at the time their licence ran out]," said Segal. "So they were going to hire Leonard Nimoy to come over and shoot a couple of weeks of second unit. Fortunately, I was able to get a hold of Leonard Nimoy. When I explained to him what they were intending to do, he obviously got cold feet and ran away."[3] That's logical.

When he wasn't stitching up the opposition, Segal was using any opportunity he could to keep his own bid in the frame – including nobbling Alan Yentob during a BBC execs' tour of the set of Amblin's *seaQuest DSV* (that's really what it was called – I haven't just left the caps lock on). While Yentob was trying to concentrate on the futuristic naval drama, Segal just kept yammering about *Doctor Who*. At the end of the tour, Segal played his trump card, and introduced Yentob to Steven Spielberg – then presumably rushed him out of the door before they could start talking about Spielberg's deep love of *Doctor Who*. ("Doctor *what*?" "No, *Doctor Who*," etc.)

In fact, Yentob was so receptive to the idea of new *Doctor Who*, he offered to put money into Enterprises' film, *The Dark Dimension*, which would now receive a BBC1 broadcast in November. This was good news for director Graeme Harper, who had previously been given a budget of just £80,000 with which to deliver an ambitious 90-minute special featuring all the surviving Doctors, numerous companions, extensive location filming, tonnes of special effects, a big-name villain (probably Rik Mayall or Brian Blessed, though David Bowie was apparently on the radar, too) and a monster menagerie including Ice Warriors, the Yeti and radically re-designed Daleks and Cybermen.

As pre-production work on the story began in May, there were rumblings on the ex-Time Lord bush telegraph about the way Adrian Rigelsford had carved up the action among the various Doctors – casting Tom Baker as the lead, with a supporting role for Sylvester McCoy and little more than glorified cameos for the rest of them. "That's fine with me – I'm just happy to be able to do my little bit," was what Jon Pertwee almost certainly didn't say when he was told.

"When the scripts arrived on everyone's doorsteps, we were all gobsmacked," said

McCoy. "It gave Tom Baker the lead role – a *vast* lead role. Everyone thought that was rather unfair, and wrong for an anniversary story."[8]

"The story worked perfectly well without us," added the Other Baker. "The whole story was centred around Tom Baker – the rest of us had a few pages each. The script itself wasn't fantastic, although it had a good villain, but those bits for Peter, Sylv, Jon and myself had clearly been bolted on. Jon Pertwee was really upset. He was deeply offended."[9]

According to Baker, Graeme Harper was full of enthusiasm for the project, and tried to talk him round. "[He said] 'Hello mate, isn't it great – we're going to be working together again'. And I had to pour cold water on it. 'I'm fond of you, Graeme, and I love you deeply, but there is no way any of us is going to do *The Dark Dimension*'. He was really disappointed. 'Can you think about it?' he said. But our thinking had been done."[8]

Unfortunately for Harper, Philip Segal had also been thinking about it. "I read the script and it was awful," said Segal. "I mean, it was really embarrassing and silly. It just felt wrong. Here we are going to reinvigorate everything, and this is coming along and it's going to muddy the waters and confuse people. I asked them if they'd put it on hold, and they did."[3]

And so *The Dark Dimension* was dispatched to an even darker dimension at the back of a BBC Enterprises filing cabinet, never to see the light of day again. "It upset a lot of people,"[3] admitted Segal. Strangely, the BBC's official line was to deny the project had ever existed. Will Wyatt, managing director of BBC Network Television, claimed it had amounted to nothing more than a few people kicking around some ideas at BBC Enterprises – conveniently ignoring the fact Tom Baker had been contracted (and was paid in full) for the special, and that a BBC product brochure had listed the story as scheduled for broadcast on BBC1 on Sunday, November 28th from 8pm-9.40pm. ("Er, that's a misprint," said Wyatt. "It should say three episodes of *Birds of a Feather*. And a bit of another episode of *Birds of a Feather*. Easy mistake to make.")

The 30th anniversary wasn't a complete write-off, however. In July, Kevin Davies, a *Who* fan-turned-director who had helmed a successful documentary about the making of *The Hitchhiker's Guide to the Galaxy*, was approached by the Late Show team with a view to making a *Doctor Who* retrospective for BBC1. At around the same time, John Nathan-Turner was asked to write a light-hearted mini-episode to be shown during that year's *Children in Need* telethon, which the ex-producer decided to turn into a *Doctor Who/EastEnders* mash-up set in Albert Square – almost certainly the only time "*EastEnders*" and "light-hearted" have ever been uttered in the same breath.

Meanwhile, Bill Baggs stepped into the breach of the canned *Dark Dimension* with his own multi-Doctor(ish) story, *The Airzone Solution*. An environmental thriller set in near-future Britain, the film stars Colin Baker as a local TV weatherman being haunted by the ghost of a murdered investigative film-maker (Peter Davison) who, along with his mysterious mentor Oliver Threthewey (Jon Pertwee) had been working to blow the lid on a powerful corporation with the help of a radical environmentalist (Sylvester McCoy).

"We had Colin Baker, and with Colin's help I managed to coerce Peter Davison," explained Baggs of the film's all-star line-up, which appeared to have come direct from Gallifreyan Central Casting. "I'd worked with Sophie Aldred and she helped me coerce Sylvester, which was lovely. And then I got a phone call, actually on the set, and it was Jon Pertwee. Jon said, 'I hear you're making a *Doctor Who* film – why am I not in it?' I didn't know what to say. I think I said something like, 'Well maybe we could get you in it?'."[2]

The Airzone Solution also boasts an early appearance by a pre-Hollywood Alan Cumming. Speaking of which, the film is notable for including a bedroom scene between Colin Baker and Nicola Bryant, which just feels a bit... *wrong* – like discovering your parents' sex tape. ("Do I get to sleep with one of my companions too?" asked Davison. "No problem," said Baggs. "I've made some calls, and Kamelion says he can do next Tuesday.")

By late summer, the BBC and Amblin were inching ever closer to an agreement. Tony Greenwood, in his new role of Director of Consumer Products International for Enterprises, sent confirmation that the deal was on from their end. But Amblin's lawyers disagreed, claiming the Corporation had failed to meet all their requirements. And there was another complicating factor, in that Universal – the studio behind some of Steven Spielberg's biggest successes – had a 50% stake in everything Amblin did, which meant a whole other set of suits to appease. So Segal and Greenwood decided to ignore them and get on with it anyway, with the producer sounding out Michael Crawford for the lead. "He was intrigued," said Segal, "but felt he was simply too old. I was also very interested in Michael Palin. Michael felt it just wasn't a character he felt he could reach as an actor."[3]

At the end of August, Jon Pertwee hit the talk shows to publicise the broadcast of The Paradise of Death, before joining the rest of the Doctors and scores of other stars from the show for that year's DWAS Panopticon convention in Hammersmith. Let's hope Tom Baker at least bought the others a drink with his Dark Dimension wages.

In September, the Time Lords were reunited again for the recording of Nathan-Turner's Children in Need short, Dimensions in Time. Most of the filming took place on the EastEnders backlot at Elstree, with some additional scenes filmed around the Cutty Sark in Greenwich. Despite having a running time of 12 minutes, the story finds room for five Doctors, 13 companions (for the record: Ace, Susan, the Brigadier, Romana II, Sarah Jane, Nyssa, Leela, Peri, Mel, K9, Liz, Victoria and Mike Yates), around 15 monsters, 11 members of the EastEnders cast and Kate O'Mara as the Rani.

"I thought it was a nice idea getting every single person who had been involved in the programme into it, but it was a bit confusing,"[10] said Nick Courtney, whose scene with Colin Baker restored his status as the only actor to have appeared alongside every Doctor.

On October 28th, the BBC made an official announcement about its co-production deal with Amblin, while several papers ran with the slightly less official news that David Hasselhoff was the new man in the TARDIS – meaning that bloke with the car from Redhill was no longer the most ludicrous name linked to the role.

BBC1's anniversary celebrations kicked off with Planet of the Daleks showing on Friday evenings throughout November, each episode preceded by a specially-shot short produced by the Late Show team. For fans, it was just like old times – especially when the story sank without trace against the unstoppable might of Coronation Street. Kevin Davies was also getting that sinking feeling, after the show's producers saw a rough-cut of his 30 Years in the TARDIS documentary – and made no secret of the fact they hated it. "They didn't understand the thrust of what I was doing,"[11] said Davies who, as well as interviewing cast and crew and celebrity fans (well, Toyah and Mike Gatting, anyway), had shot extensive material in which a small boy found himself caught up in some of Doctor Who's most iconic scenes. "What we viewed – apart from a petrified film editor – was a meandering 20-minute cut less than two weeks before transmission,"[10] countered producer John Whitson. Things got messy when both sides aired their grievances in the pages of Time Out magazine, and Davies was dismayed to learn the programme was being extensively re-cut without his input. The BBC certainly knew how to throw a party: with projects being dropped and disembowelled all over the place, fans were starting to wonder if the anniversary wasn't cursed. And then came the really crushing blow: no-one tried to cancel Dimensions in Time.

Dimensions in Time: critics hail EastEnders' most realistic episode yet

"What force for good could bring the Doctor back to TV for his 30th anniversary?" asked the Radio Times on the cover of its November 20th issue. The answer, of course, was Jonathan Powell leaving for ITV... sorry, it was Children in Need. But, pleased though they were to see Doctor Who back on the magazine's front page for the first time since The Five Doctors a decade earlier, fans couldn't help but wonder at what might have been – a full anniversary special, instead of a glorified skit split between the annual charity telethon and the following night's Noel's House Party.

The story, such as it is, opens in the Rani's TARDIS, where unconvincing models of the first and second Doctor's heads are floating about – "pickled in time" according to the Rani, "like gherkins in a jar". The fourth

Doctor isn't pickled (though give him half a chance and a lift to Soho...), but he is apparently lost in the time vortex – albeit a time vortex with a free-standing microphone that makes him look like he's in the video for a charity single. He is broadcasting a mayday call to his other selves, warning them that the Rani has already trapped "the grumpy one and the flautist" in her trap.

The seventh Doctor and Ace arrive at the Cutty Sark – but Ace suddenly finds herself in Albert Square with Colin Baker. There's a half-hearted attempt at some comedy banter with market stallholders Sanjay and Gita, before the sixth Doctor suddenly transforms into his third incarnation and, more bafflingly, Sophie Aldred turns into Bonnie Langford. (That's *got* to be worth a call to her agent.) At this point, it becomes clear how John Nathan-Turner and co-writer David Roden have got round the problem of trying to fit so many characters into such a short space of time: they haven't. Instead, various Doctors and companions appear and disappear in a puff of smoke – or a flash of white light, at least – while Kate O'Mara achieves the near-impossible by pitching it slightly too camp even for *this* nonsense. ("Say goodbye, Doctors," she crows over the cliffhanger. "You're all going on a long journey – a veeeeerrry very long journey!")

Teamed up with the seventh Doctor at Greenwich, Leela is inexplicably dressed as Pocahontas and, for a savage warrior, has suddenly started talking like Pip and Jane Baker ("she's got a menagerie of clones in there!"). According to Louise Jameson, they originally asked her to wear her original animal skins. "'No', I said. 'Two children on, I'm not going to get back into that leather leotard'."[12]

Weirdly, *Dimensions in Time* is not pitched as a spoof of the sort that would become a staple of later *Children in Need* appeals, but as a "proper" adventure with proper jeopardy, which just makes the whole thing seem even more bizarre. Oh, and did I mention it was in 3-D? So if you wore your special cardboard glasses, you could experience the giddy thrill of seeing Kathy Beale's courgettes popping out of your telly – just like a real market stall!

There's no denying the nostalgic rush that comes from seeing so many old faces back in the harness after all these years: the sight of

Tom Baker in his Season Eighteen garb, or Peter Davison back rocking the celery, punched every fanboy's buttons. But there's precious little else to recommend *Dimensions in Time*, and God only knows what the average viewer must have made of it all. (All *13.8 million* of them – yes, this was watched by more people than 95% of bona fide *Doctor Who*).

On the Saturday night, Jon Pertwee joined Noel Edmonds at his house in Crinkley Bottom to watch the second instalment, and did his best not to look mortified. Crinkley Bottom? There were certainly a few clenched buttocks among *Doctor Who* fans that weekend. Still, if it was embarrassing for the viewers, spare a thought for Elisabeth Sladen. The actress had spent the evening before filming neglecting to turn down the free wine at a BBC screening of a film her daughter was in – and was so ill the next day, she ended up throwing up all over the *EastEnders* set. Which must have looked spectacular in 3-D.

If *Dimensions in Time* had left you hungry for more – as opposed to pleading for a merciful death – the birthday celebrations continued all weekend on UK Gold, while Radio 2 aired a special documentary, *Doctor Who – 30 Years* (they must have spent ages coming up with that). Also that week, a *Who* exhibition opened at the Birmingham Science Museum, and the random Doctor/companion team-ups continued when Anne Diamond and Nick Owen were guests on *Good Morning with Sylvester McCoy and Deborah Watling*. Or was it the other way round?

But the plum in the anniversary pudding came the following week with the broadcast of *30 Years in the TARDIS* which, despite its difficult labour, still managed to distil the essence of *Doctor Who* into an entertaining hour of television, while the hardcore faithful were wowed by modern recreations of such classic scenes as the Daleks rolling over Westminster Bridge and the Cybermen marching down the steps of St Paul's. Kevin Davies even managed to achieve several money shots that were beyond the means of the original show, including the Autons smashing through shop windows on Ealing High Street, a flying Dalek on a comic strip-style hoverbout (so named 'cos they allowed them to hover... you know, about) and, most groundbreaking of all, a single tracking shot through the doors of the police box and into the TARDIS console room. Turns out it's *bigger on the inside* – who knew?

In December, The New Adventures caused another minor tabloid kerfuffle when the *Sunday Mirror* ran a story about the Doctor tripping off his nut – or taking hallucinogenic drugs, anyway – in Kate Orman's *The Left-Handed Hummingbird* (working title: *Doctor Who and Some, Like, Totally Awesome Shit, Dude*). In America, meanwhile, Universal staffer John Leekley was hired as writer and executive producer of *Doctor Who*, a move Philip Segal wasn't entirely happy with. Leekley's first job was to produce a series "bible" for use by prospective writers – an instruction he appears to have taken rather literally, eventually delivering a lavish, leather-bound volume written in the form of a message from "Cardinal Barusa (sic), Time Lord of Gallifrey" – complete with embossed Gallifreyan script and ensign faithfully copied from 1976's *The Deadly Assassin*. "This is my official insignia, and my personal glyph," begins Leekley/Barusa. "Having transcended the confines of body, I exist now amidst the crystals of the Domed City of Gallifrey, which resonate with their beautiful sounds... much like the wind chimes along the seas of the Blue Planet... the place you call Earth." He even went to great lengths to explain why the document had been written in English, rather than Gallifreyan. Frankly, it made the *actual* Bible look like a bit of lightweight fluff, and you couldn't help thinking he'd got a bit carried away. Either that, or he'd taken too much of whatever the Doctor was on in *The Left-Handed Hummingbird*.

The bible tells the story of Barusa's adventures with his grandson, the Doctor, and their search for the Doctor's father, Ulysses the Explorer. Many of these adventures seem strangely familiar, suggesting the series would re-make classic stories including *Genesis of the Daleks*, *The Talons of Weng-Chiang*, *Horror of Fang Rock*, *The Ark in Space*, *The Tomb of the Cybermen*, *The Gunfighters*, *The Daemons* and, um, *The Claws of Axos*. "I have asked my scribe to make a random selection of my adventures with the Doctor," says Barusa. "As I read through them, I am reminded of the words of the Doctor: 'Things were never dull'." Clearly,

his scribe had never told him about *The Monster of Peladon*.

Fox news

Having done their bit for *Children in Need*, it was another force that brought Jon Pertwee, Tom Baker and Peter Davison together in February 1994: cash. The three Doctors undertook a photo shoot for an ad campaign for the VW Golf Estate – pressing their noses up at the rear windscreen and marvelling at its roomy interior. (Not quite as big as the TARDIS, of course, but it did have a much better stereo.)

This didn't go down well at BBC Enterprises: "We are less than amused to see the spirit, if not the legality, of our rights to Dr Who being used in this way," said a spokesman. "But we understand the hold Dr Who has on viewers and car buyers." Still, it could have been worse: the agency behind the ad was the same one that had created the notorious, fender-crunching "Hello boys" campaign for Wonderbra. The mind boggles.

That month, Philip Segal, Peter Wagg and John Leekley headed to London for talks with BBC execs. In the first-class lounge at LA airport, the trio ran in to British film luminary Sir David (later Lord) Puttnam who, when he heard about the purpose of their trip, recommended they check out an Irish actor called Liam Cunningham who he had just produced in a film, *War of the Buttons*.

At a meeting with Peter Cregeen's successor, Michael Wearing, the Amblin team were introduced to Jo Wright, who Wearing told them would be the BBC's producer on the *Doctor Who* project. This immediately got Segal's back up: "I tried very hard to process this information clearly and professionally but, for some reason, I didn't," he recalled. "I was angry that someone else might be trying to push the project in a direction I did not want to take it."[13]

Later, the team took a cab to Alan Yentob's house, where the BBC1 controller was working from home while the builders were in. It was, by all accounts, a productive meeting, enlivened at one point by Segal falling through a wicker chair.

Casting sessions for the new Doctor took place over five days in early March. Segal and his associates saw between 15 and 20 actors a day, including such familiar TV faces as Anthony Head, Tim McInnerny, Paul Nicholas and Tony Slattery. John Sessions played both the Doctor and Napoleon during his audition, as well as improvising almost five minutes of additional dialogue. Smartarse. By mid-March, the frontrunners were Robert Lindsay and Liam Cunningham, though Segal was still holding out for Michael Crawford. When Lindsay became unavailable for the proposed late summer shoot, Cunningham came very close to being offered the job. Then Jo Wright threw a curveball in the shape of Paul McGann.

Arguably the most successful of the Liverpool-born acting clan that also included his brothers Joe, Stephen and Mark – who had been one of the hopefuls on the first day of auditions – McGann had made his name as the British deserter Percy Toplis in Alan Bleasdale's 1986 TV drama *The Monocled Mutineer*, before being cast as the eponymous "I" in Bruce Robinson's dissolute cult classic *Withnail and I*. "I think it was her agenda to cast him from the very beginning," said Segal. "It was her drive and tenacity that brought him forward. She sent me a copy of *Withnail and I*, and once you've seen that, how can you not fall in love with Paul McGann?"[13]

Unfortunately, the new series' American backers were distinctly cooler about the idea. "Paul McGann was a very good choice, we thought, because he's such a good actor, he's very good looking, he's got a great voice," explained Wright. "Everything about Paul felt right for us – and people had heard of him over here. But from Universal's point of view, they hadn't even heard of him, really, so it was difficult."[13]

While one door was opening up for the Doctor, another was finally closed. Even as Segal was auditioning potential Time Lords, the BBC informed Daltenreys – the company behind Green Light – that their licence would not be renewed when it expired in early April. The project's main financiers, Lumière, decided to cut their losses and run, leaving Peter Litten and George Dugdale with nothing more to show for their six-year mission to make a *Doctor Who* movie than a couple of props, a poster and a million-pound hole in their pockets. On the plus side, it was a really nice poster.

Also in the dead horse flagellation business

were publishers Boxtree, who announced a forthcoming book by Adrian Rigelsford called *The Making of The Dark Dimension*. As they *never actually* made *The Dark Dimension*, this promised to be quite a short read ("Met director, did a few drawings, got cancelled, The End") – though possibly still longer than some of Terrance Dicks' Target novelisations.

In the spring, Jon Pertwee went on tour with his one-man show, *Who is Jon Pertwee*. Partly performed in his Doctor Who costume, it saw him taking centre-stage to tell tall tales about his showbiz life – well, it's what he'd have been doing of an evening anyway, so he might as well get paid for it.

In the US, meanwhile, the BBC/Amblin project hit a major bump in the road when no networks expressed an interest in taking up the series. In the end, salvation – of sorts – came from Trevor Walton, another Englishman in LA who was head of movies at Rupert Murdoch's Fox Broadcasting Company (not to be confused with Emu's Broadcasting Company, which was something entirely different). Walton said he wanted to make *Doctor Who* as a movie, so Segal and Peter Wagg went to meet him at his office, where their "business negotiations" amounted to reminiscing about a few old *Doctor Who* episodes, after which Walton said it was a done deal.

There was just one small problem: the BBC wanted a series, not a film. (I'll say that again: the BBC wanted to make a series. *Of Doctor Who*. Had the fans secretly been poisoning the water supply or something?) So Segal concocted a side deal with the head of series television at Fox, who agreed to invest money into the film as a possible backdoor pilot.

On BBC Radio 4, meanwhile, listeners were transported back to *Doctor Who*'s primeval period in *Whatever Happened to Susan Foreman?*, one of a series of award-winning mockumentary "interviews" with fictional characters, in which the Doctor's granddaughter answered questions about life on, and after, the TARDIS. Jane Asher took time out from icing a Victoria Sponge to play Susan, Carole Ann Ford having apparently failed to return the director's calls, while James Grout was an older, even wiser Ian Chesterton. The programme took certain liberties with established continuity, leading to angry scenes across

Britain as despairing motorists shouted "How could Susan know about the planet Mechanus? She wasn't even *in The Chase*!" at their car radios.

After three years in which The New Adventures had proved a huge success, July saw Virgin launching a new line of Missing Adventures featuring past Doctors. Kicking off the series, Paul Cornell's *Goth Opera* – a pseudo-sequel both to *State of Decay* and The New Adventures novel *Blood Harvest* – sends the fifth Doctor and chums on vacation to Tasmania, where Nyssa accidentally gets turned into a vampire (good luck claiming that on the holiday insurance). The fanged Nyssa on the cover was supposed to have been covered in blood, until WH Smith objected that it was too gruesome for their shelves – almost certainly the first time in history that anyone has been offended by Nyssa.

Late summer proved a sad time for fans of the big screen Doctor (the one that actually made it to the screen) with the death of Peter Cushing, aged 81, on August 11th, and then Roy Castle, who lost his well-publicised battle with cancer exactly a month later. Meanwhile, two separate fan films went into production: *The Zero Imperative* was the first in a new series from Bill Baggs starring Caroline John as Liz Shaw, now working as a paranormal investigator for an organisation called P.R.O.B.E. – the Preternatural Research Bureau (the acronyms had really gone downhill since her UNIT days). A quarter of a century on from her brief time as the Doctor's mini-skirted dolly scientist, Shaw is now the one wearing the trousers – better than that, she even smokes a pipe – and has her own plucky gel assistant in the form of Lou Bayliss, played by former page 3 stunna Linda Lusardi (maybe they were aiming for a whole new demographic). The script, by actor and New Adventures novelist Mark Gatiss, also features Jon Pertwee, Colin Baker and Sylvester McCoy as three, erm, doctors ("You're just taking the piss now," said the BBC's lawyers) as well as Louise Jameson and Sophie Aldred. Then, a few weeks later, Aldred boarded *HMS Belfast* to record *Shakedown: Return of the Sontarans*. Scripted by Terrance Dicks and directed by Kevin Davies, the production was licensed by the estate of Robert Holmes to use both his potato men and their mortal enemies the Rutans (to date, this remains their only on-screen encounter), though the Sontarans had to be given a partial makeover as the BBC owned the design (and you thought it was Sir Walter Raleigh who discovered the potato). As well as Aldred, the production makes room for Carole Ann Ford, Michael Wisher and *Blake's 7* regulars Jan Chappell and Brian Croucher. It was produced by Gary Leigh of Dreamwatch Media, a production company spun out of what was formerly *DWB* magazine. (Despite this, the story manages to resist having the villain revealed to be a bearded, chain-smoking TV producer in a Hawaiian shirt.)

In early September, Paul McGann was screen tested for the Fox TV movie and, a few weeks later, a blabbermouth friend of the actor's – a certain S McCoy of Dunoon – announced him as the new Doctor at the DWAS' annual Panopticon convention. This was possibly premature, as it's fair to say McGann wasn't *quite* sold on the idea yet. "I kept saying to myself, 'I don't want to do this'," McGann recalled a while later. "And I turned it down. I said, 'this is daft, I can't do it'. You can't imagine yourself saying those things, wearing that costume... I kept saying, 'There's no way, no way. I am going to look like a tosser. And I am going to feel like a tosser'."[14] ("So shall I put you down as a maybe?" asked Segal.)

And McGann wasn't the only one proving hard to impress: Steven Spielberg didn't like John Leekley's script, describing it as "like an Indiana Jones movie". "That was the end of Steven's interest in the project," said Segal. "He just felt it was impinging on a world he'd already exploited in the movie business. It didn't demonstrate to him a fresh, unique or different character, so he rejected the script out of hand."[13] Consequently, Spielberg wanted his and Amblin's name taken off the project – a fact Segal admitted he *may* have forgotten to mention to the BBC as the film went into pre-production. (Hey, he was a busy guy – I mean, who else was going to make sure the Prydonian Seal of Gallifrey accurately matched the one from *The Deadly Assassin*?)

A new script was commissioned from Robert DeLaurentis who, in contrast to Leekley's portentous epic, favoured a wackier, more screwball approach. "My instinct is that we need a *sidekick*," he wrote in his treatment. "Dare I suggest a dog? What if the first time we see [companion] Lizzie, she's ducking through a blitz in order to save a feisty British Bulldog (Winston)?"

Yeah, what if? And why not make him a bleedin' chimney sweep while you're at it? Maybe Mr Bean or, I don't know, Princess Diana could play him? His thoughts on *Doctor Who*? (sic), incidentally: "Think Tom Hanks with a Holmesian quality. Make him *brilliant* and *bent*." Yeah, okay, enough with the British stereotypes already.

On Bonfire Night, Jon Pertwee, Lis Sladen and Nick Courtney reconvened to start recording another Barry Letts-penned radio serial, *The Ghosts of N-Space*. The cast and crew were keen to see it become a regular gig but, according to Letts, that was another avenue closed down by Philip Segal. "Phil [Clarke], Jon, Nick and Lis all wanted to do more, but we heard there was going to be a *Doctor Who* film and it was part of the contract with the co-producers that no new *Doctor Who* product should go out until the film went out."[15] Maybe they should have just done a Bill Baggs and re-named him "the Physician" or something? Speaking of which, Baggs had now reinvented his Stranger Chronicles as an audio series, while another hooky Doctor appeared on stage in a Cambridgeshire am-dram production labouring under the title *Doctor Who: Empress of Othernow* (wasn't that an early Genesis b-side?). Huntingdon Drama Club had received permission from the BBC to use the Doctor (Bob Pugh, for all you completists) and the Cybermen while the cast also included a certain Adrian Rigelsford. Look out for *The Making of The Empress of Othernow* at a bookshop near you soon. And while you're there, check out the new, happy-go-lucky seventh Doctor: in late 1994, Peter Darvill-Evans handed over The New Adventures range to incoming editor Rebecca Levene, who decided the books would benefit from a lighter touch, moving away from the existential angst of the "dark Doctor" and into less introspective territory. Thankfully, she stopped short of giving him a wisecracking bulldog called Winston.

Eric Roberts: any more at home like you?

Another year, another not-quite-*Doctor Who* spin-off. Recorded in March and April 1995, Reeltime Pictures' *Downtime* got closer than most to the real thing – a sequel to *The Abominable Snowmen* and *The Web of Fear*, it pits the Yeti against no fewer than three of the Time Lord's fellow travellers: Sarah Jane Smith, Brigadier Lethbridge-Stewart and Victoria Waterfield, as well as Professor Edward Travers (nice to see Deborah Watling was still an enthusiastic supporter of Take Your Dad to Work Day after all those years).

Marc Platt's story has the Great Intelligence planning a global takeover by infecting all the world's computers (decades before Mark Zuckerberg had the same idea) from its base in the University of East Anglia (actually it's the fictional New World University, but the UEA's brutalist concrete architecture is so familiar, it's hard to shake the feeling you might be about to meet a Yeti sitting on a loo in Norwich).

The opening scenes required Deborah Watling to play a much younger version of Victoria. "I read the script and said to the director, 'Hang on, it says here that I'm 19 years old. Well, I'm not. If you're going to film this sequence, make sure it's very dark!"[16] In the end, they shot the scenes in the London Dungeon. ("Yes okay," said Watling. "It doesn't have to be quite *this* dark.")

Directed by experienced *Who* helmer Chris Barry, *Downtime* capped a fertile few years of inventive spin-off films. "I don't think there's any other TV series in the world which has done what *Doctor Who* has done – spawned so many different writings, so many different independent productions," reflected co-producer Keith Barnfather. "It's unique in that sense."[2]

Across the pond, the *Doctor Who* TV movie was still feeling the heat in Development Hell. Robert DeLaurentis undertook a major rewrite of his script, but Fox still weren't happy, so DeLaurentis, Lizzie and Winston the bulldog all dropped out of the picture. Then Trevor Walton suggested Matthew Jacobs, who had a track record writing for shows like *The Young Indiana Jones Chronicles* and, perhaps more importantly, was British, so wouldn't try to replace the TARDIS with a red phone box in a bowler hat. In fact, Jacobs' father Anthony had played Doc Holliday in 1966's *The Gunfighters*, during which young Matthew had visited the set.

"My pitch was basically *Doctor Who Am I?*" said Jacobs. "I was completely swept away with this opportunity to invent a new Doctor."[3] Like any writer, he admitted he wanted to "bring himself to the table" and manifest aspects of his own personality in the character. "Suddenly, I could be Doctor Who!"[3] he enthused. ("That's fine," said Segal. "But I think revealing the Doctor's first name to be 'Matthew' is going a bit far.")

Whereas earlier scripts might have suggested a re-boot, Jacobs was keen to establish a single continuity between the film and the original series – and suggested they should bring Sylvester McCoy back in order to regenerate him. That went down like a bucket of cold sick at the BBC. In a memo to Jo Wright in August, Michael Wearing wrote: "Alan [Yentob] is very concerned about the idea of Sylvester McCoy being anywhere near it, and would be much happier if it was one of the old Doctors that was in it when it was a success eg. Tom Baker."

"I didn't think it was a good starting point, particularly for a project which was to have a life in the US as well as the UK," explained Yentob. "Why would anyone think that was the correct decision?"[3]

"In the end," said Wright, "I think I was the one who said to Alan, 'As long as he's only in it for a very short time, and doesn't say anything, then I'm sure it will be fine'."[3] Since they put it like that, how could he refuse?

The goalposts moved again in September when Philip Segal left Amblin to work for independent production company Lakeshore Entertainment. He took the Doctor Who project with him, and would now be working directly with Alex Beaton at Universal. Around the same time, Peter Wagg returned to England – possibly to get away from all the bloody Brits in America.

With production on the film – which had an allocated budget of $5 million – now slated to start in December, the various parties continued to wrangle over script and casting, with Segal caught in the crossfire of three separate negotiations between himself and Universal, Universal and Fox, and Fox and the BBC.

"Not one set of notes gelled with the other," he lamented. "Not one. I couldn't please anybody. I ended up trying to take as many of Jo's notes as possible, because I wanted to keep the BBC happy, and I tried to take as many of the network's notes as I possibly could. But I ignored the studio completely."[3]

As the end-of-year deadline approached, Paul McGann was slowly coming round to the idea of playing the Doctor – but Fox execs weren't. With less than a month to go before shooting was finally set to get under way, and with the sets under construction on the lot in Vancouver (Hollywood with tax breaks, essentially), the only person who had been hired to play the Doctor so far was Sylvester McCoy, which must have thrilled Alan Yentob no end.

Then, at the eleventh hour, Segal and casting director Beth Hymson suddenly threw a wildcard name into the mix. "I'll never forget the day I phoned Jo Wright at the BBC and told her we had an alternate for the role of the Doctor in case Fox didn't approve Paul," said Segal. "'Who is it?' she asked. 'Harry Van Gorkum,' I said. 'Harry *who?*' she said."[13] In fact, the unknown Van Gorkum was a political move against Fox, one designed to underscore the need to hire McGann before they had to fall back on someone like... well, Harry Who. (British-born Van Gorkum went on to a serviceable career in supporting roles in a bevy of US TV dramas and Hollywood films, including *Batman and Robin*, *The Foreigner* with Steven Segal, *Tears of the Sun* with Bruce Willis and *Avenging Angelo* with Sylvester Stallone. He wasn't bothered about the money – just as long as the projects had integrity.)

In the end, it was a combination of Trevor Walton's British passport and the promise of a big name American star as the villain that eventually persuaded Fox to agree to McGann. That villain was the Master, and that big name star was... Eric Roberts. In the 80s, Roberts had earned himself both Oscar and Golden Globe nominations, but in recent years had made more headlines for his drug-fuelled antics, which included trying to assault a police officer and, in February 1995, shoving his wife into a wall. But a big name was what they needed and, luckily for Roberts, that name happened to belong to his sister, Julia.

"The name was more important than whether they'd make a great villain," said Segal.[3] And so the deal was done. (Segal had actually wanted to approach Christopher Lloyd, but Universal said he wanted too much money. So they went with Roberts – who turned out to be more expensive than Lloyd. Go figure.)

And so, over Christmas, Segal and Jo Wright got their man, as Paul McGann signed on for the lead role. More than six years after first approaching the BBC, Philip Segal finally had his Doctor. Which was handy, as the film started shooting in less than three weeks.

The eighth Doctor: keep your hair on

By the time Paul McGann – at 36, the youngest Doctor since Peter Davison – was announced as the new Doctor, he was already in rehearsals in Vancouver. And, while all the talk in the British press was of *Doctor Who* going "glossy" and "big budget" (which, of course, by BBC standards it was), it's reassuring to know the five-week shoot was just like old times – lurching from one crisis to another in an atmosphere of barely controlled chaos.

For a start, the Canadian dollar was on the rise, and director Geoffrey Sax – a Brit (natch) who had cut his teeth on the likes of *The Cannon and Ball Show* (as well as some comedies) – found the number of allocated shooting days being whittled away by Universal's accountants, who were proving extremely slippery to pin down on the exact figure they were prepared to put into the film. To add to the problems, Matthew Jacobs' script was still being kicked around between interested parties like a football ("Don't you mean a soccer ball?" said Fox), with no-one able to agree on how the story should actually finish.

"The script was okay, but the ending still wasn't right," said Jo Wright. "We didn't really know how it was going to end."[3]

Jacobs estimated that 60-70% of the finished script was what he'd intended. "Then it all starts to unravel a bit, because everyone wanted different things."[3] "No-one was quite satisfied with what was going on," said Alan

Yentob. "It had potential for a revival, but it needed creative leadership."[3]

"It was less about me having a creative role by this point than about me being a referee stuck in the middle of it,"[3] admitted Philip Segal. On top of all that, the producer also found himself with a very nervous star. "Paul was scared out of his mind on day one," said Segal. "It turned out to be a very difficult day because he had to find the character. But Geoff calmed him down – he was a very calming influence."[3]

McGann's hair – or, rather, the lack of it – was also an issue. The last time Segal had seen him, the actor had sported long, wavy locks. Since then, though, he'd filmed a Gulf War drama in which he played an SAS officer – so arrived in Canada with a crewcut. "I was really angry," recalled Segal. "[Long hair] had really suited his face – it was the one feature of his I thought we could take advantage of. Now I see him standing in front of me and he's practically bald."[13]

McGann suggested simply playing it with short hair, but Segal was having none of it. So a stylist was dispatched to run up two curly wigs at a cost of $5,000 each. Meanwhile, Eric Roberts had a few wardrobe issues of his own: Segal had originally envisaged the Master wearing something close to Roger Delgado's Nehru suit, but Roberts claimed the costume was too uncomfortable, so opted for a long leather coat instead. Then, after filming a number of scenes wearing a pair of special phosphorescent contact lenses, he declared they were making his eyes water so, to avoid a continuity error, spent the rest of the film in dark glasses, looking less like a gentleman Time Lord than the Terminator. Finally, the prosthetics that were to be applied to his face to represent the Master physically decaying over the course of the film brought him out in a rash, so the whole idea had to be abandoned. They probably had to cut the itchy label out of his underpants too.

With costs mounting and the number of days Universal was prepared to bankroll shrinking fast, the shoot started to fall behind schedule. Even better, the script was still being rewritten on the hoof, with the climactic showdown between good and evil only amounting to six words: "Does anyone know what happens next?" (Not really, it was actually shorter than that: "The Doctor and the Master fight.")

Sax eventually brought the production in in 29 days – one less than he had originally planned, but still amounting to a £170,000 overspend that Universal tried to blame on the BBC. As a bellwether for future Anglo-American co-productions, it wasn't looking at all healthy.

The film then entered a hurried period of post-production before its scheduled May transmission while, back in Britain (where things move much more slowly and everything is still in black and white), *The Ghosts of N-Space* finally appeared on BBC Radio 2 – a full year after it was originally supposed to have aired.

Still, better late than never. That's what the producers of the non-existent *Doctor Who* feature film would have argued as, in 1996, the press reported around 20 investors in the Daltenreys consortium were launching a multi-million pound lawsuit against the BBC for "abruptly terminating" their contract to make the movie. These included art-rock lounge lizard Bryan Ferry and John Illsey, the bassist in Dire Straits – in more ways than one, since he'd ploughed $155,000 dollars into the venture. Talk about Money For Nothing.

In April, Philip Segal attended the Manopticon convention in Manchester, where he teased fans with a demo of the re-worked theme tune. Also that month, there was a chance to get another sneak peek at the upcoming movie when Bill Baggs released *Bidding Adieu*, a video diary recorded on location in Vancouver by Sylvester McCoy. If he'd been pushing his luck with The Stranger, here Baggs was really going out on a limb. "Bill rang me up and asked me if I wanted to go to Canada and cover the TV movie illegally," recalled Mark Gatiss, who served as interviewer and sometime cameraman. "We were in the strange position of Sylvester giving it his total blessing, but at the same time it was like some guerrilla operation. There were these strange negotiations going on between Sylvester and Paul about whether he would do an interview for the video. They were old friends, of course, and eventually he just said yes. It just happened one day."[17]

The film received its first official press screening at the Director's Guild in Los Angeles – the *Doctor Who* film, that is; Bill Baggs hadn't suddenly become a big Hollywood player – on May 8th, ahead of its debut on Fox on the 14th (though some Canadian stations actually showed it earlier). In Britain, it was scheduled for broadcast on Bank Holiday Monday, May 27th – before which it would be made available on BBC Video, thus giving ~~them a chance to fleece the fans for a tenner~~ devoted followers an exclusive chance to see the film before the rest of the country.

However, in the wake of the recent shooting tragedy at Dunblane Primary School in Scotland, the BBC wanted to make various cuts to the broadcast version; BBC Worldwide, meanwhile, planned to put out the Fox version – with a 15 certificate, no less – until the British Board of Film Censors stepped in and insisted both BBC versions had to be the same. The video was subsequently recalled for editing and the finished product, now re-classified as a 12, didn't hit the shelves until much closer to the TV transmission date, which had a significant impact on sales. Gary Russell's novelisation also appeared in the shops, along with a script book and a special issue of *Doctor Who Magazine*. Not exactly *Star Wars* levels of merchandise, but it was a start.

As excitement mounted, the DWAS celebrated its 20th anniversary with a special event in London, and Jon Pertwee appeared on Radio 4 discussing *Doctor Who's* enduring appeal. In recent weeks, the third Doctor had been at his most prolific for years: as well as starring in *The Ghosts of N-Space*, he had appeared on ITV wish-fulfilment show *Surprise, Surprise* presenting a Dalek to a young fan, taken part in a reunion with the cast of *The Daemons* at Aldbourne, filmed an advert in character as the Doctor for Vodafone, and completed his second autobiography, this time focussing solely on his *Who* years. So it was a huge shock when fans learned that, on May 20th, Pertwee had suffered a fatal heart attack while on holiday in Connecticut. He was 76.

The old showman would no doubt have been delighted with the ensuing news frenzy, as friends and colleagues lined up to pay tribute. "I can definitely say I was in the company of a great man", Sylvester McCoy – listed, rather touchingly, as "friend" – told one TV news crew. "Children and fellow actors alike found him delightful", said the BBC reporter on that evening's main news bulletin. "His fame never bothered him – he found it fun and funny to be fashionable. No more than a just reward for one of the country's most entertaining character actors." But it was *The Independent* which perhaps summed up the mood best when it stated simply: "It is hard to remember a time when Jon Pertwee was not on the airwaves, doing funny voices or pulling silly faces." It's true: Jon Pertwee – the Doctor Who who never stopped being Doctor Who – had been such a fixture of British life for so long, it was possible we had started to take him for granted. But when he died, a small part of millions of childhoods died with him. And that's no tall story.

Earth girls are easy?

"He's back – and it's about time!" trumpeted the publicity for the TV movie in May 1996, the BBC conveniently forgetting who it was that had kept everyone waiting so long in the first place. The film generated a lot of coverage in the UK media – despite Paul McGann, still nursing a grudge over a trumped-up story about a supposed relationship with a former A-list co-star, refusing to talk to certain sections of the British press. The *Radio Times* came with a 16-page pull-out guide to the film, and it even made the front of its downmarket rival, *TV Times* (which, despite the recent deregulation in the listings market, still generally acted as a cheerleader for ITV – hence the "downmarket").

The film, which had the official title of (wait for it) *Doctor Who*, was scheduled at 8.30pm on the bank holiday Monday – a sign, perhaps, of how the show was now viewed as having as much appeal for adults (or sci-fi weirdos, anyway) as children.

That's assuming it would appeal to *anyone*. Alan Yentob knew he was taking a big risk resurrecting a property his predecessors had written off as a busted flush. Add to that the high wire act of trying to please two audiences – one that had grown up with it, one that had never heard of it – and the endless script problems, and the potential for disaster was huge.

In the end, it wasn't a disaster – more than

nine million people tuned in to BBC1 to watch it – but it wasn't entirely successful, either. The film looks terrific: Geoffrey Sax does a great job of putting the money up there on screen and, while familiarity may have blunted its appeal, the new TARDIS interior was stunning at the time. A huge Gothic vault in the Heath Robinson / Jules Verne mode, it's the perfect home for McGann's Byronic new Doctor (Regency fop curls not model's own).

Except, when we first see him in it, he still looks like Sylvester McCoy, who has mercifully ditched that sodding jumper in favour of a tweed suit and velvet waistcoat number, and now spends his evenings reading HG Wells and listening to jazz records while surrounded by the contents of a *Doctor Who* convention dealers' room (sonic screwdriver, recorder, jelly babies – all that's missing is a K-9 plushy).

Our hero is carrying the Master's remains back to Gallifrey following his execution by the Daleks on Skaro (we know all this from the hastily added pre-titles voiceover info-dump), but the Master escapes by turning his mortal remains into a string of angry snot that forces a crash-landing in San Francisco. Here, the seventh Doctor demonstrates he's let his godlike cosmic chess player skills get a bit rusty by stepping out straight into a hail of bullets. Transferred to the local hospital, he is then finished off by cardiologist "Amazing" Grace Holloway, who clearly flunked her Time Lord physiognomy module. (Sylvester McCoy even gets a couple of lines just before he carks it – no doubt someone removed this page from Alan Yentob's copy of the script.)

Placed in the mortuary, the Doctor regenerates on the slab – bizarrely, given the $5 million budget, this is largely achieved by having McCoy and McGann compete in a comedy gurning competition – before the new Doctor kicks his way out of the freezer in a bedsheet looking like a cross between Jesus Christ and the Hulk. (There's something of a Messianic vibe to the film generally, which ends with the Master – who had previously manifested as a serpent – preparing the Doctor for his death with a hi-tech crown of thorns. Then again, given that regeneration is essentially about death and resurrection – albeit with more gurning – maybe the real surprise is no-one had ever made the allusion before.)

The Doctor then spends the next third of the movie trying to remember who he is, meaning we don't get to see him being properly... well, *Doctorish* until the last half-hour – exactly the point Matthew Jacobs' script gives way to story-by-committee, and the whole thing turns to soup. Which is a real shame because, if there's one thing everyone can agree on about the TV movie, it's that McGann is excellent: impish, impulsive and romantic on the one hand; serious, authoritative and noble on the other; he really makes those precious minutes count.

Actually, there's another thing most people can agree on, and that's Eric Roberts, who is truly dreadful as the Master (or, technically, as an ambulance driver called Bruce whose body is possessed by the snot-Master). Roberts has clearly decided camping it up is the only way to get through this weird British nonsense, but by the time he slips into his enormous Time Lord robes and starts voguing on the stairs (having declared "I always dressszzzz for the occasion"), you can't help wondering where Krystle and Alexis have got to. And this is the man who, half-an-hour earlier, had casually snapped Bruce's wife's neck (the luckless victim was played by Roberts' own wife, Eliza Garrett, which you might think is somewhat close to the bone, given recent events): it's like being asked to believe in Danny La Rue as a cold-blooded killer. Still, if nothing else, it's reassuring to know the Master's plans are just as useless as ever and that, once again, he's forgotten to find a way off the planet before he blows it up. Though, to be fair, expecting intelligent reasoning from the contents of a hankie is a big ask. (Said cataclysm is scheduled – rather conveniently – for midnight on New Year's Eve, 1999. That's midnight Pacific Standard Time, apparently, though it hardly matters, as the Millennium seems to arrive at the same moment across the world.)

After a relatively uncontroversial first half, the film gradually starts piling on the heresies. The Doctor giving Grace a smacker on the lips upset some fans, who didn't like the idea of their largely asexual hero taking an interest in, you know, all *that*. A motorbike chase on the freeway was also an Americanisation too far for some, though the use of the Pertwee-era logo – and the poignant on-screen dedication of the film to him (for UK viewers, at least) – is a reminder that this isn't *entirely* new territory. The ending, in which Grace and slightly pointless fifth-wheel extra sidekick Chang Lee (Yee Jee Tso) die, but then get brought back to life with a big temporal re-set button, is also rightly derided as a massive cop-out.

But, for many, the most controversial aspect of the TV movie is its assertion that the Doctor is half-human ("on my mother's side"). This upset a lot of people at the time – more because it contradicts received wisdom than any anger about bloody Gallifreyans coming over here and shagging or women – but, unfortunate Mr Spock parallels aside, it's not actually a *terrible* idea. You'd expect the Time Lord to bring the dominant gene to the party, which would explain why the Doctor's always considered himself an alien among us, and offers a credible motivation for his eternal fascination with our little blue galactic backwater. But it doesn't seem to be a popular notion with anyone who cares about this stuff. Then again, intergalactic mating between species is nothing compared to trying to pull off the trick of being half-British, half-American, as this strange, well-meaning but ultimately doomed experiment of a film is testament.

In Britain, the healthy ratings showed there was still a ready-made audience for *Doctor Who*. In the US, however, the film's 8.3 million viewers only gave Fox a 9% share against a brace of hit sitcoms, including *Home Improvement*, *Frasier*, *3rd Rock from the Sun* and, most damagingly, the *Roseanne* season finale in which John Goodman's Dan had a heart attack. Not that Fox had exactly killed themselves promoting it, and what publicity they did seemed misguided. The official poster foregrounded Eric Roberts, with Paul McGann peering over his shoulder in a strange echo of that *Terror of the Autons Radio Times* cover all those years ago, while the network's trailers spliced in footage of 1986's much-derided *The Trial of a Time Lord* – surely the ultimate proof that these people really didn't understand *anything* about *Doctor Who*.

The film received a largely positive response from US critics: "It manages to pull off action, wit, irony, comedy, suspense, special effects and wordplay at 90mph and still feel thoughtful," said *The New York Post*, while *The Hollywood Reporter* hailed it "one of the kickest broadcasts to hit the screen this sweeps season". (At least I *think* that's a positive review – perhaps American readers could clarify?)

Despite the movie's success back home, it was British critics who proved to be more sceptical. "In selling *Doctor Who* to the Americans (technically 'making a co-production with, but in reality flogging it to them') the Beeb has fatally wounded what would, in the hands of a sensible TV company, be a priceless asset," wrote Matthew Norman in the *London Evening Standard*. "To Americans, ignorant of the show, it must have been a baffling irrelevance, while for nostalgic fans here and through the Commonwealth, the sound of Ron Grainer's sublime theme tune emasculated by strings, and the sight of the Doctor snogging in San Francisco, was heresy."

"This film, despite a big budget and accomplished special effects, couldn't scare, or much divert, a little child," grumbled Stuart Jeffries in *The Guardian*, while the *Daily Mail*'s Max Davidson claimed the movie was "like a bad memory of childhood", adding: "I thought this absurdly inflated character had achieved his final resting place as a line in a knock-knock joke. Seeing the TARDIS again, in a vulgar American reincarnation, was too depressing for words. Do we never grow up?" (Note to non-UK readers: there's a reason the paper is commonly known as the *Hate Mail*.)

Paul McGann, though, was widely praised. Sort of. "He has the perfect touch," claimed Serena Mackesy in *The Independent*. "The part requires a theatricality and ability to ham it up that has become rare in this era of naturalism and method." On second thoughts, maybe he wouldn't put that on his résumé. *The Sun*'s Stafford Hildred, meanwhile, managed to insult everyone – including the guy he was supposedly acclaiming: "No doubt fanatical *Doctor Who* followers will hate the new Doctor for some nerdy, nitpicking reason," he schmoozed, charmingly, "but to me, Paul McGann seemed every bit as twittish as the previous Doctors – a happy return for a TV hero." Thanks for that, Stafford: you're only one vowel away from being a bit of a twit yourself.

A couple of months later, the *Daily Mirror* reported that the film's lack of success in America had killed any chance of the new *Who*

going to a series, and that the BBC were finally closing the door on *Doctor Who* – for good. That wasn't strictly true – though Fox was now out of the picture, Universal did request an extension of its agreement until the end of 1997, but, in the end, nothing came of it, and Paul McGann's claim that "I don't want to be remembered as the George Lazenby of *Doctor Who*" began to look increasingly optimistic.

Whether the film would prove to be the final nail in *Doctor Who*'s coffin, however, was a moot point. Clearly, for many at the BBC, it was a case of once bitten, twice shy. But, at the same time, the film had also shown that the British public's love affair with the badly-dressed bloke in the police box wasn't quite over yet. "It brought *Doctor Who* back into people's minds," said Jo Wright. "It showed there was an appetite for it again. Because people weren't sure there was."[3]

For Philip Segal, having his backdoor pilot slammed in his face was a bitter blow. But, unlike so many others – from Tom Baker's attempt to launch a *Doctor Who* feature film in the mid-70s to Green Light's disastrous assault on Hollywood's ramparts, not to mention *The Dark Dimension* debacle, the animated series and numerous other roads not taken – Segal had, at least, got the damn thing made. "To me that was the most successful thing,"[3] he admitted. "I was able to look at myself in the mirror and say, 'Okay see – you spent some years getting something done'. To me, it's a highlight of my career, and I think it stands as a testament to anybody in this business who has a passion project. It doesn't matter what it is – if you believe in it, if you make it about the passion, it will happen. It will happen."[3]

Doctor Who disqualified from popular vote on account of popularity

Even as they watched the chances of a new series vanishing over the event horizon, BBC Worldwide set about re-branding *Doctor Who* as a going concern. (Well, what else did they have? *Bugs*?) The Pertwee/movie logo started appearing on everything from video releases to new merchandise lines (including, thrillingly, a *Doctor Who* insert for your filofax – perfect for making yourself look like a dick twice over at your next budget meeting), and the BBC belatedly decided there was money to be made from publishing original *Doctor Who* novels, so gave notice to Virgin that their licence would not be renewed. "It was a real blow," admitted Peter Darvill-Evans. "It was a blow to me, it was a blow to my staff, it was a blow to Virgin Publishing as a company."[2]

Virgin's final book – and its only adventure featuring the eighth Doctor, *The Dying Days* – was scheduled for the following spring, after which BBC Books would pick up the reigns with *The Eight Doctors*, written by (who else?) Terrance Dicks. While other authors continued the adventures of the McGann Doctor, there would also be a range of past Doctor novels, kicking off with third Doctor caper *The Devil Goblins of Neptune* by Keith Topping and Martin Day. So, basically, they just carried on with what Virgin had been doing.

"The BBC never valued *Doctor Who*, which is why they farmed it out," said Dicks. "But they realised, in 1996, that Virgin were doing two novels a month, and making money from it, so they cheerfully stole back the whole procedure, lock, stock and barrel!"[18] Virgin, meanwhile, carried on The New Adventures with Professor Bernice Summerfield as the lead for a couple of years afterwards. "But you can't publish *Doctor Who* without the Doctor," Darvill-Evans concluded. "It doesn't work."[2]

In September, a fire with a highly developed sense of symbolism broke out and destroyed part of the *Doctor Who* exhibition at Longleat. The following month, BBC Broadcasting chief exec Will Wyatt was attending a Conservative Party dinner when Tory Parliamentary candidate and avid *Who* fan Tim Collins put him on the spot about the show's future. Wyatt blustered that the TV film had "not been right for the audience we hoped to attract" – apparently forgetting it had been a ratings hit – before concluding there would be no more *Doctor Who* because "we can't afford it". Still, that's what you get for stuffing the BBC with a load of raving pinkos, what what?

Meanwhile, Virgin continued working out its notice with the publication of *Damaged Goods*, a New Adventure from fast-rising television writer Russell T Davies. Davies' lifelong love of *Doctor Who* had manifested itself in various forms over the years, from the sublime (the acclaimed Children's BBC fantasy serials *Dark Season* – featuring a young Kate Winslet, no less – and *Century Falls*) to the ridiculous (dressing up as a Cyberman while producing school holiday staple *Why Don't You?*).

"I'd planned three months to write it, but then I got two big ITV commissions at the same time, so it turned into a nightmare," recalled Davies. "I barely slept for five weeks, bashing out that book – and it shows."[19] Granada Television were so anxious for Davies to meet his script deadlines, they lent him a researcher for the book – though, sadly, the budget didn't stretch to actually sending her into space. (Not that it would have helped – most of the novel is set on a run-down council estate full of smackheads. Keep reading for why this is significant.)

After the disappointment of the earlier false dawn, *Doctor Who* managed to end the year on something of a high when the show was voted the BBC's "all-time favourite drama" at Auntie's All-Time Greats, a special televised awards ceremony to celebrate the Corporation's 60th anniversary. Naturally, Auntie was mortified: instead of their flagship soap *EastEnders*, or acclaimed, BAFTA-hoovering serials like *I, Claudius*, *Boys from the Blackstuff* and *Tinker, Tailor, Soldier, Spy*, the idiot British public had only gone and voted for *Doctor sodding Who* – the very programme they kept telling people no-one liked any more. And as if that wasn't bad enough for Alan Yentob – on whose channel the whole shebang was being screened – who did the honours of going up to collect the award? Peter Davison – and Sylvester bleeding McCoy!

Disappointingly, both the press and the BBC chose to put the result down to a concerted campaign by hardcore fans – effectively accusing them of vote-rigging, even though the voting mechanism had been specifically designed to weed this out. The Beeb put out a press release stating that, while they "do appreciate the strength of affection of the programme's followers", in the "current financial climate, we have to try and stretch the resources we have to meet the interests of as many viewers as possible. For this reason, it is unlikely that the BBC will be producing new *Doctor Who* stories in-house in the foreseeable future." In other words, it was back to Square One. Or possibly even Square None.

But maybe, just maybe, there was a chink of hope, as Fox had scheduled a re-run of the TV movie for New Year's Eve. If enough people watched it this time around, then surely they would realise what a golden goose they had on their hands and maybe, just maybe...?

Sadly, at the last-minute, the network cancelled the repeat showing. Its replacement? *Revenge of the Nerds IV*. They really knew how to kick a Time Lord when he was down.

1997: nothing to see here

In August 1997, an American animation studio called Default Films approached the BBC about a possible new *Doctor Who* cartoon. The studio claimed to have Barry Letts on board as consultant but, after 15 crayon pictures were displayed at a US convention, nothing was ever heard on the subject again. (Though the crayon pictures were very nice – they'd stayed inside the lines and everything. Perhaps they ended up on Letts' fridge?)

The following month, the fourth Doctor embarked on a nationwide tour of 50 cities to promote his fantastically scabrous autobiography, *Who on Earth is Tom Baker?* The book was serialised in the *Daily Mail* under such licentious headlines as "She Lay on the Bed in My Dr Who Outfit and Growled 'Ok, Let's Travel Through Space'," which they had somehow decided would be more attention-grabbing than details of production problems on *Warriors' Gate*.

In December, the BBC released a Terrance Dicks-scripted computer game, *Destiny of the Doctors*, on CD-ROM (could it *be* any more 90s?). The game featured new audio contributions from all surviving Doctors, plus Nicholas Courtney, while Anthony Ainley reprised his Master one final time, appearing on-screen in a Gallifreyan get-up clearly designed to out-pimp that young upstart Eric Roberts.

And they were literally the most interesting things to happen to *Doctor Who* in 1997.

Doctor Who - The Movie (slight return)

A full two years after the broadcast of the TV movie, the first stirrings of renewed interest in *Doctor Who* were felt at the 1998 Cannes Film Festival when David Thompson, the head of BBC Films, appeared to suggest the Time Lord might be about to return in a new feature film. If you believed the press reports, the film was pretty much a done deal: it would have a budget of £12.5 million and a "politically correct" script (whatever that meant), including – this old chestnut again – the possibility of a female Doctor (presumably in a bid to combat the series' shamefully phallocentric agenda, or something).

A spokesman for BBC drama dismissed this as – and I quote – "total bollocks", adding: "It was never a statement – it was just an aside in a conversation blown into something it isn't. It's simply a gleam in the eye. We have had some preliminary discussions with a distributor, but I can't reveal who that is at the moment."[11] So perhaps not *total* bollocks, then.

A couple of months later, a rival project was mooted when Chaos Films announced it was chasing the rights to the unmade third Peter Cushing movie, based on the 1965 William Hartnell serial *The Chase*. (Philip Segal also had talks with the BBC about this around the same time – he really was like a dog with a bone when it came to this show.) The Hollywood superstar Chaos had in its sights for the project? Michael Sheard. Yes, *the* Michael Sheard – veteran of no fewer than six *Doctor Who* stories, but best known for playing tyrannical, toupéed deputy head Mr Bronson in *Grange Hill*. (For non-UK readers, he's the incompetent admiral who ends up feeling a bit choked in *The Empire Strikes Back* – hence the two volumes of his autobiography being called *Yes, Mr Bronson* and *Yes, Admiral*.) With a name like that attached, getting funding for the film was surely just a formality.

Meanwhile, prissy robot irritant K-9 was said to be sniffing out a comeback of his own in a show written by his co-creator Bob Baker – who had suddenly found himself hot property after the success of his Oscar-winning Wallace and Gromit collaborations with Nick

Park. Leaked images showed a CGI version of the metal mutt looking like a cross between a JCB and a vacuum cleaner, while the proposed series' tagline was "In space, there's only one top dog". Not if Gromit had anything to say about it, there wasn't.

The ninth Doctor (Part 1 of 3)

If *Children in Need* had been the cause that reunited the third, fourth, fifth, sixth and seventh Doctors, it took the power of Richard Curtis' international aid charity Comic Relief to pull off an even more surprising coup: bringing together the ninth, tenth, eleventh, twelfth *and* thirteenth Doctors.

For this, we can thank Sue Vertue, a producer of the BBC's 1999 Comic Relief telethon who, as well as being the daughter of Terry Nation's one-time agent (that's Beryl Vertue – not Roger Hancock), was married to the television writer and certified *Doctor Who* fanatic Steven Moffat.

Paisley-born Moffat had made his name with the acclaimed teen drama *Press Gang*, before going on to write the sitcoms *Joking Apart*, inspired by the breakdown of his first marriage (it's funnier than it sounds), and *Chalk*, inspired by his experiences as an English teacher. In the mid-90s, he'd also written "Continuity Errors", a well-regarded entry in a *Doctor Who* short story anthology published by Virgin, and was a regular fixture of the monthly *Who* fan gatherings at the Fitzroy Tavern in London.

When his wife suggested he write a *Doctor Who* sketch for Red Nose Day 1999, Moffat envisaged a two-minute bit of throwaway fluff but, as enthusiasm for the idea grew among the production team, he ended up writing more than 20 minutes of material, to run throughout the night in five and seven-minute mini-episodes.

Rowan Atkinson jumped at the chance to play the ninth Doctor, with *Press Gang*'s Julia Sawalha as his companion (and, indeed, fiancée) Emma, facing off against Jonathan Pryce's hysterical (in both senses of the word) Master. Moffat was adamant what he delivered should be a comic *Doctor Who* story, not a spoof. "The first rule was: absolutely no jokes about shaking sets, or wobbly monsters, or

crap acting, or any of those things,"[20] he said (though he did let one gag about quarries through). That means, instead of the usual rot about Daleks not being able to go up stairs, we have a script by someone immersed enough in *Who* lore to realise, for example, that the Master is utterly useless. "The Master is terrible!" said Moffat. "He doesn't notice that he always loses! He loses *catastrophically* on every single occasion that he meets the Doctor – and he's still saying, 'Ah, Doctor – you've foolishly got in the way of my fantastic plan!'"[20]

On the planet Tersurus ("planet of the bottom burps" – hey, no-one said it was Chekhov), the two Time Lords try to outwit each other by racing back in time and bribing the local architect to ignore the other's instructions. So the Master declares: "Say hello to The Spikes of Doom!", only for the Doctor to emerge from his trap on a two-seater settee with the Blackadderish riposte: "Say hello to The Sofa of Reasonable Comfort". And so on. (Comedy sketch or no comedy sketch, this is actually one of the few genuine attempts to exploit the potential of time paradoxes in the show's long history, and will become something of a Moffat trope when... oops, *spoilers!*) There is also a fantastic running gag in which the Master keeps falling down a hole, and has to spend 312 years climbing back out.

In fact, the whole of *The Curse of Fatal Death* – yes, even the title is a sly allusion to *The Deadly Assassin* – plays like an affectionate love letter to *Doctor Who*: a sentiment summed up by Emma's heartfelt description of the dying Doctor as "Too brave, too kind and far, far too silly... He was never cruel and never cowardly, and it'll never be safe to be scared again." Aaaw.

Of course, he doesn't die – he just regenerates. A lot. Once Atkinson's waspish Time Lord has felt the sharp end of a Dalek death ray, he transforms into Richard E Grant's narcissistic tenth Doctor, followed in rapid succession by a shy and bumbling Jim Broadbent, a dashing Hugh Grant and, finally, Joanna Lumley's saucy, jolly hockey-sticks take on the Time Lord.

According to Richard Curtis, attracting such a stellar cast was surprisingly easy. "Sometimes it's like pulling nails; this time it was like pulling a carrot. From soft earth. It's fun, and they get to wear a jacket... I know that Rowan, for instance, actually wanted to do *Doctor Who*. Hugh Grant thought it was a hoot, too. They were all very keen."[20]

With its star wattage, witty script and special effects and production values that, even ten years earlier, the show would have killed for, *The Curse of Fatal Death* is like the anti-*Dimensions in Time*: a celebration of the best of *Doctor Who*, and a reminder of why it matters. With boob jokes. What's not to love?

Even Hugh Grant, however, couldn't compete with the big news of 1999, when it was announced that *Doctor Who* – actual, bona fide *Doctor Who*, with the actual, bona fide Doctor – was back. And this time, it had to be heard to be believed.

That's right, so you couldn't actually *see* it. But when independent production company Big Finish won the rights to release BBC-licensed *Doctor Who* audio adventures on CD, it provided fans with a welcome chink of light in the gloom of the show's darkest days.

Big Finish had been formed by businessman Jason Haigh-Ellery and, as its producer, Gary Russell. A former child actor (he was Dick in ITV's take on *The Famous Five*), Russell had later edited *Doctor Who Magazine* and written numerous Virgin and BBC novels, including the TV Movie tie-in. In the 1980s, Russell had succeeded Bill Baggs as producer of an unlicensed series of audio stories starring fellow *Who* fan Nicholas Briggs as the Doctor. When he and Haigh-Ellery had initially approached BBC Worldwide with the idea of making official *Doctor Who* audio dramas, these creaking C90 cassettes with their hand-drawn, photocopied slip-cases probably hadn't been the most persuasive calling card. So the pair played a long game, going away and acquiring the rights to the Bernice Summerfield character, and producing a series of plays starring Lisa Bowerman (from TV swansong *Survival*) as the intergalactic archaeologist. It proved enough to convince the Beeb they knew what they were doing, and a deal was struck allowing Big Finish to produce new adventures featuring former Doctors, as long as they didn't try to continue the series beyond what had already been seen on screen. The BBC made it clear that, if anyone was going to do that, it was them. And they weren't going to.

Russell and Haigh-Ellery approached Tom Baker, Peter Davison, Colin Baker and Sylvester McCoy about reprising their roles, and all but one agreed. If you can't guess which was the odd one out, I refer you to the waxwork in a bin story from Volume I. "Tom has very definite ideas about how he should play the Doctor," said Russell. "Tom wants to do Tom, I think, rather than the fourth Doctor. Our principal belief with past Doctors is to provide reasonable facsimiles of their original television eras."[21]

The Other Baker was well up for it, though. "I'm much the same vocally – you can hardly tell the difference," said the sixth Doctor. "I may have sunk into decrepitude but, on audio, I'm still the lusty young male that I once was."[22] Crikey – let's hope he'd at least stopped biting people on the arse.

A meeting of potential writers was convened, attended by the likes of Marc Platt, Paul Cornell and Mark Gatiss (Steven Moffat excused himself early after learning Paul McGann wouldn't be available). It was here Russell announced that the first story, a team-up between all three Doctors called *The Sirens of Time*, would be written and directed by Nicholas Briggs – the Doctor himself from those 80s fan productions. Briggs had subsequently written, directed and acted in several of Bill Baggs' video productions, including The Stranger series and *The Airzone Solution*. But, unlike many in the room that day, he had never written for an "official" *Doctor Who* range. "Gary announced to all assembled that the reason I'd been commissioned was that he needed the scripts fast, and that he wanted to keep the information under wraps, so he had thought the best solution was to commission someone he knew he could trust," recalled Briggs. "There was a murmured groan around the room. No-one was pleased for me. I was really taken aback and disappointed by that lack of generosity. It was very uncomfortable for me."[23]

Despite this vote of no confidence, Briggs got down to the job in hand and, in the first week of March, Davison, Baker and McCoy entered the studios in Fulham to record the four-part story, which would see them starring in an episode apiece before joining forces for the finale. Several people on the production remarked how excited they were to be in the presence of their favourite Time Lord once again. ("Oh thank you, but I'm really just the writer on this," replied Briggs. In fact, Briggs also appears in the play, and did all the editing, sound design and even the incidental music. If you listen very carefully, you can probably hear him running the Hoover round in the background, too.)

By all accounts, there was a great rapport between the three Doctors – which is to say, being British, they ripped the piss out of each other mercilessly. "He *is* the seventh Doctor, isn't he?" asked Davison, when McCoy struggled to pronounce a difficult name. "He's not just someone who's wandered into the studio?"

Released in July, *The Sirens of Time* was snapped up by *Who*-starved fans, and further stories followed in regular succession, starting with Mark Gatiss' *Phantasmagoria*, a fifth Doctor and Turlough caper set in restoration London. Colin Baker made his solo debut battling a creature made of "pure sound" – talk about a great face for radio – in Justin Richards' *The Whispers of Terror*, co-starring Nicola Bryant as Peri, while the seventh Doctor and Ace channelled the spirit of Virgin's New Adventures by taking on both a scary monster and the political far right in Jonathan Blum's *The Fearmonger*.

More than 15 years on, all three Doctors remain Big Finish regulars, having appeared in countless more adventures than they ever chalked up on TV. (Well, you *could* count them – but, honestly, there are, like, *loads*.)

But what of *Doctor Who* with pictures and stuff? After three years of near-total silence, some fans were starting to look back wistfully on the early 90s as a positive purple patch: at least back then, someone had usually been talking about making new *Doctor Who*, while the BBC had spent a considerable amount of time talking about not making it. Now, they couldn't even be bothered to do that. But in mid-1999, the rumour mill suddenly cranked up again with a vengeance. First up, there were whispers that Russell T Davies, whose forthcoming Channel 4 drama *Queer as Folk* was creating a buzz across the industry, was being courted by the BBC – with *Doctor Who* as one of the prize carrots in the patch. "I went in there knowing more about the *Doctor Who*

situation than they did", Davies recalled some years later. "'There's a film in development with BBC Films,' I said, and they were like, 'No no, we'll sort it out'. Two weeks later, they phoned me up and went 'Oh you're right', so it died a death. I never even wrote a side of A4."[24]

The film in question was a proposed collaboration between BBC Films and Impact Pictures, the company formed by Paul WS Anderson, director of such cinematic high watermarks as *Mortal Kombat*, *Resident Evil* and *Event Horizon*. The Beeb confirmed the project was at "an early stage of development", while Gary Oldman threw his hat into the ring for the lead, saying he'd do it "if the money and the script were right". Well, at least he was honest about his priorities. According to the papers, however, Denzel Washington was top of the producers' list, with Anderson's partner at Impact, Jeremy Bolt, stating: "*Doctor Who* needs to be reinvented for a global audience, and that means casting an international name in the lead role." Translation: "That means casting an American in the lead role."

By September, Artisan – the studio behind that year's surprise film phenomenon, *The Blair Witch Project*, were also reported to be in on the deal. "We intend to make this bigger than Bond," said Bolt, while the BBC insisted "the script will be witty, suspenseful and very English". Patrick Stewart and Linus Roache were briefly touted as potential Time Lords, though how they'd gone from Denzel Washington to Ken Barlow's son in less than two months is a mystery. In November, Bolt confirmed the Master would be in the movie, which "will be new and contemporary without patronising either the new or the old audience". Tom Baker was less convinced, telling *SFX* magazine: "I don't see how Hollywood can do anything else but fuck it up, can you?"[11]

On Saturday, November 13th, Baker was in less potty-mouthed – but no less potty – form as the anchor of BBC2's *Doctor Who Night*, an evening of specially-recorded documentaries, sketches and archive stories (well, one episode of *The Daleks* and the TV Movie, anyway). It's not clear whether Baker, presenting from deep within the bowels of the TARDIS, is supposed to be playing himself or the Doctor ("I'm called Paul McGann in this one"), but as there's no real difference anyway, it hardly matters.

The undoubted highlights of the night were the comic interludes written by Mark Gatiss – fast becoming a major comedy star as one quarter of The League of Gentlemen, whose fabulously grotesque sitcom had made its TV debut earlier in the year – and co-starring fellow comedian and *Who* fan David Walliams. In "The Pitch of Fear," Walliams plays a version of Sydney Newman, selling the idea for Dr Who to his BBC boss, Mr Borusa. ("Basically, it's about a man who can travel anywhere in space and time." "Game show, is it?") "The Web of Caves," meanwhile, is a brilliantly realised pastiche of 60s *Who*, in which Gatiss finally achieves his dream of playing the Doctor, irritably trying to get rid of Walliams' hilariously ineffectual villain. (Actual dialogue: "I shall drain the world's oceans into the Earth's white hot molten core and boil them away!" "What for?" "Power!" "Power over what?" "The sea!" "When's all this likely to happen?" "Soon, Time Lord!" "Well when?" "Monday!" "You know it's a bank holiday?" "Tuesday!") Finally, in "The Kidnappers," Walliams drags a bound and gagged Peter Davison into Gatiss' bedroom ("Don't ask him about *Doctor Who*, everyone asks him about *Doctor Who*, he's going to think you're a right nutcase! Ask him about his theatre work, or composing the theme to *Button Moon*.") – a skit that culminates in the immortal line: "David, do you think it would be alright to... kiss Peter?" Cue lights out, and the sound of the tape on Davison's mouth being ripped off.

"We kept our own names for the characters," explained Gatiss, "because, give or take a prosthetic belly, it really is us. It's entirely a comment on our own madness. It's about that element of fandom that we all know and enjoy – that business of being slightly *too* keen."[25] Nope – absolutely no idea what he means.

Despite being treated as a cult concern on the BBC's second channel, *Doctor Who Night* still made the cover of that week's *Radio Times*, which reproduced a dramatic portrait of a Dalek originally used for a commemorative Royal Mail stamp issued a few months earlier. The image, one of a series of British icons commissioned by the Royal Mail to mark the Millennium, was photographed by Lord Snowdon, aka Antony Charles Robert Armstrong-Jones, 1st Earl of Snowdon; his previous subjects had included Laurence Olivier, Agatha Christie, Tony Blair and his own sister-in-law, Her Majesty the Queen – but no-one quite as famous as *this*.

Sadly, while the Royal Mail may have rated the Daleks as one of the great icons of the last thousand years, *Doctor Who* was about to enter the new Millennium with no prospect of a revival: in December, it was announced that the latest movie deal had collapsed. Again. "I worked for six months on this, brought the BBC the most exciting film company in the world, and they decide not to go with it," a frustrated Jeremy Bolt told *SFX*. "To say that I am happy would not be the case. It'll take the BBC God knows how long to sort something else out. I really don't want to talk about it any more."[11]

That, at least, was something he and the BBC could agree on.

Stephen Fry hot favourite to be bookies' hot favourite

The twenty-first century kicked off in surprising fashion with the straight out-of-left-field news that *Doctor Who* was returning to the BBC – starring Sylvester McCoy. And the *really* surprising bit? It wasn't just a feverish dream on the part of McCoy's agent, or Alan Yentob suffering from night terrors; this really was happening. Sort of. Radio 4 had commissioned a pilot for a possible new *Who* serial after being approached by Dan Freedman, a radio producer friend of Sophie Aldred who had been introduced to McCoy at the Edinburgh Festival.

With the first few stories having flown off the shelves – or out of cardboard boxes, anyway – Big Finish started releasing a new play every month from January, and scored something of a coup by securing the rights to use the Daleks. The metal mentalists were voiced by – who else? – Nicholas Briggs. ("Would you mind bringing the Dalek plunger into the studio with you?" asked his bosses. "Do you think we'll really need them for an audio production?" asked Briggs. "Oh it's not for the story – I need you to unblock the sink.") Numerous ex-companions also joined the growing rep company, including Lalla Ward, Bonnie Langford and Nick Courtney – the latter finally getting to share a proper story with Colin Baker's sixth Doctor.

Meanwhile, for those old-skool fans who still hankered after *Doctor Who* in the corner of their living rooms, Russell T Davies announced he'd been "told to wait a little longer". ("That's fine," said the fans, "we've waited this long – take all week if you have to.") Sadly, the BBC's latest statement, issued in May, suggested the wait might be somewhat longer: "The series remains in the same position as it was in 1989 when production ceased," it reported, glumly. "Nothing is cut and dried as far as this series is concerned. We appreciate that the 1996 movie was a long time coming but it may well be that there will be more of the Doctor in the future. What we cannot do is make any promises about the programme at present. If there is more to say our first action would be to issue a press release to that effect." In other words: "Stop bloody asking us about *Doctor* bloody *Who*! This press release for *Castaway* won't write itself, you know."

But if they hoped the story would eventually go away, they were going to be very disappointed. That summer, the tabloid casting carousel took another spin, with *The Sun* claiming Stephen Fry had been chosen as the new Doctor, while its Sunday sister, *The News of the World*, insisted moustachioed medallion man Tom Selleck had got the gig. Though quite what either of them would actually be appearing *in* wasn't clear: A film? A new TV series? A new series of Weetabix cards?

In retrospect, it's easy to see where the Stephen Fry confusion might have arisen, as Britain's favourite corduroy-sporting cleverclogs had, in fact, been cast in Dan Freedman's radio pilot, playing a donnish Time Lord called the Minister of Chance. "Let's be frank, Gallifrey is an English planet," Fry told *Doctor Who Magazine*. "There's something peculiarly English about the Doctor and I think in that sense, about the Minister as well."[26] None of which explained why some people thought he was about to turn into Magnum P.I.

October's Big Finish release, *The Shadow of the Scourge*, was advertised as "a side-step into Virgin territory", reuniting the TARDIS crew of '92 by teaming the seventh Doctor and Ace up with Lisa Bowerman's Bernice Summerfield. "It's been my life's ambition as a writer to fur-

nish lines for Sylvester McCoy's Doctor Who,"[27] said scripter Paul Cornell.

By November, bookmakers Ladbrokes were offering odds of 4/5 on Stephen Fry being the "next" Doctor, with *Jonathan Creek* star Alan Davies second favourite at 4/1. Footballer Gary Lineker was a lowly 100/1 but, in reality, had as much chance as anyone *since no-one was actually making Doctor Who any more anyway.*

And then, just when keeping up with who was, who wasn't, who might be and who definitely wasn't playing Doctor Who was starting to require the use of a spreadsheet, Big Finish suddenly announced it had signed a deal with Paul McGann to return as the eighth Doctor in a new series of audios the following year.

McGann claimed not to be surprised at finding himself back in the *Who* fold. "It's a job for life, isn't it?" he said. "I knew that when I originally signed up."[24] But Jason Haigh-Ellery admitted the star had taken some convincing, claiming "he was frightened that we'd turn out to be a bunch of enthusiasts with a cassette recorder". Which obviously they weren't. They were a bunch of enthusiasts with a CD recorder. Once discussions were under way, however, it was McGann who impressed the Big Finish team with his "sheer enthusiasm". "Which we honestly weren't expecting," admitted Haigh-Ellery. "Paul had never been obviously pro-*Who*."[21] Oh I don't know – I think you can read too much into someone saying they repeatedly turned down a part because they thought it would make them look like a complete tosser.

2001: a cyberspace odyssey

In 2001, the tabloids restrained themselves for a whole three days before starting a new game of Time Lord casting bingo: on January 4th, the *Mirror* "announced" that rugged slice of Sheffield steel Sean Bean had been cast in "a £250 million British film version of the sci-fi classic". Putting aside the fact this would have made it the most expensive film ever made – even *Titanic* came in at £50 million less than that – the paper went on to "reveal" that Tara Fitzgerald would play the companion, and that shooting was set to begin at Pinewood Studios in the spring. You had to hand it to them: it might have been a crock of absolute horseshit, but it was very *specific* horseshit. Then, three weeks later, blowhard BBC Films boss David Thompson was at it again, claiming: "We are talking to a famous American director and hope to be able to announce his name in the next few months." Barry Sonnenfeld was thought to be the name in question, with Kevin Kline tipped to star. You will stop me if this is getting boring, won't you?

In March, the BBC rejected Dan Freedman's *Doctor Who* radio pilot, *Death Comes to Time*, with the constructive feedback that they "didn't like anything about it". Well at least it gave them something to build on. The thorny issue of the film rights was also cited as a reason. "Trying to get *Doctor Who* off the ground is like trying to get in through the battlements of a castle," said Freedman. "You've got to wait until one of the guards on the wall has a bad prostate and goes for a piss long enough for your army to attack."[27] Whether this only applies to *Doctor Who* we can't be sure, but it would certainly explain how *Crime Traveller*[1] got commissioned.

While the seventh Doctor waited for the tell-tale tinkle of opportunity, the eighth was enjoying a new lease of life in his first series of audio adventures, teaming up with plucky 1930s adventuress Charlotte "Charley" Pollard, played by India Fisher (now best known as the voice of *MasterChef*, in which she describes recipes for Mauritian octopus salad and langoustine consommé in the style of a telephone sex line).

"The Doctor in these audios is rather more skittish, light-hearted, knockabout," explained McGann. "It's more like his more manic, camper second cousin who's nicked his mantle and gone off round the universe."[28] It speaks volumes about McGann's knowledge of the *Doctor Who* universe that his playful but measured performance could ever be described as "camp". God only knows how he'd describe *Time and the Rani*.

After making his debut in *Storm Warning* – an alien-encounter caper set aboard the doomed British airship R101 – the eighth Doctor went eyeball-to-eyehole with the Cybermen in *Sword of Orion*, which was written and directed by Nicholas Briggs. Who also played the Cybermen. Obviously.

A couple of releases later, Nick Courtney

was able to add another Doctor to his collection when he starred alongside McGann in *Minuet in Hell*, one of several re-makes of early Audio Visuals stories, except in this one Nicholas Briggs wasn't the Doctor (though he does appear as another character, Gideon Crane, who claims to *be* the Doctor). "I'm here to complete the set," announced Courtney. "I can't let the chance to work with another Doctor pass by!"[26] ("Okay," said Briggs, taking off his UNIT uniform and stick-on moustache. "But if for any reason you can't make it, you know where I am. Now, who's for more home-made flapjack?")

As fans hailed McGann's performance, the actor was already badgering Big Finish to do more (the fact that they'd agreed to record them close to his home in Bristol only added to his enthusiasm). In fact, though he may have had a screen life of barely an hour, McGann's Doctor was enjoying an afterlife few of his predecessors could have dreamed of: as well as the new audio adventures, he would eventually star in 73 BBC Eighth Doctor novels, and was the incumbent Time Lord in *Doctor Who Magazine*'s acclaimed comic strip for the best part of a decade. Not bad for the George Lazenby of *Doctor Who*.

Travelling to Bristol was one thing – but Big Finish drew the line at the demands Anthony Ainley made after they approached him to appear as the Master. "Money didn't really come into it", said Gary Russell. "He made demands that were impractical for a company of our size and turnover. They were not considerations that any other major-league *Doctor Who* actor has ever asked us for. We could have met him half-way, but he just wasn't interested."[21] Oh come on – was the blood of a first-born served in a panda's skull *so* unreasonable? (Geoffrey Beevers – aka Mr Caroline John, who'd played a cadaverous version of the Master in 1980's *The Keeper of Traken* – did the honours instead.)

In July, reports of *Death Comes to Time*'s, um, death proved exaggerated, as the pilot episode appeared in the form of an animated webcast on the BBC's new interweb thingie. The Beeb's first-ever online drama was a collaboration between Dan Freedman and James Goss, head producer for the Corporation's Cult website; arguing that, if they're sitting at a screen, people are going to expect something to look at, Goss commissioned veteran *DWM* comic strip artist Lee Sullivan to provide some (fairly rudimentary) flash animation to accompany the audio track. The script – written by Freedman under the pseudonym Colin Meek (presumably because he sounds like a genuine *Doctor Who* fan) – sends the Doctor on a mission to rescue Senator Sala, leader of the Santine Republic resistance movement fighting to protect her people from the ruthless General Tannis. In other words, Freedman appears to be the only person in the world to have watched *Star Wars: The Phantom Menace* and thought, "Yes, that's the sort of story I'd like to write one day."

The episode proved an instant success, racking up more than a million-and-a-half hits in its first two days (and remember, this was in the days when no-one over 40 knew what the internet actually was). A full series of webisodes – if it wasn't a word, then it soon would be – was hastily commissioned for broadcast early the following year, and Freedman even managed to break through the battlements long enough to pitch a full telly revival to BBC execs, with Stephen Fry once again the name on everyone's lips. "The TV pilot is potentially going to happen," Freedman told *SFX* magazine. "But it's like, until it happens, it's not happening."[11] Right – I'm glad we were able to clear that up. Freedman did claim to have "the cast, the story and the means to produce it in place," which must have come as news to Russell T Davies, who had been on hold at his desk for the best part of two years.

And before the end of the year, yet another proposal would be on the table, this time from Mark Gatiss, *Doctor Who Magazine* editor Clayton Hickman and Gareth Roberts, a former New Adventures novelist who had since moved into television, script-editing *Emmerdale* and writing two episodes of the BBC's recent re-make of cult 60s fantasy show *Randall and Hopkirk (Deceased)*. Gatiss was unapologetic about using his currency as one of comedy's hottest properties (the first series of *The League of Gentlemen* had scooped the BAFTA for best comedy, as well as four Royal Television Society awards and the Golden Rose of Montreux) to open doors on *Doctor Who's* behalf, but likened negotiations with the BBC to the Good Friday Agreement. Which was not an entirely fair allegory: one involved overcoming years of entrenched prejudice and bigotry towards a hated enemy, while all the other had to do was bring peace to Northern Ireland.

Roberts and Hickman also collaborated on December's *The One Doctor* – the Big Finish equivalent of a Christmas pantomime. Pitting Colin Baker and Bonnie Langford against an impostor Doctor played by panto regular Christopher Biggins, highlights include Mel being forced on pain of death to put together some self-assembly shelving, and the Doctor retrieving a giant crystal from a planet guarded by a very lonely jelly. God knows what Sydney Newman would have made of it.

The seventh Doctor's final story of the year, meanwhile, was wartime thriller *Colditz*, featuring a young Scottish actor called David Tennant as a psychotic Nazi (is there any other sort?) called Feldwebel Kurtz. For lifelong fanboy Tennant, it was a dream come true. "I had my knitted scarf, which my granny did, and later she knitted me a cricket jumper," he beamed. "I was an obsessive: *Doctor Who* is a big part of why I decided to become an actor – growing up agog at the genius of Tom Baker. Initially, I wanted to be a Time Lord but, as I got older, that turned into 'maybe I could be one of the people who *pretends* to be a Time Lord', and that's what got me into acting. Obviously, I appreciate Shakespeare and everything else, but my nucleus is based in long scarves and telephone boxes."[31] No doubt he didn't put it *quite* like that when, some years later, Tennant joined the board of the Royal Shakespeare Company, having won acclaim as one of the finest Hamlets of his generation. None of which really explains why I'm telling you all this.

"*Of course* we'd love to have you back at the BBC, Colin. (You were the one with the scarf, right?)"

Early 2002 brought mixed fortunes for the two most recent Time Lords: the second season of Big Finish eighth Doctor adventures got off to a confident start with Mark Gatiss' *Invaders from Mars*, which lands the Doctor and Charley in 1938 Manhattan just as Orson

Welles is sending the population into a panic with his infamous *War of the Worlds* broadcast. Guest actors Simon Pegg, Jessica Stevenson – fast-rising stars of the cult sitcom *Spaced* – and Mark Benton are a measure of the calibre of talent the range had begun to attract. And there was even better to come in February's *The Chimes of Midnight*, in which the TARDIS crew spend Christmas in a haunted Edwardian house that appears to exist outside time. An artful blend of *Upstairs, Downstairs* and *Sapphire and Steel*, Robert Shearman's story takes Big Finish's output to a whole new level in an adventure that more than earns its place among *Doctor Who*'s all-time greats.

For the little fella with the question mark brolly, though, it was game over, as the conclusion of *Death Comes to Time*, streamed in five weekly episodes throughout the spring, saw the seventh Doctor apparently killed off. Again. This time, he sacrificed himself in order to save Ace's life – which is certainly a better way to go than bumbling into a hail of bullets like an intergalactic Mr Bean.

Script editor Nev Fountain cited the defence used by Alan Moore when he killed off Superman: "This is just a story – but then again, aren't they all?" But the implications for canonicity were so grave, several *Doctor Who* fans had the entire story surgically removed from their memories ("and if you could take out *The Twin Dilemma* while you're at it...").

Sylvester McCoy was one of those under the impression Stephen Fry was being groomed as his replacement – his *other* replacement, anyway – while Fry told *Doctor Who Magazine* that, while sci-fi was generally "bollocks", he loved *Doctor Who* "with a passion bordering on insanity" (i.e. like a *Doctor Who* fan).

Death Comes to Time was judged such a success that BBCi – as the Beeb's online service was rather charmingly called in those days – immediately ordered another story. This time they went to Big Finish, who delivered a sixth Doctor-Cybermen adventure called *Real Time*. For Colin Baker, there was something of *The Time Lord Who Came in from the Cold* about it.

"There was the merest frisson of excitement because we were mainstream BB-Who," he said. "It was very special for me, given my history with the programme, having played the part during a period when the Controller of

BBC1 wanted to dump us all in Room 101. To feel that the BBC is not only happy, but presumably desirous of having me play the Doctor in the first BBC/Big Finish enterprise... That sense of pleasure that I now feel from my association with the programme, which was restored by the reaction I have had to my contributions on audio over the last few years, grew even greater with the somewhat belated sense that Auntie approved."[30] If you'll excuse me, I think I have something in my eye.

The cast also included Maggie Stables as the Doctor's unusually mature Big Finish companion Evelyn Smythe, Yee Jee Tso – aka Chang Lee from the TV Movie – Nicholas Briggs (obviously) and cult comedians Stewart Lee and Richard Herring, best known for introducing viewers to such memorable concepts as a jelly-obsessed Rod Hull impostor and The Curious Orange, Herring's citrus-based illegitimate son, in the TV shows *Fist of Fun* and *This Morning with Richard Not Judy*. Lee revealed himself to be enough of a fanboy to be able to base his performance on a specific Cyberman from a 1979 *Doctor Who Weekly* comic strip. "What I love about *Doctor Who* fans is that they really love something, and they're unapologetic about it," he said. "And the thing they love is a mixture of being great and rubbish. There's a lot of rubbish in it, and it's stupid and strange, and it's camp, but you can't knock the fact that people are actually devoted to something."[30] Er, thanks. I think.

Lee Sullivan once again provided the artwork, taking the opportunity to re-colour the sixth Doctor's migraine-inducing outfit in shades of blue. Colin Baker may have been welcomed back into the fold, but there was no way that bloody coat was getting back into the building.

World stunned by announcement that BBC Wales to make brand new *Doctor Who* series ("There's a BBC *Wales*?")

As *Doctor Who* entered its 40th anniversary year, it didn't take a genius to guess where the birthday celebrations were going to be hosted – on the screen on your desk, rather than the one in front of your sofa. Sure enough, in early 2003 the BBC commissioned Big Finish to produce a new, semi-animated version of the show's fabled lost classic, *Shada*. By use of a hand-waving, time-twisting explanation, the story allowed Paul McGann's eighth Doctor to team up with Lalla Ward's Romana and John Leeson's K-9, while the all-star cast also included James Fox, Andrew Sachs, Hannah Gordon, Susannah Harker and Melvyn Hayes. Tom Baker allegedly turned down the lead because it would have meant working with his ex-wife – though Lalla Ward had no such qualms.

"I've said to Gary [Russell] I'd be happy to do one with Tom," said the actress, now married to the evolutionary biologist and enthusiastic God-basher Richard Dawkins (to whom she was introduced by her friend Douglas Adams prior to his death in 2001). "I'd be *delighted* to work with Tom. It'd be interesting to see him again. I have no problems with it. If he does, then I'm sorry. I doubt that he does. I'm sure that it's more that he has other things to do."[26]

McGann was impressed with the quality of Douglas Adams' hastily knocked-out script. "Lalla speaks so eloquently and passionately about him, and I've come to understand why he was so well loved and respected," he said. "If you were at a blind tasting, and just shown a page or two of every script we've done, you'd easily spot that this one came from somewhere else, from a very fertile mind."[32]

By now, Big Finish was rapidly colonising other areas of the *Doctor Who* universe: it had already commissioned a spin-off series starring Elisabeth Sladen as Sarah Jane Smith, and announced plans for its own 40th anniversary celebrations in the form of *Zagreus*, an ambitious three-disc adventure featuring just about anyone who'd ever set foot in a Big Finish studio.

The story was the first to unite Paul McGann with his three predecessors – though Davison, Baker and McCoy spend most of the running time as, respectively, a vicar, a Gallifreyan provost and someone called Walton "Uncle Winky" Winkle. I'd tell you why, but the truth is Gary Russell and Alan Barnes' script is so fiendishly complicated, you could give yourself an aneurism just trying to keep up with who's who (and who's not Who). There are lots of great moments, though, including a cameo from the late Jon Pertwee, cannibalised from

lines he'd recorded for a fan film called *Devious*. (The sound was so iffy that the McGann Doctor has to keep shouting that he can't hear him properly. Bloody audiophiles.)

As if all that wasn't enough to keep them busy, Big Finish also released *Unbound*, a series of six alternative-universe stories, each featuring a different actor as the Doctor. The stellar line-up featured one-time *Who* refuseniks Geoffrey Bayldon and David Warner, regular guest star (and *Sapphire and Steel* scene-stealer) David Collings, evil anti-Doctor Michael Jayston, and *Fast Show* favourite Arabella Weir as a belching, puking Doctor who works in a supermarket and spends her nights down the pub. (Please God, let it not be canon.) Best of the bunch, though, is Robert Shearman's *Deadline*, in which Sir Derek Jacobi plays ageing writer Martin Bannister who, living out his twilight years in a care home, starts to believe he's the lead character from a science-fiction series that never got produced... It's a wonderful premise and, by presenting us with a world in which *Doctor Who* never existed, Shearman reminds us just why the 40th anniversary of this mad, ridiculous, wonderful show is worth celebrating in the first place.

As it turned out, new Doctors were everywhere you looked in 2003. As long as you didn't look at an actual telly, obviously. Following the success of *Shada*, BBCi announced another special anniversary webcast, except this one would be even more specialer than all the other specials put together because, not only would it be fully animated – with people actually moving their heads and *everything* – it would also be an *official* continuation of the TV series, with an official, brand new Doctor. In other words, *Doctor Who* was back back! *Back!* Albeit as a drawing that you'd have to try and sneakily watch at work, because most British homes were still on dial-up at the time.

The mantle of the ninth Doctor (and he really did wear a mantle) was taken up by Richard E Grant, most famous for starring opposite Paul McGann as the more dishevelled, flamboyantly alcoholic half of Withnail and I. McGann, for one, found this notion hilarious. "They're calling him the ninth Doctor!" he told *Doctor Who Magazine*. "He's official! He's in the loop!" The eighth Doctor had learned of his successor's appointment when a radio station had phoned him up and asked him for his reaction. McGann phoned his son and asked him to check online. "And there he was – the bitch! It was on the BBC website. It said 'Hail, the ninth Doctor!' or something. I thought, 'Oh my God!' It was a complete surprise."[33]

Swaziland-born Grant, whose extensive screen credits took in everything from *Gosford Park* to *Spiceworld: The Movie*, was still claiming never to have seen *Doctor Who* – despite having played the short-lived tenth Doctor in *The Curse of Fatal Death*. "I know nothing about it," he said. "I feel like a complete, I don't know, fraud... I think it's much more daunting if you're doing the film or a TV version – people see your face – whereas this is a cartoon. I don't know if it has the same import."[33] (At which point the man from BBCi thought: "Maybe we should let someone *else* do the publicity interviews?")

Written by Paul Cornell, *Scream of the Shalka* also starred Sophie Okonedo, soon to earn herself an Oscar nomination for *Hotel Rwanda*, as the Doctor's companion, Alison, alongside a cast of notables including Sir Derek Jacobi – best known for his role as Martin Bannister in the Big Finish *Unbound* series, but who had also done a bit of theatre and film work here and there – Craig Kelly, whose graphic sexual congress with a teenage boy had been so memorably intercut with the cliffhanger to *Pyramids of Mars* episode one in Russell T Davies' *Queer as Folk*, and David Tennant who, as well as being a lifelong *Who* addict, was also beer-swilling alt.Doc Arabella Weir's lodger (David tenant, if you will). Tennant found out about the production because he was recording a radio play in the neighbouring studio, and convinced the director to write him in. "I play Caretaker Two," he explained with his usual Tiggerish enthusiasm. "It's very hard not to get excited. I would kill to do more of these."[33] Hopefully it wouldn't come to that.

In late August, Lorraine Heggessy, who had been Controller of BBC1 for the past three years, was asked about *Doctor Who* at that year's Edinburgh Television Festival. "I would like to resurrect *Doctor Who*..." she began, as several hundred people leaned forward expectantly "... but the rights situation is too compli-

cated. Maybe that will happen one day." At which fans everywhere gave a collective shrug, said "Yeah, whatever", and went back to making sure the spines of their DVD collection were properly aligned.

So it was something of a bolt from the blue – to say the least – when, four weeks later, the BBC suddenly announced that *Doctor Who* was coming back. As a series. On telly. With pictures, and human actors and... well, *everything*.

"*Doctor Who*, one of the BBC's best-loved and most enduring characters, is set to return to BBC One, it was confirmed last night by Lorraine Heggessey," stated the BBC, casual as you like, in a press release issued on Friday, September 26th. "Heggessey said that all rights issues regarding *Doctor Who* have been resolved and that she has green-lit scripts from award-winning writer Russell T Davies. It is far too early in the day to discuss possible storylines, characters, villains or who might play the Time Lord," the release continued. "It is unlikely anything will be on screen for at least two years."

"*Doctor Who* is a much-loved, truly iconic piece of television history," said executive producer Mal Young. "It's time to crank up the Tardis and find out what lies in store for the Doctor. We're thrilled to have a writer of Russell's calibre to take us on this journey. However, we're at the very first stages of development and further details, including casting, will not be available for some time."

Davies himself said: "I grew up watching *Doctor Who*, hiding behind the sofa like so many others. *Doctor Who* is one of the BBC's most exciting and original characters. He's had a good rest and now it's time to bring him back!

"The new series [to be produced by BBC Wales] will be fun, exciting, contemporary and scary. Although I'm only in the early stages of development, I'm aiming to write a full-blooded drama which embraces the *Doctor Who* heritage, at the same time as introducing the character to a modern audience."

All over the world, *Doctor Who* fans had re-read the statement several hundred times before allowing themselves to believe it was true. After which they raced to the internet message boards and said: "Shouldn't that technically be TARDIS, not Tardis?"

With a whole new TV series calling tantalisingly from the future, by the time *Scream of the Shalka* crept apologetically onto buffering web connections in November, it already had the feel of a slightly disappointing sibling no-one could remember inviting to a family wedding – the Danni to BBC One's Kylie, the Eric Roberts to Russell T Davies' Julia. So to speak.

With proper(ish) animation by Cosgrove Hall, the studio behind such small screen legends as *Danger Mouse* and *Count Duckula*, Paul Cornell's tale of giant shrieking worms invading a Lancashire village has much to recommend it – though, sadly, Richard E Grant's peevish Time Lord isn't one of them. Striding about being all haughty and irritable, he makes the sixth Doctor look positively sentimental. No wonder the animators rendered him with a permanent expression of a man who's just trodden something unpleasant into the TARDIS.

"We treated *Scream of the Shalka* like the real thing, and I'm very pleased that we didn't shrink back from that and put it in its own little bubble automatically," reflected Cornell. "Obviously *history* has put it in a little bubble, and to fight against that would be silly. Mine isn't the real ninth Doctor, because the public at large have never heard of him. You wait ages for a new Doctor Who, and two come along at once."[34]

As a mark of *Doctor Who*'s place in the British cultural landscape, a celebration of the programme's 40th anniversary was hosted by the House of Commons, where MPs took time out from debating trivial stuff like Clause 28 and the war in Chechnya to ask Terrance Dicks about *The Claws of Axos* and the war between the Sontarans and the Rutans. Meanwhile, in its issue dated November 22nd, the *Radio Times* celebrated *Doctor Who*'s 40th anniversary with a choice of four collectible covers in which Tom Baker, Peter Davison, Colin Baker and Sylvester McCoy posed against a monster-packed diorama in a tribute to Jon Pertwee on the front of the first *RT* special 30 years earlier. A 16-page pull-out inside (or outside, if you pulled it out – keep up, do) revealed the results of a readers' poll, which declared Tom Baker, Jon Pertwee, Patrick Troughton, Peter Davison and Sylvester McCoy the top five doctors ("Maybe go easy on the Colin Baker cover," the editor told the printers), while Sarah Jane Smith, K-9, Ace, Leela and the Brigadier took the honours for the companions. Favourite monsters were the Cybermen, Zygons, Autons, Ice Warriors and Sea Devils (the Daleks were disqualified for being "too popular" – or possibly because the Terry Nation estate thought he should receive a fee for people writing the word "Dalek" on the voting form), while hot favourites for the new Doctor were Anthony Head, Alan Rickman, Stephen Fry, Alan Davies and Ian Richardson. "I'm hugely flattered by the readers' response," said *Buffy* star Head. Though he couldn't help notice his agent hadn't been in touch about the part yet...

The magazine – which coincided with a Doctor Who@40 Weekend on UK Gold (a special documentary, *The Story of Doctor Who*, was being saved until Christmas) – also spoke to Russell T Davies. The writer revealed he wouldn't be starting work on the new series properly until the new year, but already knew he wanted the Doctor to be "the best character ever – he should be so fascinating, he's radioactive. He's funny, clever, wild and fast. Your best friend times 500."

Asked about the show's strengths and weaknesses, Davies replied: "The strength and weakness is the same thing: the range. It's a bugger. Every episode, you could be looking at going to a new location with a new cast – which eats up money, but is simultaneously one of the most exciting things about it: you can go anywhere and do anything."[35]

And so it was that, after a decade-and-a-half of frustrations, dashed hopes and false dawns, it seemed the Doctor really was heading back where he belonged: everywhere.

⑨ Gone in 35,000 Seconds

"What do we want?" "Doctor Who!" "When do we want it?" "When all outstanding licensing and rights issues have been satisfactorily resolved!"

By 2001, the issue of who owned the rights to *Doctor Who* was starting to look less like a stock BBC excuse and more like a genuine problem. Two years after their initial chat, the Beeb were still keen to lure Russell T Davies away from the opposition, and he was adamant he wouldn't do any deal that didn't involve *Doctor Who*. At a follow-up meeting, Davies cited the BBC's own *Walking with Dinosaurs* – a sort of Discovery Channel version of *Jurassic Park* – as an example of how the technology to do *Doctor Who* properly was now affordable. Though given that *Walking with Dinosaurs* is listed in the Guinness Book of World Records as the most expensive documentary series ever made, that probably wasn't the most brilliant example, on reflection.

In the end, though, it was the rights what did for it. Again. "We tried to bring it back and the rights were tied up in movie deals and in Hollywood," said Mal Young, the Controller of Continuing Series who, according to Davies, budgeted for *Doctor Who*'s return every year – just in case. "I always felt, this isn't a movie – this is a TV show. This is an *iconic* TV show – it shouldn't feel like it's as big as a movie – it should feel like it's in the corner of the room, putting you behind the sofa again."[1]

One woman who'd been mentally clearing space behind her sofa for a while now was Jane Tranter. The BBC's Controller of Drama Commissioning was a passionate sci-fi fan who, as a teenager, had eschewed posters of David Cassidy and the Bay City Rollers in favour of William Shatner. She'd been patiently biding her time, waiting for the chance to resurrect Britain's most iconic fantasy show.

"One of the first things I was told when I took on the job of Drama Commissioner was that I had to solve evenings," said Tranter. "I was asked to find something for 8pm on a Sunday night, but all I could think about was Saturday evenings. This was my chance to bring back *Doctor Who*."[2]

The call to fix Saturdays never came, but she decided to do it anyway. "I couldn't bear it any longer. Gambling that enough of my shows were working for people not to think I was a complete lunatic for even mentioning the Doctor, I sort of shrieked *Doctor Who* at a meeting with Lorraine."[2]

Lorraine was Lorraine Heggessey, the Controller of BBC One. Heggessey was interested, but cautious, and the discussion was parked there – until Tranter, heavily pregnant with twins, was introduced to Russell T Davies at a press launch for Paul Abbott's comedy drama *Linda Green*. It was Nicola Shindler – whose Red Productions had commissioned most of Davies' recent work – who played matchmaker, telling Tranter: "You must come and meet Russell... he really wants to make *Doctor Who*."

"I nearly gave birth, right there," said Tranter. "Suddenly, in one second, everything made perfect sense. I knew that Russell was what we needed for *Doctor Who* in the twenty-first century."[2]

This chance encounter was enough to convince Heggessey to greenlight the series. "The decision was never, 'We're going to bring back *Doctor Who*'," stressed Tranter. "The decision was, 'Russell is going to write *Doctor Who*'. And that's very different."[2]

Davies is equally emphatic about Tranter's role in securing the Time Lord's resurrection. "The massive difference in 2003 was that, for the first time, the actual Drama Commissioner was chasing the show," he said. "Jane wasn't an underling. She was the boss!"[2]

Another crucial player was Heggessey herself: although not as much of an evangelist as Tranter, she was the first BBC One Controller who was genuinely sympathetic towards *Doctor Who* since... actually, she was probably the first BBC One Controller who was genuinely sympathetic towards *Doctor Who*.

"I have felt that the time was right ever since I started as Controller of BBC One," Heggessey said in 2005. "But it took some time for us to get the project off the ground for a variety of reasons. Partly because the rights were locked off and they were going to make a movie, partly to get all the ducks in a row."

Eventually, she cracked. "I just said, 'Enough, we *have* to do it, we have to do it *now* – I don't care what the situation is, just get it sorted. BBC One should now take priority, 'cos we've been waiting for this movie that hasn't yet appeared. It's BBC One that owns this brand and the British viewing public should have it as its own. And after a little bit of stamping my feet, it seemed to happen'."[1] For *Doctor Who* fans, hearing a woman talk like this was way better than anything they could get on a premium rate phone line.

"Suddenly," said Mal Young, another cheerleader for Team *Who* whose contribution can't be overestimated, "all the stars came into the right place – the new BBC One Controller wanted it back, the business side of things eased up and we got the rights back... It felt like fate was telling us now is the moment to do it."[1]

As part of the BBC's Charter commitment to push more work out to the regions, Tranter asked Julie Gardner, incoming Head of Drama at BBC Wales, to take on the show. (Well, it was often set in strange lands full of outlandish creatures, so it made sense, really.) Tranter's first job was to convince Davies – who was worried they might want to turn *Doctor Who* into some "late night, ironic, BBC Nine sort of thing" – that this was the real deal.

The Swansea-born writer's fears were largely allayed by the involvement of Gardner, and he was excited by the prospect of re-invigorating drama at BBC Wales – even if it was a long way from his home in Manchester, and the BBC's eagerness to net such a big TV fish didn't extend to anything as extravagant as relocation expenses.

And so it was that, in 2003, Davies sat down with Heggessey, Tranter and Gardner (how things had changed since the days when Verity

Lambert had rocked the BBC to its foundations by not smoking a pipe) to sell his vision for the show he'd waited his whole life to write. A vision best summed up by one, simple phrase:

"Er..."

"It's funny, even though I had all those meetings, I never thought about what I was going to *do*," admitted Davies. "I never really thought about it until it was real."[3]

Many fans, of course, knew exactly what Davies should do – and took to the worldwide web in their thousands to offer helpful advice. "Believe it or not," boggled Simon Jeffery in *The Guardian* when news of the show's return broke, "there are places online where people get together to discuss this sort of thing". (Honestly, where do they *find* these people?)

Appearing on BBC Radio 4's *Today* programme the morning after the big announcement, *Doctor Who Magazine* editor Clayton Hickman blithely informed the nation that "Russell favours Bill Nighy [as the Doctor]," before adding: "But I'm not sure I should have said that." I'm pretty sure Russell would be sure you shouldn't have. (In fact, Davies phoned Hickman up and told him not to worry.) BBC Five Live's Richard Bacon also called the gangling *Love, Actually* star a "shoo-in", but that didn't stop the papers naming everyone with an Equity card and their own teeth as likely contenders for the role, including (deep breath) Richard E Grant, Alan Davies, Alan Cumming, Ian Richardson, Sean Pertwee, Patrick Stewart, James Nesbitt, Hugh Grant, Jonathan Pryce, Timothy Spall, Stephen Fry, Ian McKellen, Michael Caine, Lenny Henry, Rowan Atkinson, Andrew Lincoln, Robert Lindsay, Paul Bettany and Shane Richie. Tom Baker, meanwhile, suggested cross-dressing comic Eddie Izzard was likely to be cast – presumably because the idea amused him for five minutes. (He also offered a typically diplomatic response to the idea of the *first* ninth Doctor returning to the part, telling one journalist: "Oh Christ no, not Richard E Grant!")

"Meanwhile," said *The Guardian* on October 7th, "rumours that Christopher Eccleston is interested and has put feelers out to the BBC remain unconfirmed after his agent resolutely refuses to return our call." *Why not just listen to his voicemails?* wondered bewildered rivals on the *News of the World*.

Among the ticker-tape parade of positive publicity, some papers managed to set the gay rights movement back 20 years with headlines like "Doctor Duckie" and idle gossip about Davies' appointment "alarming purists". This prompted *Mirror* columnist Sue Carroll to declare: "He can be Graham Norton as far as I'm concerned, provided the show still looks as if it's been filmed in a sandpit up the M25, the walls are wobbly and the Daleks still can't get up a flight of stairs." It was good to see satire wasn't dead. Just very, very unwell.

Davies offered the first clue about his intentions for the series – apart from painting the Daleks pink and turning the Doctor into a Big Gay, obviously – when he told November's *Doctor Who Magazine*: "I want the Doctor and at least one companion, whose name is probably Rose Tyler."[4]

The Doctor's name probably wouldn't be Bill Nighy, though: "I'm not going to be Doctor Who," the actor told Radio 4's *Loose Ends*. "No-one has asked me and, well… no-one has really survived *Doctor Who*." Nobody has survived *Doctor Who*? Does the Stranger video spin-off series mean *nothing* to him?

Less than two months after the jubilant announcement, *The Sun* was the first to play party pooper when it reported there were "ongoing rights issues" with the use of the Daleks. Which sounded hard to believe: I mean, it wasn't like Terry Nation's estate were the types to be difficult.

On December 8th, Russell T Davies and Julie Gardner had a meeting with Jane Tranter and Mal Young, during which Davies handed over The Pitch – a 12-page document outlining his blueprint for the show, along with story outlines for each of the planned stories (13 45-minute episodes, divided into seven standalones and three two-parters). Unlike John Leekley, he hadn't bothered to bind it in distressed leather or have it stamped with the Seal of Rassilon – but he had managed to come up with his own stories, which surely had to be progress.

The one-line pitch stated simply: "A girl meets an alien, and together they travel the universe. Forging a friendship across time and space…" The Doctor was described as "wise and funny, fast and sarky, cheeky and brave". "He should also be *sexy*," added Davies. "Not

necessarily young, but let's move on from that neutered, posh, public-school, fancy-dress-frock-coat image. He's immediate and tactile. Stand too close to him, and you could get burnt."

Teenage shopgirl Rose Tyler was described as "feisty and funny" but "idling. Life is dull. And she's so much better than this." Of her relationship with the Doctor, the document said: "She loves him, and he loves her. Simple as that. Not a kissy-kissy kind of love, this is *deeper*. From the moment they meet, the Doctor and Rose are *soulmates*."

Under the heading The Mythology, Davies wrote: "The fiction of *Doctor Who* has got forty years of backstory… Which we'll ignore. Except for the good bits." That's the mid-80s written off, then. But perhaps the pitch's most contentious aspect was Davies' assertion that "every story, somehow, should come back to Earth, to humanity": "If the Zogs on planet Zog are having trouble with the Zog-monster… who gives a toss? But if a *human* colony on the planet Zog is in trouble, a last outpost of humanity fighting to survive… then I'm interested."

(This led to an immediate complaint from the Zog Council of Great Britain: "We understood the Doctor to be an advocate in equal rights for all species, regardless of creed, colour or number of eyes on stalks," said a spokesZog. "So we were very disappointed to hear we are now being treated as second-class citizens." It was also bad news for the thousands of fans who'd already finished the first draft of *Doctor Who and the Zogs of Zog* and sent it off to Cardiff.)

Davies believed the stories should be "unashamedly high-concept": "This programme's going to be fighting in the heat of the Saturday night ratings war, so every bloody week, there should be something to grab a new viewer. Something irresistible. Big, cheeky headlines: Rose sees the end of the world! The Doctor meets Charles Dickens! Aliens invade Downing Street! The return of the Daleks! Big ideas, great characters, and real emotions. Simple as that."

The document was well received, save for a bit of wrangling over the opening story. "Initially, the BBC wanted the Daleks in episode one," said Davies. "And I was just adamant that they were wrong. I said to them, 'If you save them 'til episode six, you'll get a second launch'."[4]

In February, actress Diana Quick let slip that her long-term partner – a certain Bill Nighy – had been offered the part of the Doctor, but had turned it down, while *The People* made the unlikely claim that pint-sized trickster Paul Daniels was the man of Russell T Davies' dreams. "TV chiefs have already talked to Daniels, 65, famous for his catchphrase, 'You'll like it – not a lot, but you'll like it'," blithered the tabloid. "Paul may seem an extraordinary choice, but he would make a very entertaining Time Lord," said his agent... sorry, I mean "a source".

A few days later, Andy Pryor was announced as the show's new casting director. With extensive credits ranging from *Trainspotting* and *Our Friends in the North* to *I'm Alan Partridge*, it was good to know the show was in the hands of one of the most experienced professionals in the business. ("So tell me more about this Paul Daniels...")

Another key player joining the team was Phil Collinson who, as *Doctor Who*'s 11th producer, would oversee the day-to-day business of actually making the show. Yeah, good luck with that. Collinson was enough of a fanboy to have read interviews with all his predecessors – but, amazingly, decided to take the job anyway. "I loved *Doctor Who*, absolutely loved it," he told *Doctor Who Magazine*. "It was the only programme that my whole family watched together, and so that gives it a bit of a halcyon glow for me: dark nights, potted meat sandwiches, Mr Kipling's cakes and *Doctor Who*. My mum tells me that one of my first words was 'Drashig'."[6] (And the next three were Colour, Separation and Overlay. Truly, he was a child of the Barry Letts era.)

By now it had been decided that Davies would write eight episodes himself, with the rest to be handled by Steven Moffat, Mark Gatiss, Paul Cornell and Robert Shearman. (*State of Play* and *Shameless* writer Paul Abbott was also approached, but couldn't make time in his schedule. They also received a polite thanks but no thanks from JK Rowling, who claimed she was busy writing some book or other. "It was slightly disappointing, to say the least," said Davies.)

Moffat heard he'd got the gig when his agent phoned him at the British Comedy Awards, where he collected the Best TV Comedy gong for *Coupling*. "I don't need the rest of my life now," he quipped. Cornell, by contrast, got the call while putting some oven chips in, and was subsequently treated to five minutes of Russell T Davies riffing on the glory of frozen carbohydrates before he finally got round to popping the question. "It was the completion of my lifetime's ambition," said Cornell. Hey, come on, guys – you've both still got so much to live for!

In one of his first interviews on the subject, Moffat was asked by *The Scotsman* about *Doctor Who*'s ability to hold its own in the post-*Star Wars* landscape. "I don't think the fact we're in the post-*Star Wars* era is an issue," said Moffat. "Matching *Buffy* is. *Doctor Who* was never a space opera anyway, it was about horror: dark shadows and creepy monsters lurking around the corner."

Gatiss agreed: "Russell T Davies said to me the other day that he'd always regarded it as science fiction, but what *Doctor Who* always did best was horror, and I think that's true," he told Radio 4's *Front Row*. "From Arctic bases besieged by monsters to Cybermen on the moon, it's the creeping unknown. It's the shadows and the hand at the end of the episode; it's all horror."

By now, rumour and speculation as to who would play the Doctor had been sloshing about the internet for six months. But in late March one fan website claimed to have seen an email confirming the actor's identity, and selflessly decided to share it with their readers. This threw the BBC into something of a flap as, at the time, no contracts had actually been signed. But, in the early hours of Saturday, March 20th, a press release was issued officially naming the new man in the TARDIS. And that man was Christopher Eccleston.

"He was absolutely our first choice (after our other first choices)"

Born in Salford in 1964, Christopher Eccleston had been inspired to become an actor by such working class touchstones as Alan Bleasdale's *Boys from the Blackstuff*, Ken Loach's *Kes* and Albert Finney's performance in

Saturday Night, Sunday Morning. After graduating from the Central School of Speech and Drama, Eccleston found acting work thin on the ground and spent several years doing odd jobs on building sites and in supermarkets. His big break came in 1991 when he played the wrongly hanged British teenager Derek Bentley in the film *Let Him Have It*, but it was his role as DCI Bilborough in Jimmy McGovern's psychological crime drama *Cracker* that made him a household face, if not exactly a name – not least for his shocking, protracted and generally very harrowing death at the hands of Robert Carlyle's knife-wielding maniac early in the second series.

A leading role in Danny Boyle's *Shallow Grave* followed, but he passed on the part of violent sociopath Begbie in Boyle's *Trainspotting*, clearing the way for a career-making turn by Robert Carlyle. Let's hope Carlyle sent him a note. ("Thanks for the role of a lifetime – and sorry about the whole knifing you to death thing.") Instead, Eccleston joined the ensemble cast of Peter Flannery's epic BBC drama *Our Friends in the North*, starring alongside Mark Strong, Gina McKee and Daniel Craig. Little did they know at the time that one of them would go on to win acclaim as perhaps the definitive version of an iconic British fictional hero. And another would play Doctor Who.

In tandem with the sort of gritty TV work that had fired his youthful imagination (he was also the lead in Jimmy McGovern's docudrama about the Hillsborough tragedy), Eccleston's movie roles had included *Elizabeth*, *eXistenZ* and fender-bending Hollywood petrolhead actioner *Gone in 60 Seconds*, in which he played the lead villain, despite not having passed his driving test (even today, he's only licensed to drive automatics so, at best, could probably manage to be *Gone in About Half an Hour*).

In 2003, Eccleston played the Son of God in *The Second Coming*, Russell T Davies' ITV drama about a Manchester video shop worker who turns out to be the Messiah (thus proving that, while the Devil may have all the best tunes, God's got a better film collection). Of course, taking on the role of such a sacred figure worshipped by devout followers all over the world, many of whom had dedicated their entire lives to praising the glory of His name, was bound to be daunting. But Eccleston figured, having already done Jesus as a warm-up act, he was ready to give the Doctor a go.

"I am absolutely delighted to be playing Doctor Who," said the actor – thus upsetting his first lot of pedants before he'd even started. "I am looking forward to joining forces again with the incredible writer Russell T Davies and taking both loyal viewers and a new generation on a journey through time and space – which way is the TARDIS? I can't wait to get started!"

"We considered many great actors for this wonderful part, but Christopher was our first choice," said Davies. "This man can give the Doctor a wisdom, wit and emotional intelligence as far-reaching as the Doctor's travels in time and space. His casting raises the bar for all of us."

His casting was certainly a surprise to many: with his reputation for earnest northern grit, Eccleston wasn't exactly a natural choice for an eccentric 900-year-old alien, fancy dress or no fancy dress. "A journalist once told me the roles I played were 'comfort food for liberals'," said Eccleston. "And I guess there's some truth in that. I let him out alive, anyway. People are always telling me I'm too gloomy and can't do comedy – so taking a part in *Doctor Who* is a gamble, and I find that exciting. It could sink my career, or take it to another level."[7]

No-one was more surprised by Eccleston's appointment than the *Daily Mail*, whose first edition that Saturday morning loudly declaimed, in a page lead article, that Bill Nighy was the new Doctor Who. "After three weeks of negotiations, BBC executives whittled down the contenders to three, with Nighy finally beating off competition from Richard E Grant and *Jonathan Creek* star Alan Davies," said the paper, with all the authority and integrity for which it has become world famous.

The story subsequently earned the paper a Shafta at an awards ceremony celebrating the year's worst journalism blunders. But, unlike so many British tabloid fantasies, it doesn't appear to have been *entirely* pulled out of a reporter's backside. In 2012, Nighy told the *Huffington Post*: "I was offered the role once, I won't tell you when because the rule is that you're not allowed to say you turned that job down because it's disrespectful to whoever did it. I will say that I was approached. But I didn't want to be the Doctor. No disrespect to *Doctor*

Who or anything. I just think that it comes with too much baggage." Which is admirably circumspect – but was it perchance around the time that newspaper said you'd been offered the job, *and so did your wife?*

Publicly, Davies insisted Eccleston was the only name in the hat. "When Mal Young, Julie Gardner and I first got into the same room together in September, he was the very first name mentioned – and that's a fact", he told *SFX* in April 2004. Though that conversation could well have started "How about Christopher Eccleston if Bill Nighy says no?"

Davies later admitted that he'd also offered the part to Hugh Grant (with some sources claiming Rowan Atkinson was also approached). "Yes, well, you have to," he insisted. "Let's be honest, Christopher Eccleston would be my first choice. However, if Hugh Grant had said 'yes', of course we'd have cast him. Yes, we did make those offers, but it's not serious, because the one who was seriously interested was Chris."[8] Right. I'm glad we've cleared that one up.

"I never thought in a million years Chris would be interested in this," said Davies during an interview on Radio 2's *Steve Wright Show*. "He knows himself he's got this reputation for being tense and dour and northern, God bless him. But then he actually e-mailed me to say, 'Please put me on the list'."

Not only did he email Davies, Eccleston also offered to audition on tape, which was unusual for an actor of his standing. "Years ago, when they did the film, I was asked by my agent whether I'd want to audition," Eccleston told *Doctor Who Magazine* in his first interview about the role[1]. "I said 'no' very strongly, because I felt that I wasn't established enough, and I didn't want to be associated with a brand name that early in my career. But this time I felt experienced enough, and I felt my career was strong enough, to withstand an association like this, which can – and let's be honest here – rule you out of other parts. I felt I'd done enough to be able to surmount that, and I felt strongly enough about Russell's writing.

"The thing which sticks out for me is the Doctor himself, and the mystery of, you know, who is he?" Eccleston added. "Where does he come from? What's he thinking? What does he feel? He's got two hearts, so does that mean he cares twice as much?"[8]

In the same interview, Eccleston was in bullish mood about the series' future prospects, claiming he would be filming "seven months of the year for the next two or three years", with five months off in between.

As newspapers reported the actor had signed a £500,000 three-year contract, the reaction from fans and media pundits was generally positive – though Tom Baker was typically blunt, telling one reporter: "I've never heard of him, but I wish him well."

A less positive reaction greeted the rumour that Michael Grade was set to return to the BBC as chairman. The ever-vigilant Tim Collins, now shadow education secretary, organised a cross-party letter which stated: "Some [MPs] are concerned that, were you to become BBC chairman, the project would be derailed." (Great, thought Grade, I've not even got the job yet and the *Who* nutters are already crawling out of the woodwork. And this one could soon be in charge of the country's entire education system.)

A few weeks later, when Grade's new position had been confirmed, he told the *Sunday Express*: "I am very pleased that it is coming back to our screens – but I won't be watching it." Well, of course he wouldn't – everyone knows BBC chairmen only ever listen to the wireless.

In fact, possibly with half an eye on pleasing his new boss, BBC Director General Mark Thompson *did* ask Jane Tranter if she might consider calling the whole thing off. As diplomatically as she could, Tranter told him where to go. But the DG wasn't so easily deterred, and asked if there had been any research into whether there was much of an appetite for *Doctor Who* in the twenty-first century. The good news was that there was – BBC Worldwide had recently compiled a report on brand awareness about the show. The bad news was that it largely confirmed Thompson's fears. "It really did suggest that *Doctor Who* was going to be a failure," revealed Julie Gardner. "It said that family viewing didn't exist any more [and that] you'd never satisfy an existing fan base, because they'll want a very specific thing."[2]

So Tranter did what any responsible senior exec would do when faced with a tricky question from her boss: she lied. "I said we hadn't any research at all,"[2] she admitted. Well it was *partly* true – up until the world "we."

Before setting off on his travels through time and space, Christopher Eccleston had a slightly less exotic appointment in Leeds, where he was appearing in *Electricity*, a new[11] play by Murray Gold. As well as being a dramatist, Gold was an established composer who had scored numerous Russell T Davies productions, including *Queer as Folk* and *The Second Coming*. So it was no surprise when he was later announced as providing the incidental music for *Doctor Who* – as well taking on the challenge of updating the show's iconic theme tune for the twenty-first century.

In April, Eccleston appeared on the BBC Breakfast sofa and did his best to try to shoehorn in some plugs for *Electricity*, in between all the questions about *Doctor Who*. Asked about how he might look as the Time Lord, he said: "We're not gonna wear scarves and hats... I don't think he's going to be quite as eccentric and foppish as he was in some of his incarnations." ("I resent the implication I'm foppish," protested his predecessor, adjusting his cravat and tossing his Byronic locks.)

Eccleston was also adamant from the start he'd be playing the Doctor with his native Mancunian vowels intact. "The accent is an interesting thing," he said in the BBC's publicity pack. "The Doctor is a scientist and an intellectual, and a lot of people seem to think you can only be those things if you speak with received pronunciation which, of course, is rubbish."

This was simpatico with Russell T Davies' thoughts on the subject. "If you go online and look at any fan fiction," said Davies, "whichever Doctor they're writing for, they write it in the same voice, which is *posh*. You read it and he's always saying things like 'indubitably, my dear' and you think 'Who the hell is going to talk like that now?'"[10]

With the Doctor now cast, the tabloid guessing game turned to the subject of who would play Rose Tyler. Anna Friel, Keeley Hawes and Lou Brealey were rumoured to be hot favourites, while pop star-turned-actress Billie Piper's agent denied she had been considered for the role. So her agent must have been very surprised when, on May 24th, the BBC issued a

press release stating: "Billie Piper is confirmed to play Rose Tyler, companion to Doctor Who, it was announced today by Julie Gardner, Head of Drama, BBC Wales."

"Billie is beautiful, funny and intelligent," said Gardner. "We needed to find a unique, dynamic partner for Christopher Eccleston, and Billie fits the bill perfectly. She will make an extraordinary Rose Tyler. Doctor Who has his new assistant!"

"*Doctor Who* is an iconic show and I am absolutely thrilled to be playing the part of Rose Tyler," said Piper. "I am also looking forward to working with Christopher Eccleston and writer Russell T Davies."

Born in Swindon in September 1982, Piper's parents had originally named her Leian Paul. Six months later, they thought better of it and officially changed her name to Billie Paul Piper. Because Leian was obviously the silly bit of Leian Paul (Paul is her dad's name, if that's any excuse). She attended the Sylvia Young Theatre School before being picked, aged 15, to appear in an advert for teen pop bible *Smash Hits* ("ver Hits", to readers of a certain age). This led to a record contract and, in 1998, she became the youngest artist ever to debut at No. 1 with "Because We Want To," while follow-up "Girlfriend" was also a chart-topper.

Piper's debut album, *Honey to the B*, sold more than three million copies and, at the height of her fame, she even performed for Bill Clinton (no, not like *that*). But follow-up *Walk of Life* proved to be more like the Kiss of Death, and Piper retired from music at the grand age of 18. Eyebrows were raised when she married hard-partying DJ Chris Evans, 16 years her senior, at a ceremony in Las Vegas, after which the couple effectively bummed around the world for several years, regularly featuring in paparazzi pictures looking sozzled – but happy – in a series of exotic locations. (They also briefly owned Lionel Richie's Beverley Hills mansion before deciding, on reflection, it might be a bit on the large side for just the two of them.)

When the couple returned to London, Piper resumed acting lessons, and in 2003 earned rave reviews for her performance as a karaoke singer in a BBC production of *The Canterbury Tales: The Miller's Tale* (it was a contemporary update, in case you're wondering why you don't remember anyone doing a *Grease* medley in Chaucer's original). The following year, she won acclaim for her portrayal of a girl in care in BBC2 drama *Bella and the Boys*. She also had a leading role in *The Calcium Kid*, a 2004 film starring Orlando Bloom as a boxing milkman, which has the rare distinction of having received a 0% rating on reviews aggregator site Rotten Tomatoes. If anything, that's generous.

New TARDIS:
it's bigger on the outside

As Billie Piper prepared to take her place on the TARDIS, it was looking increasingly unlikely she'd get to face off against the series' most iconic villains. Having written numerous drafts of a story designed to reintroduce the Daleks to the nation's living rooms, Robert Shearman was informed that negotiations with the Terry Nation estate had failed, and he would need to replace the tin tyrants with a new enemy. Shearman suggested the episode's new title could be *Absence of the Daleks*, and everyone laughed. Then cried.

"The BBC offered the very best deal," said the Corporation in a statement, "but ultimately we were not able to give the level of editorial influence the Terry Nation estate wished to have."

Tim Hancock – son of the legendary Roger (and nephew of Tony) – responded by claiming the BBC was trying to "ruin the brand". "We accept the Daleks need modernising," he said. "All we ask is that they consult us on the designs. But the BBC is not prepared to."

According to one tabloid, irate fans in Southampton were planning to march in protest at this lack of Dalek action, though quite *where* they were going to march wasn't clear. Television Centre? Tim Hancock's house? Skaro? Meanwhile, *The Sun* launched a campaign for the villains' immediate reinstatement, parading their in-house Dalek (every office should have one) through New York's Times Square, for no immediately obvious reason.

Tim Collins wasn't a happy bunny either. "*Doctor Who* without the Daleks is like fish without chips," complained the Tories' frontbench *Doctor Who* spokesman. "*Doctor Who* without the Daleks would be like Morecambe without Wise or Wimbledon with strawber-

ries," weighed in Antony Wainer of the DWAS. And a quote about the Daleks without a random complementary partnership allegory would be like a clock without a wetsuit. (Hey, this stuff's harder than it looks.)

Pre-production was now in full swing, with script editors Elwen Rowlands and Helen Raynor and production designer Edward Thomas all on board. The latter worked closely with comic book illustrator Bryan Hitch, who had been hired as concept artist, while effects house The Mill, the team behind the Oscar-winning fx for Ridley Scott's *Gladiator*, were charged with bringing *Doctor Who* into the CGI era.

And then, on Sunday, July 18th, a 3'8" Scottish nightclub bouncer was spotted running down a corridor in the Cardiff Royal Infirmary dressed as a pig. A pig in a spacesuit. It could mean only one of two things: either someone had made a serious mistake with a patient's meds – or filming on the new series of *Doctor Who* had begun.

The diminutive porcine astronaut – played by Jimmy Vee, perhaps the most unlikely "doorman" since Sylvester McCoy was used as hired muscle by the Rolling Stones – was being pursued by Christopher Eccleston who, filming his very first scene for the series, must have wondered what the hell he'd got himself into. The first filming block, helmed by director Keith Boak, comprised episodes one, four and five, all of which required extensive shooting in London as well as Cardiff. The filming necessitated the closure of various roads throughout the Welsh capital, resulting in no small amount of traffic chaos. ("Bloody Time Lords," grumbled commuters.)

A few days later, a team from *Wales Today* visited the set for a report on their evening news bulletin – which is how fans as far afield as Damascus and Des Moines found themselves tuning in to watch stories about the Welsh Assembly elections and a skateboarding parrot in Blaenau Ffestiniog. For their patience, they were rewarded with the first look at the ninth Doctor in costume. That's assuming Eccleston *was* in costume, and not just doing a bit of car-clamping on the side, because his outfit was about as far from the traditional dandified Edwardian gentleman as it was possible to imagine: with his beaten-up leather jacket, v-necked jumper (with *no shirt* – surely the worst crime against knitwear since Michael Douglas' infamous clubbing gear in *Basic Instinct*), docker's boots and close-cropped hair, the ninth Doctor looked less like "your best friend times 500" than someone a slum landlord might send round to kick your door in if you fell behind with the rent. Russell T Davies had suggested he should look like "Terence Stamp after a long day on a market-stall", which suited Eccleston – though he was keen people shouldn't read his duds as a declaration of class war. "I wouldn't want to put labels on it," he said. Well of course not – clothes off the market never have labels.

Towards the end of the first week, *The Sun* managed to mess up a scene with Piper by trying to push their pet Dalek into shot, the clots, while rumours of the Autons' return were confirmed by pictures of shop dummies on the rampage in a Cardiff shopping centre. As the blank-faced automatons shuffled mindlessly around the stores in a selection of hideous leisurewear, they must have been surprised to see *Doctor Who* being filmed at the same time.

The first shots of the new TARDIS prop also started appearing online, causing thousands of fans to reach for the smelling salts when they noticed, after a casual glance lasting some 14 hours, that its proportions were not *entirely* consistent with previous models (even though none of *them* had been consistent with each other). The main gripe seemed to be that the police box was slightly fatter, and the windows were the "wrong" size. Literally *hundreds* of pages of internet chatter were devoted to this outrage; some fans even posted detailed tech specs of every previous version. It was surely only a matter of time before the gossip mags piled in, too ("Meet the LARD-IS: Full Story of the Time Machine's Battle of the Bulge!"; "TARDIS: Why I Love My New Fuller Figure" etc etc). Talk about relative dimensions.

More seriously (or not, depending on how many hours the TARDIS' windows were keeping you awake at night), rumours began to circulate of problems on the shoot. According to some, tensions on set were running high, and the production was falling hopelessly behind schedule. "That first block hit everyone for six," Russell T Davies later admitted. "We planned, we scheduled, but it was like hitting a brick wall. It was a very, very hard block for everyone. It was very hard for Keith [Boak] who actually, yes, could have planned things differently, but none of us told him to, because we were as in the dark as he was."[8]

"The show was enormous, and yet sometimes we felt like we were cobbling it together," concurred Phil Collinson. "Of course, we weren't – we were keeping hold of it, reigning in this monster – but I'm sure, at times, it seemed like it was going to be a disaster. We were learning as we went along, tripping over as we went along. Lots of mistakes were made – after filming for two weeks, we were three weeks behind. We'd misjudged how long it takes to make the show."[11]

In the middle of the second week, Collinson phoned Julie Gardner in tears. "I was crying. I'd had a budget meeting that day, and the budget was slipping away from me. It was week two, and we were in a mess already. Julie said 'I'm going to send you someone', and she sent Tracie Simpson. That's when things changed, I think."[11] As production manager, Simpson took charge of the shoot, while Collinson organised what he called "things on the ground".

The producer's literal cry for help had been made from the Brandon Estate in Southwalk. A series of 1960s tower blocks off the Camberwell Road, it wasn't the most glamorous location in the capital. Elsewhere, though, Keith Boak's crew were going all-out to capture as much of picture-postcard London – the London you see in American films, where red buses are permanently filing through Trafalgar Square and everyone carries an umbrella – as possible.

"We have a whole generation growing up steeped in American culture," explained Russell T Davies, "giving us fantasy shows like *Buffy* and *Smallville* and *Enterprise*, and I love those shows and I watch them all," – what, even *Enterprise*? – "but we're so steeped in Americana. Every single one of us knows the yellow school bus and the prom date and the graduation day and all that. And actually it's time to take that sort of fantasy material and put it in Britain. In the new series of *Doctor Who*, they are very deliberately running past Big Ben, they're on Westminster Bridge, there are red double-decker buses because it's a great big signal, right at the start, saying: this is British."[1]

At one point, filming got a bit *too* close to an iconic London landmark for comfort, when crewmembers on a motor launch bobbing about near the Houses of Parliament suddenly found themselves surrounded by armed anti-terrorist officers. But once they'd explained they were just helping to organise an alien invasion of Britain, everything was okay.

Back in Wales, Eccleston and Piper recorded their first scenes aboard the new TARDIS set – a cavernous dome supported by coral struts surrounding a central console apparently cobbled together from the contents of someone's dad's shed, and then left at the bottom of the sea for 50 years. "When I first walked into the TARDIS, it was mind-blowing," said Piper. "The size, the scale, the bits and pieces, the console – all the chess pieces and gauze and all the crazy buttons and compasses you can play with and toy with... it just looks so beautiful when it's lit."[1]

And was the Doctor similarly awestruck? "I have to be honest, and with respect to the design team, I didn't pay much attention to it because I was concentrating so hard on what I had to do myself," said Eccleston. "I think I was looking at it thinking, 'I'm going to have to fill this space and be as good as the design itself in a way'. And I've missed a lot of the locations that I've worked on because you're just head down, playing the part. You're trying to remember your lines and improve each take and you're dealing with the fact somebody wants to do a publicity interview and you've got to learn the lines for tomorrow." Alright, Captain Happiness – a simple "Yes, it looked great" would have done.

Oh No Logo

August brought good news: the militant *Doctor Who* fans of Southampton could stand down, as word came back from the front line that the war with the Terry Nation Estate was over, and the Daleks were back in business. That Tim Hancock was clearly a chip off the old block – though whether the Beeb had upped its reputed original cash offer of £250,000 isn't known (nor the validity of the rumour they were considering changing the

Daleks' famous battle cry to EX-TOR-TION-ATE!). *The Sun*, predictably, claimed it was them wot won it through their tireless devotion to rolling an old Dalek around to appear in shameless photo ops.

It was also announced that John Barrowman was to join the series as "intergalactic rogue" Captain Jack Harkness. Born in Glasgow but raised in Illinois, Barrowman had presented Saturday morning kids' TV show *Live and Kicking*, but was best known as a song and dance man in a variety of West End musicals, including the lead role in a recent revival of *Anything Goes*. And Andy Pryor and his team scored a coup by signing stage and screen veteran Simon Callow to play Charles Dickens in Mark Gatiss' Victorian-set episode. Callow was something of an expert on the great man (Dickens, not Mark Gatiss), having written extensively about him and starred in a long-running one-man show, *The Mystery of Charles Dickens*. He had also played him numerous times on screen – and, by his own admission, was in no hurry to do so again. "To be honest, when they sent me the script, my heart sank," he told *The Independent*. "As I know all about Dickens, I can say with authority that most attempts to put him on the screen are awful – and there are a lot of them. But this script is fantastic."

While Phil Collinson and Tracie Simpson spent their days wrangling Daleks, space pigs and other animals, Russell T Davies and Julie Gardner took second jobs as writer and executive producer of a BBC Three comedy drama about the life of Casanova. The serial – originally commissioned by Gardner while she was still at London Weekend Television – starred Peter O'Toole as the world's randiest librarian, looking back on his roister-doistering youth as a young buck played by none other than Big Finish regular David Tennant. Recognising a kindred spirit, Davies and Tennant spent much of the late 2004 shoot talking about UNIT dating and swapping favourite quotes from *Mawdryn Undead*. Not that Tennant was angling for a part or anything.

In October, fans had to breathe into a paper bag again when the new *Doctor Who* logo was revealed. In a devastating break with tradition, it featured the words DOCTOR and WHO on the same line and in the same font size, framed in an amber lozenge that many were quick to point out bore a striking resemblance to the sign on a London taxi cab. In possibly the worst case of industrial over-manning since the 70s, the logo was the work of no fewer than five people – three from BBC Wales' Graphic Design team and two from freelance company Insect Design. ("How about you do DOC and I do TOR? Steve, you do the WHO and Liz can do the gap in the middle. And Terry can make the tea.") Some fans were so unimpressed they emailed the designers directly to offer some constructive feedback, which was thoughtful of them.

And soon they would have not one but *two* programmes to complain about, when it was announced that the new series would be accompanied by a behind-the-scenes show, *Doctor Who Confidential*, to air immediately after each episode. And if you're wondering how something broadcast on national television could be "confidential," the answer is it was going out on BBC Three.

On November 1st, the show's good friends at *The Sun* published a paparazzi picture of a new Dalek (not an upskirt shot, mercifully) – which, to everyone's relief, turned out to look quite a lot like an old Dalek, albeit pimped with a gold paint job and accessorised with a couple of lights apparently nicked off a police car. (That explains why they'd been so reluctant to show their new designs to Tim Hancock – they hadn't bothered to do any.)

A few weeks later, executive producer Mal Young left the BBC to take up a new job as Head of Drama at 19 Television, the telly arm of Spice Girls / Pop Idol svengali Simon Fuller's entertainment empire. As 19's only previous forays into – ahem – drama were *Spiceworld: The Movie* and several series starring S-Club 7, this was perhaps an odd move. Nevertheless, as one of the driving forces behind the resurrection of *Doctor Who*, Young deserves our eternal graduate – even as he continues to collaborate with the Dark Lord Fuller to bring about the end of civilisation as we know it.

On January 1st, 2005 – with around three months to go until the planned spring launch – viewers caught a fleeting glimpse of the new-look *Doctor Who* when BBC One broadcast the coyest of teaser trailers: a camera panning across space before crashing down to Earth,

accompanied by a brief snatch of dialogue. "It's almost time...' taunted the accompanying caption, '... but not quite yet.' " After a couple of hundred viewings, most fans decided it wasn't really enough to get excited about.

There was more tabloid tittle-tattle when Billie Piper and Chris Evans announced they were breaking up, citing the time Piper was spending in Cardiff as a factor but insisting it would have happened anyway because they "wanted different things". Several newspapers claimed co-star Christopher Eccleston was "helping Billie get over the break-up" – which he probably was, but they managed to make it sound much seedier than that. Less salaciously, the BBC named UK manufacturer Character Options as the main licensee for new *Doctor Who* toys, and released details of three original ninth Doctor novels to be penned by Justin Richards, Jacqueline Rayner and Stephen Cole. It was a fair bet none of them would include the phrase "indubitably, my dear".

As the start date edged tantalisingly closer, fans began to learn more about Russell T Davies' vision for the series. "I watch a lot of other science-fiction shows and they tend to be sombre, dark, even angst-ridden, and that would just die a death on a Saturday evening," he told *SFCrowsNest* in January. "People want to be entertained at that time, so *Doctor Who* is fun, fast-paced and takes viewers on a rollercoaster ride."[12]

A couple of months later, he expanded on this theme in the pages of *SFX* magazine: "It's going out on Saturday night and that is a lively, fast, colourful slot. That's why I don't give a fuck what anyone thinks about the logo – it is brilliant when it's flying at the screen. It's big and bold and *huge* dramatically. It's almost over the top. *That* is where we're playing. We're not 9pm on BBC2. From the start, it was 'We've got to have big pictures in this'. And that's what made it so hard to make, because television isn't based around that; it's usually two people who talk."[10]

Davies is a bit of a talker himself: effusive and generous with praise but also combative, playful and provocative, he delights in tossing grenades into the more entrenched corners of fandom – or "ming mong land", as he once so delicately put it. Here's him riffing on those "big pictures" again: "I think good scriptwriting is visual. I get very, very fed up of *Doctor Who* fans saying to me, 'It's not about the special effects, it's about the script'. It's a fascinating distinction to make – are you saying scripts are just dialogue? Scripts are not just dialogue – scripts are visual things. We're *television* writers, and it's our job, as well as good dialogue, to have great images – some of which will be great science-fiction images. You're telling a story in pictures."[1]

And here's a variation on his No Zogs Rule, when discussing the Earthbound nature of the upcoming series: "If the moment the opening titles are over, you go into Scene One that's set on a purple planet with three moons, and some man in a cloak is making a villainous death threat, then the audience would switch off in their millions. I think you should set all that high-flown, end-of-the-world stuff in a very real world of pubs, and mortgages, and people."[13] It's a fair point – though you can't help wondering how *Genesis of the Daleks* would have turned out if Davies had been in charge. ("Doctor, we want you to travel back in time and stop Davros taking out a lease on a Wetherspoon's pub.")

In contrast to science fiction's inclination towards grim futuristic dystopias, Davies was also insistent the series should demonstrate a positive, optimistic attitude to the human race. "I do think that we live in an age where every day you open up the newspaper and it tells you you're dying – coffee is going to kill you and bird flu is going to kill you and genuine things like global warming are going to kill you," he said. "And I often wonder what it must be like to be eight years old, living in a climate where that is the attitude. When I was young, frankly, we used to look ahead to 2000 with optimism. Do you remember? We thought we were going to fly to the moon and have jet-packs and silver suits. It was a very optimistic attitude – even though we were living through the Cold War. I wanted to do something that said maybe there *is* a future of monorails and zip-suits and jet-packs and *fun*, and that no matter what you throw at the human race, its greatest instinct is to survive."[1]

Which was pretty good going for a man who'd just delivered a script called *The End of the World.*

First Welsh episode hit by leek

In February, BBC One Controller-turned-fanboy pin-up Lorraine Heggessey left the BBC to head up Talkback Thames, and was replaced by Peter Fincham, an experienced TV executive whose most recent job was... head of Talkback Thames. Maybe it was a game of cards that got out of hand. Anyway, for those of you keeping count, that's Lorraine Heggessy and Mal Young out, Michael Grade in. Try to remain calm.

Overseas, deals had now been signed to show the new series in Canada, Australia, New Zealand and across the BBC Prime satellite network in Europe, Asia and Africa. No US broadcaster had yet been found, with some of the major networks apparently worried it was "too British". ("Britain – that's in, like, France or somewhere, right?") But hey, at least it would be on in the Netherlands.

Two new projects were announced in early March – *Doctor Who: A New Dimension* was a 30-minute documentary scheduled to be shown on BBC One, while Radio 2 promised a two-part behind-the-scenes programme called *Project: WHO?*. Meanwhile, filming was drawing to a close, with Christopher Eccleston recording his final scenes on March 5th.

That same week, fans worldwide found themselves with an unexpected moral dilemma when the entire first episode of the new series was leaked onto the internet by an employee of a Canadian affiliate company. (Who very soon became an ex-employee of a Canadian affiliate company.) Most fans did the decent thing – i.e. illegally downloaded the episode but had the good grace to feel bad about it, while the BBC insisted it was an unfinished rough cut (which it wasn't, really).

Because normal people aren't as proficient as nerds at stealing things off the net, the first reviews inevitably appeared on geek sites like Hollywood gossip sheet *Ain't It Cool*, which offered the considered opinion: "Bottom line: excrement." Thanks for that – it was well worth the 16-year wait. Some of the press picked up on this and, despite the fact much of the feedback was really quite positive, word of the hatchet jobs got back to Christopher Eccleston. "There's been a couple of early reviews and they've... they've attacked it, and it's painful," he told *BBC News*. "You accept it, you take it on the chin. But when you've worked it out as much as we have, with so much love, you hope you'll get some back."

A few days later, the series received its official press launch at the St David's Hotel in Cardiff Bay. The celebrations got off to a high-profile start that morning when Murray Gold's revamped theme was premiered on the BBC Five Live and Radio 1 breakfast shows. Keeping Delia Derbyshire's realisation of the main "howl" proudly intact, but adding a pile-driving rhythm and a subtle counter-melody, it was generally agreed by most to be rather fabulous. Russell T Davies revealed they had considered just using the original but, when they came to listen to it, it had seemed "a bit empty and old". (His words, not mine, so don't write in.)

The slebs were out in force at the press do: as well as Davies, Christopher Eccleston, Billie Piper, Julie Gardner, Mal Young and Lorraine Heggessy – plus representatives of the old guard such as Terrance Dicks and Barry Letts – guests included Charlotte Church, Robson Green and Matt Lucas. *The Sun* sent its Dalek, which was turned away by security despite having Ms Church draped over its sucker arm. Maybe it was wearing trainers. *The Independent*, meanwhile, speculated over whether Tim Collins would choose the launch over that evening's vote on the Government's controversial anti-terror bill. "Terror debate or not, I'll be very surprised if Tim misses the screening," a colleague told the paper. "As for the rest of us, we'll have to decide which is more important: the invasion of the Daleks, or the invasion of al-Qa'ida." Yeah, I'll do the jokes, thanks.

Steven Moffat couldn't make it, so sent his mother-in-law in his place. It was here Beryl Vertue chose to reveal to the production team that she'd been the one who had originally negotiated Terry Nation's Dalek contract. ("Actually, Beryl was just leaving.")

On *BBC Breakfast* the next morning, *DWM* editor Clayton Hickman declared: "If the kids don't like that, then the kids don't deserve to have any television ever shown to them again". On BBC2's *Newsnight*, by contrast, former ITV CEO Stuart Prebble predicted the show would be a flop. "I think it looks like an attempt to sort of hark back to a 'golden age' where the whole family were willing to sit down as a

group and watch," he said. "Unfortunately, in 2005, very little television viewing is like that." He had a point – no-one had really watched family dramas since the likes of ITV and the BBC stopped making them.

On March 10th, the BBC revealed the new series of *Doctor Who* would start in just over a fortnight's time, on Saturday 26th. "It's the new November 23rd," said jubilant fans, as world leaders cancelled any motorcade appearances that week, just to be on the safe side.

In recent weeks, there had been rumblings on the internet message boards about the subdued publicity for the new series. ("What do you mean?" said the BBC. "There was that thing on *Wales Tonight* last year – what more do you want?") But in the second week of March, the Beeb's promotional machine suddenly cranked up a gear. Then it cranked up a couple more gears. And then it went absolutely batshit mental.

It began with a series of five-second teasers on BBC One showing Christopher Eccleston and Billie Piper inside the TARDIS. Then the first full trailer arrived: "Do you want to come with me?" asked Eccleston, staring straight down the camera lens. "Because if you do, then I should warn you. You're going to see all sorts of things," he promised, to a high-octane montage of Daleks, spaceships and very big explosions. "Ghosts from past, aliens from the future, the day the Earth died in a ball of flame... It won't be quiet, it won't be safe and it won't be calm. But I tell you what it will be: the trip of a lifetime." That thud you heard was several thousand *Doctor Who* fans fainting in unison.

Piper also fronted a trailer: "I've got a choice," she told viewers. "Stay at home with my mum, my boyfriend, my job... or chuck it all in for danger, and monsters, and life or death. What do you think?" I don't know – you could make a list of the pros and cons and sleep on it?

At the same time, giant billboard posters started appearing all over Britain – a dramatic shot of the Doctor and Rose that looked so damn cool, some fans couldn't even be bothered to complain about the TARDIS doors opening out instead of in.

The campaign coincided with an avalanche of media coverage in newspapers, magazines,

TV and radio. Among the more memorable were Billie Piper cavorting in her pants on the cover of men's mag *Arena* ("Dr Who's New Sidekick Fresh from the Arena Sex Tardis!" promised the strapline, subtly), and a feature on the show's huge gay following in *Attitude*. *The Sun* got so carried away it even ran an article headlined "Why Wales is so Hip it Hurts", which was surely going too far.

On March 18th, the first episode came under scrutiny by the guests on upmarket round-table pow-wow *Newsnight Review*. Host Mark Lawson, bestselling crime novelist Ian Rankin and *Sunday Times* book reviewer Professor John Carey all gave it the thumbs up (not literally – this was a much classier affair than Siskel and Ebert), but the American critic Bonnie Greer was baffled by the whole thing. "Who is this for?" she asked. "Is it for my generation? Is it for fortysomethings? Is it for babies? The acting is wonderful, the writing is wonderful, but it just looks thin. It looks cheap." "The cheapness is part of the point," countered Carey, unhelpfully. "It's very British. The fact it's done on a shoestring is very important. It's self-mocking. It's not to be taken too seriously." *That* sound you can hear? It's Russell T Davies' teeth grinding. Luckily, Rankin was on hand to note "the effects in this aren't cheap – it's a series that's been waiting for the digital age to come along", and everyone agreed Eccleston was wonderful.

The first newspaper reviews had also started appearing – with most predicting the Beeb had a monster-sized smash on its hands. "The first *Doctor Who* series for 16 years could give the BBC a much-needed hit for its ailing Saturday night schedules if the verdict of fans, critics and children is correct," said the *Daily Telegraph*, while *The Sun* predicted Davies' "sparky, witty" script would "please even the most ardent of fans". They obviously hadn't met the most ardent of fans.

Several newspapers and websites also reported that Welsh First Minister Rhodri Morgan had almost been transformed into a "tree monster" after being mistaken for a *Doctor Who* extra when he'd arrived at the BBC's Cardiff studios to take part in a political discussion show. Morgan said he had been sent to the wrong dressing room, where "a young chap from London came in and said 'Are you

the man I am making up as a tree?'" It certainly made an unusual subject for the political pages (the Welsh Assembly, I mean, not *Doctor Who*).

Five days before the start of the series, Christopher Eccleston maintained a sacred television tradition by emerging from a newly-materialised TARDIS in the *Blue Peter* studio. Later that week, he toured the radio stations, chatting to Five Live's Simon Mayo and Radio 1's Jo Whiley, to whom he described the Doctor as "a 900-year-old alien with two hearts who used to look like Sylvester McCoy". Which is probably not the feature you'd choose to highlight in a personal ad.

"If he meets something that's different from him, instead of reacting with aggression, he reacts with wonder and welcome," he added. "There's a message in there about acceptance, which is quite good when you've got eight and 12 year olds." Unless it's the Zogs from Zog, of course, in which case they can go f*** themselves.

Asked about doing a second series, Eccleston told Whiley he was "reserving judgement". He also dropped a slight hint that the scripts hadn't been *entirely* what he'd signed up for: "With any job I take, particularly in television, it's always about the writer. The main attraction was getting eight scripts by Russell T Davies. Bit naïve in a way because, to a certain extent, Russell is constrained by the fact it's *Doctor Who*. In fact he's not constrained," he corrected himself, to the sound of furious back-pedalling. "I think he's writing at the top of his form."

The actor also sounded a note of caution during a pre-recorded interview for that week's *Project: WHO?* radio documentary. "There's a kind of madness when you essentially do the same thing in each episode," he said. "I experienced it once doing a play in the West End for three months – I did the same thing every night, and you have to be very careful in the way that affects you. In a sense the Doctor doesn't develop – he does the same thing every episode, and half way through this, I found myself doing something very similar that I'd done the episode before. And I got The Fear. You think, 'Am I simply repeating myself?' The previous work I've done, it's always been beginning, middle and end drama, and this is a different animal."

Was he "in it for the long haul"? wondered interviewer Malcolm Prince. "I've done the long haul," replied Eccleston. "I've done the long haul." We'll take that as a no, then.

The star was also quoted in *The Sun* as being "not completely sure" about his future with the show. "I need to think about it," he said. "It's more than a huge responsibility to shoulder. And no, I don't want to be thought of as the Doctor to the exclusion of everything else I've done or may do in the future. So I'll have to think long and hard about it before I make a final decision to say yes or no. I am keenly aware that the whole thing could be a poisoned chalice." ("Did everybody get that?" asked the BBC press officer through a frozen smile. "Chris said it's been the greatest honour of his professional career and he's very excited to be involved. Oh look, we've run out of time. Thanks for coming.")

Elsewhere, rolls of newsprint were devoted to the question of who would win the weekend's big battle for viewers: the Doctor or conjoined showbiz twins Ant and Dec, whose *Saturday Night Takeaway* had thus far proved a ratings goliath for ITV. Perhaps rattled by all the *Who* hype, a little over 72 hours before transmission, ITV blinked first and announced it was moving the two-headed Geordie hydra forward to 6.45pm to give them a 15-minute head start on the Time Lord. They would also be wheeling out the big guns in the form of guest star David Beckham. Could Serious Actor Christopher Eccleston really hope to win a popularity contest against Goldenballs? The bookies didn't think so: "Money suggests Ant and Dec will take away the highest ratings," said a spokesman for Ladbrokes, "but we haven't seen such an intense battle for viewers on Saturday night since the finals of *Strictly Come Dancing* and *The X Factor* went head to head at the end of last year."

And still the tsunami of press coverage continued: rock bible *NME* conferred its blessing on the new series by declaring: "For the first time in its history, *Doctor Who* is about to become cool." Mind you, they said that about Shed Seven. *The Daily Telegraph*, meanwhile, struck a blow for highbrow journalism with an article headlined: "Is Doctor Who Gay?"

Honestly, just because he never dates women, likes to dress in crushed velvet and cravats and spends his life in a closet, there's no need to go leaping to conclusions.

And then, at 7pm on Saturday, March 26th, the time for speculation, conjecture and fatuous questions was finally over as *Doctor Who* returned to BBC One just 134,135 hours since the end of Part 3 of *Survival*. But hey, who was counting?

Shopgirl attacked by plastic ~~Norton~~ Auton

Rose is a deceptively clever piece of television. If it felt, to some fans hoping for a resurrection of Biblical proportions, somewhat light and inconsequential, then it probably needed to be. This is Russell T Davies being deliberately cautious, sneaking sci-fi concepts in under the radar to an audience that's been virtually starved of anything fantastical with a British accent for the best part of two decades. It's a wolf in Gap clothing.

Davies is a master of economical writing: we meet Rose, her mother and her boyfriend, and learn where she lives and works – and what she thinks about it – in the first 90 *seconds*. The rest of the team are on-message, too: Keith Boak chops up the action with fast cutting and a blur of time-lapse, while Murray Gold's skittish beats (inspired by The Pixies' *Cecilia Ann*, dontcha know – it's hard to imagine Dudley Simpson ever took his cue from scuzzy American garage rock) serves immediate notice that we're not in Kansas any more.

Then, when Rose descends into the basement of the department store where she folds jumpers for a living, we're suddenly back in old-skool *Who* territory, as shop dummies emerge from the shadows to deliver the series' first behind the sofa moment. Except... it's not actually *that* scary, because there's virtually no effort made to ramp up the tension: no sooner has the first dummy turned his head and clocked Rose than a whole gang of them are converging on her, backing her up against the wall like autograph-hunting *Doctor Who* fans at the stage door of a provincial theatre. Whether this was deliberate policy – not to frighten the kids away before they've had a chance to get comfortable – or whether Boak just fumbled it, we don't know.

And, of course, Graham Norton didn't exactly help. No, he's not one of the dummies – feel free to insert your own gag here – but, when *Rose* went out on BBC One, the excitable Irish gossip-monger could be heard blabbermouthing all over this scene after someone accidentally left an audio circuit open from the studio where he was recording short-lived reality clunker *Strictly Dance Fever*. This blunder is pretty much unheard of on British television, so the fact it occurred during the first real moment of tension in the most hyped show of the year, possibly of the decade... well, let's just say *someone's* chances of making Employee of the Month were looking a little shaky.

A few seconds later – thankfully, the feed was cut just before the timing got *really* disastrous – Rose is snatched from the jaws of death (or at least an excess of casual sportswear) by a mysterious man in a black leather jacket, who wastes no time in telling her he's engaged in a war against creatures made from living plastic. But not to worry, because he's got a big bomb. "What was your name, by the way?" he asks, shortly before blowing her workplace up. "Rose," she tells him. "Nice to meet you Rose, I'm the Doctor – run for your life!" Time check: 06:59.

As the shell-shocked shopgirl returns home, we get the measure of her mum, Jackie – and also learn something important about Russell T Davies' M.O.: "It's aged her," Jackie tells a friend on the phone. "Skin like an old Bible – walk in here now, you'd think I was *her* daughter." This doesn't really make any sense (who gets bad skin from shock?), but, for Davies, it hardly matters: it's a good gag that provides an easy shorthand for Jackie's character, and that's more important than slavish devotion to plot logic. If this bothers you, look away for several years now.

We also meet Rose's feckless boyfriend, Mickey, who is later replaced by an unconvincing plastic replica – something which Rose fails to notice, presumably on account of Noel Clarke playing the real thing like a *Scooby-Doo* cartoon anyway. To his credit, Clarke is the first to acknowledge he doesn't exactly cover himself in glory in this story: "It wasn't played straight – some of it was played for laughs," he

admitted. "I have no excuses, but I do have reasons: I had no rehearsal time, so I didn't really know the tone of what we were doing. I'd never met Chris before, or Billie, or Camille. I didn't realise it at the time, but my head wasn't where it should have been."[14] (That's literally true in *Rose*, as the Doctor pulls Auton Mickey's head off and sticks it on the TARDIS console. Where it melts.)

Rose's second encounter with the Doctor is a mixture of slapstick comic business – Christopher Eccleston gamely attacking himself with a plastic arm – and really rather wonderful dialogue. "It's like when you were a kid," says the Doctor when Rose asks who he is. "The first time they tell you the world's turning and you just can't quite believe it, because everything looks like it's standing still. I can feel it. The turn of the Earth. The ground beneath our feet is spinning at a thousand miles an hour, and the entire planet is hurtling round the sun at 67,000 miles an hour, and I can *feel* it. We're falling through space, you and me, clinging to the skin of this tiny little world, and if we let go... [He releases her hand] That's who I am. Now, forget me, Rose Tyler. Go home."

There are many such beautiful moments in this episode – Rose's first entry into the TARDIS (she bursts into tears, which is a first), Mark Benton's extended cameo as a dedicated Who-ologist ("The Doctor is a legend woven throughout history. When disaster comes, he's there. He brings the storm in his wake and he has one constant companion: death") and the Doctor's throwaway explanation for his accent ("Lots of planets have a north") among them. Tonally, though, it's all over the shop: one minute Rose is chastising the Doctor for forgetting her boyfriend has just been killed, then literally seconds later she's running hand-in-hand with him over Westminster Bridge with a grin as wide than the Thames.

And then there's the bin. In the story's most notorious scene, Mickey is eaten by a wheelie bin. It's a somewhat ludicrous idea, and filmed so as to be utterly devoid of menace, but they just about get away with it – until the moment the bin gives a satisfied belch, complete with comedy lid-pop. Davies probably had a valid point about certain fans needing to lighten up and let the kids have their fun, but this was surely better suited to a CBeebies show – in fact, it was uncomfortably reminiscent of those 70s Rod Hull and Emu skits in which the Doctor was menaced by the Deadly Dustbins – than the "full-blooded drama" we'd been promised. Or maybe I'm just a miserable old bastard.

The alien invasion story also dribbles away to a woeful anti-climax. We're told that plastic is coming to life and attacking people all over the place, but all we get are a few pedestrian – in every sense of the word – mannequins wandering about a shopping centre, like bored husbands on a day out at Bluewater. Sure, we never expected to see Rose's joke about breast implants turning on their owners realised on screen, but *something* would have been nice. Even *Terror of the Autons* managed a phone cord, a doll and an inflatable chair, and that was in 1970.

At the end of the day, though, the barely-there plot is hardly the point. As evidenced by Davies' thoroughly shameless use of "anti-plastic" as a maguffin to wrap up the whole thing without any boring explanations, *Rose* is essentially a Time Lord-meets-girl story and everything else is window dressing (literally, in the Autons' case). In that, it succeeds magnificently, with Billie Piper, in particular, lighting up the screen with a dazzling performance.

Eccleston's Doctor is slightly more problematic – give him a grandstanding emotional moment and he's captivating, and he has a nice line in snarky put-downs. But it's fair to say he's not a natural comedian, and seems visibly uncomfortable with the "heightened" acting style required in the Doctor's big confrontation with the Nestene Consciousness, which he delivers in a Sylvester McCoy-style strangulated yelp.

Nevertheless, when, in the dying moments, Rose decides to shuck off her old life and literally races into the Doctor's blue box in search of romance and adventure, it really does feel like the trip of a lifetime has begun – for her, for him, for all of us.

A few hours after the episode had aired, the BBC issued a statement apologising if Graham Norton had "affected viewers' enjoyment" (of *Doctor Who*, presumably – although they could equally have meant *Strictly Dance Fever*, I suppose). It was barely a blip on the radar,

though, as the critics tripped over themselves to lavish praise on the show's relaunch. "An alien form, called entertainment, has been discovered on Saturday nights," goggled the *Sunday Express*. "It's a thoroughly bizarre, glossy new concoction called *Dr Who*." "After such a fanfare, *Doctor Who* could hardly fail to disappoint," began *The Independent* on Sunday cautiously. "But amazingly, it didn't. Okay, the monster was feeble and the lack of a cliff-hanger ending was a shame. But Christopher Eccleston portrayed a far more complicated Doctor than we've become used to seeing, certainly since Jon Pertwee – and far more interesting as a result." "After 16 years locked in the warp-shunt fantasies of the plasters-on-specs brigade," said the *News of the World*, "Russell T Davies has breathed new life into an old favourite. The Doctor got his girl and BBC One found itself reacquainted with an old pal. Quality. Brilliant." "The new *Doctor Who* succeeded in establishing its own reality," claimed the *Sunday Telegraph*. "Skewed, sprightly and assured, without ever taking its audience's attention, or goodwill, for granted." *The Times*, meanwhile, hailed "a joyful, exuberant reinvention".

Not everyone was impressed. "The current incarnation of the Time Lord has barely moved on and the one thing the future can't afford to be is old-fashioned," grumbled the *Sunday Times*. "The new *Who* is poorly cast, badly written, pointlessly northern, relentlessly silly and, fairly crucially, the sci-fi is thoughtless and throwaway," said *The People*. And the *Daily Mail* thought it "a prodigious waste of money by the BBC". But then, they would.

These were the exceptions, though. And there was even better news to come, as overnight ratings showed the good Doctor had laid waste to the opposition in the ratings war, reaching ten million viewers to Ant and Dec's seven million. (A week later, consolidated figures would show *Rose* was actually seen by a whopping 10.81 million, making it the seventh-most watched programme of the week across all channels.) The papers went nuts again – "New Doctor Makes Dummies of Ant and Dec," guffawed the *Daily Star*; "Who's the Daddy as 10m Find Time to See the Doctor", punned *The Times* – and even the weekly gossip mags stopped laughing at celebrities' bad skin and sweat patches long enough to take an interest, with *OK!* installing Eccleston and Piper at Nos. 2 and 3 on its celebrity chart. (History doesn't record who took the top spot but, in the pre-Kardashian era, stick a pin in the general Katie Price/Peter Andre/Kerry Katona axis and you won't be far off the mark.)

Then, just four days later, Jane Tranter announced that a second series of *Doctor Who* had already been commissioned – along with a Christmas special to be shown that December. "It's fantastic news," said Russell T Davies. "It's been a tense and jittery time because the production team has been working on plans. It's particularly good for BBC Wales. This is a major flagship show for the region, and their staff and crews are the best you could find. It's a tribute to them that *Doctor Who* is returning."

For the fans, battered and bruised by so many years of disappointment and derision, it was all a bit much to take in. After a decade-and-a-half in the wilderness, and a good few years before that being shunned as an embarrassing irrelevance, *Doctor Who* was back – and everybody seemed to love it. It was everything they had ever dreamed of – and now they'd been guaranteed more of the same next year, perhaps they could finally, *finally* start to relax and just enjoy it. After all, what could possibly go wrong?

Doctor Who quits;
Pope takes it badly

In the midst of all the euphoria, on March 30th the *Daily Mirror* took a big wizz on everyone's chips when it ran an article once again raising rumours that Christopher Eccleston had been less than happy on set, and was planning to quit. What's more, the paper even named his successor, claiming that *Casanova* star David Tennant had been lined up to take over – if not now then "at some point". Other media outlets picked up on the story, which gradually built up a head of steam until, once again, the BBC found itself bounced into issuing a statement. As was customary, the press release was smuggled out onto the wires just after midnight (*Doctor Who* must have been costing them a fortune in overtime payments). And it didn't make pretty reading: Christopher Eccleston, the statement revealed, would not

be returning to *Doctor Who* for a second se… oh, you were ahead of me there.

The BBC's official line at this stage was that Eccleston had quit because he had found the filming schedule "gruelling" and that he "feared being typecast". The press release included a short quote attributed to the actor, who stated: "The audience's response for the new *Doctor Who* has been incredible. I am really proud to be part of it and I hope viewers continue to enjoy the series."

The Corporation also confirmed that talks to make David Tennant the tenth Doctor were taking place, but that other names may be put forward. "Public demand has forced us to produce a long list of possible Doctors, despite the fact that David Tennant is so hotly tipped for the role," said bookmakers Ladbrokes. But rivals William Hill refused to take any bets after being "flooded" with punters wanting to bet on Tennant. "It appears that the BBC has moved quickly to secure David Tennant's services following the departure of Eccleston," said a spokesman for the company. "It seems that the role is his should he want it, which makes it impossible for us to open a book."

The press were in uproar. "Doctor Who Do You Think You Are?" demanded *The Sun* in its front-page splash story. "It's a huge slap in the face for ten million fans who eagerly awaited the big-budget new series," wailed TV editor Emily Smith. "He's Time Lording it over us." The *Daily Mail*, meanwhile, claimed BBC bosses were "furious" after "millions" had been spent on merchandise with Eccleston's image on it. Things got so heated on Outpost Gallifrey, the world's most popular *Doctor Who* web forum, that administrators shut it down for two days in order to give everyone time to cool off. Among the most vocal protesters was former series continuity adviser Ian Levine, who unleashed a flurry of foam-flecked invective accusing Eccleston of wrecking the show's comeback and effectively pissing all over the dreams of every *Doctor Who* fan. Which was odd, because Levine was normally so calm and considered.

Peter Davison didn't pull any punches, either. "He is letting down the programme," asserted the fifth Doctor. "His commitment should have been for at least a couple, maybe three series. I'd hate to see, after all the effort that went into getting the programme back on TV, *Doctor Who* scuppered by an actor saying, 'I don't want to do this any more'."

Richard Franklin, meanwhile, fired off an angry missive to his local paper, the *Brighton Argus*, in which he accused Eccleston of using the series as a "stepping stone". "I find this insulting and ungrateful to the fans, who would have taken him to their hearts, and to the BBC, who have given him the accolade of a unique television role," raged the erstwhile Captain Mike Yates. "His departure is not much thanks for a leg-up most actors would have given their right arm for, and a glaring example of the greed, selfishness and cult of celebrity which blights modern Britain." I say, steady on, old bean. (The BBC later returned Franklin's right arm in the post, with a polite note thanking him for his interest in the role.)

It was left to new series director Joe Ahearne to spring to Eccleston's defence. "He's only done a mere ten hours of thrilling television," Ahearne wrote in a letter to *The Guardian*. "God forbid we should give him a round of applause."

A live chat with Russell T Davies scheduled for the BBC's official *Doctor Who* site to coincide with the second episode was abruptly cancelled without explanation, as was an item about *Doctor Who* on the BBC's religious affairs programme *Heaven and Earth*. To be fair, the Pope *had* died the day before – but that was hardly in the same league as Doctor Who quitting, was it?

Davies' first statement on the subject appeared in the *Western Mail*, in which he insisted: "This had all been planned. You will see the story unfold on screen and it's brilliant. We've got 13 episodes of the best Doctor in the world – he worked himself to death on that show."

And the drama didn't end there: on April 4th, the BBC issued another statement, admitting it had "broken an agreement" with Christopher Eccleston by failing to speak to the actor before revealing he was going to quit. "The BBC regrets not speaking to Christopher before it responded to the press questions on Wednesday, 30th March," said Jane Tranter. "The BBC further regrets that it falsely attributed a statement to Christopher and apologises to him. Contrary to press statements,

Christopher did not leave for fear of being typecast, or because of the gruelling filming schedule." A BBC spokesman said Eccleston's decision to leave had been made in January, but the news was supposed to have been held back until after the surprise series finale.

Oh dear. It was all a bit unfortunate, to say the least. But hey, chin up everyone – it wasn't the end of the world. That had taken place a few days earlier.

It's the end of the world as we know it (and I feel like chips)

If *Rose* had been deliberately coy about its sci-fi credentials, *The End of the World* is like a coming out party. Set aboard a space station (okay, a "viewing platform," technically) and featuring blue, green and brown aliens with names like the Moxx of Balhoon and the Face of Boe (a giant tentacled head in a tank), it's a far cry from the *Hollyoaks*-with-time travel of the previous week. And now we also knew why that Auton invasion looked so cheap – with 203 separate effects shots, this is the most technically ambitious production in *Doctor Who's* history. (Yes, even more ambitious than *Underworld*.)

Rather than whisking Rose off to Renaissance Italy or The Great Exhibition for her first trip in the TARDIS, the Doctor chooses to take her to the year Five Billion to watch her planet being destroyed by the expanding Sun. His message? "Everything has its time, and everything dies." As first dates go, it's a bit of a downer, frankly.

Among the delegates gathering to watch the cataclysm is Lady Cassandra O'Brien Dot Delta Seventeen – the last survivor of the human race, now reduced to a piece of talking skin stretched across a frame, with her brain underneath in a jar. Russell T Davies claimed to have got the idea while watching the grisly parade of facelifts and crash diets at the previous year's Oscars – though, in Cassandra's defence, she doesn't look nearly as bad as Donatella Versace or Renée Zellweger. Voiced by Zoe Wannamaker as what Rose calls "a bitchy trampoline", it's quite the campiest thing to hit *Doctor Who* since Kate O'Mara slipped into Bonnie Langford's legwarmers. (And considerably more expensive: Davies hadn't considered that every line of Cassandra's dialogue constituted an FX shot, so he cut some out and wrote a rather delightful scene with Rose chatting to a blue-faced plumber instead.)

What's particularly charming about *The End of the World* – and what sets the series up for the future, essentially – is that, while the effects may finally be punching their weight with Hollywood, Davies never lets us lose sight of the small, the domestic and the human. There's a beautiful scene where Rose phones her mum – a jump cut from the depths of space in the impossibly far future to the back of a washing machine drum in twenty-first-century south London – while the script finds room for references to, among others, Michael Jackson, the National Lottery, Ipswich and (something of a recurring motif for the new series, this) chips. There's also a great gag in which Cassandra produces an "iPod" (I know, how *very* 2005), which turns out to be an old-fashioned jukebox, and proceeds to play some "classical music from humanity's greatest composers", including "Tainted Love" by Soft Cell and Britney Spears' "Toxic" (which, pub quizzers please note, was never actually released on vinyl – so the FX boys had to make one). The idea of the Earth's continents having been restored to a "classic" model by the National Trust is also the sort of outrageous idea only Davies would have the cojones to get away with.

Again, plot logic is happily jettisoned in the name of expedient storytelling: you have to wonder why Platform One's designers thought it was a good idea to build the controls to the heat shields behind several gigantic spinning fans but, really, who cares? It's a heart-stopping action sequence, beautifully directed by Euros Lyn. And, let's be honest, it wasn't the worst trouble Christopher Eccleston had encountered with fans that week.

The story also introduces some new concepts to the show, from the relatively trivial (the Doctor now carries a wallet of "psychic paper" that allows him to project whatever credentials he needs onto them, and there's the first mention of the words "Bad Wolf," which will become a recurring allusion in this series) to the seriously game-changing: "I'm a Time Lord," the Doctor tells Rose during a truly gorgeous coda in an ordinary twenty-first-century

street. "I'm the last of the Time Lords. They're all gone. I'm the only survivor. I'm left travelling on my own, 'cos there's no one else." But he's wrong, of course. "There's me," says Rose. And then they get chips.

Ratings for the episode were down 2.5 million on the opener, but it wasn't the end of the wor... oh, we did that already. Some newspapers blamed the Eccleston fall-out for the drop (by now, Russell T Davies and Julie Gardner were sticking firmly to the party line that Eccleston was only ever going to do one series – presumably in the same way Vanilla Ice only ever intended to have one hit), but just shy of eight million viewers was still a great result, and still trounced the previously Teflon-coated Ant and Dec.

There was more good news when the professionally acidic Charlie Brooker – a man who once described the audience of *The Jeremy Kyle Show* as "so ugly they'd make John Merrick spew down the inside of his face-bag" – was suddenly seized by a spontaneous fit of *Doctor Who*-inspired joie de vivre. "I simply cannot stand by," he wrote in his *Guardian* column, "and let this week's episode, *The Unquiet Dead*, pass without comment, for the following reason: I think it may be the single best piece of family-oriented entertainment the BBC has broadcast in its entire history. TV really doesn't get better than this, ever." What – even better than *The Power of Kroll*?

As soon as Russell T Davies came up with the idea of a Victorian ghost story set in a funeral parlour, it was obvious which writer's name would be attached to it. Mark Gatiss had always had a fascination with the Grand Guignol, which is one of the reasons why *The League of Gentlemen* is almost certainly the only British sitcom to eschew sofas and kitchen tables in favour of lovingly-crafted pastiches of *The Wicker Man*, "The Monkey's Paw" and the Amicus horror anthologies of the 70s.

Throw in Simon Callow as Charles Dickens, wrapping his rich, actorly tones around words like "phantasmagoria", "cheap mummery" and "jack-o-lanterns", and Gatiss must have thought all his Christmas Eves had come at once. (The December 24th date is the only bit the Doctor gets right here – he was aiming for Naples, 1860, and ends up in Cardiff in 1869. Yes, this story is actually *set* in the city where the show is made. So naturally, they filmed it in Swansea.)

The Unquiet Dead mixes quotable dialogue ("There's a wardrobe through there," the Doctor tells Rose aboard the TARDIS. "First left, second right, third on the left, go straight ahead, under the stairs, past the bins, fifth door on your left") with strong characters (Eve Myles is terrific as Gwyneth, the servant girl with second sight) and some decent scares.

You could argue the story adds up to less than the sum of its parts, while the ending – in which the Doctor is thrown into a comedy panic by a few shuffling zombies – does its best to strip our hero of all his dignity. But there's also much to enjoy – not least the fact that, after all the awkwardness of the last ten days, the story's cheerfully macabre use of re-animated corpses helped kick up a satisfyingly old-skool scuffle about whether *Doctor Who* was too scary for children. Though the BBC press office somehow managed to manoeuvre its foot into its mouth even on this workaday matter, initially putting out a statement saying the programme was "not for children under eight", before withdrawing it and calling the previous comment "a mistake". They really were on fire. (Incidentally, the DVDs for this series would later be slapped with a 12 rating, with the BBFC citing "violence and cruelty as a way of dealing with problems" as the somewhat Delphic reason.) Meanwhile, Mark Gatiss – veteran observer of the great Whitehouse Wars of the mid-70s – declared himself "quietly thrilled" with the whole hullabaloo. And well he might.

Wanted: acclaimed Shakespearian actor (must have own sonic screwdriver)

On April 16th, 2005, the world woke up to the least surprising casting news since Lassie said "I'll play the dog," when the BBC confirmed what the newspapers had been telling everyone for ages: the new Doctor Who would be Paul Daniels. Sorry, would be David Tennant.

"Tennant, 33, will become the tenth Time Lord when filming starts on the new series in Cardiff this summer," reported *BBC News*. "Tennant said: 'I grew up loving *Doctor Who*

and it has been a lifelong dream to get my very own TARDIS. Taking over from Chris is a daunting prospect – he has done a fantastic job of reinventing the Doctor for a new generation and is a very tough act to follow. I'm also really looking forward to working with Billie Piper, who is so great as Rose.'

"Christopher Eccleston has given an exceptional performance as the ninth Doctor," added Julie Gardner. "David Tennant is a great actor who will build on the excellent work already done by Christopher in establishing *Doctor Who* for a new generation."

Born to a Church of Scotland Minister and his wife in Bathgate, West Lothian, in 1971, David John McDonald first announced his intention to become an actor at the age of three, having been inspired by the teatime adventures of a certain scarf-wearing former monk. His parents tried to steer him towards a more conventional career, until the actress Edith MacArthur – famous for her long-running role in Scottish soap *Take the High Road* – persuaded them he had a bright future on the stage after seeing him in a play at the age of 11.

McDonald made his professional debut at 16 in an anti-smoking film produced by the Glasgow Health Board. (It was so successful, no-one has smoked a cigarette in Glasgow since.) A year later, he appeared in an episode of ITV children's anthology series *Dramarama*, and was accepted into the Royal Scottish Academy of Music and Drama, where he adopted the professional name David Tennant after reading an article about the Pet Shop Boys' Neil Tennant in *Smash Hits*. (Thank goodness it wasn't an interview with Rat Scabies.)

Tennant's first role on graduating was a production of *The Resistible Rise of Arturo Ui* by agitprop theatre company 7:84, who took their name from the statistic that 7% of the UK population owned 84% of its wealth – an injustice they intended to reverse through the medium of some really quite strongly worded left-wing fringe dramaturgy. He also made an appearance in Glaswegian sitcom Rab C Nesbitt, playing a transsexual barmaid called Davina, but it was his acclaimed turn as a bi-polar hospital patient in the six-part 1994 BBC drama *Takin' Over the Asylum* that first brought him to wider attention. It was while filming the serial that Tennant met future Time Ladette Arabella Weir and, having been invited to lodge with her, set off with a knotted hanky on a stick slung over his shoulder to make his fortune in London.

In 1996, he appeared in Michael Winterbottom's film adaptation of *Jude (the Obscure)* starring Christopher Eccleston. In one scene, Tennant's drunken undergraduate challenges Eccleston's Jude to prove his intellect by naming all six segments of the Key to Time, then triumphantly declares: "See, that's why *I* should be the Doctor and not you!" (Okay, perhaps it wasn't *quite* like that.)

Tennant was also a regular performer with the Royal Shakespeare Company, specialising in comic roles, while steadily building up his screen showreel. He was one of the less well-known faces in Stephen Fry's film *Bright Young Things* and, in 2004, appeared in two BBC One serials: an adaptation of Anthony Trollope's *He Knew He Was Right* and the award-winning musical drama *Blackpool*, in which he played a leading role as wily copper DI Carlisle. By the time he was cast as Casanova, he was widely regarded as one of the hottest upcoming British screen talents, with an upcoming turn in *Harry Potter and the Goblet of Fire* as wayward, Death-Eating nuisance Barty Crouch Jr.

It was Julie Gardner who popped the question to Tennant. "She said, 'Do you want to be the next Doctor?'" recalled Russell T Davies. "I was dying to ask him myself, but she led her way into it. He laughed, and then he swore, and the third thing he did was say, 'I want a very long coat!' I thought: 'I think he wants to do it'."[8]

"I did have a few moments when I wondered if it would be a mistake," said Tennant. "Then, of course, I woke up the next day and thought, oh shut up – obviously, you'll say yes!"[8]

As with his predecessor, Tennant's name appeared in the press before the contracts had actually been signed. "It could have been fairly disastrous," admitted Davies. "His agent could have said, 'No thanks, then'. As it happens, he's got a brilliant agent who's very, very incisive. But these things are a minefield of negotiations, and it doesn't help to have it paraded across the papers like that. It was horrible."[8]

"The moment that I was announced as taking over in *Doctor Who* was sort of muddled, and fudged, and blown," Tennant lamented. "I never got to kind of go, 'Hi, it's me'. It was leaked, and gossiped about, and then just kind of slithered out."[15]

One of the first people to whom the news slithered was Mark Gatiss, who happened to appearing alongside Tennant in a live BBC Four re-make of *The Quatermass Experiment* that went out just a week after Graham Norton's similarly high wire live appearance in *Doctor Who*. As word got round the cast and crew, Jason Flemyng, playing Quatermass, slipped in a little in-joke by changing his opening line to Tennant's character, Dr Briscoe, to "Good to have you back, Doctor". Either that, or he'd just forgotten his name.

With the news now official, the fanboy in Tennant couldn't resist going on to *Outpost Gallifrey* to have a look what his fellow devotees were saying. "I just couldn't help myself," he admitted. "The first comment I read was very nice, and the next comment was terribly flattering, and then the next one said something like, 'I can't bear the sight of him'. And the one after that said, 'Who?' The one after that said, 'I'd rather have David Morrissey'. The one after that said, 'That's it, the dream is finished! Somebody who looks like a weasel could never play the Doctor! It's over!' And then I thought to myself that maybe it's best not to read this sort of thing too much."[8]

No sooner had he arrived, of course, than people began speculating about when he'd leave. "Let's get through one [series] at a time," Tennant told *Hello* magazine: "I'd love to do a hundred years, but they might sack me." The *Daily Mail*, for their part, confidently reported that Tennant would only receive half the salary Christopher Eccleston had been paid. "There was some relief that Chris went as he was so expensive", a "BBC source" told the paper.

Meanwhile, Eccleston was still earning his fee on Saturday nights. Kicking off on April 16th, the series' first two-parter, *Aliens of London / World War Three*, exists in the sparsely populated bit of Venn diagram where *Independence Day* meets *Dick and Dom in da Bungalow*. It's an epic Earth invasion story, complete with the wowiest of Davies' "big pictures" – a spaceship destroys Big Ben, Mickey blows up Downing Street – disguised as a knockabout comedy about a bunch of flatulent green aliens in which Serious Actor Christopher Eccleston is forced to deliver the immortal line "Would you mind not farting while I'm saving the world?".

The frequent guffing is a by-product of the bulky, eight-foot-tall Slitheen – a family of confidence tricksters from the planet Raxacoricofallapatorius, which is easy for them to say – having to squeeze into human body suits in order to pass themselves off as junior members of the British government as part of an elaborate plan to get their claws on the nuclear button.

Because most of the story takes place in Downing Street, the production team had to check with BBC Editorial Compliance that it was okay to broadcast it during a General Election. (They said it was, but, bizarrely, did insist on the kid who graffitis "Bad Wolf" on the TARDIS being seen to scrub it off before the end, the little bastard.) To be honest, given that Davies' initial inspiration for the story was watching Girls Aloud running riot around Number Ten in the video for "Jump," this was never in much danger of turning into a laser-sharp political satire, though there is one pointed gag in which the Slitheen bluff the UN into going nuclear with the threat of "massive weapons of destruction, capable of being deployed within 45 seconds". Cheeky.

In what will prove to be one of Davies' favourite storytelling devices, much of the action is relayed via TV news broadcasts (including a slightly over-eager cameo from BBC political pundit Andrew Marr), which the Doctor settles down to watch at the Tylers' flat, despite having just being slapped across the kisser by Jackie for kidnapping her daughter. "It hurt!" he protests. "You're so gay!" replies Rose – sparking a brief but heated online skirmish in the process.

There's a noticeably less global dimension to the second half, in which the Doctor, Rose and plucky constituency MP Harriet Jones (the wonderful Penelope Wilton) spend most of the running time trapped in the Cabinet Room talking Mickey through some basic world-saving procedures over the phone. By now, we've established that, when it suits him, Davies has a somewhat strained relationship

with plausibility – but, even so, expecting us to believe a kid in his bedroom can hack into Britain's naval defences with less hassle than it takes to re-set your Amazon password, then launch a missile strike at Downing Street feels like an ask too far. (And the fact he doesn't even need to target the missile suggests all our warheads are *already* aimed at Number Ten. Which is understandable, I suppose, when you consider most of the recent inhabitants.)

Niggles aside, this is uproarious, wittily inventive stuff – not least the idea of a fake alien invasion to distract from a *real* alien invasion, and the Slitheen plan to flog off the Earth's resources in a big post-nuclear fire sale – that fizzes with great dialogue and memorable set-pieces. ("Harriet, have a drink, I think you're gonna need it," says the Doctor, thrusting a decanter at the MP for Flydale North in the middle of a showdown with the aliens. "You pass it to the left first," she reminds him – thoroughly proper and indefatigably British even in the face of death.) It's just a pity the occasionally slapdash plotting, frequent outbreaks of children's telly acting and endless fart gags (*The Times* accused Davis of aiming show at "the eight-year-old in him" and being obsessed by bodily functions) leave such a bad smell.

With 7.63 million viewers, *Aliens of London* just had the edge over Ant and Dec's series finale. The following week, ITV returned to the fray with their much-hyped reality show *Celebrity Wrestling*, in which such superstars as Jeff Brazier, Marc Bannerman, Shauna Lowry and Tiffany Chapman (no, me neither) indulged in a bit of costumed grunt and groan for the entertainment of... well, pretty much no-one, as it turned out. Starting out with less than half *World War Three*'s near-eight million viewers, *Celebrity Wrestling*'s audience dribbled away to less than 2.5 million, at which point it was relegated to a graveyard slot on Sunday mornings. Smack and, indeed, down.

Dr Who in an Exciting Adventure with the Dalek

On May 1st, the *Sunday Mirror* arrived late to the Eccleston-kicking party with an article asking: "He quit *Doctor Who* to head for Hollywood – but is Christopher Eccleston too miserable to be famous?" As evidence, it presented an old quote from the cuttings file in which Eccleston claimed: "I'm not known for my charm ... I think I'm seen as a grumpy old sod." And, er, that was it. Channel 4's teletext service, meanwhile, examined the actor's astrological chart, and concluded: "Such a heavy Aquarian presence ensures he will never allow himself to be typecast in any way..." Wow, they really *could* see into the past.

That same week saw the hype machine powering up to 11 again for the imminent return of the Daleks. Or *a* Dalek, anyway. "It's the moment several generations have been waiting for," gasped *The Guardian* breathlessly, while the *Radio Times* came wrapped in a stunning recreation of the iconic Daleks on Westminster Bridge image in honour of the week's two biggest news events: the return of everyone's favourite Nazi trashcans and, more trivially, the British General Election. (Several years later, this would be voted the best British magazine cover of all time by the Periodical Publishers' Association.)

Loosely based on his acclaimed Big Finish adventure *Jubilee* (the audition piece that got him the gig, essentially), Robert Shearman's *Dalek* has one aim above all others: to restore the pepperpots' kick-ass reputation as the Biggest Bads in the galaxy after decades of cosy over-familiarity in Kit-Kat adverts, Looney Tunes movies, bad sketch shows and, God help us, *Destiny of the Daleks*.

And if that was *all Dalek* achieved, it would still be a triumph, because this episode proves beyond doubt that a single Dalek – one solitary, imprisoned, tortured survivor of the Time War – can be more terrifying than whole armies of the flapping, hysterical drama queens we've grown used to over the years.

Make no mistake, this Dalek is one mean sonofabitch: cunning, calculating, manipulative, relentless, unstoppable – the scenes in which it breaks its bonds and ascends from its dungeon cell to the surface, casually eliminating every obstacle in its way, are horribly compelling. Once you've seen what this guy can do with his sucker arm, you'll never make a joke about a sink plunger again. Not to its face, anyway. (Heck, even his Dalek *balls* are part of his armoury.)

The last Skarosian is the prize exhibit in a vast "museum" of alien artefacts buried half a mile beneath the Utah desert – so it's not exactly convenient for visitors, and is unlikely to have a gift shop – collected by Henry van Statten, a vulgar billionaire who "owns the internet", apparently (surely that's Google?). The contrast between the Doctor's questing thirst for discovery and van Statten's desire simply to acquire is well drawn: "I wanted to touch the stars!" he insists. "You just want to drag the stars down and stick them underground, underneath tons of sand and dirt, and label them," the Doctor replies. "You're about as far from the stars as you can get!" As is the contrast – and the uncomfortable similarities – between the Doctor and the Dalek, the only survivors of the war to end all wars. The creature brings out the worst in the Time Lord ("You would make a good Dalek", it taunts) and it's fascinating to watch as the Dalek, having absorbed Rose's DNA, becomes more human as the Doctor becomes more Dalek. (It was Christopher Eccleston's decision to play the Doctor as so angry he loses control; at one point, he flies into such a rage he flobs a big bit of spit onto his lip. Director Joe Ahearne offered to do a re-take, but Eccleston wanted it left in.)

Bruno Langley – fresh off a headline-making stint as *Coronation Street's* first major gay character – is suitably gauche as Adam, van Statten's brilliant but naive pet science geek, and the heart does sink somewhat when he joins the Doctor and Rose aboard the TARDIS at the end. Is this the new Adric?

The most impressive guest performance, though, comes from Nicholas Briggs, hired to voice the Dalek after impressing Russell T Davies with his sterling work for Big Finish. (Well, that and the fact he had his own ring modulator; the gizmo that makes him sound gravellier than Tom Waits in a gravel pit.) As well as giving the metal bastard a throaty new electronic growl, Briggs succeeds in showing a Dalek's sensitive side as the humanised creature sheds its armour casing and reaches out a tentacle to feel the warmth of the sun on its face. (Or what passes for a face on a mutant alien octopus.) It's a surprisingly tender moment in a story full of successful reinventions. After this, you'll never reach for that

Dalek bubble-bath with quite the same confidence again.

The episode garnered more rave reviews ("This new *Doctor Who* is an unqualified triumph," trumpeted the *Sunday Times*), but the best testimonial came courtesy of MediaWatch, the successor to the National Viewers and Listeners Association that had taken up the cudgels following Mary Whitehouse's death. "It depicts an evil character telling one of his henchman to 'canoodle' and 'spoon' with the Doctor's assistant, Rose," thundered the pressure group, bafflingly, before going on to complain about van Statten torturing the Doctor by "binding him to a metal crucifix". Branding the BBC "irresponsible" for using "inappropriate imagery and language", the group concluded: "This is not for children." Mary would have been proud. But Robert Holmes would have been prouder.

As the country felt the first faint stirrings of a new wave of... if not Dalekmania, then at least Dalek Extreme Enthusiasm, it fell to the next episode, *The Long Game*, to try to keep the kids interested, despite a notable absence of armoured mutant octopi. The story is aptly named: Russell T Davies had pitched it to the *Doctor Who* production team of the late 80s, which may explain why the central premise – 200,000 years in the future, the journalists of Satellite Five control the news output for the entire galaxy – feels rather old-skool.

Actually, "central premise" is overselling it: in this version, the half-hearted media satire is little more than a sideshow to the real story of new boy Adam failing to shape up as a potential fellow traveller. Which is a shame because, if the best sci-fi holds a mirror up to society, there are few diseased fruits more over-ripe for picking than the excesses and abuses of the media age. Next to that, whether some kid can deal with the concept of time travel or not feels a bit like small beer.

The set-up doesn't even make much *sense*: compressed information flows into special "ports" in the journalists' exposed frontal lobes so they become "part of the software" – though why they need a human being sitting in a dentist's chair with a gaping hole in their head to do this instead of an ordinary server isn't ever made clear. (A bit later, one of the hacks uses the same technology to mentally override Satellite Five's cooling system, suggesting it also conveniently doubles as a remote control for the air-conditioning unit. It's one way of not losing it down the back of the sofa cushions, I guess.)

Simon Pegg, fresh from the success of *Shaun of the Dead*, but yet to achieve full Hollywood velocity, is great value as the Editor – a sort of campy Bond villain who turns out to be the powerless stooge of the Mighty Jagrafess of the Holy Hadrojassic Maxarodenfoe. The latter, a ceiling-sized slug with vicious, slavering maws, may well have been written with the chairman of a certain global news corporation in mind – though does the fact the Editor calls him "Max" suggest the black arts of spin doctor-for-hire Max Clifford were also a target?

This was designed as a "Doctor-lite" episode to relieve some of the burden on Eccleston and Piper, and it's to Davies' credit that this isn't immediately obvious. Left to carry much of the episode on his own, Bruno Langley does a decent enough job but, at the end of the day, the point the script is labouring to make – that it takes a special sort of person to be the Doctor's plus one, and this kid ain't no Rose Tyler – rather serves to underline what we're missing when the real deal's not around. So it's something of a relief when the Doctor dumps Adam back in his mother's living room, complete with surgically-implanted cranial info-spike, and does a runner with Rose, because the show needed this fifth wheel rookie like a... well, like a hole in the head.

Having won plaudits for introducing Real People with Real Feelings into Virgin's New Adventures range, Paul Cornell was hired with a specific brief to wear his heart on his sleeve for the series' big weepie episode, in which Rose meets the dad she never knew, then recklessly changes history by stopping him from dying under the wheels of car. It was also meant to be the cheap episode – until Cornell added the Reapers, flying pterodactyl-like bacteria who turn up to sterilise the wound in time by wiping out the human race. As low-budget goes, it's not exactly Mike Leigh.

It's still very much a character piece at heart, though, anchored by note perfect performances from Billie Piper and Shaun Dingwall as Pete Tyler, a Del Boy-style chancer who finally gets to do the right thing by his family by sacrificing himself for the good of humanity. The scene where Rose tries to busk her way through a glowing testimonial to his future parenting skills, and he slowly realises she's lying – and why – is both subtle and utterly heartbreaking. The drama is also given an added frisson by the Doctor's boiling rage at Rose's actions ("I did it again. I picked another stupid ape. I should've known. It's not about showing you the universe. It never is. It's about the universe doing something for you!") – a rage fuelled by his own guilt at not saving his own family.

If that all sounds a bit heavy going and touch-feely for your liking, *Father's Day* also works as a straight-up adventure story, full of brilliant moments – from the surprising (the Doctor walks into the TARDIS and it's just a police box) to the comic (Jackie's immense meringue of an 80s bridesmaid's dress); the slightly queasy (Peter inadvertently hitting on his daughter) to the downright shocking (the Doctor is eaten by a Reaper – yes, really).

Cornell delivered at least 11 drafts of the script, but it was worth the effort as the love and devotion shines through every line; the result is the first *Doctor Who* story pretty much guaranteed to make you cry (and no, before you ask, *The Horns of Nimon* doesn't count).

It was testament to the series' increasingly broad church audience – which is a posh way of saying girls now watched it – that *Father's Day* earned a five star review in sleb gossip pamphlet *Heat*, which declared: "*Doctor Who* has to be the most ingenious primetime drama in years."

"Ingenious" barely scratches the surface of the series' second two-parter. According to Steven Moffat, he pitched his first story idea to Russell T Davies while a little worse for wear during a boozy lunch. Davies later emailed to say he didn't like it (especially the climactic scene where the Doctor spends 20 minutes crying and telling Rose "You're my besht mate, you are. No, sherioushly – I absholutely bloody *love* you." Possibly.). So Moffat came back with something else. Something pretty bloody astonishing, actually.

The keyword at the tone meeting for *The Empty Child / The Doctor Dances* was "romantic" – and there are few things Brits find more romantic than the genocidal slaughter of the Second World War (especially if it's got a bit of Glenn Miller stuck over the top). This is also the 2005 series' most effective horror story, and its laugh-out-loud funniest script. In isolation, any one of these elements would have been a treat – together, they result in 90 minutes of truly sublime television.

Actually, romance is something of a coy word for what Steven Moffat is really talking about. "You just assume that I don't dance," the Doctor tells Rose. "What, are you telling me you *do* dance?" she replies. "Nine hundred years old, me. I've been around a bit. I think you can assume at some point I've danced." Yes, the only "dance" being alluded to here is the horizontal hokey-cokey – but I guess calling the episode *The Doctor Shags* would have led to awkward scenes over the nation's dinner tables.

The Doctor is feeling defensive because he's just watched handsome, silver-tongued fifty-first-century Time Agent Captain Jack Harkness swoop in and rescue Rose from a particularly tight spot: hanging from the bottom of a barrage balloon during the Blitz while wearing a Union Jack T-shirt. And our "omnisexual" new friend's dancing credentials aren't in doubt – he's the sort of guy who'll light up the clock face of Big Ben in the middle of an air raid just to impress a girl.

Which is not what the kids were talking about at school on Monday, obviously. That honour falls to the Empty Child himself, a gas-masked infant with terrible, unknowable powers who wanders the rubble-strewn streets of London asking "Are you my Mummy?" in a plaintive voice. It's proper, iconic, behind-the-sofa stuff seemingly precision-built to rival "Exterminate" as the show's ultimate playground meme. In perhaps this series' most celebrated scare, the Doctor, Rose and Jack discover a tape recording of the child talking. "I'm here," says the voice. "Can't you see me? "What's that noise?" asks Rose suddenly. "End of the tape," says the Doctor. "It ran out about 30 seconds ago..." Eeek.

The story's resolution is also beautifully elegant: there are no megalomaniac invasion plans, creatures feeding off "psychic energy" or any of the other hooey we usually have to swallow – just plausible pseudo-science gone wrong as we learn that healing nanogenes (a concept carefully seeded earlier in the story) – had found the body of a child wearing a gas mask and set about "repairing" the human race in his image. To undo the damage, the nanogenes simply need to identify DNA belonging to the child's mother, leading to surely the most triumphant climax ever, as a teenage girl brings her dead son – and everyone else – back to life with a simple answer to the child's repeated refrain: "Yes," she finally finds the courage to say, "I am your mummy." It's punch the air stuff – for the Doctor, as well as us. "Everybody lives, Rose!" he declares exultantly. "Just this once, everybody lives!"

"The Mayor of Cardiff is an alien!" "As long as she's not English."

With the flame war over Eccleston's departure finally dying down, fan magazine *Dreamwatch* decided to poke the smouldering embers with a big stick by suggesting Billie Piper had only signed up for "between three and seven episodes" of the second run. "She's not doing the full series," Piper's agent told the magazine (which, to be fair, had form in this area: in its previous incarnation as militant 80s scandal-sheet *DWB*, it had been the first to break the news of Season Twenty-Three's halved episode count, despite angry denials from John Nathan-Turner). Cue another tabloid feeding frenzy, with some red-tops splashing the story across their front pages, with much feverish talk of the BBC having been thrown into chaos by the loss of both leads from its biggest new show. Never fear, though, because the crack team at the BBC press office moved fast to stamp on the story, issuing a press release with the following strongly worded rebuttal: "Billie Piper will return for the second series of *Doctor Who*. It has not been confirmed how many episodes she will be in." Er, yeah. Thanks for that.

As *EastEnders*' Michelle Ryan and *Brookside*'s Jennifer Ellison topped the tabs' wish list – sorry, "rumoured shortlist" – the *Mirror* informed readers that auditions for Piper's replacement were already under way, and the producers were looking for "a dark-haired girl with a posh accent". It's not known whether Princess Anne sent in her CV.

On June 1st, meanwhile, Eccleston himself emerged from hiding to make a rare public appearance at a school fete in Surrey. This is almost certainly the only time Christopher Eccleston has ever been to Surrey.

Michael Grade also came crawling back out of the woodwork, admitting to BBC Radio Leeds that he was "enjoying" the new *Doctor Who*, and that his son loved it. "Maybe I should ask for a blood test!" he joked. Too soon, Michael, too soon.

As the series moved towards its conclusion, one journalist of a certain age wrote in *The Guardian*: "How extraordinary at this stage in one's life to be rushing back from the coast so as not to miss even the opening credits of *Doctor Who*. Not only because Russell T Davies' reinvention with Christopher Eccleston and Billie Piper is such an exhilarating (if sometimes baffling) ride, but because, while it lasts, *Doctor Who* is once again one of the rituals which make Saturday." If press reports were to be believed, that was certainly the view shared by one man who, after becoming trapped in his car following an accident (possibly while racing home to catch the opening credits), asked the paramedic for a phone so he could ask his wife to tape that night's episode for him. ("Oh, and I'm going to need my Dalek pyjamas bringing to the hospital.")

The episode in question, *Boom Town*, is an odd fish and no mistake. A morality play about crime, punishment and personal responsibility wrapped up in a cartoon caper about a farting alien's plan to escape the Earth by blowing it up and riding the explosion on a space surfboard, it's like a bizarre hybrid of Dostoyevsky and Scooby-Doo.

Yes, the Slitheen are back – or one of them is, anyway. Having survived the obliteration of Downing Street (she landed in a skip, apparently), Blon Fel-Fotch Pasameer-Day Slitheen – Margaret to you and me – has been busy getting herself elected as Mayor of Cardiff. Despite this, she's still trying to keep a low profile and refuses to have her photo taken, lest anyone should recognise the missing-presumed-dead MI5 officer she stole her body from. (Which rather begs the question: why not just get a *different* skin suit?)

Mayor Margaret's keynote policy is demolishing Cardiff Castle and building a nuclear power station in the middle of the city, which you somehow suspect wasn't in her manifesto. Russell T Davies makes a virtue of how utterly nonsensical this is by having Margaret explain that no-one cares what happens in Wales ("God help me," she says, "I've gone native"), while the mysterious deaths of successive nuclear safety inspectors ("They were French," shrugs Margaret. "It's not my fault if 'Danger: High Explosives' was only written in Welsh") pushes the episode comfortably into the realms of broad farce.

The Doctor, Rose and Jack arrest Margaret and prepare to take her back to Raxacoricofallapatorius to stand trial – thus sentencing her to almost certain death. Acceding to his prisoner's request for a final meal, the Doctor takes Margaret out to dinner, where he nonchalantly foils several hilarious attempts on his life over the hors d'oeuvres. It's all rather a hoot, frankly.

The problem comes when Davies suddenly tries to push the story into darker, more complex territory, by having Margaret force the Doctor to face the consequences of his actions. ("I bet you're always the first to leave, Doctor. Never mind the consequences, off you go. You butchered my family and then ran for the stars.") This is, in itself, also rather wonderful – but the crunch of gears as the story moves from slapstick to serious feels a bit like dropping a fatal RTA into the middle of The Whacky Races.

The story was written as a deliberately small character piece designed to showcase the new TARDIS team, while doubling as a promotional film for Cardiff. It also offers a shot at redemption for Noel Clarke, who is so much better here as Mickey, the forgotten victim of the Doctor's reckless lifestyle. Davies pulls no punches in portraying Rose as a selfish brat who doesn't want Mickey, but doesn't want anyone else to have him either.

If anything sums up the stylistic tension at the heart of Boom Town, though, it's the scene in which a naked Slitheen sits on the toilet – even the Yeti never got to do it on telly – and decides to spare her prey after learning she's pregnant. With big sad eyes and a wistful sigh, the alien pines for her own dead family and, we assume, for the children she will never have. Which is really rather touching – for a

scene that started with another ripping great fart gag.

And then, no sooner had the ninth Doctor's travels begun, than it was the end – but the moment, to quote his fourth incarnation's dying words, had been prepared for. And I mean actually, properly prepared for. Because Bad Wolf / The Parting of the Ways introduces Doctor Who viewers to the concept of the season finale – as distinct from the old days, when series just went on until they stopped. As such, Russell T Davies goes all out to ensure everything is bigger, louder, more intense and more emotional, while also tying up loose threads from the season's various story arcs. (Arcs, of course, also being a new innovation for the show. As opposed to arks – they were ten-a-penny back in the day.)

Davies knew exactly what he wanted to fulfil the "bigger" bit of this remit: "These episodes go back to 1960s Doctor Who," he said. "The way it was in my head before I became awkward, or embarrassed or over-analytical. Those were the days when great space fleets existed, where cosmic wars happened, where the lead character could do anything – and nothing was safe, because nothing was set in stone. That's what I wanted to create: an outer-space epic."[16]

And yet, for all the fleets of spaceships and Daleks streaming through the stars in their thousands, it's the emotional content that makes the real impact. All the main characters reach a resolution of sorts in their personal journeys – none more conclusively, of course, than the ninth Doctor himself. Given the chance to carry out the final act of the Time War, the man the Daleks call the Oncoming Storm (a name with its origins in Paul Cornell's novel Love and War) finds redemption of sorts when he declines to repeat his earlier crimes. "What are you?" taunts the Dalek Emperor. "Coward or killer?" "Coward," says the Doctor, stepping away from the kill-switch. "Any day."

But he doesn't wave the white flag until he's made sure Rose is safe – tricking her aboard the TARDIS on the Game Station (actually The Long Game's Satellite Five, a couple of hundred thousand years in the future) and sending her back in time to a life of telly and chips. Denied a chance to say goodbye, the Doctor addresses Rose via Emergency Programme One – a

TARDIS-generated hologram. "If you want to remember me, then you can do one thing – that's all, one thing," says the Time Lord's flickering avatar. And then, in a heart-quickening motion, he turns and looks her directly in the eye. "Have a good life. Do that for me, Rose. Have a fantastic life." It's the outstanding moment in the series – not to mention among the most outstanding in all *Doctor Who* – and Christopher Eccleston's finest hour.

On Earth, as Jackie and Mickey witter about takeaway food, Rose refuses to accept defeat. "The Doctor showed me a better way of living your life," she tells them. "That you don't just give up. You don't just let things happen. You make a stand. You say no. You have the guts to do what's right when everyone else just runs away." It takes the words "Bad Wolf" spray-painted across a playground to make her realise how she can get back to the Doctor – even if the rest of us could be forgiven for being a bit slower on the uptake: the explanation for this season-long meme is oblique to say the least[III], but suffice to say Rose (who eagle-eyed viewers will note is wearing her red riding hoodie) is transformed into the Bad Wolf when she looks into the time vortex at the heart of the TARDIS. This gives her the power to rewrite the universe (hey, I said it was *big*), end the Time War and resurrect the late Captain Jack Harkness – who has just lost an argument with a Dalek death ray – into the bargain. But it comes at a cost: holding all of space and time in her head almost kills her, and the only way the Doctor can save Rose is to absorb the vortex energy himself through a massive wet snog. (At least he *says* it's the only way.) As he moves in to lock lips with the line "Come here – I think you need a Doctor", you'll either stand up and cheer or reach for the nearest bucket/ online forum. (Which you choose is up to you – I'm not here to judge you. But if it's the latter, then you have no soul. Just sayin')

All of which is just a little bit utterly fabulous – and a marked step up from the opening half-hour or so of *Bad Wolf*, a slightly tepid parody of reality TV that's as toothless as you might expect from a writer who makes no bones about how much he loves those shows, and whose production teams are happily in on the joke. Davina McCall (*Big Brother*), Anne Robinson (*The Weakest Link*) and Trinny and Susannah (*What Not to Wear*) even provide the voices for their android counterparts – though as they've been treated almost beyond recognition, you do wonder why they bothered. Even as the warm-up act to *Parting...*'s blockbusting, heartbreaking epic, it all just feels a bit campy and cheap. (Although it could have been worse: John Barrowman's naked butt in the Trine-E and Zu-Zana – yes, really – sequence fell foul of BBC censors, who ordered the offending cheeks to be removed. They kept in the joke about him keeping a gun up his arse, though.)

You'd forgive Russell T Davies anything for the second act, however, which packs more money-shot moments into 45 minutes than many whole seasons of old-money *Who*. Hologram aside, the best has to be the bit where a Dalek can be seen – but not heard – uttering "exterminate" in the silent void of space beyond a viewing panel, before a blast shatters the glass and it's curtains for poor *Big Brother* contestant Lynda. (It's more powerful than it sounds, because lovely Lynda is that rarest of creatures – a *Big Brother* contestant you don't *want* to see exterminated.)

Fittingly, the Doctor's big showdown with the Emperor (a supersized Dalek with the slimy organic bit bubbling hatefully away in an exposed tank) was Christopher Eccleston's final scene on *Doctor Who*, and he gives it everything. This episode is the actor's most powerhouse performance in the role, and it's great to see him bowing out on a high.

About that bow: "I absorbed all the energy of the time vortex, and no one's meant to do that," the Doctor tells Rose. "Every cell in my body's dying... I'm going to change, and I'm not going to see you again. Not like this. Not with this daft old face. And before I go..." "Don't *say* that," pleads Rose. "Rose, before I go, I just want to tell you, you were fantastic. Absolutely fantastic. And do you know what? So was I."

And then he's gone – consumed by a Vesuvius of molten light before re-assembling in the form of a somewhat startled-looking David Tennant. "Ooh, new teeth," says the tenth Doctor, tripping over his gnashers. "That's weird."

And so the trip of a lifetime rolls on.

Gone in 35,000 Seconds

Doctor Who "makes Shakespeare look shit," say critics

Even as the credits rolled at the end of *The Parting of the Ways*, the legacy of the new *Doctor Who*'s success was already becoming apparent. Jane Tranter said the series – which ended up averaging 7.95 million viewers across the 13 episodes – had been such a game-changer for Saturday nights, the BBC were now actively looking at other family dramas for that slot. And the show's own future was looking more assured than it had in decades, possibly ever. At a BAFTA screening of *The Parting of the Ways*, Tranter had announced a third series and a second Christmas special (the latter of which came as a surprise even to Russell T Davies – and he was the one who'd have to write it). It was also confirmed that Billie Piper had signed up for the whole of Series Two. You have permission to whoop.

And, all the while, the standing ovations continued. "At a time when creative leadership in television is fragile and elusive, Davies and his editors at the BBC have demonstrated that a passion for the medium, intelligently and uncynically deployed, can deliver what the contrived and compromised cannot – a big Saturday early evening audience of family viewers," gushed *The Guardian*. "It is a shame Christopher Eccleston signed up for only one series, as it is unlikely he will encounter this quality of material to interpret many times in his career – and his audience will certainly never be more gripped and grateful." At the other end of the market, *Heat* magazine hailed "a stunning climax – probably the most awesomely epic *Doctor Who* ever," and predicted "BAFTAs must rain down". "I'm soooo glad it's ending," chipped in the *Daily Star*. "I can't take any more. It's simply too good. It's spoiling the rest of my telly viewing by making it look rubbish in comparison... I'm running out of phrases to describe its magnificence."

Even former Time Lords joined in the veneration: "It was great to sit down and watch the new *Doctor Who* from the very first moment, knowing I was not in it," wrote Colin Baker in his weekly column for the *Bucks Free Press*. Crueller readers than me can insert their own punchline here.

Russell T Davies wrote a piece for *The Guardian*, which was rapidly turning into the world's most highbrow *Doctor Who* fanzine, reflecting on the success of the series and his undimmed passion for it. "I went into the first series on instinct, and that's how it should stay. But I love this show as much as ever. It has not diminished as I feared it would. I can still catch a Jon Pertwee repeat on UK Gold and be happy as a Zygon. And, as a writer, I have had a ball."

"You have to admit that the name of the programme had become a joke and its reputation had become a cheap joke at that," he added in an interview with *BBC News*. "And Chris, as one of the country's leading actors, by being willing to step up to the line and take on that part, has proved himself to be magnificent and has turned it around. So now you get actors like David Tennant, who says he wouldn't have touched it if Chris hadn't have done it, because the part had become a joke." Yeah right – let's not forget this is the guy who begged to be allowed to play Caretaker Number Two in *Doctor Who when it was on the internet*; he'd have regenerated from Wee Jimmy Krankie if he'd had to.

"It was ready for a fall," the showrunner reflected in an interview with *Doctor Who Magazine* a couple of years later. "You have to do the interview with the *Mirror* where you say it's a completely brilliant programme, but it's my job to do that. Seriously, I'm sitting there thinking, what if only two million watch? I had really big, important people saying, 'Why waste your time on that thing?' Nicola Shindler, who runs Red Production Company, is one of the people I trust most in the industry, but she was saying to me, 'It's niche, it's science fiction – it doesn't matter how hard you work, it's never going to be that big'. I was thinking, this is either going to reinvigorate the whole legacy, or prove that it deserved to be taken off the air in 1989."[9]

Christopher Eccleston's first live TV appearance after his resignation was on *Top Gear*'s Star in a Reasonably Priced Car slot, in which celebrities are challenged to throw a compact family sedan around a race track in the fastest possible time. If he'd been hoping for an enlightened discussion of his stage interpretations of Strindberg and Tennessee Williams, he was probably disappointed to be introduced as "Doctor Who, everybody!" by denim-clad petrolhead irritant Jeremy Clarkson, whose first question to the newly-bearded actor was, "Is that space fungus you've grown?"

Generally, Eccleston appeared relaxed, discussing his time on the show with good humour, though there was a tense moment for fans when Clarkson put himself forward for the tenth Doctor. Driving a Suzuki Liana automatic (one of only 40 in the UK, acquired especially for him), the rookie driver managed a lap time of 1:52.4, placing him between Sir Tim Rice and Status Quo's Rick Parfitt, which is surely not a comfortable place for anybody to be.

As pre-production on Series Two stepped up a gear, the BBC announced the return of some old enemies – the Cybermen – as well as some old friends in the form of 70s faves Sarah Jane Smith and K9. Quite a few fans went online to say they thought it was a bad idea for the show to start trading on former glories instead of driving forward with new characters and fresh ideas, which is what they thought they were supposed to say to look clever. Then they secretly did a little dance all around the house while kissing their Dapol K-9 toys and weeping fat tears of joy.

One person who wouldn't be back next year, though, was Captain Jack. "You want to go back to basics with Rose and a brand new Doctor," said Russell T Davies. "Poor old Jack gets shunted to the side because of that. We had to leave him there on Satellite Five."[5] "If I'm honest, it was like I'd been kicked in the balls," admitted John Barrowman. "Not having a go at Russell and Phil [Collinson], because they're great guys, but I got the impression that, like, to them, although they were disappointed at having to tell me something like that, it was just part of their job. That's the way the cookie crumbles. But then they told me that I'd be coming back in Series Three."[17]

In fact, he'd be back sooner than that as, in October 2005, it was announced that Captain Jack was getting his own 13-part series on BBC Three. *Torchwood* – the name is an anagram of a popular TV show (Can you guess which one? Clue: it's not *Cow Hot Rod*) – would be set in modern-day Cardiff and focus on "a renegade group of investigators".

Creator Russell T Davies described the new, post-watershed drama as "a British sci-fi paranoid thriller, a cop show with a sense of humour. It's dark, wild and sexy, it's *The X Files* meets *This Life*. It's a stand-alone series for adult audiences which will have its own unique identity". The link to *Crow Dot Ho* would be "organic", said BBC Three Controller Stuart Murphy, with the Torchwood concept seeded into the upcoming *Who* Christmas special and second series.

"*Torchwood* is sinister and psychological," added Murphy. "Russell was really keen to play with your head – as well as being very British and modern and real. But at the centre of the drama are warm, human relationships and the overcoming of adversity."

A sinister urban thriller starring West End singing sensation John Barrowman? Stranger things have happened, I suppose. Though I can't think of any off the top of my head.

Don't mention the Time War!

While David Tennant and Billie Piper got to grips with saving the universe in a corner of Wales, the Christopher Eccleston era – if era wasn't too strong a word (The Eccleston Months? The Eccleston Blip?) – cemented its reputation by winning more than ten major industry awards (considerably more if you include the Welsh BAFTAs, which surely no-one would). The first biggies came at October's National Television Awards (a sort of low-rent BAFTAs at which the winners are chosen by – good God – the public) where *Doctor Who* was named Most Popular Drama and Christopher Eccleston and Billie Piper won Most Popular Actor and Actress respectively. Eccleston did not attend the televised ceremony – much to the annoyance of *The Sun*, which demanded "Where the Ecc was he? I hope he had a bloody good excuse." (The actor's agent said he had the flu, and had also reacted badly to some travel vaccinations.) Russell T Davies collected the award, and read out a note on his behalf. "Thank you to everybody who voted for me, and to the British public for their encouragement over the last 17 years," he said. "They have always been honest with me and I'm very grateful." It sounded more like a resignation than a victory speech. Eccleston dedicated his award to the memory of Kieran Wynne, "a little boy who loved *Doctor Who* and loved life". Piper said it was the first award she'd won since bagging the coveted Most Fanciable Female in Pop at the Smash Hits Poll Winners' Party a few years earlier.

Doctor Who also won the Broadcast Magazine Award for Best Drama, while Eccleston was named Best Actor at the TV Choice Awards. In America, the show cleaned up at the Hugo Awards – the sci-fi Oscars, essentially – with Steven Moffat's *The Empty Child / The Doctor Dances* triumphing in the Best Dramatic Presentation, Short Form category (Hugo-speak for "TV show"). *Dalek* and *Father's Day* came second and third respectively, which must count as a mixed result for Russell T Davies.

The showrunner got his moment in the sun at the BAFTAs – still the most prestigious ceremony in British television by a long chalk – when *Doctor Who* covered itself in glory by winning both Best Drama Series and the audience-voted Pioneer Award, while Davies himself collected the Dennis Potter Award for Outstanding Writing for Television.

Given that a single Writer's Guild of Great Britain Award for Best Children's Drama Script in 1975 was the only major gong won by the original series during its entire 26-year-run (if you don't count the Swap Shop Awards), this was an astonishing achievement: a glowing testament to the love, care and relentless energy invested in the project by Russell T Davies, Julie Gardner, Phil Collinson, Christopher Eccleston, Billie Piper and the whole team. And also to the fact they give out a lot more awards for stuff these days.

Matched only by the first wave of Dalekmania in the 60s, and Tom Baker at the height of his imperial phase the following decade, there was a persuasive argument to be made that 2005 had been *Doctor Who*'s annus mirabilis[IV].

And yet...

There is no avoiding the fact the scrappy, awkward early exit of Christopher Eccleston had cast a shadow over the show's otherwise triumphant resurrection. Not, as it turned out, a hugely injurious shadow, but a shadow nonetheless. More than a decade on, the truth of what happened is still shrouded in mystery, gossip and innuendo. But, over the years,

Eccleston himself has let slip enough for us to know that no small amount of bad blood was involved, and that the cover story about him only ever planning to do one series was just that: a cover story.

As filming drew to a close in 2005, Eccleston told *SFX* magazine: "You can't have a life. You can't socialise. It's like having a TARDIS in your skull and every time you open your eyes you see a TARDIS. There were days when I got psoriasis, I got eczema. My face blew up in the Dalek episode. I looked literally disfigured with tiredness and poor skin. With TV, you do a 14-hour day and then you're doing your line-learning." He then added: "I loved being part of that amazing team. By and large, it was a joy."[18] Yeah, sounds like it.

In June that year, when asked by a BBC radio interviewer if he had enjoyed working on *Doctor Who*, Eccleston replied: "Mixed, but that's a long story." Speaking to the *Yorkshire Evening Post* five years later, Eccleston denied that he had left over fear of being typecast – and offered a more frank explanation. "[I] didn't enjoy the environment and the culture that we, the cast and crew, had to work in," he confided. "I wasn't comfortable. I thought, if I stay in this job, I'm going to have to blind myself to certain things that I thought were wrong. And I think it's more important to be your own man than be successful, so I left. But the most important thing is that I did it, not that I left. I really feel that, because it kind of broke the mould and it helped to reinvent it. I'm very proud of it."

He offered more hints during a 2011 acting masterclass at the Theatre Royal, Haymarket, telling students: "I left *Doctor Who* because I could not get along with the senior people. I left because of politics. I did not see eye-to-eye with them. I didn't agree with the way things were being run. I didn't like the culture that had grown up around the series. So I left, I felt, over a principle. I thought to remain, which would have made me a lot of money and given me huge visibility... the price I would have had to pay was to eat a lot of shit. I'm not being funny about that. I didn't want to do that and it comes to the art of it, in a way. I feel that if you run your career and... We are vulnerable as actors, and we are constantly humiliating ourselves auditioning. But if you allow that to go on, on a grand scale you will lose whatever it is about you and it will be present in your work. If you allow your desire to be successful and visible and financially secure – if you allow that to make you throw shades on your parents, on your upbringing, then you're knackered. You've got to keep something back, for yourself, because it'll be present in your work. My face didn't fit," he concluded. "I'm sure they were glad to see the back of me. The important thing is that I succeeded. It was a great part. I loved playing him."

During an appearance on Graham Norton's Radio 2 show around the same time, Eccleston was asked about returning to *Doctor Who* for its 50th anniversary. "I never bathe in the same river twice," he told Norton. The following year, the actor told the *Daily Telegraph* that his "conscience is completely clear" on the matter. "I know what went on and the people who were involved know what went on – that's good enough for me," he said. "I've lived my life, particularly my working life, on the basis that I have to be able to look at myself in the mirror about the way I behave. It wasn't a bold move, it was an entirely natural one. I'm hugely grateful to the children who to this day come up and talk to me about the show."

In 2015, Eccleston submitted himself to several rounds of publicity interviews for Sky Atlantic blockbuster *Fortitude* and ITV drama *Safe House*. One *Daily Mirror* journalist reported being warned by a publicist on three separate occasions not to ask about *Doctor Who*. Taking that as an instruction to steer clear of Eccleston's own time on the show, she asked him instead for his opinion on the show's current star. At which point he hung up.

A couple of months later, the actor was a guest on Radio 4's *Loose Ends*. "We've reached that moment in the interview," said host Emma Freud, seconds after dropping the *DW* word. "Here we go," said Eccleston, bracing himself. "Good luck everybody," teased Freud.

Reflecting on his performance, Eccleston said: "I think I over-pitched the comedy. If I had my time again, I would do the comedy very differently. But I think where I possibly did succeed was in the tortured stuff. Surprise surprise!," he added, laughing.

"So why did you go?" asked Freud. On receiving the standard line about the impor-

tant thing being that he did it, not that he left, she pressed the point. "It may not be important but to fans it was a bit of a shock... So that was a big decision."

"Okay," said, Freud clearly not going to take no for an answer. "But talk me through the decision to leave. Was it because you didn't work within that structure of a rigorous, show-running show?"

"Myself and three individuals at the very top of the pyramid clashed," said Eccleston. "So off I went. But they're not here to say their side of it, so I'm not going to go into detail."

So, there you go. For all his talk of being led by the scripts and not chasing "financial security", Eccleston's post-*Who* career hasn't entirely been dedicated to works of great artistic integrity. Alongside such acclaimed TV dramas as *The Shadow Line*, *Blackout* and *Accused*, some well-regarded stage work and a terrifically waspish turn as John Lennon in BBC Four's *Lennon Naked*, the actor has shilled for the multiplex buck in such conspicuously un-Oscar garlanded films as *The Seeker: The Dark is Rising*, *GI Joe: Rise of the Cobra* and *Thor: The Dark World*. He also triggered something of a geek meltdown by appearing alongside *Star Trek* legend George Takei and 90s *Who* panto villain Eric Roberts in the briefly popular US sci-fi series *Heroes*. But hey, even professional liberal comfort food providers have to eat.[V] And, in 2015, he began featuring on HBO's *The Leftovers* as a conflicted ex-reverend – exactly the sort of internal torment that Eccleston has come to specialise in.

As for *Doctor Who*, Eccleston's script remains the same: yes, he left – but before he left, he joined. And isn't that, at the end of the day, what really matters?

"The best thing about *Doctor Who* for me has been the response I've had from children," he said in a 2005 Radio 1 interview, "both in the street and the number of letters and drawings of me and Daleks, which are all over my wall at home. In the 20 years I've been acting, I've never enjoyed a response so much as the one I've had from children, and I'm carrying that in my heart, forever."

10 The Power of Squee

The Fan in the Brown Suit

Now that he'd bagged the biggest role on TV, it was only a matter of time until David Tennant's sordid past started coming to light.

The *Daily Mirror*'s Sunday magazine tracked down his old English teacher, Moira Robertson, who explained how the Tom Baker scarf that Tennant's granny had knitted for him had figured highly in the youngster's life. "It didn't matter what essay or assignment I gave him, he managed to work his granny's scarf into it," she said. "That took real ingenuity. I remember having to explain to him that the exam board wouldn't actually get the point and give him extra marks for it."

When the Doctor regenerated, so did his biggest fan, his granny stepping up to the crease with a Peter Davison-style cricket jumper. "He loved the pullover as much as the scarf," said his mum, Helen. "It was cream with a stripe. It would often be in the wash and got bigger and bigger." As a *Doctor Who* fan, this was as dangerously close to sportswear as wee David was ever likely to get.

His brother Gordon, meanwhile, recalled how the young McDonald boys had met Tom Baker during a promotional visit to Scotland. "My dad took us into Glasgow to meet him," he said. "We queued up to see him and shook his hand." (He did better than any of his predecessors, then: they had to make do with a waxwork dummy.)

Most revealing of all was an extract from a school essay called "Intergalactic Overdose," in which the teenage Tennant confessed all about the extent of his ardour: "Everyone was persistent in the belief I would 'grow out of it', but not me. I believed this was going to be a lifelong thing. When I was old enough I was convinced that I was going to play the part of the Doctor on TV. I was absolutely convinced."[1] In truth, of course, there was about as much chance of a kid from Paisley becoming *Doctor Who* as there was that bloke with the ferrets off *Tiswas*.

Two decades later, Tennant told *SFX* how it felt when that lifelong dream became a reality. "What I realised when I came to do this was that any sort of fantastic notions one might have had about this were just that – fantastic notions. When you have to come and make real decisions, it's a different thing. Actors often say that the best thing about getting a job is the phone call that says you've got it, because at that moment it is all potential, and could be anything."[2]

Ironically, Tennant's casting meant he no longer felt able to do what he'd spent so much of his life doing – watching *Doctor Who*. "I just get a bit intimidated by it," he admitted. "I don't want to see Tom Baker being brilliant!"[3] Fair enough: why not just watch *The Horns of Nimon*, then?

Tennant made his debut as the Time Lord on April 21st when a skeleton film crew snuck onto the TARDIS set to film the final moments of *The Parting of the Ways*. (The part of Rose was played by a small strip of gaffer tape placed at the height of Billie Piper's eyeline. It still gave a more convincing performance than Matthew Waterhouse.)

Despite speaking his opening lines in estuary English, the *Daily Mirror* reported Tennant would be reverting to his natural Scottish burr for the series. When asked about this on Children's BBC, Russell T Davies simply replied: "Well, every planet has a Scotland." (Come to think of it, most *Who* planets *do* look like Scotland: rugged landscape, largely empty and peopled by funny-looking natives with grey skin.)

In late June, rumours began to circulate that Stephen Fry was writing a story for the upcoming season, while returnees Stephen Moffat and Mark Gatiss would be joined by newcomers Matt Jones, Toby Whithouse and Tom MacRae. Jones was a New Adventures novelist who had written a regular column for

Doctor Who Magazine before going on to work as a script editor on *Queer as Folk* and an executive producer on *Shameless*, while Whithouse was the creator of ballsy nursing drama *No Angels*. Russell T Davies had been mentoring MacRae after the young writer had foisted some scripts on him at a signing a few years earlier. Assigned the two-part Cybermen story, MacRae was young enough to have been a fan of Sylvester McCoy, and also recalled *Silver Nemesis* fondly, which is not a sentence you hear very often. The story would also see the return of feted classic series director Graeme Harper, making his first *Doctor Who* story since 1985's *Revelation of the Daleks*.

Davies had written the Series Two outline before the first season had aired – and had even included a Christmas special, the cocky sod – but, unlike his original pitch document, there was not so much as a word on the new Doctor.

"It's amazing how little me and David talk about it," Davies admitted later. "We must have spent five minutes on 'Where do we go and what do we do?' I write it, he puts a spin on it, I watch the rushes every day, I respond to that."[4]

As *The People* reported that Tennant was getting paid less than Billie Piper (but more than the gaffer tape, presumably), the actor told *TV Times* he was "absolutely terrified" by the prospect of succeeding Christopher Eccleston. "The fact [he] has been so bloody good at it is really annoying from my point of view, because now I have to try and equal that." On the subject of doing a second series, he said: "Let's wait and see what happens. The BBC might sack me – I might get replaced by Moira Stuart."[5] (In a Berkshire recording studio, Big Finish started drawing up plans for an alternative universe audio series in which the Doctor regenerated into a slightly severe, adenoidal newsreader.)

In late July, *Blue Peter* launched a competition to design a *Doctor Who* monster. Unlike the 60s contest that had produced the legendary Steel Octopus, Hypnotron and Acwa Man, this time the winning creation would actually be written into the show by Russell T Davies. If they pulled the Zog Monster from Zog out of the hat, it would *really* ruin his day.

As principal photography got under way,

Tennant and Piper posed for publicity photos in a derelict car park next to an abandoned Beechams factory in Brentford. (They'd thought about St Tropez, but this came in slightly cheaper.) The pictures gave the world its first look at the tenth Doctor's costume, which matched a brown, skinny pin-striped suit with Converse trainers and an ankle-length coat. It was a geek chic look described by the BBC, in perhaps the most 2005 sentence ever, as "Franz Ferdinand-cum-Kaiser Chiefs". The outfit met with wide approval, with *The Guardian's* resident fashionista contrasting the first "indie Doctor" with Christopher Eccleston's terminally uncool "rocker dad" leather jacket. (Tennant later explained the inspiration for the suit-and-Converse combo had been Jamie Oliver, who had worn something similar on a recent edition of Michael Parkinson's chat show. Three decades earlier, and the tenth Doctor could well have been dressed as an emu.)

In Cardiff, Tennant had taken up residence in Eccleston's old apartment. ("Hi – instructions for the dishwasher are in the kitchen drawer, the stop-cock is under the sink and I've left the sonic screwdriver in the bedside cabinet. And sorry about the mess – left in a bit of a hurry.")

The new Doctor received *genuine* messages from his two favourite predecessors: Tom Baker sent a good luck note from the set of *Monarch of the Glen*, where he was currently in the midst of a typically fruity turn as the eccentric black sheep of Glenbogle's MacDonald clan, and Peter Davison wrote from Northumberland, where he was starring in *Distant Shores*, the ITV drama about a metropolitan doctor struggling to adjust to life in the rural North East. (Not to be confused with *Doc Martin*, the ITV drama about a metropolitan doctor struggling to adjust to life in the rural South West. ITV's drama commissioners were nothing if not consistent.)

Tennant and Piper quickly struck up a good rapport. "Chris would go away between breaks and save his energy for the performance," Piper told *Doctor Who Magazine*, "whereas, with David, we'll kind of chat, we'll have a laugh, but then, as soon as he needs to focus, he'll find his own way of doing that. He's a bit more like a – I don't know – a baby deer. He's my little Bambi!"[6]

And that wasn't her only nickname for her co-star. "I recently named him David Ten-Inch," she admitted. "I have no basis or grounds for calling him that, I just find it funny."[7] Presumably she was referring to the size of his action figure.

Meanwhile, the *Mirror* revealed the show's biggest new fangirl was none other than the Queen. According to the report, Her Maj was "hugely disappointed" when Christopher Eccleston had quit, and was planning to spend her annual Highland holiday re-watching his episodes. "'The Queen loves the series,' said a Palace source, "and has asked the BBC to send her copies so she can watch the series again during her stay at Balmoral." Typical – the richest woman in Britain, and she still won't stump up for the box set.

As filming returned to the Brandon Estate in London, the unit welcomed a visitor in the form of Peter Davison, who dropped in to say hello to the new man. This led to inevitable media speculation about the fifth Doctor returning, though in fact Davison had just brought his kids along for a day out (well, it was cheaper than Chessington World of Adventures).

By now, the show was pretty much a permanent fixture in the British press: in an average week, there were more stories about *Doctor Who* in the papers than in the entire Sylvester McCoy era. And some of them were even true.

The wildest fantasies tended to appear in the *Daily Star*, which had long since given up any pretence of being a newspaper in favour of a constant throb of titillation involving various "glamour" models, *Big Brother* babes and the occasional bona fide actress who'd misplaced her clothes. Billie Piper was a particular source of fascination: barely a day would go by without one of the paper's hacks plucking an "exclusive" from the air (or somewhere less pleasant). In August, the *Star* announced that Piper's ex-hubbie Chris Evans was being lined up to play Satan in a forthcoming episode. "We've already got some great celebrities lined up for the next series, but having Chris Evans would be the icing on the cake," said the inevitable unnamed source. "Having him as Satan would be a hoot, and we know he'd rel-

ish the role. And we're sure Billie would find it a giggle." A few weeks later, the paper breathlessly informed readers that "*Doctor Who* babe Billie Piper left toy bosses panting when they were ordered to make a doll of her – they spent hours working out the shapely star's measurements so the toy version of Rose Tyler looked just like the real thing". I guess we shouldn't be too judgmental – it can be a lonely life in the vacuum-formed toy business. Music executives at EMI Gold were also presumably left panting as they put together *The Very Best of Billie Piper*, a 15-song cash-in compilation featuring all the hits (plus 12 other songs).

Away from the spotlight, Piper's former co-star, Christopher Eccleston, was keeping busy by lending his support to the fight to save Manchester's Victoria Baths, and narrating a documentary about the city's Working Class Movement Library. Honestly, what a sell-out.

Blue Peter, meet Sad Tony

In August, David Tennant appeared on *Blue Peter* to announce the winner of the Design a Monster Competition. From a bumper 43,920 entries, the judges chose the Abzorbaloff – a "hairy Sumo" that absorbed the faces of its victims into its body, designed by nine-year-old William Grantham from Colchester. Memorable runners-up included a monster made entirely of footballs – which Tennant threatened to draw out of the hat, in order to see how Russell T Davies would cope with writing about sport – and a creature labouring under the frankly brilliant name of Sad Tony.

In Brighton, meanwhile, three people were discovered hiding in a temporary *Doctor Who* exhibition on the city's pier after escaping a raid by immigration officers. The officers would have found them sooner, but spent ages taking the names of all the illegal aliens in the building.

Two hundred miles away, one of BBC Exhibitions' longest-serving employees was readying himself for a return to action. Russell T Davies, who had already worked with K-9 on *Queer as Folk* (though the dog's sexual orientation was never discussed), had originally thought a story featuring the metal mutt and his mistress might work if the show went to a third run, by which time it would be established enough to risk the odd nod to the past. But the runaway success of the first series had emboldened him to bring it forward. And so it was that Elisabeth Sladen and John Leeson joined the cast, crew and several series writers – including Stephen Fry – at the read-through for upcoming episode *School Reunion*.

"K-9 didn't stand a chance, because Lis stole everyone's reactions," noted Davies. "Stole them like a thief in broad daylight. The read-through was quite amazing – the moment Lis said her first line, everyone was craning their necks to look down the table. I thought Stephen Fry was going to faint. I'm not kidding, you could feel the actual shiver go through the room."[8]

Toby Whithouse had seemingly anticipated this reaction in his script, which read: "The heart of every dad in the country skips a beat – it's Sarah Jane Smith". "It was quite a long process," explained Whithouse of the story's development. "They said they wanted to bring back Sarah Jane and K-9 – 'Aside from that, do anything you want'. So I went away and wrote a story and they said, 'No, that's rubbish. Do anything you want as long as it's not *that*'."[9]

Sladen had signed on after being taken out to dinner by Davies and Phil Collinson. "They were obviously planning to propose something – just as I was planning to turn it down," she wrote in her autobiography. "It wasn't because I thought their new series didn't look amazing – because it did; it was marvellous – but my time on *Who* was so precious to me that I wasn't prepared to spoil it again for a cheap ratings-boosting, blink-and-you'll-miss-me cameo."[10]

In fact, she discovered that the script under discussion had already been written – and that she was on "virtually every page". Under the circumstances, how could she say no? "Twenty-nine years after first walking away, I was going back to *Doctor Who*."[10]

Filming her first scene with David Tennant ("the loveliest, sweetest man") in a Cardiff comprehensive school was "a real goosebump moment" for the actress. "I don't think I'd appreciated how much the show had stayed with me until that moment," she said.[10] Unfortunately, while filming a chase sequence at the end of her first day, Sladen slipped on the polished parquet floor, and had to be taken to A&E. "When the doctors said I had destabilised my pelvis and torn my quad, I just wanted to cry. Back in my hotel that night, my thoughts turned as black as my leg. *They're going to hate me if I ruin this...* They'd written a whole show for me and now, like a silly old woman, I was about to wreck everything."[10]

Ever the trouper, Sladen carried on, but the pain was agonising. "The leg really alienated me, I'm afraid," she recalled. "When I wasn't on call, I was on my own packing it with ice, or resting... It was such an honour to have been chosen to return and, despite everything, I really did have an amazing time. But the leg colours everything, even today. I know we produced a fantastic episode, but it's still ingrained in my head that it was a disaster."[10]

More reassuringly, it was good to know K-9 couldn't cope with the polished floors, either. Or the tiles. Or any other kind of surface. It was like he'd never been away.

Also channelling the spirit of *Who*'s mid-70s heyday was the news that the first three ninth Doctor novels had been a huge success for BBC Books, shifting a whopping 50,000 copies – outselling the existing BBC *Doctor Who* ranges by a factor of ten to one. Three more titles were slated for release in September, with the tenth Doctor set to make his literary debut in three further books the following spring. Unlike the 70s, though, the same bloke didn't have to write them all in his lunch hour.

By now, production had moved to the Gower Peninsula to film scenes for the series opener, *New Earth*. According to *Country Life*, the peninsula boasted "the most wonderful sunset in UK", but there was precious little evidence of that when the *Who* crew arrived in a howling gale and rain storm that was so bad, filming had to be temporarily abandoned. Later, it was also discovered that the camera recording the close-ups hadn't been working. That was the official excuse, anyway – though "not working" could well be industry-speak for "forgot to press start".

David Tennant was joined by two special guests at the read-through for the second story, *Tooth and Claw* – his mum and dad. Following the previous year's Dickensian adventure, Jane Tranter had asked Russell T Davies to "kick the historicals up the arse a bit"; Davies took this literally and devised a story about "Queen

Victoria versus a werewolf and a bunch of kung-fu monks". The script was originally allocated to another writer, who failed to include either the werewolf or the warrior monks (but apart from that, it was bang on), so Davies took it on himself at short notice.

In October, Alan Davies discussed the role he had once been much fancied for in the *Sunday Telegraph*, declaring: "They worked Christopher Eccleston into the ground. He quit and the BBC put it about that he didn't want to be typecast. The truth was they just overworked him and he was exhausted." Through the pages of the *Daily Mirror*, Eccleston responded that: "Alan should keep his nose out of my business. I rang his agent and told him he had no right to say what he did." Yeah, get out of *that*, Jonathan Creek.

In an interview with *SFX*, Russell T Davies revealed that human facelift Cassandra was set to return in the new series, and claimed he already had ideas for about ten episodes of Series Three nailed down – "including that episode in Nobby's Circus Tent with the talking elephants. I think we'll transmit that live."[11] And people thought he was joking.

Early November to late January was scheduled as one big recording block that would take in the Cybermen two-parter as well as the season finale. The location filming was so cold that the Cybermen had to wear large dressing gowns to keep warm, which must really have damaged their credibility at the next Evil Monsters AGM. (And it obviously didn't work, as one of the Cyber actors got such a bad cold, he sneezed down the inside of his helmet. Nice.)

Fresh from his Dalek triumph, Nicholas Briggs was hired to create the Cybes' voices. Graeme Harper wanted something less theatrical than the rich, Vader-like tones of the 80s models, and both he and Briggs were fans of the heavily treated, buzzsaw effect from the Troughton era. Briggs offered 11 choices from his extensive menu of Cyber voices, from which Harper chose No. 7 – based on the Cybermen from *The Invasion*, for those taking notes. ("Excellent choice," said Briggs. "And would sir like extra modulation with that?")

As the first photo of the new-look cyborgs was released to a somewhat muted reception, *The Times* pined for the days when the creatures were "70% Bacofoil, with a car lamp stuck on their heads". Oh come on, that's exactly the sort of cheap shot we thought we'd got over now. If you go back and look at the original Cybermen you'd see they were actually... Er, yeah, anyway, where were we?

In November, it was announced that a special interactive mini-episode to accompany the Christmas special would be available via the BBC's Red Button service. (So named because you accessed it via the red button on your remote. The whizzkids in branding took months coming up with that one.) David Tennant was also spotted out on the town with Series Two guest star Sophia Myles – aka Lady Penelope from that dreadful live action *Thunderbirds* movie, with whom he was thought to be in a relationship. Or possibly it was just a no-strings quickie.

With Saturday night family drama unexpectedly fashionable again, ITV decided to get in on the act, releasing details of *Primeval*, a new action series about dinosaurs on the rampage in contemporary London. Like the BBC's own upcoming *Robin Hood* re-boot, the show was clearly inspired by *Doctor Who* – though not, it's safe to assume, directly by 1974's comically over-ambitious *Invasion of the Dinosaurs*. Unless someone in commissioning had got *very* drunk.

The *Daily Mirror* dropped a blonde bombshell in the middle of the month when it reported that Billie Piper wouldn't be returning for the third season, despite being "begged" by the BBC. The paper also said she had signed up to play Fanny Price in an ITV production of Jane Austen's *Mansfield Park*, which was probably true, as wild tabloid fantasies rarely involved eighteenth-century romantic literature without good reason.

Meanwhile, Stephen Fry was talking up his script, thought to be an Arthurian fable with a sci-fi twist, in an interview with *Scotland Today*: "One of the most exciting moments of my life was starting the first page and writing: Exterior: The TARDIS. The TARDIS materialises on the surface of a strange planet," said Fry – little realising that, by now, Russell T Davies had probably revised it to: "The TARDIS materialises next to a kebab van in Cardiff."

The series' adopted home gave David Tennant and Billie Piper a heroes' welcome on

November 17th when a crowd of thousands gathered to watch them switch on the city's Christmas lights. "Nadolig Llawen!", declared the duo in fluent Welsh, praying it really did mean Merry Christmas and not something indescribably offensive.

The next day, the tenth Doctor made his TV debut – somewhat earlier than anticipated – when a special Russell T Davies-scripted scene following directly on from the end of *The Parting of the Ways* was featured as part of that year's *Children in Need* telethon. That's right – forget a 3-D Kate O'Mara camping it up in Albert Square (if only we could): this was seven minutes of yer actual, genuine, canonical *Doctor Who* – and the first look at a brand new Doctor, to boot.

The scene, in which the Doctor tries to convince Rose he's the same man, before going a bit mental and setting the TARDIS on a crash course for Christmas, didn't have an on-screen title, but Russell T Davies jokingly gave it the name *Pudsey Cutaway*: a conjunction of the charity's one-eyed ursine mascot and *Dalek Cutaway*, the name used in production paperwork for the 1965 standalone episode *Mission to the Unknown*. Maybe you had to be there.

That year's appeal also offered two fans the chance to visit the set and meet the cast. The auction received thousands of bids (even if most of them were from a J. Barrowman of Cardiff).

"I don't care if you *are* Doctor Who – your mother wants to watch *Emmerdale*"

As revealed in the *Children in Need* scene, the tenth Doctor's accent was definitely a few hundred miles south of David Tennant's native Paisley, leading the *Sunday Mail* to claim fans had been "stunned" by the Doctor's "mockney Dick van Dyke" impression. Dialect issues aside, there was effusive praise from Tennant's peers, with *School Reunion* guest star Anthony Head hailing his "effortless" performance in the role. "He was literally born to play the part," Head told BBC Radio 2, describing the new man as "the best Doctor since Patrick Troughton". Harry Potter was also impressed, Daniel Radcliffe telling *SFX* his *Goblet of Fire* co-star was "so absolutely, fantastically watch-

able – I think he'll be a good Doctor Who". *Broadcast* magazine clearly agreed, putting Tennant at pole position in its Hot 100 list of trending talent.

Meanwhile, the tabloids reported that Victoria Beckham's latest Harrods shopping trip had seen her foregoing the usual designer labels and picking up a copy of the Series One script book instead. VB claimed the purchase was for her husband, who was "completely obsessed" with the show. Which sounded a bit unlikely: I mean, a footballer – reading a *book*?

At the end of November, the *Sunday Times* informed readers that Stephen Fry's episode may be delayed. According to the paper, the script was impressive and "very Stephen Fry," but simply too expensive to realise during the next run. Instead, a standby script was greenlit from Matthew Graham, whose forthcoming time travel cop show *Life on Mars* was currently generating a lot of industry heat.

December saw the show at the centre of a mild political skirmish as *The Independent* reported that *The Christmas Invasion* would contain explicit criticism of the war in Iraq, including a pointed joke about Tony Blair being George W Bush's pet poodle. Russell T Davies was quoted as saying that was "absolutely" his intention – adding that Christmas Day was supposed to be a day of peace – leaving the blowhards of *American Thinker* magazine fuming about how the "once-respected" BBC was using a sci-fi series to have a pop at America.

The British media got the chance to see for themselves at *The Christmas Invasion* press screening a couple of weeks before the big day. The praise was effusive, with *The Sun* claiming the special was "the best gift the fans could hope for", *Heat* magazine awarding it five stars and fellow sleb gossip pamphlet *Closer* telling its readers: "Prepare to be enthralled."

Making his primetime chat show debut on *Friday Night with Jonathan Ross* – one of numerous TV and radio appearances during Christmas week – Tennant said he was committed to a second series "as long as I don't get the sack". (Somewhere in Buckinghamshire, Colin Baker winced.) The actor's rising stock also earned him top place in the *Daily Record*'s Scottish Hot 100 list – surely the only time the words "Scotland" and "hot" had ever been uttered in the same sentence.

Doctor Who was also afforded the rare privilege of making the cover of the Christmas issue of Radio Times – a slot usually reserved for the likes of Santa, Rudolph and assorted snowmen and angels (but probably not Jesus – there was no need to go dragging him into it).

In The Guardian, Charlie Brooker had obviously cracked open the advocaat early, describing The Christmas Invasion as "the greatest Christmas episode of any programme ever", and reaffirming his view that Doctor Who was "the best show of 2005 by about 16 billion parsecs". "It's our first proper chance to see David Tennant in action," he added. "Thank God, then, that this doesn't disappoint in the slightest."

Indeed, it doesn't – unless you were tuning in for that first proper chance to see David Tennant in action. Because, tasked with introducing viewers to a new Doctor for the second time in nine months, Russell T Davies does the smart thing – and removes him from the picture altogether for a good two-thirds of the story.

While the Time Lord is out for the count in Jackie's flat (and Jackie's new fella's pyjamas), the Earth is subjugated by the Sycorax – an aggressive race of voodoo warriors who accessorise with the skulls and bones of their vanquished enemies – to the extent that even plucky Rose Tyler starts to lose hope. The result is that any residual resentment the kids may have been feeling towards this impostor who's replaced their hero quickly dissipates as they start willing him to wake up and save the world. What better way of establishing the new man than showing us what life would be like without him? It's almost like this Russell T Davies fella knows how to write telly.

The invasion itself is an obvious homage to Independence Day – a city-sized spaceship appears over London, and at least one major landmark (the Gherkin – or 2 St Mary Axe, for pedants) is, if not destroyed, then at least left requiring the services of a good glazier. (Another famous monument, the Tower of London, turns out to be the new UNIT HQ – though sadly there's no Brigadier, and no big give-away sign outside either.)

As well as the Sycorax, there's a subplot involving a bunch of robot Santas who want the Doctor's body. (No, not like that – though David Tennant does look quite fetching in those PJs.) In order to achieve this, they go to the effort of installing a killer Christmas tree in the Tylers' flat. Why they didn't just kidnap the unconscious Doctor while delivering the tree is a moot point but, hey... robot Santas! Killer Christmas trees!

There's a welcome return for Penelope Wilton as Harriet Jones, now promoted from MP to PM, on whose deceptively broad shoulders it falls to defend the Earth. (In the scene that so upset some American critics, she even stands up to the US President, declaring: "He's not my boss and he's certainly not turning this into a war". If you ever wanted proof that Doctor Who is pure fantasy, this is it.)

From the moment he finally makes his big entrance (having been revived by the healing power of tea – more proof that, for an alien, the Doctor is a true Brit at hearts), David Tennant owns the role completely. His freewheeling opening monologue – in which he challenges the Sycorax, works out their plan, flirts outrageously with Rose and quotes extensively from The Lion King – is a tour de force: cheeky, goofy and flippant, but with a core of steel. By the time he challenges the Sycorax leader to a duel – while still in his jim-jams – the audience is in no doubt this new man is the real deal.

Fittingly, Tennant watched his debut go out live in the place where he'd forged his lifelong love of the show: at the family home in Paisley, surrounded by his mum, dad, his sister and her kids. Whether he was wearing his scarf and cricket jumper, we can't be sure.

With just shy of ten million viewers tuning in, the special was second only to the festive (i.e. unremittingly grim, but with tinsel) edition of EastEnders as the season's most watched programme, while Gareth Roberts' interactive adventure Attack of the Graske – in which players helped the Doctor pursue an irksome gremlin through various time zones – was accessed by around half a million people.

The Christmas Invasion garnered rave reviews, with The Sun describing it as "the jewel in the BBC's crown". But right-wing propaganda sheet The Spectator was less impressed, citing the "worryingly peacenik tendencies" of the "wussie" new *Doctor Who* – a reference to the story's somewhat unconvincing final reel, in which the Doctor decides to bring Harriet Jones' premiership to a premature end as punishment for firing on the retreating Sycorax ship. The magazine appeared to have conveniently forgotten the fact the Doctor had also taken up arms for the honour of the planet – then vanquished the Sycorax leader with a satsuma. I mean, what kind of peacenik turns a citrus fruit into a deadly weapon?

Sexiest Man in the Universe: Zogs of Zog demand re-count

Russell T Davies started the New Year by topping *The Stage* newspaper's list of Movers and Shakers. "The man has achieved the almost impossible and transformed *Doctor Who* for a cynical twenty-first-century audience and made them fall in love with it again," read the citation. "He wrestled Saturday nights out of the hands of Ant and Dec and revitalised family drama." Cynical twenty-first-century audience? *Whatever.*

David Tennant came in at No. 6: "His transformation into the Time Lord has made the nation sit up, take notice and ask 'Christopher who?'" said the paper – much to the delight of a Mr C Eccleston of Salford.

Also in January, it was announced that the new series would be accompanied by a *second* behind-the-scenes show in the form of children's magazine programme *Totally Doctor Who*, while fans in the US would finally get to see the new episodes – because they absolutely hadn't illegally downloaded them off the internet or anything, honest – when the Sci-Fi Channel picked up first-run rights for Series One, with an option for Series Two. "They really did get it," said Julie Gardner of the new Stateside broadcaster. "They were happy with how British it is – they really liked the humour. They really, really got it." As Brits had famously said once before of their American cousins: better late than never, I guess.

Back home, the awards kept coming: David Tennant was voted Sexiest Man in the Universe by readers of gay interest mag *The Pink Paper* (though only Earth readers got to vote) and Billie Piper was honoured with a South Bank

Show Award for breakthrough talent to add to her BAFTA, NTA and Smash Hits trophies. Meanwhile, the *Daily Star* was up to its usual tricks, observing "just how friendly" Tennant and Piper had become while papped during a filming break. "Gorgeous Billie, 23, gazed adoringly at David, 34, before they tenderly hugged each other. And he kept a close eye on the babe, who plays the Time Lord's assistant Rose Tyler, as she burst into a fit of giggles." In other words: they must definitely be doing it.

In February, the BBC announced details of Vortext: specially recorded scenes linked to each week's episode that would be made available to download to your mobile phone. The Beeb promised the Gareth Roberts-scripted scenes would be "proper mini-dramas" (he wouldn't just be phoning it in, you know). The service would eventually go live under the name TARDISodes, having been through variations including Whosode, Who Alert and the frankly desperate Epi-mobe.

In a big month for Time Lord-related phone news, Tom Baker also became the voice of BT's home text service – meaning that, whenever you texted to a landline, the listener would receive a message in the fourth Doctor's booming, stentorian tones. ("Hello, this is a message for Dennis. Carol says would you mind popping the oven on? Jesus Christ, who writes this whippet shit?")

David Tennant was the recipient of one such call: "[Tom] phoned me up the other day," he told *Radio Times*. "Well, he didn't. I got a text message from him, which I did get ridiculously excited about. It was only to tell me my broadband had been switched on."[13]

March brought news of yet another possible *Who* spin-off, as *The Sun* claimed Sarah Jane Smith and K-9 were to star in their own series on CBBC. "It would have been a shame to put K-9 back in his kennel," an "insider" punned weakly. The BBC also confirmed that Peter Kay would be appearing in the upcoming series as the "cold and powerful" Victor Kennedy. The country's biggest comedy star had been offered the role after writing Russell T Davies a six-page fan letter about the new series.

On February 17th, New *Who* made its US debut on sci-fi, accompanied by a fanfare of press publicity. *TV Guide* listed the "slick update" as one of its 21 Shows You Gotta See, the *New York Times* remarked on its "goofy, home-made quality" and *The Hollywood Reporter* described it as "silly, sophomoric stuff that is sure to please its television audience". Which shows you what *The Hollywood Reporter* thinks about TV viewers. *Entertainment Weekly* added that, when *Doctor Who* returned to screens, the average American's response would be "it was here before?!" – thus winning the Open Goal Award for missing the world's most obvious "Doctor Who?" gag.

In the UK, Christopher Eccleston made a rare *Doctor Who*-related public appearance, chatting with a young contestant called Sam who had chosen the show as his specialist subject on *Junior Mastermind*. Eccleston described himself, with admirable candour, as an "unemployed Time Lord". (Let's hope he found a job soon as, under new rules, Time Lords are only eligible to claim benefits for the first 3,000 years.)

At the Series Two press launch at the end of the month, the new Doctor had trouble competing with Billie Piper's see-through top – an occasion recorded for posterity in that noted paper of record *The Sun* as "Doctor Who and the Bra-dis". Thanks for that. There then followed a full-on promo frenzy, with Tennant appearing on everything from *This Morning* and GMTV to *Ready, Steady Cook*, in which he competed in a kitchen battle against his dad, Sandy. ("Chicken's good – you can do stuff with chicken," observed Tennant. "And you can't go wrong with a frozen pea." Clearly, that suit wasn't the only thing he'd picked up from Jamie Oliver.)

The actor spoke to *Doctor Who Magazine* about adjusting to life in the spotlight, claiming he only really felt truly uncomfortable when people asked him for an autograph in the changing rooms at the gym. "You're standing there, literally bollock naked and sweaty... or worse, if *they're* all pink and puffy and naked. But I just go, 'Yes of course, who's it to?' – like an eejit. I don't know what's the appropriate response. Is it appropriate to go, 'This is weird – I don't want to look at your genitals while I sign an autograph?'"[12] Yes, that's probably appropriate – especially if you're in Sainsbury's at the time.

It also emerged that, ever the fanboy, Tennant had asked for his credit in the end

titles to be changed from Doctor Who, as Christopher Eccleston had been listed, to The Doctor. "As a kid it always bothered me, cause I thought, well he's not called Doctor Who," Tennant told *SFX*. "I remember as a kid when the credits changed thinking, oh good, finally they sorted it out. So I was particular about it. I mean, I wasn't going to go to war about it, but I did mention it to Phil and then on the first DVD I got of *The Christmas Invasion*, it still said 'Doctor Who' and then I moaned to Phil and he said, 'Oh sorry, I meant to change that,' and we got it re-jigged".[3] Hence David Tennant's favourite joke: "Knock knock." "Who's there?" "Doctor." "Doctor who?" "No, not Doctor Who – *the Doctor*."

The actor also admitted he had "various versions" of the theme tune and the TARDIS dematerialisation noise on his phone, but didn't have "the guts to use them as a ringtone".[3] And the magazine put his *Who* credentials to the test with a special *Mind Probe* quiz, in which he scored an impressive 10/10 by correctly answering such questions as "What's the name on the writing credit of *City of Death*?" and "Which writers created K-9?" – and even got bonus points for volunteering Gallifrey's co-ordinates from galactic centre. Just don't get him started on UNIT dating.

New Earth: not as good as the old Earth

On the eve of the series' April launch, the question of a *Doctor Who* film raised its head again, prompting Russell T Davies to lay in to his colleagues in the Corporation's movie producing arm. "I would not be desperately keen to work with BBC Films myself," the showrunner told icWales. "I'm not supposed to say this but... I can't bear them! I am in no rush to work with them whatsoever, personally." Clearly, someone was still sore about missing out on that last hash brown in the BBC canteen.

To tie in with the series' return, the BBC launched a new fortnightly magazine, *Doctor Who Adventures*. Offering a mix of comic strips, posters, puzzles and free gifts, the title was very much aimed at children – much to the embarrassment of the thousands of 30 and 40-year-old men queueing up in WH Smith to buy three copies (one to read, one to file in a presentation folder and one for spare). *Radio Times* also celebrated the show's imminent return with a fold-out cover and a 16-page pull-out guide to the new series. (Not that the fans would actually be pulling it out, of course – it's well known that *Doctor Who* issues of *RT* must be kept and filed in their entirety. That's why lofts were invented.)

BBC Three limbered up for the new series with its own *Doctor Who Night*, featuring a special edition of *Doctor Who Confidential* and repeats of *The Christmas Invasion* and *The Story of Doctor Who*, with linking presentation by *Dalek* guest star Corey Johnson. With the first TARDISode already available and the giddy, slightly over-excitable *Totally Doctor Who* launching on the 13th, the show surfed back onto screens two days later on a tidal wave of publicity and goodwill. All it had to do now was live up to the hype.

Yeah, about that...

After the deferred gratification of *The Christmas Invasion*, *New Earth* offers the first opportunity for viewers to really get the measure of the new man in the blue box. So it seems a little perverse that Russell T Davies chooses to open the season with a *Freaky Friday*-style body-swap comedy (allegedly) that forces David Tennant into some really quite undignified campery as he's possessed by the mind of stretchy suberbitch Cassandra. (I think we can safely assume this script would never have been written for the ninth Doctor – Christopher Eccleston yelling "Oh baby, I'm beating out a samba!" while wiggling his bum doesn't bear thinking about. Tennant does it rather well, of course – as does Billie Piper, poshing up as a slightly mortified Cassandra who, having taken over Rose's body, declares: "Oh my God – I'm a chav!")

If *The End of the World* was the Doctor and Rose's first date, this sort-of-sequel sees them returning to the year Five Billion (and Twenty Three) like a couple of love-struck honeymooners. But it's not all doe eyes and hand-holding: the Doctor has been summoned by the Face of Boe to a hospital in New New York, where cat nuns (as in cats, dressed as nuns – keep up) are infecting purpose-bred human lab rats with every disease in the galaxy in the name of medical research.

Once released, these plague carriers shuffle about for a bit in the usual vaguely comical zombie fashion, before the Doctor mixes up a cocktail cure – *for every known disease in the galaxy*, remember – by pouring a few bags of brightly coloured liquid into a disinfectant spray tank. This proves so instantly effective that the miracle cure can then be passed on to other disease-carriers by a simple game of zombie tag. It is, quite simply, the most heinous crime against science in the entire history of *Doctor Who*. Quite an achievement for a show in which the Doctor once managed to stop time using a wine bottle, a bunch of keys and some tealeaves (*The Time Monster*, in case it's a slow week on Netflix).

New Earth is also saddled with an ill-fitting coda in which the Doctor takes Cassandra, inhabiting the dying body of her luckless assistant, back in time so s/he can do a swan dive at the feet of her former self (Zoe Wannamaker, in the flesh this time) on the last day anyone – herself, as it turns out – called her beautiful. It's actually a very lovely scene in isolation but, as with *Boom Town*, the sudden lurch from knockabout comedy to emotional melodrama is jarring, to say the least. And, after two episodes of her being a comic (not to mention homicidal) "bitchy trampoline," suddenly being expected to care about Cassandra's wounded heart is quite a stretch – a bit like watching a re-make of *Terms of Endearment* starring Darth Vader.

New Earth looks great: the effects, production design and prosthetics (especially the cat nuns) are fantastic, and David Tennant and Billie Piper are already a winning combination. But as a comedy it's not funny enough, as an adventure it's not exciting enough and as a season opener – for a new Doctor, at that – it's a chronic misfire.

Even Charlie Brooker was downhearted. "My anticipation gland was bursting," he wrote in *The Guardian*, before admitting the episode had left him feeling "a bit... well, let down". *The Sun* also felt short-changed. "You don't think BBC1 over-sold it just the teeniest bit, do you?" grumbled its TV critic. "At best, someone has chosen the wrong opening episode. Or, at worst, we're in for a lousy series. Let's hope it's the former."

Others were more enthusiastic: "At the risk

of receiving death threats from *Doctor Who* extremists, I'd like to say that David Tennant is the best TARDIS captain in the history of the universe," gushed the *Express*, while the *Mirror* hailed "the TV event of the week by a billion light years", praising the production as "imaginative, energetic, high impact, completely bonkers, good fun, amusing, original entertainment".

The *Daily Mail*, naturally, were the first to suggest the sky might be falling in: "The first episode of the second season of *Doctor Who* drew around eight million viewers on Saturday night – nearly two million less than last season's debut," it crowed, prompting the BBC to respond that eight million people amounted to "the best drama audience figure of the year". Meanwhile, the *Sunday Mail* (no relation) claimed Sophia Myles had admitted to carrying a David Tennant action figure around in her handbag. "BBC bosses sent Sophia two of the coveted Time Lord dolls," claimed the paper, "complete with sonic screwdrivers". The winking and nudging was almost audible.

Previously, on *Doctor Who*...

Tooth and Claw sees Russell T Davies finally having a go at doing a proper *Doctor Who* horror story, and making a rather brilliant job of it. On her way to Balmoral, Queen Victoria is diverted to Torchwood House (keep an eye on that anagrammatic meme – it's this year's Bad Wolf), where she discovers it's been seized by a bunch of werewolf-worshipping ninja monks. As you do.

The monks want their furry friend (actually an alien Lupine Wavelength Haemovariform that crashed-landed in the Highlands 300 years earlier) to give Her Maj a nasty nip, thus instigating The Empire of the Wolf. She, it goes without saying, is Not Amused.

It's a bonkers premise, but Davies uses it to craft a tense, claustrophobic and action-packed thriller in which the wolf – a triumphant, Hollywood-besting creation by the CGI wizards at The Mill – stalks the Doctor and company through the isolated house in scenes reminiscent of mid-70s scarer *Horror of Fang Rock*.

Pauline Collins, returning to *Doctor Who* for the first time since passing up a TARDIS place

40 years earlier, is note-perfect as Victoria – though much of the credit resides with Davies, who avoids lazy clichés by writing the Empress of India as a formidable woman who, when she's not cutting lesser intellects down to size ("I shall contain my wit, in case I do you further injury"), proves to be no slouch as a kick-ass action heroine. Cornered by the wicked Father Angelo, she whips out a revolver from her bustle and shoots him dead – but not before putting him right on a matter of royal etiquette ("The correct form of address is *Your Majesty*"). Davies also gifts Collins a beautiful soliloquy in which the grieving widow confesses to a new-found passion for the supernatural: "That's the charm of a ghost story, isn't it?" she tells the Doctor. "Not the scares and chills, that's just for children, but the hope of some contact with the great beyond. We all want some message from that place. It's the Creator's greatest mystery that we're allowed no such consolation. The dead stay silent, and we must wait."

It's sheer TV poetry – though try telling grown-up viewers scares are just for kids whenever Tom Smith is on screen. The actor gives a truly unnerving performance as the Host – a "weakling, heartsick boy" stolen from his home in the night and slowly infected with the wolf's DNA, and now reduced to a pale, black-eyed vessel through which the alien boasts how "I carved out his soul and sat in his heart". Eek.

Tooth and Claw boasts an abundance of casually brilliant, almost throwaway ideas – from the notion of books as weapons ("We're in a library... this room's the greatest arsenal we could have") to a cheeky explanation for Victoria's mysterious haemophilia. The story's resolution is also hugely satisfying, Davies drawing all the various plot strands together to have Prince Albert save the world from beyond the grave using a giant telescope and the Koh-i-Noor diamond. Viewed objectively, it's barely less daft than *New Earth's* "magic potion" denouement, but the trick is in the way it's sold. The idea of a werewolf being killed by an excess of moonlight may be ridiculous – not least because there's no such *thing* as moonlight – but Davies' hand-waving explanation to Rose that "You're 70% water, but you can still drown" is smart and audacious enough for us to buy into it.

The end brings a final twist when Victoria knights Sir Doctor of TARDIS and Dame Rose of the Powell Estate – then promptly banishes them as punishment for "consorting with stars and magic" and thinking it "fun".

"I saw last night that Great Britain has enemies beyond imagination, and we must defend our borders on all sides," declares Her Majesty. "I propose an institute to investigate these strange happenings and to fight them. I would call it Torchwood. The Torchwood Institute. And if this Doctor should return, then he should beware, because Torchwood will be waiting. ("Oh, and could you check John Barrowman's availability for 225 years' time? I think he should be finished in *Chicago* by then.")

Figures for the episode were up nearly a million on the season debut, and the story was well received – despite the *Sunday Mirror*'s no doubt Adonis-like TV critic claiming the werewolf was not as scary looking as "demon-faced Dave" – aka David Tennant, aka The Sexiest Man in the Universe.

And not just according to readers of *The Pink Paper*. After decades of acting like a gentlemen's club – albeit a gentlemen's club where the dress code was less black tie than black jeans and un-ironed *Red Dwarf* T-shirt – *Doctor Who* fandom was suddenly being invaded by a terrifying new race of creatures known as Women. Specifically, a growing breed of fangirl whose enthusiastic online "squee-in'" at David Tennant's every move left many male fans baffled. (Although *Space Helmet*'s Diversity Officer feels compelled to point out this slightly condescending portrait of female fandom as over-excitable girlies mooning over pictures of hot boys is, in itself, perhaps indicative of how alien they were to some dusty corners of the old guard.)

On April 24th, viewers of a certain age may have been forgiven for thinking they'd fallen through a wormhole into the 1970s as the TARDIS materialised in the *Blue Peter* studio – and out stepped Elisabeth bloody Sladen. If only she'd been interviewed by Lesley Judd in a pair of floral bell-bottoms, the illusion would have been complete. As anticipation for Sarah Jane and K-9's return on Saturday built, Bob

Baker revealed he was writing a separate series starring his 'puterised pooch for cable channel Jetix Europe. Which just goes to show: no-one waits ages for a K-9 spin-off, then two come along anyway.

It has to be said that not everyone was up for a nostalgia-fest. The continuity binges of the mid-80s, when there was a widespread (though often unfounded) perception that even casual *Doctor Who* viewers were expected to come armed with a working knowledge of 20-year-old stories, had left many fans so terrified of anything even remotely referencing the past they came up with a word for it: fanwank. But the idea of ignoring the entire history – hell, let's call it a legacy – of *Doctor Who* is as absurd as asking your parents never to mention your school days. It's surely not a question of *whether* you do nostalgia, but *how*. And *School Reunion* is a textbook lesson in how to do nostalgia.

The genius of Toby Whithouse's script is how light on its feet it is. The return of Sarah Jane Smith and K-9 can't help but induce a Proustian headrush for long-time viewers, but Whithouse finds as much humour as pathos in the situation – especially the rivalry between Sarah Jane and Rose, neatly summed up by Mickey as "the missus and the ex: welcome to every man's worst nightmare". (Davies said the rivalry between Rose and Sarah Jane should be like *Sex and the City*. If *Sex and the City* was filmed in a Welsh secondary school with a talking robot dog.)

Much sport is also made of having the Doctor going undercover as a physics teacher while Rose serves the chips in the school canteen. The alien invasion stuff is relatively lightweight... the shape-shifting, bat-like Krillitane (led by a purringly malefic Anthony Head) have taken over a London comprehensive, where they're harvesting the children's creative powers in order to crack something called the Skasis Paradigm: a sort of Grand Universal Theory that would allow them to change the building blocks of the universe. Okay, so rewriting the universe isn't *that* lightweight, but we're never in any doubt that the monster-of-the-week stuff is just a framing device for the real story of the Doctor, Sarah and Rose – and Mickey, who briefly revels in his new role as the Doctor's "technical support" before coming to the hilarious realisation that "Oh my God – I'm the tin dog!" Metal Mickey, if you will.

Frothy and fast-moving though it is, when the emotional beats come, they hit pretty hard. The shot of Sarah stumbling across the TARDIS and physically recoiling in shock, as the camera reveals the Doctor standing in the shadows behind her, is punch-to-the-gut stuff, and there's a beautiful scene in a late-night café in which she reprimands him for leaving her behind. ("Did I do something wrong?" she asks him. "Because you never came back for me.") Rose demands to know if she is destined for the same fate. "You can spend the rest of your life with me," the Doctor tells her. "But I can't spend the rest of mine with you. I have to live on. Alone. That's the curse of the Time Lords."

Later, the Doctor is almost persuaded by the logic of the Krillitane plan, believing he could use it to reverse the Time War and restore his people. But Sarah, when offered the chance to live forever by the Doctor's side, stands firm: "No," she declares, in a deliberate echo of the ninth Doctor's words. "The universe has to move forward. Pain and loss, they define us as much as happiness or love. Whether it's a world, or a relationship, everything has its time. And everything ends."

And then K-9 blows up all the bat people. Seriously, is this the greatest TV show ever, or what?

At the end, 29 years after being unceremoniously bundled out of the door in Croydon (which actually turns out to have been Aberdeen), Sarah finally gets the chance for a proper farewell. "Say it. Please, this time, say it," she pleads. The Doctor grins. "Goodbye," he says, "my Sarah Jane." And several million men who are probably old enough to know better blub like children. Which that Saturday, of course, is exactly what they were.

I know that my hearth will go on

In advance of his latest episode, Steven Moffat took to the Outpost Gallifrey fan forum to warn of "story-killing spoilers" in that week's Radio Times. In truth, though, it would take a lot more than a few plot reveals to kill something as majestic as The Girl in the Fireplace.

From the moment the Doctor, Rose and Mickey (yes, the tin dog is along for the ride – and his so-called girlfriend isn't at all happy about it) discover an eighteenth-century French fireplace blazing away on board a fifty-first-century spaceship, it's clear we're in for something a bit different. And they don't need to go on the Antiques Roadshow to find out if the fireplace is genuine, because it's still attached to eighteenth-century France – specifically, the bedroom of young Jeanne-Antoinette ("Reinette") Poisson. That's her, waving from the other side in her nightdress. Hello!

Crossing time and space via the medium of a revolving hearth – well, it's no less barmy than a police box – the Doctor finds himself in Paris, 1727, where his attention is drawn to a broken clock. "Okay, that's scary." "You're scared of a broken clock?" asks young Reinette. "Just a bit scared, yeah. Because if this clock's broken, and it's the only clock in the room, then what's that?" asks the Doctor, indicating the loud tick-tock sound reverberating around the bed-chamber.

Eagle-eyed viewers may note this is exactly the same trick as the "if the tape's run out, who's talking?" scene from The Doctor Dances (and Steven Moffat had already reprised the same gimmick later that episode with a typewriter). Here, though, it has added weight by being set in a child's bedroom, at night, with the Doctor identifying that the source of the threat is hiding under her bed. Short of actually coming round and leaping out of their wardrobe, it's hard to see what more Moffat could do to tap into children's primal fears.

But don't worry, everyone has nightmares – even monsters from under the bed. "What do monsters have nightmares about?" asks a puzzled Reinette. "Me!" beams the Doctor, flashing her his most disarming smile while taking the interloper – a clockwork robot in carnival mask, periwig and breeches – for a spin in the fireplace. Monsters under the bed, and the reason we don't need to be scared of them: there is surely no scene that more perfectly crystallises the essence of Doctor Who than this one.

When the Doctor next revolves into

Reinette's room, she's all grown up – and, unlike most of his predecessors, this incarnation is not slow to notice. But it's only after she's pressed him up against the wall for a spot of tonsil tennis that one of Reinette's servants tells him who she is. "No way," he boggles. "Reinette Poisson? Later Madame Etoiles? Later still mistress of Louis the Fifteenth, uncrowned Queen of France? Actress, artist, musician, dancer, courtesan, fantastic gardener!" "Who the hell are you?" demands the servant. "I'm the Doctor," he beams, "and I just snogged Madame de Pompadour!"

The relationship between the Time Lord and the King's courtesan is the heart and soul of this story, as *Doctor Who* finally fulfils the promise – oft-cited during discussion of its "infinitely flexible format" – of delivering a genuine historical romance. In fact, our hero is so fixated with the distinguished Madame de P, he is prepared to give up his travels in favour of taking "the slow path" by her side.

This is a story worth telling – and the chemistry between David Tennant and Sophia Myles obviously didn't need much of a jump-start – but it seems odd it should be dropped right into the middle of the Doctor and Rose's ongoing will-they-won't-they romance, and even more odd coming just seven days after the Doctor made a point of explaining why Time Lords and humans are so incompatible in 'til death do us part stakes.

Still, even if you don't buy the main feature, there's plenty of other wonderful stuff going on: the clockwork robots are fantastically creepy, as is the concept of them repairing their spaceship using the crew's body parts. Plus, as you'd expect from Moffat, it's consistently laugh-out-loud funny: when Mickey asks what a horse (Arthur) is doing on a spaceship, the Doctor replies: "Mickey, what's pre-Revolutionary *France* doing on a spaceship? Get a little perspective."

The climax sees the Doctor literally riding to the rescue on a white charger, smashing through time and space – and, more specifically, a huge mirror – on Arthur and landing slap in the middle of the court of Louis XV. "This is my lover, the King of France," Mme de Pompadour tells him. "Yeah?" sniffs the Doctor. "Well I'm the Lord of Time – and I'm here to fix the clock."

Magnifique.

The inclusion of Mme de Pompadour had been a special request from Russell T Davies, who had become fascinated with her while writing *Casanova*. As research, Moffat read Nancy Mitford's 1954 biography, which included details of one of Louis XV's courtiers discovering a revolving fireplace in her bedroom, and rumbling the fact she must be cheating on him. (Either that, or she was Batman.) It was at that point the story, which Moffat had been struggling to get a handle on, finally clicked. "I just *had* to have a revolving fireplace," he said. "If there's a revolving fireplace in *Doctor Who*... well, clearly it has to be a time-and-space revolving fireplace. See, writes itself!"[14]

Talking to *Doctor Who Magazine*, Tennant revealed he hadn't made a *great* first impression on his current squeeze. "We had met once before, on *Foyle's War*, but she didn't remember that," he said. "I thought she was a bit frosty on that, to be honest, so I was a little bit nervous when I knew she was coming on *Doctor Who* – but she turned out to be a top lass."[12] Which is just as well, or all that French kissing could have been *very* awkward.

On Saturday, May 13th, episode five of *Doctor Who* Series Two, *Rise of the Cybermen*, helped ITV1 suffer the worst audience share in its history, the instalment's 9.22 million viewers amounting to 44% of the total viewing public (ITV's screening of *X-Men* could only muster three million). It was all a very long way from the late 80s, when *Who*'s blood had been splashed over the Corrie cobbles on a humiliating weekly basis.

Tom McRae's story is loosely inspired by *Spare Parts*, Marc Platt's acclaimed 2002 Big Finish drama telling how the people of Mondas found themselves the unwitting victims of cybernetic "enhancement," as seen through the eyes of an ordinary family. Platt received a credit (and a fee) for the TV version but, in reality, the two couldn't be more different. Where *Spare Parts* is tense, claustrophobic and tragic, *Rise of the Cybermen / The Age of Steel* is big, flashy, frequently ridiculous and – whisper it – actually rather dull.

For a start, this is a parallel world story, so we're not talking about the Cybermen we grew up with. That's not an issue for most of the show's target audience, of course – except, in this reality, instead of being the result of a society's last, desperate bid for survival, the Cybermen are the creation of one bog-standard mad scientist. In fairness, wheelchair-bound megalomaniac (any resemblance to another crippled mad scientist, living, dead or cryogenically frozen, is purely laziness on the part of the writer) John Lumic has the potential to be an interesting character, motivated as he is by the desire to prolong his own failing body. Unfortunately, Roger Lloyd Pack doesn't so much chew the scenery ("And how will you do that – from Beyond! The! Grave!?") as swallow it whole with a side helping of ham. He faces stiff competition from Noel Clarke, though, who decides to distinguish between Mickey and his more alpha alt.world equivalent by having the latter snarl every line through a curled lip like an angry toddler, and also from Andrew Hayden-Smith, a children's TV presenter who turns in the least convincing resistance fighter this side of 'Allo 'Allo.

Even the return of Pete Tyler – in this world, not only alive, but a self-made success – lacks impact. Despite Shaun Dingwall and Billie Piper's best efforts, their scenes together fall a bit flat, and merely serve to cheapen the memory of Father's Day.

The Age of Steel boasts one stand-out sequence in which the Doctor and fellow freedom fighter Mrs Moore encounter a Cyberman in the cooling tunnels of Battersea Power Station. When the Doctor breaks the creature's emotional inhibitor, the dying human inside – a bride-to-be called Sally – starts to regain awareness. "Why am I cold?" she asks. "Where's Gareth? He can't see me. It's unlucky the night before." It's no coincidence that this is the scene that most closely resembles a similar incident in Marc Platt's original.

There are other, occasional flashes when the story remembers what it's supposed to be doing. The Cyber-conversion scenes – all whirring blades and whining drills – would have given Mary Whitehouse palpitations (talk about teatime brutality for tots), and the decision to overlay one such sequence with "The Lion Sleeps Tonight" is wonderfully perverse. The re-designed Cybermen also look fantastic – if you can get beyond the biggest flares this side of a Slade reunion – and the art deco par-

allel London, its sky filled with zeppelins, is another triumph for The Mill.

Mostly, though, it's all just a lot of clattering sound and fury, signifying not much at all. Even Graeme Harper – one of the original series' few real auteurs – struggles to add much depth. The Cybermen marching through suburban streets makes for an iconic image, and Harper is an assured action director, but he must shoulder some of the responsibility for the fact that this all feels so relentlessly major chord.

The first episode also serves up the most bafflingly pointless cliffhanger since Sylvester McCoy went over that ledge in Dragonfire, as the Cybermen march on a country house party for no obvious reason and, instead of capturing the guests for conversion, start slaughtering everyone in the room. As a business model, it needs work.

Clearly, the mid-season two-parter had been designated the gung-ho action adventure slot (though by all accounts earlier versions of the script's many, many drafts were much darker, and much closer to Spare Parts). But while Aliens of London / World War Three had enough wit and brio to paper over all the plot holes and fart gags, this clanging dud feels emptier than the contents of a Cyberman's fridge.

"Maybe Mary Whitehouse had a point about TV"

It was indicative of just what a ratings juggernaut the show had become that the overnights for The Idiot's Lantern (a robust 6.3 million) sparked something of a public postmortem, with The Guardian asking: "Where have all the viewers gone? BBC1's Doctor Who revival has been lavished with critical praise and awards, but there are signs midway through the second series that viewers may be tiring of the time travelling sci-fi drama." The paper cited "haphazard scheduling" – including The Age of Steel being brought forward to accommodate Eurovision – but also laid into The Idiot's Lantern itself, claiming the episode "attributed all the worst attributes that have been turning the series into a smug pantomime". Yes, just because you've defied the predictions of everyone in the industry, created a monster hit out of a much-derided TV relic and single-handedly revived the concept of family viewing, there's no cause to be smug about it.

The story had started life as a Russell T Davies idea about people being taken over by rock and roll (working titles had included *Mr Sandman* and *Sonic Doom*), before Mark Gatiss had evolved the narrative into something more visual – television.

That's right: while Steven Moffat goes for monsters under the bed, Mark Gatiss takes an even more direct route to the essence of *Doctor Who* – aliens in your telly. (I know – meta, or what?)

The Wire is an alien criminal using the image of a 1950s children's television presenter – a perfectly cast Maureen Lipman – to reach out through the screen and devour the electrical activity in viewers' brains, leaving them blank-faced, barely functioning drones. A bit like a 1950s version of *The X Factor*, then.

The Doctor and Rose come roaring out of the TARDIS on a Vespa expecting New York, but instead find themselves in Muswell Hill on the eve of Elizabeth II's Coronation – which the Wire is hoping to use to gain enough TV exposure to regain corporeal form. The time travellers appear to treat the whole thing as a bit of a lark until Rose gets her face sucked off by Maureen Lipman (so to speak), at which point the Doctor gets Very Angry Indeed, with the usually faultless David Tennant sailing just a wee bit over the top in his shouty confrontation with the local plods.

He's a picture of restraint, though, compared to Jamie Foreman, who makes an early bid for Roger Lloyd Pack's Most Ill-judged Performance crown as local bully boy Eddie Connolly. Subjecting his mousey wife and repressed teenage son to a life of domestic tyranny, the character ought to be a ticking timebomb of suppressed rage and frustration, but Foreman plays him as a cartoon oaf somewhere between a Harry Enfield sketch and Windsor Davies in *It Ain't 'Alf Hot Mum*.

The story delivers some classic *Doctor Who* visuals, from the cage full of faceless victims, their 50s haircuts framing blank, featureless visages (though anyone who remembers classic 70s head-scratcher *Sapphire and Steel* will find the image familiar) to the Wire itself: a textbook *Who* monster that takes something

innocent and comforting and twists it into something dark and sinister (never have the words "Goodnight children, everywhere" been imbued with such menace). Euros Lyn, meanwhile, directs with his typical flair and imagination, channelling the 50s vibe with some striking film noir homages. (Either that, or his camera just kept falling over.)

It's a pity, then, that the story loses its way a bit in the final reel. In theory, having the Doctor hanging off the top of the Alexandra Palace transmitter, King Kong-style, should make for an exciting climax, but it's actually a bit underwhelming, while the Wire's repeated cry of "Huuunnngggrrryy!" is not so much scary as really, really annoying.

We also have to swallow an extremely pat resolution to the undercooked domestic violence storyline, as teenage Tommy – on a roll after a slightly excruciating speech to his father about the evils of fascism – colludes with his mum to chuck their tormentor out on his ear. But as Eddie shuffles off down the street with his suitcase, the Doctor and Rose convince Tommy to walk with him, because "he's still your dad". This idea that blood ties can somehow wash clean a lifetime of abuse is problematic, at best, and perhaps proof that, even in its current iteration, *Doctor Who* still struggles at times with the biggest storytelling challenge of them all: real life.

Ood, where's my TARDIS?

In late May, there was the merest rumble of a backlash when *The Independent* suggested fans were in danger of suffering from *Doctor Who* overload. "This month, the tally of new material includes four episodes of the new Saturday night series on BBC One, four instalments each of spin-offs *Doctor Who Confidential* and *Totally Doctor Who*, one issue of *Doctor Who Magazine*, two issues of the *Doctor Who Adventures* comic, two audio-only dramas on CD, three hardback novels, one paperback novella, seven mass market non-fiction books and one academic study by the Professor of Film at Leicester University. So to participate completely in the cultural practice of *Doctor Who*, you would have to devote every waking hour to it." ("Yes," said the fans. "And your point is?" Actually, you'd be surprised how easy it is to fit all that stuff in if you just cut out unnecessary functions like eating, sleeping and going to the toilet.)

After lamenting that the series was "no longer essential Saturday night viewing" and claiming "Christopher Eccleston's tenure already feels like the halcyon days", *The Impossible Planet* was enough to bring *The Guardian* back on side. "Oh but this is fantastic," gushed its preview. "It's *Alien* plus *The Matrix* divided by *The Exorcist*... thank God for *Doctor Who*." The paper also remarked on the fact that *The Satan Pit* would be broadcast on the closest Saturday to 06:06:06 – making it just four days away from being an interesting news item.

Matt Jones' two-parter is New *Who's* farthest-flung adventure so far and, true to Russell T Davies' anti-Zog manifesto, foregrounds a group of human pioneers struggling for survival in an inhospitable landscape.

The planetary conundrum in question is a barren lump of rock suspended in perpetual geostationary orbit around a black hole. While everything around it – light, gravity, time – is pulled into the dead star's singularity, this planet just keeps on circling around it like an unflushable turd (though they put it more poetically in the actual script). The crew of Sanctuary Base Six are drilling down into the planet's core to try and discover its secret – but it seems the planet's secret has discovered them first.

The keyword at the tone meeting for this story was "tough". Forget *Star Trek*-style recreation decks and tastefully upholstered lounges – Sanctuary Base Six looks more like an oil rig. It's cramped, sweaty, claustrophobic and permanently on the edge of extinction, while the bulky, grime-streaked industrial machinery is straight out of a futuristic JCB catalogue.

Filling the Zogs of Zog role are the Ood: unctuous, dome-headed aliens who look like they've been caught with their faces in the all-you-can-eat noodle bar. (Early drafts featured the Slitheen – or some of their close relatives, anyway – until Davies decided they were getting in the way of the story. He came up with the name "Ood" as a deliberate antonym to "Raxacoricofallapatorian".)

The Ood are born to serve – it makes them happy, according to the human crew – and

carry translator globes like lavatory ballcocks, which they use to talk in disquietingly polite, slightly quizzical voices. This proves particularly unsettling when they begin falling under the spell of whatever lies beneath the planet's surface, and start coming out with lines like "The Beast and his Armies shall rise from the Pit to make war against God" while dishing up Rose's dinner. (Though, to be fair, she's British, so is used to service like that.)

And it's not just the Ood who are acting strangely. Toby, the mission's archaeologist, starts hearing whispering voices in his room ("I can see you, don't turn around") – which would be pretty damn spooky even if said voice *didn't* belong to Gabriel Woolf, aka Sutekh the Destroyer from classic mid-70s frightener *Pyramids of Mars*, back in action and delivering another of the series' all-time great scares. Then, as Toby returns to his work, the hieroglyphics on the pot he has been examining vanish – and reappear all over his hands and face. It's a brilliantly spooky scene – as terrifying as *Doctor Who* gets.

Later, young maintenance technician Scooti (a pre-*Twilight* MyAnna Buring) goes looking for Toby, and finds him standing on the planet's airless surface, as the base's computer intones: "He is awake. He bathes in the black sun." The next time we see poor Scooti, her dead body is drifting, Ophelia-like, through space and into the black hole – an image at once horrific and hauntingly beautiful.

When the TARDIS disappears in an earthquake, the Doctor is forced to contemplate a more sedentary life. "I'd have to settle down," he says. "Get a house or something. A proper house – with doors and things. Carpets. Me, living in a house. Now that that is terrifying." "You'd have to get a mortgage," teases Rose, before chancing her arm: "I'd have to get one, too. I don't know... could be the same one. We could both... I don't know, share. Or not, you know. Whatever."

But the Doctor passes up this opportunity for domestic bliss – or at least an ITV sitcom – and decides to go looking for the TARDIS instead, descending ten miles below the surface in a capsule, from which he and science officer Ida Scott (the fabulous Claire Rushbrook) disembark into the new series' first actual, proper quarry. Quarries ain't what they used to be, though – this one's been enhanced with CGI to create a stunning, truly epic *Valley of the Gods*-style lost civilisation. It's a sequence worthy of Hollywood except, because this is *Doctor Who* (and therefore way more interesting than Hollywood), instead of some beefcake action hero spewing macho bullshit, we get David Tennant nattering away making jokes about the *EastEnders* Christmas special. It's the brilliance of *Doctor Who* in a nutshell.

The second act works hard to deliver on the promise of the first, not least the realisation of the titular Beast itself – a classic, fire-and-brimstone Baphomet, complete with ram's horns, rendered the size of a tower block by the CGI smarts at The Mill.

This may be the money shot, but it's not the highlight of the episode by any means. That honour must go to the quietly astonishing scene in which the Doctor ponders matters of fact versus faith while descending, alone, into the pit. He muses on whether the creature below is the one that gave rise to representations of the Horned Beast across the universe. "Maybe that's what the devil is, in the end," he says. "An idea." By now, the cable has run out, and the Doctor has only two choices: go back, or take a leap of faith. He starts unhooking the carabiners. "If you talk to Rose," he tells Ida, "just tell her... Tell her... Oh, she knows." And then he falls, silently, into the inky blackness.

It's one goose-fleshing moment among many in an exceptional 90 minutes of television, brilliantly directed by James Strong and beautifully scored by Murray Gold (whose mournful cello at times appears to be quoting Josh Whedon's highly regarded *Firefly*, another sci-fi series with a strong frontier mentality). Throw in a well-drawn, brilliantly acted cast of supporting characters, outstanding production design and the ultimate monster of the week, and this is as close to heaven as hell is ever likely to get.

"When you said you'd been in several Blockbusters..."

With a final figure of barely over six million, *The Satan Pit* was new *Doctor Who*'s lowest-rating episode to date, though the share remained strong. The BBC blamed the impact of summer, leading many to question why something this scary was being shown in the blazing sunshine in the first place – a bit like arranging a screening of *Driller Killer* for the local Saturday morning kids' cinema club.

In America, the first series finished its run on Sci-Fi, having averaged between one and 1.5 million viewers a week. No-one seemed to be able to decide whether this represented a triumph or a disaster but, a couple of months later, the channel would announce it had picked up its option on Series Two.

There was a less healthy outlook for Stephen Fry's much-delayed *Who* debut, however, as the actor/writer/presenter/smartypants announced his commitment to the ITV drama *Kingdom* meant he couldn't find "three minutes to string together" to perform rewrites in time for Series Three, so had reluctantly withdrawn from the project.

And Fry wasn't the only one who wouldn't be a part of the 2007 series. On June 15th, the BBC issued a statement confirming long-running rumours that Billie Piper would be leaving *Doctor Who* at the end of the current run.

"Rose and I have gone on the most incredible journey with Russell T Davies and the cast and crew of *Doctor Who* over the past two years," said Piper – who only weeks earlier had cheekily told GMTV she would be in "every episode" of Series Three, the minx. "It has been an amazing adventure, and I am truly indebted to Russell for giving me the chance to play Rose Tyler, and to all the *Doctor Who* fans old and new who have been so supportive of me in this amazing role. Thank you so much."

Davies said the team had a whole year to plan Rose's final scenes, and promised "a stunning exit".

The following day, *The Sun* was quick off the mark with the name of Piper's reported successor: "Former *Crossroads* stunner Freema Agyeman was last night revealed to be the frontrunner to replace Billie Piper," claimed the paper. "Freema, 26, will appear in the final two episodes of the BBC1 sci-fi's current series playing the character Adeloa... Insiders say Freema will join the Doctor in the TARDIS full-time in the third series."

Three weeks later, the BBC confirmed the former *Crossroads* stunner... sorry, confirmed the actress' appointment as the Doctor's latest sidekick, medical student Martha Jones. Agyeman had appeared in all the usual Brit drama suspects, including *Casualty* and *The Bill*, but was best known for her role as saucy skivvy Lola Wise in Channel 5's short-lived revival of a certain low-rent Midlands soap (in so much as anyone could be "best known" for *anything* on Channel 5). At the time of her casting as Martha, she was working in her local Blockbuster video shop in order to make ends meet – so, if nothing else, could at least convincingly deliver the line "Doctor, that's due back by 12pm on Thursday".

Having impressed the show's execs with her stint as Adeloa, Agyeman had been invited to audition for a role in *Torchwood*. When she arrived, she was told the *Torchwood* scripts weren't ready and she'd have to read something from *Doctor Who* – and it was only when she was recalled for a second audition it was revealed they'd actually been auditioning her for *Who* all along.

Arriving in Cardiff the night before she was due to read a scene with David Tennant, the actress found a note pushed under her door from the man himself. It said: "Sorry for all the cloak and dagger stuff, it's going to be fine – relax and have a good time." (For the benefit of younger readers, a "note" was a primitive form of communication popular in the pre-Facebook era.)

"When I first saw Freema Agyeman, she had come in to audition for the part of Adeola in Series Two," said Russell T Davies. "Watching her during filming confirmed what an exciting new talent she was, so under cover of darkness we called her back in to audition with David for the role of the new companion. It was an immediate and sensational combination."

"I've been keeping this secret from my friends for months," said Agyeman. "It's been driving me mad. It still hasn't quite sunk in, I'm sure it will slam home first day on set when I'm stood gazing at David Tennant."

Explaining her decision to leave, Piper told *Radio Times*: "The longer I stayed, the more scared I'd be of leaving because it's so comfortable and nice. I'm utterly grateful for the whole experience, but you have to take care of yourself and do what you feel is right. We filmed in Wales for nine months and I didn't like being away from home. I enjoy being domesticated, washing up and cooking dinner for my boyfriend." Which was surely the only time anyone had resigned from a high-profile job to spend more time with the washing-up.

On BBC One, Abzorbaloff creator William Grantham finally got the chance to see his creation realised on screen. His reaction? "It was supposed to be the size of a double-decker bus." At which point everyone laughed, while making a mental note to never, *ever* run another *Blue Peter* competition.

Love & Monsters finds Russell T Davies revisiting *The Christmas Invasion*'s theme of life without the Doctor. Except here David Tennant's not laid up in bed – he's off filming a different story, leaving Marc Warren to handle leading-man duties in a bottle episode that says more about our hero than many of the ones he stars in.

Warren plays Elton Pope – an endearingly sweet dreamer who forms a club of like-minded souls dedicated to tracking down the Doctor. Each member of LINDA – London Investigation 'N' Detective Agency – has their own, generally quite sad reason for searching for the mysterious man in the blue box (though Elton doesn't realise it yet, the Doctor was there the day his mum died).

Davies plays with viewers' expectations right from the get-go; the story opens with Elton tracking down the Doctor and Rose in the middle of an alien takedown – which director Dan Zeff shoots as a slapstick pantomime chase, complete with buckets of gloop. When the monster turns to the screen and goes "raar", there's a jump-cut to Elton, recording his video diary, saying "that's what it did – it went 'raar'." It's a nice postmodern wink, especially as we have to wait most of the episode to find out what happened next, the script revelling in its *Pulp Fiction*-style cut and paste chronology. It's so choppy, in fact, we get to witness the events of *Rose*, *Aliens of London* and *The Christmas Invasion* from Elton's perspective – a simple but effective idea for which they went to the effort of filming new sequences, putting Elton in the thick of the action (the Auton invasion is actually better than the one in *Rose*).

By now, LINDA has become less about searching for the Doctor and more of a social club: buns are baked, romances blossom and they even form a band in which Elton can indulge his love of the Electric Light Orchestra (whose symphonic rock classic "Mr Blue Sky" is a recurring musical signature throughout the episode).

In case you hadn't gathered by now, the story – which started out as an idea for a *Doctor Who Magazine* comic strip loosely inspired by Woody Allen's *Zelig* – is Russell T Davies' love letter to *Doctor Who* fandom, and a rather lovely one at that (the script described Elton as "a nice, ordinary bloke – not a twat, no funny voice or daft clothes"). From a vaguely comical premise, Davies weaves a touching tale of friendship, loss, loneliness, growing up and the need to belong. But poison is dripped into this wellspring of goodwill by the arrival of the mysterious Victor Kennedy (Peter Kay in a white beard and pimp hat), who admonishes LINDA for losing purpose and sets about whipping them into a more professional Time Lord-hunting outfit. He is, of course, in no-way based on any *Doctor Who* fans who enjoyed throwing their weight around and trying to spoil the fun for everyone, which they definitely didn't do in the mid to late 80s.

On Kennedy's advice, Elton manages to worm his way into Jackie Tyler's affections, offering us a revealing glimpse of life for those left behind when the Doctor comes calling for a new friend. Camille Coduri is fantastic here, all sex and sass on the surface, then slowly revealing the vulnerable, lonely widow underneath – the moment when she realises Elton has been using her is heartbreaking.

And then Peter Kay turns into the Abzorbaloff and it all goes horribly, horribly wrong. A monster that absorbs its victims into its own bloated body was always going to be a risky venture. But, as if having a load of faces staring out of your backside – some of them wearing specs, for Christ's sake – wasn't silly enough, someone also decided to give him a teeny-tiny loincloth and a comedy northern accent (Peter Kay's accent, in fact). Then Dan Zeff – whose direction up to now has been so assured – has a rush of blood to the head and films this monstrosity running through the streets in unforgiving daylight, while speeding up the film for maximum Benny Hill-style comic effect. Once the creature has met a

barely more dignified end, sinking into the pavement in a pool of gunge, all that's left is a paving slab with Elton's girlfriend's face sticking out of it. "It's a relationship, of sorts," says Elton, indicating this living souvenir. "We've even got a bit of a love life." In the years since this was broadcast, quite a few *Doctor Who* fans have tied themselves in knots to try and pass this off as anything but a blow-job gag. But they're on a hiding to nothing, because that's clearly what it is: a joke, in *Doctor Who*, about a bloke being noshed off by a paving stone. Thanks God Mary Whitehouse didn't live to see the day.

It's a shame the story should have taken such a handbrake turn for the worse in the last ten minutes because, up until that point, *Love & Monsters* was a contender for one of the most clever, funny, moving and original *Doctor Who* stories ever told. As it stands, it's still an underrated gem, anchored by a lovely performance from Marc Warren as a man who's had his share of suffering, but never loses hope or heart. "When you're a kid, they tell you it's all, 'Grow up, get a job, get married, get a house, have a kid' and that's it," says Elton. "But the truth is, the world is so much stranger than that. It's so much darker, and so much madder. And so much better."

"I don't want being trapped in parallel dimensions to come between us"

Seven days later, the Doctor and Rose returned to headline action in *Fear Her*, the episode designed to be Series Two's cheapie. Or as cheap as you can make a story that requires an entire Olympic stadium full of spectators to vanish in the blink of an eye.

Taking inspiration from Catherine Storr's children's fantasy novel *Marianne Dreams* (filmed as *Paperhouse*), it tells the story of Chloe Webber, a 12-year-old girl possessed by a lonely alien that gifts her the power to bring drawings to life, and convert people to drawings.

On – ahem – paper, it's a classic *Doctor Who* scenario. Unfortunately, writer Matthew Graham and director Euros Lyn seem to go out of their way to deliberately neutralise any scares. Instead of being set in a secret world of shadows and night terrors, the whole thing unfolds in broad daylight, while in place of the spooky, isolated house of *Marianne's Dreams*, we get an ordinary London cul-de-sac (Dame Kelly Holmes Close, no less). Sure, mixing the domestic with the fantastic is a central part of the show's M.O., but when the whole episode feels like a *Brookside* dream sequence, you've probably gone too far. (Russell T Davies originally envisaged a faintly menacing, Tim Burton-style take on suburbia, but that obviously got lost somewhere in the mix.)

For all that, a good two-thirds of *Fear Her* isn't nearly as bad as its reputation as the runt of New *Who* litter would suggest; unlike, say, *New Earth*, it's not so much actively irritating as just a bit of a missed opportunity. The episode still manages to deliver a few decent scares (like the drawings that change position between shots – creepy *and* cheap!), there are some good visual gags (love Rose being attacked by a 3D scribble, which the Doctor simply rubs out in the air) and the Isolus, an empathic alien child who looks like a tiny, delicate flower and whose only wish is to get back to its family, makes for a highly original "monster".

Unfortunately, any goodwill the story banks in the first half-hour is largely squandered by the dismal third act, in which *Doctor Who* makes an early bid for Olympic glory – and falls at the first hurdle. For a start, 80,000 spectators and 13,000 athletes wink out of existence during the Opening Ceremony, and the only response the budget will stretch to is twinkly Welsh news anchor Huw Edwards valiantly attempting to sound shocked. ("They're gone, all those people – it's a terrible, *terrible* turn of events," he laments, unconvincingly.)

But not to worry: Huw soon forgets all about said terrible, terrible turn of events in order to concentrate on the torch relay, which actually looks more like a badly under-subscribed provincial half-marathon. When the torch-bearer stumbles over a plot hole in the road, the Doctor takes up the baton and manages to trot unchallenged all the way into the Olympic Stadium and light the flame (that's G4S for you, I guess). "I suppose it's much more than a torch now," blithers Huw. "It's a beacon. It's a beacon of hope and fortitude and

courage. And it's a beacon of love!" (Utterly risible, yes – though, to be fair, this is exactly how people *did* talk throughout the whole of London 2012.)

Meanwhile, a life-size drawing of Chloe Webber's late father has come to life in her wardrobe. "Chloe, I'm coming to hurt you!" he bellows in a voice barely more convincing than the Abzorbaloff. Seriously, did no-one at BBC Wales think this might be in any way inappropriate, just slightly – tackling the issue of child abuse through the medium of a cartoon monster, while Huw Edwards talks absolute tosh on the telly?

The final scene finds the Doctor and Rose enjoying the fireworks, as the script indulges in some sledgehammer-subtle foreshadowing. "We'll always be okay, you and me," says Rose, apropos of nothing. "Don't you reckon, Doctor?" "There's something in the air," he replies. "Something coming. A storm's approaching."

Ooooh, it's like he's got second sight. Either that, or he's already fast-forwarded to the Next Time trailer.

Everyone who tuned into watch *Army of Ghosts* knew that, by the end of this two-parter, we would have said goodbye to Rose Tyler. Fittingly, the story opens with the same establishing shot as *Rose*, followed by a montage of clips (including this season's only glimpse of Christopher Eccleston – remember him, kids?) as our heroine recounts the story of how she met a man who "took me away from home in his magical box". "I thought it would never end," says Rose. "But then came the army of ghosts. Then came Torchwood and the war. And that's when it all ended. This is the story of how I died."

With a pre-titles teaser like *that*, this season finale has an awful lot to live up to. And, by and large, it doesn't disappoint. Arriving back on the Powell Estate (this is the third story in a row set in contemporary London – the Zogs must have been seriously pissed off by now), the Doctor and Rose discover the Earth has been invaded by "ghosts", who everyone – Jackie included – seems eager to believe are their loved ones returned from the dead.

Rather make these apparitions scary, or even vaguely unsettling, Russell T Davies chooses to have fun with them – by, for example, having the Doctor channel-hop between the likes of Trisha Goddard, Derek Acorah and the bloke from *Cash in the Attic* presenting ghost-themed versions of their daytime TV shows. Even Babs Windsor gets in on the act, rolling out the old "we don't serve spirits" gag from behind the bar of the Queen Vic, while the Doctor is jaunty to the point of annoying, singing the theme to *Ghostbusters* – apparently in the style of Scooby-Doo – and trying out a new catchphrase, "Allons-y!" (which, sadly, appears to stick).

Things get more interesting when the action moves to the Torchwood Institute, where Yvonne Hartman (played with arch relish by another former Queen Vic pint-puller, Tracy-Ann Oberman) and her team have stockpiled several warehouses full of salvaged alien tech. (Oddly, we're supposed to believe that Torchwood is such a secret back ops outfit even the Doctor's never heard of it, despite the fact all sorts of random Joe Shmoes have been namedropping it all season. Heck, Huw Edwards even mentioned it on *telly*.)

The prize in the Institute's collection is a giant golden sphere that, according to all known instruments, doesn't really exist. It's a vessel designed to travel through the Void – the "space between dimensions" containing absolutely nothing. "Imagine that," says the Doctor. "No light, no dark, no up, no down, no life, no time." Sounds a lot like Swindon, actually.

The sphere's arrival has splintered the whole of reality, and now creatures are bleeding through the fault lines – "walking," explains the Doctor, "from their world and into yours, with the human race wishing and hoping and helping them along".

Actually, not so much walking as stomping – as the "ghosts" turn out to be millions upon millions of Cybermen. And they haven't come alone: "The sphere broke down the barriers between worlds," explain the Cybes. "We only followed. It's origin is unknown." "Then what's inside it?" wonders the Doctor. Cut to the sphere room, where Rose watches as four Daleks emerge from the unfolding globe in a halo of golden light, promising to rain molten death down on humanity. It may just very well be *Doctor Who's* greatest cliffhanger yet. (Or, at least, it *would* have been if they hadn't included

shots of a Dalek deathray in advance publicity clips. For *Doctor Who* fans, that's as big a giveaway as calling the episode *The One Where the Daleks Turn Up at the End*.)

The first half of *Doomsday* is basically one giant fangasm in which Russell T Davies finally grants every *Who* geek's wish – first requested by the BBC as far back as 1967 – for some hot Dalek-on-Cyberman action. In practice, this turns out to be a slight case of being careful what you wish for, as Nick Briggs gamely arguing with himself in two halting voices quickly starts to wear thin, despite Davies' best efforts to turn the confrontation into a comic bitchfest. ("This isn't war," scoffs a Dalek, "this is pest control!")

For the first time on screen, the pepperpots have individual names. Thay, Sec, Jast and Caan may sound like the Dalek version of One Direction, but they're actually The Cult of Skaro: a sort of genocidal working party tasked with thinking outside their shells to come up with new and deadlier ways to be horrible to everyone. They are in possession of something called the Genesis Ark, which turns out to be a Time Lord prison that eventually unleashes millions of Daleks into the skies over London. (Could have been worse, I suppose – with a name like that, it could have unleashed millions of Phil Collinses into the skies over London.)

Graeme Harper directs the action with his usual verve but, in an echo of last year's finale, even the Dalek-Cyber mash-up ends up playing second fiddle to the emotional drama at the heart of the story. We get a taste of what's to come when Pete Tyler arrives from his own universe and comes face to face with his late wife. Davies is clever enough to bring the story to a dead stop just long enough to let the scene play out in all its glory, mixing pathos (Jackie: "Look at me, I never left that flat. Did nothing with myself." Pete: "You brought her up. Rose Tyler. That's not bad.") with humour. (Pete: "All those daft little plans of mine, they worked. Made me rich." Jackie: "I don't care about that... How rich?")

But that's just Davies limbering up for the main event, as the Doctor is forced to say goodbye to his best friend – and quite possibly the only woman he's ever truly loved.

Cheekily, Rose doesn't actually die – though

she does vanish from our world. Anyone who's read Philip Pullman's *His Dark Materials* trilogy will recognise where Davies got his idea of trapping the Doctor and Rose in parallel dimensions, but it's no less powerful for that. As Rose literally loses her grip on our reality, the Doctor is forced to watch as she is sucked into the breach between worlds, seconds before he must close it for good.

With Murray Gold adding pulsing strings to his haunting "Doctor's Theme" – a recurring musical motif whispered down the back of the neck by soprano Melanie Pappenheim – the Time Lord and the girl who stole his hearts place their heads and hands on opposite sides of Torchwood's bare white walls, as if trying to physically reach out to each other through time and space. And then, utterly defeated, the Doctor turns, and walks away.

Some time later, in the Tylers' palatial alt. world home, Rose hears a voice calling to her in a dream, and follows it across hundreds of miles until she arrives at a Norwegian beach called Dårlig Ulv Stranden: Bad Wolf Bay. There she sees a hologram of the Doctor, projecting his image across the space between realities before the last rip in the fabric closes for good. "It takes a lot of power to send this projection," he tells her. "I'm burning up a sun, just to say goodbye." (Which is surely the chorus to the best Muse song never written.)

They can't touch and, when his image fades, they will never see each other again. And then Rose (an astonishing portrayal of raw, howling, snot-and-mascara-streaked grief from Billie Piper) finally finds the courage to say the three little – and yet enormous – words she's been carrying in her heart all this time: "I love you."

"Quite right, too," says the Doctor through his own tears. "And I suppose, if it's one last chance to say it: Rose Tyler..."

And then he vanishes. Forever. Probably.

Hooray for Pontypridd

The press were plunged into mourning. "I don't think I've seen anything so affecting outside the movies of Joan Crawford or Ingrid Bergman," said the *Daily Mail*, while *The Times* lauded Piper's performance as "glorious". The finale also clocked up in excess of a million more viewers than *The Parting of the Ways*, which was enough to silence the circling vultures who'd been quick to suggest the show was losing its shiny appeal.

And the producers chalked up another small victory by managing to keep the sudden appearance of Catherine Tate in the TARDIS in *Doomsday*'s dying moments a secret from everyone. The pages featuring the comedian, who had been cast as David Tennant's co-star in the forthcoming Christmas special, weren't included in the script, and Tate had been signed into the studio under her real name, Catherine Ford, to record her scene during the series wrap party. (Listen very carefully and you might just hear 50 very drunk people singing "Hi-Ho Silver Lining" on the other side of the TARDIS wall.)

Originally envisaged for Series Two, but now promoted to Christmas special, *The Runaway Bride* entered production at the end of June – providing its guest star with a crash course in all things *Who*. (Tate confessed she knew so little about the show, she didn't realise there other aliens as well as the Daleks. What, not even the Cybermen? The Sontarans? Surely she'd heard of the Shrivenzale?!)

There were also press rumours that Sylvester McCoy would be making an appearance in the special. Yeah, right – there was about as much chance of that as there was of him appearing in a massive Hollywood blockbuster in about, ooh, six years' time.

On the streets of Cardiff, David Tennant and Catherine Tate did their best to get into the Christmas spirit despite sweltering 30C temperatures. For one scene that required cash to spew out of an ATM, the props team had provided fake bank notes featuring the faces of Tennant and Phil Collinson. Some of these later sold on eBay for £50, and are now thought to have a face value worth more than the combined currencies of Greece and Cyprus.

As digital radio station BBC7 began broadcasting the first series of Big Finish's Eighth Doctor audios, and fans wrestled with the implications of this for all manner of complex canonicity issues, the Welsh arm of the *Doctor Who* empire took up residence at their new, purpose-built studios near Cardiff. Described by BBC News as "more Pontypridd than Pinewood", the Upper Boat complex – which would be home to *Doctor Who* and *Torchwood*, along with other BBC Wales productions – was officially opened by David Tennant, who eschewed the usual outsize comedy scissors in favour of his trusty sonic screwdriver. One major advantage of the 86,000 sq ft facility was to allow the TARDIS to stay standing between production runs, as flat-packing an infinitely large time and space ship was proving annoyingly time-consuming (especially as someone had thrown away the box).

According to *The Sun*, *Footballers' Wives* star Zoe Lucker had signed up to appear as the Rani in the forthcoming series. The story was widely syndicated, but turned out to have been made up by a fan in order to put one over on the tabloids – as opposed to the usual practice of being made up by the tabloids in order to put one over on the readers.

Filming on Series Three began in early August, with Freema Agyeman recording scenes for Martha's debut story, *Smith and Jones*, at Upper Boat. "The whole focus of the episode is Martha's mad first day with the Doctor – throw everything at her and see how she survives" explained Russell T Davies.[16]

The following day, the new-look TARDIS team posed for photographs in costume, David Tennant razor sharp in a new blue suit, accessorised with a smart new assistant. Tennant and Agyeman would be seeing an awful lot of each other in the coming months – as well as being work colleagues, they were also neighbours in the Cardiff Bay apartment block that was gradually turning into Doctor Who Towers, with Russell T Davies and John Barrowman also billeted there. "Even though I don't knock on their door and go in every five minutes," Agyeman told *SFX*, "it's comforting to know they're there, should I suddenly get locked out and need a floor to sleep on".[17] Or, indeed, need saving from ravenous alien slug monsters.

In a BBC press release, Russell T Davies teased viewers with hints about the upcoming series: "The Doctor and Martha are destined to meet William Shakespeare, blood-sucking alien Plasmavores, the Judoon – a clan of galactic storm troopers – and a sinister intelligence at work in 1930s New York." The release also detailed some of the writers and directors who would be working on the series: newcomers included Stephen Greenhorn, creator of BBC Scotland soap opera *River City*, and Chris Chibnall. A lifelong *Who* devotee, Chibnall was last seen as a freckle-faced teenager giving Pip and Jane Baker what for on live TV, all the way back in Volume I. Since then, he'd written several plays and television screenplays, co-created the BBC's soothing Sunday night sedative *Born and Bred*, and was currently the co-producer and lead writer on *Torchwood*. Graeme Harper and Euros Lyn were also confirmed as returning, as was John Barrowman's Captain Jack Harkness.

As the *Sunday People* reported that David Tennant was the subject of a multi-million pound bidding war between the BBC, ITV and Hollywood, his latest co-star gave her first live television interview on BBC One's new early evening magazine programme *The One Show*. Stumbling through a painful exchange with Adrian Chiles and Nadia Sawahla beset by delays on the satellite link-up (well, she was in deepest darkest Wales, after all), the result was a bit like that *Two Ronnies* sketch where Ronnie Corbett is always one answer behind the questioner. ("How would you describe David Tennant?" "Probably the most hideous monster the series has ever seen", etc.)

At the end of the month, the *Who* crew left Wales and relocated to the Midlands to film scenes for the Shakespeare episode in Warwick and Coventry (appropriate, as Coventry's civic slogan, "The City in Shakespeare Country," is a slightly more elegant way of saying "It's Quite Near Stratford"). The local paper's headline declared "Dr Who Sent to Coventry". They must use that gag a lot in Coventry.

Production then moved to the reconstructed Globe theatre on London's South Bank, where recording had to take place during the night, as the theatre's owners considered a film crew making an episode of *Doctor Who* in the middle of a performance of *As You Like It* would be distracting for the audience.

Torchwood: "Do you come here often?" "I don't know, where am I?"

At the TV Quick Awards in September, *Doctor Who* scooped the Best Drama gong, while David Tennant and Billie Piper were named Best Actor and Best Actress. "It was very hard to step into something that had been such a success already," said Tennant. "It was very daunting and, because of that, this award means a lot." The actor was also named Coolest Man in the Country in a survey by a pizza company – a special edition David Ten-inch was surely not far behind.

Also that month, the BBC confirmed what had already been widely reported in the press: *Doctor Who* was to get a second spin-off in the form of *The Sarah Jane Adventures*. Set in present-day West London, the series – set to launch with a 60-minute special in early 2007, to be followed by a full series later in the year – would star Elisabeth Sladen alongside teenage actress Yasmin Paige as Sarah Jane's 13-year-old neighbour Maria. "Children's TV has a fine history of fantasy thrillers – I loved them as a kid, and they were the very first things I ever wrote," said creator Russell T Davies. "So it's brilliant to return to such a vivid and imaginative area of television."

"As soon as we started filming [*School Reunion*], we realised that Lis was far more than a good guest star: here was a major lead actor," Davies expanded in an interview with *Doctor Who Magazine*. "We'd already been talking to the BBC about producing a drama for them. They wanted *Young Doctor Who*, which I absolutely refused, because I thought it would damage the character – and high jinks on Gallifrey made me wince a bit. But with a slot, and the budget, and the goodwill sitting there, Sarah Jane just seemed irresistible."[18]

(Another break-out show, *Rose Tyler: Earth Defence*, got as far as being commissioned – though Billie Piper had yet to sign – before Davies decided it was "a spin-off too far". He did rather like the acronym, though.)

Elisabeth Sladen heard Davies' pitch over another slap-up dinner. In the cab on the way there, she and her agent decided it would probably be about a cameo in *Torchwood*. When they offered Sladen her own show instead, she was flabbergasted. "Slowly, it began to sink in," she said. "Over the next hour, I got the whole pitch. Nothing had been written, but Russell had all the details worked out. Sarah Jane would continue the Doctor's work of protecting Earth from alien attacks. She'd have a sonic lipstick to match his screw-

driver. And yes, K-9 would be involved. The difference this time is he wouldn't be the headline act, due to contractual issues with his creator, Bob Baker. *Oh, what a shame.*"[10]

As newsagents made room for a third Doctor Who title, trading card game-cum-comic *Battles in Time* and more original tenth Doctor novels were announced, the show's renewed momentum showed no sign of slowing down. So fans were in no mood for a pipsqueak upstart trying to steal its thunder when the 2007 edition of *The Guinness Book of Records* dared to name turgid US movie spin-off *Stargate SG-1* as the world's "longest-running sci-fi TV show" – despite the fact it had clocked up a mere 203 episodes since 1997 (a milestone, FYI, reached by *Doctor Who* with episode three of *Fury from the Deep*, all the way back in 1968). When the controversy made the papers, Guinness backed down and conceded that, while *Stargate* was the longest-running sci-fi series to have been in *continuous* production, *Doctor Who* was indeed a longer-running series, on the basis that it had been running longer. Honestly – it would never have happened in Norris McWhirter's day.

David Tennant was the subject of BBC One's celebrity genealogy show *Who Do You Think You Are?* in late September, where he was disappointed to discover he wasn't descended from nine badly-dressed men from the constellation of Kasterborous, while, in October, recording on the new series moved to Wells Cathedral in Somerset, doubling for London's Southwark Cathedral after St Paul's withdrew permission to film there at the last minute. The cathedral was set to feature in the climactic moments of Stephen Greenhorn's *The Lazarus Experiment*, in which Mark Gatiss would finally take his on-screen bow as the eponymous Professor Lazarus.

"At the back of my mind, for all these years, I've been thinking, 'Will this ever happen? Will I ever be in *Doctor Who*? And now it has," said Gatiss. "It's a funny thing to say, but I feel very much at peace with myself, 'cos finally I've done it. I feel very, *very* contented."[19] ("We're very pleased for you, Mark," said his fellow fans. "Thanks," he said. "What's that funny grinding noise I can hear?")

A week later, *Doctor Who* recorded its first-ever scenes in the US when director James

Strong, Phil Collinson, visual effects designer Dave Houghton and a cameraman flew to New York to film plate shots (including views from the top of the Empire State Building captured at 5am) for upcoming two-parter *Daleks in Manhattan*. The closest the rest of the cast and crew would get to the Big Apple was a municipal park in Cardiff (so good they named it, er, once).

The Welsh capital also took centre stage in *Torchwood*, which arrived on BBC Three in a blaze of publicity in late October. As spin-offs go, this one's a wee bit confusing, as it's something of an advantage *not* to have seen the show it's spun-off from. In *Doctor Who*, Torchwood was charged – by Royal Appointment, no less – with fending off alien invaders and scavenging their technology for the good of the British Empire, with the Doctor heading up its Most Wanted list. But forget all that, because *this* splinter group of Torchwood just isn't into all that Queen and Country scene; this one's basically a Welsh version of UNIT, with John Barrowman in the Nick Courtney role, operating from a secret lair (the Hub) beneath the Millennium Centre in ET-infested Cardiff. Except the Brigadier didn't have a pet pterodactyl flying about the office. Or shag everything that moves. As far as we know, anyway.

In addition, as a post-watershed series, expecting a substantial amount of viewers to arrive at *Torchwood* via the family-friendly *Doctor Who* was likely to result in scenes of confusion, anger, frustration and a potentially eye-popping loss of sexual innocence. Which shouldn't, in itself, be used as a weapon to beat *Torchwood* around the head with – it is its own animal, with its own set of priorities – but isn't exactly a textbook example of 360 degree branding.

In opener *Everything Changes*, we follow plucky WPC Gwen Cooper (Eve Miles) as she stumbles across the Torchwood team – Captain Jack Flash, his second-in-command Suzie Costello (Indira Varma), snarky medic Owen Harper (Burn Gorman), mousy computer genius Toshiko "Tosh" Sato (reprising her role from *Doctor Who's Aliens of London*, in which she played a, erm, medical doctor – told you it was confusing) and office manager/tea boy/dogsbody Ianto Jones (Gareth David-Lloyd) –

interrogating a murder victim they've just brought back to life with a magic glove (don't ask).

Infiltrating Torchwood, Gwen discovers that Captain Jack is immortal, Cardiff is sitting on a Rift in the space-time continuum, there are ferocious creatures called Weevils living in the sewers, and Suzie is a no-good filthy murderer. When Suzie dies, Jack invites Gwen to join his band of dysfunctional foo-fighters, which she does, without even asking about pay, holidays, private health insurance or where the hell she's supposed to park in Cardiff Bay.

Written with Russell Davies' trademark wit and brio ("*CSI: Cardiff*, I'd like to see that," says Gwen's PC partner. "They'd be measuring the velocity of a kebab."), *Everything Changes* is quite unlike anything seen on British TV before. Think *The X Files* with the kinetic energy and pace of *Spooks*, only with more jokes – and much, much more Welsh.

With 2.4 million viewers, the episode delivered BBC Three its biggest-ever audience – and the biggest audience for a non-sport programme across any UK digital channel. A further 2.8 million also tuned in for the repeat on BBC2 on Wednesday.

Sadly, though it continued to deliver strong audiences, for many the feelgood factor surrounding *Torchwood* was short-lived. About 90 seconds short, in fact, as *Everything Changes* was bundled as part of a double-bill with the second episode: *Day One*, aka *The One with the Sex Gas*. It's a laughably unsubtle and shameless affair in which the team investigate a sex-addicted alien causing the population of Cardiff to get more amorous than Tiger Woods, Charlie Sheen and Michael Douglas on a stag weekend in Amsterdam.

Of course, the sex and swearing that proliferate throughout the series aren't, in themselves, a problem. People have been known to regularly enjoy both, I believe. And we should probably cut the Torchwood team's sweaty, grunty antics some slack given that they are relatively young people in a high-stress occupation, where sweaty, grunty antics do happen. Probably. It's easy, for example, to question Gwen's intelligence when she hooks up with Owen – but it's *meant* to be viewed as a poor decision on her part. Just as Russell Davies seeded some of *Buffy* into New *Who*, the template for *Torchwood* is clearly its spin-off *Angel*: both shows have soaring shots over a cityscape (Los Angeles in the former, Cardiff – yes, I can hear you snickering in the back – in the latter), a lead who's immortal and wears a swoopy coat, and characters who do their best but fall on their faces. It's a perfectly workable framework, in theory, but often comes apart in practice, not least because the sex is so cringingly, badly written. (Sample quote: "When was the last time you came so hard and so long you forgot where you are?")

Torchwood is also the most bisexual show on television, for both good and ill. Jack is typically described as "omnisexual" (code for saying that he'd probably shag an anaconda if it knowingly winked at him), but Tosh, Owen and Ianto fall into the realm of being bi (albeit with a repellent instance of date-rape in Owen's case), and even Gwen, who is pretty resolutely hetero, kisses a woman while influenced by the mesmirising alien sex-gas. Though often confusing and annoying in implementation (Ianto starts banging Jack a mere three episodes after the man shot his girlfriend dead – with *Torchwood*, some things are not so much forgiven as forgotten), this is still something to be celebrated: if there was really a "gay agenda", as some fans insisted during Russell T Davies' reign, then good luck to it. (We *might* point to the statistical implausibility of that percentage of people swinging both ways in one workplace, but they *are* spies, after a fashion, so who knows?)

While Series One is not without its charms, overall it's one of the most bipolar pieces of television ever made. Among the stronger stories, *Small Worlds* introduces us to Estelle (endearingly played by Eve Pearce), an old flame of Jack's – and I do mean *old*, since she's easily in her 70s, while John Barrowman is, well, John Barrowman. The episode also pits Torchwood against evil fairies so powerful, it's nigh-impossible to imagine Jack and company stopping them – the twist being that they don't; Jack wins by letting his opponents accept a willing young girl into their ranks, and otherwise leave in peace. *They Keep Killing Suzie* showcases Varma (*Rome, Luther, Game of Thrones*) as a resurrected Suzie Costello, and drives home the *Torchwood* principle that there's no life after death, a justification for

Suzie's increasingly fanatical efforts to avoid it. *Random Shoes*, about a young man trying to investigate his own death, is adorably sweet, and *Out of Time*, in which a twin-prop de Havilland and its crew arrive through the Rift from 1953, has a certain romantic sweep. *Captain Jack Harkness,* meanwhile, is probably the most celebrated Series One story, bending a number of social norms when Jack and Tosh are thrown back in time to World War II, and Jack strikes up a brief romance with the doomed American officer from whom he stole his name. Even this, though, is hobbled by a reliance on some eye-wateringly implausible coincidences where the plot ought to be.

Other episodes, meanwhile, are pure filler or achingly beyond redemption. *Combat* – written by Noel Clarke – is a clumsy and forgettable attempt to do *Fight Club* with aliens; *Countrycide* is *Deliverance* done very badly in the Brecon Beacons (it also exposes how Jack's crew are terrible at their jobs, as they're hamstrung when bog-standard humans *steal their van*); and God only knows what they were attempting with *Cyberwoman*, in which Ianto's half-converted girlfriend Lisa embarks on a killing spree while wearing what looks like a metal bikini. (Yes, really.) And character-positions are reversed so fast, and developments happen so quickly and nonsensically, in the series finale *End of Days* that you'll feel like you're being pelted with a tennis-ball launcher.

This scribbled-on-a-napkin approach to continuity is also evident in the fact that, depending on who's on script duty that week, Torchwood is either a top-secret black ops unit – albeit one with its name stencilled down the side of the company car – that even the police haven't heard of, or it's so well known around Cardiff that old ladies treat it with the same weary contempt as post office queues and fortnightly bin collections.

In the final analysis, it's hard to escape the impression of everything in this series of *Torchwood* being made up on the hoof; that the show is an anagram in search of an idea, hastily greenlit because the BBC were keen to make stuff in Wales and Russell T Davies already had enough letters for the name (he could busk the rest later). It tries hard, but it's a *Countdown* conundrum stretched over 13 long weeks.

The theme music's quite good, though.

All I want for Christmas is you (and a Cyberman voice-changer helmet)

Following the success of its Design a Monster competition, *Blue Peter* launched a new contest for a viewer to win a guest role in Series Three of *Doctor Who*. ("Let's not be greedy – surely one role is enough, Mr Gatiss," said the judges. "And you're clearly over 14.") Meanwhile, Konnie Huq showed *Torchwood* fans how to make Jack and Ianto's fuck-buddy stopwatch using a Fairy Liquid bottle and some *very* sticky-backed plastic. (Okay, not really.)

At the 2006 National Television Awards, *Doctor Who* once again walked away with the Most Popular Drama gong, Billie Piper retained her Most Popular Actress trophy, and David Tennant was named Most Popular Actor. "I think if my eight-year-old self could see me at the Royal Albert Hall winning a prize for playing the Doctor on telly, he would need a stiff shot of Irn-Bru," joked Tennant. (Note to non-UK readers: Irn-Bru is a carbonated drink consisting of *ammonium ferric citrate*, sugar and more E-numbers than a Walthamstowe postcode directory. It's what Scots drink when they need a healthy alternative to whisky.)

Over the coming weeks, the series and its cast would continue racking up the honours. Tennant won the award for Best TV Performance in *Heat* magazine and Best Actor at the TV Times Awards, where *Doctor Who* was also named Best TV Show; the Doctor and Rose's farewell from *Doomsday* was voted Moment of the Year by *Radio Times* readers, and the Doctor was named one of the icons of England's heritage in a nationwide poll. Even the *Doctor Who Annual* got in on the act, knocking perennial fave *The Beano* off the top of the children's bestseller lists by shifting an incredible 271,000 copies.

On November 19th, Cardiff's Millennium Centre played host to *Doctor Who: A Celebration*, a special fundraising concert for *Children in Need* featuring Murray Gold's music from the show performed by a live orchestra. Audience members – including Freema Agyeman, Camille Coduri, Noel Clarke, Julie Gardner, Phil Collinson, Steven Moffat and Anneke Wills – were terrorised by various creatures

from the series, while David Tennant did the presenting honours on stage. An online auction of props and costumes helped bring the total raised to £75,000, with fans forking out for the likes of Tennant's trainers and Billie Piper's blouse. ("Sold! To the man in the grubby anorak from the *Daily Star*.")

As BBC America began showing the Christopher Eccleston series, filming got under way in the Brecon Beacons on *Human Nature*, a two-part adaptation of Paul Cornell's seminal New Adventures novel from 1995. "I'm doing emo-*Who* again!" joked Cornell. "I actually started it a lot further away from the book version of the story, but Russell kept saying, 'Bring it back to the book!' I think this story is my *Sergeant Pepper*, frankly."[20] Presumably that's a reference to it being his magnum opus, as opposed to him being off his head on acid when he wrote it. The filming block saw Susie Liggat taking over production duties to allow Phil Collinson a holiday. ("But surely you had a holiday in 2003?" said the woman in HR, sniffily.)

Then, in early December, David Tennant received an accolade to put all his other shiny trophies in the shade when readers of *Doctor Who Magazine* voted him their favourite-ever Doctor. "This is a real honour and I'm totally gobsmacked!" he told the magazine, as he joined a prestigious roll-call of previous winners including Tom Baker, Tom Baker, Tom Baker and, for one night only in 1989, Sylvester McCoy.

The press launch for *The Runaway Bride* in mid-December opened the floodgates on a seasonal avalanche of publicity for the special, with Tennant playing Buttons in Virgin Radio's Christmas panto among the more memorable of the week's appearances (well it's always good to have something to fall back on if it all goes wrong.) In an interview with *The Sun*, meanwhile, Billie Piper admitted she was "still crying" about leaving *Doctor Who*, and didn't know if she'd be able to bring herself to watch the new series. ("Tell me about it," sighed Colin Baker.)

If she *was* planning on avoiding *Doctor Who*, Piper would have been advised to leave the country over Christmas, as that year's festive schedules included more than 70 – count 'em! – *Who*-related programmes, ranging from *The*

Runaway Bride, Doctor Who Confidential and a screening of the Children in Need concert to episodes of Torchwood, Big Finish's Eighth Doctor Adventures on BBC7, numerous repeats on BBC Three and UKTV Gold and a three-hour Radio 1 Christmas Day special called Jo Whiley Meets Doctor Who. Meanwhile, Toys "R" Us reported that its shelves were running out of sonic screwdrivers, Daleks and other Doctor Who products, and they'd had to order more supplies from overseas. (Stories like that are how panic-buying starts – before you knew it, there'd be mile-long queues at the checkouts and the Red Cross would be dropping parcels of remote-control Daleks out of helicopters.) "It's like a Doctor Who Christmas!" declared Russell T Davies in The Guardian. "I'm very pleased, obviously, but it's a bit barmy."

Even The Archers succumbed to Who-mania, as warring brothers Eddie and Will Grundy – the Oasis of Ambridge – put aside their differences to watch Doctor Who together while, on New Year's Day, The Vicar of Dibley's dippy verger Alice wore a tenth Doctor costume for a Doctor Who-themed wedding. Frankly, Fiona Bruce could have read the Ten O'Clock News dressed as the Kandyman and no-one would have batted an eyelid.

Wincy wincy spider

And the main event? The Runaway Bride is two Christmas Day films for the price of one. The first – a knockabout screwball comedy with David Tennant and Catherine Tate in the Tracy/Hepburn roles – is rather fabulous. The second – a sci-fi B-movie about an invasion of killer spiders – is, well, less fabulous.

Tate plays Donna Noble, a gobby temp from Chiswick whose big day is ruined when she disappears halfway down the aisle and pitches up aboard the TARDIS instead. Cue much hilarity as the Doctor attempts to get the hysterical bridezilla back to the church on time while getting sidetracked into various scrapes, including an audacious set-piece in which he has to fly the TARDIS down a motorway in pursuit of a taxi-driving robot Santa.

Russell T Davies has a ball with the leads' verbal sparring: "Haven't you got a mobile?" asks the Doctor. "I'm in my wedding dress!" snaps Donna. "It doesn't have pockets. Have

you ever seen a bride with pockets? When I went to my fitting at Chez Alison, the one thing I forgot to say is 'give me pockets!'" And duplicitous groom Lance's despairing monologue about Donna is priceless. ("I was stuck with a woman who thinks the height of excitement is a new flavour Pringle. Oh, I had to sit there and listen to all that yap yap yap. Oh, Brad and Angelina. Is Posh pregnant? X Factor, Atkins Diet, Feng Shui, split ends, text me, text me, text me. Dear God, the never-ending fountain of fat, stupid trivia.")

But the story also makes time for moments of reflection, including a lovely, tender rooftop two-hander between Tennant and Tate, a scene in which the Doctor explains what's going on using the contents of Donna's desk ("I'm a pencil inside a mug?" "Yes you are – 4H, sums you up.") and, best of all, an awe-inspiring sequence in which the pair stand on the threshold of the TARDIS and witness the creation of the solar system. "We're just tiny," sighs Donna. "No, but that's what you do," the Doctor tells her. "The human race makes sense out of chaos. Marking it out with weddings and Christmas and calendars." Then they watch as the Earth itself begins to form from the dust, coalescing around a spaceship belonging to an ancient race known as the Racnoss.

Which is where things start to go a bit pear-shaped. As the Empress of the Racnoss, a giant half-spider, half-humanoid creature that looks impressive until you realise it can't actually move, Sarah Parish dials her performance up to 11 – and then dials it up some more. (Though, in her defence, she doesn't exactly have a lot of choice, as the script forces her to spend most of the story's last act shrieking and wailing in a manner that must have come as a rude awakening for anyone enjoying a post-turkey slumber. Plus, she's clearly losing the battle to make herself understood through giant joke shop fangs.)

At the climax, the Empress' spider-babies begin to wake and start scrambling up from the centre of the Earth – though we have to take her word for this, as the budget won't stretch to actually showing us – until the Doctor uses the Thames to flush them all back down the plughole. Cue more hysterical shrieking – "No! No! My children! No! My children! My children!" – as the nation desperately gropes about on the sofa for the mute button.

The story closes with a lovely little postscript in which the Doctor uses "basic atmospheric excitation" – fired from the TARDIS lamp like a Roman candle – to make it snow. As the flakes fall on their heads, he asks Donna to join him on his travels, but she declines, admitting: "You scare me to death." And so the Time Lord prepares to depart, alone. A somewhat bleak ending for Christmas Day, perhaps, though at least viewers had the death of Pauline Fowler in *EastEnders* to lighten the mood.

As *The Times* declared that *Doctor Who* had usurped the Christmas visit to Walford as "the flagship of the Christmas schedules", *The Sun* did its best to play Grinch with its latest "Tennant quits" story, this one elevated to front-page status, despite claiming the tenth Doctor wouldn't actually leave until mid-way through the fourth series.

On New Year's Eve, Paul McGann was joined by Sheridan Smith as chippy northern sidekick Lucie Miller in *Blood of the Daleks*, the first of a new series of eighth Doctor stories specifically commissioned by BBC7. "When I auditioned, she was a generally brash, feisty, northern bird," said Smith, at the time still best known for propping up the BBC Three schedules with endless repeats of shouty sitcom *Two Pints of Lager and a Packet of Crisps*. "She's horribly rude to the Doctor at first, but her caring and sensitive sides do come out."[12] "I think there's a really good rapport," enthused McGann. "Sheridan is fantastic. Long may the fun continue."[21] The eighth Doctor's previous significant other, India Fisher, was gracious in defeat. "Ah yes, the other woman," she told *Doctor Who Magazine*. "I was told that they were moving to BBC7, and for that they would need a new companion. It was a blow, after playing it for several years, but Sheridan is a brilliant actress."[22]

The next day, another of the Time Lord's fellow travellers found herself promoted to star billing as BBC1 broadcast *Invasion of the Bane*, a 60-minute bank holiday special to introduce *The Sarah Jane Adventures*.

When 13-year-old Maria (Yasmin Paige) and her newly-divorced dad move into Ealing's Bannerman Road, the teenager is determined to discover more about the mysterious woman over the road – who she swears she saw talking to an alien in her front garden. Before long, the duo have formed an alliance to stop the Bane, a race of giant squid creatures led by Mrs Wormwood (Samantha Bond), who are controlling the human race using Bubble Shock!, an addictive fizzy drink containing secretions of the Bane Mother. (Yes, I know – but it's still nicer than Irn-Bru.)

Accompanied by Maria's chippy new friend Kelsey (Porsha Lawrence-Mavour), they squish the squids and rescue the Archetype (Tommy Knight), a human child grown as part of the Bane's DNA experiments, who Sarah Jane adopts as her son. (She calls him Luke, but only after considering Harry and Alistair – just one of the episode's numerous subtle nods to Sarah's time aboard the TARDIS. Her attic, in particular, looks like a *Who* fan's bedroom circa 1977. Minus the posters of Louise Jameson in a leather bikini, obviously.)

K-9 makes a brief cameo inside Sarah's safe, where he's busy containing a singularity that threatens to destroy the Earth ("Your best friend is a metal dog with its bum stuck in a black hole?" asks Kelsey, memorably), while Alexander Armstrong is the voice of Mr Smith, a slightly pompous, steampunky supercomputer who appears to be the closest thing to a man in Sarah's life.

With its themes of love, loss and loneliness – Sarah admits she spent years grieving for her days with the Doctor ("Space, and time. Then it came to an end. Suddenly, I was back to a normal life. Electric bills, burst pipes, bus tickets... and rain"), this supposedly kiddie-friendly arm of the rapidly-expanding *Who* franchise is, ironically, often more grown-up than the frequently adolescent shock tactics of *Torchwood*. It's certainly much more charming, with Lis Sladen – finally getting to be top dog 25 years after *K-9 and Company* – in winning form as an initially quite spiky, brittle Sarah Jane whose emotional firewall gradually comes down as she forges new friendships and embarks on her biggest adventure since she left the TARDIS: motherhood. "I saw amazing things, out there in space," she tells her newly-formed Scooby gang. "But there is strangeness to be found, wherever you turn. Life on Earth can be an adventure too... you just need to know where to look."

Just short of three million viewers knew exactly where to look; few would have felt short-changed.

The plastic figure-ness of being

David Tennant kicked off 2007 as guest host of raucous Channel 4 comedy *The Friday Night Project*, and was one of the great and good honoured with an entry in the new edition of *Who's Who* (no pun intended – they don't really go in for that sort of thing in *Who's Who*).

On set for *Human Nature*, Tennant was soldiering manfully on with a terrible cold, but finally admitted defeat and took a day off after losing his voice completely. Meanwhile, *The Guardian* reported on rumours that Brit beefcake lunk Jason Statham was being lined up as the next Doctor in a bid to "sex up" the show. ("Are you suggesting I'm not sexy?" asked Tennant, wiping a big dangly bit of snot off the end of his nose.)

At the read-through for Chris Chibnall's episode, *42*, Gary Russell – who'd now graduated from Big Finish to a script-editing job at BBC Wales – stood in for the recovering Tennant by reading the Doctor's lines. ("It's no biggie," he shrugged. Then ran around the streets of Cardiff shouting the words to Jon Pertwee's "I am the Doctor!" in the faces of passing shoppers.)

By mid-January, Tennant was fighting fit again – just in time to film in a disused Monmouthshire paper mill in sub-zero temperatures. The constant fog of frozen breath was a particular problem as the mill was supposed to be doubling as a spaceship flying into the heart of a sun; to simulate sweat, the actors had to be lathered in baby oil. Which sounds pretty sexy – and it might have been, if they hadn't been in a disused Monmouthshire paper mill in the middle of winter.

Towards the end of the month, it was announced that the second series of *Totally Doctor Who* would feature weekly instalments of a new animated adventure, *The Infinite Quest*, featuring the voices of David Tennant, Freema Agyeman and Anthony Head. *Totally* and *Confidential* producer Gillian Seaborne

had the idea after seeing some images pinned up in *Scream of the Shalka* producer James Goss' office. Goss suggested Big Finish regular (and former *Doctor Who Magazine* editor) Alan Barnes as scriptwriter, while Gary Russell was the "only choice" to direct, according to Russell T Davies. Meanwhile, it was a slow made-up news week at the *Daily Star*, which claimed "Pop babe Britney Spears is set to take on *Doctor Who* – playing a raunchy bunch of sex-mad aliens. Blonde Brit, 25, will be cast as an entire race of lusty cloned creatures who all look identical to the twice-wed beauty." Still, at least now we know where the *Star* gets it stories – direct from the slightly clammy dreams of 14-year-old boys.

A few days later, *The Sun* stated that a character played by Sir Derek Jacobi would be revealed to be the Doctor's arch-nemesis the Master, after which he would regenerate into John Simm – which sounded *less* like a 14-year-old boy's dream. Simm later dismissed this as "speculation". So it was definitely true.

In fact, by late February, the *Life on Mars* star was already on-set as the Master, and wielding a "laser screwdriver" that left David Tennant feeling somewhat... inadequate. "David said it was outrageous to discover that John Simm's was bigger than his sonic screwdriver," Russell T Davies told *Radio Times*. "Truly, I was getting texts from him: "Have u seen the size of his screwdriver?"[23] Yeah, but you know what they say: it's not the size, it's how you resonate longitudinal compression waves with it.

And there were more saucy shenanigans – or not – when the Digital Spy website reported that a scene featuring Freema Agyeman in her undies had been cut after being deemed "inappropriate". By that measure, they ought to have deleted every story Katy Manning ever appeared in.

Just after midnight on March 11th, a cake was handed round to celebrate John Barrowman's 40th birthday. With his usual relentless *joi de vivre*, Barrowman wasn't about to let the fact he was in a quarry in Merthyr Tydfil in the middle of the night spoil the celebrations. The actor was back on board for the final three episodes of the series, including the two-part finale directed by Colin Teague. Or, at least, directed by Teague until he fell down the stairs at his home and ended up in hospital, after which Graeme Harper gamely stepped in to finish the shoot.

On the BBC's Comic Relief telethon, David Tennant guest-starred in a Catherine Tate sketch in which stroppy teenager Lauren "am I bovvered?" Cooper winds up her new English teacher so much, he whips out his sonic screwdriver and turns her into a Rose Tyler action figure. A separate sketch saw Tate playing the character opposite Tony Blair. At time of writing, Blair's sketch has been watched just over 1.5 million times on YouTube, while Tennant's has racked up more than ten million views – thus proving that David Tennant is at least six times more popular than the former Prime Minister. Especially in Iraq.

By now, the hype machine for the launch of Series Three at the end of the month was in full swing, with Tennant, Freema Agyeman, Russell T Davies and John Barrowman all doing the sofa-shuffle around various TV and radio studios. Talking to *TV & Satellite Week*, Tennant reflected on how the role had changed his life: "This show is a bit of an all-consuming beast, but in a good way. It's unlike anything I've done before or will ever do again. Just the scale of it, the plastic figure-ness-of it, the birthday cake-ness, the jigsaw-ness of it. It's thrilling and terrifying to be at the pointy end of all that. I'm aware that it's potentially the first line of my obituary.

"Being presented with a plastic model of yourself is a weird, out-of-body experience. It does flatter a strange corner of your ego that's probably best left unflattered. It's crazy... but mostly good crazy."[24]

The series press launch was a suitably starry affair, with the likes of Jonathan Ross, Dawn French, Celia Imrie, Jo Whiley, Arabella Weir, Charlie Higson and Adam Woodyatt joining members of the *Who* cast and crew. (Okay, so *EastEnders'* Ian Beale wasn't exactly Hollywood A-list – but these launches had come a long way since it was just Sylvester McCoy and a waitress out of '*Allo 'Allo*.)

The *Mirror's* coverage of the launch included a claim that David Tennant had "agreed a £1 million deal" to stay with the show. Either that, or he was definitely leaving. Or he may not have made up his mind yet. Anyway, whichever it was, it was definitely going to happen. Unless it didn't. In the *Daily Telegraph*, Sam

Leith had his mind on more rarefied matters, examining the "deep, underlying melancholy" at the heart of *Doctor Who's* reinvention: "Mr Davies has taken a rickety old 1970s science-fiction series and, by applying a little psychological seriousness to the premise, has turned it into an extraordinary study of loss," said Leith. "Its deep theme is loneliness... The Doctor is described at one point as a 'lonely god'. He has something close to the perspective of a god: he can munch, if he so chooses, his breakfast bagel shortly after the Big Bang and have supper the same day in the Restaurant at the End of the Universe. But he does not have the power of a god: he can't go back and change the course of events. So everybody he cares about or ever will care about is always already dead; every companion he picks up will, sooner or later, be gone. I've mentioned before, in connection with this, TS Eliot's notion that if 'all time is eternally present, all time is unredeemable.' Eliot was interested (inter alia) in the theology of this; Russell T Davies in the psychology." Blimey, that's pretty deep stuff for a show whose most recent episode featured Doctor Who and Catherine Tate fighting some giant space spiders.

Lunar hospital fails to meet outpatient attendance targets

Four days before the new series' launch, Freema Agyeman appeared on *Blue Peter* – arriving by TARDIS, natch – and claimed she used to watch the show when Sylvester McCoy and Bonnie Langford were in it. And there aren't many people who can openly say *that*. She also admitted to *The Sun* that she'd been a huge Trekkie[1], and was looking forward to her first *Doctor Who* convention.

"I was really into *Star Trek: The Next Generation*," Agyeman told that month's *SFX* magazine. "I used to go to conventions. Yeah, really, I went to two. So I can fully appreciate that programmes can sometimes go beyond you just sitting there and watching it one night a week. It touches your life in a different way. I went to fancy dress parties... I dressed up as Dax from *Deep Space Nine*."[17] And in the minds of a thousand adolescent boys, a cosplay fantasy is born...

That week's *Radio Times* came wrapped in a

choice of two *Doctor Who* covers while, in *The Times*, columnist-turned-superfan Caitlin Moran reported on a set visit to Cardiff, during which David Tennant revealed he and Billie Piper had let it be known through their "people" that they'd like to present a BRIT award – and had been knocked back: "They turned down the Doctor and Rose!" he chortled. "Famous across the universe!"

The series build-up concluded with a special edition of *The Weakest Link* that saw eight *Doctor Who* celebrities (and Andrew Haydn-Smith) facing interrogation by Anne Robinson, with the surprise result suggesting that Jackie Tyler is smarter than the Doctor, Captain Jack and K-9. Mother knows best, I guess.

Smith and Jones, which kicked off 13 weeks of new adventures on March 31st, sees Russell T Davies sticking firmly to the template established in *Rose*, introducing viewers to the new companion, while also giving us the chance to see the Doctor anew through someone else's eyes.

If anything, it's an even more assured and confident production than the Series One opener, as Davies no longer feels compelled to shy away from big sic-fi concepts: in this case, an entire London hospital is ripped out of the ground and transported to the moon. Before that, though, we're introduced to medical student Martha Jones and her dysfunctional family: flinty divorcee Francine, siblings Tish and Leo, wayward dad Leo and his bimbo trophy girlfriend Annalise. And we've already seen Martha meeting the Doctor, who bowls up to her in the street in the opening seconds, takes off his tie and says "see?," much to her (and our) bafflement.

By the time the two are reacquainted, the Doctor – sitting up in a hospital bed in his PJs, grinning like a Cheshire cat – claims to have no knowledge of this encounter. But the explanations will have to wait, because the rain outside is falling upwards, the hospital is rocked in what appears to be an earthquake and then, suddenly, it's dark outside. While her colleagues flap around wondering how it could have gone from lunchtime to night, Martha quickly gets a grasp of the situation. "We're on the moon," she says. "We're *on the bloody moon!*" (the first time anyone's ever sworn on *Doctor Who* – unless you count TOMTIT, the matter transmitter from *The Time Monster*).

Martha's powers of deductive reasoning – working out something must be supplying them with oxygen because the windows aren't airtight – piques the interest of Tie Man, who emerges from behind a curtain in a sharp new blue suit and challenges her to step outside with him. "We might die," he warns. "We might not," she replies. It's a typically brilliant Russell T Davies scene, establishing Martha's credentials as a worthy TARDIS traveller with maximum economy and wit.

As the new friends talk on the balcony in the Earthlight – beautifully captured by director Charles Palmer (son of jowly sitcom curmudgeon Geoffrey) – a fleet of towering vertical spaceships thunder overhead and dispatch their crew. The phalanxes of tiny figures marching across the lunar surface like ants is one of several classic images in this story – prime among them, of course, the sight of a brutalist concrete hospital standing *on the bloody moon*.

The new arrivals are the Judoon – rhino-headed, leather-clad guns for hire with orders to execute a vampiric Plasmavore criminal thought to be hiding in the hospital (which they have relocated to "neutral territory" using a rain-based "H20 scoop". Hey, it could happen.)

The Judoon are fantastic: thuggish and physically imposing, with brilliantly articulated features, they're pretty terrifying but also really funny. ("You will be catalogued," barks the platoon captain, shining a torch-like device into the eyes of a petrified junior doctor. But it turns out to be nothing more sophisticated than a marker pen, which he uses to draw an X on the medic's hand, complete with comedy squeak effect.)

The Plasmavore is another memorable creation, as it's taken the form of a pensioner (the superb Anne Reid) in her dressing gown, and sucks its victims' blood with the aid of a straw. Only in *Doctor Who*.

The creature's climactic confrontation with the Doctor is a bit silly (even by the standards of a story set in a hospital on the moon) and appears to rely on a standard MRI scanner packing the same wallop as an atomic bomb. But it's a small niggle in a wonderful episode, full of Davies' patented chutzpah. It's exactly the sort of funny, frothy opener *New Earth* should have been, and a fantastic showcase for the new team of David Tennant and Freema Agyeman, both of whom are fabulous.

Back on Earth, the Doctor rocks up in the middle of a typically explosive Jones family gathering and offers Martha a ride in his magic box. She refuses to believe he's got a time machine, so he disappears in the TARDIS, and re-emerges a few seconds later with his tie in his hand. "Told you," he says with a wolfish grin. When she challenges him for not warning her against going into work this morning, the Doctor tells her "crossing into established events is strictly forbidden – except for cheap tricks". Actually, it's a classic Davies trick – covering up plot holes by making a joke of them, and getting away with it.

Eventually, Martha agrees to take a quick spin around the universe ("Your spaceship's made of wood!") – though the Doctor insists it's a strictly platonic date. Talk about mixed signals. "Welcome aboard, Miss Jones," he says, closing down the gravitic anomaliser, firing up the helmic regulator and releasing the handbrake. "My pleasure, Mr Smith." And new adventures await.

With 8.7 million viewers, the new season was off to a solid start – and the critics were unanimous in their praise for Freema Agyeman, with the *Mirror*'s "She's So Dalektable" summing up the mood in true tabloid fashion.

Arriving on screens seven days later, the year's celebrity historical takes the maxim that Shakespeare was the rock star of his day and runs with it, Dean Lennox Kelly playing the Bard with the swaggering braggadocio of a more evolved Liam Gallagher.

The story exists in a highly stylised, theme-park version of Elizabethan London that looks absolutely gorgeous on screen, while The Mill work miracles turning a handful of extras into a cast of thousands for the scenes inside the Globe Theatre.

The story opens with a young man serenading a beautiful young woman, Lilith (Christina Cole) who actually turns out to be a hideous old hag (he wouldn't be using *that* online dating site again). She then introduces him to her two cackling "mothers", who devour him

whole. (He definitely should have checked the small print.)

Later, Lilith enchants Shakespeare into writing a new ending to his latest play, *Love's Labours Won*, which, when spoken aloud inside the Globe's 14 walls, will release her species, the Carrionites, from their eternal prison. Meanwhile, the Doctor is treating Martha to a trip to the theatre, 1599-style – but she's worried about the butterfly effect: "What if, I dunno, what if I kill my grandfather?" she frets. "You planning to?" asks the Doctor, incredulously.

Gareth Roberts' script is full of such witticisms – not least the (obvious, but well deployed) running gag of the Doctor and Martha constantly putting words into Shakespeare's mouth by quoting his own plays at him before he's written them.

The story also delves into darker territory, including the Master of the Revels choking to death on dry land, a grim visit to Bedlam Asylum and Shakespeare talking about the son he lost to the Black Death. But you're never more than a couple of lines away from the next killer gag.

For all his cocksure bravado, Shakespeare is also portrayed as a man of genuine intellect and insight. "How can a man so young have eyes so old?" he asks the Doctor. "And you," he tells Martha. "You look at him as if you're surprised he even exists. He's as much of a puzzle to you as he is to me."

As you'd expect in a story about history's greatest writer, there is much emphasis on the importance of language, and Roberts manages to make the Carrionite idea of words instead of numbers as the building blocks of the universe sound vaguely plausible. It isn't, of course, but if you're going to blur the lines between magic and science, what better place to do it than a Shakespearian tale of sorcery and witchcraft?

The resolution also depends on the power of language to save the day. As a black whirlpool of wraiths fills the skies above the Globe – another stunning set-piece courtesy of The Mill – the Doctor tells Shakespeare only he can find the words to close the portal that's letting them through. When the Bard stumbles over a suitable rhyme to finish his improvised stanza, Martha steps up with a cry of "Expelliarmus!", Roberts seemingly equating JK Rowling with

Shakespeare. Which, for this show's target audience, of course, she is.

It's a measure of the New Who's confidence by this stage that it can comfortably pay tribute to what is, in effect, a rival franchise. But then, *everything* about *The Shakespeare Code* demonstrates as much self-assured swagger as its celebrity guest. It would probably be going too far to say it's a script worthy of Shakespeare himself. But it does have much better jokes.

The following week's episode brought heightened tension as, if the afternoon's FA cup semi-final went into extra time, transmission of *Doctor Who* would be delayed a week. Perhaps for the first time ever, *Doctor Who* fans were suddenly interested in the football results: they didn't care who won, just as long as *someone* did. In the end, Manchester United treated Watford to a 4-1 drubbing, leading to much jubilation on the *Who* terraces. ("Thank you, Man U / Now we won't miss *Doctor Who* / Fergie's the man / Though not quite as good his namesake Michael Ferguson, director of *The Ice Warriors*, among other vintage classics" – as a chant, it needed work.)

The third of Russell T Davies' Year Five Billion trilogy, *Gridlock* is New *Who's* most outré experiment yet; inspired by Davies' love of *2000AD*, it cocks a snook at convincing world-building in favour of a heavily stylised comic book sensibility, while the central conceit – people stuck in traffic for decades on end – jettisons plot verisimilitude for an extended metaphor about... well, traffic jams.

The cars' occupants are all vividly cartoonish, from the bowler-hatted civil servant (clearly based on *2000AD's* Max Normal) and a pair of nudists to Brannigan, a "human cat" played with a roguish Irish twinkle by Ardal O'Hanlon, and his human wife, who gives birth to a litter of talking kittens. Asimov this ain't. (Brannigan's feline Biggles look was taken from Ratz, an animated cat in flight helmet and goggles who'd appeared on *Live and Kicking* in the mid-90s. You may wonder what place a daft comedy character from Saturday morning kids' telly has in *Doctor Who*, but this is not the place to get into a discussion about John Barrowman.)

Gridlock is one of *Doctor Who's* most visually stunning achievements (even if New New York's CG cityscape does look suspiciously like *Star Wars'* Coruscant) and the Doctor's "vertical chase" down through the lanes of traffic is an audacious set-piece. The Macra look pretty cool, too.

Hang on, rewind... did I just say the *Macra*? That's right, do not adjust your sets: the outsized, largely unloved, near-forgotten alien crabs, last seen in Patrick Troughton's debut season in 1967, are *back!* Briefly. "I just thought it was cute for once to being back one that nobody would remember"[25], said Davies of the creatures' extended cameo lurking in the fumes beneath the motorway. (Next week: Doctor Who meets the Mechanoids and one of the beardy old men from *The Savages*. Possibly.)

For all its lurid, funny-book aesthetic, *Gridlock* also finds room for more contemplative moments: the scene where all the cars' occupants join in with a city-wide rendition of "The Old Rugged Cross" is quite lovely, as is the Doctor's evocation of Gallifrey which, with its burnt orange skies and slopes of deep red grass, heavily quotes from Susan's description in *The Sensorites* a whole 43 years earlier. And then there's the death of the Face of Boe. You might think it's hard to get emotionally involved with a giant head in a jar, but seeing that big old boatrace gasping his last on the floor is strangely moving. Before he goes, though, he must deliver his long-held promise to impart one final message to the Doctor. Those famous last words? "If you've had an accident at work, you may be entitled to claim compensation." No, not really, it's:

"You are not alone..."

Sec's in the City

Occupying the now traditional mid-season kiddie-friendly action adventure slot, *Daleks in Manhattan / Evolution of the Daleks* is, if anything, even more of a misfire than the previous year's Cyberman two-parter. Helen Raynor takes a seemingly bulletproof premise – Skaro's meanest on the loose in Depression-era NYC – and turns it into an incoherent mess that undoes all Series One's good work by reverting the Daleks into just another routine monster-of-the-week. And not a very convincing one at that.

The plot is full of narrative blind alleys. The Daleks have spliced human and pig DNA to create boiler-suited porcine servants – why? Presumably because someone thought pig-men would look cool. (Which they don't – especially when deployed for a cringey, *Beauty and the Beast*-style "will you still love me even though I look like Babe?" romantic sub-plot.) And the ending, which Raynor admits she struggled with for weeks, involves the pepper-pots mixing human and Dalek DNA using energy from a lightning-style "gamma strike" on the Empire State Building. (Would it have killed them to Google what a gamma ray actually is?) But don't worry, the Doctor manages to scupper this plan by putting his own DNA in the way – a complex scientific process that involves hugging the lightning conductor on the top of the building. Don't try this at home, kids. Because it won't work.

The part one cliffhanger, in which the collaborator Diagoras emerges from the shell of Dalek Sec as the prototype Dalek-human hybrid, proved highly controversial after the *Radio Times* featured a close-up of the creature on its cover four days before the episode aired – a major spoiler that was pretty hard to avoid. "We love a *Radio Times* cover," Russell T Davies told the magazine. "You want to give away a certain amount to draw people in... What we try to protect are the endings of plots. That's the important thing."[26]

In truth, though, the problem isn't that the surprise was spoiled so much as the fact it looks ridiculous in the first place. The prosthetic – complete with vaguely obscene flesh dreadlocks – doesn't really work, and the sight of an octopus-headed man in a suit and two-tone brogues is just too silly to be shocking or scary.

The 30s art-deco design work is nice, but the lack of New York street scenes is painfully obvious: everyone is forced to spend half the running time skulking in the sewers, with the story actually feeling rather small and stagey as a consequence. There's also something uniquely grating about British actors doing Broadway musical-style Noo Yoik accents (though LA-born future webslinger Andrew Garfield acquits himself well, and Miranda Raison's Betty Boop turn as showgirl Tallulah is endearing). Hugh Quarshie, as community leader Solomon, comes off particularly badly, not least because the script saddles him with some truly excruciating grandstanding speeches. ("See, I've just discovered this past day, God's universe is a thousand times the size I thought it was. And that scares me. Oh yeah, terrifies me right down to the bone. But surely it's got to give me hope. Hope that maybe together we can make a better tomorrow!" If that isn't a cue for a song, I don't know what is.)

Pulpy, disjointed and fatally unconvincing, *Daleks in Manhattan* takes a silk purse of an idea and makes a right pig-man's ear of it. That said, it's still worth watching for the priceless scene in which two Daleks are seen nattering in the sewers like a pair of old fishwives – particularly the moment when one of them furtively checks over what passes for its shoulder before imparting the next piece of scurrilous gossip. Or maybe they're just bitching about the script.

In late April, *The Sun* indulged in one of its occasional fantasy casting sessions with a story claiming pocket-sized pop saucestress Kylie Minogue was being lined up to appear in this year's Christmas special. "Don't be stupid," was Russell T Davies' blunt response. "I haven't even written the script yet, and a woman like that is booked up two years in advance."[27]

A few days later, the same newspaper reported a string of bets had been placed on unknown actor Julian Walsh to become the next Doctor. The 37-year-old Mancunian was best-known – which is to say, not known at all – as a child star from 80s kids' football drama *Jossy's Giants* (created by Sid Waddell, the only darts commentator with a degree in Modern History from Cambridge, fact fans), and was currently to be seen in an advert for Warburton's bread. "Julian might not look the part as he's a bit squat and bald," said a spokesman for bookies Paddy Power, "but he's the one people have been trying to back in the last 48 hours." Walsh's agent claimed: "He is bemused by all of this. Nobody has approached us yet." You have to love the optimism of the "yet" at the end of that.

More Kylie speculation followed over the coming weeks, with the star having apparently confirmed to a celebrity magazine that she was doing *Doctor Who*, while *The Sun*, clearly on a roll now, weighed in with a report that Woody Allen would also be in the Christmas special, playing Albert Einstein, which sounded like nonsense=bullshit[2].

Lazarus: "I'll be back"
"I thought you'd say that"

Russell T Davies' two-word pitch for *The Lazarus Experiment* was "mad scientist" – specifically, the sort of genetically modified super-boffin from the pages of Marvel and DC Comics.

The eponymous Professor Lazarus' mission is to "change what it means to be human" by unlocking the secret of immortality. Emerging from his rejuvenation pod 40 years younger, his experiment appears to have been a huge success – give or take the odd side-effect, like turning into a giant scorpion monster (that's why you should always read the label).

Mark Gatiss is suitably loathsome as both versions of this creepy genius, and the make-up job to make him look like a septuagenarian is a triumph – in fact, Gatiss looks a lot more convincing as an old man than he does playing his own age, thanks to a dodgy blonde wig he supplied himself from his League of Gentlemen dressing-up box. The script also calls for him to snog Mavis out of *Coronation Street* (77-year-old Thelma Barlow) – and the pair really go for it. "I said, 'What are we going to do about the kiss?'" recalled Gatiss, "and Thelma said, 'Let's see where the passion takes us!'"[19]

The paper-thin plot is over and done within a brisk 30 minutes, after which Lazarus comes back from the dead ("I should have known, really," sighs the Doctor) and we do it all again. It's worth it, though, for the terrific cathedral climax: the set-piece confrontation between Lazarus and the Doctor is a wonderful piece of writing from Stephen Greenhorn, with brilliantly intense performances from Gatiss and David Tennant.

The evolutionary science may be hokum (so what's new?) and there's no real central message beyond "don't mess with nature". But Greenhorn delivers a pacy romp peppered with punchy dialogue and thoughtful philosophical asides ("Some people live more in 20 years than others do in 80 – it's not the time that matters, it's the person"). Plus the Doctor gets to reaffirm the central tenet of the series

when he tells Lazarus: "There's no such thing as an ordinary human."

Next up, *42* is a Jack Bauer-riffing real-time race against the clock in which the Doctor and Martha have the episode's running time to stop a spaceship[II] and its crew crashing into the heart of an alien sun. Except, being *Doctor Who*, the solution to saving the ship lies beyond 29 password-sealed doors that can only be opened by answering trivia questions in what amounts to the world's most high-stakes pub quiz. Seriously, in which other show would avoiding a sci-fi cataclysm depend on knowing who had more UK number ones: Elvis or the Beatles?

Clearly contemporaneous with *The Impossible Planet / The Satan Pit*, from which it borrows much of its chunky, industrial aesthetic, a strong guest cast is led by ex-East-Ender Michelle Collins, carrying off the Bruce Willis, sweat-soaked vest look rather convincingly. But the real eye candy is provided by The Mill's superb VFX work: the shots of the ship being pulled inexorably towards the churning, broiling red orb are breathtaking, especially on a television budget.

There are proper scares, too, as the crew – and then the Doctor himself – are gradually possessed by the sentient sunlight (just go with it, okay?), their eyes like pools of fire as they they deliver the monster catchphrase of the week: "Burn. With. Me!"

Graeme Harper is in his element directing all this ripped-action stuff – though the stand-out scene is one of those minor chord moments *Who* does so well, as Martha and a member of the ship's crew are cast adrift in a jettisoned escape pod. In an echo of Rose's call to Jackie in *The End of the World*, Martha phones her mother to say goodbye, Harper deftly contrasting the silent void of space with an ordinary suburban kitchen.

Chris Chibnall's work on *Torchwood* didn't exactly inspire confidence, but the former DWAS Mersyside Local Group mainstay doesn't disgrace himself at all with his *Who* debut. While no classic, this is a solid, robust, high-octane actioner that sustains its momentum across 42 frenetic minutes.

And the answer, in case you're wondering, is Elvis – but only if you include that JXL remix.

Paul Cornell does himself a disservice

describing his second contribution to the series as "emo-*Who*". That conjures images of kohl-eyed adolescent angst or, worse, those mooning vampires of The Twilight Saga – when, in fact, *Human Nature / The Family of Blood* is one of the most intelligent, thoughtful, nuanced and grown-up pieces of work ever to go out under the `1 banner.

The high concept at the heart of the story is that, in order to escape a vengeful band of marauding aliens who want to steal his future regenerations, the Doctor becomes one of us. A human. Specifically, John Smith, a teacher at an English public school in 1913. This disguise, which goes all the way to the molecular level, is so effective even *he* doesn't know who he really is, allowing David Tennant to prove his acting chops all over again with a characterisation entirely different from the norm. Whereas the Doctor is cheeky, cocky and loose-limbed, Smith is starchy, buttoned-up, contained – the awkward Clark Kent to the Doctor's breezy Superman.

Only Martha, faithful keeper of the flame, knows Smith's real identity (which is hidden in a fob watch), and in order to watch over him, she is reduced to the role of a maid, forced to scrub floors while witnessing Smith engage in a stumbling courtship with school nurse Joan Redfern (the terrific Jessica Hynes).

As a character piece, this story demonstrates an emotional maturity rarely seen in *Doctor Who* – the script pulls no punches in portraying even the heroes, like Smith and Redfern, as products of their time. He authorises a beating, while she will accept aliens and monsters before she'll accept that Martha, a black woman, could be training as a doctor.

Of course, it's not only a meditation on the human condition, it's also a rollicking sci-fi adventure. Once they've assimilated a few locals, the Family of Blood prove to be a chilling enemy; Harry Lloyd, in particular, excels both as public school bully boy Baines and the terrifying Son of Mine who takes over his body – never has someone made a simple sniff seem quite so sinister. Daughter of Mine, meanwhile, appears as a young girl dispensing death with a single red balloon.

But the Family are positively cuddly compared to the army of animated scarecrows they press into service as footsoldiers. In one aston-ishing sequence, these straw men march on the school to face a defensive line of terrified, tearful young boys armed with rifles. As the youngsters blast the stuffing out of the enemy to the strains of "To be a Pilgrim," the shadow of the coming war that has loomed large over the story finally crystallises into focus. That something could be at once so scary and moving, so fantastical and so real, is testament to the quality of this richly textured production.

Nor does the script shrink from the consequences of the Time Lord's actions – the slow re-emergence of the Doctor leaves Joan, already a widow, grieving for the loss of another man. Both she and Smith are granted a cruel glimpse of what might have been on the road not taken: marriage, children, normality – a whole John Lewis ad of a life in flash-forward. "Could you change back?" she asks him. "Yes," he says. "Will you?" "No."

And it's not just their tragedy – as she surveys the carnage wrought on her sleepy corner of England, Joan asks: "If the Doctor had never visited us, if he'd never chosen this place on a whim, would anybody here have died?" It's a question *Doctor Who* has rarely addressed so unflinchingly. Even then, though, the issue is far from black and white. As the Doctor metes out a peculiarly baroque form of punishment – Son of Mine is forced to live as a scarecrow, his mother is imprisoned in the event horizon of a collapsing galaxy, while his sister is trapped in every mirror in the world – it becomes clear he wasn't hiding from the Family to save his life, but theirs. "We wanted to live forever," Son of Mine says, "so the Doctor made sure we did".

Director Charles Palmer rises to the occasion in style. As well as drawing fine performances from the whole cast – Freema Agyeman has rarely been better – Palmer has a keen eye for the mise en scene, making full use of the Brecons' bleak winter beauty (and how nice to see *Doctor Who* back in its spiritual heartland, the British countryside, after the urban bias of recent years).

The story is also full of delightful, almost throwaway grace notes. There's the *Journal of Impossible Things*, in which Smith logs his feverish dreams of monsters and demons and travel inside an impossible box (among the journal's sketches are impressions of several former Doctors, including – brace yourselves – Paul McGann, which surely had to nail those "is he canon?" arguments once and for all); Smith naming his parents as "Sydney and Verity" from Gallifrey ("Is that in Ireland?"); and the moving, perfectly judged present-day epilogue in which the Doctor and Martha watch an aged Timothy – the schoolboy who all those decades ago had found the soul of a Time Lord inside a fob watch – salute his fallen comrades at a Remembrance Day ceremony.

"I've seen him," Timothy had once told Joan Redfern of the Doctor, after looking inside the watch. "He's like fire and ice and rage. He's like the night and the storm in the heart of the sun. He's ancient and forever. He burns at the centre of time and he can see the turn of the universe. And he's wonderful." And this is a wonderful piece of television.

Cornell won much acclaim for his scripts – *Radio Times* called the story "rich, complex, resonant and BAFTA-worthy", and he would later earn a second Hugo nomination for his troubles. All of which appeared to be somewhat to the chagrin of Russell T Davies who, in one of many unguarded moments in his confessional 2008 book *The Writer's Tale*, stated: "I had a whole Sunday of people saying 'That was brilliant' and, specifically, 'What a brilliant script. Paul Cornell is a genius.' Which he is. But I'm thinking: if you only knew how much of that I wrote! But I stifle myself, so it all goes inwards. It festers. People know that I polish stuff, but they think polishing means adding a gag or an epigram, not writing half the script. I know I shouldn't, but it drives me mad. How selfish."[28] Not really – it's just human nature.

Rumours of companion departure "absolute rubbish" says BBC spokesman (with fingers crossed behind back)

In late May, Kylie Minogue was photographed carrying around a to-do list which included the words: "When Dr Who script arriving? Russell's number." With careless security leaks like that, she could get a job with the British secret service. Meanwhile, Freema Agyeman guested on BBC One's *Friday Night with Jonathan Ross*. When Ross made the presumption Martha would be back for the

following series, Agyeman visibly slumped in her seat, and offered a diplomatically vague answer.

The following day, *The Sun* was less circumspect. Under the sensitive heading "Exterminate! Freema Axed," the paper claimed Agyeman had been dropped from the next series. "Pretty Freema, 27, only joined the BBC1 sci-fi hit as the Timelord's (sic) new companion Martha Jones at the beginning of the current series," wrote TV editor Ally Ross. "We told how the struggling actress scooped the role after Billie Piper quit. But show chiefs think her performance is not as strong as in her earlier episodes. And they are planning a storyline where the Doctor, played by David Tennant, will lose her and travel through the universe searching for her.

"The decision to dump Freema comes as a bolt from the blue after her performance for the first couple of episodes was praised. A source said: 'Freema is very talented but we don't think she is just right on *Doctor Who*. None of this is being done with any malice. Freema's a lovely girl.'"

A BBC spokesman described the story as "absolute rubbish", but would not comment on "future storylines". A week later, Agyeman was named Best Newcomer at *Glamour* magazine's annual Women of the Year awards, where she admitted she'd been upset by the tabloid reports, but insisted: "I'm not axed, I haven't been sacked. You know you're not going to get 100% of the people all the time. What's important is the fans are enjoying it."

Meanwhile, *The Sun* had gone even further, claiming *the entire show* was to be cancelled at the end of the fourth series. "Boss Russell T Davies has decided to axe the BBC1 sci-fi drama and concentrate on other things," claimed the paper, demonstrating a shaky grasp of the TV commissioning process. "He and senior staff have hatched a plot to hand in a group resignation in 2008." Well of course, that made total sense. I mean, it's not like there were any other suitable candidates waiting in the wings who could possibly take over...

In entirely unrelated news, the next episode of Series Three is written by Steven Moffat. It was never the plan for Moffat to write the series' Doctor-lite bottle episode. He'd originally been offered the Dalek two-parter, then another episode earlier in the run, but his commitments on *Jekyll* – a contemporary reimagining of Jekyll and Hyde starring James Nesbitt – meant he had to keep deferring.

In the end, he volunteered to do the "cheap" episode as compensation for "jerking them around". With the clock ticking, he turned to a short story, "What I Did on My Christmas Holidays by Sally Sparrow," that he'd originally written for the *2006 Doctor Who Annual*. "I had so little time to write, I needed to be able to tell them what I was up to, sharpish," said Moffat. "And giving them a page reference saved time. It was my desperate attempt to keep a toehold in Series Three, really."[29]

In the original story, 12-year-old Sally had helped rescue the ninth Doctor after discovering a message from him under the wallpaper in her bedroom. *Blink* opens with a similar scene in which Sally – in this version a young woman, played with winsome charm by a pre-Hollywood Carey Mulligan – discovers the words "Beware the Weeping Angel" written beneath the wallpaper in an abandoned house she has broken into. She pulls more paper off to reveal the message "Oh and Duck! Really, Duck! Sally Sparrow Duck, Now" – seconds before a heavy object smashes through the window and whizzes past her head. The message is signed "Love from the Doctor (1969)". Cue titles.

Do we have your attention?

From the first frame to the last, *Blink* is a brilliant, glorious puzzle-box of a story. Moffat has always been the writer with the keenest interest in the possibilities of time travel, and here he delves into a dizzying bag of tricks in order to exploit those possibilities to their full potential. "People assume that time is a strict progression of cause to effect," explains the Doctor – who, perhaps uniquely in fiction, has taken the form of a DVD Easter egg – "but actually from a non-linear, non-subjective viewpoint, it's more like a big ball of... wibbly-wobbly, timey-wimey stuff."

Later, he will prove this point by having a conversation with Sally – despite being nothing more than a series of zeroes and ones on a disc – because he already knows exactly what she is going to say; as she gradually fills in all the blanks in a conversation previously only heard from one side, the Doctor's earlier picaresque ramblings suddenly make perfect sense, to us as well as her. "Okay, let me get my head round this," says Sally. "You're reading aloud from a transcript of a conversation you're still having?" "Yeah," says the face on the screen. "Wibbly wobbly, timey-wimey."

But Moffat doesn't just use time for cheap tricks – he packs an emotional punch with it, too. When cocksure copper Billy Shipton disappears before Sally has even had the chance to go on a first date with him, she tracks him down to a hospital ward where, now a dying old man, he tells her he has until the rain stops. "It was raining when we met," remembers Billy. "It's the same rain," says Sally.

The cause of all this temporal disruption are the Weeping Angels – stone statues who feed on "potential energy". "Fascinating race, the Weeping Angels," explains the Doctor from his exile in 1969. "The only psychopaths in the universe to kill you nicely. No mess, no fuss, they just zap you into the past and let you live to death. The rest of your life used up and blown away in the blink of an eye. You die in the past, and in the present they consume the energy of all the days you might have had. All your stolen moments."

The Angels can't move while they're being observed – which means you can't see them moving either. Look away even for a fraction of the second, and they will be upon you, their beatific stone faces twisted into a hideous, fanged leer – hence the Doctor's repeated warning: "Don't turn your back. Don't look away. And don't blink."

"You start with the playground game," explained Moffat of the creatures' origins. "You start thinking about the game of statues – and the fact children are a little bit frightened by statues. What you've got with the Weeping Angels is *Doctor Who* monsters that are permanently imminent. You never actually see them do anything; they're just always *about* to attack. They're frozen in the moment of being the most terrifying."[30]

Moffat also delivers his usual high gag quota – when Sally's friend Kathy jokingly suggests they set up an investigations agency called Sparrow and Nightingale, Sally dismisses it as "a bit ITV", and there's a great in-joke at the expense of a certain stripe of online *Doctor Who* fan when Billy describes the TARDIS' police box disguise as a fake because "the phone's just a dummy and the windows are the wrong size". Take that, ming mongs.

Despite his much-reduced physical presence, Moffat cleverly ensures the Doctor makes his presence felt by having him pop up, Zelig-like, on TV screens throughout the episode, while director Hettie MacDonald makes a confident *Who* debut, playfully referencing everything from Hitchcock to German expressionist cinema.

For a story that Moffat originally submitted with no higher aspiration than "getting away" with a Doctor-lite episode, *Blink* has proved to have quite a legacy. Among its haul of awards, it earned its writer a third consecutive Hugo and, even more impressively, saw Moffat taking home the 2008 BAFTA for Best Writer, beating off heavyweight competition from Tony Marchant (*The Mark of Cain*), Jimmy McGovern (*The Street*) and Heidi Thomas (*Cranford*). A poll by the BBC and *Doctor Who Adventures* magazine proclaimed the Weeping Angels that year's scariest monsters – beating even the Daleks – while, five years later, the creatures were voted the greatest *Doctor Who* monsters *ever* by more than 10,000 *Radio Times* readers.

In 2009 – and again in 2014 – *Blink* was voted the second best *Doctor Who* story of all time in a *Doctor Who Magazine* poll which asked readers to rate every adventure. "I suppose *Blink* is probably the most successful thing I've ever written, if I'm honest," said Moffat in a *DWM* interview. "I've never written anything that has won so many awards – a ridiculous number for a single episode – and it's the one thing that everyone I meet always mentions to me. I didn't think, when I handed it in, it was my best, although Julie Gardner immediately said that it was. I thought, 'Don't be silly – it's not got Doctor Who in it!'"[31]

Maybe not. But in every other sense, *Blink* is the perfect *Doctor Who* story.

Utopia: it's not ideal

In mid-June, *Blue Peter* broadcast a *Doctor Who* special under the name *Doctor Blue* (not really, that would have been rubbish – it was *Who Peter*). The programme's main function was to reveal the winner of the show's casting competition, with Russell T Davies phoning nine-year-old John Bell from Kilmacolm in Renfrewshire to give him the good news. The cameras then followed Bell filming his scenes for upcoming story *Utopia*, with David Tennant declaring his young co-star to be the most professional actor on set, while John Barrowman revealed he had nicknamed him Little John. (At least we *hope* he was talking about Bell – you can never tell with Barrowman.) Barrowman then joined Gethin Jones in the BP greenhouse to construct a model of the TARDIS console room using household items including a yoghurt pot, some curtain rings and, oh yes, a washing-up liquid bottle, and revealed that he often runs on to the TARDIS set for a play when no-one is looking. Which surprised absolutely no-one.

For a good two-thirds of its running time, *Utopia* is as flimsy as that jerry-built TARDIS. Having stopped to refuel his ship in Cardiff (he says it's a good source of Rift energy, but may just be trying to avoid paying London prices), the Doctor and Martha run into Captain Jack, whose complicated dead-man-walking status causes the time machine to throw a hissy fit and leg it to the end of the universe, with Jack clinging to the outside like a frisky puppy on a dimensionally transcendental trouser leg. I guess some people just can't take a hint.

The end of the universe, it turns out, bears a striking resemblance to a Welsh quarry ("I still flinch slightly at the quarry at night," admitted Russell T Davies, "because it shows how difficult an alien planet is to achieve – it feels very old school"[32]) and is home to the Futurekind: fanged, primitive types who look like they've stepped off the set of Duran Duran's "Wild Boys" video. They spend their days trying to break into the silo where the last remnants of humanity are building a rocket, in order to reach the fabled sanctuary world of Utopia.

Sir Derek Jacobi, no less, is quite adorable as Professor Yana, the deceptively bumbling scientist on whose shoulders the survival of humanity rests. In a way, he's like a throwback version of the Doctor (he even dresses like William Hartnell), complete with his own adoring companion, Chantho (Chipo Chung) – an insectoid female who has to start every sentence with "Chan" and end it with "tho".

Chan which is quite sweet at first, but probably gets quite irritating after a while tho. The silo is also home to Creet, the smudge-faced street urchin played John Bell who, for a competition winner, acquits himself rather well.

It is, frankly, all a teensy bit *Blake's 7* – until the 33 minute mark, when Martha discovers the Professor owns a fob-watch (identical to the one the Doctor used to disguise his identity in *Human Nature*, with the same Gallifreyan script engraved on it) and the episode suddenly shifts up through about five gears at once. As the Doctor sees the name YANA flashing on the screen, and suddenly understands the meaning of the Face of Boe's dying words – "You Are Not Alone" – the Professor flips open the watch and, with the sound of Roger Delgado and Anthony Ainley's demonic laughter ringing in his ears, finally remembers his real identity.

"The Professor was an invention," he tells the terrified Chantho. "So perfect a disguise that I forgot who I am." "Chan then who are you tho?" she asks. And with black eyes burning like coals, a live cable sparking in his hands, he bears down on her with a triumphant: "I – am – the – Master!"

It's exhilarating stuff, brilliantly played by Jacobi, whose sudden switch from maladroit grandfather figure to vengeful demon is utterly convincing. So much so that you can't help but feel a bit cheated when, moments later, he is shot by the dying Chantho and regenerates into – can you guess who it is yet? – TV's John Simm.

"Did you hear me say that I didn't like the Master and didn't want him back? Well, I was lying!" chortled Russell T Davies. "Actually, I was delaying, 'cos I needed a couple of years to work out how to write him."[29]

Sir Derek Jacobi claimed that being in *Doctor Who* – as in actual, proper *Doctor Who*, on the telly – was one of the "few ambitions" he still had left. "I have a friend I didn't know was a fanatic and when I told him, he just went hysterical. When I said I'd be playing a character that becomes the Master, he thought it was the pinnacle of my career! It can never get better for me than this. I was told that what I was going into was tremendously important to millions of people, and actually that contributed greatly to my approach, knowing that I

was entering a kind of legendary world. No pressure, then!"[29]

The imminent series finale saw another big publicity push, with all the usual hoopla – radio and TV interviews, multiple *Radio Times* covers, rainforests of press coverage – fans had now come to expect. Among the more memorable was Freema Agyeman's appearance on Christian O'Connell's Virgin radio show, during which a fan called Derek called in to say he was going to buy "Freda"'s action figure, but claimed he wasn't too keen on the current Doctor, David Eccleston, who was "a bit rubbish". Eventually, Agyeman rumbled that Derek was, in fact, David Tennant, punking her live on air. Though 90% of the other callers probably *were* called Derek and probably did own Freda's... sorry, Freema's action figure.

As BBC Worldwide reported a 24% leap in profits, largely fuelled by *Doctor Who*, *Top Gear* and David Attenborough's *Planet Earth* series, the *Daily Mirror* claimed the Doctor would definitely be accompanied by a new companion for the next series. The paper reiterated its red-top rival's story about Russell T Davies quitting at the end of the fourth series, but reported Head of Drama Jane Tranter as promising "*Doctor Who* will be around on BBC One for years to come".

While viewers enjoyed a compilation repeat of animated adventure *The Infinite Quest* – an enjoyable, kinetic romp that's all about location, location, location as the Doctor and Martha caper across alien deserts, jungles and icescapes in search of the keys to a fabled spaceship said to be capable of granting people's hearts' desires – plans were also announced to show the series' final episode on a big screen in Trafalgar Square as part of the weekend's major Gay Pride celebrations. In the end, the plan was scuppered by technical problems – which is a shame, as it would quite possibly have been the campiest thing anyone had seen all day.

Harold Saxon: worst prime minister since the last one

How you feel about *The Sound of Drums / Last of the Time Lords* will largely depend on how much of a hoot you think John Simm's Master is. Russell T Davies clearly thinks he's an absolute *scream* – so much so that he writes David Tennant out of the second episode (that's the *series finale*) almost completely, using the Master's laser screwdriver to reduce the Doctor to a wizened CG elf. In a bird cage. Part Gollum, part Dobby the House Elf, part Tweety Pie – whichever way you slice it, it's not dignified.

Davies has said the key to unlocking his writer's block on the Master was realising that, just as Roger Delgado was the suave, urbane foil to Jon Pertwee's velveteen dandy, so the twenty-first-century model had to be a mirror image of the tenth Doctor: quick, funny, mercurial, likes the sound of his own voice... Except, where the Doctor is a bit manic, the Master is a total fruit-loop. "The whole thing suddenly clicked – he's insane!" explained Davies. "And I don't mean that lightly; I don't mean ha-ha barking mad; I mean genuinely, profoundly, clinically insane, a psychopath, or more probably a sociopath, and a high-functioning one at that. As soon as I understood that, then I was dying to write him."[29]

Simm's interpretation of this is like Heath Ledger's Joker crossed with Jim Carrey: wise-cracking goofball one minute, cold-blooded killer the next. He is also the British Prime Minister. Harold Saxon is a name that had been seeded throughout the series since *The Runaway Bride*, and now he's been elected, thanks to some hypnotic trickery over the mobile phone network, to Downing Street – though he's not what you'd call a consensus politician, as evidenced by the fact he gasses his entire Cabinet to death at their first meeting (even Margaret Thatcher never went quite that far).

He also has a wife, Lucy (Alexandra Moen) who, in one of those uncomfortable shifts in tone Davies likes to throw at us occasionally, he physically abuses. And, *of course*, he wouldn't be the Master if he hadn't entered into an alliance with a bunch of dodgy aliens. In this case, the Toclafane, spinning, giggling, flying metal balls which are revealed to contain the heads of the last humans in the universe – an evolutionary last gasp after *Utopia* turned out to be not quite as advertised in the brochure. The moment one of these shells is cracked open to reveal the wizened skull inside is truly horrific, as is the notion they have devolved into giggling, amoral, infantile cyborgs driven only by a reckless desire to have fun – the by-product of a failed attempt by humanity to regress to childhood. (Davies originally created the creatures in 2004 to replace the Dalek in Robert Shearman's Series One script; if negotiations with the Terry Nation estate had broken down, you might be squeezing your bubble bath out of a Toclafane to this day.)

The Master announces that first contact with his new friends will take place aboard the *Valiant* – a flying UNIT aircraft-carrier that appears to have flown in from an episode of *Captain Scarlet*. He then proceeds to assassinate the US President live on television, though this seems barely more than a blip in the rolling news cycle in Davies' hyper-accelerated reality.

As a rift opens and millions of Toclafane fall to Earth and lay waste to entire cities – an event the Master chooses to soundtrack with Rogue Traders' "Voodoo Child" ("So here it comes, the sound of drums") – the fate of the world rests in the hands of one woman: Martha Jones. With the Doctor and Jack at the mercy of the Master, Martha watches London burning and declares: "I'm coming back."

Picking up the story a year later, *Last of the Time Lords* finds the Earth living under the tyrannical yoke of the Master, whose Saddam-style totems dominate the landscape. Yes, after all those bungled, back-of-a-fag-packet schemes of the 70s and 80s, this time he's only gone and bloody won. And to complete the Doctor's humiliation, he keeps him in a tent with a dog bowl outside, and wheels him round the *Valiant* deck in a wheelchair while singing along to the Scissor Sisters. It's hard to imagine Roger Delgado ever doing *that*.

At dead of night, Martha returns to England by boat, having travelled the world, so we're told, collecting the parts for a special Master-killing gun. If that seems like a maguffin too far, even for this show, it is. What she's really been doing is spreading the story of the Doctor; creating a new folklore in whispered stories of heroic deeds. This is a lovely idea, so it's a pity it ends up being in the service of the hokiest denouement imaginable, as Martha uses the Master's psychic phone network against him to restore the Doctor using the

Power of Hope. As Tweety Pie is set free from his cage, David Tennant is physically carried across the room on invisible wires for a biblical resurrection that's as close to a literal dues ex machina as you're ever likely to get. Then the Master is shot by his wife, and refuses to regenerate, just to annoy the Doctor. You've got to hand it to him, the guy knows how to bear a grudge.

This is a big, busy two-parter that strains to be epic, but is constantly hobbled by an excess of silliness. There are plenty of memorable moments: the cliffhanger is *massive*, the new series' first look at Gallifrey – a magical snow globe of citadels and burnt orange skies – doesn't disappoint, and no long-term fan can fail to enjoy the Master watching *Teletubbies* (a lovely nod to Roger Delgado chuckling at *Clangers* in *The Sea Devils*). The episodes also doubles as a Master origin story, including the rather wonderful revelation that his insanity – forged when he stared into the "untempered schism" of the time vortex – is soundtracked by a constant four-beat drum pattern exactly matching the intro to Ron Grainer and Delia Derbyshire's Doctor Who theme tune.

John Simm risked a glance into the untempered schism himself when he dared to go on to the *Doctor Who* forums to see what fans were saying about him. "I think some of the online community thought it was too jokey, too fun, too camp," he said. "But who gives a toss what they think? It's 200,300 people on the internet."[33] Fair enough.

Like Christopher Eccleston, Simm – better known for his working class northern everyman repertoire – is perhaps odd casting for an eccentric and, yes, campy alien aristocrat. But he attacks the role with vigour, and appears to be having a ball. That's surely no excuse, though, for sidelining your leading man – a hero to millions at the height of his powers – in his own season finale. When it's Tennant's name above the door, that just feels like bad business.

Captain Jack fares little better: having waited two years to return, he spends most of the second episode strung up in chains. And then there's the indignity of the strong hint that Captain Jack will one day evolve into gnarly old big 'ead the Face of Boe – surely an alarming thought for someone who moisturises as

much as John Barrowman. (Maybe it's short for the Face of Botox.)

Last of the Time Lords is, at least, a fitting swansong for Freema Agyeman. This is Martha's story, and Agyeman seizes it with both hands. Which only makes the decision to write her out at the end of it all the more puzzling. Davies claimed he'd painted himself into a corner and had nowhere else to go with Martha's unrequited love story, but that doesn't ring true. If the man feted for putting emotions at the heart of *Doctor Who* can't sustain a (fairly minor) subplot like that in the background to another series of adventures, then things have come to a pretty sorry pass. Even less convincing was Davies' assertion that the Jones family are so damaged by what they've seen the Master do that Martha "has to stay with them. That decides Martha's fate. You can't just sail off happily."[34] Well you *could*, given the massive re-set button at the end of the story that means none of the last year ever happened. But we'll let it go.

On July 2nd, the BBC issued a press release stating that Freema Agyeman was "set to make a triumphant return" in the fourth series. "Freema, who gained rave notices for her portrayal of Martha Jones, is also set to join the cast of *Torchwood*, where she will continue to play the character in three new episodes before returning to *Doctor Who* in the middle of the fourth series.

Russell T Davies was quoted as saying: "Series Three has gained outstanding reviews and Freema has been a huge part of that success, gaining rave notices for her portrayal of Martha. Now we are taking the character of Martha into brand new territory with a starring role in *Torchwood*."

As "triumphant returns" go, three episodes of *Torchwood* and a handful of New *Who*s perhaps left something to be desired. It's a bit like being called in to your boss' office to be told about your exciting forthcoming leaving do.

Who knows: maybe Martha was *always* intended as a one-series deal. Perhaps something happened behind the scenes that the rest of us aren't privy to. Or perhaps they decided she just wasn't working out. If it's the latter, then the viewing public clearly decided differently. But by that time, of course, it was too late, leaving Freema Agyeman's TARDIS exit second only to Christopher Eccleston's as *Doctor Who*'s biggest question mark. (Or third, if you count that big red question mark brolly Sylvester McCoy used to carry around.)

Kylie and the Doctor: "I'm very excited to be working with such a huge gay icon" (says Kylie)

On July 3rd, the BBC officially confirmed the least surprising antipodean casting news since the part of Skippy went to a kangaroo, as Australia's favourite boiler-suited grease monkey-turned-showgirl pop diva was announced as David Tennant's co-star in the 2007 Christmas special, *Voyage of the Damned*. Or, as they used to say in *Smash Hits*: Corks o'reilly, it's Kylie!

Ms Minogue was no stranger to *Doctor Who* in one way, as her best friend and creative director – yes, this is the first person ever to appear in the show who was famous enough to have her own creative director – William Baker was a massive fanboy, and had used the series for inspiration in some of Kylie's previous live shows. Her 2006 *Showgirl: The Homecoming Tour* had featured a variation on the Cybermen, while 2002's *Fever* shows had featured dancers inspired by the Raston Robot from *The Five Doctors*. At this rate, it was surely only a matter of time before Baker started dressing her as Susan Engel in *The Stones of Blood*.

"It's true, Will is my dear friend, and an absolute super fan of *Doctor Who*," Kylie (I'm sorry, it just doesn't feel right to call her Minogue) told *Doctor Who Magazine*. "We're talking a convention-goer here! Even before its recent revival, I was always hearing about it. I was very flattered to be invited to be part of the show – especially the Christmas episode."[35]

According to Baker, the idea for what would be Kylie's first acting role since her well-publicised battle with breast cancer had been hatched at the Series Three press launch. "My friend Mark Gatiss took me to the launch and Julie Gardner asked me if I thought Kylie might be interested. I knew that she'd enjoy the experience. Kylie wasn't 'a fan,' but knew *Doctor Who* through me and was aware of its success. She was really excited, but for her it was much more about getting back into acting

– and being part of such a quality production." Kylie had discussed the role over dinner with Gardner and Russell T Davies, during which she claimed she "just fell in love with the two of them".[35]

On the same day as Kylie's appearance was confirmed, the BBC Trust and BBC Executive issued their annual report, in which they stated that *Doctor Who* had "exceeded all expectations" and had become "a national talking point", adding that the show had made a significant contribution to a 19% uplift in worldwide TV sales. And then, on July 4th, the Corporation issued its third major *Doctor Who* casting announcement in as many days when, out of the blue, it was revealed Catherine Tate would be returning as Donna Noble for the whole of Series Four.

According to Jane Tranter, Tate had been invited to a meeting to discuss future BBC projects, and wouldn't stop talking about how much she'd enjoyed her stint on *Doctor Who*. Tranter then got on the phone to Julie Gardner and said she thought Tate might be up for doing a full series. Gardner arranged to travel up to London to meet her two days later, with Russell T Davies staying in Cardiff because, by his own admission, he didn't believe the talks would come to anything. By now Davies had already decided that the new companion would be a feisty northerner called Penny, so swapping her for a gobby temp from Chiswick wouldn't be too much of a stretch.

"I genuinely couldn't believe they'd asked me," said Tate. "I love the show and I love working with David, so I just thought it was a fantastic opportunity."[18]

Some fans genuinely couldn't believe they'd asked her either, with many taking to the message boards to bemoan the return of that shrill harpy from *The Runaway Bride*.

"I think it's a bit horrific," said Davies of the reaction in some quarters. "Of course people are free to say whatever they want, but it seems they're even freer when the subject is a successful woman. Successful women are considered to be fair game, especially by female columnists. Women beware women – that's the truest phrase ever said.

"The problem is that a lot of journalists go online to find their material, quoting the internet forums and that area of fandom that reacts as if the world is ending, as though by casting Catherine we're destroying the show. That's embarrassing, quite frankly. To be absolutely blunt, it's the only moment in my entire four years that I was actually ashamed of fandom. I'm not talking about fandom full stop; I'm talking about those dark corners that react in that way."[37]

By the end of the week, another unlikely name had entered the casting fray, with tabloid reports that 60s counterculture icon Dennis Hopper was in talks to join David Tennant and Kylie Minogue in the Christmas special. Russell T Davies later confirmed they had been in negotiations with the *Easy Rider* star, but the deal fell through and the part ended up going to Clive Swift instead. Say what you like about *Doctor Who*, but there aren't too many shows that would consider gas-huffing, obscenity-screaming Frank Booth from *Blue Velvet* and Richard Bucket from *Keeping Up Appearances* for the same role.

As Series Three kicked off on Sci-Fi in the US, the *Daily Mail* reported that David Tennant was in talks to play Hamlet for the Royal Shakespeare Company the following summer. This sent fans into another tailspin as they tried to digest the implications of Tennant playing the Prince of Denmark when he should have been filming *Doctor Who*. Was he leaving? Was the show being postponed? Cancelled? To be or not to be – that was the sodding question.

That week, Tennant could also be seen as a guest presenter at the Live Earth charity concert. If he really was re-joining the RSC, he would surely have the distinction of being the only Hamlet in the company's history to have introduced the Pussycat Dolls on stage at Wembley Stadium.

Colin Baker welcomed on to set of *Doctor Who*; BBC chairman orders immediate inquiry

As recording on *Voyage of the Damned* commenced in Cardiff, *The Guardian*'s annual Media 100 list of industry movers and shakers put Russell T Davies at No. 15. "The highest ranking TV producer in this year's 100, Davies has the ability to walk into any commissioning

editor's office and get any project he wants off the ground," said the paper. In with a bullet at 24, David Tennant was also considered to be "the most powerful actor in television".

That must have seemed like a very empty blandishment when, in late July, recording of the Christmas special was delayed so Tennant could attend the funeral of his mother, Helen, who had died of cancer on the 15th. In a show of compassion and unity far removed from the "dark corners" Russell T Davies had spoken of, fans across the world came together to raise more than £6,000 for the ACCORD hospice in Paisley.

"The fans' response when my mother died was... well, it puts it all into perspective, really," said Tennant. "People on the internet started raising money for the hospice that she died in, without any prompting, without me saying anything, just because of a job that I do. The fact that it obviously means so much to people, and that they want to do something like that for someone they've never met, is very humbling and terribly, terribly moving."[35]

The first publicity still from *Voyage of the Damned* showed David Tennant, resplendent in a tux, with Kylie Minogue in character as waitress Astrid Peth. According to *BBC News*, the costume led to some confusion when Kylie was mistaken for a real waitress by an elderly customer outside a Swansea hotel. One eyewitness said: "Kylie is an international star, but this old dear obviously didn't know who she was. She said to Kylie, 'Excuse me, love, is it too late for a cup of tea?' Kylie saw the funny side and laughed." Unlike the pensioner, presumably, when the tea failed to appear.

Night filming on the streets of Cardiff involved a major security operation, with large barriers being erected to keep unwanted visitors out. In the end, though, one of the only people who turned up to watch was Colin Baker, who was appearing in *Bedroom Farce* at the city's New Theatre – and, in a notable break from former BBC policy, they let him stay. In fact he stayed for hours, enjoying what Russell T Davies called "a lovely old chinwag". "I must confess to a moment of quiet envy seeing David, impeccable in his tuxedo, surrounded by bizarre aliens, doing his Time Lord thing," Baker wrote in his weekly column for the *Bucks Free Press*.

In August, Russell T Davies attempted to do what many *Doctor Who* producers had tried and failed to do before him – take a holiday. Inevitably, he ended up sitting around the pool doing script rewrites. (So if an upcoming episode featured a monster wearing speedos and flip-flops, that's probably why.) Back home, meanwhile, thoughts turned to Davies' possible successor, as *The Sun* claimed Steven Moffat was being lined up as the next show-runner, with James Nesbitt tipped as the eleventh Doctor.

Moffat took to *Outpost Gallifrey* to rubbish the story – or part of it, at least. "The James Nesbitt story is a total fabrication," he wrote. "Made up. A fantasy. Just a guy sitting at a desk and inventing stuff." Which was a bit rich, coming from him.

A few days later, another super soaraway *Sun* "exclusive" claimed that Sir Ben Kingsley was in "final negotiations" to play Davros in the upcoming series. A nice idea but the story, like Davros, didn't have legs.

Shortly afterwards, the BBC released details of some of the things that *would* be in the series, including a visit to the Ood's home-world and an encounter with Agatha Christie. "What a brilliant idea that Agatha Christie and Doctor Who should meet!" said Mathew Prichard, Christie's grandson. "Two characters whose contribution to British entertainment is absolutely unrivalled. As far as I know, my grandmother, Agatha Christie, never saw *Doctor Who*, but I am sure she would have been intrigued, excited and above all flattered by all this attention in 2007." (Do you think he always says "my grandmother, Agatha Christie"? I know I would.)

Though Susie Liggat would handle production duties on the story, the idea to include the world's best-selling novelist was Phil Collinson's. National Theatre regular Fenella Woolgar was cast in the coveted role at the suggestion of her friend, David Tennant, with whom she had appeared in Stephen Fry's Twenties-set *Bright Young Things*. "I suggested her for the part because I knew she would be fantastic," said Tennant. "It's the first time the producers have ever listened to any of my casting recommendations!"[38] (In fact, the episode would also feature Tennant's dad, Sandy, in a non-speaking role. "I came down to see David,"

he explained. "We'd been having a difficult family time, which has passed, and I felt it would be good for us to get together."[39])

The tabloid fantasy casting bingo continued with Joan Collins apparently in the frame for the Rani, according to the *News of the World*. "She's perfect for the role," said the inevitable "insider". "Like Alexis Colby with a sonic screwdriver." Honestly, you couldn't make this stuff u... oh, you just did.

Meanwhile, Sylvester McCoy told a New Zealand convention that Peter Jackson had told him Peter Davison was to return to *Doctor Who*. As casting rumours go, a major Hollywood director telling one Doctor about another Doctor was at least original.

Not to be outdone, *The Sun* weighed in with a report that David Bowie was to play a villain who kidnaps Agatha Christie. Bowie described the story as "tish and tosh" – which doubtless gave Russell T Davies a great idea for a spin-off starring Martha's sister and the computer geek from *Torchwood*.

Filming for *Planet of the Ood* required a quarry to be covered in fake snow, but the weather was so hot that David Tennant and Catherine Tate had to wear dark glasses to reduce the glare, and some of cast got burned from the sun reflecting off the white ground. "It's just one of the quirks of filming," mused Tennant. "Whenever you're meant to be hot, it's freezing cold. And whenever you're meant to be cold, the sun is beating down on you."[40]

At the end of August, the Royal Shakespeare Company confirmed that David Tennant would indeed be joining the company for its summer 2008 season in Stratford, playing Berowne in *Love's Labour's Lost* and Hamlet in, um, *Hamlet*. That same evening, Tennant followed in the footsteps of Jon Pertwee and Tom Baker when he switched on the annual Blackpool illuminations in front of a crowd of thousands of screaming fans. (They do love their Shakespeare in Blackpool.)

Readers with long memories and even longer evenings may recall a mini-drama all the way back in Volume I, when Baker and company forgot to bring the sonic screwdriver along. Tennant went one better by getting held up in traffic on the M6, at which point a police escort arrived to blue-light him into the town. Yes, while actual doctors on their way to medical emergencies had to sit on the motorway, TV's Doctor Who was rushed through for his date with Natalie Imbruglia, Natasha Bedingfield, Gareth Gates, McFly and Dale Winton. That's showbiz.

Rome burns down. Again.

September kicked off with Steven Moffat picking up his second[III] Hugo Award for *The Girl in the Fireplace*. "The best thing about winning a Hugo is that it's for *Doctor Who*," Moffat told the BBC's *Doctor Who* website. "'Cos years ago, when I was a tiny little *Doctor Who* fan, I bought this American magazine called *Starlog*. It was all about *Star Wars* and *Star Trek* (whatever those are) but the reason I bought it was a tiny box in the corner that said *Doctor Who*. I was so excited that this big important American magazine had an article about my favourite show! And it broke my heart. Because in the article it said, 'In all fairness, *Doctor Who* is unlikely ever to win a Hugo...' Two Hugos, I've got! Two Hugos for *Doctor Who*! And I'd say more, but I'm off to the *Starlog* offices to dance around and flick v-signs."

A couple of days later, the BBC issued a press release giving details of *Doctor Who's* short-term future: "After months of speculation, BBC One can confirm that the BAFTA-award winning *Doctor Who* will return for a fifth series in spring 2010," it chirruped, happily. "In 2009, *Doctor Who* will return with three specials starring David Tennant, with head writer, Russell T Davies. Jane Tranter, Controller, BBC Fiction, says: '*Doctor Who* is one of the BBC's best loved and most successful dramas. Its journey over the past three series has been one of the most ambitious and exciting that we have had, and I'm delighted to be able to confirm not only three exciting specials for 2009, but a fifth series in 2010.'"

Some fans, naturally, were less delighted by the idea of a "gap year", with just three specials instead of 13 episodes, resulting in another online bunfight. Others were more phlegmatic, pointing to the BBC's obvious long-term commitment to *Doctor Who*, to which the Chicken Licken fraternity responded with a considered "la la la can't hear you".

Behind the scenes, the BBC had pushed for a full series, but Davies and company stuck to

their guns so that Tennant could return to the stage and Davies could have at least a couple of days off. That was the plan, anyway.

The announcement coincided with *Doctor Who* winning Best Loved Show (again) and Tennant being named Best Loved Actor (again) at the TV Quick and TV Choice Awards. "Yeah, whatever," said Tennant in his acceptance speech. (Not really – but it *was* becoming something of a habit.)

That month saw the *Who* crew departing for the new series' first full overseas shoot at Rome's Cinecittà studios, which boasted a large-scale recreation of the city during, erm, Roman times, as featured in the HBO series, um, *Rome*. Can you guess where this particular *Doctor Who* adventure was going to be set? That's right: Pompeii. Well, when in Rome...

Plans to film at Cinecittà had almost been wrecked earlier in the summer when a huge fire had swept through the studio. "We woke up on the morning of the [second] recce to the news that Cinecittà had burnt down," recalled Phil Collinson. "Half of it had been destroyed, including some of the streets that we'd recced and wanted to use. But there was still enough standing to make it work, by slightly rethinking a few things."[41] So, they'd lost the lot – but not all of the lot. Just a lot of the lot.

David Tennant and Catherine Tate travelled out to Rome in a small party of five, including 19-year-old actress and model Karen Gillan, who was playing the minor role of a soothsayer. "It was such a great experience," said the teenager. "I got to know David and Catherine a little bit better than I would have if we'd just done it in Cardiff. They were really, really lovely and made me feel at ease."[42] You might even say that, for the duration of that flight, Gillan was *the Doctor's travelling companion*. If you wanted to.

Danny Hargreaves, the show's resident pyromaniac, had a less enjoyable journey, when the special effects truck got held up at customs at Calais. Honestly, you can't even drive a lorry full of explosives through an international border these days without the police getting all twitchy.

Late September marked the launch of the first series of *The Sarah Jane Adventures*. With Daniel Anthony's Clyde replacing the pilot's short-lived Kelsey, the series sees the

Bannerman Road Scooby Gang battling Slitheen in the classroom (let's be honest, Raxacoricofallapatorius' flatulent first family were always a shoo-in for this CBBC show), Gorgon nuns in a monastery and alien warriors in the local Laser Quest centre. It is, frankly, all rather a hoot. The standout episode – for grown-ups, anyway – is undoubtedly Gareth Roberts' *Whatever Happened to Sarah Jane Smith?*, in which our heroine is hoiked out of time and her place taken by Jane Asher (which was bad news for the Earth's chosen defender – though, on the plus side, the quality of her cakes improved dramatically). The flashbacks to Sarah Jane's 60s childhood are hugely rewarding for long-term devotees of the character, while monster-of-the-week the Trickster is a terrifying creation – especially for five o'clock in the afternoon. By turns poignant, heartwarming and chilling, the story – and the series in general – feels like a welcome return to a golden age of British children's telly.

"I have to say we were shocked by the response," said Lis Sladen. "Consistently number one in the timeslot, and well reviewed everywhere... Not bad for a pensioner, as my daughter kept reminding me."[10]

"The first series surprised everybody with just how good it was," said head writer Phil Ford. "We were blown away by how great it looked. Everything worked. The scripts worked, the actors' performances were brilliant, the special effects were great. It was a real thrill ride for kids. Kids hadn't really seen, for quite some time, a show like that."[37]

Meanwhile, another actress once in the frame for her own CBBC *Doctor Who* spin-off made her debut in a series definitely *not* for children: based on the real-life memoirs of the pseudonymous "Belle du Jour", *Secret Diary of a Call Girl* starred Billie Piper as a high-class London hooker servicing the peccadilloes of various kinky clients in scenes that didn't overly stretch the costume budget. In the first episode, Belle is hired by a man with a farmyard fetish, and ends up riding him like a horse, complete with saddle. As a way of shedding her *Who* girl image, it made Katy Manning's photo shoot with that Dalek look like a page from the *Blue Peter Annual*.

"It's high time someone didn't make another *Doctor Who* movie"

As Elisabeth Sladen rekindled adolescent stirrings in men of a certain age, October brought news of the return of another childhood favourite – the subject of Sarah Jane's First Contact, no less – as it was announced the Doctor would face the Sontarans in Series Four.

In Cardiff, the series opener was currently before the cameras – during which it became clear that Howard Attfield, reprising his role as Donna's father from *The Runaway Bride*, was too ill to continue. "Howard's agent had warned us that he'd been ill, but I don't think we realised quite how ill until he turned up at the read-through," said Russell T Davies. "It was chemotherapy. Howard recorded [scenes with Catherine Tate], and he was absolutely brilliant in them, but then it became clear he couldn't carry on. We went through a terrible few weeks of trying to see if we could shoot his scenes [for the series] in advance, but then he broke his leg, and that's when his wife said, 'I'm sorry, but I don't think he can continue'. I thought, should Donna's father die? Should I refer to this in the script? Or is that in bad taste? Howard was such a nice man."[37]

Attfield sadly passed away a few weeks later. Rather than re-cast the role, it was decided to introduce Donna's grandfather, Wilf – and Phil Collinson knew just the man for the job. Bernard Cribbins – crinkly-eyed friend to a generation of children thanks to his work on *The Railway Children*, *Jackanory* and as the voice of The Wombles – had just recorded a cameo for the upcoming Christmas special. Davies instinctively knew he'd be right for the role of Wilfred Mott – and so it was that 78-year-old Cribbins found himself back in the *Who* family, a full 41 years after helping Peter Cushing defeat the Daleks on the big screen.

Cribbins would perform many of his scenes with Jacqueline King, returning to the show as Donna's mother, Sylvia. "Wilf's relationship with Sylvia and Donna is absolutely brilliant," said Cribbins. "A nice rapport, too, with the Doctor. David is a total pro... It's important to me, because I'm a very, very old pro now. If people start pissing about, I get very cross."[43] Memo to production manager: please keep Cribbins away from John Barrowman.

After a fallow period in which it had let *The Sun* do all the running, the *Daily Star* suddenly piped up again with a variation on that old tabloid warhorse: the *Doctor Who* movie. According to the red-top, Tennant would be reunited with – but of course – Billie Piper. Which was handy, as the paper just happened to have several thousand file pics of Piper in her underwear. "It's all been hushed up," said a "source", "but yes, it's definitely happening." Or, to put it another way, it hasn't been hushed up, and it's definitely not.

Clearly on a roll, the paper was back a few days later with a report that Billie Piper – look, here she is and, oops, she's forgotten to bring her clothes again – and the Tyler family would be joining Martha, Sarah Jane, K-9 and Captain Jack to fight Davros in the upcoming series finale. Sounds like *someone* was having trouble letting go.

On October 15th, Freema Agyeman scooped the Female TV Star Award at the Screen Nation Film and TV Awards, and was also shortlisted, alongside David Tennant and the show itself, for the 2007 National Television Awards. "It means a lot that the public have taken so well to Martha Jones," said Agyeman.

The following day, *The Sun* took it upon themselves to reveal pretty much the entire plot of *Voyage of the Damned* – including the ending. They also revealed that Kylie would be "planting a smacker" on the Doctor. "BBC bosses have been desperate to keep it a secret – but *The Sun* has seen a copy," crowed the paper. It's good to see investigative journalism isn't dead – Woodward and Bernstein would be proud –

Later that month, the BBC confirmed what Peter Jackson had told Sylvester McCoy, who'd told a convention audience, who'd told the papers, was true: Peter Davison was indeed coming back as the fifth Doctor. Sort of. Davison was to star alongside David Tennant in a special Steven Moffat-scripted scene as part of that year's *Children in Need* telethon. "It is an honour for me to be able to make the connection between the fifth Doctor and the tenth Doctor," said Davison – even if, by his own admission, he could no longer do the buttons up on his old coat.

The suggestion to use Davison had, in fact, been Tennant's: he pitched the idea to Moffat when the pair ran into each other at an open air concert in London, and the writer signed up to the idea immediately. "He's one of my favourite Doctors," Moffat told *Radio Times*. "Until then, the Doctor had been a middle-aged man... even Tom Baker was your grumpy dad in a way... a funky, grumpy dad, but nevertheless the voice of authority. And suddenly the Doctor was dashing about, youthful and reckless. There's a strong argument to say he's the first of the modern Doctors. It was the end of the Gandalf Doctor, and more your genius-but-unreliable mate."

Recording on the TARDIS set, Tennant was so in awe of his childhood hero, he had to send a text afterwards apologising for being "tongue-tied". "We were probably feeling the same, in a way, for different reasons," said Davison. "You do obviously get a sense of coming home," he added. "But it was very much the new series.... There was a moment at first when I walked on, and felt that my costume was a little out of place in the surroundings. But as I grew into it again after an hour or so, that disappeared."[44]

Filming on the Sontaran story was now under way, the production team having scoured the country to find enough five-foot tall people to fill out the ranks of the clone army (Davies said he wanted to see "hordes of them, in war, in battle, fighting and loving it"[45]). The "nasty, brutish and short" aliens certainly had Catherine Tate fooled – it was only after working with them for several days she realised there were actually people inside. "I didn't know they were real!" she told *Radio Times*. "I thought they moved by electricity or something!"[46]

The story would see Freema Agyeman returning to the parent show following her stint on *Torchwood*. "It's a darker, harder show," said the actress of her experience in the Hub. "Coming back to *Doctor Who*, it's lighter-hearted, a lot more optimistic at heart." A year on, Martha was now a medic with UNIT. "I would describe her as having an older head on young shoulders," said Agyeman. "The Doctor is this benevolent being who's surrounded by violence. Wherever he goes, a certain amount of destruction follows. It's never fluffy bunnies and flowers, is it?"[43] She's not kidding: for one scene, Agyeman had to sit in a bath of gloop and emerge from beneath the surface; during filming, she mistimed her breathing and ended up with load of the foul stuff up her nose. Anyway, welcome back.

At the National Television Awards, David Tennant picked up his second Best Actor trophy, and the show was named Best Drama for the third consecutive year, but Agyeman lost out to *EastEnders'* Lacey Turner – rapidly becoming something of a national treasure herself – in the Best Actress category. Tennant dedicated his award to his mother and, talking to the press afterwards, spoke out in support of the recently deposed BBC One controller Peter Fincham and Head of Publicity Jane Fletcher, who had been forced to resign over a storm in a royal teacup in which a trailer for the documentary *A Year with the Queen* had given the impression Her Majesty had stormed out of a photo shoot (The issue appeared to be that the scenes in the trailer weren't in strict chronological order. Which they weren't. Because it was a trailer.) "Peter and Jane were fantastic supporters of our show and brilliant at their jobs," said Tennant. "It is a real shame they have gone." This presented the popular press with something of a quandary: David Tennant, the most popular actor in Britain, slagging off the knee-jerk trial-by-tabloid career execution they had themselves brought about. There was only one thing they could do: ignore it and print another picture of Billie Piper in her pants.

In November, Tennant and Agyeman celebrated the release of the Series Three DVD box set with a signing at HMV in Oxford Street. As people queued from dawn to get in, the store handed out wristbands to restrict access and avoid a crush. It was just like Beatlemania, but with way, way more carrier bags.

Five meets Ten: David Tennant goes wibbly-wobbly at the knees

With David Tennant and Peter Davison gracing the cover of that week's *Radio Times*, November 16th saw the long-awaited meeting of the tenth and fifth Doctors during the night's *Children in Need* appeal.

Steven Moffat must have been like a kid in a sandpit writing *Time Crash* which, as well as resurrecting a hero from his youth, allows him to have fun with all the wibbly-wobbly, timey-wimey implications of two Doctors bumping heads.

In among all the gags and nostalgia, there's time for a proper mini-adventure as the collision of two TARDISes threatens to blow a hole in the space-time continuum the size of a Belgium (the *exact* size of Belgium, in fact). But the real fun, as always with these occasions, is in the interaction between the two Time Lords. In this case, beaming Ten is overjoyed to see his old self, while the more waspish Five is irritated at the interruption to his day by this skinny young upstart.

Despite the gentle piss-taking ("Brave choice, the celery. But fair play to you: not many men can carry off a decorative vegetable."), this is an unashamed love letter to the Davison years. "You were *my* Doctor," says Ten – speaking, let's be honest, less for himself than the ten-year-old David Tennant and teenage Steven Moffat. Then, all too soon, it's time to go. "To days to come," says Five, doffing his panama hat. "All my love to long ago," grins Ten.

It's a lovely, funny, touching little scene guaranteed to bring a lump to the throat of anyone who ever missed youth club to follow the midweek adventures of the fifth Doctor. Though, to be honest, they had us at "Peter Davison" in the opening titles.

The scene – which leads directly into the Christmas special, with the RMS *Titanic* apparently crashing through the TARDIS wall – was watched by 11 million viewers, with another two million watching the repeat in the early hours of Saturday morning. The evening's other entertainment included Kylie performing a new track called "2 Hearts". (It's not what you think – the chorus is a disappointingly generic "2 hearts, beating together, I'm in love, I'm in love"; though I bet Will Baker tried adding a line about a binary vascular system as well.) John Barrowman also belted out a version of "Your Song", but, even so, it was still a night to remember.

Three days later, *Doctor Who* scooped the

Writers' Guild of Great Britain Award for Best TV Series. (Significantly, this was the only major award won by the series during its original run – and that had been for best children's series, whereas this one beat off all the competition from grown-up telly, too.)

Paul Cornell, Gareth Roberts and Steven Moffat collected the trophy on behalf of the Series Three writing team. Though the latter could ill-afford a night out: as recording of his Series Four two-parter began, Moffat was still working on his script for Steven Spielberg (CLANG!) and Peter Jackson's (CLANG!) new Tintin movie – so had only written the first half. "I remember Euros Lyn coming up to me and saying 'Soooo... broadly speaking, what happens in the rest of the show?'" said Moffat. "I had to give him a list of all the things and settings, which were in my head. I only had ten pages written, but I knew what I was going to do."[41]

On November 22nd – almost 44 years to the day since she had finally launched Doctor Who after a heroic battle with her BBC bosses – the television world was saddened to learn of the death of Verity Lambert. Russell T Davies was among the flood of talent paying tribute to a genuine TV pioneer. "When you start a new programme, a million things can go wrong," he said. "But when you look at what she did with that first episode, every decision she made was right. That is so rare. I think only that and the very first episode of Coronation Street are landmark pieces of television because, over the decades, the programmes still haven't basically changed from the first episode. And that's extraordinary.

"Their ambition was massive. In 1964, they had The Dalek Invasion of Earth! They conquered the planet with Daleks in a corner of Lime Grove! Nothing daunted her."[47]

Davies – who, along with David Tennant, had been due to present Lambert with the Lifetime Achievement Award at the Women in Film and Television event a couple of weeks later – gave a speech about his predecessor before the next script read-through. Among the cast was David Troughton, whose father had been an early beneficiary of Lambert's pioneering vision for the show. (The second Doctor's son, last seen in 1974's The Curse of Peladon, was a late replacement for 'Allo 'Allo star Sam Kelly, who had broken his leg in a car accident.)

On the streets of Cardiff, meanwhile, there was another blast from the past as fans spotted Billie Piper on set during filming for the new series. Shortly afterwards, an announcement on the BBC's Doctor Who website stated: "Following a series of unconfirmed reports, we're delighted to confirm that Billie Piper will return as Rose Tyler in Series Four of Doctor Who. Anything you may read elsewhere about when, how or for how long Rose returns to Doctor Who should be treated as pure speculation at this point." Especially if it's in the Daily Star.

"I knew I was coming back when I knew I was leaving," Piper later told Doctor Who Confidential. "We all made a little pact that I'd come back and do a few more. I really love lying to journalists... I'm sorry that I lied to fans, but I think it was a surprise worth waiting for."[48]

Someone taking a less circumspect approach to their career was Sean Pertwee, who placed a £50 bet with his local bookie on him succeeding David Tennant in his father's old job. With odds of 12-1, others soon started placing similar bets. "I'd definitely do it if I was asked," Pertwee told ITV Teletext, adding that his five-year-old son Alfred was a big fan of the show. Well, he certainly had the genes for it – not to mention all those old props his dad had nicked for him.

As a Voyage of the Damned trailer was shown in cinemas across the UK, David Tennant and Kylie Minogue posed in Leo and Kate mode for a Titanic-riffing Radio Times cover. Then Kylie posed in homage to another iconic image when she was photographed draped over a Dalek for a special Doctor Who Magazine cover shoot. Unlike the Katy Manning Girl Illustrated pics the shoot was designed to pastiche, Kylie kept her dignity covered with a shiny gold mini-dress – though it was still, by some way, the sexiest DWM cover ever (though issue 81, featuring three wizened old geezers from Shada, is pretty smokin', too). Unsurprisingly, the issue, which boasted an exclusive chat with Kylie, was the magazine's biggest-selling issue since its early days as Doctor Who Weekly (hey, even Kylie can't compete with free transfers).

In mid-December, the BBC announced that

Julie Gardner was to leave BBC Wales in January 2009; her replacement as Head of Drama – and the new executive producer of *Doctor Who* – would be multi-award-winning producer Piers Wenger, who until recently had been Head of Development at Granada Drama. "Working with Julie on *Doctor Who* over the next year will provide an invaluable insight into the secrets and success of the series," said Wenger. "I couldn't have a more inspiring leader."

That week's *Radio Times* included a notable first as a 90-second trailer for *Voyage of the Damned*, scheduled for December 15th, was given its own listing. In *The Guardian*, Charlie Brooker looked back over the TV highlights (and lowlights) of 2007, hailing *Blink* as "simultaneously the best piece of sci-fi and horror the BBC has produced in a decade," while, in the US, BBC/HBO's *Extras* Christmas special had its world premiere. The Ricky Gervais comedy – about a struggling "supporting artiste" – featured a cameo from David Tennant, whose Doctor confronted a slug monster (Gervais) called Shlong. He didn't win all those Emmys for just writing any old shit, you know.

There was a pleasing symmetry to the latest snippet of casting news, as Peter Davison's daughter, Georgia Moffett, was announced as appearing in Series Four. Davison recalled that, after he'd finished recording *Time Crash*, he'd phoned her up and said, "Right, that's it – it's your go." Asked by *Doctor Who Magazine* what it was like having a Time Lord for a dad, Moffett said: "I've never known any different. Funnily enough, I became good friends with Colin Baker's daughter – pure coincidence, actually – but then I sort of thought *everyone's* dad was Doctor Who!"[41] "I never really watched *Doctor Who* when I was younger," she added in an interview with *Radio Times*. "Because I'm a girl."[49] Fair enough.

The press screening for *Voyage of the Damned* was another starry affair, with David Tennant joined by John Simm, Elisabeth Sladen, Camille Coduri, Noel Clarke and guest stars Geoffrey Palmer, Clive Swift, Bernard Cribbins and Russell Tovey, as well as Richard Curtis and Nick Cave. That's right, Nick Cave – the high priest of heroin-chic gothic murder-blues and Bernard Cribbins, together at last. (Kylie

couldn't make it, unfortunately – she was busy being impossibly famous and glamorous in Japan.)

By now, Russell T Davies was less concerned with *this* Christmas than the next one. He'd already abandoned several ideas for the 2008 festive special, including one in which he hoped to persuade JK Rowling to guest-star as herself. David Tennant was concerned that the story, which would have seen the Harry Potter author transported back to a Victorian world of wizards and witches, seemed too much like a spoof, and persuaded Davies to drop the idea. With the script due in February, Davies hadn't come up with a suitable idea for replacement, and was starting to get a bit of a sweat on. Julie Gardner told him that, in a worst case scenario, they could forego a Christmas special next year, but both producers were conscious of not wanting to upset the new BBC One controller, Jay Hunt (they'd obviously seen his letter to Santa).

Thankfully, Catherine Tate stepped in to give everyone something else to worry about instead when, appearing on Jonathan Ross' Radio 2 show, she casually dropped into conversation that she thought the next season would be David Tennant's last. As press speculation whipped up into a frenzy, Tennant – ranked third in a list of The Coolest Men in Britain in that week's *Zoo* magazine, just behind Noel Gallagher and Steven Gerrard (Sylvester McCoy was scandalously overlooked yet again) – attempted to play it down, saying he'd made no decisions about the 2010 series. "Catherine Tate stitched me up good and proper," he told *BBC News*. "I started getting all these phone calls on Saturday lunchtime saying, apparently you're leaving *Doctor Who* – Catherine Tate's just announced it on Radio 2. 'Thanks, Catherine!' I said to her on Monday morning, 'Did you know you've caused a minor diplomatic incident?' She was completely oblivious."

There was another mild hoo-ha a few days later when a Christian evangelical group complained about the use of Messianic imagery – specifically a scene in which the Doctor ascends through the air in the arms of angel-like robots – in the forthcoming Christmas special. "The Doctor would have to do a lot more than his usual prancing around to be a messiah," said Stephen Green from *Christian Voice*. "He has to save people from their sins." Prancing around? He's not the one in a dress, mate.

And the Christians weren't the only ones who were upset. According to the *Daily Record*, the last survivor of the *Titanic*, Millvina Dean, was unhappy with the use of the doomed ship in *Voyage of the Damned*. "The *Titanic* was a tragedy which tore so many families apart," the 95-year-old told the paper. "I lost my father and he lies on that wreck. I think it is disrespectful to make entertainment of such a tragedy." A spokesman for the BBC insisted that no offence was intended, adding that the story was set on a spaceship called *Titanic*, rather than the actual ship. Though he was pretty sure someone *had* made a movie about that as well at some point.

Finally, Russell T Davies got into the Christmas spirit – which, this year, appeared to be "needless controversy" – when, asked which figure from history he thought would make a good Doctor, replied: "Hitler. He was stern and strong. He would be great." ("Okaaaay..." said the fans, cautiously. "Well it's better than David Hasselhoff, I suppose.")

Starship *Titanic*: what could possibly go wrong?

Two days before Christmas, David Tennant followed in Christopher Eccleston's skid marks (so to speak) as *Top Gear*'s Star in a Reasonably Priced Car. Tennant threw a Chevrolet Lacetti around the track in 1:48:8 – nearly four seconds faster than Eccleston, but .5 of a second slower than Billie Piper. Just in case you want to update your spreadsheet.

In *The Times*, an exclusive feature by superfan Caitlin Moran followed the evolution of *Voyage of the Damned* over the course of a year. Highlights of the piece included Julie Gardner announcing at the read-through that a *Sun* photographer had been found hiding downstairs in a cupboard, and Kylie taking one look at the dismal hotel bar reserved for her farewell drinks, declaring "This is awful – everyone follow me!" and leading the whole party, Pied Piper-like, to a different bar. "Ms Minogue would like to move her bar-tab to this bar," said one of her people. "There isn't a problem

with that that, is there?" Moran also witnessed Gardner, Russell T Davies and Phil Collinson in abject despair after watching the first edit of the special ("Too slow, it's too slow!" shouted Davies. "I feel like tearing my hair out by the end of every scene!"), with Gardner claiming that director James Strong – who'd recently become a dad – was suffering from physical exhaustion. By the end, of course, all three producers are cock and, indeed, a-hoop with the result, and a Merry Christmas for all was guaranteed.

Or was it? As an exercise in *Doctor Who-does-disaster* movie, *Voyage of the Damned* must be considered a success... as it's 71 minutes long, and a bit of a disaster.

Okay, that's harsh. There's fun to be had from seeing the standard disaster film tropes given a sci-fi twist. But in sticking so closely to one particular source – it's The Poseidon Adventure in Space, basically, with the survivors of a meteor strike making their way through the crippled spaceliner SS *Titanic* before it crashes into the Earth in a nuclear fireball – there's a danger the audience will feel like they've seen it all before.

Part of the problem is the characters. Yes, we know the party of survivors needs to include certain archetypes – the big-hearted loser, the self-serving shit who won't listen to reason, the miniature cyborg with a face like a red conker (okay, that one's new) – but the problem is they feel *so* much like archetypes, it's hard to believe in them as people, or care much whether they live or die. (In the event, Davies dispatches three of them in the same scene; maybe he was getting fed up of them as well.)

Astrid Peth is a curiously muted presence, too. Russell T Davies is normally brilliant at writing women – and here he had the advantage of writing for a specific actress. But Astrid – a waitress who dreams of adventure among the stars – offers precious little for the episode's big star to get her teeth into. And, it should be said, it takes a special sort of skill to make someone as beautiful as Kylie Minogue look that... well, daggy, but that Lily Savage "do" isn't doing her any favours at all. And then, to top it all, she has to share her heroic death scene with a bright yellow forklift truck, like an unusually tragic episode of *Bob the Builder*.

Unlike most disaster movies, this one has an

antagonist in the form of cruise line owner Max Capricorn, who is planning to destroy the *Titanic* – and the Earth – as part of an insurance scam. (Quite a high stakes one, as it turns out, since he's *on the ship*.) Capricorn is of such advanced years, he's now little more than a head poking out of a life-support system, a risibly cheap-looking prop not helped by George Costigan's mugging performance – or, indeed, his preposterous death on the end of Kylie's forklift.

But the worst is yet to come, as the *Titanic* is on a collision course for – wait for it – Buckingham Palace. With the Doctor pulling on a big comedy lever, the ship misses the royal household by inches, leading to perhaps the most misjudged scene in all *Doctor Who* as the Queen – in curlers and pink fluffy dressing gown – stands on the palace roof shouting "Thank you, Doctor, thank you. Happy Christmas!"

There are some nice touches. Clive Swift is good value as Mr Copper, an alien historian who gets all his facts about Earth wrong; the reveal that London is deserted following the previous two years' Christmas Day disasters is a good gag; the Heavenly Hosts – think the art-deco droids of 1977's *Robots of Death* doing a Nativity play – are an impressive creation. And hey, look everybody, it's Bernard Cribbins! There is also a lovely postscript in which the Doctor tries – and fails – to bring Astrid back from the dead (what was that about him having a Messiah complex?). "She's just atoms, Doctor," says Copper. "An echo with the ghost of consciousness. She's stardust." So the Doctor sends the stardust out into space. "You're not falling, Astrid," he tells her. "You're flying." How's that for a bit of Christmas magic?

Sadly, it's too little, too late. Lacking a real sense of urgency to drive the story forward, and saddled with cardboard cipher characters, a woeful villain and an underused superstar guest (not to mention HRH in her bloody curlers), *Voyage of the Damned* is holed below the waterline. Or spaceline. Or whatever.

According to Phil Collinson, Astrid's death scene had presented more than a few practical problems. "The main difficulty is you've got an actress who has to drive a vehicle, and she's not able, for safety reasons, to drive that vehicle," he explained. "It's Kylie Minogue, so you're not

exactly going to say, 'Would you mind going off for three weeks to get an HGV licence?'"[50] Well, you know what they say, Phil: don't ask, don't get.

The special garnered mixed reviews. The *Mirror's* Jim Shelley complained "the plot was a mess... and it descended into noise and bluster". Tim Teeman in *The Times* went further: "Here's a bit of seasonal sacrilege," he wrote. "*Doctor Who* sucks." Ouch. On the other hand, the story was enough to convince another self-confessed *Who*-sceptic, the *Daily Telegraph's* James Walton, of the error of his ways: "I can't imagine how this episode could have done its job any better," he admitted.

The big news, though, was the ratings. With the seemingly irresistible combination of Kylie Minogue and David Tennant bringing in a truly – oh go on then – titanic 13.31 million viewers, *Voyage of the Damned* was the second-most watched TV programme *of the whole year*. (The most watched, for those who care, was the same day's episode of *EastEnders*, in which freckle-faced cuckold and self-confessed *Doctor Who* fan Bradley Branning found out his wife Stacey had been cheating on him with his own father. It wasn't so much the betrayal that bothered him as the fact that, in all the uproar, he'd forgotten to tape *Voyage of the Damned*.)

Torchwood: the second coming

On New Year's Day, David Tennant was a guest at Billie Piper's wedding to the actor Laurence Fox. Declining big money offers for exclusive pics from the celeb gossip mags, the couple tied the knot in a low-key ceremony at a small parish church in Eastbourne, before decamping for a few drinks and a bite to eat at the local pub. As well as Tennant, the wedding party included Piper's first husband, Chris Evans, and numerous members of the Fox acting dynasty.

One famous fox who wasn't on the guest list was Basil Brush (boom and, indeed, boom), but the 70s Saturday teatime TV staple *was* back on telly with his own show which, from early January, included a new spoof segment called *Dr Why? The Ultra Inquisitive Time Fox*, in which Basil dressed as the tenth Doctor. Thirteen million people watching the

Christmas special was one thing – but a *Doctor Who* sketch on *The Basil Brush Show*? It really was a return to the golden age.

January's issue of *Doctor Who Magazine* was notable for a fractious interview with *Voyage of the Damned* guest star (and celebrated Dennis Hopper avatar) Clive Swift, in which journalist Benjamin Cook gets off to a disastrous start with the irritable thesp. "Hello, Clive. I'm recording this interview on tape, if that's okay," Cook begins, to which Swift replies, "I think you'll find that *proper* journalists know short-hand," and it all goes downhill from there.

"I'm quite aggrieved," grumbles Swift. "Why should I do this? I'm not getting paid, am I?" Cook attempts to win him back with some innocuous questions about his character in the Christmas special, to which the actor snaps: "Have you read the script? That's what I perform. *You* can tell them about my character. What a silly question."

Having stumbled through the rest of the encounter – and been treated to a lengthy hard-sell for Swift's one-man show – Cook attempts to wrap up with a final question. "There's no reason why I should talk to you at all, so you shouldn't push it," warns Swift. "I know that you all think that this is a big world, this *Who* business. But it isn't. There are much bigger things than this."

Well, that's us told.

As the *Who* showrunner discussed his life and career on the set of the TARDIS for BBC Four's *Mark Lawson Talks to Russell T Davies*, the Corporation announced that its new iPlayer catch-up service had been accessed more than a million times since its Christmas launch, with *Voyage of the Damned* taking the top spot. The freedom to watch *Doctor Who* whenever and wherever you wanted would have been beyond the wildest dreams of fans in the 70s and 80s, when a well-thumbed Terrance Dicks paperback was the nearest you could get to TV on-demand. And, for that matter, it made it easier to watch *Torchwood* (or harder to miss it, depending on your point of view).

The second series of adventures for Cardiff's much-tolerated alien bug-hunters is a significant improvement on its predecessor, in that you don't get quite the mercurial rise and fall of quality that vexed Series One. *Kiss Kiss, Bang Bang* by Chris Chibnall relies upon the not-so

original idea of "What if *Buffy*'s Angel and Spike were lovers?", but it's an entertaining 45 minutes, including a rousing bar-fight between John Barrowman and guest star James Marsters. Helen Raynor's *To the Last Man* – in which Tosh finds love with a cryogenically frozen World War I soldier – is way more affecting than anything with that premise deserves to be; told largely in flashback, Chris Chibnall's *Fragments* is a satisfying origin story of how the Torchwood team were recruited; and *Exit Wounds*, in which Tosh and Owen die, is surprisingly moving. (Before they go, they even clear up some important continuity issues from *Aliens of London,* which is thoughtful.)

Elsewhere, though, the old problems remain. The Torchwood players are deplorably bad at their jobs; Gwen fails to grasp the concept of a *secret* alien-hunting organisation, and tries to spill the beans about Torchwood's true mission with a depressing regularity; Owen is still so unlikeable that, even when he's killed and spends the rest of the series as a dead man walking, it's hard to care; Freema Agyeman is largely wasted during her three-episode stint as Martha Jones; and a sometime-inability to grasp basic plot-structure metastasizes in *Adrift*, which is almost spellbinding in the way calamity ensues because Jack refuses to tell Gwen, for no sane reason, at all: "Sometimes, people come back through the Rift damaged, and I've set up a hospital to help them."

The theme music is still great, though.

If *Torchwood*'s mix of sex and spacemen often seemed uneasy, it was nothing compared to the latest effort from fan-producer/director Bill Baggs. At the end of the 90s semi-professional video boom, Baggs had directed three *Auton* films (the first featuring a young Reece Shearsmith) pitting the Nestene Consciousness against UNIT. In 2003, he had resurrected another classic 70s monster for a film tentatively (and, indeed, tentacledly) titled *Zygon*, before deciding he was unhappy with the results and shelving the project. Following script changes and a re-write, the pithily named *Zygon: When Being You Just Isn't Enough* was finally released in early 2008, earning the distinction of being the first *Doctor Who* spin-off to be marketed as an erotic thriller. In reality, it struggles to be either of those things, but does feature a fair amount of nudity and some tepid humping. Technically, of course, it's not the first time we've seen a Zygon naked – it's their default state – but it *is* the first time we've seen them like that while taking human form. Which version you prefer is your own private business.

By the time he'd finished with Series Four, Russell T Davies had just three weeks to write the 2008 *Doctor Who* Christmas special. Then more rewrites on later episodes in the series were required. And then he got ill with chickenpox and bronchitis. But apart from that, it was all going really well. In late January, it was revealed that *ER* star Alex Kingston would be guest-starring in Steven Moffat's Series Four story as the mysterious River Song. "Alex Kingston is a proper, big, sexy star who makes you feel like a fat, clumsy, Scottish git just by being in the same room," said Moffat. "Or that could just be me. I introduced myself to her on the set, and she smiled at me, and parts of my face *actually melted*."[41] It still wasn't as sexy as meeting Peter Davison, though.

Meanwhile, the call sheet for filming on the series' epic finale was starting to look like a Who's Who of New *Who*, as David Tennant and Catherine Tate were joined by Billie Piper, Freema Agyeman, Elisabeth Sladen, John Barrowman, Camille Coduri, Noel Clarke, Adjoah Andoh, Bernard Cribbins, Eve Myles, Gareth David-Lloyd, Tommy Knight, Penelope Wilton, John Leeson and Alexander Armstrong. "We were bringing together all the people that I've had a good time with," said Tennant. "It's as though it were written just for me! I think everyone genuinely loves the characters that they play, so was just keen to be part of it. There were some big personalities in there. Everyone sort of bounced off each other."[43]

Elisabeth Sladen admitted she "adored" John Barrowman. But did he, asked *Doctor Who Magazine*, live up to his reputation and... you know... "Expose himself? Not to me," said Sladen. "To everyone else, but not to me. I'm taking it as a compliment."[51]

"No way am I going to whop it out for Sarah Jane Smith," insisted Barrowman, gallantly. "It'd be like whipping it out for the Virgin Mary! I did get it out quite a few times, but she was looking the other way."[43] And they say chivalry is dead.

As a specially-shot trailer for the new series debuted in Cineworld cinemas, the BBC announced Phil Collinson would be taking up a new role as Head of Drama at BBC Manchester. "Phil has been the secret hero of *Doctor Who* for the past four years," said Russell T Davies, "and we'll miss him more than I can say."

Those ace investigative reporters at *The Sun*, meanwhile, had managed to get hold of two complete Series Four scripts, using all their journalistic powers of opening the post. "Top brass hit the roof after hearing about our leak," thundered the tab. "An insider said, 'Bosses are fuming – this is the last thing they would want to happen'. But they needn't worry – we won't be ruining it for the show's 14 million fans by serving up all the twists and turns of the plot." Unlike last time, then.

And in *EastEnders*, things were looking up for Bradley Branning. As part of her efforts to make amends for her infidelity, Stacey had decided to treat her husband to a day out at a *Doctor Who* exhibition called The Time Lord Revisited. Look, I know she shagged his dad and everything, but even she surely didn't deserve *that*.

Richard Dawkins questions existence of Tom Baker

Russell T Davies finally started writing the 2008 Christmas special on March 4th – a full six days before production on it was due to start. He eventually handed it in on the 17th – then immediately had to start work on the next series of *Torchwood*. (Not as a punishment, you understand – although "I must not be late handing in my *Doctor Who* assignments" written 500 times *would* have been one of *Torchwood*'s better scripts.)

On the same day, prominent Labour Party supporter David Tennant introduced Prime Minister Gordon Brown at a gala fundraising dinner. "When I was told I was going to be introduced by a man who spent a lot of time on another planet who comes from another century, I thought it was Boris Johnson," joked the PM, with his trademark comic flair.

At the end of the month, the Series Four wrap party doubled as Phil Collinson's and Catherine Tate's leaving do – though there were still outstanding odds and sods to be filmed, including one of this year's by now obligatory episode twelve celebrity cameos from evolutionary biologist, prolific God-rubbisher and, lest we forget, the current Mr Lalla Ward, Professor Richard Dawkins. "People were falling at his feet," Russell T Davies told *Radio Times*. "We've had Kylie Minogue on that set, but it was Dawkins people were worshipping."[52] Yes, because he does so love a spot of worship.

Doctor Who was now scheduled to return to BBC One on Saturday, April 5th at the new, earlier time of 6.20pm. Attending a television conference, Russell T Davies made no bones about the fact he thought the Beeb had "cocked up" the scheduling, and predicted it could cost the show around a million-and-a-half viewers. "The BBC says it will do well," he grumped. "Well, we'll see, but I think I'm right." (The following week, it was reported that later episodes would be moved to a later slot. File under: job done.)

Launch week saw the *Radio Times* offering a choice of four different *Doctor Who* covers – they certainly knew a completist geek when they saw one coming; the issue also contained details of Saturday's BBC Four Verity Lambert tribute evening, made up of *The Naked Civil Servant*, three episodes of *The Daleks* and episodes of *Minder* and *Jonathan Creek*, alongside a special documentary on her life and work.

As Tennant and Tate threw themselves headlong into the pre-season publicity merry-ground – including an appearance on *Friday Night with Jonathan Ross* in which Tennant struggled to get a word in – Tate explained a bit more about her character. "She's lost none of her feistiness, but she's better for knowing the Doctor," said the actress. "The writers have rounded her out from a shouty fishwife to someone vulnerable and emotional."[38]

SFX, meanwhile, asked Russell T Davies to explain his contrasting statements that the new series was going to "lighten up", while also offering "some of the darkest stuff we've ever done". "Easy – I just say whatever I fancy on the day!" beamed Davies. "You must realise this about interviews – you just say whatever you fancy. But also, underneath that, all those things are true as well. How much did I know by saying, 'We're going to lighten up,' how many fans that would piss off? I love that! That's not proper fans, just a small corner of

fandom, the ming mongs. You know that the ones who'll be upset at me anyway will be more upset, so that's fine by me – marvellous! But nonetheless, there's a truth buried there. If you take *Human Nature* and *Blink* as a template and then it gets darker from there, you've got nowhere left to go. You've actually got the wrong show for seven on a Saturday night."

The magazine also asked him if he'd been surprised by the Catherine Tate backlash. "Not really," he shrugged. "Successful woman in comedy. Guaranteed, absolutely guaranteed, to polarise. Tabloid critic fodder. It was vitriolic. What are you going to do? Cast someone according to what the message boards are going to say? I'm not sure [Catherine] would even be aware that it exists – and quite right too."[53]

In the *Daily Telegraph*, two journalists fought it out in an inter-generational Time Lord smackdown to answer the pressing question of who was the greatest Doctor Who: Tom Baker or David Tennant?

"David Tennant woos his audience like a young man standing in a downpour proffering a bouquet – the gesture, however well meant, is more about him than its intended recipient," wrote Dominic Cavendish, advocate for the man in the stripy scarf. But Sarah Crompton argued the fourth Doctor was simply "too strange". "Baker's performance, though vivid, is so mannered and eccentric it is hard to care about him... But Tennant brings real intelligence to his portrayal... he is capable of expressing everything from love to awe to the chill of fear at planetary extinction."

Clearly, there was only one way to solve this once and for all: fiiiiight!

In *Partners in Crime*, David Tennant and Catherine Tate reprise *The Runaway Bride's* screwball comedy partnership for another light-on-its-feet series opener designed to lure unsuspecting sci-fi-phobes in with some gentle romping. (No, not *that* sort of romping. After a year of Martha making doe eyes across the TARDIS, Donna makes it very clear she's not interested in getting it on with a "long streak of alien nothing".)

It's not as good as *Smith and Jones*, mainly because the Big Concept – people's excess fat "literally walks away" after being turned into cute little alien critters called the Adipose – is just too twee, and lacks menace. But, sticking firmly to the rules laid down in *Rose*, that's not really what the episode is about – it's about establishing the relationship between the Doctor and his new significant other. And in that it works beautifully.

When we last took our leave of her, Donna had resolved to change her life – to stop wittering about Posh and Becks and Pringles and generally *carpe diem*. Eighteen months on, it hasn't really worked out that way: "I did try," she says, in one of those lovely Davies soliloquies that succeed in nailing the human experience in an almost offhand manner. "I went to Egypt. I was going to go barefoot and everything. And then it's all bus trips and guidebooks and 'Don't drink the water', and two weeks later you're back home."

So now she's turned detective to seek out the only man who can offer her a taste of *real* adventure. After some comic near-misses, Tennant and Tate's first scene together – an elaborate, semi-improvised mime in the middle of a hostage situation – is among the funniest set-pieces in all *Who*.

Main guest star Sarah Lancashire is deliciously arch as the villainous Miss Foster, "outer space Supernanny" (according to Donna) to the waddling little lumps of lard (the Adipose crowd scenes were the first TV application of technology developed for *The Lord of the Rings* trilogy). When the creatures' impressive, *Close Encounters*-style mothership (geddit?) arrives to collect the kids, Miss Foster's services are dispensed with by dropping her off the side of a building – for which the law of gravity is temporarily replaced by the Wile E Coyote Principle. (To wit: An object will remain hovering in the air until such time it makes the mistake of looking down.)

As an action-adventure, *Partners in Crime* is a bit lightweight. As a satire on the weight-loss industry, it's a bit toothless (unlike the Adipose, who each have one adorable, iddy-biddy little fang). But as a shop window for the new TARDIS team, it's a blast, with Catherine Tate instantly proving her critics wrong as an older, wiser, less shouty, less... *fishwifey* Donna, who Russell T Davies clearly adores writing for.

The story also foreshadows some of the recurring themes of the fourth series, including the disappearance of the Adipose breeding planet, and the fact the bees are all vanishing. But the real jaw-on-the-floor revelation comes moments from the end, as Donna leaves a message with a blonde woman in the street, who then turns to the camera and reveals herself to be... Rose Tyler. O and, indeed, MG.

Piper's surprise cameo was removed from press preview copies of the episode and, according to Russell T Davies, all three producers spent the whole day fretting that the trimmed version was the one they'd broadcast. Thankfully, someone remembered to press the right button, and so Billie Piper's return was seen as scheduled by 9.14 million viewers, making *Doctor Who* the highest-rated nonsoap of week. In his Cardiff flat, Russell T Davies sat down to eat his words, with plenty of relish. The figures – and the episode in general – generated loads of positive media coverage, suggesting that, four series in, the *Doctor Who* bubble was not about to burst any time soon. Even Michael Grade was overcome by a fit of enthusiasm: "The whole thing is absolutely magical," he told Five Live. "I love it! It's brilliant." Shameless, absolutely shameless.

That week, it was announced that the show would be the subject of a special concert as part of the summer's Proms series at the Royal Albert Hall – mixing the music of Murray Gold with celestial works by lesser composers such as Holst and Prokofiev. Meanwhile, the Cybermen were spotted in a snow-covered graveyard during filming for the Christmas special. That's April in Cardiff for you.

By now, planning had also begun on the 2009 specials, with Gareth Roberts commissioned to write the first one – likely to be broadcast around Easter, even though, privately, the production team had serious concerns about the turnaround time if recording didn't start until January. Phil Ford, who was now *The Sarah Jane Adventures'* co-producer, was also pencilled in for one of the slots. The original plan had been for Russell T Davies to write all the specials – until BBC One had thrown a spanner in the works by commissioning a *Torchwood* mini-series for 2009. (That's right: *Doctor Who's* runtish, weirdly popular sibling was getting promoted to the flagship channel. What next – a K-9 and Company feature film?) Julie Gardner insisted Davies take a co-credit on the stories, both to reflect his input and also to help attract big name guest stars on what would be a reduced budget.

Series Four's sophomore episode, meanwhile, was written by newcomer James Moran, a long-time *Who* fan who had been commissioned on the strength of his horror comedy *Severance*, with a specific brief to explore the ethical dimensions of time travel. Hence *The Fires of Pompeii's* skilful blend of *The Aztecs* – *Doctor Who's* original discourse on the moral implications of changing history – and *Asterix. The Azterix*, if you will. Or not.

For her first (proper) trip aboard the TARDIS, the Doctor attempts to take Donna to ancient Rome, but ends up in Pompeii, the day before Vesuvius flips its lid. (He really is rubbish at first dates.) Using the old maxim that one death is a tragedy, a thousand deaths a statistic, Moran cleverly lifts the event out of school textbooks[IV] and into the realm of real human drama by focusing on one ordinary Pompeiian family. (Positively a sitcom family in fact, complete with domineering mother, hen-pecked father – the always fabulous Peter Capaldi, last seen in Volume I bombarding the *Doctor Who* production office with sackloads of fan mail – and feckless teenage layabout son. Though, granted, the daughter turning to stone never happened in *My Family*.) If that makes the story sound small and domestic, it's anything but: this is as close to Hollywood blockbuster mode as *Doctor Who* gets. Animated stone warriors the Pyrovile are a literally petrifying CG creation, the Cinecittà sets look fabulous and the Vesuvius money shot doesn't disappoint.

It's also another great episode for Donna. Whether ingratiating herself with the locals ("You got mates? Do you go hanging about round the shops? TK Maxximus?") or berating the Doctor ("Oi, don't get clever in Latin!"), she's a scream. But Tate also proves she's much more than comic relief – in the Barbara Wright role as the Doctor's conscience, she is stunning, refusing to accept his assertion that he can't change a "fixed point" in time and literally begging him through her tears to save someone: "Please. Not the whole town. Just save *someone*." And the fact Donna has no choice but to help the Doctor actively *cause* the

eruption is a great twist that adds another layer to the drama.

Funny, scary, exciting and ultimately rather moving, *The Fires of Pompeii* is surely what twenty-first century *Doctor Who* was born to do: match Hollywood visuals with the series' trademark subversive wit and big, beating heart. The result is irresistible.

"My brain hurts" "I think you're sitting on it"

Planet of the Ood's mission is to explain how everyone's favourite noodle-noggined ballcock wranglers can be such a subservient race. And, er, that's about it, really. (Dig deep enough down into the subtext of the story, and you'll find there's also a subtle allegory about slavery tucked away in there somewhere. If it hadn't been for 95% of the dialogue, it would have slipped right under my radar, too.)

Of course, the Ood weren't born to be slaves – as the Doctor points out, no race that subordinate would ever be able to evolve in the first place. Trouble is, it's not really a good idea to draw attention to a race's potential evolutionary handicaps – and then reveal they carry their brains around in their hands like teenagers welded to their smartphones. I mean, where do they put them when they're doing... well, anything? ("Just hold my brain for a minute, will you love, I need to reach the biscuit tin.") You'd think they might at least have invented some revolutionary form of brain-housing device – like, ooh, I don't know, a breast pocket?

And speaking of brains, the episode puts a lot of effort into building up the riddle of what's inside the mysterious Warehouse 15. It's obvious from the script it's some kind of Ood central brain thing – a bit like the Nestene Consciousness – but as it's kept so tightly under wraps until the big reveal, you can't help but wonder exactly what this big, world-shattering secret is going to be: a returning enemy? A remnant of old Gallifrey? Colin Baker's lucky underpants? But no: turns out it *really is* just a massive brain – I mean, you might think Stephen Hawking and Mr Spock have big brains, but they're like Homer Simpson next to this thing.

The scene in which oily corporate slavemaster Klineman Halpen learns he's been drinking Ood DNA in his hair restorer tonic is also quite the silliest thing since 50s crooner Billy necked a glass of Chimeron juice back in 1987's *Delta and the Bannerman*. I mean, I'm no biochemist, but I suspect it would take a hell of a special brew to transform a human being's entire physiognomy into a complete alien species without him noticing until the moment his face falls off and he vomits up a new cerebral cortex. (Don't get me wrong, we've all brought up some pretty nasty things after a night on the poison, but this is something else.)

Despite all that, there's a lot about *Planet of the Ood* to like – the planet of the Ood itself being one. Cos everyone loves an ice planet, right? And there's no denying the brilliant white vistas of the Ood-Sphere mark a welcome change of location from Cardiff city centre. Though the show, as always, is careful to keep its feet on the ground – where else would you find people on a distant planet in the far future talking about Persil balls and doing Homer Simpson impressions? (For more on this, see Professor Jon Pertwee's paper, "If The Yeti Won't Come to the Loo in Tooting Bec, You have to Take the Loo in Tooting Bec to the Himalayas", Cambridge University Press, 1974.)

There is also something pleasingly old-skool about the early scenes, in which Tate and Tennant basically wander about looking at stuff. (It's shades of director Graeme Harper's *Revelation of the Daleks*, too, in the scene in which the Doc and his companion discover a dying but feral creature in the snow – except, this not being an Eric Saward story, Donna doesn't pick up a massive stick and batter the Ood about the brains with it like Peri did.)

The episode was written by Keith Temple, who had served his apprenticeship on the likes of *Emmerdale*, *Heartbeat*, *Casualty* and *EastEnders*. Susie Liggat had worked with him before, but hadn't realised he was a *Doctor Who* fan. "That was good, to have Keith out of the closet," she said, before clarifying: "As a *Doctor Who* fan. He's probably one of the only straight boys on the show, bless him."[54]

Sadly, Temple's script seems to run out of steam somewhere around the midway point, padding out the second half of the episode with endless shots of people running around a factory shouting and firing guns, intercut with the occasional Poignant Bit that might as well have a caption saying "Cry now!" plastered across the screen. Catherine Tate duly obliges by turning on the waterworks again, while listening to the Ood's *Les Mis*-style big choral number. (Did I mention it's also a musical?) Still, I guess if you're going to carry your brain around in your hand, wearing your heart on your sleeve is no great shakes.

In late April, David Morrissey was unveiled as the Christmas special's main guest star. Best known for roles in the likes of *State of Play* and *Blackpool* (where he starred opposite a rising talent called David Tennant), and for playing Gordon Brown in TV film *The Deal* – not to mention trying to live down his turn as the male lead in *Basic Instinct 2* – Morrissey was one of Britain's most in-demand actors. Though it's fair to say the tabloids weren't as excited by him as they had been by Kylie, and demand for a photo shoot with him draped provocatively over a Dalek was noticeably thin on the ground. (According to some sources, and later confirmed by his agent, Martin Clunes had originally been cast in the Morrissey role, apparently pulling out just days before filming began. Maybe he was still smarting about the skirt they'd made him wear in 1983's *Snakedance* – a fashion faux pas that continues to pop up on those Look How People Used To Be Slightly Different shows on an almost weekly basis.)

On BBC One, the omens for *The Sontaran Stratagem / The Poison Sky* weren't good, publicity shots of the Sontarans in garish, plasticky-looking blue armour and the fact that the early season action double bills had so far tended to err a bit on the rubbish side conspiring to dampen expectations. But, for the first episode-and-a-half at least, this is actually pretty good. From the perfectly-formed pre-titles teaser – in which a journalist digging the dirt on the company behind a revolutionary SatNav system ends up taking a long drive off a short river bank – to the audacious sight of the Sontarans performing a haka, this may be "frothy nonsense", as Ricky Gervais memorably described *Doctor Who* in the *Extras* Christmas special, but it's frothy nonsense of a gloriously superior stripe.

Certain fans will no doubt find the treatment of the Sontarans lacking in due reverence, but to these ears, the script strikes a fine balance between slyly building on their mythology while not being afraid to poke them in the eye occasionally. After 35 years, it's refreshing to hear someone finally acknowledge the baked potato in the room, while dialogue like "Words are the weapons of womenfolk" wouldn't have disgraced Linx – Robert Holmes' original toad-face – himself. (Are we to infer from this, incidentally, that there are female Sontarans? And what role do they play, exactly, in a clone race that's grown in a big bath of gloop? No wonder they're such a belligerent lot – they're clearly getting even less than the Doctor.)

The episode also has a genuine sense of momentum, not least in the way it keeps our hero on the move across different locations. And it's nice to see Martha's back... sorry, to see Martha back – though the scene in which her evil duplicate rises naked from the clone-soup is as tentatively erotic as *Doctor Who* ever gets (even if it is a stunt-back).

There are also some cheeky satirical sideswipes at everything from Guantanamo Bay to the exploitation of East European migrant workers (not bad for a show that could easily have been called *Attack of the Killer Potatoes*). And, for the ultimate proof that Russell the T is lightening up and embracing his inner fanboy, we even get a UNIT dating joke that would have brought a smile to the faces of literally hundreds of viewers.

Of course, this being big, daft old *Doctor Who*, there is also much about *The Sontaran Stratagem* that is Too Silly For Words. It's particularly sobering to see the Last of the Time Lords, the Oncoming Storm, the man who led the battle in the Last Great Time War and saw a hundred thousand ships burning in the sky (or something), defeated by a car window any scally with a brick or a bit of coat hanger could have sorted out in seconds flat. And UNIT, gratifyingly, remain the world's least convincing elite fighting force, especially now all their troops look as if they've just started shaving.

It's still a decent 45 action-packed minutes of adventure, though – unlike *The Poison Sky*, which falls of a cliff quite spectacularly in the final reel, with both Raynor's script and Douglas Mackinnon's direction struggling to build up any tension or sense of a gathering threat. As the Sontarans fill the skies with toxic gas, the story becomes all tell and no show. From *Newsnight*'s Kirsty Wark to dear old Bernard Cribbins, everyone works hard to persuade us the end is nigh, but it's hard to take them seriously when all we get is some dry ice and the odd plate shot of smog-choked London (which, let's be honest, could have been *actual* shots of London most days).

Everywhere you look, people are gamely stepping up to compensate for the lack of anything actually happening. The Doctor flaps about doing his student peacenik shtick, Donna blubs for the third story running and Murray Gold is clearly ignoring what's on screen and scoring a much more impressive movie running in his own head. And, for *Doctor Who Confidential* viewers, Russell T Davies is on hand to tell us that, despite all available evidence to the contrary, the scenes with Donna alone aboard the Sontaran spaceship are "really scary".

Raynor also cements her reputation as the undisputed queen of the shameless deus ex machina. After *Evolution*'s DNA/gamma interface travesty, this time we get the Doctor burning up the skies – *of the whole world* – with a small patio heater. Built by a teenager. Ah well, it was good while it lasted.

Meanwhile, on *Doctor Who Confidential*, Douglas Mackinnon let viewers in on the secret of filming a big explosion: "The trick with these sequences," he explained, "is to make them look dangerous, but not *be* dangerous." I hope you're writing this down.

Jenny from the Doc

When *Lazarus Experiment* writer Stephen Greenhorn told *Doctor Who Magazine* that one of the biggest challenges of writing the Doctor is that, fundamentally, he never changes, Russell T Davies decided set him a challenge: write something that *would* change him.

Greenhorn's response was *The Doctor's Daughter*. (Well it was either that or *The Doctor's Sex-Change*.) Some of the most effective New *Who* episodes – *School Reunion* and both of Paul Cornell's contributions among them – are the ones seemingly extrapolated from a simple, one-line emotional pitch: "What if the missus met the ex?" "What if Doctor were human?" In that sense, then, "What if the Doctor had a daughter?" seems like a bit of a no-brainer. But when the entire story ends up tying itself in knots and jumping through hoops in a desperate attempt to sketch in enough background to support this initial premise, you do wonder if the tail isn't wagging the dog just a little.

So yes, playing Who's the Daddy is a good wheeze. But it's hard to escape the sense that everything about this story – set-up, characters, situation – are just cogs and pistons grinding noisily away to deliver the Doctor a daughter, and then dispatch her, in 42 perfunctory minutes.

For a kick-off, she's not really his daughter: "Jenny" is, in fact, the product of a DNA-extracting "progenation machine" that the Doctor sticks his hand into. And any attempt to introduce this idea in a convincing, measured and emotionally resonant manner has to be sacrificed to the exigency of having her arrive fully-formed before the title sequence kicks in. Surely they could, at the very least, have had the Sontarans and Evil Martha popping casually out of a pod last week and saved the bubbling bath of gloop for this one? That way we might have got some sense of a new life being brought into the world: something gasping, shivering, disoriented, frightened and generally a bit less... well, perky. Instead, we get Jenny Who stepping out of what appears to be a tanning booth with a grin and a cheesy "Hello Dad!". Which raises several nagging questions, like: who created her fetching tight T-shirt and leather pants combo? Who did her make-up? Who put her hair in a ponytail? (Is that scrunchy part of her DNA?) And is this the first example in television history of what can only be described as gratuitous non-nudity?

The big reveal that the war between the humans and the Hath – scaly, fish-like humanoids with a bubble machine for a mouth – that everyone thinks has been going on for generations is actually only a week old is too daft for words. Does that mean the grizzled general – an instantly forgettable villain-of-the-week turn from Nigel Terry – is really only supposed to be a few hours old? In which case, how had he become leader of an army? Why does he look so knackered and dishevelled? Why does he have a West Country accent? And, sorry, what was his name again? (I just looked it up in the Radio Times and it's Cobb – probably on account of it being quite a small role. Small roll, see? Oh never mind.)

But even if this is a bit of a pony tale, there is still much to enjoy. Like Stephen Greenhorn's script for Series Three, the best thing about *The Doctor's Daughter* (apart from Georgia Moffett in that tight T-shirt) is the dialogue. Though lacking a set-piece showdown to rival the Doctor and Lazarus' electrifying dialectic on humanity, this should still comfortably fill a page or two of *The Doctor Who Bumper Book of Quotations*. The Doctor being outwitted by his own progeny on the question of whether he is a warrior is beautifully conceived, and there are a couple of successful passes at distilling the essence of the tenth Doctor ("Not impossible – just a bit unlikely" and "You talk all the time, but you don't say anything") into handy soundbites. Not to mention a sly tribute to the magic of *Doctor Who* itself ("It can be terrifying, brilliant and fun, all at the same time").

Catherine Tate, meanwhile, continues to steal every scene in sight. Donna's teasing the Doctor over his "dadshock" (Him: "You can't extrapolate a relationship from a biological accident" Her: "Child Support Agency can") is a prime example of exactly the sort of sparky interplay Tate was hired to provide, while her eagerness to deploy her feminine wiles to distract a soldier – only to be knocked back by the Doctor in favour of a clockwork mouse – is priceless.

With its underground humans praying to false totems, the plot, such as it is, contains echoes of sixth Doctor adventure *The Mysterious Planet* – not to mention the countless other *Who* stories in which a godhead is unmasked as only a slightly more sophisticated version of the Wizard of Oz standing behind a curtain pulling some levers. (And yet, weirdly, people still insist on holding seminars about Christianity in *Doctor Who*. Discuss. Actually, don't.)

In the end, Jenny Who takes a bullet for her old man – a sacrifice crunchingly telegraphed the moment she starts talking about joining him aboard the TARDIS – before regenerating(ish), stealing a rocket and going off to have her own adventures. This led to much online speculation about where we might see her next – in the season finale? In her own show? Or, given all that Time Lord DNA, going rogue and returning as the Rani? Like everything else about *The Doctor's Daughter*, that wouldn't be impossible – just a bit unlikely.

In May, the British Broadcasting Corporation was rocked to its very foundations when it was discovered that a woman known as Mazzmatazz had been handing out patterns for an Adipose doll to members of her knitting circle. When some of these woolly wonders started turning up on eBay, the suits at BBC Worldwide threatened to take their creator to court for breach of copyright. The case was taken up by freedom of expression campaigners the Open Rights Group, and the Corporation eventually agreed that, rather than banning the patterns, it would adopt them as a "limited edition" licensed product. ("How many do you think we should produce for this limited edition?" they wondered. "Shall we say, none?")

On Five Live, Eamonn Holmes courted controversy when, during a rave about how good the current series of *Doctor Who* was, he branded the 80s episodes "boring" – prompting a phone call from listener Mr C Baker of Buckinghamshire, who wasted no time in taking him to task live on air. Though, to be fair to Holmes, he was probably just trying to keep in with the current BBC chairman.

Arriving on BBC One like an early English summer, *The Unicorn and the Wasp* is such a reverential parody of the works of Agatha Christie – and the country house murder mystery in general – it's in danger of meeting itself on the way out of the billiard room with the candelabra. Being *Doctor Who*, of course, it goes one further and makes the loving element of homage the fulcrum on which the entire plot revolves – the Big Bad, it turns out, is *deliberately* working to the pattern established in Christie's novels, thus allowing Gareth Roberts licence to run riot in the equivalent of an Agatha Christie theme park.

In many ways, Roberts is on easy street here – chucking in a grab-bag of familiar tropes from even the sketchiest Christie primer was exactly what the project demanded and, ultimately, what gifts the episode so much of its charm. (Though, for the aficionado, the dia-logue is riddled with Christie titles – the product of a competition between Roberts and Russell T Davies to see who could shoehorn the most in.) Far from being mere window dressing, it's the period trappings that prove crucial: imagine, for a moment, that Pip and Jane Baker had turned in a reasonable murder mystery pastiche for 1986's *Terror of the Vervoids* (I know, I know, but try); the fact it was set aboard a white plastic spaceship filled with people in casual 80s sportswear would still have damned it to being on the back foot when trying to present a satisfying whodunnit. But give us gramophones, sun-dappled lawns, mahogany trim and a pink gin and we're up for anything, what what?

Ultimately, though, comic episodes stand or fall by one criteria: is it funny? And *The Unicorn and the Wasp* is an absolute blast. David Tennant simply excels at this sort of light comedy, bounding from parlour to dining room to library dropping bon mots like cake crumbs and devouring Roberts' witty wordplay with the relish of a Trappist monk who's just been given leave to tell a particularly filthy joke.

It's obvious from the get-go that this is a script custom-built for the man in the brown suit (see, it's catching), and it's impossible to imagine any other Doctor having quite the chutzpah to carry it off. The poison sequence, in particular – in which the Doctor tries to detoxify his body by drinking half the contents of the larder – is hilarious, Tennant's blustery exasperation at Donna's inability to find the right ingredients matched tic-for-tic by Catherine Tate's boneyard dry sarcasm. Tate is also particularly suited to her role as the sleuthing Doctor's plucky gel assistant, moving easily between girlish enthusiasm and a sort of withering Greek chorus ("Professor Peach. In the library. *With the lead piping?*"). She can't run in heels, though.

Elsewhere, the story's parade of familiar archetypes is well served by a strong cast, including a pre-Hollywood Felicity Kendal and fan treasure Christopher Benjamin (aka *The Talons of Weng-Chiang*'s Henry Gordon Jago). It's a shame the ensemble nature of the piece reduces most of the talent to little more than glorified cameos, but it's entirely appropriate that the one performer who really gets a chance to shine is Fenella Woolgar as Christie herself. Previous sleb historicals have opted for a familiar name in the pivotal role, and the temptation to indulge in a spot of stunt casting must have been strong, but Woolgar – a dead ringer for the young Christie – is just perfect. If anything, her chemistry with Tennant is even stronger than Tate's – the scene in which she admonishes him for enjoying all the murder and mayhem too much ("How like a man") is delightfully played by both actors.

If you're looking for the one major element that lets *The Unicorn and the Wasp* down, the clue's in the title – and it has nothing to do with horny horses. Many *Who* fans would love to see the producers have the confidence to go monster-free occasionally but, hey, we've read the memo on keeping those damned kids happy, so we understand why this perfectly enjoyable time travel caper had to have a ruddy great alien wasp plonked in the middle of it. It's just a pity the Vespiform couldn't have taken the guise of something a bit more organically linked to the setting – a giant Victoria sponge, perhaps? Okay, maybe not. (The transformation effect, incidentally, is a spectacularly cheap affair – ask the actor to say "zzzzzz" while shining some coloured lights on him. But if you care about that sort of thing, you're probably reading the wrong book.)

There are other irritations. It isn't just the Doctor who is breezily cavalier about death (witness how quickly Lady Eddison gets over the murder of her own son) – although to be fair, from Christie to *Cleudo* to *Midsomer Murders*, the genre has always worn its tragedies somewhat lightly. The sci-fi elements of the plot – alien wasp man absorbs works of Agatha Christie through a necklace, or some such gubbins – are also flimsier than usual (and that's saying something). But what the heck. It might be ironic that, in a tribute to the first lady of plotting, the plot itself barely has time to simmer, let alone thicken, but with so many other giddy distractions on offer – including the rather unforgettable notion of Felicity Kendal shagging a wasp (yes, really) – it would be churlish to grumble too much. As a gay old treat to be enjoyed over a Mint Julep as the shadows lengthen on the lawn, this is the cat's pyjamas.

Britain's Got Tennant

On May 20th, the BBC announced, casual as you like, that Russell T Davies was to step down as executive producer of *Doctor Who* after the 2009 specials, with Steven Moffat taking over for the fifth series.

BBC Fiction (that's Drama in old money) controller Jane Tranter said the past four series of *Doctor Who* had been "brilliantly helmed" by the "spectacularly talented" Davies. "As lead writer and executive producer, he has overseen the creative direction and detail of the twenty-first century relaunch of *Doctor Who* and we are delighted to have his continued presence on the specials over the next 18 months," she added.

"I applied before, but I got knocked back 'cos the BBC wanted someone else," joked Moffat. "Also, I was seven. Anyway, I'm glad the BBC has finally seen the light and it's a huge honour to be following Russell into the best – and the toughest – job in television.

"I say toughest 'cos Russell's at my window right now, pointing and laughing."

The announcement was treated as a major news event. "The *news!*" boggled Davies in an email to *The Times'* Caitlin Moran, adding: "Though the next headline was, They Still Haven't Moved That Skip." Even so, it was never like this when Derrick Sherwin left.

A week later, Moffat gave his first interview on the subject to the Scottish *Big Issue*: "I was speaking to David [Tennant] a few weeks before I was offered it, and I said, 'It must've been great when you were offered *Doctor Who*, you must've jumped at the chance'. He said, 'You know, when it really happens, it's not like that'. It's kind of weird, it's almost like it's not *supposed* to happen. You're not supposed to be a grown-up that gets offered his childhood favourite."

Which is why, when the call had finally come in July 2007, Moffat took months to come to a decision – even offering to write more episodes per series if it would convince Davies to stay. He was eventually persuaded when his father – who'd never been in any doubt he'd take the job – sent him a picture of his 11-year-old self reading a Target *Doctor Who* novel.

"It was fairly easy for me to be the favourite,

because I was the only one who'd been around since the beginning and turning up every year," mused Moffat. "I was kind of the other contender, which puts me kind of in the position of Gordon Brown. And look how that turned out. The surly Scot comes in and it all goes to fuck!"

Back in the present, the threat to the latest Moffat-penned *Doctor Who* story had less to do with the surly Scot who'd written it than the preening, Cuban heeled, eccentrically trousered media mogul on the other channel. *Britain's Got Talent* was Simon Cowell's end-of-the-pier alternative to *The X Factor* – a gaudy cavalcade of dancing dogs and singing pensioners that was proving to be a ratings juggernaut for ITV. Not to worry though, because *Doctor Who* had an ace up its sleeve: "Space! Library!" beamed the never knowingly under-effusive Russell T Davies in that week's *Confidential*. "How can that not be commissioned? It's a must!" (Blimey, if we'd known that was all it took, we'd have sent in our own one-line pitches – "Post Office! Under the sea!" – years ago.)

As *Who's* scarifier in chief, Moffat brings a wonderfully unrepentant zeal to his mission to leave no bed un-wet, delighting in poking about in the corners of our primal, atavistic fears, be they creepy statues, monsters under the bed or, erm, gas masks. This time, he takes the plunge and goes straight for the biggie – chapter one, page one of the Big Book of Scary Things: darkness itself. "Almost every sentient species in the universe has an irrational fear of the dark," says the Doctor, who has developed a habit of speaking in movie taglines. "But they're all wrong. It's not irrational..."

Because that big dark patch in the corner of your bedroom? Turns out it might not be shadows after all, but the Vashta Nerada ("the shadows that melt the flesh"): a swarm of microscopic creatures who, in large numbers, are indistinguishable from shadows, right up to the point they strip the flesh from your bones.

In many ways, Moffat would have been an ideal writer for the budget-stretching "classic" series, sticking as he does to the edict that it's the things unseen that inspire the most dread. After all, why pay The Mill a fortune to produce a giant pink brain, or go to the effort of stitching Peter Kay into a comedy It's A Knockout suit, when all you have to do is position a few lamps to throw some spooky shadows around the place? (It also allows Moffat to add a new lick to his favourite "if the tape's finished, why is he still talking?" / "the clock's broken, so what's ticking?" riff, as the Doctor notes: "You said there are five people still alive in this room – so why are there six [shadows]?" Some may call this laziness; I prefer to think it's the sort of signature trope Hitchcock might have relished in his pomp.)

When he's not messing with your head, of course, Moffat is never happier than when messing with time: the man has wibbly wobbly, timey wimey stuff where the rest of us have DNA. I bet he even writes his shopping lists backwards (after he's got back from the supermarket, probably). Here, the chief timey-wimey element is supplied by Alex Kingston's Professor River Song, an archaeologist from the Doctor's own future – a future in which, apparently, the two of them are *very* chummy indeed. The fact she knows everything about him – heck, she even knows his real name – and he hasn't a clue who she is affords us the chance to see the Doctor genuinely on the back foot for once. Moffat, naturally, has great fun with this wonky dynamic ("We go way back," says the professor. "Just not *this* far back"), while cheekily taking advantage of the show's unique relationship with chronology to forward date his CV and tell us that, hey, if you think this show is cool *now*, you ain't seen nothing yet.

"With a stake in the future of *Doctor Who*, I thought it would be good to have a character who's coming along and saying 'Aaah, the Doctor I knew, he was *really* great'," Moffat told *Doctor Who Confidential*. "So instead of, 'This show used to be fantastic', you're saying 'Oh, you wait until you see the next guy!'"[55]

Rather than simply pick up where the cliff-hanger left off, *Forest of the Dead* re-sets the story with Donna, now assimilated into the library's digital archive, living a hyper-accelerated alternative life, complete with a husband and two children. When reality begins to intrude, and she realises her happy existence is a lie, it's genuinely upsetting. But there's a happy ending, of sorts, for River who – despite dying to save the man she loves – finds an afterlife in this virtual reality. In the episode's closing moments, she puts her children to bed (including, significantly, the little girl whose mind was powering the library all along – chalk that up as another child who stops wreaking havoc the moment she finds her mummy) and wishes them, and us, sweet dreams. That's right: the master of nightmares, the man responsible for more bed sheets going into the wash than Russell Brand, is tucking us up and telling us to sleep soundly. Because it's okay – the Doctor has saved the day again.

And how. Where most screen heroes would pull out a gun, the Doctor puts the lengthening shadows of death to flight with a simple: "I'm the Doctor and you're in a library – look me up." It's a thrilling moment in a typically inventive Moffat script, full of delicious chills (the concept of "data ghosting" – which allows people who've just died to keep on talking, is beyond creepy) and witty wordplay ("If you understand me, look very, very scared"), while River is a great addition to the series' mythology. "When you run with the Doctor, it feels like it will never end," says the professor. "But however hard you try, you can't run forever. Everybody knows that everybody dies, and nobody knows it like the Doctor. But I do think that all the skies of all the worlds might just turn dark, if he ever, for one moment, accepts it."

Sadly, none of this was enough to overcome the force of nature that is Simon Cowell, with *Silence in the Library*'s audience slipping to just 6.3 million – around half the audience watching ITV1 at the same time. It was *Doctor Who*'s first defeat since Survival Part 3 went down in a hail of Corrie bullets way back in 1989. But, against less formidable opposition, *Forest of the Dead* was seen by almost eight million viewers, putting the show firmly back on track. And besides, while Cowell may have won the day, people will still be watching *Silence in the Library* (probably in "classic flat-o-vision" or some such) in a hundred years' time, which is approximately 99.5 years after anyone outside his immediate friends and family will have given more than a passing thought to *BGT*'s breakdancing "sensation" George Sampson. (Remember him? Exactly.)

Britain's got talent? You bet your life it has.

Doctor Who officially more popular than Turkey v Czech Republic

In June, Russell T Davies was awarded the OBE in the Queen's Birthday Honours (blimey, she really *had* enjoyed that box set). "I'm delighted to accept and I hope it does the whole industry a bit of good, for the writing of television drama to be recognised," said Davies.

The honour was well timed, as that week's episode of *Doctor Who* is a masterclass in the art of scripting – albeit one that would work just as well on the stage as on screen. Davies has described *Midnight* – a late replacement for a Tom McRae script that was considered too similar to the Agatha Christie story – as the "anti-*Voyage of the Damned*" in which, instead of pulling together and standing shoulder-to-shoulder in a crisis, everyone turns on each other in order to save their own sorry skins. Though, on the plus side, no-one drives a fork-lift truck or tries to land a famous historical passenger liner on Buckingham Palace.

By *Doctor Who*'s standards, the premise is refreshingly simple. The Doctor joins a tour party on a journey across the beautiful but deadly surface of the planet Midnight, where their transport comes under attack from an unseen creature with the power to take possession of anyone on board. With suspicion and paranoia running out of control, lynch mobs are formed against anyone perceived to be acting strangely and, as the witch-hunts intensify, the Doctor learns that the dark side of human nature is the one monster he can't defeat. The moral of the story? Never take a coach trip with a party of *Daily Mail* readers.

A dark inversion of the show's usual sunny view of human potential, this claustrophobic psychological thriller – set largely in one room, with a small cast and minimal effects – is bold new territory for *Who*. It's not so much scary as unbearably *tense*, never more so than in the sequences where possessed characters start mimicking their fellow travellers' speech patterns – a simple but effectively disturbing device for ratcheting up the tension.

Well, simple unless you have to act it, of course, and props to Lesley Sharp and David Tennant for eating up and spitting out pages of machine-gun dialogue – including learning the square root of pi to several dozen decimal places – and making it look easy. Sharp is also capable of doing more with one scary look than some "monsters" manage with whole episodes of puffed-up threats, while the show's lead proves he's still capable of reaching into new places as a Doctor stripped of all his usual cocksure confidence and magic tricks.

"Filming was very intense," said Tennant. "It was a cramped set, and one scene lasts 45 pages, which we played in 12 to 15-minute takes. That's unheard of in television drama – let alone *Doctor Who*. It's the closest I've ever felt to doing theatre on television."[39]

"It was impossible to keep up with David," said Sharp. "His speech pattern, the rate at which he speaks, is phenomenally fast. He learns pages, and pages, and pages, and the rate at which he speaks is the rate at which he thinks. Russell explained to me that David's Doctor has a lot to say because that's David – he's so bright."[51] Maybe – but he still got beaten by Rose's mum on *The Weakest Link*.

With 8.1 million viewers, *Midnight* was the fifth-most watched programme of the week, even beating coverage of Euro 2008. Yes, *Doctor Who* was now officially more popular than football, prompting geeks everywhere to do an awkward high-five. (Though, to be fair, the show might not have done quite so well against a tournament England had actually managed to qualify for.)

On Sky One's *50 Ways to Leave Your Lover*, the Doctor and Rose's parting in *Doomsday* was voted the all-time greatest love split, even though Paul Simon had never mentioned getting trapped in a parallel dimension in his original song (it certainly makes a change from "it's not you, it's me," though.)

Those famous spoiler-phobes at *The Sun*, meanwhile, appeared to have forgotten their pledge not to "ruin it for the show's 14 million fans" when the paper printed a photo of the new-look Davros it had successfully managed to be sent. There was no mention of Ben Kingsley, strangely. This time, the man in the mask was Julian Bleach, who had co-created the Olivier award-winning musical *Shockheaded Peter*, and had subsequently been cast as the villainous Ghostmaker in *Torchwood*. Bleach would later describe the Dalek creator as "a

cross between Hitler and Stephen Hawking". ("None taken," said Professor Hawking.)

Series Four's Doctor-lite bottle episode, *Turn Left*, is Russell T Davies' take on an *It's a Wonderful Life*-style "what if?" alternative time-line wheeze. Specifically, it imagines how events might have unravelled if Donna Noble, unwittingly given the chance to re-write history, took a right turn at a road junction instead of a left, and never met the Doctor. And Donna wasn't the only one changing direction that week: while the temperamental temp was dooming the world – and the Doctor, who doesn't survive his encounter with the Racnoss – with a casual flick of her indicator, Russell T Davies was slamming on the brakes, locking the wheel and executing a complete 180. Or at least that's how it looks, as the man who never wasted an opportunity to remind us how vulnerable the average *Who* viewer is to the lure of ITV's big shiny floors goes charging pedal to the metal through four years' worth of backstory, collecting space-ships, spin-offs and supporting players from Sarah Jane to Sarah Parish like bugs on his windscreen.

As late as 2007, Davies was still claiming that only a small percentage – two million, tops – of his audience were regular viewers, while the rest was made up of casual floating voters who wouldn't know an Exxilon from an egg sandwich. *Turn Left* – and Series Four in general – suggests the big man has either decided to give these fair-weather followers the finger, indulge his own fanboy fantasies and leave Moffat to deal with the fall-out or, more likely, has realised there's a hardcore audience of at least five million who would stay in and watch this show even if a nuclear-powered replica of a giant ocean liner *was* about to land on their heads.

Yes, in *Turn Left*'s reality, the Doctor is not around to stop the *Titanic* landing on Buck House, and the whole of London goes up in smoke. Which is a bit odd, tonally: a healthy dose of retconning's all very well, but dignifying *Voyage of the Damned* with this sort of dark apocalyptic vision – in which the whole of southern England is an irradiated no-go zone, and foreign nationals are carted off to labour camps – is a bit like making a Holocaust drama out of *Bedknobs and Broomsticks*.

And yet, somehow, it works. Well, most of it works. This episode has so many ideas that some – like the gratuitous implication of gassing immigrants, which only serves to cheapen a very real atrocity – are bound to fall short. And some elements seem only to have been included in a bid to paper over previous mistakes and inconsistencies (while haplessly throwing up a few more into the bargain – wasn't London supposed to be deserted during *Voyage of the Damned*, for starters?). But it's always better to have too many ideas than too few and, in *Turn Left*, Davies' scattershot imagination fires new (and, indeed, old) faces, locations, concepts and mysteries at us like an ADHD-afflicted Raston Robot who's missed his Ritalin shot.

What's also striking about the story is how, even though David Tennant is the beating hearts and wheezing-groaning engine of this show, he isn't really missed. And you can put that down to Catherine Tate, who is amazing. Again.

And then there's Rose. Or "Roshe," as she seems to have become. Billie Piper had admitted struggling to find the accent again, but here – in her first full episode since *Doomsday* – she seems to have developed a fully-fledged speech impediment. In an episode filled with flying ocean liners, killer fat and the ghost of Earl Mountbatten haunting the Boat Show (you think I just make this stuff up, don't you?), Rose's voice is by far the oddest element. Still, I guess at least she's good for recycling old Sean Connery jokes ("Shall I meet you at 10ish?" "Tennish, I thought we were playing golf" etc).

That aside, it's still a thrill to have Billie back, even if she is reduced to playing a supporting role to Catherine Tate and the continuity researcher. It would have been all too easy to construct an entire episode around Rose's return, but it seems Russell T Davies just has too many stories to tell right now – stories about mothers and daughters (the scene in which Donna tells Sylvia "S'pose I've always been a disappointment", and Sylvia just replies with a dead-eyed "Yeah" has to be among the bleakest, most brutal moments in *Doctor Who* history) and grandfathers and destiny and darkness and death and triumph and hope. It's a big, bold vision that, for all its occasional over-reaching and over-ambition, has never looked bigger or bolder. And this is one of the *cheap* episodes.

"In the event of breakdown, please stay with your planet and await assistance"

With viewing figures staying north of eight million, *Turn Left* was the fourth-highest rating programme of the week – *Doctor Who*'s second-best-ever chart placing (after *Voyage of the Damned*). Clearly, the show was on a roll, even before the epic two-part finale and its attendant media circus hove into view.

Featuring just about anyone who'd ever been anyone from the past four years – apart from that grumpy bloke with the ears and the leather jacket (Christopher something?) – and stuffed with so many nods to the past it's in danger of pulling a muscle, *The Stolen Earth / Journey's End* is like a giant wrap party for the whole of the Russell T Davies era (even if there were still a few specials hanging around like stragglers refusing to go home).

After the lo-fi thrills of the previous two episodes, it's obvious from the start what Davies has been saving his pocket money for, as the entire Earth is wrenched from its orbit, its skies now a crowded vista of planets, moons and fleets of Dalek ships, while the Doctor and Donna, Cap'n Jack's Torchwood gang, Sarah Jane's Scooby gang, Martha Jones' UNIT gang, Rose and Mickey – not to mention Sylvia, Wilf, Jackie, Francine and even Harriet Jones – team up as a distinctly mixed-ability resistance movement. Even the opening titles roll call – David! Catherine! Freema! John! With Lis! And Billie! – reads like the world's most exciting Powerpoint presentation.

Perhaps inevitably, the story struggles to accommodate this much continuity-porn (even *Voyage of the Damned*'s Mr Copper gets a look in) while the plotting is Davies at his most devil-may-care. (Twenty-seven planets aligned to create a universe-destroying "reality bomb"? Yeah, why not? The Doctor and Donna tracking down the Earth by following a swarm of intergalactic bees? Stranger things have happened. Probably. Sarah Jane accessorising with a miniaturised "warp star" around her neck?

You can laugh, but you'll all be wearing them next year.)

Oddly, Davies' handle on some of his own characters seems a bit shaky. Faced with a minor set-back to his plans, the Doctor simply decides it's all hopeless and chucks in the towel; Jack and Sarah are similarly defeatist, completely going to pieces at the sound of a Dalek voice, while Jack abandons Gwen and Ianto to their fate during an attack on the Torchwood Hub without a second thought. More unforgivably, the Rose-Doctor reunion – which ought to be the pivotal moment of the story, even the whole series – gets lost in the mix, sacrificed for the expediency of an (admittedly knockout) cliffhanger, after which they don't get so much as a single scene alone together.

Some of the dialogue is unintentionally hilarious as well. (Martha: "I'm medical director on Project Indigo." Jack: "They got that working?" Martha: "Indigo's top secret – no-one's supposed to know about it!" Yeah, well you might want to stop blabbering about it, then. Or at least change your Facebook status from "Martha Jones is now medical director of top-secret Project Indigo".)

The much-feared Shadow Proclamation – darkly invoked as the most powerful force in the universe as far back as *Rose* – also proves to be a damp squib, amounting to little more than an under-staffed intergalactic police station, apparently based in a Victorian public toilet. The Daleks fare better: Dalek Caan – now a half-destroyed, quivering, giggling lunatic dispensing cryptic, sing-song prophesies like an octopoid Mystic Meg – is an unsettling creation, brilliantly voiced by Nicholas Briggs. And the Supreme Dalek, with his red livery and extra armour, is clearly destined for the shelves of a Toys "R" Us near you in the run-up to Christmas.

And then there's Davros. It was fashionable for a long time to criticise ol' blue eye for having stolen all the Daleks' thunder, but that's a bit like accusing The Beatles of making Cliff Richard look a bit lame – a better alternative came along, that's all. Davros is everything the Daleks aren't – creepy, repulsive, insidious, and capable of holding his own in genuinely thrilling confrontations with the hero. And Julian Bleach has clearly nailed it right out of the traps – the perfect synthesis of Michael Wisher's cunning and Terry Molloy's barely contained hysteria, he just might turn out to be the daddy of them all. (Is it just me, though, or is there something inherently funny about Davros being played by a bloke called Julian? Or is it actually slightly less ridiculous than his real name being Terry?) And who can't help but feel a shiver echoing down the years when Davros first clocks Sarah Jane? ("Impossible – that face... You were there on Skaro, at the very beginning of my creation.")

Oh, and the cliffhanger's a bit of a doozy, too. As the Doctor runs towards Rose in the street for what ought to be their emotional reunion, he's struck down by a Dalek death-ray in an extreme case of coitus interruptus, and starts regenerating...

With 8.8 million people tuning in on an early evening in late June, the episode matched *Voyage of the Damned*'s chart placing as the second-most watched show of week in Britain. More than that, it created a national talking point, as the cliffhanger sparked fevered speculation across newspapers, websites, TV and radio that the Doctor would regenerate into a new body at the start of the following episode.

In the days running up to the finale, *Who* stars past and present lined up on everything from *GMTV*, *This Morning* and *BBC Breakfast* to *Richard and Judy* and even the *Six O'Clock News* to speculate about what might happen on Saturday. "None of us saw that coming," admitted Russell T Davies. "I think the entire country realised, consciously, how much they love David Tennant."[37]

Meanwhile, Sky One's Pointless Lists season continued with the Top 50 Showbiz Comebacks, which placed Billie Piper at 23 and *Doctor Who* itself at a lofty No. 2. (Take That took the top spot, controversially beating both *Elvis' '68 Comeback Special* and the return of the Macra.)

Of course, the Doctor *doesn't* regenerate. Instead, he fires all the regeneration energy into his spare hand (the one that Jack's been carrying around since it got lopped off all the way back in *The Christmas Invasion* – keep up, do), from which Donna inadvertently grows a clone Doctor that's half Time Lord, half human. Half Donna, in fact. And Donna's half Doctor.

The Doctor-Donna: with *that* brain attached to *that* mouth, it doesn't bear thinking about.

There's a powerful idea struggling to make itself heard among all the noise and bluster of *Journey's End*. As the Doctor's friends come rallying to his aid, Davros taunts him for turning them into warriors: "This is the truth, Doctor. You take ordinary people, and you fashion them into weapons. Behold your Children of Time – transformed into murderers. I made the Daleks, Doctor. You made this."

Even more powerful is Donna's fate. Dalek Caan has prophesied that one of the Children of Time will die, but what happens to Donna is arguably worse. Unable to contain the Doctor's mind in her own, the only way he can save her is to wipe her memory of their entire time together, effectively re-setting her to the shrewish airhead we met in *The Runaway Bride*. "But she was better with you," says Wilf, heartbroken. "I just want you to know," replies the Doctor, "there are worlds out there, safe in the sky because of her. That there are people living in the light, and singing songs of Donna Noble, a thousand million light years away. They will never forget her, while she can never remember. And for one moment, one shining moment, she was the most important woman in the whole wide universe."

Next to this, the resolution to the Doctor-Rose arc – in which she gets to settle down and have babies with the half-human version – is pat and unsatisfying, only serving to diminish the iconic scene on the same beach two years earlier.

Still, at least they're largely talking in English by then, which comes as a relief after a 50-minute assault of almost relentless technobabble. Four years ago, Davies started out studiously avoiding sci-fi bafflegab in favour of simple concepts like "anti-plastic"; here, he seems to be on a spellcheck-bothering mission to cram as much head-scratching nonsense into one script as humanly possible. Highlights include: "biomatching receptacle" (translation: talk to the handy plot device); "Project Indigo" (teleportation device developed from scavenged Sontaran technology – full name: Project Indigo Here and Outdicome There); "instantaneous biological metacrisis" (device that allows David Tennant to charge a double fee); "zed neutrino energy" (Dalek power source, possibly also early 90s rave band); "extrapolator shielding" (TARDIS security system, built using an intergalactic surfboard disguised as a model of a Welsh power station – true story); "TARDIS base code numerals" (if you lose these, you'll never get the stereo to work again); "Osterhagen key" (big bomb); "warp star" (a warp-fold conjugation trapped in a carbonised shell, *really* big bomb); "planetary alignment field" (arrangement of planets that allows Daleks to detonate reality bomb – with thanks to the show's new scientific adviser, Russell Grant); "time lock" (developed by Tosh, appropriately enough); "spatial genetic bioduplicity" (complicated way of providing unnecessary explanation of why woman from *The Unquiet Dead* looks like woman from *Torchwood*); "biometric damping field with retrograde arse inversion" (well that's what it *sounds* like, anyway)... Seriously, can you imagine the size of the prop Jon Pertwee would have needed to write all this stuff down on?

Ultimately, though, how you feel about *Journey's End* can probably be summed up by how you feel about one particular scene, in which the Doctor and all his chums use the TARDIS to tow – yes tow – the Earth back across space to its correct position, with only a few swinging light fittings to show for the cosmic upheaval. It is, by some measure, quite the silliest thing seen in *Doctor Who* since... well, since something last week, probably. And yet, as our heroes take their places around the console – Sarah and Rose and Martha and Donna and Jack and Mickey and Jackie, all grinning at each other like loons to the accompaniment of a Welsh male voice choir – you'd need a heart of stone not to feel a certain sense of euphoria. After all, if you can't be silly with your best friends, who can you be silly with?

With just shy of 11 million viewers – triple ITV1's audience – and an AI of 91, all the week's hype had clearly paid off. But the episode's place in history was cemented by another statistic. After a long, slow, frequently rocky climb of some 45 years, seven months and 13 days, *Doctor Who* had finally made it to the top as the UK's most-watched television programme of the week.[V] Even the auld enemy, *Coronation Street*, was left eating its dust. The 2008 run of stories may have been inconsistent, but, in terms of popularity and profile, the show was reaching new heights – and mounting a serious challenge to 60s Dalekmania and Tom Baker's imperial reign for the title of *Doctor Who's* Golden Age. For anyone who lived through the dark days when an article in John Craven's *Back Pages* – or even a Bill Baggs video spin-off – was about as exciting as it got, these were heady times indeed.

And in David Tennant's crackling, kinetic, lightning rod of a Doctor, the show had its most popular leading man since Baker had hung up his scarf nearly 30 years earlier: a rock-star Doctor who seemed perfectly at home fronting comedy panel shows and announcing bands on stage at Wembley, but who was also about to open as Hamlet for the Royal Shakespeare Company.

Tennant's partnership with Catherine Tate had also proved irresistible to viewers – and to Tate herself, who confessed to a certain amount of separation anxiety when it was all over. "It's such a wonderful atmosphere, such a close-knit cast and crew," she said. "And then suddenly, it all stops. I miss it like crazy, I really do... Had there been the potential for Donna to stay on for another series, I must confess I'd have said yes like a shot. I would have jumped at the chance to go back. I know that it's going to be a job in my career that I'm going to look back on and measure other jobs by. Most definitely. In every respect."[56]

It was the end of an era, too, for Phil Collinson – the man who had ridden this crazy mule from the start, and had the bruises to show for it, was heading back north. "In the initial few months [after leaving], it does feel like someone's died," Collinson told *Doctor Who Magazine*. "There's suddenly a massive part of your life that isn't there any more. It's awful. I've cried. It's a very strange thing to be in your late 30s, and know that what you'll be defined by forever, probably the most exciting job you'll ever do, is behind you. It's very disconcerting. I've had to come to terms with that.

"When I first started, I did feel intimidated by all the illustrious names who had held the job before me – Verity Lambert, Barry Letts, Philip Hinchcliffe, John Nathan-Turner. I felt I couldn't live up to those people. But you know what? I feel that I have. I did the job. I lasted.

They didn't sack me. I no longer feel like I don't belong there."[57]

Tennant "finest Hamlet of his generation" (and the fish and chips aren't bad either)

Steven Moffat's career choices came under scrutiny when the *Daily Mail* claimed he had turned down a £500,000 movie deal from Steven Spielberg to become showrunner on *Doctor Who*. Moffat had already delivered a draft of the Tintin movie to Spielberg and Peter Jackson, but had apparently passed on the proposed sequels in favour of playing with Daleks in Cardiff. "I hope you won't make it sound too dramatic," Moffat told the paper. "I talked to Steven and he understood completely." (After all those years listening to Philip Segal banging on, what Spielberg probably actually thought was: "If another dorky Brit wants to throw his life away on that dumb TV show, knock yourself out.")

In Stratford, David Tennant opened in *Hamlet* to glowing reviews. "Tennant is an active, athletic, immensely engaging Hamlet," said Michael Billington in *The Guardian*. "This is a Hamlet of quicksilver intelligence, mimetic vigour and wild humour: one of the funniest I've ever seen." "Funny, clever and with sudden flashes of deep emotion, Tennant's Time Lord strikes me as a pretty good jumping off point for the most famous and challenging of all Shakespearean characters," wrote Charles Spencer in the *Telegraph*, noting that the production had "become universally known as the *Doctor Who Hamlet*, with even the local fish and chip shop promising to 'exterminate' its patrons' hunger". (Co-star Patrick Stewart, playing Claudius, was not honoured with any such take-away tribute – Bream me up, Scotty? – thus proving conclusively that, in the catering trade at least, *Doctor Who* was now more popular than *Star Trek*. So there.)

On July 27th, an army of villains including Cybermen, Judoon, Ood, Sontaran, Daleks and Davros marched on the Royal Albert Hall for the *Doctor Who Prom*. Hosted by Freema Agyeman, with help from Catherine Tate, the performance was the most over-subscribed of the Proms season, with 6,000 tickets sold and half that number again on a waiting list for cancellations. On the big screen, David Tennant starred in a seven-minute mini-episode, *Music of the Spheres*, getting into bother with a pesky Graske which then escaped into the Albert Hall and started soaking the audience with a water pistol. Something for the organisers of that week's Rimsky-Korsakov recital to consider, perhaps.

In late August, a panel of journalists and industry execs voted the series Best Programme at the 2008 Edinburgh International Television Festival. A few weeks later, *Doctor Who* was named Best-Loved Drama for the third year running at the TV Quick/TV Choice Awards, where David Tennant also collected his third consecutive Best Actor gong, and Catherine Tate was named Best Actress.

On BBC One, Elisabeth Sladen faced a rematch with the first alien race she'd ever encountered, way back in 1974, when *The Last Sontaran* kicked off the second run of *The Sarah Jane Adventures*. Yasmin Paige's Maria bowed out after the first story, to be replaced by Anjli Mohandra as Rani Chandra. The actress told *Doctor Who Magazine* that the first thing she did after being cast was "take all the really bad photos of me off Facebook, in case any seven-year-olds find my profile".[58] I don't think it's the seven year olds you need to worry about, love.

Once again, the series highlight – for grown-ups, anyway – is a Gareth Roberts episode delving into Sarah Jane's past. *The Temptation of Sarah Jane Smith* is effectively a rehash of *Father's Day*, with our heroine rewriting history to save her parents from being killed in a car crash. But, as rehashes go, it's rather wonderful. It's season finale *Enemy of the Bane* that really punches fan buttons though as, in addition to an encore for Samantha Bond's Miss Wormwood, the story sees the return of Nicholas Courtney as a certain retired Brigadier. The character was a late replacement for Martha Jones, who had to be written out when Freema Agyeman landed a regular role in ITV drama *Law and Order: UK*. "I think I had about five days' notice," said Courtney. "I don't know what they'd have done if I'd said no!"[59] (At which point there was a loud cough from John Levene and Richard Franklin, who were lurking in the corner.)

Despite being 78, Courtney still plays the Brig with his familiar twinkle, in what would prove to be his last outing in the role. Courtney died a little over two years later – a loss felt keenly by fans across the world. Over the years, they had taken the actor – who for many years had been Honorary President of the *Doctor Who* Appreciation Society – into their hearts, as he had taken them into his. For many, it felt like losing a friend.

Weevil Rock You

October brought an unexpected development – to say the least – when the production team were approached about the possibility of staging *Torchwood: The Musical* – with Bjorn and Benny from ABBA apparently keen to write the music. "Bjorn and Benny love *Torchwood*," claimed the BBC producer acting as go-between. ("We'll think about it," said Russell T Davies, cautiously. "I've booked flights to Stockholm," said John Barrowman.)

Davies also made headlines that month when, during an appearance at the Cheltenham Literary Festival, he called Prince Charles "a miserable swine" for turning down a cameo in *Doctor Who*. Which was awkward, as Davies was due to collect his OBE from the Prince of Wales the following month. Davies was at the festival promoting *The Writer's Tale*, a hefty volume of emails between himself and *Doctor Who Magazine* journalist Benjamin Cook. Conducted over the course of a year, the book offers a detailed – and, at times, unflinchingly candid – insight into the creative process behind Davies' *Doctor Who* scripts. For all his breezy bonhomie and lofty demolition of his critics, Davies actually emerges as a rather tortured soul, forever doubting his own abilities and frequently racing towards deadlines in a blur of nicotine and blind panic.[VI] (So, just like every other *Doctor Who* writer in history, basically.)

That year's National Television Awards should have been enough to silence the demons in his head, at least for a night or two. For the fourth year on the trot, *Doctor Who* was voted Most Popular Drama, while David Tennant collected a third Outstanding Performance trophy. Accepting the award via video-link during the interval at Stratford, Tennant thanked the viewers for their support

– and then dropped the mother of all bomb-shells by resigning live on air.

"In January, I go back to Cardiff to make four new specials which will see *Doctor Who* all the way through 2009," he told a shocked nation. "But when *Doctor Who* returns in 2010, it won't be with me. The 2009 shows will be my last playing the Doctor."

To audible gasps from the audience in the Albert Hall, he continued: "I love this part and I love this show so much, that if I don't take a deep breath and make the decision to move on now, then I simply never will. You would be prising the TARDIS key out of my cold dead hand. This show has been so special to me, I don't want to outstay my welcome."

Tennant explained how he'd "always thought the time to leave would be in conjunc-tion with Russell T Davies and Julie Gardner" but had been "sorely tempted" to stay when he'd heard Steven Moffat's plans for the show. In the end, though, he'd stuck to his original plan.

"I will be there, glued to my TV when his stories begin in 2010," he added. "I feel very privileged to have been part of this incredible phenomenon, and whilst I'm looking forward to new challenges, I know I'll always be very proud to be the tenth Doctor."

The announcement was the culmination of weeks of covert planning by the production team, working under the codename Operation COBRA (the name used by the Government for matters of considerably less national impor-tance, like terrorist attacks and flu pandemics). It was a high-wire act fraught with risks – not least because it relied on Tennant actually win-ning – that saw Julie Gardner play M to Tennant's Bond in a crossfire of secret emails and, on the day, frantic text updates. True to form, the BBC's own press office nearly blew the whole thing wide open by accidentally issuing the press release early – the story briefly appeared on *The Guardian's* website, before being taken down – but, in the end, all the *Spooks*-style espionage paid off.

"It was always in the back of my mind that I'd do three series, and maybe a few specials," Tennant told *Doctor Who Magazine* afterwards. "Once I realised Russell and Julie were going, it seemed the obvious stepping-off point. But then I fluctuated. I wobbled a couple of times.

I came closer to doing another series than I ever thought I might. When I started speaking to Steven, it all seemed too tempting to miss – because it was Steven, I suppose, who I'm such a fan of."[33]

"I was talking to David on the set of *Silence in the Library*," recalled Moffat. "I was saying, 'You have to make up your mind.' I wasn't going to sit down and write it until I knew whether I was writing for a brand new Doctor or the same old Doctor. I was saying 'I'm writ-ing it on Monday, you're going to have to tell me now.' He stuck to his original decision, which I completely understand."[60]

Speculation immediately turned to who might replace him, with David Morrissey, Paterson Joseph, James McAvoy, James Nesbitt and Robert Carlyle the favourites, according to the press. Morrissey, in particular, attracted a lot of attention as, by now, the title of the Christmas special had been revealed as *The Next Doctor*. "Hopefully that creates a bit more intrigue, and hints at interesting developments in the show's future," said Russell T Davies, the big tease. "Let's just say that regeneration is a complicated process."

By now Julie Gardner had agreed to throw her lot in with Jane Tranter at BBC Worldwide in Los Angeles and, privately, Davies had also resolved to join them there. More immediately, the execs had a firefight on their hands when the second of 2009's planned specials was thrown into doubt by the imminent collapse of Woolworths, the ailing high street fixture that was the BBC's partner in its home entertain-ment arm, 2 Entertain. When Woolies went into receivership, BBC Worldwide was forced to reduce its funding commitments, including the chunk it was contributing towards *Doctor Who*. Gardner explained to David Tennant that their first priority was to safeguard his two-part finale, which might mean writing off one of the other stories. Also, he ought to brace himself for a severe shortage of pick 'n' mix in the catering truck.

As press speculation about the eleventh Doctor continued, one name seemed to have risen above the pack as a clear bookies' favour-ite. Paterson Joseph, who had previously appeared in the Series One finale and would soon be seen alongside Freema Agyeman in a re-make of Terry Nation's post-apocalypse drama *Survivors*, told the BBC he would "love the challenge" of playing the Time Lord, but refused to be drawn further. "I'm afraid I can't make any comment on it," he said. "I'm not a gambler. And I don't approve of gambling, unless it's for the Grand National."

Having just been told by Julie Gardner that the second special was back on, Russell T Davies made his way to Buckingham Palace to collect his OBE from the Prince of Wales. Continuing his charm offensive on the heir to the throne, Davies asked him if his ears were real, while Charles insisted he'd only just heard about the cameo offer. (And actually, now he came to think about it, wasn't there now a vacancy for a more substantial role...?)

The next day, Davies appeared at the Inside the World of *Doctor Who* event at the London Children's Film Festival, where he improvised a story, based on audience suggestions, set on Venus featuring Davros, the Daleks, Sarah Jane Smith, a hurricane, a stepladder and an aardvark. Suddenly, *Journey's End* started to make a lot more sense.

As *TV Times* readers voted David Tennant the Sexiest Male on TV, the actor was forced to pull out of *Hamlet*, which had now transferred to London, for an operation on a prolapsed disc in his back. Fans flooded him with get well messages – specifically: get well in time for January, because that's when filming starts on *Doctor Who*. "We'll be very careful," promised Russell T Davies, speaking at the press launch for the Christmas special a few days after Tennant's successful surgery. "I don't think we'll be swinging him from a wire on his first day back." He wasn't making any promises about day two, though.

New Doctor Who "nearly old enough to remember Paul McGann"

Some of *Doctor Who*'s finest hours, from *The Talons of Weng-Chiang* and *City of Death* to *Tooth and Claw* and *Midnight*, were the product of last-minute scripts bashed out in a fug of cigarette smoke and black coffee. Unfortunately, *The Next Doctor* is not one of them.

The 2008 Christmas special's biggest disappointment is its failure to commit to its intriguing premise: having raised the mystery of who David Morrissey's future Doctor – complete with his own companion, TARDIS and dandy wardrobe – might be, Russell T Davies briskly dispenses with the whole thing less than half way in, with the underwhelming reveal that he's just an ordinary bloke who *thinks* he's the Doctor. Yes, there's some nice stuff about how the Doctor can inspire ordinary mortals to great deeds and yadda yadda yadda but, really, why bother? It's less a tease than an outright cheat.

In fact, everything about the production smacks of a missed opportunity. Cybermen on the rampage in snowy Victorian London? You'd have to work pretty hard to make that lack atmosphere. But somehow they manage it, largely by having the tinheads star in a gloopy re-make of *Oliver!* – you'd just swear the smudge-faced urchins operating the Cybes' cartoon steampunk factory are going to break out into "It's a Hard Knock Life" at any moment. (And yes, I'm aware that's from *Annie*, so don't write in.) From this Willy Wonka-esque sweatshop there eventually rises the Cyber King – a somewhat impractical spaceship in the shape of a walking, Japanese-style mecha robot with a factory in its chest, which stomps about for a bit until the Doctor talks it to death from a hot air balloon.

The Cybershades are another case in point: savage cybernetic beasties, like a cross between a Cyberman and a wild animal, they ought to be terrifyingly feral creatures. But the result looks like someone in a cheap gorilla suit wearing a Cyberman mask. Probably because it is someone in a cheap gorilla suit wearing a Cyberman mask.

The graveside funeral massacre is probably the most impressive set-piece – though it's Dervla Kirwen, a vision in vivid scarlet against the white snow, who stands out more than the Cybermen. Kirwen is deliciously arch as the devilish Miss Hartigan, the ultimate embodiment of a woman scorned, while the Two Davids make the best of the thin material. There's also a fan-pleasing slideshow of all the previous Doctors (Julie Gardner's idea, apparently – and, yes, it does include Paul McGann).

Ultimately, though, this feels like a rough sketch of a much more satisfying story waiting to emerge. In later years, Steven Moffat would retcon this episode in a bid to explain why no-one remembers the day a 200-ft robot went rampaging through Victorian London. Really, though, he needn't have bothered. *The Next Doctor* does a pretty good job of being entirely forgettable on its own.

There was no arguing with the numbers, though – with a barnstorming 13.1 million viewers, *Doctor Who* was the second most-watched show over Christmas, beating all the soaps and only being outperformed by Wallace and Gromit's latest claymation caper.

And there was more excitement to come. On January 2nd, the BBC announced that the following day's special BBC One edition of *Doctor Who Confidential* – billed as a guide to all ten Doctors – would in fact see the eleventh Doctor unveiled live on air, and also on the Beeb's giant screens in cities across Britain. As big announcements go, all that was missing was a plume of white smoke from the roof of the Broadcasting House.

"We are so pleased to have been able to cast this person as the new Doctor," said new exec producer Piers Wenger. "We believe the actor is going to bring something very special to the role and will make it absolutely their own – I just can't wait to tell everyone who it is. It has been a nail-biting Christmas trying to keep this under wraps!"

Discussing the announcement the next morning, BBC entertainment correspondent Lizo Mzimba ran through the usual list of suspects, but also threw in a hitherto unmentioned name in the form of 26-year-old Matt Smith, previously seen alongside Billie Piper in the TV adaptations of Philip Pullman's *Sally Lockhart Mysteries* and, more recently, in the BBC's underperforming (but really rather good) Westminster drama *Party Animals*.

The *Confidential* special kicked off with a lengthy discussion of the first ten Doctors with David Tennant, Russell T Davies and Steven Moffat, before the camera suddenly cut to a slightly shellshocked-looking young man peeping sheepishly out from beneath of an unruly tangle of hair. Matt Smith. The eleventh Doctor.

The actor – who had only signed his contract a few hours before the interview – had been one of the first people Moffat, Piers Wenger and casting director Andy Pryor had seen for the part. "He was just spot on, right from the beginning," said Moffat. "The way he said the lines, the way he looked, his *hair*. We just thought, 'Oh, that's him'. Trouble is, it's the first day. Trouble is, it's one hour into the process and you've been bracing yourself for months, so you can't believe it. We thought we had to go and keep going and keep looking and keep finding people."[62]

"I got an email from Steven at 4.30 one Saturday afternoon," recalled Wenger, "where he basically said, 'It's Matt, isn't it? And it kind of always has been'."[62]

"There is something quite old about him," observed Moffat. "He looks old and young, and I think that's terribly important."[62]

And the man himself? "How do I feel? I'm flabbergasted," said Smith. "I haven't slept, to be honest. Truthfully, I haven't."[62]

He also produced a letter, written to him by David Tennant. Smith declined to read the letter aloud on air, but Tennant later said it referred to the Doctor as "the greatest part – you get to do everything and be everything, and you get to save the universe on a weekly basis. It doesn't get much better than that." Aaaw, how sweet. I wonder if he'd copied it from Christopher Eccleston's handover note?

In a press release issued immediately after the broadcast, Moffat said: "The Doctor is a very special part, and it takes a very special actor to play him. You need to be old and young at the same time, a boffin and an action hero, a cheeky schoolboy and the wise old man of the universe. 2010 is a long time away, but rest assured the eleventh Doctor is coming – and the universe has never been so safe."

It had been Russell T Davies' idea to make the announcement live on television – after Operation COBRA, he was obviously getting a taste for all this cloak and dagger stuff. Matt Smith's name was never referred to in emails, and his first photo shoot – in the basement of Television Centre on Christmas Eve – was shrouded in such secrecy, even the photographer didn't know what it was for (the TARDIS was added into the shots later, as it may have been something of a giveaway).

The *Confidential* programme was seen by a remarkable 6.30 million viewers. "We got higher viewing figures than *The Daemons*!"[63], chortled Russell T Davies. Which is not actually true: *The Daemons* averaged 8.3 million viewers, while its Christmas 1971 repeat got an astonishing 10.5 million – the highest-rated *Doctor Who* story since *Galaxy Four*, way back in... oh, you've gone. Was it something I said?

The New Year's next bit of publicity was less positive, as *Guardian* journalist Gareth McLean filed a biting op-ed piece based on rumours that the first of 2009's *Doctor Who* specials was going to be filmed in Dubai.

"That's the Dubai that isn't a democracy," he wrote. "Dubai with its dubious human rights record, appalling treatment of migrant workers and flagrant disregard for the environment. Dubai, *where you can be arrested for being gay* and jailed for up to ten years. To that list, you can now add – because you can be sure the emirate's tourist board will – Dubai: location for BBC1 hit drama *Doctor Who*. Come! Bring your children!

"It's a move that totally goes against everything that the Doctor as a character stands for. At best, filming *Doctor Who* in Dubai is stupid. At worst, it's hypocritical – and it's hypocrisy fuelled by hubris at that. What would the Doctor do?"

On the plus side, the weather was lovely at that time of year.

When production resumed on January 19th, David Tennant admitted it took him a while to remember how to do the Doctor's voice. Though, unlike Billie Piper, he at least managed to remember *before* they started filming. With broadcast slated for Easter, the first episode – inspired by the image of a tube train (now changed to a bus) in the desert that Russell T Davies remembered from co-writer Gareth Roberts' 90s New Adventures novel *The Highest Science* – would require one of the quickest turnarounds ever attempted.

Guest stars for the story were announced as former EastEnder (and short-lived Bionic Woman) Michelle Ryan and slapstick stand-up Lee Evans. Meanwhile, *The Sun* claimed the Doctor would be teaming up with Martha Jones for at least one of the specials, despite the "fact" Freema Agyeman had "reportedly annoyed *Who* chiefs" by signing up for *Law and Order: UK*, after which Davies was "forced to tear up scripts for *Who* spin-off *Torchwood*, in which she'd been given a starring role".

At the end of the month, the production team heard news from the Middle East that the red Routemaster bus they'd shipped out for filming in the desert had been damaged while being unloaded in Dubai. Director James Strong was leaving his house when he got a call from Julie Gardner telling him "It's a disaster – the bus is fucked". "When I got into the office, I was handed a photograph, and my initial reaction was absolute horror. A crane had dropped a massive cargo container on top of our beautiful bus, and completely smashed it up."[64]

An emergency meeting was called, but Russell T Davies shrugged the whole thing off. "I actually laughed and laughed," he said. "There was frantic work for a lot of people, but I just thought of the solution in about a minute flat. That's just what happens when a bus goes through a wormhole, it looks a bit worse for wear. You won't even notice the re-write."[65]

For continuity purposes, the team in Cardiff had to find another bus – and then smash it up to match the one in Dubai. It was the most extreme act of vandalism committed by members of the *Doctor Who* production team since Pip and Jane Baker rewrote the end of *The Trial of a Time Lord*.

When David Tennant – fresh from winning the Critics' Circle Award for Best Shakespearian Performance – and Michelle Ryan arrived in Dubai, their minibus was pulled over by armed police and the driver forced to pay a "fine", while another crew driver took a wrong turn in the desert and ended up heading for Oman.

But the worst was still to come. On the morning of the first day's shooting in the desert, the crew awoke to a raging sandstorm. "This massive desert landscape – you couldn't see it," said James Strong. "I mean, we could have been in a car park in Upper Boat. Also, sand was being blown in our faces, constantly. The actors couldn't open their eyes. They all looked like they'd been tarred in sand and dragged through a hedge."[66]

On the plus side, the episode was the first *Doctor Who* story to be filmed using high-definition cameras – so at least viewers would be able to see all that sand in pin-sharp detail.

"There were moments when we thought, 'We're not going to be able to do this'," said David Tennant on the episode's DVD commentary. "We've finally been defeated by circum-stance."

As plans were frantically being drawn up to film on a Welsh beach instead, the sun suddenly came out, and Strong was able to complete all the shots he needed – though he did have to contend with a gang of dune bikers riding across his supposedly deserted alien vista. Maybe *The Guardian* had a point about Dubai.

"Please note Travelcards are not valid for journeys to planets outside Zones 1-6"

In late February, the main guest star for the second special, set on Mars and scheduled for broadcast around Hallowe'en, was revealed. Russell T Davies had written an older female lead with Helen Mirren in mind, and had also heard that Judi Dench might be interested. In the end, though, the role went to 58-year-old Lindsay Duncan, whose illustrious stage and screen career had seen her win two Olivier Awards and a Tony, not to mention being made a CBE in that year's New Year honours. All of which paled in comparison with the high watermark of her career, voicing the android TC-14 in *Star Wars Episode I: The Phantom Menace*.

By this time, Davies was hard at work on the tenth Doctor's swansong. He had already abandoned several ideas, including a small, deliberately low-key story about the Doctor dying saving a family on a stranded spaceship, before developing a much bigger narrative involving a rematch with the Master and (drum roll please) the return of the Time Lords. The latter was a request from Julie Gardner, who was inspired by hearing Murray Gold's Gallifrey theme performed at the *Doctor Who Prom*. "I dreaded writing them," admitted Davies. "I got rid of them for a reason: I used to worry that those scenes would be like the RSC green room, and I tried everything to counter that. I tried writing young, sexy Time Lords. Or fast, flip, *Buffy*-esque dialogue. Or weird, surreal, mime-type faces. You name it. But in the end, you've got to be honest. They are what they are. They're grand, and powerful, and dress like it's opera season."[66]

Davies – who cheekily turned up to a tone

meeting for the story sporting his OBE – had also planned to use the Daleks, and asked Steven Moffat what he thought. Moffat said he'd rather wait and re-launch them in the 2010 series, and Davies deferred to his request. Isn't it nice to see two young Doctor Who fans playing so nicely together and sharing their toys?

In March, the *Daily Mirror* reported that the new Doctor was to get a new TARDIS – let's hope the bloke they sent round to measure up got the bloody windows right – while David Tennant was one of the hosts of that year's Comic Relief telethon, during which he snogged Davina McCall live on air. And there aren't many award-winning members of the Royal Shakespeare Company who can say that. The evening also included a special Sarah Jane Adventures sketch, written by Gareth Roberts and Clayton Hickman, and starring Ronnie Corbett as a pint-sized Slitheen who clamps K-9, before being despatched back into space ("and it's goodnight from him", etc).

By April, Russell T Davies was already talking up David Tennant's departure. "I think it's going to be a brilliant piece of television," he told *SFX*. "And let's be honest, David is one of the hugest stars in the land, and his Doctor has been a massive figure for an entire generation. So in a way it's a piece of television history. It's not the invention of colour, but you'll have eight-year-olds remembering it, just like we remember the regenerations, forever. I love that, and I know exactly how to do it."[63]

How? asked *Time Out*. "An elephant falls on his head," said Davies. "Death by circus."[65] Just his little joke. Probably.

David Tennant and Michelle Ryan were also doing their share of publicity for the upcoming Easter special. Tennant once again co-hosted Jonathan Ross' Radio 2 show with Catherine Tate (which included several memorable impressions of guest John "Music! Music! Music!" Barrowman) and Ryan rolled her sleeves up to bake a cake on *Blue Peter* – which surely qualifies her as a canonical *Doctor Who* companion in its own right. On *BBC Breakfast*, meanwhile, Davies described the story as "the last chance to have a great big romp of an adventure before the darkness".

Like *The Next Doctor*, *Planet of the Dead* starts with an interesting premise – a London bus and its passengers are stranded on an alien world after driving through a wormhole on the North Circular, like you do – but then doesn't really know what to do with it. The desert location looks stunning – especially in HD – and brings a new widescreen sensibility to the show. But that will only get you so far. There's such an ambling lack of urgency or jeopardy to the whole caper, you feel Michael Palin might wander on at any moment for some gentle comic business with a camel.

The bus passengers are a fairly unmemorable bunch – including, sadly, Michelle Ryan as one-shot companion Lady Christina de Souza, a rather stiff aristo jewel thief who's just a bit too smug to warm to, and fails to ignite any real chemistry with David Tennant's Doctor. (She's not even very *sexy* – Ryan is a very beautiful woman, but those leathers are less Lara Croft than Sunday morning fry-up down the biker caff.)

It's left to Noma Dumezweni and Lee Evans, as UNIT's Captain Magambo and scientific advisor Malcolm Taylor, to try to inject a bit of life into proceedings. Some may balk at the idea of a slapstick comedian better known for pratfalls and silly voices as UNIT's scientific adviser, but this is no place to get into a debate about Jon Pertwee. Let's just say how you feel about Malcolm will pretty much depend on how you feel about Lee Evans. (And at least he's *trying* to make us laugh – elsewhere, this is surprisingly mirth-free for a script with Gareth Roberts' name on it.)

The episode's Big Bad – a swarm of giant metallic stingrays who can devour whole planets and rip a hole in the fabric of space – are a pretty cool idea, though somewhat undermined by the fact the Doctor and Christina can outrun them *in sand*. And the Tritovores – twittering humanoid flies in jumpsuits – are a fun addition for the kids, even if they don't actually get to do very much.

The story is bookended by two sequences that push the implausibility needle dangerously into the red. The first is a silly chase sequence in which Christina bribes her way onto a London bus with a stolen diamond (even though it's probably worth less than an Oyster card), which persuades the driver it's a good idea to try to outrun the police.

The second comes right at the end as the Doctor flies the bus over London, *Chitty Chitty Bang Bang*-style, and spins its back end out in order to swat a stray stingray. Not only is it very silly, it's also very badly executed. Maybe it was a victim of the production's rapid turnaround, but it has to be a contender for the least convincing effects shot since the show's revival.

Despite this, *Planet of the Dead* isn't bad so much as just a bit... meh. And that's the one thing *Doctor Who* – especially an episode serving as viewers' only fix in 11 long months – surely can't ever afford to be.

True to Davies' assertion that this is the last opportunity for a frothy romp before things get serious, there's some spooky foreshadowing of things to come when psychic Carmen, a bus passenger who claims to have the gift of second sight, tells the Doctor: "Your song is ending. It is returning... Through the dark. He will knock four times."

Wow – she obviously has some pretty awesome psychic powers. Though not awesome enough to stop her getting on the bus in the first place.

Planet of the Dead was promoted as *Doctor Who*'s 200th story, and the bus has the route No. 200 in honour of this fact. It was *Doctor Who Magazine* editor Tom Spilsbury who pointed out this milestone to Russell T Davies – though it takes some fairly tortuous leaps of logic to reach that conclusion, including counting the unfinished *Shada* as canonical, lumping *The Trial of a Time Lord* in together and, least plausibly, counting *Utopia*, *The Sound of Drums* and *Last of the Time Lords* as a single story. Even though they're clearly, you know, *not*.

As fans began counting off the days until the next special – revealed at the end of *Planet of the Dead* to be called *The Waters of Mars* – the new Doctor Who production team was confirmed, with Steven Moffat and Piers Wenger joined by fellow exec Beth Willis, producer of hit *Life on Mars* spin-off *Ashes to Ashes*, while Tracie Simpson and Peter Bennett, fresh from production duties on *Torchwood*, would handle the day-to-day running of the show.

Taping had now begun on David Tennant's final story, which the *Daily Mail* reported would feature actress Claire Bloom as the Doctor's mother, no less, while *The Sun* claimed former 007 Timothy Dalton would play "a baddie" in the episodes.

In fact, Dalton was already in Cardiff and had started filming. "Russell's script is one of the most extraordinary scripts that I've ever read," he said. "He's blended the imaginatively outrageous with the ordinary and prosaic, and moves between them with ease."[67] Blimey, that's not a quote, that's a *review*.

"He's every inch the movie star," observed David Tennant of Dalton, "but without any of the grandness that might come with that. He said, 'I'm proud that not only am I James Bond, I'm also a Time Lord', so I think he was quite happy to notch up the icons. I remember us comparing the James Bond and *Doctor Who* theme tunes. There's a certain similarity of bassline there."[67]

Dalton was also one of the cast and crew – which included everyone from David Tennant, Billie Piper and John Simm to the show's drivers, sparkies and even a bunch of dancing Adipose – who filmed a special version of The Proclaimers' "(I'm Gonna Be) 500 Miles" to be shown at Russell T Davies and Julie Gardner's farewell party. Even funnier was a second video, "The Ballad of Russell and Julie," a spoof of Victoria Wood's most famous witty ditty starring Catherine Tate as Gardner, singing in a Welsh accent: "Let's do it, let's do it, I've had a really good idea / We'll revamp, make more camp, a sci-fi show from yesteryear / I've had banter, with Tranter, your written word will be hailed as a ming mong mantra." Then David Tennant appears as Davies claiming, among other things: "I can't block out, please lock out, images of Johnny B getting his cock out, I can't do it, I can't do it toniiiiiight!" And thanks to YouTube, this delightful little tribute is now available for us all to enjoy at our leisure.

On May 12th, David Tennant entered the TARDIS set at Upper Boat to film his regeneration. When the time came to call Matt Smith from his trailer, the studio was cleared of non-essential personnel so as not to faze the new man. "To clear the studio, everyone goes outside," recalled Russell T Davies. "And how does Matt Smith get to the studio? Oh, by walking through all the people who have been cleared to avoid him!"[68]

The showrunner admitted he was "thrown" by seeing Smith in Tennant's brown suit.

Having thanked Davies for his good luck card, the new Doctor walked on-set, introduced himself ("Hello everybody, lovely to meet you all – I'm Matt Smith") and posed for pictures with his predecessor, before getting down to the business in hand.

"As I walked off," recalled Tennant, "I heard [director] Euros Lyn turn to Matt and go, 'Anyway, what we do now is...' I thought, wow, so that's how it works? And of course it does. One knows that's what will happen. Suddenly, what becomes important is getting the next scene done, and I'm not in the next scene. That's it, cheerio. That, more than anything, was a reminder that it was all over."[67]

Tennant recorded his final scene – as opposed to his *final* scene, which he'd recorded the previous week (I hope you're following this) – on May 20th. The sequence – some flailing about on wires in front of a green screen – perhaps lacked the appropriate gravitas required for such a momentous occasion, but that's television for you.

Shortly afterwards, he was called back to the studio for a "lighting reference", at which point Peter Bennett announced: "That's a golden wrap on the tenth Doctor, Mr David Tennant", and the set was showered by a cannon of pink confetti. Tennant couldn't help shedding a tear, after which he joked that he'd changed his mind. "I'm very proud of everything we've done," he told the assembled crew. "Thank you very, very much."

And that was that. Allons-y.

"Just because I used to go to school dressed as your dad, it doesn't mean this has to be weird"

Except it wasn't, quite – for a man who'd just regenerated, the tenth Doctor was kept pretty busy over the next few months. The week after his golden wrap on *Doctor Who*, David Tennant was back in the stripy suit recording a guest slot on *The Sarah Jane Adventures*. "Instead of finishing like an amputation from *Who*, it was an easier kind of slide," mused Elisabeth Sladen. "Instead of just 'Finish!', he knew he was coming to do this."[10]

Tennant was pleased to do his bit for *Doctor Who*'s sister show – but it still didn't provide him with a more dramatic final moment. "The last line I say as the Doctor is 'You two, with me, spit-spot'," he told reporters. "They were the last words I uttered in this suit. So I guess it was robbed of any epic quality."

Meanwhile, John Barrowman – who seemed to be on TV more than the news these days – was fronting BBC One Saturday night wish-fulfilment show *Tonight's the Night*, which had recently run an Alien Talent Search in a bid to find a new monster to star in a short *Doctor Who* mini-adventure. The winning entry was from viewer Tim Ingham, whose creation Sao Til was basically a man wearing a trilby hat and a blue sock over his face. Russell T Davies dutifully scripted a three-minute scene in which Til tries to pass himself off as the new Doctor, but Captain Jack sees through his sock... sorry, through his disguise. When Til threatens Jack, David Tennant walks onto the TARDIS set, in his civvies, and tells Barrowman to stop mucking about. According to Davies, the piece was originally supposed to be a straight drama, featuring Tennant in character, but he couldn't bear for it to be the last thing he wrote for the tenth Doctor, so turned it into a sketch instead.

Finally, in late May, the BBC announced that a new animated *Doctor Who* adventure, *Dreamland*, would be shown later that year on the Corporation's Red Button service. Tennant had recorded his contribution earlier that month, accompanied by co-stars David Warner and Georgia Moffett, who Tennant was now dating.

Yes, you read that right. The tenth Doctor was now in a relationship with the fifth Doctor's daughter. Which, if it ever led to marriage, would make him his own father-in-law. What's more, she had played *his* daughter on TV, which... actually, let's not go there.

According to Peter Davison, Tennant may have been "the sexiest man on TV," but he was still rubbish at chatting up girls. "[Georgia] said, 'I don't understand – if he's interested, why doesn't he just ask me out?'" Davison told *Reader's Digest*. "'He's playing Doctor Who!' And I said, 'It doesn't really make any difference. You're either that sort of person or you're not.' It doesn't matter if you're the most famous."[69] Also, let's not forget that he was, at heart, still a *Doctor Who* fan, so talking to girls didn't come naturally.

Across the pond, *Variety* reported that this year's *Doctor Who* specials would debut on BBC America, not the Sci-Fi Channel (or SyFy, as it had now been irritatingly rebranded). Having previously been outbid, BBC America were delighted to finally have first-run rights to the show. "If I'd been here, we wouldn't have sold it," said the channel's bullish new president, Garth Ancier. Ooh, get him.

May's big news, though, was the announcement of the new companion who would accompany Matt Smith's Doctor. Actress and model Karen Gillan, 21, had already appeared in a minor role in the previous year's *The Fires of Pompeii*, but now she'd been promoted to full-time TARDIS traveller.

"The show is such a massive phenomenon that I can't quite believe I am going to be a part of it," said Gillan. "Matt Smith is an incredible actor and it is going to be so much fun to act alongside him."

Steven Moffat described the Inverness-born actress as "funny, and clever, and gorgeous, and sexy. Or Scottish, which is the quick way of saying it. A generation of little girls will want to be her. And a generation of little boys will want them to be her too."

As *Torchwood* prepared for its promotion to primetime BBC One in early July, Captain Jack and company appeared in perhaps an even more surprising new guise: taking over three Afternoon Play slots on Radio 4. We can only wonder at what the station's audience of tweedy *Telegraph* readers made of their traditional Aga saga fix being replaced by John Barrowman fighting aliens in Cardiff, but it's safe to assume There Would be Letters.

The auspices for *Children of Earth* were not good. Despite the promotion to BBC One, budget cuts had seen the episode count slashed from 13 to five – something John Barrowman had publicly protested felt like a "punishment" – and the story had been afforded a graveyard slot in the middle of summer, albeit stripped over five consecutive nights in a bid to give it more Event status. Against all the odds, though, it proved to be the making of *Torchwood*. And then some.

Children of Earth is a conspiracy thriller that takes a hammer to the established *Torchwood* set-up, destroying the Hub and turning Jack and company into fugitives, on the run from their own government. By stripping out everything familiar and comfortable, it succeeds in removing the excess of silliness that dogged the first two series, and pushing it into a wholly more interesting shape.

The central premise is a doozy: over the course of two days, every child in the world suddenly stops, and begins chanting – at first just the word "we," then "we are" and finally: "We. Are. Coming". The British Government suspects the involvement of an alien race known as the 456, after the wavelength they use to communicate. In 1965, the 456 had secretly offered the government a cure to a deadly new strain of flu destined to wipe out 25 million people, in exchange for 12 children. The incident was subsequently hushed up, but now the Home Office orders the assassination of everyone involved with the first contact – including one Captain Jack Harkness.

This time, the 456 have upped their demands: hand over 10% of the world's children, or they will destroy the Earth. Secretly, the world's governments agree they have no choice but to comply, and the British cabinet, along with the US Army and UNIT, begin drawing up plans to round up millions of children under the cover of giving inoculation shots in schools.

Which is where it gets really interesting... having rejected the idea of a random lottery, the government uses school league tables to identify which children are considered to be more expendable, turning what had been a straight action thriller into a thoughtful meditation on eugenics, social engineering and the value of life. (It's perhaps significant that most of the best scenes revolve around Peter Capaldi's tragically compromised Home Office Permanent Secretary, with Jack, Gwen and Ianto often feeling like a distraction in their own show.)

The 456 are a *terrifying* creation – what we can see of their ambassador, housed in a smoke-filled isolation tank in Thames House, suggests a giant, three-headed hydra given to fits of rage in which it smashes violently (and bloodily) against the glass. Even more terrifying is their motivation: their desire for human children is not driven by an instinct for survival or a quest for power or any of the usual sci-fi staples, but because they crave the chemicals in their bodies as a recreational drug. The moment the dead-eyed, shrivelled husk of one of the children from 1965 appears in the tank is probably the darkest and most disturbing the *Doctor Who* universe has ever got.

Torchwood's efforts to intervene and blow the government's plan wide open end in disaster, poisoning everyone in Thames House, including Ianto, who dies in Jack's arms. Jack does eventually save the day, of course, after realising the 456 are vulnerable to a certain frequency of audio signal. However, this requires a child to act as a focal point for the transmission, and Jack is forced to sacrifice his own grandson for the cause.

After such a strong build-up, this pat sci-fi solution is both lame, and in questionable taste, the inherent shock value of a child's death acting as a lazy shorthand for a more satisfying dramatic denouement. (Within the context of the drama, let's be clear, Jack's actions are entirely forgivable, noble even. I'm just not sure the writer's are.) It's a rare misstep, though, in a really quite astonishingly good piece of television from Russell T Davies, James Moran and newcomer John Fay. And a bona fide hit, too: the viewing figures were so strong – averaging around 6.5 million viewers – that the somewhat surprised Controller of BBC One rang Davies up to thank him.

Producer "touched" by Most Thieving Fanbase accolade

On July 20th, a publicity photo taken on the first day of Series Five filming showed Matt Smith and Karen Gillan – now revealed as playing a character called Amy Pond – in their new costumes. Smith's tweed jacket, bow tie and rolled-up trousers got the thumbs up from *Esquire* and *GQ* magazines, and an enthusiastic endorsement from the chairman of the Harris Tweed Authority. *The Guardian* accused the Time Lord of trying too hard to be on-trend, while *The Sun* said he was "dressed like a geography teacher" with a "preppy, old-fashioned look". Either one of them was mistaken, or geography teachers had got a *lot* more stylish recently.

Paparazzi photos taken on Southerndown Beach – previously used as Bad Wolf Bay in

Doomsday and *Journey's End* – showed Smith and Gillan accompanied by Alex Kingston (described by *The Sun* as "The Doctor's wife") in a glamorous frock, as well as the new TARDIS, which was painted a deeper shade of blue and sported the St John Ambulance badge not seen since the 60s. Frock or no frock, if Kingston thought she was going to get a look in on the *Doctor Who* forums alongside *that*, she had another thing coming.

In America, David Tennant, Russell T Davies, Julie Gardner and Euros Lyn appeared at Comic-Con in San Diego – Glastonbury for geeks, basically – where they received a rock-star reception, generating considerably more heat than several major Hollywood movies also plying their wares at the event. Trailers for all three specials were screened to fans, while Davies received a plaque commemorating *Doctor Who*'s second Guinness World Record, this one for Most Successful Science Fiction Series Ever, a calculation based on sales, merchandise and downloads both legit and illegal. "Close the doors!" shouted Davies. "Don't let *Star Trek* in!" And everyone laughed, as if he was joking.

A few weeks later, *Doctor Who Magazine* confirmed that David Tennant's final episode would be called *The End of Time*, for which the Doctor's main companion would be Bernard Cribbins as Wilfred Mott, with Catherine Tate and June Whitfield also among the cast. "I didn't have to think twice," said Cribbins. "I was delighted to be asked to come and do these two specials, especially since I was a companion, as it were, and actually got to go into the TARDIS. I hadn't been in the TARDIS for – I don't know – 40-something years."[33] Since it last had a St John Ambulance badge on it, in fact.

In October, the world held its breath as the new *Doctor Who* logo was revealed. Rendered in metallic blue letters not dissimilar to the Pertwee/McGann font, the script was accessorised by the letters DW in the shape of the TARDIS. "A new logo – the eleventh logo for the eleventh Doctor," said Steven Moffat, like an Apple exec launching a new phone. "Those grand old words, Doctor Who, suddenly looking newer than ever. And look at that, something really new – an insignia! DW in TARDIS form! Simple and beautiful, and most impor-

tant of all, a completely irresistible doodle. I apologise to school notebooks everywhere, because in 2010, that's what they're going to be wearing." (I think he's seriously underestimating the timeless allure of your classic cock-and-balls there, but we'll move on.)

The same week, *Blue Peter* launched its latest competition to design a TARDIS console. Any suspicions the BBC was simply using children as cheap labour were dispelled when the producers explained the console wouldn't actually be the main one used in the new TARDIS – but would make an appearance in the show at some point.

On October 9th, the *Who* world bade farewell to another of its most stalwart friends when Barry Letts passed away, aged 84. "The whole of the *Doctor Who* production team took pause, when we heard this sad news," said Russell T Davies. "None of us would be here without Barry's brilliant work in the 1970s. As a child, his show filled my eyes and my heart and my mind; he fostered the imagination of an entire generation, and his work will never be forgotten." Amen to that.

As evidence of Letts' continuing legacy, the same week saw the launch of the third series of *The Sarah Jane Adventures*, a twenty-first century hit based around a character he had helped create – and fronted by the actress he had cast – some 35 years earlier.

The run was the strongest yet, particularly Joseph Lidster's *The Mad Woman in the Attic* – an affecting tale of friendship that also sees K-9 released from black hole-bunging duties to join the Bannerman Road foo-fighters proper – and *The Eternity Trap*, a genuinely chilling haunted house tale that's scarier than 90% of "grown-up" *Who*. And then there's *The Wedding of Sarah Jane Smith*, in which the surprise nuptials between Sladen's eternal singleton and silver-tongued lothario Nigel Havers are rudely interrupted by a certain skinny wedding crasher in a stripy suit. Sadly, the planned meeting of the tenth Doctor and the Brigadier had to be called off when Nicholas Courtney proved too ill to appear, but it's still a thrill to see David Tennant interacting with the *SJA* gang – including K-9 – and it's almost certainly the only thing on children's telly that year to contain a reference to *The Armageddon Factor*.

The Waters of Mars: "Anyone mind if I grab the first shower?"

At the press launch for *The Waters of Mars*, Russell T Davies announced that the special, to be broadcast in mid-November (on a Sunday, no less), would be dedicated to the memory of Barry Letts. "He was an extraordinary figure in *Doctor Who* history and in pop culture," said Davies, "so, of course, we wanted to have that tribute to him on screen."

David Tennant's publicity duties for the new story included co-presenting Absolute Radio's breakfast show for five days with his mate Christian O'Connell, while press interviews included a joint conversation with Tennant and Davies in *SFX*. Did having more time to write the specials mean less pressure, wondered the magazine? "Nah, he just leaves it to the last minute!" joked Tennant. "Well of course someone said, 'Will you completely reinvent *Torchwood* from top to bottom?'" grumbled Davies. "So that was all my spare time gone."[70]

Having evolved the basic idea of a human base on Mars, Davies and Phil Ford found their story shaped by real-life events. "The day that we sat down to talk about this was actually, believe it or not, the day that NASA announced that they had discovered evidence of water on Mars," said Ford, "so there was a certain synchronicity that day between science and science fiction."[71]

As the script took shape, the idea of water began to assume a more sinister purpose. "Wouldn't it be cool," wondered Ford, "if the element that was crucial to humanity's survival was also the thing that could destroy it?"[71]

Cool, yes – but complicated, as having water constantly spewing out of characters' mouths proved to be the most challenging practical effect ever attempted by the team. In the end, they developed a system of pumping water through two tubes taped to the actors' cheeks. The scary contact lenses, meanwhile, were supplied by Specsavers. (It wasn't so much the quality that attracted the production team as the free prescription sunglasses with every pair.)

One element Davies was keen to include in the script was the idea of the Doctor going rogue – the notion that, as the last of the Time Lords, he now felt there was no-one to stop him buggering about with the Laws of Time as much as he bloody well liked: pride before the approaching fall.

Much of the pre-publicity focused on story's fear factor. The *Radio Times* invoked the spirit of the late Mary Whitehouse by questioning the episode's suitability for children, while its coverline asked if this was the scariest *Doctor Who* story ever.

Probably not, is the answer. But it's pretty bloody scary all the same. And it's certainly the show's most adult treatment of, for want of a better word, zombies. Forget the shuffling, vaguely comical plague-carriers of *New Earth*: here the victims of a waterborne Martian virus are transformed into animalistic killers with cracked, almost reptilian skin and faces fixed into hideous leers, from which a torrent of water pours constantly through blackened lips. The effect is deeply unnerving – as is the fact that, unlike the glacial pace the undead normally move at, these unstoppable predators can run at full pelt.

Water is even harder to outrun – and that's what really ratchets up the terror. "Water is patient," warns the Doctor. "Water just waits. Wears down the clifftops, the mountains, the whole of the world. Water always wins."

And win it does: *Doctor Who* is a show that, on the whole, faces danger with a song in its heart and a spring in its step. This, by contrast, is grimly fatalistic as, one by one, the crew members of Bowie Base One succumb inexorably to the virus; the moment when technician Steffi desperately fights a losing battle to keep control of her humanity while a video message from her young daughter plays on a screen in front of her is heartbreaking – and as bleak as *Doctor Who* gets.

Lindsay Duncan is fantastic as no-nonsense mission leader Captain Adelaide Brooke – a woman who will go down in history as one of Earth's great spacefaring pioneers. She's so important, in fact, that this is one if those tricksy "fixed points" in time that the Doctor is forbidden to – as the original series proposal for *Doctor Who* memorably put it 46 years earlier – "monkey with". He knows that Adelaide and the rest of her crew have to die, here, on Mars, today. Told you it was grim.

Except...

The Doctor has had enough. After walking away from the base with the screams of the crew ringing in his ears, our hero has an epiphany – and turns back. Because, he realises, he's not just the last survivor of the Time War, he's the winner – "the Time Lord Victorious". So who exactly is going to stop him rewriting any bit of history he chooses?

This is a potentially fascinating idea for the series to develop. The problem is, it comes from nowhere in the last act, and then stretches credulity beyond breaking point by having Captain Brooke, who the Doctor has just returned safely to Earth, take her own life in order to set time's needle back in its groove – even though the Doctor has already assured her it probably won't make any difference. Are we really expected to believe anyone would forsake the chance to see their own children and family again by shooting themselves dead on the basis of something a nutter with a blue box casually mentioned earlier, and then changed his mind about anyway?

However implausible, Adelaide's suicide has the desired effect of making the Doctor see the error of his ways, thus reversing the story back out of the Time Lord Victorious cul-de-sac before the credits have even rolled. That's a whole plot arc, from transgression to penitence, wrapped up in under ten minutes, with the consequence that the whole thing feels like a bit of an afterthought, and makes Adelaide's sacrifice seem strangely hollow.

Which is a shame as, up until the 50-minute mark, The Waters of Mars is by far the stand-out entry in this run of specials: a classic Doctor Who base-under-siege story that evokes a very real, very palpable sense of dread.

In the closing seconds, our guilt-ridden hero turns and finds Ood Sigma – last seen leading the rebellion on the planet of the Ood – projecting across time and space to a London street in the snow. "Is this it?" asks the Doctor, haunted by the gathering portents of doom. "My death? Is it time?" To which Ood Sigma offers no answer, and simply fades away. But don't go reading anything into that – it was probably just a bad signal.

The story benefited from its winter slot (which, let's face it, is where Doctor Who belongs) to capture almost ten million viewers

(and would later net the show its fourth Hugo Award in as many years). Over on the Red Button, meanwhile, David Tennant's CG avatar had an alien encounter in the Nevada desert in Dreamland. Shown in six parts, followed by a BBC2 compilation repeat, Phil Ford's Men in Black-meets-Them! homage is Doctor Who's first real attempt at 50s-style pulp American sci-fi, complete with Roswell greys, Area 51 and a US Army blowhard who wants to use alien tech to nuke the Reds. (Sadly, a sub-plot featuring a certain Private Presley was cut for timing reasons. Pity, as it would almost certainly have been one of Elvis' better movies.)

"Basically, it's the kind of story we would always love to do on Doctor Who on the telly, but could never do because of the budget," said Ford (who seemed to have forgotten that it was on the telly). "A big kind of 1950s monster movie. It's almost a B-movie, in the best of ways. It's full of aliens and flying saucers – this is Doctor Who if it had been filmed in 1958. This is drive-in movie Doctor Who!"[67]

In December, David Tennant flew to LA to star in the pilot for a proposed new US comedy drama, Rex is Not Your Lawyer, about a hotshot litigator who starts suffering crippling panic attacks, and so has to coach his clients to represent themselves. With a hilarious premise like that, it surely couldn't fail to get picked up for a series. Right?

Office "Master race" joke gets out of hand

Despite being more than 5,000 miles away, David Tennant somehow still managed to be more ubiquitous than Santa throughout December – even replacing the big bearded fella on BBC One's Christmas idents, which featured the tenth Doctor goofing about with a reindeer, and digging the TARDIS out of a snowdrift.

As The Waters of Mars won BBC America its highest ever primetime rating, with 1.1 million viewers tuning in, in the UK The Times ranked Doctor Who at No. 5 in its Top 50 TV Shows of the Noughties. (The Sopranos took the top spot, but Caitlin Moran's citation for Who suggested she thought this was an injustice: "I don't care what anyone says about The Wire or The Sopranos," she wrote. "This is a kids' show, made in Wales, by gays, about a scorchingly hot nerd travelling through time and space. That's clearly the best show ever. F*** off.")

In the *Daily Mirror*, Russell T Davies was quoted as saying the Tories would "exterminate" the BBC if they won the 2010 General Election. Though he probably didn't actually use the word "exterminate". In the same interview, he admitted to getting a bit blubbery while writing the tenth Doctor's farewell: "I shed a tear when I finished writing it. It is emotional. Saying goodbye, for me and David, has been a long process. If it had happened overnight, I'd be bereft and grieving, but we've had a long time to get used to the idea."

Sadly, as a Christmas Day special – and the first part of the tenth Doctor's final bow – *The End of Time Part One* is a crashing non-event. It's an extended runaround in a scrapyard, interspersed with the occasional comedy interlude (June Whitfield squeezing David Tennant's arse, that sort of thing) or out-of-left-field emoting (there's a painfully overwrought scene in a cafe in which the Doctor starts blubbing like someone who's just been dumped by text message). The Master's resurrection – in which he's brought back to life by the cast of *Prisoner: Cell Block H* using lipstick and some magic potion – is Russell T Davies at his most shameless, while the Doctor's conflicted emotions about his old enemy feel just as forced and unconvincing as the last time round. The message seems to be, yes, he's a genocidal maniac with the blood of millions on his hands – but, really, you gotta love the guy. Just look at that adorable smile!

Given her tragic fate in Series Four, Donna starting to remember details of her travels with the Doctor also ought to be a major emotional beat. Instead, despite his repeated insistence they will kill her, her memories have the opposite effect of turning her into a super-powered weapon capable of firing a massive, Master-blasting energy wave from her head instead. Which is just silly.

The cliffhanger, meanwhile, in which the Master manages to turn everyone on the planet into copies of himself, strives to be epic – but it's hard to focus on the death of humanity when John Simm is camping it up in an assortment of dresses and ladies' trouser suits. Imagine *28 Days Later* crossed with *Tootsie* and

you'll have a rough idea of where this went so horribly wrong. (One scene had required John Simm to make more than 30 costume changes. "The tights are a big pain", he lamented. Honestly, call yourself a Scissor Sisters fan...)

Luckily, Timothy Dalton turns up in the dying seconds to explain why it's more exciting than it looks. "This was far more than humanity's end," he booms (producing a really quite impressive amount of spit in the process). "This was the day on which the whole of creation would change forever. This was the day... the Time Lords returned!"

Yeah, okay – you got us there.

On Boxing Day, David Tennant and Catherine Tate resumed their semi-regular gig presenting Jonathan Ross' Radio 2 show, where their guests included Bernard Cribbins and Peter Davison. Or Dad, as Tennant liked to call him these days. A few days later, Tennant's Zelig-like presence as the new face of Christmas was co-opted by the *Daily Mail* as part of its ongoing hate campaign against the BBC. "He is about to make his final bow after nearly five years as one of the most popular incarnations of Doctor Who," said the paper. "But it seems the BBC are squeezing as much as they can out of the success of David Tennant. By the end of the Christmas period, the actor will have made 75 appearances in three weeks on the Corporation's TV channels and radio stations.

"As well as his two-part farewell as the time-traveller in *Doctor Who: The End of Time*, the 38-year-old has starred in a production of *Hamlet*, been a presenter and panellist on celebrity quiz shows and read stories for a children's programme. He has also been featured as a guest on *Desert Island Discs* and even popped up on a programme about the Open University – all between December 14th and January 3rd.

"Just 28 of his appearances come in new programmes, while 47 are repeats. Tennant has also appeared regularly in BBC1's promotional 'idents' in between shows.

"Yesterday, the BBC came under fire for freezing out young acting talent by giving audiences an overdose of Tennant." The paper then turned to rentagob Tory MP Nigel Evans, a member of the Culture, Media and Sport select committee, to provide some flimsy cover for their hatchet job.

"The BBC's public service remit was always about bringing on fresh talent," blithered Evans – clearly ignoring the fact Tennant himself had been largely unknown at the time of his casting, and Matt Smith was hardly Tom Hanks. "Sadly, they seem to have got themselves stuck in the rut of chasing ratings and going populist.

"Relying on such an overkill of one particular person is freezing out a lot of opportunity for a lot of up-and-coming people. Even the most dedicated fan might have thought that the BBC was turning into the David Tennant Corporation."

Yeah, they might – if you replaced the word "dedicated" with the word "stupid".

On New Year's Day, no doubt much to the irritation of the Right Honourable Member for the Ribble Valley, Tennant even replaced the BBC's continuity announcer to introduce his last hurrah. "This is the Doctor," he told viewers. "And now, the end of time is nigh."

The End of Time Part Two is a big improvement on the opening instalment – but it's still a bit of an unholy mess at times. Neither cohesive nor especially coherent, it lacks an obvious dramatic through line. There are so many unnecessary distractions from the main job of giving David Tennant a good send-off that at times it feels like Davies started out writing one story, got bored and then started writing an entirely different one. Several times over.

Even the Time Lords are a victim of the previous week's over-selling. Although there's a brief glimpse of Gallifrey in its full ceremonial pomp, mostly the Lords of Time are represented by a dozen people sitting around a table arguing (and flobbing, in Timothy Dalton's case).

Then Rassilon (yes, Dalton is playing the daddy of all Time Lords, who's gone a bit rogue over the millennia) comes up with an idea to use the Master to help them escape the Time War – a plan that appears to involve "triangulating" the drumming in the Master's head, then throwing a small diamond into a hologram of the Earth, which then makes Gallifrey appear in the sky somewhere over Chiswick. Search me.

There are good bits, most of them involving Bernard Cribbins. And the "he will knock four times" prophecy comes with a neat twist, as it's

actually good old Wilf – gently tap-tap-tap-tapping on the glass of an isolation chamber – who the Doctor has to sacrifice himself to save. (Though, memo to the engineer: a chamber designed to be flooded with a massive dose of gamma rays probably ought not to have large gaps around the door.) The appearance of Doctor's mother – never named as such on screen, but confirmed by Davies in *The Writer's Tale* – as part of a silent Greek chorus of Time Lords is also nicely underplayed, as she covers her eyes in shame at what her people have become.

Faced with sucking up a lethal hit of radiation in order to save his friend, the Doctor is unusually petulant, raging against the dying of the light with a little tantrum about how Wilf is "not remotely important. But me? I could do so much more. So much more! But this is what I get. My reward. And it's not fair!" At which point, he mans up and accepts his fate with a resigned: "Oh, I've lived too long". Like the earlier scene in which the Doctor and Wilf look down on the Earth from space ("It's dawn over England, look. Brand new day. My wife's buried down there. I might never visit her again now"), it's these quieter moments of reflection that linger in the mind, not the Doctor falling hundreds of feet out of a spaceship – with only a few cuts and bruises to show for it – or the Master flying about and chucking laser bolts from his hands like a reject from *Heroes*.

The story's most egregious crime, though, is the way it encourages John Simm to steal all of David Tennant's oxygen – *again*. This was bad enough in the Series Three finale. In what is supposed to be the tenth Doctor's heroic last stand, it's unforgivable.

Fortunately, the extended postscript – in which the dying Doctor claims his "reward" by dropping in to check up on his old friends – is quite lovely. He pulls Luke Smith from in front of a car as a parting gift to Sarah Jane, sets Captain Jack up with a hot date in a bar (the script names the location for this scene as the "city of Zaggit Zagoo on the planet Zog" – *at last*), buys Donna a winning lottery ticket on her wedding day, and even drops in on the strangely familiar Verity Newman (Jessica Hynes) as she signs copies of her book, *The Journal of Impossible Things*, based on the diaries found in her grandmother's attic. He also saves Martha and Mickey from the sharp end of a Sontaran laser by clanging him on the probic vent with a hammer (that's *gotta* hurt) – during which we learn that Smith and Jones are now married. Talk about a rebound relationship.

And finally, of course, there is Rose Tyler, who the Doctor visits on the Powell estate in the early hours of New Year's Day. "What year is this?" he asks. "Blimey, how much have you had?" she smiles. "2005, January the first." "2005," says the Doctor. "Tell you what. I bet you're going to have a really great year." It's a simple but enchanting idea: to take it back to where it all started, before the man in his impossible box came to transport her – to transport all of *us* – away from our ordinary lives to a place of magic and monsters and adventure and wonder.

Then, as the Doctor collapses in the snow, Ood Sigma appears and, to the accompaniment of one of Murray Gold's most haunting scores, tells the Time Lord: "We will sing to you, Doctor. The universe will sing you to your sleep. This song is ending, but the story *never* ends." It's a goose-fleshing moment, one of Davies' finest pieces of writing.

After that, Tennant's final line – a wobbly-lipped "I don't want to go" – is curiously unheroic; the tenth Doctor reduced to the level of a reluctant child at the school gate. But the regeneration itself – a primal burst of raw energy that destroys the TARDIS control room – is thrilling stuff, and Matt Smith and Steven Moffat successfully undercut any lingering lachrymosity with a fast, funny bit of business ("Blimey!" says the new Doctor, as he discovers his generous new chin) that reinforces Ood Sigma's final message. The tenth Doctor's song may have ended, but the story goes on.

Later that evening, BBC One viewers were treated to a minute-long trailer for Series Five. "Okay," said the eleventh Doctor to his TARDIS. "What have you got for me this time?" The answer – if the ensuing rush of Daleks, Weeping Angels, sexy vampires and full-on snogging was anything to go by – was quite a lot. "In 2010," promised the closing caption, "the end... is just the beginning."

In fact, the New Year kicked off in tepidly controversial style when the BBC received 140 complaints about the eleventh Doctor's line "still not ginger" while checking out his new appearance. "We would like to reassure viewers that *Doctor Who* doesn't have an anti-ginger agenda whatsoever," said a very patient spokesman, through a fixed grin. "This was a reprise of the line in *The Christmas Invasion*, when David Tennant discovers that he's not ginger, and here he is, missing out again."

Poor Steven Moffat. Only a handful of lines written as the new showrunner, and he was already in trouble. Welcome to *Doctor Who*.

"My father was Doctor Who, like my mother's father before him"

The End of Time proved another ratings blockbuster, chalking up more than 11.5 million viewers for both episodes. For Russell T Davies and Julie Gardner, it was a fitting testament to their tireless work in making the new *Doctor Who* a smash hit and then, contrary to all the laws of attrition that usually eat away at something when it stops being shiny and new, building it up into an even bigger hit. In 2005, viewers had willingly invited the Doctor back into their homes. What no-one could have predicted was how he would find such a lasting hold on their hearts.

"I've always loved *Doctor Who*, and always thought it was the best," reflected Davies. "And now, for once in my life, everyone agrees. That never happens! It's been an enormous pressure and I won't miss that but, when we get it right, as I believe we have, it's like a form of folklore – and that's the greatest compliment of all. In 70 years' time, there will be old folk saying 'Do you remember Rose Tyler and the Doctor on the beach?' and 'Do you remember when the four knocks came?' And that's the best legacy I could ever hope for."[67]

And, in David Tennant, Davies had had a guiding hand in minting a bona fide new National Treasure. Whether holding court on the apron of the RSC stage, goofing about on a comedy panel show or saving the universe on Saturday teatimes, Tennant was adored by millions, a hero to a generation in a way not seen on British TV for decades and, by all accounts, the Nicest Man in Showbusiness to boot.

When *Rex is Not Your Lawyer* failed to win a

re-trial, America's loss proved Britain's gain. In the years immediately following *Doctor Who*, Tennant established himself as a permanent fixture on stage and screen. He won plaudits for his role as a man struggling to raise five children after the death of his partner in 2010's affecting BBC drama *Single Father*, gave a sensitive portrayal of Manchester United coach Jimmy Murphy in *United* (a TV film about the 1958 Munich air disaster) and was the brilliantly deadpan narrator of painfully funny Olympics comedy *Twenty Twelve* and its BBC-teasing sequel, *W1A*. He voiced Charles Darwin in Aardman Animation's hit *The Pirates! in an Exciting Adventure with Scientists*, and a talking acorn in CBeebies' *Tree Fu Tom*, alongside Sophie Aldred. (We'll draw a discreet veil over misfiring 2011 film *The Decoy Bride*, a romcom that was neither rom nor com.) In 2013, Tennant took the lead in Chris Chibnall's *Broadchurch*, a huge critical and commercial smash that won ITV its biggest midweek drama audience for more than a decade (even if the follow-up was a bit rubbish). Two years later, he earned a People's Choice Award for playing a purple-clad, mind-controlling rapist in the Marvel/Netflix series *Jessica Jones*.

On stage, he was reunited with Catherine Tate for a celebrated sell-out run of *Much Ado About Nothing* at London's Wyndham Theatre in 2011, and in January 2012 was appointed to the Royal Shakespeare Company board. He returned to the RSC the following year in the title role of *Richard II* at Stratford.

Tennant married Georgia Moffett in December 2011. Their first daughter, Olive, was born earlier that year, and Tennant adopted Moffett's son, Tyler. Two more children – Wilfred and a second daughter – followed in 2013 and 2015. The chances of at least one of them going into the family business of being Doctor Who are surely quite high.

In 2015, a decade after he first stepped into the TARDIS, a somewhat shell-shocked Tennant received the Special Recognition honour at that year's National Television Awards. Leading the tributes, Billie Piper called him "a special actor and a decent human being", adding: "He is a very gifted person, but he is also able to be a human within that." His *Broadchurch* co-star Olivia Colman described him as "an utterly, utterly good human being

– you'd love him". "He's witty and he's sharp," said Catherine Tate. "He can be a clown, a statesman, a king and a pauper."

In 2016, Tennant reunited with Tate for a series of tenth Doctor and Donna audios for Big Finish – reaffirming, as if there had ever really been any doubt, that a part of him was perfectly happy to view *Doctor Who* as a job for life.

Five years earlier, in January 2010, *Doctor Who* had been named Best Drama for the fifth time at the NTAs, while Tennant collected his fourth consecutive Best Drama Performance statuette. "I've loved *Doctor Who* since I was tiny," Tennant told the audience. "I was slightly obsessed, never missed an episode. So about five years ago, when it became a more central part of my life, there was a fear it might have been some sort of anti-climax or disappointment. But because of the brilliant people who work on it – Russell T Davies, Julie Gardner, the incredible cast who I've worked with over the last five years and the exceptional people who make the show down in BBC Wales – because of that, the whole thing exceeded my expectations.

"So if you're a kid who's fallen in love with *Doctor Who* recently like I did then, or if you're a grown-up kid who loves *Doctor Who* now like I have always done, or even if you just tune in now and again, thank you very, very much. I've had a blast. Thank you."

No, said fans everywhere, thank *you*. Because David Tennant is not just the scarf-wearing kid who grew up to be a Time Lord. In the eyes of many – including a nationwide 2013 YouGov poll commissioned to mark the show's 50th anniversary – he is nothing less than the ultimate Doctor Who.

Sorry, I mean the ultimate Doctor *in Doctor Who*. He's very particular about that sort of thing. And quite right too.

11 Bow Selecta!

"Hello, is that Doctor Who? Can you put your dad on?"

History records that the eleventh Doctor Who was cast at 3.42 on the afternoon of Friday, December 12th, 2008. That was the exact time that Steven Moffat, sprawled on the sofa with his laptop balanced on his chest, sent an email to his colleagues that concluded with the following words: "It's Matt, isn't it? Of course it's Matt, it's always been Matt."

This came as something of a shock to one man in particular – *Doctor Who* showrunner Steven Moffat who, some weeks earlier, had fired off another email, having received the names of the actors lined up for the first casting day and discovered that most of them were barely old enough to shave. "Just looking at the latest list [of] The Boy Doctors, I twitch!", he wrote. "I twitch every time we discuss the really young ones, you've probably noticed. I'm just not sure, can't quite convince myself. Mysterious stranger! Dangerous past! And 27? He's going to be playing scenes with Amy and *not* look like her boyfriend, 'cos that's not how I'm writing it. In my new one, he's got scenes head to head with River Song, all sexy and tense. These boys might get stuck in her teeth."

But an hour in the company of 26-year-old Matt Smith – a winning mix of lantern-jawed action man and klutzy mad professor – was all it took to change Moffat's mind. "My idea was that the person was going to be between 30 to 40 years old, young enough to run but old enough to look wise," the showrunner admitted. "Then, of course, Matt Smith comes through the door and he's odd, angular and strange looking. He doesn't come across as being youthful at all, in the most wonderful way."[1]

"I tried to make it as funny as it should be," Smith recalled of his audition. "But it's a bit like Hamlet. It has to be your version. The Doctor is so committed, whoever plays him. So I tried to be creative and artistic, and silly, and crazy, and also the cleverest man in the world, and part of that is there's a rapidity to the way he speaks. He's an intergalactic genius, a superhero-ish, mad, fumbling, bumbling science geek. He's everything you can pluck from any universe and put into him."[2]

Born in Northampton in 1982, Matt Smith was all set for a career as a professional footballer – he signed as a youth player with Northampton Town, then Nottingham Forest and Leicester City – before a back injury put paid to his lifelong dream. Thankfully, one of his teachers at Northampton School for Boys, Jerry Hardingham, saw his potential as an actor and signed him up for a production of *Twelve Angry Men*. Smith failed to turn up for a rehearsal and, later, refused to attend a drama festival, but Mr H persevered – even supplying his protégée with forms for the National Youth Theatre (which, naturally, Smith didn't bother to fill in).

In the end, the teacher's persistence paid off. Smith was accepted at the NYT, and was quickly signed up by an agent; he went on to study drama and creative writing at the University of East Anglia, having brokered a deal that allowed him time off for professional acting engagements instead of attending lectures. ("That's fine," said his tutors through gritted teeth. "But I don't see what you could possibly learn from Nicholas Hytner at the National Theatre that you couldn't learn from my PowerPoint presentation in Norwich.")

Early stage performances included gobby student Lockwood in Alan Bennett's *The History Boys*, while he made his West End debut in *Swimming With Sharks* opposite Christian Slater. His first TV role was as chirpy cockney office boy Jim Taylor in the BBC's adaptations of Phillip Pullman's *Sally Lockhart Mysteries*, where he became good friends with leading lady Billie Piper (with whom he later got up close and *very* personal in an episode of *Secret Diary of a Call Girl*, the dirty dog).

In 2007, Smith won acclaim on stage for his

role as Henry in Polly Stenham's *That Face*, starring Lindsay Duncan, and on screen as parliamentary researcher Danny Foster in BBC2 politico-drama *Party Animals*. None of which brought him as much attention as his sister Laura managed by gyrating sweatily about in a leotard as one of the dancers in Eric Prydz' pneumatic "Call on Me" video.

When told he'd bagged the biggest part on television, Smith was so excited he walked for miles around London listening to Frank Sinatra on his iPod, feeling "on top of the world"; which is appropriate, as Ol' Blue Eyes used to like nothing better than walking around New York listening to the LP of *Genesis of the Daleks*. Probably.

Smith wasn't allowed to tell anyone about his appointment, which started to drive him slightly mad. Eventually, he phoned his father and said, "Dad, just call me the Doctor" – leading to an inevitable comedy misunderstanding about whether he was ill or not. (That was one chat show anecdote in the bag already.)

When his casting was announced live on BBC One on January 2nd, 2009, Smith was in Brazil with his girlfriend Mayana Moura – a singer from Ipanema who was a regular on New York's punk circuit. The couple had met the previous year at fashionable Rio nightspot Club 00 – which, on balance, is probably slightly cooler than meeting on *The Tomorrow People*, like Peter Davison and Sandra Dickinson did.

Back home, it was all kicking off, as the media pored over every detail of the new Time Lord – including (did we mention?) his sister's appearance in *that* leotard. "I feel proud and honoured to have been given this opportunity to join a team of people that has worked so tirelessly to make the show so thrilling," Smith said in a pre-recorded interview made available on the BBC's *Doctor Who* website. "David Tennant has made the role his own, brilliantly, with grace, talent and persistent dedication. I hope to learn from the standards set by him. The challenge for me is to do justice to the show's illustrious past, my predecessors, and most importantly, to those who watch it. I really cannot wait."

Although, if you pushed him, he could probably manage a couple more caipirinhas on the beach first.

New Doctor films first scenes on new TARDIS, totally smashes it

Having won over Steven Moffat, Matt Smith's next big challenge was to convince a far more important audience: Moffat's children. During a meeting at the showrunner's house in early 2009, Moffat's eight-year-old son Louis asked if Matt would be *his* Doctor; Smith responded by taking Louis to the shops, and chatting with some of his friends they met along the way. Which just goes to show that while, for most kids, the idea of having "their" Doctor is a matter of generational identity – when you're the boss's son, you can take things slightly more literally.

Having grown up in *Doctor Who*'s Wilderness Years, Smith hadn't had a Time Lord to call his own, but threw himself wholeheartedly into researching the role with a stack of DVDs. Having worked his way through the new series, he began going further back, finding a particular connection with Patrick Troughton and Tom Baker, citing *The Tomb of the Cybermen* and *City of Death* as his favourite serials.

In a bid to get into the mindset of this cosmic genius he'd been tasked with playing, he also put his creative writing degree to good use penning a series of short stories featuring the Doctor and Albert Einstein, including one set in ancient Egypt during the building of the pyramids. It was the most extensive piece of *Doctor Who* fiction by an actor in the title role since Tom Baker last went through a script with his blue pencil.

In February, *The Sun* claimed Smith would be trousering £200,000 a year as the Doctor, guaranteed for three years. (Everyone in *The Sun* "trousers" money, even if they're being paid by Bacs.) The following month, the *Daily Mirror* revealed the TARDIS interior was to get a makeover, while *The Sun* reported that Smith was "scared stiff" of following in David Tennant's footsteps, based on a *Doctor Who Magazine* interview in which he'd conspicuously failed to use either the words "scared" or "stiff."

By now, auditions were under way for the role of the eleventh Doctor's companion, Amy Pond. Steven Moffat was impressed by a tape from Scottish actress Karen Gillan, but told his colleagues it was a shame she was so "wee and dumpy". He agreed to see her anyway, and was stunned to find she was, in fact, a stunning redhead measuring 5'11" – at least 5'10" of it leg.

"I knew that the audition was for the part of the companion, but I wasn't allowed to tell anyone about it," Gillan recalled. "They even had a code name for the role because it was so top secret. The code name was 'Panic Moon'; an anagram of companion, which I thought was really clever." (Which it was – though some members of the production team had held out for Camp Onion.)

Like her co-star, Gillan was sworn to secrecy after being told she'd got the part. "I wasn't allowed to tell anyone, but my boyfriend was with me when I found out, so there was rather a lot of screaming!

"I decided not to tell my parents as I didn't want to spoil the surprise, but when I finally did tell them, I made a special day of it and my mum took a day off work. She just couldn't believe it when I told her. She was doing the dishes and she literally stopped in her tracks and cried. She's a huge fan of the show, has been a fan for years. She even has Dalek bubble bath at home!"[1]

Born in Inverness in 1987, Gillan studied acting at Telford College in Edinburgh, before joining the Italia Conti school in London. Her first TV role was in an episode of *Rebus*, and she also worked as a model to pay the bills. She displayed her versatility in sketches for *The Kevin Bishop Show* between 2007 and 2009, during which time she also had a practice run at *Doctor Who* in *The Fires of Pompeii*.

In the summer, Smith and Gillan upped sticks to Cardiff, ready for photography to start in July. Smith moved into the flat previously occupied by David Tennant and Christopher Eccleston, making them the only three Doctor Whos to share a bed. As far as we know, anyway.

With Moffat talking up a "fairytale" vibe for the new series – leading to much online speculation that *Doctor Who* was about go emo, *Twilight*-style – Adam Smith, director of the first block, spent time with the two new leads discussing their characters, and even insisted they go on a "real adventure together". (They considered searching for a Holy Relic among the lost tribes of the Amazon but, time being short, settled on a speedboat ride around Cardiff Bay instead. The movie rights are still available, if anyone's interested.)

Though scheduled as episodes four and five, Moffat's two-part reprise for the Weeping Angels was the first story to go before the cameras. Stepping out onto Southerndown Beach in Glamorgan for their first scenes, Smith and Gillan were amazed that the fans and the paparazzi had found them so quickly – as was Steven Moffat, who claimed some photos made their way onto the internet so fast, he was still standing in the same position when he saw himself online, staring at his phone. The Weeping Angels hadn't moved very far, either.

Filming on that first day had to be abandoned when the tide came in unexpectedly early (translation: someone misread the tide table) at 3pm, while the second day saw such torrential rain that Moffat had to rewrite scenes on the hoof to relocate them from the beach to the TARDIS. "I did slightly wonder if this would be the shape of things to come," he told Five Live. At which point, he could swear he heard a faint Welsh guffaw drifting across the Atlantic.

For Matt Smith, the reality of actually doing the job triggered a crisis of confidence. "I just thought, I'm not in control of it," he admitted later. "I didn't know if I was coming or going. I rang up my dad and went, 'I don't know how to do this, what the hell am I going to do?' He said, 'You've just got to keep going. I know you'll get there'."[3]

At least he was happy with his costume: what the fashionistas hotly debating the eleventh Doctor's new duds ("geography teacher meets Hoxton clubkid", according to *Esquire*) didn't know at the time was that Smith had pretty much thrown together the ensemble himself. "We're talking 20 minutes before the end of the day, on the final day before we had to unveil something," recalled Steven Moffat. "He asked if he could put his braces on, so he put the braces on. And I think the jacket is either his or one very like his, with the elbow patches, and I was thinking, well it's alright... And then he said – and I knew this was coming, because he'd become so obsessed with Patrick Troughton and *Tomb of the Cybermen* when he'd seen it; he spent 20 minutes on the phone to me – he said, 'Can I try a bow tie'? And I said, 'No, no, that's just the most ridiculously retro, child's eye view of what Doctor Who wears. But still he put on the bow tie he'd brought with him, and he did look really good.

"And we signed off on it – mainly because Matt was leaping around the room with a pen, pretending it was a sonic screwdriver, saying, 'I'm Doctor Who!'"[4]

They drew the line at the stovepipe hat, though.

By August, production had moved on to Mark Gatiss' contribution to the new series, which promised a heady combination of Winston Churchill and the Daleks. Among the special effects required for the episode was a fake cigar for Ian McNeice to puff as Churchill, as new anti-smoking legislation didn't permit the real thing. This was particularly ironic, as the scenes in the Daleks' spaceship were filmed in Freeman's Cigar Factory in Cardiff, where they had to scrub the walls to get rid of the tobacco stains. (They may be genocidal Nazis, but even the Daleks draw the line at breaking no-smoking laws.)

The other story in the second production block was Steven Moffat's *The Beast Below*, which involved Matt Smith and Karen Gillan – in her nightie – spending a day sloshing about in what amounted to the world's biggest compost bin to simulate the inside of a giant whale. Was it their imaginations, or were people a bit less forthcoming with the showbiz hugs that day?

Season opener *The Eleventh Hour* (see what they did there?), which went before the cameras in September, required a young actress to play the seven-year-old version of Amy Pond. Having drawn a blank so far, casting director Andy Pryor asked Karen Gillan if she had any family members who might be suitable. Gillan told him she had a cousin who looked "identical" to her, was the right age and had the right accent, so nine-year-old Caitlin Blackwood was auditioned – and totally smashed it. (The read-through for the episode was actually the first time the two cousins had met, as Blackwood had grown up in Ireland and only moved back to Inverness after Gillan had left for London.)

One scene for the story involved Matt Smith holding his sonic screwdriver in the air while a small explosive charge was triggered. Smith managed to burn his hand, flinch and break the prop in two. This surprised no-one, as he was rapidly developing a reputation as the clumsiest man on a *Doctor Who* set since Katy Manning last ran into a wall without her specs on.

"He just knocks things over the entire time, falls over, permanently," mused Steven Moffat. "You veer away from him if you see him carrying a coffee, because you're going to wear it. He's quite an athlete, though. He was a great footballer when he was young, so he can do the action stuff, but there's something quite shambling about him, with his bandy legs – sorry, Matt – and his wee short jacket. He can go from being quite a cool action hero to being really quite Stan Laurel, which is adorable."[4]

As summer turned to autumn, it became clear the effects-heavy series finale would need longer in post-production if it was to make the proposed spring TX date. So a schedule switcheroo saw the two-part story brought forward to become block six instead of seven, throwing Steven Moffat into self-confessed "deadline hell."

Hallowe'en saw Bob Baker's K-9 spin-off make its debut on the Disney XD channel. A collaboration between Disney and Australia's Network 10, the Brisbane-made caper starts out with the metal mutt (voiced by John Leeson) as the bulky box-on-wheels we all know and... well, that we all know, before he "regenerates" into a funky new flying model that looks like a cross between Pluto and a Hoover attachment. A total of 26 episodes have been made to date, though few among even the most die-hard *Doctor Who* fans – the sort of people who will happily watch an extended cut of *Dimensions in Time* – will admit to having seen any of them.

In December, the *Doctor Who* crew decamped to Croatia, where the walled Adriatic town of Trogir – a designated UNESCO World Heritage site – was doubling both for sixteenth-century Venice and nineteenth-century Provence. There was some concern about two female cast members having to jump into the freezing water, so exec producer Beth Willis volunteered to double for them if necessary. In the end, the actresses, including main guest star Helen McCrory, agreed to take the plunge, but

Willis tested it for them beforehand: "It was cold, but it was doable," the producer told *Doctor Who Confidential*. "I think if I'm asking anyone else to get in the water, I have to be able to say whether or not I think it's okay. And now I do."[5] (That's nice, thought Matt Smith and Karen Gillan – though they couldn't help notice she'd been less forthcoming when they'd spent the day swimming about in rotting cabbage.)

Series Thingymabob or Series Oojamaflip?

One week after the eleventh Doctor had arrived in a blaze of fire on New Year's Day 2010, the writers for his first series were announced. Steven Moffat would pen six episodes, Chris Chibnall two and Mark Gatiss, Gareth Roberts and Toby Whithouse one apiece. Comedy writer Simon Nye – creator of none-more-90s lad comedy *Men Behaving Badly*, among others – was a surprise choice for a further episode, but the real headline news was the inclusion of Richard Curtis in the line-up. The nation's most successful screenwriter, who had practically kept the British film industry afloat with the likes of *Four Weddings and a Funeral*, *Notting Hill* and *Love, Actually*, was a terrific coup for New *Who*. And any fears he might try to mould the show to his formula, rather than vice versa, were allayed when it was announced his story would be set in a North London bookshop and follow a shy and bumbling alien (Hugh Grant) as he attempted to win the girl of his dreams, despite having three heads (and three lots of floppy hair). Okay, not really.

There was some confusion, though, about what the new series would actually be called. Most had assumed it would be Series Five, based on the not-unreasonable premise that it followed on from Series Four. But the production team were referring to it as Series One. As well as the obvious confusion this might cause on Amazon ("People who bought the Series One box set also bought the, er, other Series One box set"), it presented a doomsday scenario for fans' careful filing systems. Just what in the name of Clom, asked a baffled *Doctor Who Magazine*, was going on?

"How do you number a series of *Doctor Who*?" retorted Steven Moffat. "I fess up, the whole Series One thing came about when I had to give a speech to the various licensees, explaining why they should be excited about *Doctor Who*. The message coming back, before I went into the meeting, was that 'Series Five means an ageing brand.' And it struck me, my God, Series Five is a very, very boring number. But there are other numbers you can use – Series Thirty-One or Series One.

"It's Series Thirty-One of *Doctor Who*, and Series One of Matt Smith's Doctor. Those are both real numbers. I submit that 'Series Five of *Doctor Who*' means nothing unless you really believe that Matt Smith is the third Doctor. Everyone knows he's the eleventh Doctor, so that means it's definitely not Series Five. Whichever one you choose, Series Five is the one that's flawed. But never mind all that, I was saying to them, you can't go away saying 'Series Five, ageing brand', cos it's Series Thirty-One – it's epic and immortal!"[6]

In February, production on Series Five (shut up, yeah?) continued with the cast and crew being given exclusive access to film at Stonehenge for the finale, while Arthur Darvill was announced as playing Amy's boyfriend, Rory. As a teenager, Darvill had presented continuity links on Children's ITV, and had made his TV acting debut opposite Sooty and Sweep. After graduating from RADA, he earned a Best Newcomer nomination at the 2007 Evening Standard Theatre Awards for his performance in *Terra Haute* at the Vaudeville Theatre, where he later appeared in *Swimming With Sharks*, alongside a certain Matt Smith. He was also a talented musician and composer – something he'd inherited from his dad Nigel, who had played keyboards for 80s soul-pop sensations Fine Young Cannibals; his mother Ellie, meanwhile, had been the voice and puppeteer behind the Why Bird on tots' TV show *Playdays*. So if you ever saw a giant, rainbow-coloured bird playing piano to "She Drives Me Crazy" on *Top of the Pops*, you knew someone had taken the wrong bag to work.

Studio sessions for the series finale saw the construction of the biggest set ever used in *Doctor Who* – a huge underground vault with giant doors inspired, according to director Toby Haynes, by *The Tomb of the Cybermen*. For a 43-year-old story, the Troughton scarer was surprisingly fashionable this season. Haynes also wanted an Indiana Jones vibe and suggested flaming torches – though there were some concerns about Matt Smith's legendary clumsiness ending in the biggest set ever built for *Doctor Who* being reduced to a pile of cinders before lunchtime. The team were also interrupted by... sorry, were also delighted to receive a visit from *Doctor Who* legend (at least that's what it said on his badge) John Levene.

Haynes took it upon himself to direct some scenes while sitting in the base of a Dalek – which is where he was when the Controller of Drama Commissioning, Ben Stephenson, arrived to show a group of visitors around. (Or that's how the story goes, anyway – but see Aggedor, Holy Fucking Cow, Reaction To under Volume I.)

Accepting an award at that month's SFX Weekender convention, fantasy icon Neil Gaiman – the man behind such acclaimed comic books and novels as *Sandman, Neverwhere* (which featured a character, the Marquis, inspired by the Doctor), *Coraline* and *Stardust* – declared: "In about 14 months from now, which is to say, not in the upcoming season but early in the one after that, it's quite possible that I might have written an episode [of *Doctor Who*]." This caused much excitement among the sci-fi community, to whom Gaiman was considerably more famous than the bloke who wrote *The Vicar of Dibley*.

In fact, Gaiman – who had once admitted "the shape of reality, the way I perceive the world, exists only because of *Doctor Who*" (specifically *The War Games*; Patrick Troughton really was bang on-trend right now) – had originally written the episode for the 2010 series, but had just been told it was being deferred a year because they'd run out of money to do it justice.

And in another back-door announcement, Scottish actress Neve McIntosh let slip a juicy detail about Chris Chibnall's upcoming two-parter when she told the *Perthshire Advertiser*: "I play twins, they're big lizard warrior women. They're one of the Silurian tribes that have been undisturbed under the Earth." But don't go reading too much into that, said the production office. It could be *any* race of subterranean Silurian lizards making a comeback.

"All of time and space, anywhere and everywhere – where do you want to start?" "How about Sunderland?"

Were the kids losing interest in *Doctor Who*? That was the question when figures for the second half of 2009 showed that sales of *Doctor Who Adventures* magazine had slumped to 45,000 – down from a whopping 155,000 two years earlier. A spokesman for BBC Worldwide said they expected to see an improvement when *Doctor Who* was actually on telly again. (Adding: "Yes, I'm looking at you, Russell T Davies.")

At least you could rely on *Blue Peter* to keep the faith: its competition to design a console for the TARDIS saw Matt Smith surprising winner Susannah Leah by popping up on a big screen in Leeds city centre to give her the good news. What he didn't mention was that her winning effort – a junkyard lash-up featuring a coat hanger, skipping rope, hair curlers and a karaoke mic – was for Neil Gaiman's story, so she might have quite a wait to see it on screen.

Meanwhile, scandal threatened to bring down the BBC as the media worked itself into a frenzy over the political subtext of tepid 80s satire *The Happiness Patrol*. (For those of you who skipped Volume I – still not judging – this involved McCoy era script editor Andrew Cartmel being hauled onto *Newsnight* to answer the charge that the *Doctor Who* production team of the late 80s had been a "nest of anti-Thatcherite subversives". It followed a comment from Sylvester McCoy about Sheila Hancock's none-too-subtle Thatcher impression in said story, which the press had failed to pick up on the time because it was the late 80s, and they didn't know *Doctor Who* was still on.)

Back in the present day, pre-publicity for Series Whatever shifted up a gear with the release of a specially-shot 3D TV and cinema trailer featuring the Doctor and Amy falling through the vortex surrounded by Daleks, Weeping Angels and other meanies, with a voiceover from the Time Lord asking: "All of time and space, everywhere and anywhere, every star that ever was – where do you want to start?" The trailer was poorly received by fans, who claimed it looked "cheap" – despite the fact it had cost an arm and a leg. Or a plunger and a wing, anyway.

In late February, *The Sun* revealed that *Gavin & Stacey* star James Corden was to guest star in an upcoming episode. "We normally keep our guest stars under wraps," said a "show insider", "but you can't hide a bloke like James." Nice – Corden may be a little on the large side, but he's not Godzilla.

Like Matt Smith, Corden had made his name in the National Theatre production (and later the film) of *The History Boys*. As one of the original cast, he had transferred to Broadway with the show, while Smith had undertaken a UK tour. "He's constantly going on about how he was doing *The History Boys* in New York while I was doing it in Milton Keynes," Smith told *Radio Times*.[7]

As filming wrapped in March, the build-up to the eleventh Doctor's debut began in earnest, with Matt Smith and Karen Gillan posing for a spectacular 3D *SFX* magazine cover, and BBC America announcing the series would debut in the US on April 17th. Canadian viewers would be able to watch it on Space on the same date, while ABC in Australia also confirmed an April start. As yet, there was no word on a UK broadcast date, but it was safe to assume it would air at some point.

The BBC also unveiled details of a special *Doctor Who* bus tour, with Belfast, Sunderland and Salford – plus Matt Smith and Karen Gillan's home towns of Northampton and Inverness – each hosting a regional premiere of *The Eleventh Hour* attended by the two stars. "Matt and Karen will travel around the UK on a specially themed *Doctor Who* bus, featuring the new TARDIS logo and iconic imagery," stated the press release of what the cast and crew had already christened The Wengerbus, in honour of Piers Wenger and 1998 Europop travesty "We Like to Party (The Vengabus)" by Dutch combo The Vengaboys. Maybe you had to be there.

"The focus of the tour is targeting hard to reach and relatively under-served communities by the BBC," said a spokesman for the Corporation, which was under pressure to show greater commitments to the regions, including – good God – the North as part of its Charter renewal conditions. The tour would be followed by events on big screens in major cities like Swansea, Manchester and Plymouth. ("They have TV there now, right?," asked execs in White City nervously.)

As *Doctor Who* was named Best Drama Programme at the Television and Radio Industries Club Awards, the UK launch date was confirmed as April 3rd. At the press screening of *The Eleventh Hour* at Cineworld in Cardiff on March 18th, visitors were greeted by the sight of the TARDIS laying on its side on the grass – which was either a clue to the events of the episode, or Charlotte Church had been out on the lash with her mates again.

As a measure of their confidence in the new man, Piers Wenger announced at the launch that a 2010 Christmas special and a sixth series in 2011 had already been commissioned, both of which would star Matt Smith. The new Doctor was in ebullient form, telling reporters: "To my mind, it's the best part on British television and I'm fortunate to have it and I'm going to keep it." And the critics appeared to agree, with the screening creating a positive press buzz summed up in fine tabloid style by *The Sun's* "Just What the Doctor Ordered." Which was a relief, as they'd already written the headline and couldn't think of a decent one if he'd turned out to be rubbish.

"He is still the same man, but I think my Doctor is a bit more reckless," said Smith in the accompanying BBC press pack. "He's a thrill-seeker and addicted to time travel. He is the mad buffoon genius who saves the world because he's got a great heart, spirit and soul, but he also doesn't suffer fools. I hope all of these things come across, but I think I've also injected a bit of my own personality into the role."

Karen Gillan also gave her view of Amy Pond to that month's *Doctor Who Magazine*. "I know that 'feisty' is a really typical word for *Doctor Who* companions," she said. "Every single one of them has been feisty! But it has to be used, because Amy really is feisty. She's kind of got this inner confidence, I think, which makes her quite sassy. She can give the Doctor a run for his money and all that. But what's really interesting about her is that, underneath all that, somewhere inside, she's kind of like this lost little girl. She's almost stuck as a little girl, in a way. She's got these two sides to her, which are almost contradictory. That's interesting to play."8

The BBC publicity material also included an interview with Steven Moffat in which he outlined his vision for the show, and how it might differ from his predecessor's. "I've never done anything differently, at least not deliberately," he said. "I just try and think of all the best and maddest *Doctor Who* stories I want to watch, and get them made – there are worse ways to make a living. You could say that I'm more into the clever plots; I like the big twists and the sleight of hand. I like playing around with time travel, but I don't think it should be at the front of *Doctor Who* in every episode.

"However, I do think it should happen more often and reinforce the fact he has an odd relationship with time. If you look at the stories I've written so far, I suppose I might be slightly more at the fairytale and Tim Burton end of *Doctor Who*, whereas Russell is probably more at the blockbuster and Superman end of the show."

He expanded on this in an interview with *The Guardian* the same week, claiming his instinct led him towards a more "storybook quality". "For me, *Doctor Who* literally is a fairytale. It's not really science fiction. It's not set in space, it's set under your bed. It's at its best when it's related to you, no matter what planet it's set on."

In *The Times*, Moffat admitted he wouldn't necessarily have allowed the burping wheelie bin from *Rose* to make the cut, but added: "You know, kids laughed. I'd quite happily do things to make children laugh. The thing is, *Doctor Who* isn't just Hammer Horror or sci-fi. It's also a little bit *The Generation Game*, a little bit showbiz. It's a weird show. It's half scary Gothic castle, half shiny floor show. And that's part of it. Any show can be one or the other, but *Doctor Who* manages to be both and have a burping wheelie bin and an absolutely heartbreaking scene in the same episode."

Stirring stuff – but perhaps his definitive statement came in the *Daily Telegraph* when, asked what his goal for the new series was, Moffat replied: "For it not to be shit." Well, you can't argue with that.

Moffat was acutely aware he wasn't just writing a TV show, but had been entrusted with one of the BBC's most valuable golden geese.

"The precise worth of the brand is a closely guarded secret," said *The Guardian*, "but according to BBC Worldwide, the drama has been sold to over 50 territories and has shifted more than 3.3m DVDs, more than 7m action figures and, in 2009 alone, around 300,000 books. And then there are the pencil cases and folders, Cyberman and Dalek masks and the deal, reputed to be worth £10m, to bring *Doctor Who* to Nintendo DS and Wii. Meanwhile, David Tennant's final outing as the Doctor secured BBC America's highest primetime rating and *Doctor Who* is BBC Worldwide's top-selling download on iTunes in the US."

Impressive – but that didn't mean the show was protected from the "efficiencies" being applied across the board at the BBC, which had been ordered to make an eye-watering £400 million worth of budget cuts. According to a *Private Eye* report at the time, the *Doctor Who* production team had been "incensed" to discover that BBC Marketing had blown a million quid on the 3D cinema trailer – enough to make an entire new episode, with change to spare. The magazine quoted a production insider as saying: "Look for some amazing found-at-the-back-of-the-cupboard monster cameos towards the end of the season."

Piers Wenger responded by saying *Doctor Who* was subject to the same production constraints as every other drama, but he hoped it wouldn't show on screen. Speaking to the *Daily Telegraph*, Steven Moffat was more bullish: "This is going to sound pious," he said, "but the original TARDIS was a budget cut. It was. They couldn't afford to make a spaceship. They couldn't even afford to do a magic door. So someone came up with, why don't we do a police box? And it's bigger on the inside. That's the single best idea, I think – though I am a bit prejudiced – in all of fiction."

The week running up to the series launch found Britain battered by another tsunami of *Who* hype: Matt Smith talked to anyone who'd listen (and, in the case of *Friday Night with Jonathan Ross* and *The One Show*, some who wouldn't); he made a TARDIS bird feeder with Helen Skelton on *Blue Peter*, toured the offices of *The Sun* and the *Daily Mirror* with Karen Gillan, popped up across every BBC radio station in a series of specially-written trails, and charmed local reporters on regional TV and radio stations from Northern Ireland to Northampton during the three-day Wengerbus tour. The new Doctor graced the front of the *Radio Times* – whose gatefold cover revealed the new TARDIS interior for the first time – and the cover of a *Who*-themed issue of *Gay Times*, which must have left some married completists with some explaining to do.

Publicity pictures from *The Eleventh Hour* of Amy Pond dressed as a policewoman kissogram / strippergram (depending on the quality of the paper you were reading) caused an entirely predictable kerfuffle, with the *Daily Mail's* Allison Pearson asking: "Since when was *Doctor Who's* assistant supposed to be sexy." Er, shall you tell her or shall I? "What next?" she added, "Cybermen become Cyberchicks with metal boobs"? (So she'd never seen *Torchwood's* Cyberwoman episode either. Lucky her.)

Similar stories were splashed across the other tabloids ("I'm the sexiest sidekick *Doctor Who's* ever had!" Karen Gillan apparently told the *Mirror*), but the most salacious gossip was provided by the *Sunday Mirror* in their thrilling story, "Dr Who Girl Karen Gillan Buys Bonsai Trees With New Boyfriend". Phwooooar!

But what of the new Doctor? Where did he rate on the TARDIS crump-o-meter? Pretty highly, according to Alex Kingston. "David was brilliant, but very, very straight – quirky, but straight down the line," River Song told *SFX*. "Matt is quite... sexy. I shouldn't say this, but he is. Quirky and mad professorish, but also quite sexy."[9]

Steven Moffat had a slightly different take on his leading man: "I always think he's a kind of *Bo' Selecta!* caricature of a handsome man," he told the same magazine. "He's strikingly handsome, but he's like a cartoon of handsome, with his big sweep of hair. The first time he came in, that's what he looked like, and you just think, 'You're the Doctor, you are'."[4]

On Saturday, April 3rd, Karen Gillan and her boyfriend, photographer Patrick Green, returned to Gillan's home in Inverness so she could watch her debut as Amy Pond with her family. Steven Moffat and Matt Smith invited their respective clans to a viewing party at Moffat's London home – though both later admitted they'd watched it, if not exactly behind the sofa, then at least through a crack in the door. At the initial read-through for the episode, Moffat had warned the assembled cast and crew this would be "the most scrutinised hour" of their lives. Now that hour had arrived, with the future of *Doctor Who* largely dependant on how the public reacted to the following 60 minutes. No pressure, then.

Cometh the Hour...

There can be few fans who haven't mentally rehearsed how, if given the chance, they'd reinvent *Doctor Who* to match the perfect version of it that's always existed in their head. At the heart of Steven Moffat's vision is a fairytale, and at the heart of that fairytale is a girl: seven-year-old Amelia Pond, an orphan with a mysterious crack in her bedroom wall who prays for salvation, until salvation arrives one Easter in the form of a wheezing, groaning sound outside her window.

In the night garden, Amelia discovers a mysterious blue box lying on its side. There are sounds from inside, then a hand appears, then another and finally, there he is: a strange, raggedy man, hauling himself out of the box and into her life, babbling nonsense about apples and swimming pools in libraries.

As entrances go, this is pretty much perfect, with all the totemic icons – engines, TARDIS, Time Lord – delivered in the right order, in the perfect context of a child discovering the magic, the fear and the wonder of *Doctor Who* for the first time.

Russell T Davies once said the reason *Doctor Who* is so complicated to write is because, unlike most drama, it isn't just two people sitting talking in a kitchen. And here comes Steven Moffat to turn two people talking in a kitchen into some of the best material in the entire *Who* corpus, riffing on *The House at Pooh Corner* (haycorns is really what Tiggers like best) in an enchanting sequence in which the Doctor makes little Amelia go through the contents of her fridge while he tries to find something his new mouth can eat. He eventually settles on fish fingers dipped in custard. Yum.

It's an extraordinary scene, loaded with memorable Moffat one-liners ("You're Scottish, fry something"; "I hate yoghurt, it's just stuff with bits in") which Matt Smith milks for maximum comedy effect – until Amelia tells him she's not scared of being left alone in the house, at which point his voice drops several octaves and he is suddenly deadly serious: "Course you're not," he says, all crinkly-eyed compassion. "You're not scared of anything. Box falls out of the sky, man falls out of box, man eats fish custard, and look at you, just sitting there. So you know what I think? Must be a hell of a scary crack in your wall."[1]

The problem, it transpires, is not so much as crack in a wall as a crack in the universe – two points in space and time that should never have touched. And someone – something – has escaped through it. But the Doctor hasn't got time to fix it right now, because the TARDIS cloister bell is tolling doom. Amy wants to come with him, but it's too dangerous. "Five minutes," he promises. "Give me five minutes, I'll be right back." "People always say that," she says, doubtfully. "Am I people?" he smiles. "Do I even look like people? Trust me. I'm the Doctor." And so little Amelia Pond packs her favourite teddy in her suitcase, and sits in the garden to wait for her raggedy man to come back.

Which he does, of course: five minutes later, just as he promised. Except, in her world, little Amelia Pond isn't little Amelia Pond any more. Twelve years – and four psychiatrists – later, she's all grown up. And mad as hell.

It's a simply magical framing device for the new series, bringing a brilliant new dynamic to the central pairing. And Matt Smith and Karen Gillan attack the material for all it's worth: from the moment he first emerges, hauling himself out of his upended police box, soaking wet from an unexpected dip in that pool, Smith – old yet young, serious yet silly, heroic yet daft, cool yet klutzy – appears entirely born to the part.

Gillan, too, is dazzlingly assured. Yes, Amy is "feisty," but she's also vulnerable, confused and not a little bit damaged, and Gillan takes all this and runs with it – so far as anyone *can* run in a micro-skirt that tight. Arthur Darvill, meanwhile, is hugely endearing as long-suffering boyfriend Rory, whose presence Amy barely appears to acknowledge when her raggedy man finally returns and starts doing his thing.

The setting – a picture-postcard English village, complete with duckpond – provides a

marked contrast with the urban milieu of the Russell T Davies years. But, for all that, it's still very identifiably the same show that brought us space rhinos and cat nuns and the *Titanic* falling on Buckingham Palace and John "Hi, I'm John Barrowman" Barrowman; Moffat had spent months in the run-up telling people that, if they were expecting a radical reboot, they were going to be disappointed. Even so, when the story-of-the-week does kick in (the Doctor has 20 minutes to locate escaped intergalactic criminal Prisoner Zero before the alien Atraxi toast the planet), it's a surprise to see Moffat taking leaves – and, at times, tearing whole chapters (it's the same plot as *Smith and Jones*, for a start) – out of the Russell T Davies Book of Frothy Caper Season Openers. *The Eleventh Hour* is fast, frantic and funny, includes a scene in which a man swaps voices with his dog, and culminates with the Doctor crashing through a window in a stolen fire engine. As *Space Helmet* has been moved to note before: Asimov, it ain't.

Perhaps what's most surprising, given its author's track record, is how unscary it is. It's all there in the set-up – the lonely child, the big spooky house, the mysterious crack, the secret room you can only see out of the corner of your eye... But the execution seems deliberately geared towards neutering any night terrors in favour of a frenetic, against-the-clock runaround. (Or, as 12-year-old Daniel Purdie from Hove put it in *The Observer*, the episode was "on the verge of being scary, rather than actually scary.")

As runarounds go, though, it's hard to imagine one that's smarter, or more fun. Or a better showcase for the new man with his name above the title. Having saved the world with seconds to spare – and while "still cooking", too – the raggedy man helps himself to some new duds (in tribute to both the third and eighth Doctors, they're nicked from a hospital locker room), then summons the Atraxi back to Earth, just to tell them to clear off... or else. It's a fantastic, grandstanding speech (and a surprisingly late addition the script) that ends with the Doctor stepping through a holographic playback of his former selves, adjusting his new bow tie as he emerges from David Tennant's face and declaring: "I'm the Doctor. Basically... run."

In the space of one short hour, Smith has

taken ownership of the role utterly (assisted in no small part, it should be said, by Murray Gold, whose pulse-quickening "I am the Doctor" signature tune will quickly come to challenge even Ron Grainer's legendary theme as this era's most iconic musical motif). So it's no surprise Amy is ready to drop everything and run away to the stars with him, still in her nightie. (Amy, of course, is Wendy Darling, and the Doctor – the ageless creature who went back to visit the child and found her all grown up – her Peter Pan.) What she doesn't tell him is that tomorrow is supposed to be her wedding day. And what he doesn't tell her is that he has his own reason for wanting to steal her away in his magical box – something related to Prisoner Zero's prophetic warning that "The universe is cracked. The Pandorica will open. Silence will fall."

All these things are waiting for the Doctor and his new best friend. But, before that, there are adventures to be had. "There's a whole world in here, just like you said," boggles Amy, standing inside that impossible cabinet of dreams at last. "It's all true. I thought... well, I started to think that maybe you were just, like, a madman with a box."

"Amy Pond, there's something you'd better understand about me, because it's important, and one day your life may depend on it," warns the Doctor. And then a grin: "I am *definitely* a madman with a box."

BBC whales

The critics were unanimous in their praise for the episode – and the new Doctor. "From the moment he appeared, dangling from the architrave of his time machine, the new boy demonstrated that he can more than fill the shoes of his predecessor," said Matthew Sweet in *The Independent*. "Matt Smith fights aliens. He wears tweed. He loves custard. He is the Doctor. And he might be more the Doctor than anyone who was the Doctor before."

The *Telegraph's* Benji Wilson gave Smith (and the casting director) an A+, while Sinclair McKay in the *Mail* was equally smitten. "By the end of the episode, in his tweed jacket and bow tie, like an indie-band Professor Quatermass, you have forgotten all about his illustrious predecessor. Indeed, Smith might

turn out to be one of the best Time Lords of the lot."

"You can all relax," said Kevin O'Sullivan in the *Mirror*. "After a fine performance in an encouragingly expensive and slick special-effects packed opening salvo, it's crystal clear that Mr Smith is certain to be a sensation."

And with more than ten million viewers tuning in to watch – despite the new, considerably earlier timeslot of 6.20pm – it was clear the new era was off to a flying start. Heck, even the *fans* seemed to enjoy it – and everyone knows *Doctor Who* fans weren't put on this Earth to go around enjoying *Doctor Who*, thank you very much. Short of firing £50 notes out of the telly, it's difficult to imagine how *The Eleventh Hour* could have been better received, frankly.

A few days later, further encounters with the Doctor and Amy Pond were announced in the form of *The Adventure Games*, giving viewers the chance to control the action in a series of four, Matt Smith and Karen Gillan-voiced "two-hour dramas" (i.e. computer games) commissioned by BBC Vision's Multiplatform team. (Hey, they sound like fun guys to work for. And in-no-way first in line for those £400 million budget cuts.)

Seven days after their triumphant debut, the New *Who* team's bubble was, if not exactly burst, then at least found drifting perilously close to a very sharp object as their sophomore offering hit the screens.

A queen in a red riding hood. A girl who's crept out of bed for a magical adventure in her nightie. Carnival masks. Nursery rhymes. A castle in the sky. Vanishing children. And a journey into the belly of a giant whale. They certainly weren't lying about the new series having a fairytale vibe; by the end of *The Beast Below*, viewers wouldn't have been surprised if the Doctor had ridden to the rescue on a white charger through a magic mirror. Except he already did that in one of Steven Moffat's earlier stories.

In retrospect, a show about a mysterious man in a magic box was always ripe for this sort of treatment. What's intriguing is that, in all the years of chatter about *Doctor Who's* infinitely flexible format, we never had this version on our radar; the usual litany decrees the show can be "anything from sci-fi to horror to space opera to historical romance", but did anyone ever think of it as a fairytale, until it was presented to us as one?

Sadly, while *The Beast Below* is filled with fascinating ideas and delightful notions – the Queen of England as a gun-totin', streetwise Cockney descendant of the House of Windsor, hiding out in a room entirely filled with glasses of water being just one memorable image – we need to talk about the elephant in the room. Or, more specifically, the space whale in the room.

Seriously, has there ever been a more bonkers premise for a *Doctor Who* story than the UK's plan to escape global catastrophe by strapping the entire country to the back of a 50,000 tonne galactic sea cow? We can only imagine the meeting they called to discuss the project:

"Okay, listen up everyone, we've put our heads together and this is what we've come up with. Basically, the idea is to build a sort of mini-version of the country on the back of a massive whale, and then float off into space. Any questions?"

"Erm, yes. Why not just build a spaceship?"

"That's what we're doing. A space whale ship."

"No, I mean, just a normal spaceship. With an engine and everything."

"Riiiiight. And where would we put the whale, exactly?"

"Forget about the whale, there is no whale."

"I'm sorry, I'm not sure I follow you."

The plot also pivots on the Doctor *not knowing* the Starship UK is powered by a giant whale – so it's just as well he and Amy materialise directly above it, in the one spot for 500 miles around where you can't see the ruddy great thing. And how rubbish are the TARDIS instruments that give the whole history of the ship, but fail to mention (or detect) the colossal Cetacean swimming about underneath it? What's the Doctor got as his memory bank homepage these days, Wikipedia?

They're pulling punches on the scares again, too. The Smilers – leering, fairground-style mannequins – are a very creepy idea, but woefully under-exploited, especially in the scene where they climb out of their booths and advance on the Doctor and Amy. This should be a memory-searing classic monster moment,

but they're only on their feet for about two seconds – not long enough to even begin to affect a menacing advance – before Liz 10 comes along and pops a couple of caps in them. (Though her line "I'm the bloody Queen, mate – basically, I rule" *is* rather fabulous.)

Matt Smith gives us a surprisingly different take on the Doctor from *The Eleventh Hour* – odder, more angular, more awkward (in a good way), as if he'd deliberately played his debut as a hybrid of David Tennant and himself. He also has incredible wrists – they seem to be about a foot too long, emerging from the end of his sleeves like a cross between Jarvis Cocker and a Slitheen. (I bet he has no trouble nicking crisps out of vending machines.) And Karen Gillan once again proves she's a fine character actor stuck in the body of a supermodel – not too shabby a combination, when all's said and done.

The Beast Below has many charms – not least Sophie Okenodo's pistol-packing monarch – but, ultimately, the whole thing creaks and strains beneath the 50,000 tonne dead weight at its centre. Yes, whales have been the stuff of myth and legend as far back as the Old Testament – referenced here in the scene where the Doctor and Amy end up inside the creature's mouth (hence Matt Smith and Karen Gillan spending a day sloshing about in a pool full of treats from the BBC canteen slop bin). But, in this instance, it's hard not to be reminded of the poor, doomed sperm whale who suddenly blinks into existence among the stars in *The Hitchhiker's Guide to the Galaxy,* the product – like much of this script – of an Infinite Improbability Drive.

In mid-April, Matt Smith, Karen Gillan and Steven Moffat flew out to New York for the series' US launch. After the giddy heights of Sunderland and Northampton, NYC seemed a bit of a comedown, but they tried to make the best of it.

The Eleventh Hour was due to be shown to fans at the Paley Centre for Media, followed by a second event at the Village East Cinema on 2nd Avenue, where the queues started at 6.30am for the 7pm screening. BBC America had funded an impressive publicity campaign, and Smith and Gillan were amazed to find themselves staring down from billboards and the sides of buses across Manhattan. But not as amazed as Smith's predecessors would have been – the only way Colin Baker or Sylvester McCoy would have found themselves on the side of a New York bus was if they'd accidentally stepped out into heavy traffic.

The fuss generated plenty of coverage back home, with many tabloids focusing on Karen Gillan's choice of outfits. But that's red-tops for you (the tabloids, I mean – not Karen Gillan).

The good times kept rolling when it was revealed *The Eleventh Hour* had set a new record for the BBC's iPlayer, with 1.27 million requests in the first week since its transmission. A similar number also tuned in to the US broadcast, delivering BBC America one of its best-ever figures.

A fortnight after its last cover, *Doctor Who* was back on the front of the *Radio Times* on April 13th to promote the return of the Daleks. In a tribute to its iconic cover of five years earlier, the pepperpots were once again tied in to that week's UK General Election, with a choice of three suspiciously portly-looking Daleks sporting the red, blue and yellow liveries of the three main political parties. That's pretty funny, thought the fans. Imagine if they really did look like that – LOL!

Then they tuned in on Saturday.

Victory of the Daleks is not the worst New *Who* story by a long chalk – but it's definitely the flimsiest episode we've seen since the show's revival, in the sense that the "story" (basically a series of confrontations in which the Doctor and the Daleks shout perfunctory plot points and empty threats such as "I won't let you get away!" at each other) isn't so much bad as missing. Give it even a gentle poke, and it collapses like a Heston Blumenthal helium soufflé.

Which is a shame, as the premise is fabulous. In the Cabinet War Rooms, the Doctor discovers Winston Churchill has co-opted a range of armoured soldiers called Ironsides into the fight against the Nazi peril. And now the Doctor has to convince him that what he sees as his best hope of winning the war isn't the invention of his pet scientist, Bracewell, but a race of deadly alien mutations called the Daleks.

Not only does the story fail to do anything interesting with this open goal of a set-up, it rather makes a mockery of it by dooming the

whole thing to exist only as part of the most pointless plot device imaginable – a trap for the Doctor so head-twistingly convoluted, even the Master would have written it off as a bit of a faff. The Daleks have a maguffin that will allow them to take an evolutionary leap forward (i.e. create a whole new range of Daleks for BBC Worldwide to fill the shelves of Toys "R" Us with) – but the maguffin refuses to recognise them as Dalek because they're not "pure." (Why they're not pure is never explained; presumably it's a reference to the "stink of humanity" introduced into the race in *The Parting of the Ways*, but it's surely asking a bit much for the kids to remember an incidental plot point from five years ago.) Their solution to this identity crisis? Get the Doctor to recognise them instead – a bit like when you get your GP to countersign your passport. And the way they choose to go about attracting their greatest enemy's attention is thus (you might want to write this down):

Travel back to 1941. Build a Scottish robot (Bracewell). Get the Scottish robot to build some Daleks. Introduce the Daleks to Winston Churchill on the off-chance he might become suspicious enough to call in the Doctor, who will then recognise them as Daleks, thus reactivating the Progenitor device and ensuring the survival of the Dalek race. Or something. Wouldn't it have just been quicker to show the Doctor a Dalek Top Trumps card and say, "What's that?"

Incredibly, though, this is not even the dumbest thing about the episode. That dubious honour has to go to the sequence in which Bracewell equips a squadron of Spitfires for space flight, and then launches them into battle on the far side of the moon. Again, nice idea, but what ought to be a triumphant moment – the classic totem of British wartime moxie taking on the might of the Daleks – is ultimately rendered preposterous by sloppy scripting and editing that suggests the entire process, from drawing board to dogfight, is achieved in less than five minutes. Five minutes! It would take the pilots longer than that just to wax their moustaches.

After that, the story just fizzles out, with the Daleks switching some lights on over London apparently serving as the dramatic climax. Even the Doctor seems embarrassed by the lack of a decent ending: "So this is your big plan, is it?" he snorts, as his mortal enemies announce their diabolical scheme to, er, bugger off and leave everyone alone. (They do leave a parting gift in the form of Bracewell, who turns out to be a ticking timebomb as well as an android. Fortunately, Amy is able to diffuse him with some light flirting.)

What's disappointing about *Victory of the Daleks* is not just that it's a mess, but that it promised so much more. The Daleks in Churchill's bunker is a solid gold concept for a cracking *Doctor Who* story. Sadly, Winston and the war end up being mere window dressing for a far less interesting story Mark Gatiss chose to tell instead. Surely the man voted the greatest Briton deserved better for his *Who* debut than that?

Oh, and the new Daleks are a bit rubbish, too.

Reviewing the story in the *Mirror*, lifelong fan David Quantick lamented that, "this week *Doctor Who*, for the first time in recent memory, was really not very good". But most of the attention focused less on the shortcomings of the story than the, um, widecomings of what were already being dubbed – admittedly not hugely cleverly – the Fatleks.

"We talked at the first meeting about making them more like the Daleks from the 60s movies, which I've always loved," Mark Gatiss told *Radio Times*. "The sheer boldness of those colours and the size of them just gets to you."[10]

To look at what happened next, it certainly got to some people. "Angry *Doctor Who* fans claim a shock redesign has turned the Daleks from cold, menacing metallic killers into brightly coloured TELETUBBIES," shrieked *The Sun* on Monday morning. "The new, bulkier exterminators which made their debut on Saturday have also been accused of looking fat. A fan called DiscoP wrote on a web forum: 'Why have they got such huge backsides?' Aneechick added: 'They looked like disabled toilets. Others claimed their coloured panels make the Doctor's armoured foes appear SPONGY.'" (Love the caps on that, as if SPONGY is the worst insult you could possibly level at something.)

And it wasn't just random crazies on the internet who were unimpressed. In *The Guardian*, Charlie Brooker dismissed them as "furious crayons", while *SFX* reckoned they looked "comical" and "cartoony". Though I bet they still wouldn't have said it to their faces.

Interviewed by *Doctor Who Magazine* a few months later, Mark Gatiss admitted to some retrospective regrets over the New – to use their more generous handle – Paradigm Daleks. "When I saw the designs, I loved them in every respect apart from the hump. I said, 'I think the hump is dodgy', because whatever has happened to the Daleks over the years, the fundamental pepperpot design has not been altered. It works. It's a design classic. What you've got now is... I think it's pushed just a little too far. They look fat. From the side, it looks as if they're slouching. Maybe if the head were bigger, to be more in scale?

"I think it's sad that the Daleks' new look has become the disproportionate focus of ire," he lamented, "because I love everything else about them. If it weren't for that hump, they'd be exactly what I wanted."[11]

Amazingly, the press restrained themselves from a "*Doctor Who* Writer Gets the Hump with New Daleks' headline. Maybe it was because he didn't mind the fact they were so SPONGY.

Angel delight

If the Daleks' Victory had proved hollow, matters were made worse for them by the fact everyone seemed to love this year's model of their mortal enemy. And Matt Smith fans were handed a bonus ball when it was announced that the eleventh Doctor would be appearing in an upcoming instalment of *The Sarah Jane Adventures*, in a story that would see Russell T Davies writing for Smith's incarnation for the first time. ("Great, what's it called?" asked a delighted Steven Moffat. "*Death of the Doctor*," replied Davies. That'll learn 'im.)

On April 21st, commuters in Sheffield found themselves being terrorised – if that was still the right word – by the Daleks as Skaro's most colourful death machines invaded the city to promote the upcoming release of the first of the Doctor Who Adventure Game, *City of the Daleks*. Nick Briggs was on hand to provide the voices, and even took over the station's PA system, thus bringing an unusually human and sympathetic quality to the day's litany of delays and cancellations.

The Daleks also met snooker ace John Parrot, who was in the city for the World Championships, but declined to take him on in the green baize, figuring they'd suffered enough humiliations lately.

Matt Smith and Karen Gillan were also scheduled to be there, but were still stuck in the US as planes were grounded in the aftermath of the Eyjafjallajökull volcano eruption. As he hung out at California's achingly hip Coachella festival, watching Gorillaz and Vampire Weekend with his supermodel girlfriend, Daisy Lowe, Smith must have been gutted to miss out on the Sheffield rush-hour.

The volcanic ash cloud created a more pressing problem for Steven Moffat, though, who found himself writing the *Doctor Who* Christmas special while stuck in a bakingly hot Los Angeles. "Two days of writing nothing, and I took emergency measures," Moffat told *Radio Times*. "I downloaded every Christmas song I could find, closed all the curtains, and turned up the air conditioning to Doctor Zhivago, and sat at my desk in a big coat and mittens."[12] Still, at least he didn't let the location affect his writing (though the surfing scene with the Beach Boys soundtrack did seem a *bit* out of place).

After a bumpy couple of weeks, the relaunch was back on track – and then some – with *The Time of Angels*, the brilliant first instalment of Steven Moffat's rematch for the Doctor and the Weeping Angels.

And not just the Angels: River Song is back, too, literally flying into the TARDIS in a packed, Bond-riffing pre-credits sequence and then engaging in some sparky, flirtatious banter with the Doctor that gives Matt Smith and Alex Kingston a chance to do their best Hepburn/Tracy routine. ("It didn't make the noise," the Doctor gripes when River lands the Ship. "It's not supposed to make that noise," she tells him "You leave the brakes on.")

River has taken the Doctor and Amy to Alfava Metraxis, where – a stunning matte shot, this – the burning wreck of the space cruiser *Byzantium* has embedded itself in the rocks rising up from the beach.

As the Doctor grumbles about not being a taxi service ("I'm not going to be there to catch

you every time you feel like jumping out of a space ship") and Amy teases him about his sour mood ("Are we all Mr Grumpy Face today?"), it's hard to believe these scenes were the first Matt Smith and Karen Gillan ever filmed, as the tide moved in on one side and the paparazzi closed in on the other. Have any other Doctor-companion combo ever nailed it so instinctively from – quite literally – day one?

"There's one survivor," says River, indicating the *Byzantium*. "There's a thing in the belly of that ship that can't ever die... What do you know of the Weeping Angels?"

And then, in trademark Moffat fashion, the playful, sitcom-tooled exchanges segue via an effortless key change into full-on horror territory in a *Ring*-inspired sequence in which Amy is trapped in a small room with a video of an Angel on a monitor. "That which holds the image of an Angel itself becomes an Angel," warns the Doctor – as the stone creature literally starts coming out of the screen. Having terrified children with monsters under the bed, creeping shadows and cracks in the wall, here Moffat pulls off the ultimate *Doctor Who* scare: the monster that comes *out of your TV*. It's such a simple, obvious thing to do – and yet no-one else in half a century had thought to do it. (Well, Mark Gatiss sort of did, but Maureen Lipman camping it up on a Bakelite set isn't quite the same thing.)

Events take an even darker turn – literally – when the Doctor, Amy, River and a small platoon of armed clerics (forget whist drives and summer fetes; the church is seriously kickass in the fifty-first century) enter the Maze of the Dead, a network of tomb-lined catacombs filled with statues that they eventually deduce are not memorials to the native departed, but atrophied Weeping Angels who are slowly being restored to life by the radiation leaking from the crashed ship. And they're completely surrounded.

The ending is exceptional. "Oh, big mistake," the Doctor taunts the Angels. "Huge. Didn't anyone ever tell you there's one thing you never put in a trap? If you're smart, if you value your continued existence, if you have any plans about seeing tomorrow, there is one thing you never, ever put in a trap." He fires a gun into the air. "*Me*."

If Matt Smith was feeling first week nerves – which we know he was – it's certainly not obvious here, as he nails his first cliffhanger convincingly with a confident, compelling delivery. In fact, if not for Graham Norton, it would have been pretty much perfect.

Yes, that's right: the pug-faced Irishman – last heard blabbing over the opening minutes of *Rose* – manages to make another unscheduled appearance at a critical moment. This time, the miscreant was Norton's animated avatar, seen prancing about over the bottom half of Matt Smith's face in a crassly-timed trail for upcoming reality talent search *Over the Rainbow*.

Having received more than 5,000 complaints, the BBC issued a statement apologising to fans "whose enjoyment of the show was disrupted. We recognise the strength of feeling that has been expressed," it added, "and are taking steps to ensure that this mistake will not happen again". In the opening monologue to his BBC One chat show broadcast a couple of weeks later, Norton proved himself a good sport by telling viewers: "Recently, I achieved a lifelong ambition – I appeared on *Doctor Who*. Yes, I secured the prestigious role of Man Ruining the End of the Episode." By way of an apology, he allowed his avatar to be exterminated by a cartoon Dalek (that is, an animated Dalek, as opposed to one of those cartoony new ones from the show itself).

April ended with a mixed message about the place of *Doctor Who* in the nation's hearts. A report by the market research agency YouGov claimed that viewers had found the recent election debates between the three main part leaders "more interesting" than *Doctor Who* – so expect those Gordon Brown action figures and Nick Clegg lunch boxes to hit the shelves any day now – while, on the plus side, Topman reported sales of bow ties had increased by a staggering 94% since the eleventh Doctor's TV debut. Which meant they had now sold 94 of them.

Meanwhile, on Alfava Metraxis, the Doctor had successfully managed to get rid of Graham Norton – but the Weeping Angels were proving more persistent. Steven Moffat had previously spoken of his vision for *Doctor Who* being inspired by "fairytales before Disney defanged them". *Flesh and Stone* is a fairytale with fangs alright, and never more so than when young Amelia Pond – who's wearing a red hood, just in case we missed the allusion – is left lost and alone in the middle of an enchanted forest. (A fake forest aboard a spaceship, for sure, but none the less enchanted for that. And it was filmed at a place called Puzzlewood, so even the location manager's sticking to the fairytale brief.)

Moffat really puts Amy through the ringer in *Flesh and Stone*: seeing her subjected to various forms of torture across these 90 minutes feels a bit like watching a pre-watershed version of *Saw*. ("Let's see, we'll have her all alone in the middle of a forest full of Angels where the one thing you can't do is blink... Nah, too easy, instead of saying she can't close her eyes, let's say she can't *open* them." I'm surprised he didn't tie her shoelaces together while he was at it.)

"Part of the mission statement of writing a script for *Doctor Who* is how bad a time can you give Amy Pond?" Moffat told *Doctor Who Confidential*. "What if it were a situation where if you open your eyes, you'll die? Imagine forcing yourself to keep your eyes shut when you're surrounded by scary monsters."[13]

Karen Gillan's leading man also got in on the act when, in a scene where the Doctor bites Amy on the arm, Matt Smith chose to go a bit... method. "I didn't know Matt was gonna do that at the time," said Gillan. "And it was really hard."[13] Still, at least it was the arm and not the arse – Colin Baker, please note.

If there's one thing that keeps *Flesh and Stone* simmering just under all-time, top five classic status, it's the feeling that it's less than the sum of its parts: a sequence of ruthlessly, even sadistically, well-engineered scares strung together like the world's most brilliant ghost train, but which don't entirely hang together as a story.

The Weeping Angels don't escape with their reputations entirely intact, either. In one sense, this new, deadlier strain – who do a lot more than just send you back in time and let you live to death – are much more terrifying than the ones in *Blink*. But telling us the Angels now want us to look at them – in other words: *do* close your eyes, *do* turn away and *do* blink – does rather muddy what was previously a very elegant and highly effective premise. The

Weeping Angels encouraging you to keep your eyes open feels a bit like the Daleks joining a rainbow alliance, or the Ice Warriors installing central heating.

But these are minor niggles in an otherwise extraordinary piece of television which, like all the best *Doctor Who*, manages to be both scary and funny, often at the same time. ("What if the gravity fails?" asks Amy. "I've thought about that," the Doctor assures her. "And?" "And we'd all plunge to our deaths. See, I thought about it.") River Song, meanwhile, is warming up to be quite the mystery woman who, when she's not gallivanting about with the Doctor, is locked up in a maximum security prison for killing a man: "A very good man – the best man I've ever known." Can't think who she means, can you, readers?

Oh, and then there's the sex scene. Or the nearly sex scene, in which Amy pushes the Doctor up against the TARDIS in her bedroom and tries to rip his clothes off, before draping herself across her bed and inviting the Time Lord to investigate her crack a little more closely. The eleventh Doctor, however, isn't quite as smooth as his tonsil-wrapping predecessor. "I'm nine hundred and seven!" he protests. "This can't ever work." "Oh, you are sweet, Doctor," purrs Amy. "But I really wasn't suggesting anything quite so long term." (Oh yeah? Well, memo to Pond: trying to tempt someone to a no-strings quickie in a room full of Barbie and Ken-style dolls of the two of you together – products of a lifelong obsession with your "raggedy man" – could be considered something of a mixed signal.)

"I'm just going to come right out and say it," said *Guardian* blogger Dan Martin. "*Flesh and Stone* can lay credible claim to being the greatest episode of *Doctor Who* there has ever been." But try telling that to the *Daily Mail*, who hooked up with Mediawatch – the heirs to Mary Whitehouse's high horse – in a bid to whip up a storm over the Amy seduction scene. The pressure group's director, Vivienne Pattison, claimed the sequence "sailed pretty close to the wind", while the article also picked up on the sexy vampire girls in their nighties from the Next Time trailer. In reality, though, there were only 43 complaints from a total audience of 8.5 million. But they were very *shrill* complaints.

In Cardiff, Matt Smith was busy recording his contribution to *The Sarah Jane Adventures*, alongside Elisabeth Sladen and her Scooby gang – and one Katy Manning, no less, returning to the role of Jo Grant a full 37 years after we last saw her disappearing up the Amazon to look for spores. "It's absolutely fricking amazing!" squealed Manning, with her trademark reserve. "It's like one of those extraordinary things in life, isn't it? You can never guess what's going to happen next. Normally when I do something, I talk to lots of people – it's a Libran thing – then I make up my mind. But I mean – Russell! Hello! And Matt, who is just such an extraordinary, creative actor. Obviously Lis, because she's such a dear, sweet soul. We've always been friends, even though we've never actually worked together. I actually didn't do the Libran thing – I made up my mind by myself within seconds."[14] (It was a yes, in case you're wondering.)

City of Death in Venice

A refugee alien disguised as a human cooks up an elaborate plan to avert the destruction of its race while hiding out in a romantic European tourist destination, while the Doctor makes himself comfy in a fancy chair and engages in some sparky banter with a haughty bit of aristo-crumpet. There are many – oh, so many – good jokes, and the whole thing is eventually resolved in a matter of seconds.

Sound familiar? What I'm saying, and not very subtly, is that if you don't like *The Vampires of Venice*, then you surely can't like its 70s spiritual antecedent either. And anyone who doesn't like *City of Death* is hereby ordered to report to the *Space Helmet* admin office to hand in their psychic papers/library card[II].

In *Vampires of Venice*, the jokes come thick, fast and funny. Crucially, many of them are also uniquely *Doctor Who* jokes: where else would you find a sixteenth-century Venetian gondolier in a stag-do T-shirt, or hear words like "Ofsted" deployed to kick the legs from under an otherwise wholly convincing bit of Hammer glamour lusty vamp action?

This verisimilitude is important – the comic anachronisms only work because the production around them is so handsome, so sumptuously cinematic, so credibly Venetian. When the sets, costumes and acting also felt like part of the joke – as in some of those hyper-inflationary knockabouts of the late 70s – it's no wonder we started pining for the Gothic chills of the Holmes and Hinchcliffe years. But when witty, vibrant, cheeky scripts get the production values they deserve – as they did in *City of Death*, or *The Talons of Weng-Chiang*, or *Tooth and Claw* – that's when *Doctor Who* feels properly, treasurably unique. (Especially when you throw in some Gothic chills and thrills as a bonus. Did I mention the hordes of lusty, busty vampire girls in their nighties already?)

Like its Parisian forebear, *The Vampires of Venice* isn't perfect. In fact, the two share some common faults, including credibility-stretching human disguises for the alien Big Bads (in this case, a bunch of alien fish led by Helen McCrory) and a plot resolved by a simple punch to the head/flick of a switch (though Duggan's right hook in *City of Death* was infinitely more stylish, as a deliberate gag carefully seeded over four weeks, whereas here the Doctor literally just switches the story off at the end).

There are the usual messy plot holes, too: Why would disguising yourself as a vampire make you susceptible to sunlight? That's like a Playboy bunny getting myxomatosis. How do you transform one species to another through a blood transfusion? More fundamentally, why go to all the trouble of sinking an entire city to create a new home for your fishy species on a planet that's 70% covered in water already? Or does this whole episode revolve around the fact that, like their Earthly, tank-bound cousins, the Fish from Space just want some nice underwater ruins to swim around in? (And if someone wouldn't mind dropping a few pellets of fish-food into the ocean every couple of days, that would be lovely, thanks.)

The Doctor's thrilling, semi-flirtatious confrontation with McCrory's Rosanna, ending with our hero promising to "tear down the house of Calvierri stone by stone" is exhilarating stuff (even if, in the end, he manages to do it with a small brass light switch instead). Despite moving with the natural grace of a camel on roller skates, Matt Smith once again manages not to put a foot wrong, though he faces serious competition from Arthur Darvill's deeply loveable Rory. Together, the two of them give us one of the show's most memorable pre-title sequences, in which the Doctor pops out of a cake at Rory's stag-do in place of the planned stripper ("Lovely girl – diabetic"). If they ever introduce a BAFTA for popping-out-of-cake acting, Matt Smith surely has it in the bag.

In its review, *Metro* claimed "Matt Smith has so quickly inhabited the character, it's now a case of David Who?", while *The Independent* described the story – and its vampiric finishing school – as "a Hammer Horror wet dream."

"You can't really give the licence fee-payer any more than 18 scantily clad vestal virgins with Barbarella hair and fangs, can you?" mused Helen McCrory in an interview with the *Daily Telegraph*. Oh I don't know, thought Mediawatch's Vivienne Pattison. How about an omnibus edition of *Songs of Praise*, with that nice Aled Jones?

As pre-production began on the Christmas special, the team welcomed new production designer Michael Pickwoad, replacing the outgoing Edward Thomas. Thomas had been one of the key architects of *Doctor Who*'s 2005 revival – but Pickwoad's dad, the actor William Mervyn, was in *Doctor Who* (*The War Machines*) in 1966, so he wins on points. The episode also had a new producer in the shape of German-born Sanne Wohlenberg, fresh from her recent success with the BBC's adaptations of Henning Mankell's *Wallander* novels.

Simon Nye was also new to *Who*, but an old friend of Steven Moffat's, whose wife's mother, Beryl Vertue, had produced *Men Behaving Badly*. Best known as a comedy writer, but with dramas like *Frank Stubbs Promotes* on his CV too, Nye brings his trademark wit to the quietly brilliant, smart but un-showy seventh episode, *Amy's Choice*. (Being a fellow sitcom writer, Moffat obviously had no problem with Nye turning up the funny – just as long as he stayed away from the mother-in-law jokes.)

Amy's Choice may be a bottle episode clearly made with whatever loose change they could find down the back of the Upper Boat sofas after they'd spent all the cash on the season finale, but it's none the worse for that. Part psychological thriller, part zombie romp-com, this little gem puts our heroes at the mercy of the Dream Lord, a Zelig-like mischief-maker, played with puckish relish by Toby Jones, who presents them with two alternate realities (Amy and Rory's sleepy Gloucestershire village under siege from aliens disguised as pensioners[III], and the TARDIS drifting towards a frozen cold star) and challenges them to decide which is real and which is fantasy, on pain of death.

Rory has a vested interest in the near-future Leadworth scenario being real, as Amy has chosen settling down with him over adventuring with the Doctor, and is heavily pregnant. That version turns out to be the dream, of course – which is just as well for him, as it turns out, because he gets killed in it.

The script is as droll as you'd expect from Nye – certainly, it's hard to imagine a line like Amy's "If we're going to die, let's die looking like a Peruvian folk band" in an era before they started hiring sitcom writers. And if all this had just amounted to a bit of knockabout fun – a sort of *Old Men Behaving Badly* – it would have been more than entertaining enough. In the event, though, the comedy turns out to have a razor-blade inside it: "If you had any more tawdry quirks, you could open up a tawdry quirk shop," the Dream Lord taunts the Doctor. "The madcap vehicle. The cockamamie hair. The clothes designed by a first-year fashion student. I'm surprised you haven't got a little purple space dog, just to ram home what an intergalactic wag you are."

The sly reveal that the Dream Lord is really nothing more than a piece of psychic cosmic fluff feeding on the shadows within the Doctor's soul, and all that bile and hatred is actually directed towards himself, is a powerful insight into the shame and self-doubt in the hearts of the Time Lord ("Nobody else in the universe hates me as much as you do," observes the Doctor – which does make you wonder what blood is on those twitchy hands), and all the better for being done with such a deft touch. A deceptively light comedy with a heart of darkness, *Amy's Choice* is an experimental story about nightmares that works like a dream.

Proving that *Doctor Who* really was the new rock and roll, mid-May brought news of an ambitious arena tour to be staged at cities across Britain in the autumn. *Doctor Who Live* promised a feast of monster action, spectacular effects and, best of all, no-one trying to play "something off the new album".

"This is everything I ever wanted since I was 11," said Steven Moffat. "A live show, with all the coolest *Doctor Who* monsters, a proper story and brand-new screen material for Matt Smith's Doctor! I'll be writing scenes for it, and probably attending every single night."

The tour was scheduled to kick off on October 8th at Wembley Arena – something of a step up from the last *Doctor Who* stage show 21 years earlier, where the venues for *The Ultimate Adventure* had included The Congress Theatre in Eastbourne and the Theatre Clwyd, Mold.

Live and Let Dai

The Hungry Earth/Cold Blood is Steven Moffat and Chris Chibnall's love letter to the early 70s vision of Barry Letts, Terrance Dicks, Derek Sherwin and John Devon Roland Pertwee, adoringly riffing on everything from *Inferno* (big drilling project) to *The Daemons* (remote community cut off by force field) and *The Green Death* (Welsh mining village). Oh, and for those who are really paying attention, there's the odd tip of the hat to *Doctor Who and the Silurians* in there, too.

Okay, so it virtually *is* *Doctor Who and the Silurians*. And that's a significant departure for twenty-first-century *Who*: Steven Moffat has explicitly acknowledged the timeless brilliance of Malcolm Hulke's premise ("One of the best ideas that *Doctor Who* ever had – the former owners of the planet reclaiming it," Moffat told fans in New York) and the result is the first New *Who* story that feels less like a re-invention and more like an actual re-make for a new generation of viewers. (Chibnall, for his part, claimed to be more inspired by Hulke's novelisation, *Doctor Who and the Cave Monsters*, from which he lifted the phrase "Homo reptilian".)

All of which is fair enough, but it does leave old-skool fans frequently asking "Yeah, and..?" For anyone even on nodding terms with the original, none of the mysteries presented here are very mysterious at all. Why are people being dragged underground? (That'll be the Silurians, then.) Why are there so many empty graves? (Yep, Silurians again.) And who's that drilling upwards towards the surface from beneath? (Fifty quid says it's not a giant mole.)

Not that you'd necessarily recognise them, as the Eocenes are the latest design classic to have undergone a radical makeover. Sydney Newman would no doubt approve – the Silurians are no longer bug-eyed monsters; now they're just, erm, eyed monsters. (Though they *do*, bizarrely, wear B.E.M. masks on top of their lizard faces when going into battle. It's not clear why: maybe they were a free gift with *Doctor Who Adventures*. Or maybe they're just really into cosplay.)

The first 20 minutes or so of *The Hungry Earth*, then, have a gently nostalgic, bucolic quality that's rather appealing. How lovely to see rolling valleys and country churchyards in *Doctor Who* again. Some people complained that Russell T Davies and company didn't make Wales look enough like alien planets; you could equally argue they didn't make it look enough like *Wales*. But here it is in all its lush, green, picture postcard glory. The idea of focusing on an ordinary family is also a nice one – though it does raise the question of why what we're assured is the world's most ambitious drilling operation is being project managed by a group of people who look like they should be running the village post office instead. It's as if a couple of local families have clubbed together to roll back the frontiers of subterranean exploration.

Unfortunately, things start to fall apart when the main plot kicks in. Or, rather, when it becomes clear it isn't really going to. Back in 2005, Russell T Davies warned that, in the new era of 45-minute stories, a single *Radio Times* billing was in danger of giving away the entire plot. That's never been more true than here. If you know it's about humans drilling down into the Earth while something else – something rhyming with Nilurian – is drilling upwards, then you've pretty much got it covered. That's not a story, it's a see-saw. Though the scene where Amy gets pulled under the ground is pretty scary stuff – if not quite *Drag Me to Hell* scary, then at least *Drag Me to Heck*.

In *Cold Blood*, the Doctor ventures underground into the Silurian city, and immediately proves himself the most rubbish peace envoy since Tony Blair, as the first thing he blurts out is: "I met some of you lot before – the humans

blew them up and now they're all dead." Nice one, Kofi Annan. Later, when things are looking a bit hairy (or scaly, technically), our hero is moved to refer to the situation as "super squeaky bum time". Which doesn't seem very dignified for a Time Lord. I mean, just think how many times over the years he's been in a bit of a fix, and not once has he felt the need to refer to the fact he might just shit himself. (Imagine, for example, if *The Deadly Assassin* had opened with Tom Baker portentously intoning: "Suddenly, and terribly, the Time Lords faced the most dangerous crisis in their long history... yes, it really was Brown Trousers Time on Gallifrey.")

Amy, meanwhile, is proving too clever by half. Throughout this series, she's had a habit of being one step ahead of the Doctor, and here she instantly deduces everything like a ginger Sherlock Holmes; when she asks, "Have you never picked a lizard man's pocket before?", you get the impression she really has done it hundreds of times. A bit of plucky sang-froid is all very well, but where's the awe, where's the wonder? For someone who spent her whole life dreaming of the man in the blue box, she's awfully blasé about the whole experience.

And Rory? Rory's dead. Again. Except it's worse than that because, thanks to the timey-wimey properties of that crack in the universe, he's also ceased ever to have existed. So no sooner has Amy finished grieving over the body and begging him to live – a wonderful performance from Karen Gillan, all snot and tears and denial – than she's forgotten all about him. Even for a doormat like Rory, that's harsh.

And that's that. We never do find out what that massive drill is actually for, so we can only assume it's for boring the ruddy great holes in the plot.

After the episode had finished, Karen Gillan received a tearful call from her mother, who was utterly distraught at Rory's death. Maybe she'd already bought a hat for the wedding.

But life, for some at least, went on. In the *Radio Times*, Richard Curtis explained how he'd come to write the following week's episode of *Doctor Who*. "My kids absolutely love it," he said. "We all watched the Christmas special two years ago and my children said I had to do one. Scarlett, our eldest, pointed out that while I'd always promised I would write a children's movie, by the time I do it she won't be a child any more. And the great thing about telly is how swift it is, compared with films."[15]

In fact, one of the reasons the family had gathered to watch *The Next Doctor* that Christmas was because David Morrissey was their next door neighbour – and Curtis' partner Emma Freud is the cousin of Morrissey's wife Esther, who was in 1985's *Attack of the Cybermen*. Are you following this, or do you need a diagram?

As with Simon Nye, Steven Moffat knew Curtis through his wife Sue, a producer on Comic Relief – which you may recall is how Curtis came to commission Moffat's first-ever *Doctor Who* script, *The Curse of Fatal Death*. According to Moffat, he had since drunkenly asked Curtis to write for *Doctor Who* on numerous occasions, but "he never exhibited the slightest interest in it".[16]

The man who changed his mind was Vincent van Gogh. While Curtis was no *Doctor Who* expert, he was passionate about the Netherlands' favourite gloomy post-Impressionist, and thought a time-travel story might be a good way to correct a historical injustice and allow van Gogh – in fiction, at least – finally to have some recognition for his work in his own lifetime. Hence the text Moffat received from Curtis stating he wanted to do "a story about van Gogh and depression". (He had to admit, it didn't *sound* like a barrel of laughs for six o'clock on a Saturday night.)

Talking to *BBC News*, Curtis admitted he had started out writing the Doctor in that florid, vaguely Dickensian way that Russell T Davies had worked so hard to eliminate, prompting Moffat to explain that he didn't really talk like that any more. The showrunner also thought the script was too slow, and the first meeting between the Doctor and van Gogh too clunky. "Steven said normally he would give people a note saying, 'Make it more like what happens in Richard Curtis films where something cute happens when they meet'," Curtis told *The Guardian*. "So he said, even though it's you, you have to do better."

And did he? Yes and no. The clue to understanding *Vincent and the Doctor* is in the title. There's no ambiguity about who gets top billing here – and it's not the fella with the bow tie and the bandy legs.

So Curtis saw *Doctor Who* as the perfect vehicle for finally tackling the van Gogh story he'd had buzzing about in his head for years like a bee in a bottle. Which, indeed, it might have been, if he'd succeeded in weaving his love letter to the artist into the fabric of *Doctor Who*, or vice versa. What we get instead is a perfectly charming, if slightly hagiographic portrait of the great man, with a mildly incongruous *Doctor Who* creature-feature somewhat clumsily bolted on to the side like a lean-to shed.

Or maybe that wasn't how it happened, but it's certainly hard to shake the notion that the entire Krafayis plot – in which what appears to be a giant space parrot left stranded on Earth by its brethren causes merry havoc in nineteenth-century Provence, before dying a rather pitiful and pointless death at the hands of our heroes – was a bit of a dutiful afterthought, and that Curtis would much rather have done a straight van Gogh story. Or at least a very simple, monster-free Doctor-meets-Vincent story, a bit like those superannuated school text books they stuck Tom Baker's face on in the 70s; *Doctor Who Discovers the Impressionists*, anyone?

Even in the main Vincent-meets-Doctor through line, there is evidence of the romcom king gingerly feeling his way through an unfamiliar genre. Surely no-one with a working knowledge of the grammar of time-travel stories – particularly its "celebrity historical" variation – would have knowingly recycled so many familiar genre tropes, or seemed quite so pleased with themselves for doing so. The way in which the Doctor and Amy bring their influence to bear on the creation of various van Gogh masterpieces, in particular, fails to bring anything new to a well-worn gag. Compare, if you will, the pay-off shot here – a simple "For Amy" daubed on those Sunflowers – with *City of Death*, written more than 30 years earlier, in which we ended up with six Mona Lisas bearing the legend "This is a Fake" in felt-tip pen. Now that's good value storytelling.

The gags are disappointingly subdued, too. Maybe Curtis was too conscious of his baggage as a comedy writer and felt the need to exercise restraint; there are some great lines – "Is this how time normally passes?" grumps the Doctor, "Really slowly, in the right order?" –

but on the whole, it's surprising to see this end up with a lot fewer laughs than this year's Moffat, Nye or even Whithouse scripts.

And yet...

... despite all this, *Vincent and the Doctor* is easy to love, actually. Partly because director Johnny Campbell gives it an easy, languid charm that suits the Provence sunshine, while demonstrating a keen eye for the mise en scene, especially in those sly (and occasionally not so sly) recreations of van Gogh's paintings. And partly because, for all the lack of cohesion and structural integrity, the story is redeemed by three of the most extraordinary scenes in the entire *Doctor Who* canon.

The first is when Vincent welcomes the Doctor, Amy and the viewers into his mind to give us a privileged glimpse of the world through the gaze of an artistic genius; to show us the Starry Night as he saw it in his head, the dark canopy above us transforming into the brilliant whorls of his magnum opus before our very eyes. What an honour.

The second revelatory moment is an unflinching study of van Gogh in the very pit of his depression, in a scene where the Doctor encounters him curled up on his cot in the depths of wretched despair. There's a very real sense of *Doctor Who* coming of age here, tackling real human emotion and frailty in a way it's never quite been brave enough to do before. And what's most striking is the Doctor's reaction, his sense of helplessness. Because this is the one monster the Time Lord doesn't know how to fight: the black dog of depression at the heart of a broken man. The Doctor has always been about seeing, and sharing, the joy and boundless wonder of the universe. Yet here is a man who looks at the universe and sees only darkness.

Or does he? Because the final extraordinary scene of the episode is one of redemption, in which the Doctor and Amy take Vincent into the future to see how his work will become appreciated, in an effort to lift the terrible burden of failure from his shoulders. It's a beautiful sequence soundtracked – to the ire of some purists – by a rather lovely song from anthemic indie types Athlete, and anchored by a wonderful speech from Bill Nighy, in an uncredited cameo as an art expert: "Pain is easy to portray. But to use your passion and pain to portray the ecstasy and joy and magnificence of our world – no-one had ever done it before. Perhaps no-one ever will again."

This, when you think about it, is a Big Idea for the little show designed to fill the gap between the pools results and *Juke Box Jury*. "The way I see it," the Doctor tells Amy when she realises all their efforts failed to stop Vincent killing himself, "every life is a pile of good things and bad things. The good things don't always soften the bad things, but vice versa, the bad things don't necessarily spoil the good things or make them unimportant. And we definitely added to his pile of good things."

Three extraordinary scenes, then. Add those to the three luminous central performances from Matt Smith (love the knowing wink of Eleven looking in the mirror and seeing Patrick Troughton), Karen Gillan and Tony Curran as van Gogh, and that's half a dozen items Richard Curtis has added to *Doctor Who*'s pile of good things right there.

The closing titles advertised a helpline number for any viewers who had been affected by the programme, a first for *Doctor Who* (though God knows, some of Pip and Jane Baker's stories would have benefited from one).

Coming so hard to America

After a critical dry period – during which he had frequently been accused of peddling a preppy, sentimental fantasy view of Middle England – *Vincent and the Doctor* was Richard Curtis' most lionised script in years, with *The Times*' Caitlin Moran describing "Van Gogh and Doctor Who v the budgie of doom" as "a beautiful story of mental illness". *The Guardian*'s Mark Lawson hailed "an exceptionally good" episode, while Peter Bradshaw claimed: "Richard Curtis is back with a bullet, his mojo apparently restored by one of our great small-screen institutions. If you haven't seen it yet, settle down to his terrifically clever, funny, likeable, wildly surreal episode of *Doctor Who*."

"Clever," "funny" and "likeable" were three words rarely used about *Torchwood* – at least, not until *Children of Earth* came along. But the success of 2009's blockbusting mini-series proved enough for BBC One to commission a fourth run – and this time the Americans fancied a slice too. "The sci-fi drama will air a ten-part run following an international partnership between the corporation and US premium network Starz Entertainment," said the BBC in a statement. "Russell T Davies will continue to write the series. It has also been revealed that plots are to go beyond Cardiff to locations worldwide."

"We have a long history of working with many US networks, but it is incredibly exciting to be working with Starz for the first time, as well as to be reunited with the best of British in Russell, Jane [Tranter] and Julie [Gardner]," said Ben Stephenson, controller of BBC drama commissioning. "*Torchwood* will burst back onto the screen with a shocking and moving story with global stakes and locations that will make it feel bigger and bolder than ever."

The BBC had originally entered into discussions with Fox TV but, when that deal fell through, turned their attention to Starz, the US movie cable network that had recently been trialling original drama such as the lurid swords, sandals and shagging grunt-fest *Spartacus: Blood and Sand*. HBO, it wasn't.

And so to *The Lodger*. Look, *Space Helmet* isn't one for scurrilous gossip – much – but all we're saying is, it must have been one hell of a pre-season writers' party in 2009 because, somehow, Richard Curtis ended up going home with Gareth Roberts' celebrity historical, Toby Whithouse got off with Mark Gatiss' Gothic comedy and Roberts, the dirty bugger, found himself sharing a cab with both Curtis' romcom and Simon Nye's flatshare caper. With the result that, while Roberts' story may not be the greatest *Doctor Who* story ever made, it's difficult to remember a more thoroughly irresistible 45 minutes of shamelessly showboating entertainment.

The story has its roots in Roberts' 2006 *DWM* comic strip of the same name, in which the tenth Doctor crashes into Mickey Smith's life, with disastrous consequences. When he read it, Steven Moffat emailed Russell T Davies to say: "That's so an episode," but Rose and Mickey were being written out, so the idea was never taken any further.

Shortly after accepting the *Doctor Who* job in 2008, Moffat asked Roberts to develop "The Lodger" for television – then promptly forgot all about it and asked him to write something else instead. But when it became clear a "budg-et" episode would be needed towards the end of the 2010 run, Roberts suggested *The Lodger*, which he happened to have sort of accidentally written anyway – just, you know, in case.

In the TV version, Mickey is replaced by James Corden's loveable loser Craig Owens, who the Doctor invites himself to live with after the TARDIS belches him out of the door in downtown Colchester. As he works out a way to get his Ship – and Amy – back, the Time Lord has to deal with a mysterious entity luring people to their deaths in the flat upstairs, not to mention playing matchmaker to Craig and his would-be should-be girlfriend Sophie (Daisy Haggard). But his biggest challenge is trying not to look like a total mentalist in front of his new friends.

The real masterstroke here is that, in exploiting the comic potential of the Doctor's total bewilderment at lives less extraordinary than his own, Roberts delivers a format-expanding episode that feels new and fresh and different, but which is also fundamentally true to the spirit of *Doctor Who*. In fact, its alien-among-us premise is thematically not that much of a stretch from the show's own ground zero, *An Unearthly Child* – except we never saw William Hartnell playing footie or running about in a small bath towel. (You can't help thinking all that grunty stuff with the cavemen would have been a lot more fun if we had.)

So this is the perfect showcase for everything that's special about the Doctor – because, just as that Yeti sitting on the loo in Tooting Bec is scarier than one in the Himalayas, so a Time Lord in a flat in Colchester is more alien than one in the Panopticon on Gallifrey. More than that, it's the perfect showcase for *this* Doctor. Ironically, given its origin as a tenth Doctor strip, this story wouldn't have worked nearly as well with David Tennant; with all that blokeish charm, he'd have fitted in far too convincingly. But Smith's angular, awkward young fogey is a more obvious outsider, ripe for mining fish-out-of-water comic potential in the spirit of *Mork and Mindy*, *My Favourite Martian*, *3rd Rock from the Sun* and *ALF* (with whom, let's face it, Smith bears more than a passing resemblance).

Our man seizes this opportunity with both hands. From mistaking a toothbrush for his sonic to his hilarious regurgitating wine act to his bonkers take-over of the call centre ("Hello, Mr Jorgensen? Can you hold, I have to eat a biscuit"), Smith's performance is a comic tour de force. James Corden – who three days earlier had made headlines for an altogether less pleasant encounter with a sci-fi icon after being insulted on stage at an awards ceremony by a somewhat refreshed Patrick Stewart – is also fabulous, proving he's big enough to play the straight man and let Smith get on with the crowd-pleasing comic business.

The story's horror element is also surprisingly effective, from the plaintive, disembodied voices luring hapless passers-by through the intercom to the shadowy figures at the top of the stairs (these scenes very much channelling the spirit of *Sapphire and Steel*, the elemental puzzler that remains the gold standard for creepy British fantasy television).

And the secret of the top of the stairs turns out to have a satisfying pay-off, mining that domestic / fantastic mix yet again with a huge, impossible time machine hidden inside a flat. In – let me say again – Colchester. (The villain of the piece is eventually revealed to be the ship's emergency crash program, but early versions of the script had featured Meglos – the homicidal cactus from Tom Baker's final series – as the Big Bad, with less-than-serious suggestions for the story's title including *Meglos 2* and, from Steven Moffat, *Mrs Meglos*. Amazingly, Zolfa Thura's most maniacal pot plant survived a full five drafts, and was only dropped because his spiky face was considered too similar to the Vinvocci in *The End of Time*.)

The deft manner in which the romcom element is hardwired into the sci-fi resolution is also extremely elegant: love literally saving the world courtesy of some well-seeded gags about Craig's stubborn attachment to his sofa. Who needs biological metacrises or Whitepoint stars and all that bafflegab, when the only words needed to save the day are: "For God's sake, kiss the girl!" Wonderful.

Ironically for a story with more midfield action than the rest of *Doctor Who* put together, *The Lodger* got hammered in the ratings by England's World Cup game against the USA, which pulled in 13 million viewers, despite both teams muddling their way through to a thrill-free 1-1 draw. But those who did tune in may have got more than they bargained for,

according to the tabloids, with the *Mirror* and the *Star* both suggesting the Doctor might have revealed a lot more than his sonic screwdriver during the episode. "As Matt, 27, rushed from the bathroom, a blue towel covering his modesty slipped," claimed the *Star*. "It was a blink and you'll miss it moment that lasted a fraction of a second... Cheeky fans posted the exact time of 15 minutes and 10 seconds into the show that the Doctor's lunchbox appeared, and urged others to freeze frame." A BBC spokesman wearily pointed out that Smith had, in fact, "been wearing an item to protect his modesty". He didn't specify what the item was – but let's hope it was a pair of BHS Tom Baker underpants.

As the two-part season finale approached, *Doctor Who* bagged its third *Radio Times* cover in a little over two months, this time foregrounding "Saturday Night's New Sensation", Karen Gillan. "Amy is likeable, I hope, but she's not ordinary," Gillan told the magazine. "She's quite complicated and there are layers to explore. So I was taking a few risks with her, and I think it works."[17]

Stephen Fry was no doubt delighted to see Gillan and Matt Smith staring out from the newsstands once again. At that week's 2010 Annual Television Lecture at BAFTA, the man who once described writing a *Doctor Who* script as "one of the most exciting moments of my life", laid into the "infantilisation" of television, stating: "The only dramas the BBC will shout about are *Doctor Who* and *Merlin*. They are wonderful programmes, don't get me wrong, but they are not for adults. It's children's TV."

Asked about Fry's comments at a BAFTA preview of episode twelve a couple of days later, Steven Moffat responded: "Let's be fair to Stephen Fry, he's the biggest *Doctor Who* fan in the world. He's just trying to sound grown-up. *Doctor Who* was designed specifically to be a family programme. That's what it is. It's a junction between children's programmes and adult programmes. It's the one that everybody sits and watches. It is for adults, it is for children. It's a rather brilliant idea: why don't we make a programme that everybody wants to watch? We should do that more often." Yeah, stitch that, Stephen Fry. Also, *Kingdom* was rubbish.

Talking up the finale on Radio 1, Matt Smith

admitted he watched *Doctor Who* go out live every Saturday: "I do, because I'm a complete geek. Or just terribly vain. I watch it every week. I love the ceremony of it, really. You sit down. And I've become a real fan." Karen Gillan went one better by claiming that, not only did she watch it every Saturday, she liked to dance around her living room to the theme tune.

In the opening salvo of the two-part series finale, the Doctor goes to Stonehenge and finally discovers the secret of the Pandorica. It's a prison, designed to contain the greatest threat there has ever been to the universe, which turns out to be... himself.

Before that, though, there's much Indiana Jones-style adventuring as the Doctor, River and Amy explore the secret cavern beneath the ancient druidic shrine and encounter, among other things, a Cyberman's head skittering across the dust on its own spidery innards before opening up and popping out a big, grinning skull, and Rory Williams, the recently deceased Gloucestershire nurse who now appears to be a Roman Centurion. Though he's really an Auton. It's that sort of story.

In the skies above the henge, meanwhile, an alliance of all the Doctor's most feared enemies gathers to spring their trap: Daleks, Cybermen, Sontarans, Terileptils, Slitheen, Autons, Drahvins, Sycorax, Zygons, Atraxi, Haemogoths, Draconians, Judoon, Silurians, Roboforms, Weevils... "Everyone that ever hated you is coming here tonight," says River. "You can't win this. You can't even fight it."

He's going to have a bloody good go, though. Mounting the altar stone, the Doctor rigs up a makeshift PA system and addresses the circling fleets: "The question of the hour is, who's got the Pandorica? Answer, I do. Next question. Who's coming to take it from me? Come on! Look at me. No plan, no back up, no weapons worth a damn. Oh, and something else. I don't have anything to lose! So, if you're sitting up there in your silly little spaceship, with all your silly little guns, and you've got any plans on taking the Pandorica tonight... just remember who's standing in your way. Remember every black day I ever stopped you, and then, and *then*, do the smart thing... Let somebody else try first."

This is probably the most gloriously grand-standing moment the Doctor has ever had, in any of his incarnations. It's his *Henry V* St Crispin's Day speech – and Matt Smith totally nails it, in what will probably stand as his signature moment in the role.

Not that it does the Doctor much good. Before long, he's surrounded by the ultimate Axis of Evil, and about to be locked away forever, in a thrilling cliffhanger that director Toby Haynes chooses to present partly in slow motion. We've had pomp and bombast before – Russell the T loved a bit of that – but has *Doctor Who* ever been more grandly, more thrillingly operatic than in the climactic shots of our defeated hero being dragged, Christ-like, to his final humiliation? It's stunning stuff, especially when intercut with equally heart-breaking scenes in which Amy finally remembers who Rory is, as he struggles to exert his own will over his Nestene programming... and shoots her dead. And then, for an encore, the TARDIS explodes, and every star in every universe goes out. But apart from that, everything's pretty much fine.

As viewers held their breath for the finale, tabloid tipsters confidently predicted the episode would see the return of Omega – last seen running round Amsterdam after losing an argument with a box of Rice Krispies, way back in 1983. Meanwhile, *The Sun* claimed NASA had spotted Series Five's motif crack in the middle of the Milky Way in an infrared image from Spitzer telescope. (Which meant either the whole of time was fracturing, or there was a crack in the lens.)

As the *Daily Express* asked "Are Smith and Gillan the best Doctor and assistant in history?", the pair's second Adventure Game, *Blood of the Cybermen*, received its official launch at Gavinburn Primary School in West Dunbartonshire, Scotland. Apparently, BAFTA was fully-booked that day. Or it may have been something to do with the fact the head teacher, Gillian Penny, just happened to be Steven Moffat's sister.

The new Big Bang: even better than the first one

According to calculations made by the Doctor as far back as *Flesh and Stone*, June 26th, 2010 is the date the universe ceases to exist. *Doctor Who* fans probably knew the feeling as they anticipated the last episode of their favourite show for six long months.

The Big Bang takes Steven Moffat's timey-wimey tricksiness to a whole new level, brazenly resetting every button he can think of while galumphing through the previous 13 weeks to bring new light and new meaning to all manner of half-glimpsed, throwaway moments. (One scene in particular, in which the Doctor talked to the stricken Amy aboard the *Byzantium* in *Flesh and Stone*, had prompted eagle-eyed viewers at the time to question the significance of the Doctor appearing to wear a jacket, when he'd previously been in his shirt sleeves. It's a measure of the quality of this show that we would immediately assume some clever-Trevory over a mere continuity blunder. And then be proved right.)

At Stonehenge, Rory the surprisingly emotional Auton ("a lump of plastic with delusions of humanity") is grief-stricken at having just murdered the love of his life. If only he could turn back time... And then the Doctor appears, in a fez, with a mop. Given that the last time we saw our hero he'd just been locked away for eternity by an alliance of all his greatest enemies, this sudden comic, vaudeville reappearance – with props – totally subverts our expectations.

He's got a plan to save Amy, too: just pop her in the Pandorica on a slow heat, and she should be back to health in around... ooh, 2,000 years' time. A blink of an eye to a Time Lord with a vortex manipulator on his wrist, of course – but Rory chooses to take the slow path, standing vigil over the woman he has sworn to protect for two millennia. The boy who waited. Talk about an epic fairytale.

When everyone is reunited in a museum in 2010, Moffat cuts effortlessly between jaunty, chronology-crunching shenanigans ("It's a fez," the Doctor says, by way of explanation for his new headgear. "I wear a fez now. Fezzes are cool.") and cold, clammy scares. The stone Dalek exhibit powering up in the darkness echoes the latent menace of 2005's reputation-rescuing *Dalek*, while the moment a future eleventh Doctor suddenly appears out of the air and collapses dying into his own arms is shocking, to say the least.

Having finally lost an argument with a Dalek

death ray, the mortally wounded Time Lord reveals his plan to fly the Pandorica into the exploding TARDIS and "reboot the universe". This is clever stuff – not so much jargon as anti-jargon, bringing the biggest Event of all time down to the level of everyday Windows frustrations. And for all its crazily epic scale, the idea that all you need is a few atoms to grow a universe is a very elegant sci-fi concept; after all, your basic periodic table of elements provides all the building blocks you need.

A new universe means a new start: Amelia asleep on her suitcase in the garden. The Girl Who Waited. And this time, he really does come back. Scooping up the child, the Doctor puts her to bed and pulls up a chair. "When you wake up, you'll have a mum and dad," he says. "And you won't even remember me. Well, you'll remember me a little. I'll be a story in your head... The daft old man who stole a magic box and ran away. Did I ever tell you that I stole it? Well, I borrowed it. I was always going to take it back. Oh, that box. Amy, you'll dream about that box. It'll never leave you. Big and little at the same time. Brand new and ancient, and the bluest blue ever. And the times we had, eh? Would have had. Never had. In your dreams, they'll still be there. The Doctor and Amy Pond, and the days that never came." Now that's what I call a Doctor with a bedside manner.

Matt Smith is simply exceptional in these scenes[IV], his expression turning from sadness and love to mortal dread as he turns to look at the crack in Amy's wall closing up, calling him to his doom and concluding: "I don't belong here any more."

As Amelia sleeps, twinkling lights begin to appear in the sky: her reward for wishing upon a star. Then the sun comes up and... it's Amy, all grown up. And Amy has a family. With a little tiny dad! In *The Doctor Dances*, everybody lived. Here, even people who were already dead get to live. Seriously, how many little surprises can one episode throw at us?

Quite a few, as it happens. Because the Doctor's words about that box – "brand new and ancient at the same time, and the bluest blue ever"? Turns out this wasn't just a lump-in-the-throat stuff, it was clever coded message. A way for Amy to remember something

– someone – important that she ought never to have forgotten:

"I found you!" she declares, standing up in the middle of her wedding reception as a wind starts to whip up, the glasses start to rattle and a strange, wheezing-groaning sound fills the air. "I found you. I found you in words, like you knew I would. Something old. Something new. Something borrowed. Something...

"... blue."

And there it is, right in front of her: the TARDIS. And inside, back from the dead: "Hello, everyone," beams the Doctor, looking dapper in topper and tails. "I'm Amy's imaginary friend. But I came anyway." The most triumphant, punch-the-air moment in *Doctor Who* history? It just might well be.

After a spot of dancing – in which Matt Smith busts a move now popularly known as the Drunk Giraffe – the bride and groom steal away, not in the traditional car decorated in tin cans, but aboard an impossible mazarine box that promises the most eventful honeymoon in history.

According to the Doctor, an Egyptian goddess is loose on the Orient Express. In Space. Which suggests that, somewhere in a parallel universe, Russell T Davies is still writing the Christmas specials. But in ours, Steven Moffat is the man with the power to make and break realities, to reboot universes and give little lost girls the gift of stars. He is the custodian of the greatest story ever told, with the greatest hero who ever lived, and died, and lived again. And in Matt Smith, he has found his perfect muse, and may very well have given us the perfect Doctor Who.

"I'll be a story in your head," the Doctor had told Amy. "That's okay – we're all stories in the end. Just make it a good one, eh? Because it was, you know. It was the best."

Boy, was it ever.

No shit, Sherlock

Sadly, this television masterpiece didn't quite get the audience it deserved, as baking hot temperatures across most of Britain took their toll on the overnight figures, which were almost a million down on the previous week. "Fans Ditch *Doctor Who* to Enjoy Sunshine," squawked *The Sun*'s headline (which shows just how little they know about *Doctor Who* fans).

The final figure, of course, would correct that injustice. And the reviews were the sort you might frame and put up in the downstairs loo. "This series has been a feat of virtuoso storytelling by Moffat and acting by Smith, the 27-year-old who now looks ageless in the role," wrote Andrew Billen in *The Times*. "There is no more assured drama on British TV." In *The Guardian*, Sam Wollaston described the episode as "fantastically moving, and beautiful, and thrilling, even if you (or I) don't really have a clue what the hell is going on." The *Mirror*'s Jim Shelley declared the whole series a "dazzling, entertaining triumph", adding that "Smith has perfected the ultimate Doctor Who trick of being classically old-fashioned and futuristically timeless."

Asked by *Doctor Who Magazine* what part of his first series in charge had worked best, Moffat had no hesitation in stating: "Matt, Karen and Arthur. We got that so shockingly right. I'll never get anything as right as that again. Matt's new Doctor was brilliant. I don't think any new Doctor has had as universally positive a reception, especially given that he was following the most loved Doctor of all time. I don't think I'll ever be prouder of any piece of television that I'm involved in than I am of *The Eleventh Hour*."[18]

At the end of June, Matt Smith cemented *Doctor Who*'s new-found rock star status when he appeared onstage during Orbital's Glastonbury performance, donning the electro duo's trademark LED glasses and hammering away at a keyboard during their traditional set-closer: a kinetic, techno take on the *Doctor Who* theme. "Yes, Glastonbury – way out baby!" yelled Smith, giving the crowd his now traditional Churchillian salute. "Let me hear you cheer, let me hear you roar, for Glastonbury!"

It's fair to say that, if any single moment crystallised *Doctor Who*'s journey across the cultural Rubicon over the past five years, it was this one. It's hard to imagine what the Glasto crowd would have made of Sylvester McCoy or Colin Baker in similar circumstances. And it's an even bigger stretch to envisage William Hartnell up there on The Other Stage, waving his cane to Flanagan and Allen's "Underneath the Arches".

Having said that, Matt Smith wasn't entirely living the rock and roll lifestyle: a couple of days after his Glasto triumph, the 27-year-old left for a well-earned holiday. With his parents. Bless.

In mid-July, the guest stars for the Christmas special were announced as theatrical knight of the realm Sir Michael Gambon and, making her acting debut, mega-selling Welsh mezzo-soprano Katherine Jenkins. "We're going for broke with this one," promised Steven Moffat. "It's all your favourite Christmas movies at once, in an hour, with monsters and the Doctor and a honeymoon and... oh, you'll see."

"I'm the first to say I don't really consider myself an actress," admitted Jenkins. "So I asked if I could go in and read for them, and I thought, 'Well, if I'm rubbish they won't give it to me, will they?' So I read to them, and they called me on my 30th birthday and offered me the part."[12] After her audition, Jenkins drove 200 miles to a hotel in Somerset, where the first person she saw in the lobby was... Matt Smith.

Less than a month after Glastonbury, Smith was back on stage – this time in the more rare-fied surroundings of the Royal Albert Hall – for the 2010 *Doctor Who Prom*. Like David Tennant a couple of years earlier, Smith appeared on screen in a specially-scripted scene, telling the audience the venue was in danger of being blown up. Then he declared he'd have to come and fix the problem in person – at which point he popped up, in character, in the middle of the audience and co-opted a young fan into helping him carry out some comedy business with a prop and an invisible wire. Hosted by Karen Gillan, with help from Smith and Arthur Darvill, the concert was a triumphant celebration of Murray Gold's enormous contribution to the success of the new series, with his electrifying "I am the Doctor" being one of the show's highlights. But, said the *Daily Telegraph*, Smith's "rock star welcome" proved that, for many, no amount of flugelhorns could ever be a match for an appearance by the good Doctor himself.

A couple of days later, *The Sun* claimed that Smith would be quitting after the next series for – you've guessed it – "a Hollywood career".

This was later put down to somebody in the newsroom accidentally sitting on the Doctor Who Quits For Hollywood Story Generator button.

Popular though Smith was, however, he was about to get some serious competition for the role of the nation's favourite Sexy But Slightly Odd Looking Cleverclogs Genius With Great Hair in a Steven Moffat Production. That's right: from now on, the Doctor wouldn't be getting all Daddy's attention, as there was a new kid in town – and his name was Sherlock Holmes.

Conceived during train journeys between London and the Doctor Who production base in Cardiff, Moffat and Mark Gatiss' contemporary re-imagining of Conan Doyle strips the world's greatest detective of his usual gas lamps and Hansom cabs paraphernalia and transplants him into a world of smartphones and GPS. A 60-minute pilot recorded in 2008 had been scrapped and the series re-tooled as three 90-minute films. With industry whispers suggesting the BBC had an expensive disaster on its hands, the show was eventually launched into a less than propitious midsummer slot – where it proved to be an instant smash, dazzling the critics and pulling in more than nine million viewers. Leading man Benedict Cumberbatch, meanwhile, was transformed from a vaguely familiar TV face to a bona fide global superstar for his waspish, borderline Asperger's take on Baker Street's finest.

Matt Smith had nothing but goodwill towards BBC Wales' latest success, having struck up a good friendship with Cumberbatch while both series were filming in Cardiff. "We have lovely mornings where we go, 'Hi Sherlock! Hi Doctor!'" Smith told *The Times*. "I think they should do an episode with him: these two great minds going 'Ding-ding-ding, watcha got?'"

For Moffat, the success of running two of Britain's biggest TV shows came at a price. "There is no way of balancing this," he told Den of Geek. "The last year has been extraordinary. I've had about four days off, and that includes Christmas Day. I work every weekend, I get up early in the morning, I go to bed late at night. It's been extraordinary, but it's great fun, too. Great fun, so long as it doesn't kill me."[19] In August, Moffat departed with his family for a "holiday" in Greece. Yeah, let us know how that works out for you.

As new figures showed *Doctor Who Adventures* had clawed its way back up to 53,559 weekly sales, it seemed the kids weren't giving up on *Doctor Who* just yet. Or the grown-ups, for that matter: reporting its first-ever ABC figure, *Doctor Who Magazine* was shifting an average of 35,374 copies a month. For a publication that had soldiered on through the dark days when a new Bernice Summerfield novel was the height of excitement, these were high-rolling times indeed.

At Hamleys in London, meanwhile, there was a bit of a ding-dong when Karen Gillan made an appearance to sign copies of the Amy Pond action figure, and only 250 of the 400 people who turned up got to meet her. A spokesman apologised, explaining that Gillan had already stayed an hour longer than planned (and anyway, aren't some of you a bit old to be playing with dolls?).

At the annual Edinburgh Television Festival, Steven Moffat announced that the 2011 series of *Doctor Who* would be split into two, with half the episodes broadcast in the spring and half in the autumn. "The split series is hugely exciting because viewers will be treated to two premieres, two finales and more event episodes," said Moffat in a BBC press statement. "For the kids it will never be more than a few months to the next *Doctor Who*! Easter, autumn, Christmas!"

"What this show needs is a big event in the middle," Moffat told Five Live. "So what we're going to do this year is make it two series." Promising an "enormous, game-changing cliff-hanger" in the middle, he added: "The wrong expression is to say we're splitting it. We're making two separate series." That's Series 6A and 6B. Or was it 32A and 32B? Or 2i and 2ii? Maybe they'd just wait and see what they put on the DVDs.

In September, new term for the *Doctor Who* team got off to a leisurely start when the read-through for Mark Gatiss' latest story took place over food and wine on a warm summer's evening at Steven Moffat's house. A few days later, it was back to Cardiff to run through Neil Gaiman's episode, with the writer in attendance to hear his delayed *Who* debut finally get an airing.

Based in the US for many years, Gaiman had been passed DVDs of the new series by Jane Goldman – aka Mrs Jonathan Ross – who had co-adapted his novel *Stardust* for the screen. Impressed, Gaiman contacted fellow comics scribe Paul Cornell, who put him in touch with Steven Moffat. When Moffat was announced as Russell T Davies' successor in May 2008, Gaiman was one of the first people hired by the new showrunner – in fact the story now going before the cameras was the first eleventh Doctor script written after *The Eleventh Hour*. The main guest star for the episode, meanwhile, was announced as Suranne Jones – most famous as *Coronation Street*'s sharp-tongued, soft-hearted hellion Karen McDonald – who was cast after Gaiman had requested someone "beautiful but strange-looking". A girl could take offence, you know.

At the TV Choice Awards, Series Five earned its first stripes when *Doctor Who* was named Best Family Drama, with Steven Moffat and Karen Gillan accepting the trophy at the Dorchester Hotel in London. "This is the first award we've ever received for this generation of *Doctor Who*, so it means a lot," beamed Gillan. "We feel incredibly relieved and pleased that we're carrying on winning awards," added Moffat. "That's what the show is for, frankly. Big audiences and big awards."

Later that week, Matt Smith continued the trend when he was named Best Actor at GQ's Men of the Year show at the Royal Opera House. Smith attended the ceremony with his supermodel girlfriend Daisy Lowe, and collected his award from Brit art provocateur Tracey Emin, while his fellow winners on the night included *Mad Men* beefcake Jon Hamm, grime star Dizzee Rascal and fashion guru Georgio Armani. It was all a very long way from the days when the best a Time Lord could hope for was a Swap Shop Award from Maggie Philbin. The same week, Smith was also recognised as youngest actor to have played the Doctor by Guinness World Records – a feat he put down to a rigorous training schedule, a high-carb diet and being born in 1982.

Of all the things *Doctor Who* fans who endured the Wilderness Years never thought they'd live to see, it's fair to say a sequel to *Carnival of Monsters* at Wembley Arena must have been pretty low on the list. But that's what they got when the curtain went up on the first night of *Doctor Who Live* in London, as 12,000 people – Matt Smith, Catherine Tate, Richard Curtis and Murray Gold among them – packed in to the cavernous North London hangar to watch Nigel Planer's Vorgenson unleash a parade of monsters from inside his "Minimiser," just as his father had done with his Miniscope 37 years earlier.

With Steven Moffat busy with... well, everything, Gareth Roberts was drafted in to script the show – a sort of rock opera version of the *Doctor Who Prom*, with the orchestra replaced by a 16-piece band and a loose narrative employed to keep things moving between monster mashes. Matt Smith was originally scheduled to record around five minutes of footage, but eventually contributed closer to 15, including a clever bit of trickery in which he appeared to be trapped in a box on stage. Some fans grumbled that £40 was a bit steep to watch a glorified clips show (which may explain why one Glasgow performance was cancelled for "logistical reasons"), but most were happy just to see the kids excited by the monsters and soak up the communal experience of enjoying *Doctor Who* in the way, a long time ago in an Odeon far, far away, we once enjoyed *Star Wars* – pretty thrilling if, until recently, your only experience of *Who* on the big screen was several hundred middle-aged men watching a grainy VHS of *The Daemons* in a hotel room in Coventry.

What Katy did 37 years later

As the Time Lord continued his tour of tramshed venues around Britain, the BBC revealed that his next trip would be somewhat farther flung, as the sixth series would open with a Steven Moffat-penned two-part story set – and partly filmed – in America.

"The Doctor has visited every weird and wonderful planet you can imagine, so he was bound get round to America eventually," said Moffat. "And of course every Doctor Who fan will be jumping up and down and saying he's been in America before. But not for real, not on location – and not with a story like this one! Oh, you wait!"

The same press release hailed 2010 as "a breakthrough year for the *Doctor Who* fran-

chise" in the US, with the show earning record ratings for BBC America and taking the number one spot on iTunes' Top TV Seasons chart. That's little old *Doctor Who* – No. 1 of all TV shows in America. Whodathunkit?

In typical timey-wimey fashion, Moffat explained his plan was to "start with a finale" to hook viewers for the whole series – and his epic story demanded an epic location. The original plan had been to film in Florida – until they checked it out and realised Florida in November looked a lot like Cardiff (must be those famous Bristol Channel everglades), so they decided to go for the iconic, John Ford-hymning sandstone buttes of Monument Valley instead.

After just two *Doctor Who* production blocks, Sanne Wohlenberg returned to see Kenneth Branagh through some more existential Nordic brooding in *Wallander*, and was replaced by Marcus Wilson, whose CV included stints on *Cutting It*, *Life on Mars* and *Taggart*. And if anything was good preparation for being the producer of *Doctor Who*, it was finding the budget to realise life on Mars – then cutting it.

On CBBC, the fourth series of *The Sarah Jane Adventures* kicked off in creepy style with Joseph Lidster's *The Nightmare Man*, with Julian Bleach clocking up a franchise triple as the eponymous dream-botherer. Other stories in the run included *The Vault of Secrets* – in which Rani's parents join a paranormal investigation group called B.U.R.P.S.S. (aw c'mon, at least this time it's on kids' telly) and *The Empty Planet*, in which Rani and Clyde discover the entire population of London has disappeared. (Weirdly, they react as if this is a bad thing.)

But the headline event was Sarah Jane Smith's latest encounter with you know Who – this time looking less than half her age, and sporting a natty bow tie, to boot. And it wasn't just Sarah getting to grips with the new man in the TARDIS – *Death of the Doctor* also gives us Russell T Davies' take on the eleventh Doctor, not to mention a certain Mrs Josephine Jones, formerly known as myopic, knicker-flashing, ham-fisted bun vendor Jo Grant.

"I knew exactly what I wanted to do with Jo," said Davies. "Gary Russell told me there's a lot of fan fiction, or fan theories, that would have us believe Jo's divorced, or that she ended up all alone in a cottage in North Wales, that sort of thing. All of which was utterly unfaithful to her character, to the poignancy with which Barry Letts and Terrance Dicks left her in our minds. *The Green Death* does not end with a woman heading for bitterness and loneliness, don't be ridiculous! That would be violating the past; I felt very strongly that we had to adhere to what Katy and that brilliant production team created back in 1971 – a character full of joy and smiles and trust, with a wonderful lack of cynicism."[14]

Rather sweetly, the Doctor reveals to Jo that he checked up on *all* his companions in the dying days of his tenth body – the bits we saw in *The End of Time* were just the edited highlights. Sarah Jane also updates us on some of the Doctor's fellow travellers: "There's a woman called Tegan in Australia, fighting for Aboriginal rights. There's a Ben and Polly, in India, running an orphanage there. There was Harry. Oh, I loved Harry. He was a doctor. He did such good work with vaccines. He saved thousands of lives. And there's a Dorothy something. She runs that company, A Charitable Earth. She's raised billions. And this couple in Cambridge, both professors. Ian and Barbara Chesterton. Rumour has it, they've never aged. Not since the sixties. I wonder..." ("And then there's Adric," she might have added. "Word is they're still scraping bits of him off the Cretaceous Age.")

Amidst all the planet-hoppin' and body-swappin' and alien vultures (the Shansheeth are a classic Russell T Davies anthropomorphic number), *Death of the Doctor* is a sweet, touching little tribute to our hero's place in the universe – and in the hearts of the people who love him. Seeing Jo Grant and Sarah Jane Smith on screen together for the first time is a guaranteed crowd-pleaser for fans of a certain age; you could get light-headed from the frequent rushes of warm nostalgia as these women swap stories of their adventures with their funny alien friend. And, although no-one knew it at the time, the Doctor's final farewell to the Bannerman Road gang would turn out to be loaded with a special, heartbreaking significance.

Couple place £325k on Sylvester McCoy to win the Epsom Derby

With *Doctor Who Live* having barely wrapped up, November brought news of yet another spin-off venture in the form of the *Doctor Who Experience*, described by Steven Moffat as "a fan's dream come true – a fully interactive adventure that will allow viewers of the show to get as close as possible to some of the scariest monsters from the series". (Many fans' real dream come true, of course, would have been to get as close as possible to Amy Pond or Captain Jack, but we'll let it go.)

The project, scheduled to open in London in February, would also bring together sets and props from all eras of the show's 47-year history, many of them being seen for the first time. "And never mind that," said Moffat. "This is the day the Doctor teaches you how to fly the TARDIS through time and space, and takes you into battle with all his deadliest enemies in a brand new adventure. So steady your nerves and bring your own sofa – the Doctor needs you." (Let's hope no-one took this last invitation literally, as several hundred people trying to manhandle couches around an exhibition was bound to contravene all *sorts* of health and safety rules.)

Meanwhile, Channel 4 quiz show *The Million Pound Drop* – in which contestants who give the wrong answers see their cash disappear off the table faster than a late 70s *Doctor Who* budget meeting – found itself embroiled in controversy when a couple lost £325,000 after failing to identify the longest-serving Time Lord. Faced with a choice of Sylvester McCoy, Paul McGann, Christopher Eccleston or David Tennant, husband and wife Johnny and Dee split their remaining £650,000 between McCoy and McGann, only for host Davina McCall to inform them the answer was Tennant. Cue an army of *Doctor Who* fans rushing to point out that, while Tennant may have made more episodes, McCoy was *technically* the incumbent Time Lord for longer.

This was enough to force a capitulation by Channel 4, who said: "Having spoken to the *Doctor Who* production team at the BBC, *The Million Pound Drop* producers have confirmed that the correct answer to this question was

Sylvester McCoy and not David Tennant. We apologise for this oversight and as a result, the contestants, Johnny and Dee, will return to the show to finish the game this Friday or Saturday at 10pm on Channel 4 with the £325,000 they placed on McCoy."

Which was fair enough. But anyone who thinks Paul McGann might have been the longest-serving Doctor Who clearly needs to get out less.

Before departing for filming in the States, Matt Smith and Karen Gillan hosted two children to tea on the TARDIS set for *Children in Need* and, the following day, were joined by Arthur Darvill – plus Bob the Builder, Wendy and Spud – to switch on Cardiff's Christmas lights. Smith thanked the 15,000-strong crowd for making the *Doctor Who* team so welcome in the city, which he had come to look on as his second home. He was only sorry he couldn't spend the *whole* winter in Wales but, if they'd excuse him, he had a plane to LA to catch.

The Doctor's first house call Stateside was an appearance on *The Late, Late Show*, CBS' long-running post-Letterman talk slot now hosted, probably as much to his surprise as anyone else's, by Scottish comedian Craig Ferguson. A lifelong *Who* fan, Ferguson was joined by Smith to record an opening skit-cum-interpretive dance number to Orbital's version of the *Doctor Who* theme – which then had to be cut from the broadcast version because no-one had thought to clear the music rights.

From LA, Smith boarded a charter plane that deposited him on an airstrip in the middle of the desert at 11.30pm – only to find he was still two hours from the location hotel. They don't call it the Big Country for nothing, you know.

As filming began on the Series Six opener, cast and crew were warned to watch out for venomous snakes and scorpions, which wasn't normally a problem in Wales where, at best, they might be troubled by an inquisitive sheep. In the end, though, they encountered nothing more harmful than a few *Doctor Who* fans, who weren't about to let a small detail like being a hundred miles from anywhere stop them getting in on their hero's US filming debut. (Smith was amused to find someone proffering a tablet device for his electronic signature. Which was either evidence of a very organised auto-graph hunter, or he was about to be the victim of major identity fraud.)

Joining the three regulars for the shoot was Alex Kingston, returning once again as River Song. Steven Moffat promised that the new series would see River's identity revealed once and for all. "I want to explain who she is, not explain away who she is," he said. "If you don't deliver on most people's expectations, and you just say, 'Oooh, she's a specially programmed android who believes she's the Doctor's wife', people will go, 'Well that's a cheat, you can't do that'."[20]

Back home, a Cyber platoon marched on London to publicise the *Doctor Who* Experience, recreating the famous St Paul's steps sequence from 1968's *The Invasion* as well as boarding a Jubilee Line train, where some commuters presumably got to experience what it's like having your face jammed into a Cyberman's armpit.

By late November, the Arizona desert felt like a distant memory for the cast as they filmed in freezing conditions at Caerphilly Castle for Matthew Graham's new two-parter. Director Julian Simpson slipped and injured his ligaments on the frozen pavement outside his apartment, and spent the rest of the shoot on crutches, downing painkillers. And then the roof fell in – literally – as a collapsing ceiling sequence proved a bit too convincing for comfort. He knew he should have taken that job on *Holby City* instead.

In December – as figures showed *The Eleventh Hour* had hung on to its top spot as the year's most requested programme on iPlayer, racking up a mighty 2.2 million hits, with the rest of Series Five averaging 1.5 million hits per episode – the weather got so bad the cast and crew were sent home for Christmas early, though Matt Smith and Karen Gillan were kept busy talking up the Xmas special to anyone who'd listen. And, for the hard of listening, Gillan stripped down to her undies for a saucy cover shoot for *ShortList* magazine that sparked much interest in the tabloids. It's a long shot, I know, but I'm guessing those pictures may still be available on the internet somewhere if you look really hard.

A shark is for life,
not just for Christmas

A Christmas Carol and Steven Moffat is a marriage made in heaven – or at least in whichever bit of the time vortex passes closest to it. In hindsight, what else was Moffat ever going to do for his first festive special (the Feast of Steven, if you will) than riff on Dickens' seasonal time-twister? Charlie, you had him at "ghost of past, present and future".

Doing the Scrooge honours is Kazran Sardick, an ulcerous old miser played with snarling relish by Michael Gambon. He is the less-than-benevolent dictator of Sardicktown, a steampunky city on the planet Ember into which an enormous spaceliner^V is about to crash. Sardick has the power to save the ship and all its passengers and crew – including honeymooners Amy and Rory – but can't think of a compelling reason why he should. And so it falls to the Doctor to play both Marley and Santa, Matt Smith tumbling soot-faced into the story down Sardick's chimney and proceeding to steal the show from under Sir Michael's nose with a bravura opening routine in which he bamboozles Sardick with a mix of comic bluster ("Santa Claus – or, as I've always known him, Jeff") and withering sarcasm ("In 900 years of space and time, I've never met anyone who wasn't important").

Sardick's sourness is largely the product of his abusive father and his great lost love, Abigail (Katherine Jenkins), who he keeps cryogenically preserved in the hope of one day being able to cure the illness that would have killed her if he hadn't shoved her in the freezer first.

All the Doctor needs to do, then, is rewrite Sardick's history – give me the boy, and I'll show you the man who won't let a spaceship full of people die, sort of thing. Some fans have a problem with this, arguing it undermines the drama if all the Doctor ever has to do is nip back and change the past. But it *is* kind of the point of Dickens' original – and you can't deny there's something rather magical about the Doctor walking into the TARDIS while Sardick watches old home movies, then reappearing seconds later in scratchy black and white on the screen in front of him.

Much of the middle section is concerned

with the Doctor, Abigail and the young Kazran meeting up every Christmas Eve for adventures in the TARDIS, during which the Doctor accidentally gets engaged to Marilyn Monroe. Like you do. This script mentions Christmas more than any festive special so far (a whopping 54 times, to save you counting), and yet, even with everything covered in snow, it doesn't really *feel* all that Christmassy, on account of being set on a different planet, with its own, like-ours-but-not-really-ours version of Christmas. (It's quite an *alien* alien planet, too: there are fish swimming in the fog, and Katherine Jenkins sings a lullaby to a flying shark. You don't get that on the *Emmerdale* Chrimbo special, do you?) It's romantic, and surreal, and magical, and rather wonderful in its own way. But I'm not sure I'd watch it with *It's A Wonderful Life* and *White Christmas* to get me in the festive mood.

As guest villains go, Michael Gambon is pretty much as good as you can hope for, while Katherine Jenkins is suitably winsome as Abigail, despite being saddled with the worst wig since Kylie (what is it with these awful festive makeovers of perfectly beautiful superstars?). Karen Gillan and Arthur Darvill (who now joins his co-stars in the opening credits) are reduced to little more than extended cameos – though having Amy and Rory emerge from their honeymoon suite in their policewoman/Roman Centurion outfits is a good, cheeky gag. It's Matt Smith's show, though – his skittish, curiously childlike Doctor is just made for Christmas, and Smith lights up the screen every time he appears.

In the end, of course, Sardick sees the error of his ways, and everyone stands round while Katherine Jenkins guides the spaceship to safety with a lovely Murray Gold aria. "We've had so many Christmas Eves together, Kazran" says the dying Abigail. "I think it's time for Christmas Day." And so they take to the skies for one last sleigh ride, soaring over the rooftops in a carriage, pulled by a flying shark. Dickens would be gutted he never thought of that.

Debuting on both sides of the Atlantic on December 25th, *A Christmas Carol* was a ratings smash, attracting 12.11 million viewers and garnering strong reviews. *The Guardian* hailed "a thing of great ingenuity, beauty and imagination", while the *Mirror's* Kevin O'Sullivan said it was "the most festive *Doctor Who* ever", though his colleague Jim Shelley admitted he found it "bewildering".

Matt Smith and Karen Gillan both spent Christmas at their family homes, with Gillan making an appearance as Grotty Totty in *Beauty and the Beast* in Inverness. (Presumably this was for charity, or a personal favour, rather than a paid engagement. Though there were a few ex-*Who* girls who'd have been grateful for the work, frankly.)

In Northampton, Smith was busy granting Christmas wishes as the local paper arranged for him to visit seven-year-old *Who* fan Alfe Game, who'd spent the previous Christmas in hospital with cancer and, since going into remission, had dedicated much of his time to helping other sick children.

"My mum mentioned this to me and as I was going to be around in Northampton, and I thought 'Why not?'" Smith told the paper. "It was a pleasure to do it. I'm really pleased we came. Alfe was lovely and they're such a nice family. It's nice to see how inspired children are by *Doctor Who* and how much of a difference it can make sometimes, when you hear about them meeting in hospital, talking about it and bonding over it. This has been a wonderful experience."

"It's not the winning, it's the taking part. And then winning"

If he'd managed to avoid any family rows over Christmas, Steven Moffat started 2011 with a potential bust-up when his two favourite sons (apart from his *actual* sons, obviously) were revealed as going head-to-head for the Best Drama Performance prize at that year's National Television Awards.

A late schedule change meant the cast weren't available to attend the National Television Awards ceremony on January 26th. Which was just as well as it turned out, as it was the first year since the show's return that *Doctor Who* went home empty-handed. Many pundits had predicted that the presence of *Doctor Who* and *Sherlock* would end up splitting their respective votes, so it was no surprise – and no real injustice – when the Drama Performance award went to twinkly-eyed national treasure Sir David Jason. But the Best Drama honour for sub-*Grange Hill* school soap *Waterloo Road* was a bit of a travesty, frankly – though Steven Moffat was generous in his praise for the show.

"I didn't like [the awards] at all," the show-runner later told *Doctor Who Magazine*. "It felt hugely uncomfortable. It made me quite grumpy, actually. I didn't really want to go. I'm very close to all the people – one of them's my wife, but Matt and Benedict have become very good friends, too.

"My attitude towards award ceremonies has changed slightly. I keep saying, 'What on Earth does *Doctor Who* and *Sherlock* need an award for? They've already got the audience. The shows are beloved. I don't really care about the school prize-giving.' Sue gets quite grumpy with me for being that way. If you've got two shows nominated in the same category, all I kept thinking was 'I can lose twice' – which I did – 'or I can lose once. Either way, I lose'."[18] Loser.

To make things slightly more galling, the *Doctor Who* production team had collaborated with the NTAs on an elaborate, Gareth Roberts and Clayton Hickman-scripted opening sequence in which the Doctor helps host Dermot O'Leary get to the ceremony on time via comic encounters with Ant and Dec, Dot Cotton, Bruce Forsyth and numerous other small-screen royalty. After all that, the least they could have done was rigged the vote for them.

The next story before the cameras saw the *Who* crew buckling the swash aboard a schooner in Charlestown harbour, Cornwall, for a pirate adventure from new writer Steve Thompson. An award-winning playwright, Thompson had been commissioned by Moffat to share writing duties with himself and Mark Gatiss on *Sherlock*, and had made a good enough fist of it to rewarded with a shot at the boss' Other Show.

The cast for the story included Hugh Bonneville, star of ITV's smash hit new period drama *Downton Abbey*, and supermodel-turned-actress Lily Cole, who had somehow managed to fit in the job between modelling assignments, film roles and studying for a History of Art degree at Cambridge University. "It is a great script and a fun character, and I am glad to be involved," Cole was quoted as telling *The Sun*, while our old friend "an insider" added: "Lily's a big fan of the show and jumped at the chance to appear. She will play a sea creature in an episode based around a well-known tale. It's a real ocean adventure." To illustrate this point, *The Sun's* finest Photoshop-wranglers mocked up a picture of a Sea Devil sporting the actress' fiery red hair – though its readers would probably have preferred a picture of Lily in a Sea Devil's string vest. @HughBonn, meanwhile, was getting very excited, tweeting: "I can't believe it. I'm in *Doctor Who*! It's so much fun! I'm a 47-year-old boy!"

Another excited schoolboy, David Walliams, was also reported by the tabloids to have bagged a part in *Doctor Who*, having button-holed Matt Smith backstage at *The Graham Norton Show*. "I kept on saying to my agent, 'Have they asked me to do *Doctor Who* yet?'," admitted Walliams, reported to be playing an "alien mole-like creature," "because everyone else has been in it'."[21]

In fact, Walliams had already started work on the show, having overcome initial concerns that he wouldn't be able to express himself through the heavy alien prosthetic. The long hours in the make-up chair meant the comedian was always the first to arrive and the last to leave, prompting Karen Gillan to admit a few months later that she had "only ever met David when he's been dressed as a mole". Either that, or he'd had way too much Botox.

In London, Matt Smith came face-to-face with a slightly scary-looking waxwork model of himself at the official opening of the *Doctor Who* Experience at Olympia. For the most part, the attraction delivered on its promise of dropping fans into the middle of a *Doctor Who* adventure: after stepping through the crack in the universe, visitors found themselves aboard the *Starship UK*, where the Doctor – Smith making his presence felt on a series of video screens – enlisted their help in freeing him from the Pandorica. Through clever use of lights and misdirection, the TARDIS literally materialised in front of your eyes, the doors opened and – well whaddayaknow? – turns out it really is bigger on the inside. As children were encouraged to take the controls of the timeship, the floor of the console room lurched

and rocked, tipping the audience headlong into a Steven Moffat-scripted walk-through adventure featuring the Daleks, the Weeping Angels and an impressive 3D video sequence. The experience ended with a sizeable exhibition of props and costumes from the whole run of *Doctor Who*, including the original ninth and tenth Doctor-era console room, an army of monsters and, most terrifyingly for parents, a well-stocked gift shop. It was, frankly, all a very long way from the days when a trip to a *Doctor Who* exhibition was seeing K-9 mouldering in a stable block at Longleat House.

On February 22nd, fans had cause to pause and reflect on hearing of the loss of Nicholas Courtney. The actor's death at 81 brought tributes from every corner of the Whoniverse. "There was a certain innocence in his personality that was utterly endearing," wrote his good friend Tom Baker. "He was very easy to tease, and I did my share, which made him shake his head in disbelief when he realised he had been had." "I only met Nicholas Courtney once and very briefly," said Steven Moffat, "but he was as kind and generous and funny as his reputation suggests. And on screen, his perfectly pitched performance as the Brigadier carved a very special place in the history of *Doctor Who*. Somewhere out there, the Doctor just got a little lonelier." Mark Gatiss, meanwhile, paraphrased the Brigadier's oft-quoted tribute to the Doctor: "Splendid chap. All of him."

I would go out tonight, but I haven't got a thing to wear

In March, the BBC announced that Piers Wenger was to step down as head of drama at BBC Wales, to be replaced by Faith Penhale, currently creative manager at independent production company Kudos. In a statement, the Corporation said Wenger would continue as "creative leader of a range of key shows", including *Doctor Who*, but that Penhale would have overall responsibility for the strategic direction of the drama department. Two months later, Wenger announced he was leaving the BBC for a new role at Film4 Productions. So that was the end of the Piers show.

At the Royal Television Society's annual Programme Awards, Steven Moffat collected the Judges' Award in recognition of his work on *Doctor Who* and *Sherlock*. It must have slipped his mind that he didn't like school prize-givings any more. Meanwhile, experimental theatre group Punchdrunk announced an "immersive" adventure (there were a lot of them about these days) called *The Crash of the Elysium*, to be staged as part of that summer's Manchester International Festival. Steven Moffat and Tom MacRae were officially on board, so it was no surprise when it later turned out to be a *Doctor Who* story featuring video contributions from Matt Smith, who was making so many extra-curricular appearances as the Doctor these days, it was a wonder he had any time to film the actual show.

And here was another one – or another two, in fact – as the Doctor, Amy and Rory appeared in two special mini-episodes (if you want to call them minisodes, I won't judge you) as part of that year's Comic Relief telethon. I guess once Richard Curtis has you on speed-dial, it's hard to say no. *Space* and *Time* add up to a fun, typically timey-wimey and really rather saucy confection from Moffat, who takes advantage of the later timeslot to have Rory looking up Amy's skirt, Amy flirting outrageously with a future version of herself and Rory... well, you can probably imagine what Rory is thinking by that point.

At the end of the month, the BBC also announced the Script to Screen project – a competition open to schools across the UK to write a Doctor Who scene, which would be filmed for inclusion as part of *Doctor Who Confidential*. ("Sounds fun," said Matt Smith, as he considered moving out of his flat and just bedding down on the TARDIS set.)

As the new series launch date approached, the BBC dropped the mother of all teasers: in the opening episode, one of the four regulars would be killed off. *Doctor Who Magazine* got in on the act with four collectors' covers – you could take your choice of the Doctor, Amy, Rory and River – bearing the headline "Marked for Death". "You reckon that's hyperbole, don't you?" asked the magazine. "Yeah, well – it's not. One of the TARDIS crew will breathe their last before the credits roll."

At the April 4th press screening of the opening two-parter, *The Impossible Astronaut / Day of the Moon*, Steven Moffat asked journalists not to reveal the identity of the unlucky victim.

With three weeks left until transmission, it was a big ask – but the press duly played along. What's more, they were falling over themselves to rhapsodise about the story. "Family viewing doesn't get smarter, scarier, wittier or more thrilling," said Michael Hogan in the *Telegraph*. In the *Mirror*, Mark Jeffries declared "the most eagerly awaited drama of the year is back with an explosive Whodunit", and both he and *The Guardian's* Jon Plunkett agreed it was the "darkest" *Who* yet. "This is the scariest and most shocking start to a *Doctor Who* series ever," said Dan Menhinnitt in *The Sun*. "It's world-class teatime science fiction. And there's a real feeling that no-one's safe."

"Steven Moffat's line for this series is, 'If last year was the funfair, this year's the ghost train',"[22] Marcus Wilson told *SFX*, while Moffat himself told *Doctor Who Magazine* it was "time to stop pretending that people don't watch the show. We've developed a weird humility where we say, 'We'd better remind everybody what's going on," he added. "Around eight million people watch this show every week! And then watch it on iPlayer. And then it's splashed all over the papers. Everybody knows. I wanted to exploit that this year."[18]

UK hype machine fully lubricated, the *Who* team flew out to New York for the series' US launch, where a screening at the Village East Cinema proved so popular a second one had to be arranged. Quite what happened on the rest of that trip isn't widely known – what happens in New York, stays in New York – but, a couple of months later, several British tabloids related a bizarre story about Karen Gillan being found naked, and in a state of confusion, in the corridor of a Manhattan hotel after a night of "riotous partying". A BBC Worldwide spokesman said: "We're unaware of this alleged incident." (But if anyone had any further details, he'd *love* to hear them.)

In the UK, the publicity blizzard intensified as the series launch date approached: highlights included a special issue of *Time Out* with six – count 'em! – collectible covers, and Arthur Darvill being reunited with Sooty on Fern Britton's chat show. The host was keen to know what it was like playing sidekick to a famous orange screen star who didn't wear any clothes, but Darvill thought Karen Gillan's private life was her own business.

A tear, Sarah Jane

With just four days to go until *The Impossible Astronaut* premiered in Britain, the US and Canada (Australia would have to wait another week), excitement among fans was at fever pitch. But on the evening of Tuesday, April 19th, reports began circulating on Twitter that seemed too shocking to believe. And then came the confirmation from the BBC: Elisabeth Sladen – the timeless, ageless Sarah Jane Smith – was dead.

The 65-year-old had kept the fact she had cancer a secret from all but her closest family and friends. Recording on the fifth series of *The Sarah Jane Adventures* had been delayed mid-way through when it became clear the actress was ill, but the production team had been hopeful of picking up where they left off when she'd recovered.

"We're reeling at the moment," Russell T Davies told *BBC News*, "thinking of all the children who will need a hug from mum and dad at breakfast when they wake up and hear the news." The story made the evening bulletins, as tributes began flooding in on Twitter from the likes of Stephen Fry, Jonathan Ross and many members of the extended *Doctor Who* family.

"Sarah Jane Smith was everybody's hero when I was younger, and as brave and funny and brilliant as people only ever are in stories," Steven Moffat told the BBC. "But many years later, when I met the real Sarah Jane – Lis Sladen herself – she was exactly as any child could ever have wanted her to be. Kind and gentle and clever; and a ferociously talented actress, of course, but in that perfectly English, unassuming way."

"What struck me about Lis was her grace," added Matt Smith. "She welcomed me, educated me, and delighted me with her tales and adventures on *Doctor Who*. And she also seemed to have a quality of youth that not many people retain as they go through life. Her grace and kindness will stay with me because she had such qualities in abundance and shared them freely. I will miss her, as will the world of *Doctor Who* and all the Doctors that had the good pleasure to work with Lis Sladen and travel the universe with Sarah Jane."

David Tennant reflected the thoughts of fans across the world when he said: "I just can't believe that Lis is gone. She seemed invincible. The same woman who enchanted my childhood, enchanted my time on *Doctor Who* and enchanted generations who have watched her and fallen in love with her – just like I did. I feel very honoured to have shared a TARDIS with Sarah Jane Smith, and I feel very lucky to have shared some time with Lis Sladen. She was extraordinary."

On *BBC Breakfast*, Tennant added: "I think what's wonderful... not that anything about this is wonderful... but to know she had that renaissance and was loved by a new generation of kids in the same way that my generation of kids just adored her."

Thursday's papers were full of more tributes to the woman *The Sun* called "the greatest *Doctor Who* girl". Across a double-page spread, the paper ran a moving eulogy from Tom Baker that the actor had posted on his website the previous day: "Sarah Jane dead? No, impossible! Impossible. Only last week I agreed to do six new audio adventures with her for Big Finish Productions," he wrote. "She can't be dead. But she is, she died yesterday morning. Cancer. I had no idea she was ill; she was so private, never wanted any fuss, and now, gone.

"A terrible blow to her friends and a shattering blow for all those fans of the programme whose lives were touched every Saturday evening by her lovely heroic character, Sarah Jane Smith."

Baker wrote of "those sweet memories of happy days with the lovely, witty, kind and so talented Lis Sladen", concluding: "I am consoled by the memories. I was there, I knew her, she was good to me and I shall always be grateful, and I shall miss her."

Don't get clever, Trevor

Interviewed by the *Daily Telegraph* in late April, Matt Smith found himself drawn into an escalating war of words with veteran TV actor Trevor Eve, following the latter's bellyaching about *Doctor Who* getting an unfair share of Auntie Beeb's affections. "They're obsessed with it," said Eve, who was miffed after his soporific crime drama *Waking the Dead* was axed after a mere nine interminable series. "It gets all the budget and all the attention," he grumped. Still, not to worry Trev – if anyone knows how to make programmes on a Shoestring budget, it's you. Cheers.

"If we all listen to Trevor Eve, then we're in trouble," was Smith's response in the *Telegraph*. "Thank you very much, Trevor, we appreciate your opinion, but that's ridiculous. *Doctor Who* is brilliant. That's why it attracts some of the best writers in the country, and some of the best actors. Trevor, try telling that to Sir Michael Gambon. Show me any other series that can tackle this many big issues, appeal to this broad a range of people, and still have a laugh along the way, and I will say, 'You can't.' That's what I'd say to Trevor Eve. At least we're never predictable. At least we're inventive. This whole show is testament to Steven Moffat, and his ambition and his scope, and that's a privilege to be part of. It's as simple as that."

For *Doctor Who* fans, this was analogous to one of Churchill's wartime broadcasts. And if Matt Smith needed to raise an army, they'd be there for him. Just as long as they were back by Saturday teatime.

Waking up on the morning of April 23rd, fans were horrified to find the UK sweltering in a heatwave, which meant families would be off enjoying the bank Holiday weekend at the beach or the park or whatever ridiculous things normal people got up to in the sunshine. (And, with a 6pm start, the new series was scheduled even earlier than the previous year's, leading sceptical fans to complain that, instead of being given a slot to maximise its own audience, *Doctor Who* was being used to prop a weak Saturday night line-up. There would, it's safe to assume, be letters.)

Three weeks on from the press screening, the media had been true to their word and not revealed any major plot details. So it was somewhat astounding that, after all the cloak-and-dagger secrecy, the BBC took it upon themselves to release two massively spoilery promotional images just hours before the first episode was due to go out. The pictures – apparently showing the the Doctor mid-regeneration – gave the tabloids free licence to speculate on the possibility of the eleventh Doctor's death, and the cat was not so much out of the bag as sitting on the top of Television Centre holding a big sign saying "It's the Doctor wot dies".

Which he does. Just seven minutes into the new series, the Time Lord is shot dead – blasted in the chest by the eponymous spaceman – then doused in petrol and pushed out into the water on a flaming funeral pyre. (Reading the script, Matt Smith had to admit his long-term future with the firm didn't look promising.) Killing off your leading man when the opening credits have barely rolled is quite a bold move, especially with 13 episodes still left to go. But even before his body's stopped smoking, there he is again: a younger version of the same Doctor, grinning like a Cheshire Cat and rhapsodising about his special straw (it adds more fizz, apparently) and clearly oblivious to the fate that's awaiting him in, as it turns out, 200 years' time.

After that attention-grabbing opening, the action moves to the White House, where the Doctor, Amy and River team up with former FBI spook Canton Delaware III (played with twinkly charm by genre telly staple Mark Sheppard) to help President Richard Milhous Nixon (Stuart Milligan in an outrageous putty-nosed prosthetic) trace a mysterious child who has a hotline to the Oval Office and has been creeping out the Commander-in-Chief with cryptic messages.

The Doctor confounding POTUS and his security goons is a joy ("These are my top operatives," he explains, as Amy, Rory and River pile out of the TARDIS, "The Legs, The Nose and Mrs Robinson"), but things turn a few shades darker when the monsters of the week show up. The Silence are a terrifying creation: Munch's the Scream dressed for a funeral, these suited-and-booted aliens – who we learn have been "standing in the shadows of human history since the very beginning" – dispense death from their fingertips with a look of orgiastic pleasure on their hideous, mouthless faces. But the most chilling thing about them is their ability to melt into the shadows without trace: using post-hypnotic suggestion, the Silence have the power to make you forget about their very existence the moment you turn away, thus forcing our heroes to adopt all sorts of *Memento*-style tricks – including tally marks on their skin – in order to remember exactly what it is they're supposed to be fighting. You might say it's Steven Moffat playing the same old riffs – it's certainly not a million miles away from the whole blink/don't blink scenario – but it's no less scary for that.

Moffat delights in piling on the questions throughout this two-parter. Who is the little girl on the White House phone, and why does she end up inside the Apollo spacesuit? Why, in the final scene, does she appear to be regenerating? Who is the mysterious woman with the eye-patch who appears, apropos of nothing, looking at Amy through a door? And is Amy really with child? She says she is, then claims it's a false alarm, while the TARDIS – which appears to come with a built-in home pregnancy testing kit – can't make up its mind.

You might be waiting a long time for answers, though – if, indeed, they ever come at all. *The Impossible Astronaut / Day of the Moon* is a fascinating, infuriating jigsaw puzzle of a story with many wondrous elements that don't quite fit together. Or at least, you suspect they *might* fit together, but it would be handy to be able to see the picture on the box. The action chops and changes so much, it's not obvious what the main narrative through line is supposed to be; the scenes in which Amy and Canton visit a creepy, abandoned orphanage one storm-lashed night are a case in point, almost appearing to belong in a different episode of a different show. Or possibly an 18-rated horror movie.

The second episode, in particular, leaves more dangling threads than an Axon's jumper. While Amy, Rory and River hunt the Silence, the Doctor spends three months sitting in Area 51 growing a big beard. This later turns out to be a bit of misdirection to put the government's agents off the scent – but why bother, if he's in cahoots with the President? Couldn't RMN just write a memo, or something? It's almost as if the Doctor just fancied an excuse for a nice sit down.

The resolution is also a frustrating mixture of the brilliant and the really quite dumb. The Doctor's idea of inserting a clip of the Silence into TV coverage of the moon landing – thus ensuring no-one has a chance to forget them – is genius, but does rather rely on one of the creatures helpfully suggesting "you should kill us all on sight" at the precise moment it's being filmed on a camera phone. (What would have happened if it had said "You should take us all

to Chessington World of Adventures" instead?) The subsequent global uprising against the Silence also leaves many unanswered questions – like, once the deed has been done and the human race have returned to a life of blissful ignorance, won't they start to wonder what those millions of dead aliens are doing lying about in the gutters?

But hey, since when did *Doctor Who* ever make sense? And there are so many great ideas and retina-searing visuals here, it's certainly never a dull ride. The Apollo astronaut rising from the lake in the middle of the Utah plains, in particular, is an iconic image to stand up alongside the Cybermen emerging from their tombs or the Sea Devils surfacing from beneath the waves, while the Doctor's body being pushed out into the water on a floating funeral pyre is both haunting and beautiful. (Elsewhere though, the US location filming feels strangely underused. Sure, Monument Valley looks cool – how could it not? – but it's not exactly *The Searchers*.)

The script is also peppered with great lines, from the racy ("Don't worry, I'm quite the screamer," River promises the Doctor saucily) to the strangely poignant: "Swear to me," the Doctor tells Amy. "Swear to me on something that matters." Her response? "Fish fingers and custard." In how many shows could those four words constitute a major emotional beat?

The Impossible Astronaut also boasts a line which casually encapsulates the joy of *Doctor Who* in a nutshell. "Time isn't a straight line," explains the Doctor. "It's all... bumpy-wumpy. There's loads of boring stuff, like Sundays and Tuesdays and Thursday afternoons. But now and then there are Saturdays. Big temporal tipping points when anything's possible. The TARDIS can't resist them."

Well, who could?

Even the death of the Doctor couldn't match the poignancy of real life, though as, for many, the most gut-twisting moment of the episode was the simple caption card at the very start, dedicating the episode to the memory of Elisabeth Sladen.

Once again, the good weather put a severe dint in the episode's ratings, with overnight figures showing a slightly underwhelming 6.52 million people had drawn the curtains to watch *The Impossible Astronaut* live. *The*

Guardian's "Doctor Who's Return Wilts in the Heat" was typical of the bad headlines this generated, though there was better news from across the pond, where the episode's 1.28 million viewers sent yet another BBC America record tumbling. (The simultaneous UK and US transmission date was designed to clamp down on internet piracy. Presumably they weren't worried about pirates in Australia, where viewers had to wait an extra seven days. Maybe that's how long it takes the internet to reach Australia.)

In contrast to the bouquets thrown the story's way after the press launch, the post-broadcast press reaction saw the faint rumblings of discontent beginning to emerge. The Observer likened the episode to "a four-year-old's bedtime story as made up on the hoof using string theory", the Mirror claimed it was "impossible to understand" and "strictly for sci-fi nerds only" and The Guardian's Sam Wollaston admitted that he didn't understand it, but the kids probably did.

But the real story came later that week when, after 48 years and 11 Time Lords, Matt Smith became the first Doctor to be nominated for a Leading Actor BAFTA for his performance in the role. The 28-year-old was shortlisted alongside Jim Broadbent, Daniel Rigby and – you guessed it – Benedict Cumberbatch for Sherlock. Steven Moffat, presumably, had already made plans to wash his hair that night.

At the end of the month, principal shooting on Series Six wrapped – though naturally Matt Smith had to stay behind to film his Crash of the Elysium scenes, as well as some special shorts for the DVD box set, co-starring Alex Kingston. He was allowed time off for the series wrap party, though – after which, according to The Sun, he fell over in his Cardiff flat and split his head open. The implication was he must have been a bit worse for wear – though it's equally possible he was just demonstrating the Drunk Giraffe again.

"Now Doctor Who scares off another one million viewers", blurted the Daily Mail in its Tuesday edition, in reference to Day of the Moon's overnight figure of 5.1 million. In The Guardian, meanwhile, two dads debated that old hoary chestnut, "Is Doctor Who now too scary for children?" Ho-hum.

Thankfully, the week also brought some news to silence the doubters, when the consolidated ratings for the season opener came in at a whopping 8.86 million – almost 2.5 million up on the overnight figure, and an incredible 4.11 million more than the number who watched it go out live, making The Impossible Astronaut officially Britain's most recorded TV show of all time. All of which suggested viewers hadn't been so much "scared off" as just... you know, out.

The Doctor's Wife: ("Do I look bigger on the inside in this?")

"Yo ho ho!" cries the Doctor, popping up from the hold at the start of The Curse of the Black Spot. "Or does nobody actually say that?"

Well, no, they probably didn't – but that's not necessarily a problem if you're going to go all pistols blazing for a full-throated pirate pastiche – which is what Steven Moffat had apparently asked for. But Stephen Thompson's story doesn't really seem to have its heart in that, either.

The story is a "celebrity historical" in so much as Captain Henry Avery was a real pirate, even if most of the audience wouldn't know him from Henry's Cat. In real life, rape, torture and murder were all in a day's work for this Naval officer-gone-rogue, but Hugh Bonneville's interpretation is more cuddly bear than cutthroat mercenary.

Arriving aboard Avery's becalmed privateer, The Fancy, the Doctor and company find the crew under siege from a mysterious sea siren with a taste for blood. Rory, naturally, is quickly marked for the death by the titular black spot, while Amy proves far more adept at buckling the swash than anyone else on board: "What kind of rubbish pirates are you?" she asks, echoing the thoughts of millions of viewers as she cuts a swathe through the motley crew with some surprisingly deft cutlass work.

With her otherworldly beauty, Lily Cole is perfect casting as the Siren – though why a sea sprite would be swimming about in a ruched two-piece number isn't clear; I guess that's what you get when you hire an actress with her own stylist. (In the battle of the skyscraping redhead actress-models, incidentally, Space Helmet says Karen Gillan wins by a fetching tricorn hat.) Sadly, as villains, Avery's sorry bunch of faceless buccaneers are way more forgettable than the Silence – literally, in the case of Lee Ross' Botswain, who simply disappears from the story midway through without explanation.

Despite having schlepped all the way to Charlestown, the episode feels stagey, cramped and static, with no sense of the high (or even becalmed) seas. It's also very dark, with all the action taking place at night, which makes the decision to swap it with episode nine in order to get a bit more light and space into the early part of the run frankly baffling.

In the third act, the script abandons ship for a futuristic alien spacecraft, where the Siren is revealed not to be a Siren at all, but an emergency medical program caring for injured humans. Avery decides to commandeer this new vessel for himself, and expertly pilots it off for new adventures among the stars without so much a glance at the owner's manual. Because how different from a seventeenth century privateer can a spaceship *be*, right?

This is just one of the many credulity-stretching moments in a sloppily-plotted, confused and confusing mess that does no favours to anyone involved. Even the normally dependable Matt Smith seems a bit – ahem – at sea here, his performance in danger of slipping into fully-fledged Frank Spencer territory at times. There's a great *Doctor Who* pirate story waiting to be told. But this – the show's first attempt at a proper swashbuckler since 1966's *The Smugglers* (which also featured a different haul of Cap'n Avery's stolen booty, technically making this a sort-of-prequel, but not really) – is a rum do, and no mistake.

In America, *Doctor Who* received a major publicity boost when Meredith Vieira, anchor of NBC's iconic *Today* programme, presented a report about a cameo she'd filmed for the series finale as part of a strand called Anchors Abroad (did not *one* person in the whole building suggest Anchors Away might be a better title?) designed to throw the spotlight on "some of the world's hottest TV shows". Vieira reported back to her colleagues on the "very unassuming" soundstage on which the series was made – a diplomatic way of saying she'd travelled five-and-a-half thousand miles to spend the day in a draughty warehouse in Wales.

Slightly less positive publicity followed when Steven Moffat was accused of "attacking" the show's fans who leaked spoilers online. Having mithered about a so-called fan revealing the entire plot of *The Impossible Astronaut / Day of the Moon* following the New York press screening in his *Doctor Who Magazine* column, Moffat had been asked about the subject during a backstage interview at BAFTA with BBC Five Live journalist Colin Paterson. "It's heartbreaking in a way, because you're trying to tell stories and stories depend on surprise," he said. "To have some twit get into a press launch, write up a report in the worst English you can imagine and put it on the internet... I just hope that guy never watches my show again."

From Five Live, the story was picked up by Radio 2 and was the subject of a live discussion between Paterson and *DWM*'s Benjamin Cook on *BBC Breakfast*, before the tabloids weighed in with their own considered take ("Dr Who Boss Launches Verbal Attack at Fans," screamed the *Evening Standard*).

"Finally heard my own rant," Moffat later tweeted. "Grumpy sod. I had a mic stuck in my face in the middle of a party." It sounded a bit like an apology – though why it was Moffat in the stocks, as opposed to the idiot who'd blabbed in the first place, wasn't really clear.

Away from such squabbles, it was a good week for remembering two of the most important women in the Doctor's life. On Monday, BBC Four broadcast her 1976 swansong *The Hand of Fear* as a tribute to Elisabeth Sladen while, on Saturday, viewers finally got to meet the Time Lord's missus[VI]. Sort of.

At times, *The Doctor's Wife* feels less like Neil Gaiman's take on *Doctor Who* than *Doctor Who*'s take on Neil Gaiman – closer in tone to the surrealist fantasy of *Coraline* or *Neverwhere* than the show's usual diet of domestic sci-fi horror. Initially, this is a bit disorienting: the early scenes with Auntie and Uncle – a Frankenstein-style double act apparently assembled from random body parts and dressed like extras from a Cure video – the enigmatic Idris (Suranne Jones) and their Ood servant Nephew are full of cryptic, abstruse dialogue that makes no concessions to the Saturday night "shiny floor" crowd.

Thankfully, the episode has a bulletproof

central premise that delivers way more than even its deliberately tarty title promises. Because, unlike the somewhat mis-sold *The Doctor's Daughter*, this really is about our hero's most Significant Other – and just because she chooses to spend most of her time disguised as a police box... well, who are we to pass judgment on other people's lifestyle choices?

Giving the TARDIS human form is a simply brilliant idea, and this is a wonderful celebration of the Doctor's relationship with his only constant companion: part smouldering sexual attraction ("She's a woman and she's the TARDIS," smirks Amy. "Did you wish *really* hard?"), part bickering married couple ("I'm the TARDIS" "No you're not, you're a mad bitey lady"), it's a relationship beautifully sold by Matt Smith and Suranne Jones' glorious performances.

Best of all, Gaiman casually retcons the entire history of *Doctor Who* with an almost throwaway exchange in which the Doctor harrumphs that "You didn't always take me to where I wanted to go," to which the TARDIS responds: "No, but I always took you where you needed to go." And with that deft flick of the pen, all those years of stories where the Doctor just happens to arrive moments before everything kicks off suddenly make perfect sense. Bravo.

We also get a closer look at the TARDIS' nooks and crannies (no, not like *that*, I mean the actual vessel) as Amy and Rory are pursued through the Ship's corridors by a feral Ood and House, a sentient asteroid that's possessed the ship and keeps buggering about with its internal dimensions (cue a surprising reprise for the Tennant-era console room).

There's some pretty dark stuff here, not least the death of Rory (yes, *again* – he's rapidly turning into the *Who* equivalent of Kenny from *South Park*), who carks it after waiting a lifetime for Amy to come back for him. (His "I hate Amy" graffiti, daubed on the TARDIS walls after he thinks she's abandoned him, is as bleak as the show gets.) And Amy reaching out in the darkness for her husband and being rewarded with a handful of Ood tentacle instead is just... eeeuw.

The one element of *The Doctor's Wife* that doesn't work is House. For a start, why go to the trouble of hiring an actor as good as

Michael Sheen for a bog-standard "threatening monster" voice that's so heavily treated, it could be Susan Boyle for all we know? (It isn't, I checked.) And the ending, in which the TARDIS fights back against its assailant while Sheen goes "Ooh, ah, no, stop that, gerroff" like a disembodied Frankie Howerd is plain ridiculous – albeit partly salvaged by a thrilling exchange in which House boasts, "Fear me, I've killed hundreds of Time Lords", to which the Doctor replies, darkly: "Fear me. I've killed all of them."

The final conversation between the Doctor and the Idris TARDIS also ensures the story goes out on a high: "I've been looking for a word," she says. "A big, complicated word, but so sad. I've found it now: Alive. I'm alive."

And then it's time to go. "There's something I didn't get to say to you," says Idris. "Goodbye?" asks the Doctor. "No, I just wanted to say hello. Hello, Doctor."

Hello, I must be going: I guess that's just the way things roll when you hitch up with a time machine.

The Headless Monks: "Sorry, we didn't think"

On the cover of the *Radio Times*, Matt Smith squared off against Benedict Cumberbatch as the magazine heralded "Sherlock V The Doctor – the Battle of the BAFTAs." Inside, Kathryn Flett argued that "while neither is a cookie-cutter pin-up, with their jolie-laide angular faces and gangly limbs, both are quirkily sexy, accomplished actors with a compelling on-screen presence and energy". Which I think is a posh way of saying she fancies them.

On BBC One, Matthew Graham's latest two-parter offered a shot at rehabilitation after the critical drubbing handed out to *Fear Her*. And *The Rebel Flesh / The Almost People* does have the makings of a decent sci-fi thriller – or at least, it would have if it wasn't fatally harpooned by sloppy plotting and basic continuity errors that render the whole thing a frustrating, incoherent muddle.

The set-up is sound: on a remote island monastery in the twenty-second century, human acid miners use expendable duplicates – known as Gangers – made from "programmable flesh" to do the dangerous, dirty work.

But when the Doctor and company arrive, they find themselves in the middle of a revolution, as a bunch of these skinsuits rise up to demand better conditions (not being melted down and made into a candle when they've outlived their usefulness, that sort of thing). "It's *Made in Dagenham* meets *The Thing*!" declared Graham, not inaccurately.

There's also a hefty chunk of *Blade Runner* in there, as the story's philosophical core revolves around questions of identity and what it means to be human; namely, if the Gangers share the same thoughts, memories and feelings as their human templates, do they not also deserve the same rights? "I'm not a monster," pleads "Jennifer" (Sarah Smart), "I'm me, me, me!", while Jimmy and his Ganger show the same depth of feeling towards "their" son.

As an added bonus, we get two Matt Smiths for the price of one, as the Doctor not only gets his own Ganger, but forms something of a comedy double-act with him. When you're always the smartest guy in the room, I guess it's nice to have someone to talk up to. (Listen carefully and you'll also hear Tom Baker and David Tennant in the mix as the Ganger struggles to replicate an organism as complex as a Time Lord.)

The Rebel Flesh is, for the most part, pretty solid stuff, energetically directed by Julian Simpson, who makes great use of the fabulous location at Caerphilly Castle. It's in the second part that things start to unspool, as internal logic is thrown out of the window in favour of plot expedience (Jen's Ganger inexplicably mutates into a giant spider-giraffe monster, for no immediately obvious reason), while whoever's in charge of continuity appears to have nodded off (the Doctor throws his sonic to his Ganger, then whips it out of his pocket in the next scene, while Dicken – a character who otherwise barely speaks – does a Significant Sneeze three times, for reasons that are never followed up). The ending, meanwhile, is pure *Acorn Antiques*, as two of the Gangers make the most pointless sacrifice since Adelaide Brooks, spending what feels like an eternity holding back a door while insisting they don't have time to make it to the TARDIS, despite the fact it's clearly only two steps away.

There's no doubting the shock value of the story's postscript, though, in which it's revealed

that Amy has been a Ganger this entire series, while the real thing is being held prisoner and is about to go into labour, with Frances Barber's creepy eyepatch lady – a repeated meme throughout this year's run – acting as midwife. But even this big reveal is flawed as, having spent the entire story acting as a passionate advocate for Ganger rights – he's the Martin Luther King Jr. of fleshbots, basically – the Doctor suddenly has no compunction about taking his sonic to Amy's double and splattering her across the TARDIS like a balloon full of porridge. Still, at least he's consistent in one way: like exploding Amy, this story is all over the place.

On May 22nd, Matt Smith, Steven Moffat and Mark Gatiss donned their best bib and tucker for the BAFTA Television Awards. Both Smith and Benedict Cumberbatch lost out on the Leading Actor statuette to Daniel Rigby, for his performance as another great British institution, Eric Morecambe, in BBC biopic *Eric and Ernie*. But it was a good night for *Sherlock*, which bagged both Best Drama Series and a Best Supporting Actor gong for Martin Freeman. (By the end of the night, a confused Moffat can't have known *what* he thought about awards ceremonies any more.)

Talking to *Radio Times*, Moffat made an aside about "resting" the Daleks this year, which led to yet another tabloid feeding frenzy ("Daleks Get the Chop!"). Maybe it was time to consider a new career as a Trappist monk. In the *Daily Mirror*, meanwhile, Matt Smith revealed he was "going over to Los Angeles to dip my head in the pond". Feel free to fill in your own Karen Gillan joke.

Ponds are at the heart of *A Good Man Goes to War*, Steven Moffat's supremely confident mid-season finale. Even by Moffat's standards, the pre-title teaser is audaciously brassy: aboard the asteroid space station Demons Run, Amy Pond cradles her baby daughter, Melody, and tells her that "There's someone coming... There's a man who's never going to let us down – and not even an army can get in the way."

Twenty thousand light years away, the Cybermen report an intruder aboard one of their ships. "He has a name," continues Amy, "but the people of our world know him better as... The Last Centurion."

"I have a message and a question," says Rory,

facing down the Cybermen in full Roman battle dress. "A message from the Doctor and a question from me: Where. Is. My. Wife?"

"What is the Doctor's message?" asks the Cyberleader.

Outside the ship, the rest of the Cyber fleet explodes in an enormous fireball. "Would you like me to repeat the question?" asks Rory.

It's a jaw-dropping entrée that sets the tone for what follows, in which the Doctor calls in a few favours[VII] to raise an army against one-eyed space bitch Madame Kovarian and her partners in crime.

Chief among the Doctor's allies are Madame Vastra – a Silurian adventuress living in Victorian London – and her faithful retainer Jenny. "Jack the Ripper has claimed his last victim," says Vastra, arriving home in a Hansom cab. "How did you find him?" wonders Jenny. "Stringy," replies Vastra, removing her Samurai sword. (As well as being surprisingly handy in a fight, Jenny turns out to be more than a housemaid in other ways, too. "I don't know why you put up with me," Vastra says, moments before lashing out at an enemy with her enormous reptile tongue. That's right, an actual cunnilingus joke. In *Doctor Who*. But then, once you've done a gag about sticking your dick in a living pavement, I guess all bets are off.)

Then, on an alien battlefield, we meet Strax – a disgraced Sontaran serving his penance as an army field nurse. "Captain Harcourt," he tells his patient, "I hope some day to meet you in the glory of battle, when I shall crush the life from your worthless human form. Try and get some rest."

On Demons Run, meanwhile, are the Order of the Headless, a bunch of laser sword-wielding monks in hooded cowls. Rumour has it they're so named because they follow their hearts not their minds... until it's revealed that, no, they really *are* headless, literally tied off at the neck with a neat little knot, like sausages. All except one, that is, as – a whole 19 minutes into the episode – one of the monks pulls back his hood to reveal you know Who. "Surprised?" asks the Doctor. Not really, to be honest – but it's still a punch-the-air moment, as he and Rory stage a daring rescue of mother and baby.

The triumphalism is short-lived, however, as the whole set-up turns out to be a trap – and

Melody a Ganger copy of the real thing. After everything we've just witnessed – especially Rory's heroic rescue act – watching that tiny baby explode in a shower of gloop in its mother's arms seems almost too cruel to bear.

Except their daughter is still with them, after a fashion – because, in the language of the forest, Melody Pond translates as something else: River Song. "It's me," says River. "I'm Melody. I'm your daughter."

And on that *Dallas*-style bombshell, *Doctor Who* bows out for the summer, with the Doctor embarking on a mission to find Amy and Rory's baby, and an animated caption promising that our hero will return in the autumn in... wait for it... Let's! Kill! Hitler!

It's a bold, cheeky ending to a bold, cheeky episode, packed to the gunwales with great lines and mind-stretching concepts. ("Doctor – the word for healer and wise man throughout the universe," says River. "We get that word from you, you know." That's quite a big idea for an offhand comment, mentioned almost in passing.) As a story, *A Good Man Goes to War* doesn't really go anywhere – least of all to war (it's more of a mild skirmish in a loading bay). And the mid-season cliffhanger isn't quite the game-changing shock we'd been led to believe, either. But the quality of the dialogue, the vivacity of the direction and performances and the sheer chutzpah of Moffat's ideas more than make up for any shortcomings, resulting in 45 minutes of confident, positively swaggering adventure from a writer with the world at his feet.

Less is more.
Or do we mean less?

With the dust barely settled on the mid-season finale, the question of *Doctor Who*'s future suddenly exploded like a Ganger's trousers all over the worldwide web.

It started with a report in *The Guardian* stating that "14 new episodes of *Doctor Who* starring Matt Smith have been commissioned" by the BBC. This was in response to a *Private Eye* story – which a BBC secretary had apparently persuaded *Eye* editor Ian Hislop to read out over the phone – that BBC Wales were proposing not to make a full series in 2012, and instead air four specials.

So, 14 episodes. Matt Smith. So far so good. But the rub came in *The Guardian*'s claim that "a good chunk" of the 14 episodes would be airing next year, which set alarm bells ringing among fans that they might indeed not be getting a full series in 2012. What, they asked philosophically, constitutes "a good chunk"?

Sam Hodges, the Beeb's Head of Communication, tried to close the *Eye*'s story down, tweeting: "#DoctorWho is returning. Fourteen new episodes have been commissioned with Matt Smith as The Doctor #bbc1"

Which didn't really answer the question about what was happening *when*. "The new commission is a big commitment," insisted a BBC spokesman. "Not many other shows have such a commitment so far in advance. ["Too bloody right," grumbled Trevor Eve.] We do not know yet how many will air in 2012."

Steven Moffat added his own contribution via Twitter, stating: "14 eps + Matt DEFINITELY. I've got a plan and I'm NOT TELLING YOU WHAT IT IS. Now hush or River shoots you with her Spoiler Gun. #formaqueue"

At a conference the following week, BBC One Controller Danny Cohen attempted to pour water on the flames – without realising he'd accidentally brought along lighter fuel instead. "The tricky thing to explain to your kids," said Cohen, "is that the same man who writes *Doctor Who* also writes *Sherlock*, and there's only so many hours in the day he can be awake. We're very keen that *Sherlock* comes back too, so he needs enough time to get that done and then start work on the next series of *Doctor Who*. There will be some episodes, but there won't be a full series, so we won't have a 13-part run. And there'll be more episodes again in 2103 – which I think is the 50th anniversary of *Doctor Who*, so that will be a big year." (He *thinks*? Shouldn't he at least have something in his Outlook calendar about this?)

His comments subsequently appeared in a *BBC News Online* article headed "*Sherlock*'s Success Means Less *Doctor Who* in 2012." Neil Gaiman then sent a tweet to Steven Moffat, asking: "Er... is it my imagination or are you being shafted by BBC online news?" "It's not your imagination," replied Moffat. "Unbelievable, unacceptable."

In a follow-up tweet, Moffat insisted: "The scheduling of Dr Who has got NOTHING to do with Sherlock." Citing "misquotes and misunderstandings", he added: "I'm not being bounced into announcing the cool stuff before we're ready. Hush, and patience."

Reflecting on the whole sorry saga a few months later, Moffat told *SFX*: "That made my life very awkward for a day – because I'm married to the producer of *Sherlock*!"[23]

Though, inevitably, the pressure of running both shows *was* taking its toll. Moffat completed work on the opening script for *Sherlock*'s sophomore series in late June, then ploughed straight into the *Doctor Who* Christmas special, which he later told Five Live was "the highest pressure I think I've ever had". Having turned around his Christmas script in three weeks, Moffat decided to take his first day off in months – which is when he came down with a stinking cold that hung around for weeks. But apart from all that, he had absolutely no regrets about turning down all those piles of money from Steven Spielberg.

If the BBC were hoping things would calm down after a choleric couple of weeks of backbiting, July brought two new potential disasters. The first was the announcement of Beth Willis' departure from BBC Wales, which was seized upon in a typically diplomatic and sensitive piece from *Private Eye* that decency (and a touch of good old-fashioned cowardice) prevents *Space Helmet* from repeating.

And the second misfire? Say hello to *Torchwood: Miracle Day*.

Despite its shortcomings, *Torchwood* had somehow proved enough of a success to make the leap from BBC3 to BBC2 and, finally, to the main channel, where it had managed not to make the place untidy by suddenly Being Unexpectedly and Consistently Good.

And now here it was, all grown up and doing its own thing in America, with Proper American Money and Proper American Film Actors. And John Barrowman. Which meant *Torchwood* now made less sense than ever because, while it might have been a silly show about alien takedowns, the fact the alien takedowns happened in Splott instead of Sacramento at least gave it a certain quirky USP. But now they'd relocated it to LA, which did seem to miss the point of the joke, rather.

The first striking thing about *Miracle Day* is

its demonstration of how far *Torchwood* had now fallen from the tree of *Who*, as its opening seconds introduce the rape and murder of a 12-year-old girl as a pivotal plot point. In 2005, Captain Jack Harkness and his time-travelling chums foiled a flatulent green alien's plan to ride away from an exploding planet on an intergalactic surfboard. Here he's up against a child rapist. For *Doctor Who* fans, that's an idea so repellent, it feels a bit like JK Rowling writing a Harry Potter sequel in which Ron Weasley is placed on the sex offenders register. That said, the previous story – the highly acclaimed *Children of Earth* – had entailed soldiers moving in to seize millions of schoolchildren and hand them over to aliens as prepubescent drug reservoirs. And it was never intended that *Doctor Who* and *Torchwood* would play by the same rules. But whatever their shared DNA might once have been, it was clear that, today, they'd barely qualify for a "frequently bought together" recommendation on Amazon.

The central narrative hook of *Miracle Day* is that dying has suddenly been suspended across the whole of Earth, denying people the sweet relief of shuffling off this mortal coil. The turn of events owes to some Illuminati-types, the Three Families, who lucked out in acquiring Captain Jack's blood in the 1920s, and are leveraging that resource in an attempt to crash and burn the global economy, then rebuild it to their liking. Being a US co-production, the cast includes some familiar faces from American film and TV, including Bill Pullman (*Independence Day*), Wayne Knight (*Seinfeld*, *3rd Rock from the Sun*), Mekhi Phifer (*ER*), Lauren Ambrose (*Six Feet Under*) and *Star Trek*'s Nana Vistor and John de Lancie.

But if there's one thing that threatens to turn *Miracle Day* stone cold dead, it's the format. *Children of Earth* was a taut and racing five-parter, but *Miracle Day* is double that length, and simply doesn't contain enough story to justify ten episodes. Watched week to week, it's a slog to get through all the digressions – episode two kills time with Jack being poisoned on an airplane, without Leslie Nielsen or Peter Graves to lighten the mood with deadpan jokes – and then matters just plod along before episode seven (in an arresting flashback to 1927, by seminal *Buffy* writer Jane Espenson)

finally starts to reveal the secret history behind these events, i.e. *what the hell is actually going on*. It's a shame, because *Miracle Day* begs some interesting questions about life and death, but those get washed out amidst all the padding.

Miracle Day opened with 4.8 million UK viewers, and was lucky to only lose a million of them over the weeks that followed. In the US, 1.5 million tuned in for the opener, but the audience soon slumped under the magic million mark (although it had the impediment of being on Starz, one of those US networks that it's easy to forget exists). Those aren't the sort of numbers that demand immediate cancellation, but neither do they warrant an automatic renewal. And any thoughts of Starz funding more *Torchwood* became complicated when Russell T Davies moved back to the United Kingdom in 2011 to care for his partner, who was stricken with brain cancer. Prior to this, *Torchwood* been a fairly resilient property, but *Miracle Day* – a show about people refusing to die – would ironically prove its death knell on television.

In mid-July, Matt Smith spent another Saturday in the TARDIS, taping the winning entry of the Script to Screen competition, *Death is the Only Answer.* (Wow, primary school kids are *bleak* these days.) The same day, Karen Gillan and Alex Kingston dipped a toe in the world of organised fandom with an appearance at the London Film & Comic Con, alongside the likes of Sylvester McCoy and John Leeson. As well as taking part in an audience Q&A, there was a chance to share a photo op with Gillan's telescopic legs and microscopic skirt, for the princely sum of £15. (Or a tenner if you agreed to have Sylvester McCoy in it, too. Just kidding – love that guy.)

"A Ford Focus and a fish supper on Friday? You're Mr Average (and Dr Who is probably your favourite show)." That was the headline in the *Daily Mail*, reporting the results of a survey into British lifestyle choices which revealed that, after years of being labelled geeks and outcasts, *Doctor Who* fans had finally risen to the heady heights of being average. In Manchester, meanwhile, the young audience at a performance of *Crash of the Elysium* got a shock when, instead of video inserts, Matt Smith – the hardest working

Time Lord in show business – appeared in person for his scenes as the Doctor.

Shortly afterwards, Smith boarded a plane to San Diego, where he and Karen Gillan received a hero's welcome at Comic-Con 2011. The pair appeared on a panel alongside Toby Whithouse – deputising for Steven Moffat, who had a few thousand other things on that weekend – and outgoing execs Piers Wenger and Beth Willis. In Cardiff, Wenger and Willis' replacement was confirmed as Caroline "Caro" Skinner, whose CV included the acclaimed *Five Days* and BBC Three's fantasy horror drama *The Fades*. (Loved their first album.)

Ending the summer break on a high, at the 69th World Science Fiction convention in Reno, *Doctor Who* scooped its fourth Hugo Award when *The Pandorica Opens / The Big Bang* took the honours for Best Dramatic Presentation (Short Form). It was the fourth such award for Steven Moffat, whose mantelpiece now boasted more Hugos than the Tory backbenches.

(Modesty also forbids us pointing out that *Chicks Dig Time Lords* – "a celebration of Doctor Who by the women who love it", published by Mad Norwegian Press – also won a Hugo that year, for Best Related Work. So we won't do that. But you should read it anyway.)

Let's kill Hitler! Or, failing that, let's at least lock him in a cupboard for a bit

Another month, another *Doctor Who* premiere, as the first episode of Series Thingie was confirmed for broadcast on August 27th, meaning the seven-episode run would be all wrapped up by the start of October – much to the disappointment of fans who'd been hoping to see the show returned to a winter slot.

Let's Kill Hitler is a misleading title in more ways than one. Not least because, by crashing the TARDIS through the window of his office, the Doctor actually *saves* Hitler – just as he is on the point of being assassinated by a robot Nazi containing 423 miniaturised humans (just go with it for now, okay?).

This dramatic entrance is caused when Amy and Rory's wayward childhood friend Mels – a spunky performance from Nina Toussaint-White – fires a gun in the TARDIS, having told

the Doctor: "What the hell: you've got a time machine, I've got a gun – let's kill Hitler!" Which is fair enough, I suppose. When their arrival in 30s Berlin has the opposite effect, Rory does at least get to utter the immortal line "Shut it, Hitler", before locking the Fuhrer in a cupboard. And that's the last we see of him. (Which is another way in which the title is something of a misnomer: in reality, this story is as much about Hitler as *The Green Death* is about Kermit the Frog's funeral.)

When Mels takes a Nazi bullet, she surprises everyone – except perhaps viewers who have been paying attention – by regenerating into River Song, who is part-Time Lord because her parents conceived her in the TARDIS. Apparently. (Sounds like someone needs to sit down and have a conversation with Steven Moffat about the birds and the bees.) This proves a gift for Alex Kingston, who never knowingly underplays the part, and here gets to make great sport with suddenly finding herself in a body with a whole new set of curves and a runaway mouth. "I was on my way to a gay Gypsy bar mitzvah for the disabled," she tells a group of Nazi officers, "when I thought, 'Gosh, the Third Reich's a bit rubbish, I think I'll kill Hitler'."

Unfortunately, River has been conditioned by the Silence (long story) to kill the Doctor instead. Which is where the whole thing begins to derail somewhat.

Firstly, the method of execution – lipstick poisoned with the sap of a Judas tree – is deeply silly, as River apparently fatally poisons the last of the Time Lords, beyond any hope of regeneration, through the most chaste brush of the lips (small boys have kissed their hairy-lipped grannies with more passion and enthusiasm than that). And it does rather raise the question of why River herself, who is slathered in the stuff, is apparently immune.

This makes it rather hard to buy what follows: half-an-hour of Matt Smith flailing about doing comedy pratfalls as he gradually loses function in his limbs. Whereas the Doctor's impending death in *The Big Bang* was heroic and heartbreaking, this one's just mildly irritating, and leaves you wondering what happened to that story about Hitler we were promised.

And then, after all that faffing about, River has a dramatic change of heart and burns up all her future regenerations to bring the Doctor back from the dead. It's meant to feel like redemption; instead, it just makes you wonder what the point of the last half hour has been, exactly. Still, at least the script acknowledges this with typical Moffat wit: "She did kill me," says the Doctor. "Then she used her remaining lives to bring me back to life. As first dates go, I'd say that was mixed signals."

About that robot: the *Teselecta* is a Justice Department Vehicle capable of transforming its exterior to resemble living beings, crewed by a militarised – and, indeed, miniaturised – vigilante squad whose mission is to track down famous war criminals and "give 'em hell". As an M.O., it's certainly original: built yourself the perfect shape-changing robot assassin to send into battle? Why not add an unnecessary element of danger by shrinking yourself to the size of a Twiglet and hiding inside it? If you're not now getting an image of the Numbskulls from *The Beezer*, you obviously didn't grow up in Britain in the 1970s or 80s. (The *Teselecta* does give rise to the best gag of the episode, though, when it assumes the form of Amy, leading Rory – who is regularly getting all the choice lines these days – to note: "Okay, I'm trapped inside a robot replica of my wife. I'm really trying hard not to see this as a metaphor.")

After a strong start – including a fabulous pre-titles sequence in which Amy and Rory use a Mini to spell out "Doctor" in a cornfield ("You never answer your phone!") – *Let's Kill Hitler* wanders off the point rather spectacularly. Its biggest misstep, though, is its failure to follow through on the dramatic revelations of *A Good Man Goes to War*. Amy and Rory barely seem bothered by their missing baby: Amy admonishing the Doctor about having had "all summer to find Melody" is more peeved than desperate – and is the revelation they grew up with Mels supposed to make everything okay? To somehow compensate for being denied the chance to raise your child? If *Doctor Who* is going to play with grown-up themes, it surely needs to do them in a grown-up way. By the end of *Let's Kill Hitler*, Amy and Rory are back in the TARDIS and ready for more larky adventures, any thoughts of looking for their baby apparently abandoned. As

parents, they make Darth Vader look like Atticus Finch.

"Giddily thrilling entertainment" was the *Telegraph*'s verdict on the episode while, in the US, *Entertainment Weekly* called it "marvellously energetic, funny, clever, noble". The *Daily Mirror*, though, appeared to be on a bit of a *Doctor Who* downer these days, dismissing the story as the "usual ball of nerdy confusion". That was nothing to compared to *The Sun*'s latest dispatch, however: its finest investigative journalists had once again used all the skills in their arsenal to look at Steven Moffat's Twitter feed for their piece, "*Doctor Who* Boss' Blast at Net Fans". "PRICKLY *Doctor Who* boss Steven Moffat has been threatened with a BEATING by idiotic fans," said the report. "The famously grumpy exec, who also oversees *Sherlock*, took to Twitter yesterday to blast brainless so-called fans angry at his changes to the BBC1 show. He told how one rude tweeter abused him, while another 'wanted to beat me up'. Fans have taken offence to Moffat's new direction for the show, which has seen it become more complex. He's also decided to 'rest' the Daleks, annoying purists.

"He tweeted: 'I'm tired of being threatened and sworn at. Behind your back is freedom of speech. To your face is an attack.

"Moffat caused an online stir among fans earlier this year after he laid into them for discussing storyline spoilers. He seethed in May: 'You can imagine how much I hate them. It's only fans who do this, or they call themselves fans. I wish they could go and be fans of something else.'"

Oh dear. At least *The Independent* was sending out positive vibes. In an op-ed piece entitled "The Best Future Would be One Imagined by *Doctor Who*", Laurie Pennu wrote that, "over three generations, 32 series and 11 leading actors, and especially since the show was re-imagined in 2005, the BBC's flagship drama has been the closest we come, on this godless little island, to a national act of devotion. Occasionally, you meet people who don't get excited when they hear the wibbly-wobbly timey-wimey whoosh of the TARDIS, but they are a bit like Cybermen: soulless and efficient, their humanity ripped out and encased in cold, clanking metal, and fundamentally not actually people at all. Right now, we need

Doctor Who more than ever." Amen (or whatever its godless equivalent is) to that. And, with perfect timing, here's Mark Gatiss to reinforce the message with perhaps the most quintessential *Doctor Who* story ever made.

For his latest contribution, Steven Moffat had asked Gatiss to write something along the lines of *Crooked House*, his spooky BBC Four anthology series, but with a modern setting. Gatiss was keen to show he didn't just do period dramas, and suggested a story set in a hotel where people's phobias came to life – at which point Moffat told him this was pretty much the *exact* plot of Toby Whithouse's upcoming story.

Instead, Gatiss retreated to what he described as "the scariest place in the universe": a child's bedroom. With the result that, not only is *Night Terrors* fantastic, you could argue it is *the* archetypal *Doctor Who* episode – the show's ur-text, if you want to get all media studies about it – showcasing an average day at the office for the man who fights the monsters under your bed and behind your sofa. (Fans often canvass each others' opinion about the best story to introduce *Doctor Who* to a newcomer; to which the short answer, if you're sensible, is: Step. Away. From. The. Remote. But if you *are* going to try, this feels like as good an overture as any.)

Because, let's face it, *Night Terrors* chucks well-worn fantasy, horror and literary tropes about like an industrial trope dispenser (ghostly children's laughter, nursery rhymes, doll's houses, pyjamas, Edwardiana – aw c'mon, you didn't think it was *all* going to be contemporary, did you? Gatiss would find a way of working muttonchop sideburns and a Hansom cab into *Flash Gordon*). They're all here, and all used slyly and knowingly to create the right atmosphere and punch the right buttons.

When the Doctor receives an intergalactic distress call from a little boy who's afraid of the dark, he pays a house call on an inner-city London tower block, where eight-year-old George (Jamie Oram) is driving his parents (Daniel Mays and Emma Cunliffe) mad with worry.

Later, it transpires that George is actually a Tenza, one of a cuckoo-like alien race who used his empathic powers to home in on a couple desperate for a child. But this psychic ability proves highly volatile when combined with the irrational fears of an eight-year-old boy, making nightmares reality – most vividly in an extended sequence in which Amy and Rory become trapped in a dolls' house, where they're menaced by terrifying, crudely finished peg dolls. (Gatiss claims to have had a fear of such coarse, rough-hewn faces ever since he saw a neighbour wearing a Hallowe'en mask made from eggboxes. He also claimed that he'd always been frightened of dolls, "particularly china-faced Victorian dolls with the hair missing and those holes where the hair is punched in and terrible glass eyes"[24]. He's a big wuss, basically.)

In pure story terms, *Night Terrors* can be seen as very much a companion piece to 2006's much unloved *Fear Her*, but the presentation couldn't be more different, and gives us a glimpse of how much better that story might have been if they'd taken a more obvious route and set it at night, with scary monsters and taffeta petticoats, and no Huw Edwards. *Fear Her* was a cautionary example of writer and director pulling in different directions, but here Richard Clark serves Gatiss' vision with great sensitivity, particularly in the lighting and grading – the doll's house scenes immersed in spooky shadow, the council flats the colour of gruel and broken dreams. Murray Gold is also singing from the same hymn sheet (not literally – not this time, anyway), most notably in the quite lovely way he underscores the Doctor's showdown with Alex (Mays) in the kitchen.

And what a showdown. If *Night Terrors* is made of pure *Doctor Who* DNA, here's where we get to unravel its sequencing: "Whatever's inside that cupboard," warns the Doctor, "is so terrible, so powerful, that it amplified the fears of an ordinary boy through all the barriers of time and space; through crimson stars and silent stars and tumbling nebulas like oceans set on fire. Through empires of glass and civilisations of pure thought and a whole terrible, wonderful universe of impossibilities. You see these eyes? They're old eyes. And one thing I can tell you, Alex: monsters are real."

Besotted fanboy that he is, Gatiss is clearly staking his own claim for a pull-out entry in *The Quotable Who* here, and it's all the more effective for the way he neatly undercuts any pomposity with Alex's wonderfully bathetic response: "You're not from social services, are you?"

If anything is likely to lose *Night Terrors* points with some viewers, it's the ending, in which love saves the day as Alex decides that, just because his son is actually an alien parasite, it doesn't have to get in the way of playing happy families. (Incidentally, this is the third bit of father-son bonding this series, after Cap'n Avery and his stowaway son in *The Curse of the Black Spot* and Ganger Buzzer adopting Dead Buzzer's child. This one, thankfully, is much more convincing – for those keeping score, then, that's Real Dad Fake Kid 1, Fake Dad Real Kid 0.)

But when Alex says, "Whatever you are, whatever you do, you're my son," he's doing more than loving the alien: he's vocalising the unconditional love of so many parents on this earth. Which makes this a very easy story to love, unconditionally.

The ongoing rumbles about whether *Doctor Who* had become too complicated were picked up by the *Daily Express* in David Stephenson's piece: "*Doctor Who*? What the hell is going on?" The article quoted Matt Smith as admitting he sometimes had to read the scripts a couple of times to get his head round them, but launching a robust defence of his boss: "Isn't it good to raise questions?" he asked. "Isn't it brave to have a TV show on at half-past six that challenges audiences, challenges children, that doesn't set out to spoon-feed anyone? I'm so tired of TV that's patronising and simple."

Moffat himself was quoted as saying: "I think if something's good, people won't mind if they don't completely understand it. Who says we have to understand everything? You either enjoy it or you don't. I didn't understand a word of *The West Wing*, but I loved it all the same. Or even what's going on in any given day. I understand about an eighth of it. It doesn't matter. Do you like it or don't you?"

On September 6th, Smith collected more silverware at the GQ Men of the Year Awards at the Royal Opera House, this time walking away with the Most Stylish Man title (so maybe fezzes *are* cool). On BBC One, meanwhile, it was Karen Gillan who took centre-stage in *The Girl Who Waited* – a salutary reminder that

Doctor Who is often at its best when the ideas are in inverse proportion to the budgets. With the smallest cast since *The Edge of Destruction* a full 48 years earlier, it's effectively a three-hander between the regulars – and even then Matt Smith doesn't get much screen time, his scenes mostly confined to the TARDIS as he was busy filming episode twelve. That leaves Karen Gillan and Arthur Darvill with plenty of room to shine, an opportunity they seize with both hands – or, in Gillan's case, all four hands.

Confused? When the TARDIS arrives at a hi-tech quarantine facility, Amy accidentally stumbles into a different time stream to the Doctor and Rory – one that's running at dubbing speed in order to allow dying patients to live their entire lives in a day (you can see why Steven Moffat was initially worried Tom MacRae's script might be "too timey wimey", even for him).

With the Doctor confined to quarters (conveniently, it's a plague that only affects beings with binary vascular systems), Rory mounts a rescue mission to recover his wife. The only problem is, she's now 36 years older – and mightily pissed off with waiting around. What's more, she refuses to accept the Doctor's plan to spool back the decades and rewrite history, arguing that all those years surviving alone have made her into who she is.

And that's the philosophical pearl in the oyster here, MacRae asking whether a sad and lonely life is better than no life at all. It's a very grown-up question – and, with only the local robot population and a bit of slo-mo Samurai sword action to distract them, the episode is quite a big ask for younger viewers. But, for the rest of us, this is heady stuff – especially as Gillan sells the concept so brilliantly. It's not just that the make-up job is astonishing (and it really is). It's the way Gillan subtly shifts her performance – voice, eyes, body language – to fashion a whole new character. This is never more evident than in the scenes where Amy meets her younger self – to come face-to-face with the woman you used to be (especially one as ravishingly beautiful as this) and then see the way your own husband used to look at you is the sort of tragic scenario only *Doctor Who* can do, and Gillan's bitter jealousy is expertly played.

Arthur Darvill, too, rises to the occasion as a

man forced to choose between two versions of the woman he loves. And, ironically, it's also a fabulous showcase for Matt Smith who, despite his limited contribution, is integral to the story – and not always in a way that makes for comfortable viewing. "I hate the Doctor," says Older Amy. "I hate him more than I've ever hated anyone in my life." Ouch. And when Rory asks why the Doctor can't take simple precautions to keep his friends from trouble, and is told "that's not the way I travel", he gives full vent to his fury, screaming at the Time Lord: "Then I do *not* want to travel with you!" Finally, the Doctor betrays everybody when, having promised them there's room for all three Ponds on the TARDIS, he coldly slams the door in older Amy's face.

Though the ending strains to be more poignant than it actually is (after everything they've been through lately, losing an aberrant Amy to ensure the real one lives a happy life doesn't feel like *such* a big sacrifice), *The Girl Who Waited* successfully blends hard sci-fi with emotional intelligence, demonstrating just how much MacRae has grown as a writer since his previous *Who* credit.[VIII]

Director Nick Hurran makes a virtue of the invisible budget with effective use of clinical, antiseptic white sets, which only serve to contrast the scenes in the facility's garden area, a sumptuous, *Alice in Wonderland*-style Eden that finally delivers on the Doctor's oft-heard promise to take his companions somewhere breathtaking (usually made shortly before he lands in a disused Welsh paper mill).

But the episode really belongs to Arthur Darvill and, in particular, Karen Gillan. Originally envisaged as a role for another actress, Gillan fought hard to be allowed to play the older Amy herself; it was a bold gambit, but she pulls it off – and then some.

Later that week, *Doctor Who* once again came home heavy-handed from the TV Choice Awards, winning Best Family Drama and Best Actress for Karen Gillan, while recording began on the Christmas special, with a starry guest cast including Claire Skinner, Bill Bailey, Alexander Armstrong and David Tennant's former landlady, Arabella Weir. During a break in filming, Matt Smith was enjoying a quiet drink in a hotel in Llanelli when he was somehow persuaded to join a meeting of the town's rotary club. Seriously, would the poor man never be allowed five minutes to himself?

Meanwhile, tabloid skirmish No. 5,422 saw John Barrowman embroiled in a spat over some rather timid gay sex scenes[IX] in *Torchwood: Miracle Day*. Responding to a complaint about "too much gay content" in the series, Barrowman told *iVillage*: "We kissed, we held each other, we lay on top of each other in bed... and there were lots of complaints about that. Nobody complained that I was shot in the head four times, they were burning people in ovens, that I was stabbed by a mob of 50 people hundreds of times and I was hanging dripping my blood in a pit. So that's what confuses me, because you're not complaining about gay sex, you're complaining about two men kissing."

The BBC declined to comment, probably.

The (Oh) God (That's) Complex

The Shining meets *Crossroads,* with a spooky side plate of *Sapphire and Steel, The God Complex* finds the Doctor checking into a hotel that leaves him wishing he'd read those TripAdvisor reviews more closely. Because, in these rooms, there's a lot more to worry about than the mini-bar prices. Behind each door is a terrifying secret specifically attuned to the phobia of one of the guests – the cue for a series of visually arresting tableaux including a sad clown with a red balloon, a restaurant full of leering ventriloquist's dummies and, in one case, the Weeping Angels. Even the Doctor gets a glimpse of his own darkest fear, peeking through the door of Room 11 (see what they did there?) and remarking: "Of course... who else?" Oh, and did we mention there's also a Minotaur on the prowl around the corridors? (Either that, or there's a stag party in.)

Steven Moffat specifically told Toby Whithouse he wanted a tacky, 80s-style hotel as opposed to a looming Gothic pile, and director Nick Hurran makes great use of the location, his cameras prowling along the miles of migraine-inducing carpet, Kubrick-style, as the luckless guests gradually get picked off one by one. (It's relentlessly grim in that respect: the Doctor spends a lot of time reassuring everyone he'll save them, but ends up having to watch impotently as the hotel bar is turned into a makeshift mortuary.)

Hurran employs all manner of visual trickery to add pace to what could have been a rather stagey chamber piece, using quick-cutting, time-lapse, CCTV and text overlays to create a suitable sense of disorientation, while his framing on the hotel staircase is pure Hitchcock. He's aided by an excellent ensemble cast, most notably Amara Karan as Rita, a nurse who outsmarts just about everyone – until she gets killed, anyway – and is such potential companion material that the Doctor even points it out. David Walliams is also great value as Gibbis, one of a race of mole-like aliens who are so cringingly subservient, their planetary anthem is called "Glory to [Insert Name Here]."

Viewers of a sensitive disposition might want to look away when it comes to The Science Bit, in which it's revealed the hotel is actually a virtual reality prison for the Minotaur (a close cousin of 70s platform-heeled disco bulls the Nimon, apparently) which drifts through space snatching people with belief systems and converting their faith into, er, food for the creature. (Whatever you say, Toby.) Amelia Pond's faith, of course, is in a certain madman with a box, which the Doctor has to break in order to save her; it's such a strong idea, we can overlook the fact it's been used before (in 1989's The Curse of Fenric).

And then the Doctor decides he can't travel with Amy and Rory any more, so he gives them a house and runs off. The End.

Woah, back up a minute: where did that come from? Yes, this is a story in which, despite his empty promises, the Doctor is unable to save people. But even so, after nearly 50 years of jaunting about the universe putting his friends in mortal danger every Saturday teatime, this sudden realisation that travelling with him is a wee bit on the dangerous side feels a bit out of left field – especially as we know full well Amy and Rory will be back for the series finale. And it's not helped by Amy telling the Doctor, "If you bump into my daughter, tell her to visit her old mum sometime". Really? That's all we're going to get? You've lost your baby but you've got a sporty red softop instead, so that's okay?

This dizzying handbrake turn aside, The God Complex is a clever, scary and beautifully made story that, unlike the hotel, earns itself a solid four stars.

There was something of a bucket-of-water-in-the-face moment when overnight viewing figures showed the episode had been outperformed by an edition of All Star Family Fortunes – featuring Trevor Nelson, Cheryl Baker and their respective broods. (So less All Star Family Fortunes than just... Family Fortunes, really.) "Fans Switch Off Doctor Who," was The Sun's stark headline over a story that re-hashed the "is it too complicated?" line yet again. (They'd kick themselves when they realised they'd failed to make a pun out of the episode's title. No such oversight here, you'll notice.) The article also included a tweet from Family Fortunes' toothsome host Vernon Kay, in which he gloated: "Wow! The Time Lord can beat the Daleks but not Family Fortunes! Great!" (It goes without saying that when the final figure came in ten days later, Doctor Who's very respectable 6.77 million amounted to more than a million more than All Star Family Fortunes. But by then, the news cycle had long moved on.)

The Guardian, meanwhile, was slightly late to the party with yet-another article headlined "Has Doctor Who Got Too Complicated?". "I don't think the problem is that Doctor Who has become more complicated," said Toby Whithouse in the piece. "Surely it's the fact that the rest of television has become more simplistic. The themes and plots are no more complex than some classic Who stories. The only problem is, Tom Baker's Doctor wasn't jostling in the schedules against Red or Black?" Or, indeed, Cheryl Baker's nan.

On the whole, fans in the US were spared all these attempts at performing a post-mortem on a perfectly healthy body, as the show continued to deliver unprecedented audiences for BBC America, and Doctor Who began to chip away at the national consciousness to a degree that not even Tom Baker had managed at the height of his PBS-fuelled pomp. The series was regularly referenced on hit sitcom The Big Bang Theory, and now NBC's campus comedy Community introduced viewers to Inspector Spacetime, a fictional long-running British TV show about a time-travelling alien known only as the Inspector, much beloved by obsessive film studies geek Abed. (Yes, so Doctor Who largely got referenced by characters some way along the autism spectrum, but you take it where you can find it, right?)

Back home, Matt Smith made the ultimate sacrifice in the name of his ambassadorial duties by taking a trip to Basingstoke. Yes, I know. The actor was joined by an Ood and Steven Moffat (though not necessarily in that pecking order) to surprise pupils at Oakley Junior School during a special assembly screening of their winning Script to Screen film, in which, gratifyingly for Smith, his Doctor finally gets to meet Albert Einstein. At the end, everyone clapped, and Smith got a gold star for working extra hard at being Doctor Who all week.

From Basingstoke to Colchester, there was a sneaking suspicion the Doctor wasn't making the best use of his unlimited time and space travel pass this week. A sequel to *The Lodger* (*The Lodger II*? *The Lodger Strikes Back*? *Lodge Harder*?), *Closing Time*'s title alludes to the fact it's the Doctor's last day before he must finally face his death on the shores of Utah's Lake Silencio. And also to the fact he spends it working in a shop.

Relatively speaking, it's been 200 years since the events of *The God Complex* and the Doctor (who hasn't changed his clothes – no wonder they call him the Oncoming Storm) drops in on old chums Craig and Sophie as part of his farewell tour. Except Sophie's gone away for the weekend, leaving Craig holding the baby – literally. And as if that wasn't challenging enough, the Doctor discovers some old enemies hiding out in a crashed spaceship beneath a department store – hence the story's working title, *Three Cybermen and a Baby*. (Yes, really.)

If *Closing Time* doesn't *quite* win our hearts in the way *The Lodger* did, it's only because there are more scenes where it deviates from its predecessor's gold-plated Smith/Corden comedy bromance template. Because we could watch that stuff all day – or, at least, you can't help thinking Matt Smith's Doctor trying to interact with normal human beings has enough legs to sustain a full series, sort of like The UNIT era crossed with *Mork and Mindy*; the way he ingratiates himself with his co-workers in the store, all childlike innocence and fumbling intimacy, is adorable. (Should the

Oncoming Storm *be* adorable, do you think? Who cares – he is.)

It's a measure of Smith's impact on the show that they can construct a whole episode around his skills like this. It's hard to imagine the tenth Doctor pulling off working in a toy shop (badge: Here to Help) – a hip second-hand record store maybe, but not toys and small children. ("Why a shop? Why not a nuclear power station?" the Doctor asks at one point – possibly anticipating the question being asked by those old-skool fans who preferred *Doctor Who* when it was set in Magnox reactors, not toy departments, and had less kissing and jokes and stuff.)

Also, brilliant as Tennant was, it's fair to say Smith does the whole "burdened by the weight of so many deaths and departures" shtick a lot more subtly than his predecessor, and it's all the more affecting for it – as showcased in a poignant cameo from Amy and Rory (who, lest we forget, the Time Lord hasn't seen for a full two centuries). And if it's a bit of an unlikely coincidence he should run into them in a Colchester department store, Gareth Roberts covers himself – sort of – by explaining that "coincidence is what the universe does for kicks". So that's okay.

Smith is particularly brilliant when left alone in the nursery with Craig's child. He starts out as Frank Spencer cooing at baby Jessica, before effortlessly shifting gear into universe-weary sadness and resignation. The Doctor is a gear-shift part, and Smith never crunches them. "It was funny," someone remarks of him in this story. "He seemed so happy, but so sad at the same time." Which is spot on, really.

The ending of *Closing Time* is, let's be honest, entirely ridiculous. Having apparently been fully converted into a Cyberman (doesn't that involve, like, cutting out your cerebral cortex and stuff?), Craig somehow manages to reverse the process after hearing baby Alfie's cries over the in-store CCTV system. So yes, love saves the day. Again. And it's a father's love for his son. *Again*. But what the hell, hard sci-fi concepts aren't really what an episode like this is about. And you can't help but admire Roberts' chutzpah in having the Doctor act as his own Greek chorus, cheekily pointing out the resolution is "grossly sentimental and over-simplistic". Besides, simplicity and sentimentality are occupational hazards when, unlike most action series (yes *Torchwood*, we're looking at you), the show's brains-over-brawn advocacy means you can't just solve everything by blowing things up. *Closing Time does* end with something blowing up – the Cyber ship – but it's very deliberately a controlled explosion that keeps the story contained and domestic. Or as contained and domestic as you can get in a story about a Cybermen invasion. Perhaps for this reason, the Cyber presence feels a bit awkwardly grafted on to the wider buddy movie/sitcom, making this even less convincing as a Cyberman story than *The Next Doctor*. But it doesn't really matter because, unlike that particular Christmas turkey, the main event is so funny and winsome and generally – that word again – adorable, it succeeds in distracting you from its shortcomings with the sheer weight of its charm. And, for what it's worth, it's almost certainly the most fun you can have in Colchester on a Saturday night.

Sadly, it was closing time, too, for *Doctor Who Confidential*, with the surprise announcement that the following weekend's instalment of the behind-the-scenes show would be the last. Producer Gillian Seaborne and her crew only found out about the decision in the middle of a night shoot while covering the Christmas special – for a programme that wouldn't now be shown. *The Guardian* claimed the move was down to cost-cutting, while a BBC Three spokeswoman said *Confidential* had "been a great show for BBC Three over the years, but the priority is now to build on original British commissions, unique to the channel." Commissions, since they brought it up – and these are real – such as *Extreme OCD Camp*, *Britain's Worst Teeth* and *Help Me Anthea, I'm Infested*.

The Wedding of River Song: honeymoon cancelled after bride shoots groom dead

Cars fly over London on hot air balloons. Steam trains thunder past the Gherkin. Roman legionaries march down Oxford Street, and pterodactyls swoop on the children in Regent's Park. On the *BBC Breakfast* sofa, Charles Dickens talks up his latest Christmas TV special while, at Buckingham Senate, Emperor Winston Churchill is attended by his physician. Who's a Silurian. And this is all before the titles have even rolled. Either Steven Moffat is pulling out all the stops for the season finale – or someone's forgotten to take their Ritalin shot.

You can't accuse *The Wedding of River Song* of lacking ideas. Or sumptuous visuals. Or moments of jaw-dropping bravado. There are plenty of *other* accusations you can throw at it but, as Steven Moffat has almost certainly never said: one thing at a time.

Told largely in flashback, the story's first act follows the Doctor as he searches for the truth about the Silence, enlisting the help of an unwitting Dalek (rumours of their demise had clearly been exaggerated) a heavily-disguised Mark Gatiss (credited as Rondo Haxton, in tribute to acromegalic B-movie actor Rondo Hatton, whose roles included the Hoxton Creeper in 1944's Sherlock Holmes film *The Pearl of Death*) and black market hustler Dorian Maldovar. Dorian (a wonderfully fruity turn from Simon Becker-Fisher) was first seen in *A Good Man Goes to War*, where he had the misfortune to be amputated from the neck up. Despite this minor setback, he's still alive and kick... well, he's still alive, anyway, in the form of a disembodied head in a box.

This is all about the Doctor raging against the dying of the light – refusing to accept this season's oft-repeated assertion that he's fated to die in Utah because it's a "fixed point in time" and taking the game to the enemy instead. "Time has never laid a glove on me!" he declares defiantly, before having the fight knocked out of him in the most unexpected way: phoning to speak to the Brigadier, he is told by a nurse that his old friend has passed away – Steven Moffat's tribute to the late Nicholas Courtney serving a genuine plot purpose, as well as being achingly poignant in its own right. "It's time," says the Doctor, putting the phone down, defeated at last. "It's time."

Fortunately for him – and us – the women in his life have other ideas. As the Doctor and Churchill are menaced by a huge colony of Silents hanging from the roof – a truly blood-freezing image – a platoon of soldiers enters into the room led by a flame-haired woman sporting an eye-patch (actually an "eye-drive" creating a neural link to constantly remind the wearer about those big creepy bald dudes in the suits[X]) and a big gun.

It's Amelia Pond, who whisks the Doctor off on a night train to Cairo where, inside a pyramid requisitioned by the US government, the Silence are held in flotation tanks – another memorable visual from an episode that's packed with iconic images. There, the Doctor is reunited with River, and implores her to set time back into its groove by finishing the job she started at Lake Silencio. (Because River is the Impossible Astronaut, see? I hope you're all following this.)

As the Silence break out of their watery prisons, and our heroes flee, Amy *finally* addresses the elephant in the room by turning her gun on the captive Madame Kovarian: "You took my baby from me and hurt her," she says. "And now she's all grown up and she's fine, but I'll never see my baby again." When Kovarian sneers that she wouldn't dare kill her and risk disappointing her precious Doctor, Amy re-attaches her prisoner's eye-patch – now turned by the Silence into a deadly weapon – and, over Kovarian's dying screams, coolly tells her: "River Song didn't get it all from you, sweetie."

And now if you'd please be upstanding for the entrance of the bride, as the Doctor takes this moment to make an honest woman of River. She is refusing to touch him, because she knows it will short out the time differential and land them back in Utah, but the Doctor insists, telling her they are "the ground zero of an explosion that will engulf all reality". So they get married – by Rory, on top of a pyramid full of aliens (let's hope it's fully licensed) – and River finally concedes that the Doctor may kiss the bride, thus fulfilling the universe's cosmic destiny and setting time back on the right track. Which would be everyone's idea of a happy ending if the Doctor wasn't... you know, dead.

Except... Except... You'll never believe this. He's not dead! Not really, because it wasn't him! Which is to say, it *was* him by the shores of the lake that day, but he was hiding inside a robot replica of himself. That's right kids, it was the *Teselecta* all along! I bet you never saw that coming, right? Or at least, you wouldn't have done if the *Teselecta*'s first appearance

hadn't been crudely crowbarred into the "previously on *Doctor Who*" recap at the start of the episode, thus kind of giving the whole game away. As River is so fond of saying: Spoilers!

If you're confused about what the hell's going on by this point, believe me you're not alone. So let's take a moment to review the evidence.

For reasons we're not yet entirely privy to, the Silence need to kill the Doctor. In order to achieve this, they came up with a plan. The plan went something like this: create a doppelgänger of Amy and substitute it for the real Amy, keeping the real Amy in captivity until she gives birth to a Time Lord hybrid (that she and Rory, er, instigated while in the TARDIS). Then create a doppelgänger baby and substitute it for the real baby, raising the child and training it to wear a homicidal exoskeleton disguised as an Apollo 11 astronaut suit. Wait a few decades until the next available "fixed point" in time, then kidnap the trained assassin all over again, strap her back inside the homicidal Apollo 11 astronaut suit and stick her at the bottom of a lake – that's right, a lake – until the Doctor arrives. Then kill him. Job done. Sounds so simple when you put it like that, doesn't it?

What is never explained in any of this is *why* it has to be River. If the spacesuit is the one in control, making her shoot the Doctor against her will, surely *anyone* could have done it? In fact, the suit could have done it on its own. In *fact*, why bother with the bloody suit in the first place – let alone going to all that effort of breeding the killer from scratch. Why not just shoot the Doctor, or zap him with one of those Silence lightning bolts or, I don't know, drop a piano on his head or something? And did it even *need* to be a fixed point thingummy in the first place? Presumably not, as they'd already tried bumping him off in 1930s Berlin?

And, since we're on a roll, how exactly did the Doctor and River touching re-set the universe – since it was actually the *Teselecta* she was snogging? And how come everyone is still talking like they really did get married, even though one of them was a robot and it happened *in a deleted timeline*?

And herein lies the rub about this whole series of *Doctor Who*. In the newspapers and on the forums, all the chatter was about whether the show had got "too complicated". But that isn't the problem: complicated's fine, complicated's good, as long as your hard work is rewarded. The problem with this season-long arc isn't that it's complicated – it's that it doesn't make *sense*. At all. There are some terrific stories along the way – the second half is particularly strong – and Matt Smith, Karen Gillan and Arthur Darvill have proved adept at papering over the bits that don't quite work. But the series' dramatic through line – and the frankly cack-handed treatment of Amy and Rory's kidnapped baby – shows that, put under enough pressure, even the most assured writer *Doctor Who*'s probably ever had can get himself into a bit of a fix sometimes.

But hey, onwards and upwards. The ending of *The Wedding of River Song* suggests something of a reboot for the series – and its hero – as the Doctor decides he's just got too big and too noisy, and resolves to slip back into the shadows and let the universe think he's dead. Not that his latest enemies have given up the fight quite yet: "Silence will fall," Dorian warns him, "when a question older than the universe is asked. The question that must never be answered, hidden on plain sight. The question you've been running from your whole life..."

The question? What else but:

Doctor Who?

Joy as most of *The Underwater Menace* remains undiscovered

While fans nursed their wedding hangovers, the time for another goodbye drew near as *The Sarah Jane Adventures* started its fifth, sadly truncated run. In Phil Ford's opener, Sarah finds a baby on her doorstep who has an ability to create power surges. Sky (Sinead Michael) is a member of the alien Fleshkind race, bred by her mother as a weapon in her people's war against the Metalkind – so naturally SJ adopts her into Ealing's most intergalactically diverse family. The second story, also by Ford, sees Clyde subjected to a curse that makes everyone hate him ("Is there an antidote?" asked Piers Morgan, hopefully), and the series draws to a premature close with Gareth Roberts' *The Man Who Never Was*. A pulpy tale about an alien race's attempt to brainwash TV

viewers with a mind beam, it's not one of Roberts' better scripts, and certainly not the ending Russell T Davies and company would have envisaged in better circumstances. But a closing montage of highlights from all five series of *The Sarah Jane Adventures*, as well as Sarah's travels with the Doctor, can't help but bring a lump to the throat, and makes for a fitting farewell to a much-loved TV icon.

In the *Radio Times*, Sladen's daughter, Sadie Miller, talked movingly about her mother, and the comfort the family had taken from the outpouring of affection that had followed her death.

To cheer everyone up, *The Observer* came straight out and asked "Is time up for *Doctor Who*?". Bizarrely, this took the form of a "debate" between two self-confessed fans – *The New Statesmen*'s Helen Lewis-Hasteley and Andrew Harrison from *The Word* magazine – neither of whom seemed in any real danger of justifying the headline question. "When you look at the figures, the idea that *Doctor Who* is fading just doesn't stand up," said Harrison. "This season averaged about 7.5m viewers (a little down on David Tennant in his rock-star pomp, but hardly a collapse) and between 1.5m and 2m people watch it on time shift. In September, four out of the five most-requested shows on iPlayer were episodes of *Doctor Who*. These are figures that TV executives dream of."

So that's an end to that, then. Oh no, my mistake, here's Five Live's Tony Livesey hosting another debate, "Have you had enough of *Doctor Who*?" For which Andrew Harrison – shortly to be appointed editor of rock bible *Q* – once again stepped up to defend the show's honour, while Andrea Mullaney, TV editor of *The Scotsman*, acted for the prosecution, claiming the stories had got too (wait for it) complicated.

Steven Moffat addressed the issue head-on in the second *Brilliant Book of Doctor Who*, published that autumn. "To be honest, I was a bit nervous because I know my own love of Byzantine complexity," he admitted. "I worry that I do it too much. I have to keep pulling myself back. But it's worked. I don't know if it would have worked even two or three years ago. When *Doctor Who* came back, in a series that now probably seems to us all quite simple, it was the only fantasy show around. People had to get used to the grammar of it. Now, having paved the way for other shows, *Doctor Who* has to stay out in front. It has to be the show that makes people go, 'Woah, what's going on?' I like it when people say that. When people say, 'I had to talk to my kids' or 'my kids had to talk to me about what was going on', I'm thinking, 'Why is that bad? Show me why that's wrong.'"[25]

Moffat was similarly defiant in an interview in October's *SFX*, telling the magazine: "Feedback about it being too complicated doesn't exist in our audience research at all. Not one piece of it. Nothing."

Under forensic interrogation by Nick Setchfield, Moffat admitted to being at the centre of "a very, very small press siege", but insisted: "So long as the press are printing stories about us, we're clearly okay. Even if they're printing stories about our ratings supposedly falling. The day we know our ratings really are falling is the day they don't bother to run that story."

Setchfield also pressed the producer on the truth behind those "less *Who* in 2012" stories. "The truth behind the delay next year is: why are we killing ourselves, and risking compromising the show, in order to go out in the middle of summer?" said Moffat. "I'm sick of it. I'm sick of standing in the blazing sunshine with a barbecue fork in my hand, knowing that *Doctor Who* is coming on any minute. While our catch-up performance and iPlayer performance are extraordinary, they do suggest that *Doctor Who* isn't on at the time people want it to be."

So *Sherlock* wasn't being favoured over *Doctor Who*?

"Of course not," Moffat insisted. "We're making three more episodes of *Sherlock*, and 14 more episodes of *Doctor Who*. You do the math.... If people are saying 'Steven Moffat is a bit tired', I don't mind, because my reply would always be, 'Well you go and have two hit shows and see what it's like!'"[23]

In mid-October, Matt Smith clocked up some more air miles when he returned to the US to accept the trophy for Best Science Fiction Actor at the Spike TV Scream Awards at Universal Studios, beating off competition from fellow nominees Harrison Ford and Daniel Craig. So *Doctor Who* was now officially

better than Indiana Jones and James Bond. Just sayin'. Smith told VH1: "I've got another year of *Doctor Who,* but then I'm certainly going to give [America] a shot. I'd love to hang out in LA." Insert your own "Doctor Who Quits for Hollywood Career" headline here; the British tabloids certainly did.

As Karen Gillan started a well-received run in John Osborne's *Inadmissible Evidence* at the Donmar Theatre, Steven Moffat donned a tin hat and ventured out to attend the premiere of the Tintin film he'd written several hundred years earlier. Asked about the cancellation of *Doctor Who Confidential*, Moffat admitted he found the decision a bit baffling, leading to the inevitable *Sun* headline: "*Doctor Who* Chief Blasts the BBC". From now on, maybe he should just pretend to have lost his voice? Moffat did break ranks in his Production Notes column for *Doctor Who Magazine*, though, writing: "[It] seems hard to grasp. All shows have their time, and all shows end, but not, in all sanity, while people still watch and love them. I'm not supposed to say it, but I'm going to anyway: bad day, bad decision."

If he thought that was a bad decision, we can only imagine his reaction when he saw the report in that week's *Variety* that Harry Potter director David Yates was working with Jane Tranter and BBC Worldwide on a *Doctor Who* movie, which sources claimed would be a reboot with a new, Hollywood-friendly Doctor. (Actually we don't need to imagine his reaction – stay tuned, folks.)

On November 19th, *Doctor Who*'s traditional contribution to *Children in Need* saw the Time Lord auctioning the shirt off his back – as well as the rest of his costume, as his holographic clothes disappeared one-by-one, leaving a very sporting Matt Smith wearing little more than a pair of braces and a shocked expression. The eleventh Doctor's outfit eventually sold for an astonishing £50,000 – one of the highest bids ever received in a *Children in Need* auction.

The following day, *Doctor Who*'s executive producer and head writer celebrated his 50th birthday by hosting a party at his home attended by a trio of Time Lords: Matt Smith, David Tennant and Peter Davison. He may have had a few uncomfortable moments this year but, at the end of the day, how many fans got to stage their own personal version of *The Three*

Doctors, complete with wine and nibbles? (Imagine having three Doctor Who's queuing to use your loo, though: "I'd go forward in time five minutes if I were you.")

Throwing himself into another energetic round of publicity – this time for the Series Six box set – Matt Smith told BBC Breakfast: "I saw David on Saturday [at the party]. I was like, 'It's Doctor Who!' I saw Peter Davison as well. Steven was very excited that there was more than one Doctor there. And I can't help but go, 'Oh my God. It's Doctor Who!' But then I realise I'm the Doctor." So if you ever hear Matt Smith suddenly shout "Oh my God. It's Doctor Who!", you know he's either met one of his predecessors – or he's caught a glimpse of his reflection in a shop window.

Special features on the DVD set included a series of five specially-recorded scenes under the umbrella heading Night and the Doctor, which revealed, among other things, the Doctor and River sneaking off to have adventures while Amy and Rory were in bed. As well as Matt Smith, Karen Gillan and Alex Kingston, there is also a scene featuring James Corden and Daisy Haggard, while the Queen of England is played by a goldfish. Long story.

The Sun managed to squeeze one final Doctor Who-related rumpus into the year when it ran a story claiming £50,000 had already been spent on the Christmas edition of Confidential before it got canned. The BBC insisted all material would be used – though not necessarily on yer actual telly.

Put on the spot by MTV at a BAFTA event in LA, David Yates said the proposed Doctor Who movie was still "a long way away". "To clarify," said Steven Moffat on Twitter, "any Doctor Who movie would be made by the BBC team, star the current TV Doctor and certainly not be a Hollywood reboot. David Yates, great director, was speaking off the cuff, on a red carpet. You've seen the rubbish I talk when I'm cornered."

And besides, talk of scheduling and Hollywood re-boots would have to take second place to the month's big news: the discovery of two previously lost episodes of Doctor Who, recovered from a private collector who had apparently bought them at a school fete in Southampton in the 1980s. Like you do. Sadly, neither episode was exactly a classic – episode two of The Underwater Menace does little to restore that particular serial's benighted reputation, while "Air Lock", from 1965 season opener Galaxy Four, is mainly of interest to that special interest group who've long been kept awake at night wondering what the Rills looked like. (Like a warthog made for a primary school art project, since you ask.) Nevertheless, every find that chipped away at those gaps in the archive was welcome, and the episodes received a rapturous reception when they were unveiled at the BFI's Missing Believed Wiped event (even though, technically, they were now neither).

Interviewing Matt Smith in The Observer, Euan Ferguson applauded the actor for pulling off "the near impossible and not being in any way a disappointing follow-on to David Tennant". Smith once again stressed how much he'd fallen in love with the show, and the character. "I just like him," he said. "His lack of cynicism. He's like a baby. He wants to sniff, to taste, everything... If he had a bath, it would be filled with rubber ducks which could talk or something. He'd find a way to reinvent the common bath. And I admire that."

Joining Smith on Richard Bacon's Five Live show to talk up the Christmas show, Steven Moffat was cagey about his exact plans for the 50th anniversary, but promised: "You will not be short of material." Afterwards, Bacon chaired a Q&A at a press screening of the episode at Television Centre which, much to the horror of Doctor Who fans, among others, was in the process of being sold off as part of a plan to close a £2 billion black hole in the BBC's finances. The screening took place in TC1, where no fewer than 30 Doctor Who stories had been taped, from The Wheel in Space to Dragonfire. Among the audience was the chancellor, George Osborne.[XI] Maybe they were hoping to tap him up for the missing £2 billion on the way out.

Moffat used the occasion to make a big announcement: "Amy and Rory will be re-joining us next year and joining the Doctor back on the TARDIS," he declared. "But," – and it was a big but – "the final days of the Ponds are coming. It's during the next series – I'm not telling you when and I'm certainly not telling you how. But that story is going to come to a heartbreaking end." Oh, and Merry Christmas everyone.

In fact, the search for the next companion was already under way, with Caro Skinner and Andy Pryor seeing around 45 actresses, who were apparently auditioning for a show called *Men on Waves* – an anagram of Woman Seven. So expect to see a spin-off starring John Barrowman as the head of an elite foo-fighting, all-male Californian surf team any day soon.

Throughout December, Matt Smith and Karen Gillan could be seen regularly on BBC One sporting garish Christmas jumpers while playing Twister with a Cyberman. Sadly, this wasn't a clip from the upcoming special, but their contribution to the channel's star-packed festive trail. (Note to Cyber strategists, though: you might not be able to defeat the Daleks in battle, but you'd definitely kick their arses at Twister.)

In Christmas week, it was announced that *Crash of the Elysium* would be revived as part of the following year's London 2012 Festival celebrating the Olympics. Which was obviously a huge honour, even if, instead of the Olympic Stadium, it would be staged in a car park. In Ipswich.

Once again, the *Who* regulars returned to their home towns to watch the Christmas special with their families, while Arabella Weir watched it at David Tennant's house, where eight-month-old Olive was enjoying her first Christmas with daddy (Doctor Who), granddad (Doctor Who) and mummy (Doctor Who's daughter, and wife). Modern families are complicated.

The Doctor, the Widow and the Wardrobe: not as scandalous as it sounds

After the previous year's Dickens homage, no prizes for guessing the literary inspiration behind *The Doctor, the Widow and the Wardrobe*, in which our hero tries to save Christmas for a wartime widow and her two children, by way of a trip through a magic portal to a snowbound, fairytale kingdom.

When Madge Arwell (Claire Skinner) rescues the Doctor after a fight with an exploding spaceship, he asks her to let him know any time he can return the favour. Three years later, when she receives a telegram stating that her husband's plane has been lost over the Channel (Alexander Armstrong looking right at home in his RAF flight suit after several series of Armstrong and Miller's "chav airmen" sketches), Madge doesn't have the heart to tell her son and daughter their father is dead before the family decamp to a relative's country pile for Christmas.

There they encounter "the Caretaker" – a madman in a bow tie whose efforts to give the children the perfect Christmas include lemonade in the taps, a "sciencey wiencey workbench" and "dolls with comical expressions" – but no beds ("I couldn't fit everything in – there had to be sacrifices"). And under the tree sits the ultimate present: a whole other, Narnia-esque world inside a gift-wrapped box....

Impressive disintegrating spaceship prologue aside, *The Doctor, the Widow and the Wardrobe* is short on high-octane thrills, long on fairytale whimsy and wonder. Matt Smith is simply wonderful in the scenes where he shows the children around the house, demonstrating his handiwork with Wonka-esque glee, while the always-fabulous Skinner proves the perfect foil as the only grown-up in the building.

The CS Lewis influence looms large in the scenes in which our heroes explore the snowy forests of the world inside the box, and it's entirely in keeping with the fairytale aesthetic that the main villains – if you can even call them that – should be a King and Queen carved from wood, adding a touch of Lewis Carroll to the classic children's literature vibe.

Bill Bailey and Arabella Weir's extended comic cameo as a party of tree-harvesters from Androzani Major[XII] (yes – the very same) feels a bit underwritten, but their chunky, *Star Wars*-style walking platform is pretty cool, even if it stretches credibility that a 40s housewife could work out how to drive it. (That would apply equally to 40s househusbands, of course, so don't write in.)

Fans of "serious" sci-fi will no doubt hate the tooth-rottingly saccharine finale, in which trees are transformed into starlight and a mother flies a spaceship through the time vortex – and brings her husband back from the dead into the bargain – using only the Power of Love. (And then, for good measure, the Doctor pays a Christmas Day visit to Amy and Rory, during which he remembers how to cry.) *Doctor Who* has never been so unashamedly sentimental, and you wouldn't want it like this every week. But as a Christmas Day film – complete with snow, stars, fir trees and a little boy lost in the woods in his chequered, Snowman-style dressing gown – it's really rather magical.

With 10.77 million viewers, the episode was the third most-watched festive offering behind twin titans *EastEnders* and *Coronation Street* – and even saw off the seasonal shenanigans at *Downton Abbey*. So *Doctor Who* was clearly in crisis, then.

In the *Daily Telegraph*, Michael Hogan applauded "the kind of broad fairytale fun that unites the generations", while the *Mirror*'s Jim Shelly declared it "not a classic *Doctor Who*, but a good one, and a perfect piece of English whimsy". But Graeme Archer, in a separate *Telegraph* piece, launched a bizarre, abstruse rant headed "I'm sure Harriet Harman enjoyed that *Doctor Who*, but did anyone else?", accusing "Labour supporter Steven Moffat" of using "every trite left wing cliché" in the book. Maybe he just really, really hates wardrobes.

On Boxing Day, Colin Baker – currently appearing in *Jack and the Beanstalk* in Mansfield – took part in a special pantomime-themed edition of the hit reality show *Come Dine With Me*, in which he cooked shoulder of pork for Linda Nolan, Bianca Gascoigne and *Big Brother*'s "Nasty" Nick Bateman. It wasn't his dream job, by any stretch, but he'd done worse. (Did someone just mention *Timelash*?) David Tennant, meanwhile, started the New Year in style by marrying Georgia Moffett at a ceremony at the Globe Theatre attended by Patrick Stewart, Stephen Fry, Derren Brown, David Morrissey and former PM Gordon Brown. ("Didn't you used to be the most powerful man in the country?" asked the other guests. "Oh I don't know about that," said Tennant, with his usual modestly.)

In Cardiff, Steven Moffat was plotting a radical divergence from the previous year's labyrinthine story arcs. Having ascertained from Marcus Wilson that two stand-alone episodes wasn't necessarily any more expensive than a two-parter, he resolved to make every

story in the seventh series a "big, movie-sized idea".

"When we had the pitch meetings for the various stories," Moffat later told the Edinburgh Television Festival, "I would say 'Tell me the movie poster, tell me the title, what's on the poster and what's the log-line... Let's have a blockbuster every single week... Let's not have the cheap episode. Let's just made them *all* huge'."

It had now been decided that the 2012 run would comprise just four episodes instead of the usual 13. ("But hey," said the fans. "We're just grateful to have any *Doctor Who*, at all. It's no biggie." Oh no, my mistake; they went absolutely batshit.) Moffat's plan was to use the mini-season to draw the Pond era to a close, with a new companion joining at Christmas, and the rest of the season following in early 2013.

The showrunner had originally envisaged the Daleks for the Ponds' finale, then decided to use the Weeping Angels in that slot, bumping the Daleks up to the season opener instead. His aim, he said, was to reintroduce fear to the creatures and remind people they were "insane tanks" as well as Plushies your kids took to bed. What's more, to start the series with a bang, he'd cooked up a plan to use Daleks from every era of *Doctor Who* (yes, even those new ones that no-one liked).

Gonzo 2006 actioner *Snakes on a Plane* provided the inspiration for the series' next one-line movie pitch idea. Moffat told Chris Chibnall that the does-what-it-says-on-the-tin *Dinosaurs on a Spaceship* should be "big, fun and loud" (if the tone meeting had a key word, it was probably "Barrowman") and make maximum use of the available budget.

For the third story, the team planned to make the first *Doctor Who* Western since 1966's much-unloved *The Gunfighters* had effectively put the kibosh on all historical stories. Caroline Skinner claimed the Doctor in a frontier town was a naturally irresistible idea, but Steven Moffat told *BBC News* he had a different agenda: "Matt Smith on a horse in a proper Western – surely those bandy legs were made for horse-riding? That's why we did it."

When a fifth episode was added to the run, Chibnall was asked to deliver a second script at short notice. The writer agreed, even though he'd just been commissioned to create a major new crime drama for ITV. The finale, meanwhile, would be set in New York, Steven Moffat having decided it was the perfect backdrop to Amy and Rory's farewell while trapped with his family in a diner there during a blizzard in early 2011. So don't be surprised to see the Ponds written out after suffering Death by Chocolate.

In mid-January, Matt Smith appeared as the Doctor on *Blue Peter* asking for ideas for a new Script to Screen competition, this time with an Olympic theme. The Doctor broadcast his message from the Land of Fiction, much to the delight of all those eight-year-old fans of 1968's *The Mind Robber*.

The New Year also saw Tom Baker making his debut for Big Finish in a series of adventures for the fourth Doctor and Leela. Producer David Richardson said he wanted recreate the spirit of 1977 – though, thankfully, that didn't include Baker being an utter shit to Louise Jameson.

In other product news, BBC Books announced the latest addition to its roster of *Doctor Who* novelists in the form of chick-lit author Jenny Colgan. Despite her previous bestsellers including such titles as *Do You Remember the First Time?*, *Where have All the Boys Gone?* and *Amanda's Wedding*, Colgan insisted her eleventh Doctor adventure, *Dark Horizons*, would be "proper" science fiction (apart, of course, from that bit where Amy gets a job in a publishing company, and has to take a working trip to Milan with the arrogant but dangerously handsome head of marketing).

As awards season began cranking into gear, *Doctor Who* got off to a flying start, winning five categories in the Virgin Media TV Awards, including TV Show of the Year, and well-deserved recognition for Arthur Darvill, as Rory was named TV Character of the Year (in your face, Sooty!). Karen Gillan won twice – once for being a good actress and once for being "hot" – while Matt Smith was a runner-up in *Zoo* magazine's Britain's Coolest Man poll, eventually losing out to John Levene (not really – it was street magician Dynamo).

And then the biggie: after leaving empty-handed last year, Smith and Gillan both triumphed at the National Television Awards at London's O2 Arena. Smith beat off competi-

tion from John Barrowman, Martin Clunes and David Threlfall to scoop the award for Outstanding Drama Performance (Male), while Gillan's success in the equivalent female category came at the expense of Eve Myles, Suranne Jones and Jaye Jacobs from *Waterloo Road* (whatever *that* is). The show itself lost out in the race for Most Popular Drama to *Downton Abbey*. Typical bloody aristocratic sense of entitlement.

Speaking afterwards, Smith told *Radio Times* he had "one more year of *Doctor Who* left", after which he wanted to try his luck in Hollywood. Shortly afterwards, he clarified to *BBC News* that he had no plans to leave.

Gillan, meanwhile, used both her award-winning acting and hotness skills to good effect in *We'll Take Manhattan*, a BBC Four film about 60s supermodel Jean Shrimpton's relationship with photographer David Bailey. As part of the project, Gillan undertook a photo shoot for *Vogue* with the real Bailey, where she found his challenging reputation was no exaggeration. "He's a funny one," she told *Radio Times*. "He plays mind games to provoke his subjects. He seems to build up your confidence, but then knock it back down again. He kept on saying to me, 'You're pretty, but pretty girls are like red buses'."[26] (When they heard, Steven Moffat and Matt Smith sympathised with their co-star over this rather glib assertion that there'll always be another pretty girl along in a minute. Then they had to leave for Television Centre, where they had loads of pretty girls lined up to audition as Woman Seven.)

Fort Apache: You've had some right cowboys in here

This time, the try-outs for the new *Doctor Who* companion were such a cloak-and-dagger affair, they took part in a basement, to ensure absolutely no-one would get a whiff of what was going on. At least, that was the plan. "We did the auditions down in the bowels of the BBC," Matt Smith told *Radio Times*. "It was meant to be top secret – which was ridiculous, because we'd been going for about four hours when we heard a cough behind a partition. And there was this security guard with his feet up."[27]

As work got under way on *Dinosaurs on a Spaceship* – the first story of the 2012 series to go before the cameras – Smith told the BBC it was "thrilling and exciting to be back and working with two of my closest friends". The story itself involved the construction of the largest set ever built for *Doctor Who*. Naturally, it was a corridor. A really, *really* big corridor. Also on-set was a full-size triceratops, known to all as "Tricey", which Matt Smith was required to ride like a horse – with the aid of padded underpants ("It wasn't great on the goolies," the actor admitted to the BBC's *Doctor Who* website).

Chris Chibnall had also been asked to write in a pair of robots, after the producers were offered the use of a couple that had been created for a 2010 CBBC show. (Since the show had been cancelled, the robots had experienced trouble finding work, and been spending their days hanging round the BBC bar getting lubricated.)

At the end of February, Matt Smith became the third – and fastest – Doctor to drive a test lap for *Top Gear*, powering a Kia Cee'd around the track in 1:43:7 – putting him just above Tom "Days of Thunder" Cruise on the leaderboard. A few days later, the cast received the script for the 2012 series finale, *The Angels Take Manhattan* – which Karen Gillan refused to look at, later claiming to be in "some weird form of denial". After two weeks, Matt Smith and Arthur Darvill eventually persuaded her to read it, arguing it would probably help her with saying the lines.

By that time, cast and crew had decamped to Spain to film Toby Whithouse's cowboy caper at Fort Apache in Mini Hollywood, Almeria. Constructed in 1965 for Sergio Leone's original Spaghetti Western, *For a Few Dollars More*, the lot had been purchased by extras who'd worked on the film and its follow-up, *The Good, The Bad and the Ugly*, and was now operated as a theme park. ("Yee-Who: *Doctor Who* Films Wild West Special on *The Magnificent Seven* Set' claimed *The Sun*, proving their fact-checking was as poor as their puns.) Recording also took place at another disused set, Fort Bravo, which had been bought by Clint Eastwood's stunt double (that was *The Fall Guy*, surely?).

The cast included Ben Browder, famous for his recurring roles in sci-fi staples *Farscape* and *Stargate SG-1*. The actor, who had trained in England and was married to an English actress, was so keen to be in *Doctor Who* that he flew in from LA for the job, even though it was the middle of pilot season. Also on the call sheet was Garrick Hagon – who was unrecognisable from his last significant *Who* role as Ky the giant insect in *The Mutants*. Then again, it *was* 40 years ago.

Inspired by a book he'd been reading about the making of *The Empire Strikes Back* in Norway, Marcus Wilson realised that the Spanish location was only a couple of hours away from the snow resorts of the Sierra Nevada mountain range, which would be perfect for scenes in the Dalek opener. Director Nick Hurran and his director of photography flew out with the cast for a couple of days "guerilla filming" at short notice, while Wilson stopped to pick up a Dalek eyestalk during a flying visit back to Cardiff. I'd like to have seen him explaining *that* at Customs.

On March 12th, BBC Worldwide unveiled its "massively multiplayer" online *Doctor Who* game *Worlds in Time*. Robert Nashak (Executive Vice President, Digital Entertainment and Games) said the game offered players "a multitude of elements and opportunities to socialise – from introducing beloved characters and progressive storylines to presenting additional guild play". ("Can you explain what 'guild play' means?" asked the non-gamers. "Can you explain what 'socialise' means?" asked the gamers.)

The same day saw the official opening of BBC Wales' shiny new media village at Roath Lock in Cardiff Bay – the main walkway of which had been named Russell T Davies Alley, in honour of the former showrunner. And for anyone expecting a filthy joke at this point – shame on you. (That comes later.)

The week also saw the publication of Douglas Adams' legendary lost story, *Shada*, in the form of a novel by Gareth Roberts. "The BBC have been asking us for years," explained Ed Victor, literary agent for the Adams estate, "and the estate finally said: 'Why not?'"

But the really hot news for March was that, after all the whispered conversations, coded messages and fevered arguments over shortlists in smoke-filled rooms, the biggest secret in *Doctor Who* was finally revealed: the winner of the 2012 Script to Screen competition was Ashdene Primary School in Wilmslow, Cheshire. And, in other news, Jenna-Louise Coleman was the new companion.

New *Who* girl dumped me for the Doctor, says heartbroken avocado

Unveiled to the media on March 21st, the Doctor's latest sidekick was already well-known to TV viewers, having played – the tabloids delighted in reminding us – Teenage Lesbian™ Jasmine Thomas in *Emmerdale*, and class hardnut Lindsay James in (whisper it) *Waterloo Road*.

"I'm beyond excited," beamed the Blackpool-born 25-year-old. "I can't wait to get cracking; working alongside Matt I know is going to be enormous fun and a huge adventure."

"It always seems impossible when you start casting these parts, but when we saw Matt and Jenna together, we knew we had our girl," said Steven Moffat. "She's funny and clever and exactly mad enough to step on board the TARDIS. It's not often the Doctor meets someone who can talk even faster than he does, but it's about to happen. Jenna is going to lead him his merriest dance yet. And that's all you're getting for now. Who she's playing, how the Doctor meets her, and even where he finds her, are all part of one of the biggest mysteries the Time Lord ever encounters. Even by the Doctor's standards, this isn't your usual boy meets girl."

Coleman told the press conference *Doctor Who* was "her grandma's favourite show" (*that's* how young *Doctor Who* companions are these days) and, in an interview for *BBC News*, recalled what she'd been doing when she heard she'd got the part: "I was in Marks and Spencer holding an avocado, having the debate of what goes best in a salmon salad, when I got the call from my agent. It was kind of a bewildered, excitement, confusion... All sorts of emotions. After I hung up I thought, I really can't carry on shopping, so I just put the basket down and left M&S and just went for a little walk and tried to digest." (The news, not the avocado – that was history by this point.)

But while Coleman was excited about the journey to come, her predecessor was having trouble letting go, struggling with the read-through for *The Angels Take Manhattan*. "I had my hand on Kazza's back, trying to help her get through it," Arthur Darvill told *Radio Times*, adding. "I didn't want the actors who'd come in for just one episode to think we were really self-indulgent, because we were all crying. It must have been really weird for them."[27]

"To be honest, though, you'd have to be dead inside not to cry at it," added Gillan. "Steven Moffat knows exactly what he's doing when he's tugging on the old heartstrings."[27]

On March 24th, Moffat joined his three leads at the Millennium Centre in Cardiff for the first-ever official *Doctor Who* convention, staged by BBC Worldwide. In total, 3,000 fans attended across the two days, getting the chance to meet the stars and learn behind-the-scenes secrets – if such a thing still existed after six years of *Doctor Who Confidential*.

Down the road at Roath Lock, a Dalek army was assembling as props from across the decades were pressed into service for filming on the series premiere. Among the original and fan-made casings was a *Genesis of the Daleks*-style replica loaned by Russell T Davies. The Dalek had been in Davies' hallway in Manchester for years, and the former show-runner was thrilled that, having now "acted" on screen, his trusty sentry would no longer be a mere copy but an official, canonical Dalek. And, as a memento of the event, a souvenir photo was taken of Davies' Dalek being pushed up his own Alley. (There – happy now?) Steven Moffat also tweeted a picture of Matt Smith and Karen Gillan with a vintage model, declaring that, "After extensive deliberation, THE DOCTOR HAS SPOKEN. Matt Smith likes the 60s Dalek best."

During a trip to London, meanwhile, David Yates was asked about the state of the proposed *Doctor Who* movie. "Yes, I'm definitely doing a *Doctor Who* movie," he told *Bleedin' Cool*, "but I think where everyone got confused was that we're not making it for five years, or six years – it's a very slow development."

Of the current, Steven Moffat-helmed show, Yates added: "Steven's a genius. I love his work, I think he's incredibly clever. I love what he's done with *Doctor Who*, love his Sherlock Holmes. He's such a gifted man. But this is something that's a very slow burn and I'm hoping to sit down with him at some point and have a chat. It's just something that we've been talking about for a little while... But I'm very excited about it, very excited about that world." So there you have it, folks: watch this space. For at least six years.

While Yates was reigniting the discussion about whether *Doctor Who* should ever go to Hollywood, the Time Lord had already arrived Stateside to record *The Angels Take Manhattan* – which, unusually, was actually being filmed where it was set.

The first day's shoot brought the three regulars to Central Park, where large crowds – and no small amount of paparazzi – gathered to watch. Gratifying though this was, it proved something of a struggle for Matt Smith, who had to film a particularly intense scene in which he reads a final goodbye message from Amy Pond. Karen Gillan had made a promise to her friend to read the passage aloud off-camera – whether she was required on set that day or not. In the end, she had to make sure she did it without anyone overhearing, while the page in the book the Doctor was supposed to be reading was replaced with a dummy page in case anyone tried to photograph it.

Smith prepared as best he could, listening to Pavarotti's *Nessun Dorma* to help him find the right emotional space, then proceeded to record one of the most intimate and personal scenes of his career, in front of an audience of hundreds.

"This was *Doctor Who!*" boggled Steven Moffat. "The show I'd grown up with, the show I'd loved all my life, and here it was, for two nights in New York, surrounded by screaming crowds. Think about that for a moment. Who'd have thought this could happen? Remember that long, 15-year gap when our show disappeared? If you'd been told about this in those long, dreary years, would you have believed a word? *Doctor Who* didn't just come back, it came back huge. And, miracle of miracles, it just keeps getting *bigger*."[28]

By the time filming moved to a night shoot at 30s skyscraper Tudor City, word-of-mouth had caused the crowd to swell even bigger. "I knew we'd get a degree of attention," said Moffat. "But when we rocked up outside Tudor City and turned the corner to find a thousand

people waiting for us... Even the Americans, who are used to crowds turning up for Julia Roberts or whoever, were taken aback."[28]

Smith, Gillan and Arthur Darvill went out to sign autographs – and to ask the crowd to keep quiet during filming. "One of the oddest days of my life," concluded Darvill.

Not that the stars necessarily minded the attention. In fact, Smith later admitted he and Gillan had visited a *Doctor Who*-themed bar in the city. "It shows the appalling limits of our vanity that we wanted to go to a *Doctor Who* bar," the actor told the *Daily Mail*. "But our curiosity got the better of us. You could have heard a pin drop when we strolled in." It's one way of getting a free drink, I guess.

Back home, Colin Baker made further inroads into reality TV with a guest appearance on *Get Your House in Order*, in which he attempted to help obsessive hoarder Barry Phillips offload some of his extensive collection of *Doctor Who* memorabilia. Phillips had so much *Who* merchandise in his house, he had nowhere left to eat his dinner. But hey, who needs food when you've got a mint condition LP of *Doctor Who and the Pescatons*?

"It's such an honour to share this stage with so many of my illustrious successors. (Security, can we get these people removed?)"

Though scheduled fourth in the run, Chris Chibnall's second Series Seven script – fittingly titled *The Power of Three* – would be the last story to be recorded by the long-established team of Smith, Gillan and Darvill. Along for the ride was Jemma Redgrave as Kate Stewart – who had dropped the "Lethbridge" from her name before going into the family business of running UNIT. Chibnall devised the character as a tribute to Nicholas Courtney, unaware – or so he claimed – that the Brig's daughter had previously appeared in various video and book spin-offs under that very name (Kate, not Nicholas). While filming on the story continued, Matt Smith and Karen Gillan took time out to tape the winning Script to Screen entry, *Good as Gold*, in which the TARDIS is invaded by an Olympic athlete being chased by a

Weeping Angel. Team GB's training methods had obviously got a *lot* more hardcore in recent years.

May 10th marked the final scenes to be filmed at Upper Boat, *Doctor Who's* home for the past five years, while the following day brought a more significant departure: the last day of the Ponds had arrived. "Me and smith dawg. Wandering around set all nostalgic. It's a special day," tweeted Karen Gillan. "@RattyBurvil get on set."

In a corner of a Welsh hospital[XIII] dressed to look like a suburban garden, Gillan and Ratty Burvil... sorry, Arthur Darvill prepared at 7:30 pm to record their final scene which, more by luck than judgement, just happened to be the Doctor, Amy and Rory piling into the TARDIS, and closing the door behind them.

"It was a weird, serene day where everyone was feeling it," said Gillan during an appearance at the Cannes Film Festival. "Matt closed the door for the last time and we were in darkness. We hugged and started crying. It was kind of tears of happiness. It was a feeling of, 'Look what we've done'. It was lovely."

At the golden wrap, Steven Moffat gave a speech and presented his departing stars with gifts – specifically, giant portraits of themselves. "It's awkward," said Gillan, "because I don't know what to do with it. It kind of dominates a room."[27] And tricky to re-gift, too.

At the BAFTA Television Craft Awards, Steven Moffat received another Writer trophy to place alongside the one for *Blink* – except this time it was for the other woman in his life (the *Sherlock* episode *A Scandal in Belgravia*) – while BBC Worldwide served up yet another *Doctor Who* game into an increasingly crowded marketplace: featuring performances by Matt Smith and Alex Kingston, *The Eternity Clock*, released for PC and Playstation, met with poor reviews by gamers, who claimed it had more bugs than *The Web Planet*.

May 22nd marked the first day of filming on "Series 7B"[XIV], with Jenna Louise-Coleman making her debut in front of the cameras as the Doctor's as-yet unnamed new companion (though, as it turned out, it wasn't *quite* the first day in the office many assumed it to be...). Meanwhile, as part of the build up to London 2012, an Olympic Torch Relay was currently making its way around Britain, bringing the flame of hope and courage and, you know, *whatever* to towns and cities across the UK. As well as local community champions, high-profile celebrities were being drafted in to give the parade a bit of TV glamour – which is how that notable West Country son of the soil will.i.am came to be running through Taunton in Somerset one Monday afternoon – and Matt Smith was drafted in to do the honours for the Cardiff leg. (This despite an apparently serious campaign by some *Who* fans for David Tennant to do it, in costume as the tenth Doctor, in a bewildering attempt to bring some sort of narrative legitimacy to 2006's *Fear Her*.)

"It's a great privilege to be involved," said Smith, as thousands gathered to see his early morning run through Cardiff Bay. "I can't quite believe that people have actually turned up – I thought I'd just be carrying it around, waving to the ducks!

"It's one of those once-in-a-lifetime things, and for me personally to have the privilege of carrying it... It's one of those rare opportunities that has nothing to do with me and everything to do with the fact that I play the Doctor." More surprisingly, he even managed not to drop it.

At the weekend's BAFTA Television Awards, Steven Moffat was the recipient of that year's Special Award. "Steven has had an outstanding year with *Doctor Who* and *Sherlock*, not to mention the feature film *The Adventures of Tintin*, and we are delighted to honour his contribution to television and the arts," said BAFTA chairman Tim Corrie. "He is one of the finest exponents of his craft and his award, presented in honour of the late, great Dennis Potter, is very well deserved indeed."

The award, previously won by Russell T Davies in 2005, was presented to Moffat on stage at the Royal Festival Hall by the fanboy dream team of Matt Smith and Benedict Cumberbatch. Smith – himself flush with the success of having just been named Favourite Doctor in *Doctor Who Magazine's* annual readers' poll – told the audience that Moffat's scripts, though usually late, were "brilliant". "But impossible to learn," added Cumberbatch, drily.

"That's Sherlock Holmes and Doctor Who

– giving me an award," beamed Moffat. "That is absolutely brilliant!"

A week later, the slightly less glamorous surroundings of a football stadium in Milton Keynes was the location for a no-less seismic team-up as, for the first time, the fourth, fifth, sixth, seventh and eighth Doctors appeared on stage together, at a sci-fi signing event.

Asked what it was like having the Doctor as a son-in-law, Peter Davison admitted: "I'm waiting for him to call me dad. I asked my grandson, 'Who's your favourite Doctor?'", he added, "and he said 'David Tennant' and I said 'Who's your second favourite Doctor?' and he said 'Tom Baker'. So I said: 'Who's your third favourite Doctor?' and he thought about it and said 'I haven't got a third favourite'."

Speaking a few days later, Colin Baker credited the "clever" (i.e. devious) organisers with getting all the Doctors in the same room. "Tom didn't realise until he got there, otherwise I think he might have feigned a diplomatic illness!" Baker told the *Cambridge News*. "He's a bit of a loose cannon. But I think he's mellowed over the years. He was very entertaining, certainly."

Baker suggested that, while there was a certain esprit de corps among the ex-Time Lord's club, they didn't necessarily find strength in numbers. "I don't think we're actually competitive," he said. "What it is – and I think this is true of all of us – we find it easier when we're on our own. Because when you're answering questions and there are five of you there, some people are a bit self-effacing, others are not, some want to share it out, others don't; it's tricky striking a balance. So basically we all sat back and let Tom talk, really. It's easier!"

Sadly, on June 5th, the *Who* family lost another much-loved member when Caroline John – aka Cambridge's leggiest physicist, Liz Shaw – died of cancer at the age of 71. Colin Baker was among the stars who paid tribute to the "lovely, talented, wise and gentle" actress, who was survived by her husband, one-time Master actor Geoffrey Beevers, and their three children.

After years keeping a low profile and raising her family, John had been persuaded to join the *Doctor Who* convention circuit in the early 90s, where she'd been overwhelmed to discover the affection she was held in, and belat-edly came to realise her performance in the show wasn't the disaster she'd somehow convinced herself it was. "When I saw [*Doctor Who and*] *the Silurians*," she said after viewing her sophomore serial for the first time in more than two decades, "I thought, 'Well they were bloody lucky to get me!'" And they were.

Less than a month after leaving *Doctor Who*, Karen Gillan and Arthur Darvill were back in character to record a series of prequels, called *Pond Life*, for the new series. The pair were also contracted to film pick-up shots for the series proper, including new dialogue for a substantial rewrite of the end of *The Power of Three*, and additional work on their final scene in *The Angels Take Manhattan*. So it's probably just as well they hadn't been rude about anyone in their leaving speeches. Gillan was also named Fashion Icon of the Year at the 2012 Scottish Fashion Awards, beating off stiff competition from Calvin Harris, Emeli Sande, Gerard Butler, Tilda Swinton and Edie McCredie from *Balamory*[XV]. Meanwhile, John Barrowman kept the boys' end up by being voted Britain's Rear of the Year. "I'm sorry, but I think objectifying my body in this way fatally compromises my integrity as a performer," is what he almost certainly didn't say.

On Twitter, the BBC announced that Dame Diana Rigg and her daughter Rachael Stirling were to appear on screen together for the first time in a Mark Gatiss-penned *Doctor Who* adventure to be broadcast in 2013.

Gatiss had appeared with Rigg in *All About My Mother* at the Old Vic in 2007, and five years later was starring alongside Stirling in *The Recruiting Officer* at the Donmar Warehouse. The three of them went out to dinner, and the next day Stirling was explaining how she and her mother had received lots of offers to work together, but had never found the right project. "Well a little devil got into me," said Gatiss. "I said, 'Do you think your mum would do a *Doctor Who*, if I wrote it for her? For you both?' Rachael went 'Oh f*** yes!'."[29]

The BBC revealed that the pair would play "a mother and daughter with a dark secret" in the Yorkshire-set story, which would begin filming the following week in the same production block as the 2012 Christmas special, with which it would share some cast members.

Arriving in Cardiff for a considerably longer

engagement, meanwhile, was the *Doctor Who Experience*, which transferred from London to new, purpose-built premises in the Welsh capital, where it was expected to remain for at least five years. The success of the interactive adventure was just one of the ways in which *Doctor Who* helped BBC Worldwide report an 8% profit increase in 2012, with *Torchwood* also listed among the top-selling brands, having achieved success in more than 100 markets. *Doctor Who* also helped BBC America achieve its highest-ever ratings, according to Worldwide's annual report, with Series Six setting new records for the channel. And the show's global reach was never more in evidence than during July's annual pilgrimage to the Geek Mecca that is Comic-Con, where Matt Smith, Karen Gillan and Arthur Darvill wowed the crowds with an impromptu rendition of "Bohemian Rhapsody," before joining Steven Moffat and Caro Skinner for a panel in front of 6,500 – count 'em! – fans. Imagine Question Time taking place at Madison Square Gardens, and you'll get some idea of just how mad this is. While Gillan and Darvill talked up their imminent departure, Smith reiterated his love for Patrick Troughton, and said his dream episode would be one in which their Doctors met (sort of like 1985's *The Two Doctors*, but less shit).

Another sign of the show's increasing US traction was its appearance on the cover of *Entertainment Weekly* – with an estimated readership of 8.2 million, by far the country's most popular entertainment magazine. Its cover story, "How a British Sci-fi Series Became a Global Geek Obsession," examined the *Who* phenomenon via everything from worldwide ratings to the series' regular shout-outs on shows like *Community*, *Grey's Anatomy* and *The Late Show with Craig Ferguson*.

Back home, Karen Gillan began filming the lead role in romcom *Not Another Happy Ending* – shot, of all places, in the Scottish town of Moffat – while Matt Smith's most recent extra-curricular activity, the feature-length Olympic rowing drama *Bert and Dickie*, was broadcast on BBC One. Then, on July 27th, *Who* fans were left reeling at the news that yet another much-loved companion, Mary Tamm, had died of cancer, aged just 62.

"She was a darling companion and wonder-fully witty and kind," said Tom Baker, who had just finished working with Tamm – albeit, for logistical reasons, in separate studios – on an as-yet unreleased season of adventures for Big Finish. "I'm so sorry to hear of her death."

On Twitter, a "shellshocked" Colin Baker talked warmly of a "funny, caring, talented, lovely and down-to-earth lady", while Anneke Wills recalled "a brave, beautiful woman". "It's an obit every month in *DWM* these days," Paul Cornell lamented, summing up the mood for many. "How terrible." "Another tragedy – what an awful year it's been to be a *Doctor Who* fan," added former *DWM* editor Gary Gillatt. "This terrible silence, slowly rolling over it all."

Tragically, Tamm's husband, Marcus Ringrose, would survive the love of his life by less than a fortnight, collapsing and dying several hours after giving a moving eulogy at her funeral. The cause of death was given as sudden adult death syndrome, with acute emotional stress as the possible trigger. The couple are survived by a daughter, Lauren – and, in Tamm's case, a legacy of one of the most exquisitely-judged companion performances in *Doctor Who* history.

Lack of Doctor Who in opening ceremony ruins Olympics for everybody

Under the title *Isles of Wonder*, Danny Boyle's much-lauded opening ceremony to the London 2012 Olympics was an audacious, idiosyncratic celebration of the best of British, showcasing everything from Brunel and Bond to The Beatles and Mr Bean to a worldwide audience of hundreds of millions. And, if you listened very, very carefully, you might just have heard *Doctor Who*'s contribution: a snatch of the TARDIS materialisation sound during a dance routine to "Bohemian Rhapsody." In the technical rehearsal, a video montage of all 11 Doctors accompanied by Ron Grainer's theme had been included, but was later dropped for timing reasons. Either that, or they'd all failed a drug test.

While the rest of Britain skived off work to watch the Greco-Roman wrestling, photography began on the *Doctor Who* Christmas special at Cardiff's Coal Exchange, with Matt Smith and Jenna-Louise Coleman joined by

Richard E Grant as the guest villain. "I played Doctor Who in the digital animated *Scream of the Shalka*," said Grant, "and I'm honoured to be in the Christmas special." Which was his way of saying: "Yes, I now know what *Doctor Who* is."

Of equal – if not more – excitement to die-hard fans was the announcement that the BBC was to make a special 90-minute drama chronicling the origins of *Doctor Who*, to be broadcast during the show's 50th anniversary year. *An Adventure in Space and Time* – which followed in the footsteps of the Beeb's acclaimed *The Road to Coronation Street* – had been written by Mark Gatiss, who said: "This is the story of how an unlikely set of brilliant people created a true television original. And how an actor – William Hartnell – stereotyped in hard-man roles became a hero to millions of children. I've wanted to tell this story this for more years than I can remember! To make it happen for *Doctor Who*'s 50th birthday is quite simply a dream come true."

More immediately, Steven Moffat had five new adventures to launch. In publicity interviews issued by the BBC, the showrunner spoke of the trauma of saying goodbye to Amy and Rory. "They have been with the Doctor since I took over show – they're part of the landscape for me," he said. "Karen and Arthur have become friends, and I still can't get my head round the fact that I'll never find them on the set again. Brilliant performers and warm and lovely people – the best of the best."

Asked to sum up his departing friends, Matt Smith plumped for "stupid dancing, stupid faces and stupid everything". But he meant it in a nice way. "There were points when we wouldn't even have conversations, but just make noises at each other," he said. "We had a laugh and that really informed the energy and spirit of the show. The relationship between our characters on screen and off screen really blurred."

Smith also revealed that he would often make Gillan scream by hiding in her trailer and jumping out. "She is a real screamer," he added. Let's move on, shall we?

Scheduled to launch on September 1st, the new series was given a primetime 7.20pm slot – a full 80 minutes later than the previous season premiere. And, once again, the Time Lord would find himself going head-to-heads with Ant and Dec's latest ITV vehicle, *Red or Black*?

Though *Who* had a history of besting the Geordie duo, the Doctor did lose one ratings feather in his cap in late August, when it was announced that, after clinging on for more than two years, *The Eleventh Hour* had finally lost its position as the most accessed programme on the BBC iPlayer. Its usurper? The Olympic Opening Ceremony. Clearly a *lot* of people had been desperate to hear that TARDIS noise.

During an appearance at the Edinburgh International Television Festival over the August bank holiday weekend, Steven Moffat was asked about persistent rumours that *Doctor Who*, like the rest of the BBC's drama output, had had its budget slashed from the hay-making days of the Russell T Davies era. "The schedule and the pressure of trying to do *Doctor Who* on any budget – including *Avatar*'s – is horrific," said Moffat, diplomatically. "I am never, ever going to say I've got enough money – that's like asking, 'Would you like to be more happy?' [But] *Doctor Who* is incredibly well looked after by the BBC – they are incredibly aware of its crown jewel status, that it's not merely a show that's successful now. I truly believe it could be a show that outlives everybody in this room. It could carry on that long, so it doesn't just make money now – it'll make money forever. Of course I'd like more money," he added – just in case any BBC accountants were in the audience – "just as I'd like to be happier, thinner and more handsome." A happy, thin and more handsome *Doctor Who* fan from Renfrewshire? He basically wanted to be David Tennant.

Publicity for the new series saw Karen Gillan doing most of the heavy lifting, including a memorable appearance on *The One Show* in which she shared her impression of a Dalek ordering chips and mushy peas, and also revealed that the series wrap party had ended up back at John Barrowman's flat – which is surprising, as he usually prefers a quiet night in. The show also featured Nicholas Briggs using his Dalek voice to terrorise passengers at the railway station and a Tesco store in Slough (twinned with Skaro).

In the *Radio Times*, Gillan revealed she'd

been texting Jenna-Louise Coleman "bits and bobs" about Matt Smith. "What I wrote is a secret," she said. "That's the code of the companion." But presumably some advice about checking the wardrobe when you walk into your trailer would have been useful.

Asylum of the Daleks: You don't have to be mad to work here, but it helps

September 1st – series launch day – saw Matt Smith splashed across the front of the *Daily Mirror* in the latest attempt to extrapolate an "I quit" story from a perfectly innocent remark – in this case, an interview in *Empire* magazine in which Smith admitted he probably wouldn't play the role as long as Tom Baker. The BBC swiftly issued its standard "Doctor Who Quits" Story Rebuttal Statement, and everyone got on with their lives.

Somewhat more creatively, *radiotimes.com* got into the spirit of the occasion with a downloadable Dalek bingo card, designed to help fans tick off every iteration of the metal meanies during the evening's episode ("Two fat paradigm Daleks, 88!" etc).

In *Doctor Who Magazine*, Matt Smith admitted that *Victory of the Daleks* hadn't *quite* been an unalloyed success. "I never felt that we got the Dalek episode right first time round, and I don't think we got the Daleks right," he said. "And I really feel like we have now, so I've fallen in love with them a bit more."[30]

And for the rest of us? The first thing to note about *Asylum of the Daleks* is that anyone tuning in with that bingo card to hand was going to be sorely disappointed. Despite the hype promising "every Dalek ever", any pre-2005 models are reduced to little more than background artists, often deep in shadow and covered in dust and cobwebs (though, on the plus side, the 2010 models don't get much of a look-in, either).

After an attention-grabbing opening inside a giant, Saddam-style stone Dalek effigy on a ravaged Skaro, the Doctor and the Ponds find themselves transported to the Dalek Parliament, where the dishonourable members are having a spot of local difficulty with the Asylum: a planet-sized repository for millions of Daleks so insanely genocidal, they make

your regular Daleks look like the cast of *Rainbow*. To that end, a motion has just been passed to the effect that This House Believes the Dalek Asylum has been Breached and the Doctor and His Companions Ought to Bloody Well Sort It Out for Us. ("You're going to fire me at a planet?" asks the Doctor. "That's your plan? I get fired at a planet and expected to fix it?" "In fairness," points out Rory, "that is kind of your M.O.")

Landing in the snow – director Nick Hurran making his guerrilla shooting day on the Spanish slopes really pay its way – the Doctor and Amy discover some of the occupants of the crashed starliner that breached the asylum's defences. Unfortunately, they've been dead for a year – but that hasn't stopped the local nano-genes rewriting them with Dalek DNA, leading to a truly horrific sequence in which our heroes are menaced by rotting corpses with Dalek eyestalks emerging from their split skulls. And Mary Whitehouse thought *The Deadly Assassin* was teatime brutality for tots.

There is one actual survivor, though, in the form of Oswin Oswald, the ship's entertainment officer, who has somehow managed to evade Dalek capture for a whole year, barricading herself in and passing the time making soufflés. "Soufflés, against the Daleks?" grins the Doctor. "Where do you get the milk?"

And here, ladies and gentlemen, is the story's coup de grace: because, while it might have cheated us out of Every Dalek Ever, what we get instead is a surprise early appearance by none other than Jenna Louise-Coleman, whose turn as Oswin – sassy, flirty and drop-dead gorgeous in a livid red mini-dress – brings a welcome dash of colour and buckets of charm to what is, at times, a somewhat grim and downbeat season opener.

To rescue Oswin, the Doctor has to pass through intensive care – home to survivors of the wars on planets including Spiridon, Kembel, Aridius, Vulcan and Exxilon. "Ring any bells?" asks Oswin. "All of them," says the Doctor, grimly. "These are the Daleks who survived me."

Sadly, this attempt to punch fan buttons just results in more frustration as *all* the Daleks in intensive care are twenty-first century models who look nothing like they did when those adventures were on telly in the 60s and 70s. But that's soon forgotten as the Doctor finally reaches Oswin – and learns the horrifying truth. "It's a dream, Oswin. You dreamed it for yourself because the truth was too terrible. Because you are... a Dalek."

And there she is, fully revealed – not a hot, flirty girl in a mini-dress after all, but an insane octopus in a tank; a full conversion job designed to harvest Oswin's genius in a racially acceptable manner. That explains the eggs and the milk for the soufflés, the Doctor tells the Dalek. "Eggs," it replies. "Terminate." (Yes, Moffat really does go there.)

Except the Doctor will live to fight another day, because there's just enough residual trace of the real Oswin Oswald left for her to help him escape. "Run you clever boy," she tells him. "And remember."

What's missing here is a hand-waving explanation of how everyone hears Oswin as a spunky young woman and not a grouchy old Dalek. But we'll let it go, because the whole concept is a brilliant, audacious bit of trickery that sets up an intriguing scenario for Jenna-Louise Coleman's return at Christmas. It also helps add lustre to a story that might otherwise have fallen victim to a case of over-selling. Then again, you could argue it's Steven Moffat's job to keep pushing *Doctor Who* forward with new ideas and new mysteries, rather than simply wheeling on a load of old dustbins for the sake of it. If that left some people feeling a bit short-changed... well, I guess you can't make a soufflé without breaking a few eggs.

Though the overnight rating of 6.4 million was a little disappointing for such a plum timeslot, by now everyone – or everyone except the British press, anyway – was wising up to the increasing irrelevance of such figures and, sure enough, when the final numbers came in, the story had attracted a sizeable audience of 8.33 million, placing it comfortably within the week's top ten programmes. In the US, meanwhile, the episode's 1.5 million viewers once again set a new ratings record for BBC America (do stop me if this is getting boring), and the programme was also the second-highest rated show in the history of Canada's Space network. In Australia, *Asylum of the Daleks* premiered on the on-demand iView

player where, predictably, it also set a new record.

The story was warmly reviewed by most critics, with *The Guardian*'s Sam Wollaston hailing "a lovely episode, overflowing with Moffatism and, well, *Who*-ness" (he must have spent hours coming up with that), the *Radio Times* declaring it "absolutely stunning" and *SFX* claiming the "strong, cinematically-minded opener" had left them with "a smile the size of a small galaxy".

Sun readers, meanwhile, declared Jenna-Louise Coleman the Doctor's "sexiest-ever sidekick", with the new girl taking 50% of the vote in an online poll. ("And did we mention she once played a Teenage Lesbian™ in *Emmerdale*?")

Once again, Steven Moffat was full of admiration for everyone who had been complicit in keeping the episode's big secret under wraps. "There were four screenings, and on each occasion we just asked them not to say anything," he said. "What's remarkable is that literally nobody did. Every single fan there, every single member of the audience, every single newspaper responded brilliantly."[31]

Actually, that wasn't *entirely* true: the *Financial Times* had inadvertently blabbed about the Doctor's new companion making "a brief appearance today" in its Saturday TV preview. Fortunately, about as many people read the *FT* for its TV previews as read *Doctor Who Magazine* for its in-depth analysis of changes to personal taxation thresholds.

In Chicago, *Doctor Who* was once again the toast of the global sci-fi glitterati – or as glittery as you can get in room full of black T-shirts and leather trench coats – when *The Doctor's Wife* bagged the show its sixth Hugo Award at the 70th World Science Fiction Convention. Neil Gaiman's story – which had recently also won the 2011 Ray Bradbury Award for Outstanding Dramatic Presentation at that year's Nebula Awards – saw off competition from a shortlist of four that also included Tom MacRae's *The Girl Who Waited* and Steven Moffat's *A Good Man Goes to War*. During his acceptance speech, Gaiman revealed he was writing a second *Doctor Who* story: "Only a fool or a madman would try to do it again," he joked. "So I'm on the third draft."

Having already appeared in *Vogue*, Karen

Gillan's latest modelling assignment found her puckering up for rival glossy *Marie Claire*, in a project featuring some of the UK's brightest stars in iconic London locations. Granted permission for the first-ever fashion shoot in Downing Street, the magazine photographed Gillan on the steps of Number Ten, wearing lace-up PVC boots and leaning insouciantly on a policeman. It's a look Margaret Thatcher never quite managed to carry off, somehow.

Dinosaurs on a Spaceship: oldest creatures on a spaceship since original *Star Trek* crew

Dinosaurs on a Spaceship is *Doctor Who* as theme park ride – a galumphing great comedy adventure that starts with the big CG pictures and works backwards to build a workable story around them.

In a hyperactive opening sequence, the Doctor rounds up an unlikely gang of chums consisting of Queen Nefertiti of Egypt (like you do), a square-jawed big game hunter called Riddell and the Ponds – complete with Rory's dad Brian – to investigate a giant spacecraft that's on a collision course with the Earth.

On board, they're surprised – and, in the Doctor's case, giddily excited – to discover the ship is crawling with Cretaceous creatures, including a friendly triceratops, some distinctly less friendly raptors and, in a fabulous set-piece filmed on a rainswept Southerndown beach doubling for the ship's wave-powered engine "room", a flight of pterodactyls.

The craft, it transpires, is a Silurian ark, launched from the Earth just before the devastating asteroid strike that's thought to have wiped out the dinos – a clever idea that both honours and embellishes Malcolm Hulke's original story.

Sadly, the Silurians are long dead[XVI], ejected during cryo-sleep by Solomon, a ruthless black market space raider – played with gimlet-eyed relish by David Bradley – who's keen to offload his precious dino haul to the highest bidder. (Despite Chris Chibnall being encouraged to go for broke, in the end budget constraints necessitated limiting the dinosaurs' screen time – hence the humanoid villain, who Chibnall conceived as a mix of businessman and Somali pirate.)

It's fairly broad stuff: "You don't have any vegetable matter in your trousers do you, Brian?" asks the Doctor, as a triceratops sniffs Pond Sr's crotch. "Only my balls", says a terrified Brian, removing two grassy golf balls from his pocket. While Mark Williams is utterly adorable as the TARDIS' latest accidental traveller, the Mitchell and Webb-voiced comedy robots are possibly a gag too far – especially when one of them gets so scared, he wees a bit of oil. Laugh? Not so much.

That said, you'd have to be pretty miserable not to crack a smile at this Jurassic lark. This is *Doctor Who* cutting loose and showing off with some shameless one-upmanship (*Snakes on a Plane*? Don't waste my time) – a showcase for the sort of wham-bam spectacle the show spent years having to write its way around. It's fast, funny and frenetic, and the dinos – both CG and animatronic – really do look terrific. You wouldn't want the show to be like this every week but, taken on its own mad terms, *Dinosaurs on a Spaceship* is stomping great fun.

The story was well received ("Slight and fluffy and silly, and tonally spot on," said *SFX*) and, with 7.57m viewers, helped *Doctor Who* maintain a toehold in the top ten. And the good times kept rolling at that week's TV Choice Awards, where the show was named Best Family Drama for the third year running, beating *Glee*, *Merlin* and – oh, rotten luck – *Waterloo Road*.

Next up, *A Town Called Mercy* has its boots planted firmly in the dust of the spaghetti western – philosophically as well as physically, tacking as it does instinctively closer to the brooding, drifter aesthetic of Sergio Leone (not to mention its obvious debt to 70s sci-fi classic *Westworld*) than the simple-minded Saturday matinee shoot-outs of your classic cowboys and injuns picture.

In frontier country, the Doctor, Amy and Rory find themselves caught in the crossfire of a final showdown between an alien war criminal and one of his own cyborg creations. While the townsfolk have adopted the surgeon Kahler-Jex (Adrian Scarborough) as the local sawbones, the half-man, half machine Gunslinger (Andrew Brooke) waits patiently beyond the perimeter of the town, having sworn to exact revenge on the man who experimented on him, but determined to do it without the loss of innocent lives.

This stand-off sets the scene for a slow-burning, occasionally ponderous morality play, in which questions of honour, redemption and the capacity of war to make good men do bad deeds are earnestly chewed over like a spittoon full of tobacco.

At times, the moral dilemmas feel a mite overcooked. The Doctor's righteous anger when the nature of Jex's crimes are revealed seems particularly forced; of all the villains he's encountered over the years, it's not clear why this one – who insists he only acted to stop a more widespread slaughter – should suddenly turn him into judge, jury and trigger-happy executioner. (It's possible Jex reminds him of his own actions during the Time War, but that's not a thread the script chooses to pull on.)

Quite what the kids must make of all this yakkin' and yammerin' we don't know, but at least the Gunslinger – a towering bionic predator with a laser cannon for an arm – is a memorable, genuinely scary "monster", even if his M.O. seems a bit muddled. After a whole episode of refusing to enter Mercy and risk civilian casualties, the Slinger suddenly has a change of heart, thinks "Sod this for a game of cowboys" and marches into town in order to give the story its requisite *High Noon* moment. (Maybe he realised there was only ten minutes of the episode left.)

Nitpicking aside, this is satisfyingly meaty stuff, leavened – as we've come to expect from Toby Whithouse – with some killer gags: "He's called Joshua," a preacher tells the Doctor when he hijacks his steed. "It's from the Bible. It means the Deliverer." "No, he isn't," the Time Lord rebukes him. "I speak horse. He's called Susan – and he wants you to respect his life choices."

It's also beautifully filmed, director Saul Metzstein extracting maximum value from the Almería location to give the story a widescreen quality that, as the Gunslinger shimmers through the heat-haze of the desert, feels more like America than the previous year's episodes that were actually shot there.

It's to *A Town Called Mercy*'s credit that it manages *not* to feel like a pastiche, while at the same time not short-changing the audience who expects to see certain boxes dutifully ticked. So yes, the Doctor rides a horse, proves he's quick on the draw and causes the piano player to stop when he pushes through a pair of saloon doors. But this is no *Blazing Saddles* – and it's definitely no *Gunfighters*. And so, a mere 47 years after its first abortive attempt, *Doctor Who* finally earns its spurs as a proper Western. Or as proper as you can get with aliens, spaceships and a horse called Susan.

The episode benefited from the return of sequinned hoof-off *Strictly Come Dancing* as its lead-in, delivering *Doctor Who* a rating of 8.41m – the show's best audience since *The Impossible Astronaut*. The seventh most watched programme of the week, it was seen by twice as many people as Ant and Dec's *Red or Black?* (which, just to add an extra dash of schaden-freude, was produced by the Prince of Darkness himself, Simon Cowell) and marked the first time *Doctor Who* had ever achieved three top 10 placings in a row. But apart from all that, the show was, like, totally on the skids.

The series could also boast an influential fan in the form of the BBC's new Director General, as George Entwistle cited *Doctor Who* as one of major international properties that could help build the BBC as a global brand. In an interview with *Radio Times*, the (as it turned out, very short-lived) DG recalled how the show had been one of the programmes that had inspired his love affair with TV drama as a child. "Jon Pertwee was my Doctor," he said. "I was a bit sceptical about the Tom Baker regeneration." But not as sceptical as Jon Pertwee had been.

The 2012 MediaGuardian 100 list of influential movers and shakers saw Steven Moffat moving up five places from 92 to 87. "To have one hit BBC One drama may earn you a place on the MediaGuardian 100," said the citation. "To have two on the go seems a bit like showing off." Moffat's workload was the reason cited for his sudden disappearance from the Twittersphere. "For all asking," tweeted his wife, Sue Vertue, "@stevenmoffat is well and currently having a family lunch but he's got a huge amount on and Twitter was proving a distraction." When fans pointed out the Twitter account she'd referenced was a fake, Vertue responded, "Obviously the new @stevenmoffat is an imposter and not The Moff. It's just these sort of idiots that ruin Twitter for the majority of users" – leading many to suspect her husband's vanishing act had been at least partly influenced by his exasperation at abuse by trolls. Or fans, as they sometimes preferred to be known.

As Matt Smith appeared on *Alan Carr: Chatty Man* – where discussion turned to the recent sad loss of legendary Northampton budget prostitute "50p Lil" – John Barrowman and his sister Carole were doing the sofa shuffle to promote their new Torchwood novel, *Exodus Code*. On ITV1's *This Morning*, Barrowman was asked if he missed playing Captain Jack. "Of course I do," he said. "Jack changed my life; the fans have changed my life, and this book is dedicated to all the fans, and I've always said, if I'm asked to play Jack again of course I would – I would do it at the drop of a hat." Which was funny, as a hat was usually the last item of clothing to drop when JB was around.

Later, on Radio 2's *Steve Wright in the Afternoon*, Barrowman addressed the question of whether *Torchwood* was history: "It's been over a year now since *Miracle Day*. We haven't been told no, it's not going to happen ever again, but we haven't been told yes, and consequently that's why I spoke to Carole and we spoke to the BBC. I wanted to keep Jack alive, and that's why we wrote the book." (Also, he'd inadvertently found himself with 25 minutes between TV appearances, so was at a loose end anyway.)

New Yorkers discover shocking truth about Statue of Liberty (she's French)

"Every time we flew away with the Doctor, we'd just become part of his life," explains Amy Pond at the start of *The Power of Three*. "But he never stood still long enough to become part of ours. Except once. The Year of the Slow Invasion. The time the Doctor came to stay."

Steven Moffat described this late addition to *Doctor Who's* 2012 run to the *Radio Times* as "halfway between an alien invasion movie and *The Man Who Came to Dinner*" – the story of "a

nice young couple who happen to have a bow-tied lunatic from space staying in their spare room". The "slow invasion" idea, meanwhile, has its roots in the unfortunate fate of the container ship *MSC Napoli*, which ran ashore and spilled its cargo near Chris Chibnall's Devon home in 2007, prompting an unseemly scavenger hunt in which the local populace grabbed everything they could fit in their hands (and brought a wheelbarrow along for the stuff they couldn't).

In *The Power of Three's* case, the booty takes the form of millions of identical black boxes which suddenly appear all over the Earth one night. "Invasion of the very small cubes," muses the Doctor. "That's new."

And it is: following a story over the course of a year offers a marked contrast to the show's usual working method, where – as the seventh Doctor once noted – there's usually time for a quick adventure before tea. Though *The Lodger* and its sequel have robbed the idea of a domesticated Doctor of some of its novelty value, there's still great fun to be had in watching the Time Lord trying to adjust to daily life chez Pond during his least favourite kind of global crisis: one where nothing really happens. (His ways of passing the time while everyone else sits around eating cereal include mowing the lawn, creosoting the fence, doing four million keepy-uppies and becoming addicted to the Wii.)

It's not long before he comes to the attention of the authorities, though, prompting an early morning home invasion by a UNIT squad. "There are soldiers all over my house," complains a half-dressed Rory, "and I'm in my pants." UNIT and gratuitous underwear? It's like Jo Grant never left. And to complete the 70s vibe, there's a Lethbridge-Stewart in charge – except Kate Stewart has ditched one barrel of her father's surname, along with his shoot first, ask questions later approach to alien incursions. She's also the first Lethbridge-Stewart to kiss the Doctor. Talk about UNIT dating.

Just as the mysterious boxes have started to become a fixture of everyday life – with Lord Sugar and Professor Brian Cox popping up in cute, cube-related cameos – they suddenly turn nasty, causing millions of people across the world to go into cardiac arrest.

Which is where *The Power of Three* – up to

this point the undisputed jewel in this mini-season's crown – starts to look a bit tarnished, as the Doctor and Amy track down the brains behind the scheme to a spaceship that, usefully, just happens to be accessed through the lift at Rory's work. On board, Steven Berkoff goes through the motions as a representative of the Shakri – a race of deeply unmemorable alien "pest controllers" determined to stop the "human contagion" before it spreads across the galaxy.

After a tepid defence of humanity, the Doctor simply sonics the ship's computer into reverse: "The Shakri used the cubes to turn people's hearts off. Bingo! We're going to use them to turn them back on again," he "explains". So that's that. Oh, and as a side effect, he also blows up the ship and all the poor comatose human captives still on board. But no-one else seems worried about them, so why should we be?

Damp squib finale aside, though, this is a refreshing and hugely enjoyable new twist on the *Doctor Who* format. As a commentary on consumer society and tech fetishism, it's not exactly subtle (Kate even compares a cube to an iPad, just in case we didn't get the message). But that's not really the point: the point, in their penultimate adventure, is to give us a glimpse of what real life might be like for Amy and Rory – if only it could just get started.

Amy estimates it's ten years since she first stole away in the Doctor's magic box, and there's a real sense that, for both her and Rory, the pull of a life more ordinary – a life of work and shopping and opticians' appointments – is getting stronger. And their funny friend knows it, leading to one of the all-time great Time Lord-companion exchanges:

"I'm not running away," says the Doctor when Amy accuses him of having pathologically itchy feet. "But this is one corner of one country in one continent on one planet that's a corner of a galaxy that's a corner of a universe that is forever growing and shrinking and creating and destroying and never remaining the same for a single millisecond. And there is so much, *so much* to see, Amy. Because it goes so fast. I'm not running away from things, I am running *to* them before they flare and fade forever. And it's all right. Our lives won't run

the same. They can't. One day, soon maybe, you'll stop. I've known for a while."

"Then why do you keep coming back for us?" she asks.

"Because you were the first," he tells her, tenderly. "The first face this face saw. And you're seared onto my hearts, Amelia Pond. You always will be. I'm running to you, and Rory, before you fade from me."

It's a beautiful moment, made all the more affecting by the ominous foreshadowing of events to come. When Brian – a welcome reprise of Mark Williams' endearing Pond Sr – asks what happened to his previous companions, the Doctor admits: "Some left me. Some got left behind. And some, not many but... some died." But he insists that won't happen this time: "Not them, Brian. Never them."

At the end, Brian takes the Time Lord at his word and encourages Amy and Rory to delay real life just that little bit longer, and go off and have more adventures. "Just bring them back safe," he tells the Doctor.

Of course he will, Brian – I'm sure you've got absolutely nothing to worry about. Though, to be on the safe side, you might want to give the Next Time trailer a miss. Just sayin'.

Her *Doctor Who* duties complete, Karen Gillan had done what so many successful British actors do, and relocated to a poolside villa in LA. Okay, not really – she'd moved back home to live with her parents in Inverness. "It's a really funny thought having all these crazy experiences on *Doctor Who*, then always seeming to end up back in my old childhood bedroom, with my childhood posters," she told the *Daily Record*. "I've got a Muse one, from when I was like an angsty teen. And I've got a Daniel O'Donnell calendar, which I thought would be really funny when I was younger, from 2004 or something. I lie there and I am like, has all that just really happened? Or did I just imagine it?"

Yes, it really happened – and here's your final curtain call to prove it...

The Doctor doesn't like endings. In fact, he hates them so much, he rips the last page out of all his books. But, when you're a thousand years old, endings are hard to avoid – and this one's going to bruise more than most.

From its opening film noir pastiche, in which a hardboiled gumshoe describes New

York as "the city of a million stories – half of them are true; the other half just haven't happened yet", *The Angels Take Manhattan* revels in its iconic, Chandler-esque imagery, in which pulp fiction is punched out on typewriter ribbon, our crumpled investigator rides a bird-cage elevator, and our heroes are invited to take a ride by hoodlums with Roscoes.

Though Team TARDIS start out in 2012, it's not long before Rory has been whipped back in time, where he ends up as a character in a detective thriller written by one Melody Malone – aka River Song, aka his daughter. Using the book to track them to the 1930s, the Doctor and Amy find Rory and River are prisoners of mob boss and art collector Julius Grayle, whose haul of stolen booty includes a fully-grown Weeping Angel and several giggling Cherubs.

This latter variation on a theme – inspired by a photo director Nick Hurran had taken of the statues on the Bethesda Fountain in Central Park – are a terrifying invention, even by Steven Moffat's standards, especially when Rory is thrown into a dark cellar with a bunch of the snickering gargoyles, one of which uses its chubby little cheeks to blow out his match. Gulp.

Upstairs, the Doctor engages in some weapons-grade flirting with his on-off squeeze ("She's got ice in her heart and a kiss on her lips," summarises Amy) before following the trail to Winter Quay – a tenement block-turned-Angel battery farm (in Battery Park, ho ho), where Rory witnesses an aged version of himself gasp his last. Well, one more death for the road can't hurt, can it?

When River says the only way he can destroy the Angels is to create a temporal paradox, Rory resolves to take matters into his own hands – and jump off the roof. But not if the Statue of Liberty stops him first, the world's most famous neoclassical Goddess having loosed her moorings and stomped across town like Godzilla in sandals. "I always wanted to visit the Statue of Liberty," gulps Rory. "I guess she got impatient." (It's an arresting image, this colossal demon, but it does beg the question: has the statue *always* been an Angel? And does it often go walkabout? 'Cos it would be kinda hard not to notice, even in New York. Plus, as

any Poindexter will tell you, she's actually made of copper, not stone.)

Amy, of course, is not just going to let Rory jump to his death – not on his own, anyway. "What the hell are you doing?" demands the Doctor, as his best friends cling to each other on the ledge. "Changing the future," says Amy. "It's called marriage." And then they take a leap of faith – falling, entangled together, in slow motion, in a sequence that's clearly striving to be huge and operatic but, sadly, ends up looking vaguely comical.

Luckily, it's a false ending designed to set up the real farewell – and this one's a proper three-hankie job. In a cemetery on the edge of town, Rory discovers his own grave, which tells us he died, aged 82. And then, unable to escape destiny after all, he promptly vanishes. A distraught Amy knows the only way she can reach her husband is through the touch of an Angel – but it means she will never see the Doctor again. (The TARDIS can't get back to 30s New York because it's full of "time distortion", apparently. And yes, we could quibble about what nonsense this is, the plot groaning at the seams to tear our heroes apart – if the TARDIS can't go back to NYC, why not meet them in Paris or Milan or Swindon or something? Or just visit a few years down the line? – but it's played with such conviction, they just about get away with it.)

"Raggedy man," says Amy, before turning away from the Angel to look the Doctor in the eye one last time – the look that will seal her fate. "Goodbye."

And then she's gone – now nothing more than a dead woman's name on a headstone: Amelia Williams, aged 87. But there's a postscript – an afterword in River's book, written by Amy especially for her madman with the box.

"Hello, old friend," she writes. "And here we are, you and me, on the last page. By the time you read these words, Rory and I will be long gone. So know that we lived well, and were very happy. And above all else, know that we will love you always. Sometimes I do worry about you, though. I think once we're gone, you won't be coming back here for a while, and you might be alone, which you should never be. Don't be alone, Doctor. And do one more thing for me. There's a little girl waiting in a garden. She's going to wait a long while, so she's going to need a lot of hope. Go to her. Tell her a story. Tell her that if she's patient, the days are coming that she'll never forget. Tell her she'll go to sea and fight pirates. She'll fall in love with a man who'll wait two thousand years to keep her safe. Tell her she'll give hope to the greatest painter who ever lived, and save a whale in outer space."

And then, beneath Gillan's voiceover, the final shot of the series – the final shot of the Pond era – is a fantastic, audacious punchline two-and-a-half years in the making: a reprise of a fleeting, puzzling scene from *The Eleventh Hour*, which hadn't made any sense in its original context, of the young Amy, sitting on her suitcase in that garden in Leadworth, looking up in surprise and, for reasons unknown until now, grinning from ear to ear. "Tell her this is the story of Amelia Pond," says Amy. "And this how it ends."

The Bush Tucker Trial of a Time Lord

Steven Moffat described writing the episode as "torment and hell". "The end of Amy Pond and Rory Williams was one of the hardest things I've ever written," he told the Press Association. "I must have rewritten it 20-odd times. I kept changing my mind about the exact way they'd leave – alive or dead? One or both of them? Their fates kept changing every five minutes until I hit on what I thought was right."

His blood, sweat and tears were rewarded with 7.82m viewers – 13th for the week – further vindicating the decision to move the show to a later slot at a time of the year when the actors weren't having to compete with the sound of ice cream vans in the street. The reviews were generally positive, if not exactly gushing: the *Telegraph* rhapsodised about "a powerful, taut, compelling, filmic, emotionally punchy affair", while the *Mirror* described Amy and Rory's fate as "beautiful yet terrible, believable without ever being mawkish... a true statement of love between two characters who – let's face it – we've all come to love just a bit over the last two and a half years of *Who*". But *SFX*'s Dave Golder was typical of the critics who loved it – up to a point: "On one level it's a glorious, daring, gutsy, high-concept and hugely entertaining slice of *Who*, with individual moments of the show at its best: creepy, funny and visually arresting," he said. "On another level, it's downright baffling..."

But as one door closes, another opens. A few days after the Ponds' emotional farewell was broadcast, Matt Smith was on-set for the story that would officially introduce his latest side-kick, a Steven Moffat adventure entitled *The Bells of Saint John*. The filming included a high-profile shoot in London, with motorbike stunts being performed on the South Bank and Westminster, and further action taking place by the city's newest landmark, The Shard. With the principle shoot wrapped, director Colm McCarthy and his director of photography embarked on *Doctor Who*'s most globetrotting adventure ever, shooting scenes for the story in Paris, San Francisco and Tokyo during a seven-day long-haul marathon. So if the episode included scenes of two men in shorts and Crocs giving the thumbs up in front of the Eiffel Tower and the Golden Gate Bridge, you'd know why. Afterwards, production moved onto the second episode of the 2013 run, written by Neil Cross, the British-born, New Zealand-based creator of the BBC's hit Idris Elba vehicle, *Luther*.

During pick-up shots for Mark Gatiss' episode on October 28th, Matt Smith was surprised on-set with a TARDIS cake to celebrate his 30th birthday, with a video released by the BBC showing the cast and crew – including Jenna-Louise Coleman – donning cardboard Matt Smith masks for the occasion. Either that, or it was a story about the Doctor being cloned, and the budget cuts were worse than feared.

The following week saw the read-through for Neil Gaiman's latest story, which the BBC announced would feature the return of the Cybermen, as well as guest turns from ex-EastEnder Tamzin Outhwaite and *Star Wars*/*Harry Potter* actor Warwick Davis, most recently seen as a pint-sized Ricky Gervais manqué in the sitcom *Life's Too Short*.

Following the read-through, someone managed to leave their copy of the script in a taxi. Fortunately, the next customer – Cardiff University student Hannah Durham, who was dressed as a skeleton at the time – returned it to the BBC, its secrets un-spilled. Gaiman later tweeted "a world sized pat on the back to @ hannahldurham," adding: "You're a good person and I'm thrilled you did it the right way." (*Space Helmet* is not the sort to cast aspersions about *who* might have left the script there in the first place – we will simply note that Gaiman had already had to abandon one draft of the story after leaving his MacBook on an aeroplane. Just sayin'.)

Talking up the story, Steven Moffat described the Cybermen as *Doctor Who's* "scariest monsters" – but that was nothing compared to what a former Time Lord was about to face, as Colin Baker was announced as one of the stars of that year's televised trial by testicle-chewing, *I'm a Celebrity... Get Me Out of Here!*

The sixth Doctor told reporters he'd been persuaded to do the show – which involved being dropped in the Australian jungle surrounded by such poisonous creatures as snakes, spiders and bitchy 80s pop stars – by his four daughters. "They are fans of the show and the programme is on incessantly every year," he said. "They told me I had to go on and they are so excited – 'Can't wait to see you chomping on a giraffe's buttock!' There's no sympathy at all, it's all 'Ooh can't wait, can't wait!'

"I wouldn't say I am excited," he confessed. "It's a mixture of intrigue, a feeling of resigned and interested to see how I am going to react. I haven't a clue as I have not done anything like this ever before. For me, this is pushing back the boundaries. I think I'll be able to deal with anything that comes up in the jungle. After all, I've met aliens from the planet Zog [bloody hell, don't tell Russell T Davies] and I have encountered the fans at conventions – all of whom are wonderful but can be a bit alien! There is one trial in particular that I'm terrified by, and I'm not going to tell you what it is." Well whatever it was, it surely couldn't be as bad as *The Trial of a Time Lord*. And, let's be honest, he's had worse things in his mouth than a kangaroo's anus – there's Pip and Jane Baker's dialogue, for a start.

Baker's campmates would include Charlie Brooks (*EastEnders*), Helen Flanagan (*Coronation Street*) and Linda Robson (*Birds of a Feather*), comedian Brian Conley, Pussycat Doll Ashley Roberts, darts ace Eric Bristow,

boxer David Haye, some posh bloke from reality show *Made in Chelsea* and bonkers Tory MP Nadine Dorries. Even the spiders were scared of *her*.

The 2012 gong show continued for Steven Moffat when he collected the Special Award for Outstanding Writing at The Writers' Guild of Great Britain Awards. Okay, so it was for the *other* show again, and he had to share it with Mark Gatiss and Stephen Thompson. But it still counts. *The Sarah Jane Adventures* was also honoured, with Series Five's *The Curse of Clyde Langer* nabbing Phil Ford the Best Children's TV Script trophy.

Filming on Series Seven was now entering its final phase with a head-spinning schedule, as one unit worked on Block 11, overlapping for a week with Block 10, while a second unit double-banked making inserts for numerous other episodes, alongside various special projects. On any given day, the principal cast might find themselves working on up to three separate stories, while slipping in some DVD bonus material in spare moments. So now we know why the Doctor never changes his clothes.

As was now traditional, November's *Children in Need* appeal featured a first look at the trailer for the *Doctor Who* Christmas special – revealed to be called *The Snowmen* – alongside a special mini-episode, *The Great Detective*, in which the Doctor's old chums Vastra, Jenny and Strax attempt to coax the Time Lord out of retirement. Perhaps even more memorable, though, was Terry Wogan's description of co-host Fearne Cotton as "the Bonnie Langford to my Colin Baker". Surely that's no way to treat a friend and colleague.

"The Doctor at Christmas is one of my favourite things," explained Steven Moffat in BBC publicity for the special. "But this year it's different. He's lost Amy and Rory to the Weeping Angels, and he's not in a good place; in fact, he's Scrooge. He's withdrawn from the world and no longer cares what happens to it. So when all of humanity hangs in the balance, can anyone persuade a tired and heartbroken Doctor that it's time to return to the good fight? Enter Jenna-Louise Coleman..."

And exit Colin Baker: after 15 days in the jungle, the happy camper packed his bags and left *I'm a Celebrity...* after losing a head-to-head trial with Eric Bristow. During his stint, Baker had fallen out of a canoe, learned to rap and been viciously assaulted by a psychotic crab. He'd also shed a whopping two stone – losing weight being one of his prime motivations for entering in the first place – and earned a reputation as the nicest man in camp. But, for many, the highlight of his jungle caper was the chance to see the sixth Doctor shaking his booty to "Don't Cha" with one of the Pussycat Dolls. Once seen, never forgotten. And God knows, we've tried.

December saw *Doctor Who's* US profile being cranked up another notch when *Good Morning America* – the nation's coast-to-coast breakfast show – announced the winner of the annual TV Guide Fan Favorites Cover Poll, in which readers vote for their favourite show to grace the cover of America's iconic weekly listings mag. Despite strong competition from the likes of *Fringe, Parks and Recreation, The Vampire Diaries* and *The Walking Dead*, it was plucky British import *Doctor Who* wot won it, with Matt Smith looming large on the front of the pre-Christmas double-issue published a week later.

Smith was also joined by Jenna Louise-Coleman on the cover of *Radio Times*, inside which he raved about his new costume: "I've got a whole new Christmassy outfit and the best hat! There's a lot of purple this year, which is nice. I've always wanted something purple, but they were always reluctant. It's taken three years to get a jaunty hat and a purple coat!"[32]

Discussing the new duds – which, as seen in recent publicity photos, would revert back to a more traditional frock coat and waistcoat ensemble, even after the Christmas Victoriana had been dispensed with – Steven Moffat admitted: "We did fight shy of it. I think we were terribly aware, Russell in particular, of not looking like somebody dressing up as Doctor Who. We were all quite paranoid about that. But it's progressing. We started very, very dour with Chris' Doctor. Very quickly he's got the stupid coat and the stupid hair when David takes over. And we were very close to a frock coat when Matt came in, because he just looks good in them. Then we liked the tweedy jacket. It's sort of a different phase of his life now – it felt right for him not to be wearing the same clothes. He's a bit more grown-up now,

he's a bit more the daddy Doctor. He's more Pertwee-like, really, and it just suited him. Matt's a bit of a clothes horse – you can put him in anything. It really came down to what he felt like wearing."[32]

Smith was one of the celebrity gang show pressed into service for the BBC's Christmas trails (theme: "It's Showtime!") with the eleventh Doctor being chased by a mistletoe-wielding Miranda Hart, while Brendan O'Carroll (false-bosomed matriarch of inexplicably popular sitcom throwback *Mrs Brown's Boys*) was seen departing in the TARDIS, presumably on a joke-finding trip to the 1970s.

For the many fans hoping *The Snowmen* would herald the start of the new series – or the second half of the old series, depending on how you looked at it – there was bad news courtesy of *Doctor Who Magazine*, who announced the show wouldn't be returning until Easter. In other words, all the upheavals and delays involved in moving to a winter slot had apparently been in vain.

A year earlier, discussing *Doctor Who's* 2012 schedule with *SFX*, Steven Moffat had stated: "It's not even a ratings thing: it's an aesthetic thing. Six o'clock on a sunny Saturday is the middle of the afternoon, whereas six o'clock on a winter or autumn Saturday is dark and exciting. The show is all about people running down corridors, with torches. You want to be able to see it without sunshine streaming through your window and onto your TV screen."[23]

Somewhere in Kew, a TV showrunner was currently measuring up his house for blackout blinds.

1200-year-old Time Lord takes early retirement

As Murray Gold played an impressive seven-night residency at Sydney Opera House with the *Doctor Who Symphonic Spectacular* (a variation on the *Doctor Who Prom* that had already extended its run twice), Steven Moffat expanded on his hero's current state of mind in the Christmas *Radio Times*.

"The Doctor has retired. He's withdrawn from the world and hidden himself away in his battered old TARDIS. No more friends, no more world-saving, no more heartbreak. What could it possibly take to bring him back into the world again?

"That's a brilliant idea. And I can say that without a hint of arrogance, because it's not mine. The greatest writer ever to have turned his genius to *Doctor Who* was, of course, the mighty Douglas Adams. And he pitched that story, *The Doctor Retires*, many, many years ago. Back in the late 1970s the production office said no, but I remember reading about it and thinking it sounded so great that, if I ever had the chance, that would be one hell of a story to tell."[33] (Recycling old Douglas Adams ideas was nothing new, of course. It's just it was normally Douglas Adams who did it.)

The magazine also spoke to Jenna-Louise Coleman about life on the *Who* roller coaster "Every day has been surprising," she said. "You walk into the studio every few weeks and whole new sets have been built. You open the TARDIS doors and you're suddenly in a different era. It's very technical but also fun and adventurous, and it's okay to run down a corridor shouting and being as silly and ridiculous as you like. It makes me feel like a big kid. It's like magic."[33]

The actress also told CNN in America that she'd previously auditioned for the role of Mels – aka River Song – in *Let's Kill Hitler*. Her *Who*-mad gran had been devastated when she hadn't got the gig, but was delighted by the recent turn of events and – according to Coleman – very much looking forward to meeting Matt Smith. Somewhere on a dining room table in Blackpool, there was clearly a meat and potato pie with his name on it. Her co-star's promo duties, meanwhile, included an appearance on *The Graham Norton Show* where he was coerced into snogging a member of the audience by Dustin Hoffman. Like you do.

In many ways, *The Snowmen* is Steven Moffat's most quixotic fairytale offering yet. Newbie Coleman – as a governess who ascends into the clouds on an umbrella, and claims to have been born behind the clock face of Big Ben – is essentially Mary Poppins with dimples, while the Doctor now wears a crumpled, Artful Dodger-style topper, and lives on a cloud. That's right, a cloud. But, unlike previous festive confections, this one isn't so throwaway as it first appears – in fact, it amounts to

the biggest re-boot of the show since the Moffat-Smith takeover of 2010.

Firstly, there's the obvious stuff: new titles (a thrilling, kaleidoscopic tumble through vaporous clouds and spiralling nebulas that – oh be still our beating fanboy hearts – finally reintroduces the Doctor's face to the opening credits), new theme (actually a lot like the old theme, with some added steam valve sizzles and pops) and new TARDIS interior (this apparently arose after Steven Moffat decided it had all got a bit quirky, so gone are the brass taps and ketchup dispenser, replaced by a more sober, compact affair with a more mechanical, almost clockwork aesthetic). But these are just window-dressing: more substantially, the episode also lays down the groundwork for the future direction of the series, in which the Doctor must discover why different versions of the same person – Oswin Oswald in *Asylum of the Daleks*, Clara Oswald here – have apparently been scattered throughout time and space. And he gets a new gang of mates to help him in Vastra, Jenny and Strax: his own Baker Street (or Paternoster Row, technically) Irregulars, ready to enter the fray whenever the script needs pepping up with a bit of lesbian lizard action.

Though the Doctor has been deaf to Vastra and company's please to involve himself in local difficulties in Victorian London – preferring to sit in his TARDIS in an epic sulk since losing the Ponds – Clara is intriguing enough to tempt him out of retirement to investigate the mysterious case of homicidal snowmen suddenly rearing up out of the ground and eating people. This frosty army, with their razor-sharp piranha leers, is commanded by the mysterious Dr Simeon, played by Richard E Grant in exactly the same way he played the abortive ninth Doctor a decade earlier: i.e like he's got a particularly bad smell under his nose. Thankfully, this time that's exactly what's needed. ("I said I'd feed you," he sneers at his workforce, contemptuously, as the snowmen circle. "I didn't say who to.")

But Simeon is really just a patsy for the real villain of the piece, which turns out to be the Great Intelligence – the ancient, formless sentience behind the second Doctor's run-ins with the Yeti all those years ago. (Here, the Doctor is revealed to be the architect of one of those adventures, when he gives the Intelligence a lunchbox with a 1967 London Underground map on it. How *very* careless.) Currently housed in a giant talking snow globe (an uncredited voice cameo by Sir Ian McKellen), the Intelligence is on a quest to find a useful corporeal form with which to establish itself on Earth – and the prime candidate is the body of a wicked governess lying dead in the frozen pond of a stately home, who duly rises from her icy tomb and comes back to haunt her young charges, Moffat seasoning the general air of whimsy with a dose of creepy, *Turn of the Screw*-style nursery horror.

Having already seen Jenna-Louise Coleman as the whip-smart Oswin, here we get two Claras for the price of one, as our heroine starts out as a sassy cockney barmaid, all hand-on-hip gorblimey cheek, before a quick-change act in the back of a Hansom cab sees her transformed into a posh governess for the children whose previous duenna met such an unfortunate end. Coleman excels as both variants, and her sparky, quickfire interplay with Smith's Doctor is everything Moffat promised it would be. (Smith cheekily claimed the pair's inevitable kiss was his favourite *Doctor Who* scene so far, not least because Coleman really went for it. "It was a case of, better to grab him and just do it," said the actress. "I shocked Matt, actually. That kiss, we did the most amount of takes... We were doing it so many times, I think Saul, the director, got a bit uncomfortable."[34])

In the episode's stand-out sequence, Clara follows the Doctor up an invisible spiral staircase into the clouds. Framed against the moon, with a Dickensian, Christmas card London laid out beneath her, and serenaded by one of Murray Gold's most magical compositions – like a choir of angels lifting her into the sky – it's as enchanting a moment as any in the last 50 years.

Later, Clara returns to the cloud and, after subverting the Doctor's (and our) expectations by declaring the TARDIS "smaller on the outside" (we love her already), is offered a place on board. "Why?" she asks, as he dangles a key in front of her. "I never know why," he says. "I only know who." But the moment is short-lived as the Time Lord's new BF is dragged falling to the earth below by the ice governess, receiving fatal injuries in the process.

After this, your tolerance for sentimental whimsy may be sorely tested, as Clara's dying swan act generates enough blubbing from her young charges to defeat the Intelligence and win the day. "It's not raining, it's crying," says the Doctor, as the heavens literally weep for the lost girl. So there you have it – last year Christmas was saved by a mother's love, this year it's children's tears. Next year, don't be surprised if Bambi is called in to help out.

But it would be churlish to grumble – on this of all days – when *The Snowmen*, sumptuously directed by Saul Metzstein, delivers such rip-roaring, heart-swelling festive entertainment. As well as being magical, romantic and thrilling, it's also Moffat's funniest script in ages. Many of the best gags come courtesy of Dan Starkey's "psychotic potato dwarf" Strax, clearly still struggling with having been exiled from the glory of battle in order to serve as a butler ("Do not attempt to escape or you will be obliterated! May I take your coat?").[XVII] There's also a delicious sequence in which the Doctor dons a deerstalker in order to impersonate Sherlock Holmes, Moffat cheekily riffing on his *other* adopted British icon in a scene that plays to Matt Smith's strengths as he conspicuously fails to emulate the Great Detective's powers of deductive reasoning. ("Do you have a goldfish named Colin?" "No." "Thought not.") But the real knockout line is reserved for Neve McIntosh's Madame Vastra who, when asked who she is by a befuddled housekeeper, declares: "I am a lizard woman from the dawn of time – and this is my wife."

By the end titles, Moffat has all his ducks neatly lined up in a row. The Great Intelligence has adopted Richard E Grant's milky slab of a face as its own, the Paternoster Gang are waiting in the wings for further adventures and, most tantalisingly of all, the mystery of Clara Oswald – the impossible girl – is out there, waiting to be solved. "Run, you clever boy," she tells him once more. "And remember." And off he runs, spinning and pirouetting around his spaceship like an excitable, thousand-year-old schoolboy.

The chase was on. And, as it prepared to enter its landmark golden anniversary year, *Doctor Who* – the British institution-turned-global phenomenon – had scarcely looked in ruder health.

With a final audience figure of 9.87 million, *The Snowmen* was almost a million down on the previous Christmas – though much of that was probably down to its 5.15 timeslot; the earliest *Doctor Who* had been scheduled since the Colin Baker era. Despite this, it was still the fourth most-watched programme of the day, beaten by *EastEnders*, *Call the Midwife* and *The Royle Family*, but managing to slay such big beasts as *Coronation Street*, *Strictly Come Dancing* and *Downton Abbey*. In the US, the episode attracted 1.4 million viewers – a 54% rise on the previous year's Christmas special. Back home, with less than six million having watched it go out live, *The Snowmen* set a new record for the UK's most recorded TV show.

While *The Guardian* hailed it "easily the finest Christmas special under this regime", other reviews were of the grudgingly positive variety: "Through sprout-engorged eyes and a brandy befuddle, it's a great piece of entertainment, but it doesn't hold up to much sober fanboy scrutiny," declared the *Mirror*, before confusingly declaring it "miles better than anything else on". *The Daily Telegraph*'s Dominic Cavendish, meanwhile, felt it "an enjoyable enough romp" but cautioned: "If Moffat doesn't rein in his tendencies to make every script a brain-teaser of Sudoku-like complexity, his young audience will melt away, fast."

On Boxing Day, the Royal Mail announced it would be producing a set of 11 special stamps to commemorate *Doctor Who*'s 50th anniversary, giving fans everywhere the chance to lick the back of their favourite Doctor (stamps are self-adhesive these days, of course, but you know what some are like).

And the best bit? Imagining all those bills piling up on Michael Grade's doormat with Colin Baker's face grinning out from them.

History in the remaking

In early January 2013, Big Finish popped the 50th anniversary's first champagne cork when it announced Tom Baker, Peter Davison, Colin Baker, Sylvester McCoy and Paul McGann would be teaming up for a "fully-fledged multi-Doctor" audio adventure called *The Light at the End*. (Just don't tell Tom that's

what it is – he probably thinks the other four are from catering.) The British Film Institute also kicked off their own celebrations with the first in a sold-out series of Southbank screenings of stories featuring every Doctor.

At the end of the month, the BBC unveiled the actor chosen to play William Hartnell in *An Adventure in Space and Time*. At 70, David Bradley was a full 15 years older than Hartnell when he signed on for *Doctor Who*, but the physical resemblance was remarkable, and Bradley's distinguished CV – from an Olivier Award-winning King Lear to choleric Hogwarts caretaker Argus Filch in the Harry Potter films, not to mention his splenetic turn in the previous year's *Dinosaurs on a Spaceship* – made the casting seem at once inspired and, in the best possible sense, kinda obvious. An "absolutely thrilled" Bradley said: "When [Mark Gatiss] asked if I would be interested, I almost bit his hand off! Mark has written such a wonderful script not only about the birth of a cultural phenomenon, but a moment in television's history. William Hartnell was one of the finest character actors of our time, and as a fan I want to make sure that I do him justice."

As the first Doctor prepared to return to the BBC ("Bill always said that one day he'd come back," tweeted Mark Gatiss), his most recent successor was about to make the leap onto the big screen, as *Variety* reported that Matt Smith had been cast as the male lead in *How to Catch a Monster*, the directorial debut from current Hollywood wunderkind Ryan Gosling. With co-stars including Eva Mendes and Christina Hendricks, it was possibly the most achingly hip thing anyone associated with *Doctor Who* had ever been asked to do. (Unless you count Colin Baker's spot alongside Tom O'Connor on x-word themed quiz show *Crosswits*.)

In February, Mark Gatiss was channelling the spirit of 60s *Who* at every turn. As the Daleks rolled over Westminster Bridge to recreate an iconic scene for *An Adventure in Space and Time*, *SFX* magazine revealed the writer was also set to bring back everyone's favourite Martians, the Ice Warriors, in an upcoming story. Meanwhile, the not-so-jolly green giants' first appearance was being readied for release on DVD, with the missing second and third episodes presented with new animation. With William Hartnell's long-lost final episode also about to get the same treatment, it seemed there were more people working on recreating 1960s *Doctor Who* than there were making new *Doctor Who*. (And to think viewers used to moan about "bloody repeats" – now they actually employed people to *make* the bloody repeats.)

While Patrick Troughton and company were being made two-dimensional, it was revealed that *Doctor Who's* 50th anniversary special would be made in glorious, eye-popping 3D. After which, said the BBC, they wouldn't be making anything else in 3D, because it was a waste of time and money, and no-one likes wearing those stupid glasses and, basically, everyone thinks it's a bit shit. Anyway, enjoy!

With the launch of Series 7B confirmed for March 30th, Steven Moffat talked up the new adventures in a BBC press release, promising "If this wasn't already our most exciting year it would be anyway!" A promotional image showed the Doctor and Clara on a motorbike crashing through The Shard, to promote series opener *The Bells of St John*, a capital-set thriller which promised "something sinister in the Wi-Fi" and a new nemesis called the Spoonheads. Having done scary statues, creeping darkness and monsters under the bed, was Moffat now having to fall back on evil cutlery?

The BBC also unveiled plans to host a three-day 50th anniversary *Doctor Who* Celebration Weekend in November at London's ExCeL. It promised to be just like the legendary 20th anniversary celebration weekend at Longleat House, except this time they'd probably ask you to buy a ticket in advance and not just rock up on the off-chance with 40,000 mates.

Amidst the air of celebration, the eve of the Ides of March brought bloodshed on the steps of BBC Wales, with the rather sudden announcement that, after 15 episodes, Caroline Skinner was leaving *Doctor Who* to take up a BBC drama role in London. Head of Drama at BBC Wales, Faith Penhale – now stepping in as a late replacement exec producer on the 50th anniversary special – praised Skinner's work on the series, but *Private Eye* claimed the producer had been told she was being "erased from *Doctor Who* history". She wouldn't be the first person to be erased from *Doctor Who* history, of course – perhaps one day a copy of her would turn up at a Nigerian TV station.

Doctor Who's contribution to the 2013 Comic Relief appeal saw the Time Lord pitching up in the middle of a mash-up of *Call the Midwife* and *One Born Every Minute* – twin planks of the current, strangely obstetrics-obsessed TV landscape. Afterwards, Matt Smith appeared in the studio fending off the advances of presenter Claudia Winkleman, while David Tennant repeated his snog routine of four years earlier, this time sucking the somewhat more lived-in face off Scouse comedian John Bishop, with hilarious consequences, probably.

The following Friday, the BBC paid tribute to its soon-to-be former spiritual home with a night of programmes dedicated to Television Centre, which was due to close at the end of the month. Among those taking a valedictory turn around the famous White City doughnut were Colin Baker and Sylvester McCoy, who emerged from the TARDIS for a brief exchange of anecdotes with Chris Evans, who then – sixth Doctor fans of a sensitive disposition look away now – turned directly to one Michael Grade, who Evans proceeded to interview *while wearing Baker's multicoloured nightmarecoat*. The irony was not lost on fans – nor presumably on Baker and Grade, though it must have been tempting for the latter to order Evans to change into McCoy's outfit, just for old times' sake.

McCoy was back on BBC1 a few days later, teaming up with Sophie Aldred for a *Doctor Who*-themed edition of quiz show *Pointless Celebrities*, a sort of reverse *Family Fortunes* in which celebs have to guess the least popular correct answers given by a survey audience. The other teams were made up of a classic companions pairing of Frazer Hines and Louise Jamieson, a Noble family reunion of Bernard Cribbins and Sylvia King, and a sixth Doctor team boasting Nicola Bryant and, um, Andrew Hayden-Smith. (The *Rise of the Cybermen* guest star was actually a late replacement for Colin Baker, who was busy eating crock cocks in the Australian jungle at the time.) Cribbins and King eventually prevailed, proving the wisdom of ages by answering questions on everything from the periodic table to the plays of Terrence Rattigan, while showing a healthy ignorance of anything to do with *Torchwood*.

Doable trouble

In recent years, the BBC had found itself under constant siege by its enemies in the press. Jealous of their rival's unique, publicly-funded role in British life, the likes of the *Daily Mail* and the Murdoch-owned *Sun* and *Times* kept up a constant barrage of Beeb-bashing "stories" designed to propagate a view of the Corporation as a nest of Communist vipers intent on undermining such great British values as honesty, decency and an innate suspicion of foreigners.

But in 2013, the BBC suddenly found itself with a very real crisis on its hands that couldn't be written off as mischief-making by its enemies. In October 2012, an ITV documentary presented compelling evidence that the recently deceased Sir Jimmy Savile – a mainstay of the Corporation's schedules for more than 40 years – had been a predatory sex offender and paedophile whose crimes had been an open secret in the industry. Most damningly for the BBC, it seemed many of Savile's hundreds of possible victims had been abused on BBC premises amid a constant chorus of whispers that, astonishingly, had never translated into a serious criminal investigation.

Launched by the Metropolitan Police in the light of the documentary's claims, Operation Yewtree would eventually extend its scope to encompass complaints about numerous other well-known fixtures of British television and radio, resulting in jail sentences for the likes of Stuart Hall and, most shockingly, erstwhile national treasure Rolf Harris.

It was into this febrile atmosphere that, in the spring of 2013, former *Blue Peter* editor (and erstwhile *Doctor Who Magazine* scribe) Richard Marson launched his controversial book *JN-T: The Life and Scandalous Times of John Nathan-Turner*, a warts-and-all (and then some) biography of the late *Doctor Who* producer.

Assembled from scores of interviews with just about every key figure from Nathan-Turner's time in charge – including the three men he cast as the Doctor and all their respective companions – Marson's book is a triumph of reportage that has won plaudits from all quarters, from *The Times* ("the definitive behind-the-scenes portrait of the show in the

Eighties") to Sophie Aldred ("scurrilous, fascinating, hilarious and naughty") to Russell T Davies, who praised its author for making "something elegant and even beautiful out of such a wretched mess".

And a wretched mess it was. Marson's account of JN-T's final years, in particular, is almost unbearable to read. Shunned by the industry he had loved, a pariah at the BBC, terrified of losing his long-term partner Gary Downie to cancer, and pinning his last show-biz dreams on a doomed plan to open a vaudeville theatre in the Spanish mountains, the heavy drinker suffered a long and painful decline through liver failure, including a partial amputation of his leg. During his last decade, Nathan-Turner had also burned bridges with many of his old friends, spurred on by the toxic Downie, memorably described by Ian Levine as "the black widow spider, spouting venom into his ear"[35]. The ex-producer's estrangement from his former leading lady, Nicola Bryant, was particularly shocking: at a *Doctor Who* convention in the mid-90s, Nathan-Turner walked up to Bryant backstage and, in a jealous rage over some paranoid idea she had slept with a gay friend of his, spat in her face. They never spoke again.

But the chapter of Marson's book that inevitably made headlines in March 2013 was the one entitled "Hanky Panky" – a title that alludes to Nathan-Turner's oft-repeated quote that "there's no hanky panky in the TARDIS", while revealing there was an awful *lot* of hanky panky going on outside it. In particular, Marson adds substance to the rumours, long circulating in fandom circles, that Nathan-Turner and Downie used their influence to seduce young men, with Downie acting as the talent scout, cruising convention floors to identify – to use his charming idiom – "doable barkers".

It gets worse. Marson himself enters his own narrative when he recalls how, on a visit to the BBC's Union House to collect some photographs for *Doctor Who Magazine*, he was pounced upon by Downie in a lift, and had to run away and hide under a desk. Luckily for him, there was no-one else there, though it wasn't unknown for people to be found squatting out of sight in BBC offices. In perhaps the book's most vividly indelible tale, former

DWAS exec member Mark Sinclair recalls how he crouched under Nathan-Turner's desk, dutifully administering a blow job while the producer was on the phone to legendary *Blue Peter* editor Biddy Baxter. (I bet at ITV, they could at least afford a proper casting couch.)

With "Doctor Who Sex Scandal" splashed across its front page (alongside a picture of Nathan-Turner and Colin Baker who, a very small caption pointed out, "is not involved" in the allegations[XVIII]), the *Daily Mirror* reported that, "still reeling from the Jimmy Savile sex scandal, the BBC was last night rocked by more claims of sleaze among its ranks". All things being equal, it was hardly the sort of publicity push the BBC had had in mind for the show's 50th anniversary year. Thankfully, the world seemed to greet the story with a collective shrug. Marson, meanwhile, grappled with the elephant in the room by asking: "Was John Nathan-Turner a paedophile?" He believes not: "However dim a view today's BBC management might take of John's activities, there is no evidence whatsoever that he was a Savile-esque character. John was clearly attracted to young adults – but not children."[35] His targets may often have been below the homosexual age of consent – which was not brought in line with heterosexuals until 2000 – but to condemn him for that, argues Marson, would be to punish him simply for being a promiscuous gay man in less enlightened times.

We now return you to *Space Helmet for a Cow*, where there will be jokes about funny monsters and petty arguments about whether things are canon.

Tennant's extra

On March 25th, there emerged news of a scandal that was *really* worth *Doctor Who* fans getting in a lather about: a three-minute mini-episode called *Demons Run – Two Days Later*, explaining how Strax had survived the events of *A Good Man Goes to War*, was made available via Amazon and iTunes... but only in North America. That's right, *Doctor Who* that *British* people – British *licence-fee payers* – weren't allowed to watch. (If only the same had been true of *Torchwood: Miracle Day*, thought viewers, wistfully.)

Not to worry, though, as the imminent return of *Doctor Who* proper was signalled by a rush of promotional activity, with Matt Smith and Jenna Coleman talking up the new series across the world, from British breakfast telly to the *New Zealand Herald*. In the US, the show made a quick return to the front of *Entertainment Weekly*, which came wrapped in a choice of two *Who* covers and featured a contribution from one Peter Jackson, who revealed his desire to direct an episode. "They don't even have to pay me!" the Hobbit-wrangler insisted. "But I have got my eye on one of those nice new gold-coloured Daleks. They must have a spare one (hint, hint)." Sounds like a pretty good deal for the BBC (provided there's a favourable Dalek exchange rate).

Interviewed by *The Times*, Matt Smith revealed that his granddad helped his mum open his fan mail – and had once got more than he bargained for. "So he gets this letter and it opens with, 'I want to... you know...' Well there was sucking and... all that stuff. It was pretty graphic. But anyway, she was about 40 or 50 and asked me to go to her house in Essex, I think it was, and 'take care' of all these things she was describing. My granddad wrote back: 'Matt isn't available, but I'm his grand-dad and I am'." Down boy.

Jenna-Louise Coleman spoke to *Radio Times* about her character's "challenging" relationship with the Doctor – "Matt describes it as a dance, but to me it's such a ping-pongy kind of dynamic"[37] – and her own partnership with boyfriend Richard Madden, aka Robb Stark in HBO's phenomenally popular fantasy epic *Game of Thrones*. (The cosplay implications don't bear thinking about. Or maybe they do.)

In *Doctor Who Magazine*, Steven Moffat outlined his vision for the upcoming run of episodes. "It's a lighter version of the story arc, I suppose, than we had last year," he mused. "I'm keen to have big, standalone stories – but of course there's a mystery running throughout the year."[36] *SFX*'s shorthand notes from the Series 7B press junket, meanwhile, revealed Caro Skinner rhapsodising about the "utter, utter joy" of the job, adding: "I just feel very excited. It feels as if I've probably got the best job in television this year."[37] Oh dear.

There were mixed fortunes – that's putting it kindly – for FX house Mill TV when it was nominated for a BAFTA for its work on *Asylum of the Daleks* – in the same week it announced it was shutting up shop owing to the "volatile trends present in the film and TV industry". Happily, six of the Mill team would subsequently re-open for business as a new visual effects company called Milk, with one of their first major contracts being the *Doctor Who* 50th anniversary special. So it just goes to show, there's no point crying over spilt... well, you get the idea.

In Georgia, USA, *Doctor Who* was honoured at the 72nd Annual Peabody Awards ("The World's Oldest Awards for Electronic Media", dontcha know). The presiding committee stated: "Seemingly immortal, 50 years old and still running, this engaging, imaginative sci-fi/fantasy series is awarded an Institutional Peabody for evolving with technology and the times like nothing else in the known television universe." Quite an honour – now all they needed to do was decide which person from the last 50 years should keep it in their loo.

And then, on Saturday, March 30th, *Doctor Who* returned to BBC One for a shiny new series of adventures starring Matt Smith and Jenna-Louise Coleman which promised to take viewers on a roller coaster from modern-day London to the depths of the ocean, the far reaches of space and on a journey to the heart of the TARDIS. Except, by 6.15pm, everyone was already talking about something else entirely. Namely, the cast for the 50th anniversary special, which had leaked out when subscription copies of the latest issue of *Doctor Who Magazine* were mailed out early, plopping onto doormats that very Saturday morning. Not for the first time, the BBC found itself bounced into making an official announcement on the fly – namely, that David Tennant and Billie Piper would both be back for the celebration shindig, along with special guest star John Hurt. Exciting stuff, to be sure – but Tennant and Piper were probably not the hot couple Moffat wanted people talking about as he launched his new TARDIS team on their latest escapades.

The Bells of Saint John was born out of Moffat's desire to do a proper *Doctor Who* urban thriller. "We usually do our most epic stuff in outer space," said the showrunner. "This time, we're doing it in the middle of the

city, and that somehow makes it more exciting. I thought, if you could bring outer-space production values to twenty-first century London..."[36] According to Caro Skinner, the season premiere may also have been at least partly inspired by another British screen icon who had just celebrated his 50th birthday in spectacular, award-hoovering style: "He probably watched *Skyfall* and thought, right, how do I top that?"[37] Skinner told *SFX*.

Possibly. But *The Bells of Saint John*'s opening sequence, hymning the modern London skyline beneath a blur of html, shares as much – if not more – DNA with Moffat's reinvention of Sherlock Holmes than Sam Mendes' take on 007. While *Sherlock* largely fetishises technology, though, here Moffat takes a more cautionary approach, finding menace in the ever-present thrum of wi-fi just as, five decades earlier, Kit Pedler had issued a similarly modish warning about the Post Office tower in 1966's *The War Machines*. Or possibly it's just a grumpy middle-aged man – and recent social media refusenik – moaning about all that dreadful new-fangled technology: "Human souls trapped like flies in the worldwide web, crying out for help," muses the Doctor. "Isn't that basically Twitter?" asks Clara. The bad guys, meanwhile, are ultimately betrayed by their Facebook statuses.

The biggest of these bads turns out to be the Great Intelligence (and you do have to wonder what *its* FB profile must look like: "The Great Intelligence updated its status from Psychic Snowflake to King of the Yetis"). This time, Richard E Grant has employed a frontwoman for his plan of uploading human souls to the internet ("It's like immortality, only fatal") in the form of Celia Imrie's deliciously arch Miss Kizlet.

One chosen method of upload is the "spoonheads" – portable Wi-Fi terminals capable of cloning human beings, albeit human beings with a ruddy great dent in the back of their skulls. To be honest, they're not destined to be great monsters, though the one that takes the form of a little girl from Clara's book (written by one Amelia Williams, no less) is pretty spooky.

But all the episode's giddy pleasures – even the silly-but-thrilling set piece where the Doctor rides a motorbike up The Shard – are really just a sideshow for the real story here, which is *Doctor Who*'s latest twist on the patented boy meets girl, boy turns out to be time traveller with dimensionally transcendental police box formula. In a wonderful, very Moffatian set-up, Clara – modern, twenty-first-century Clara, a northern girl working as a live-in nanny in London – calls for help with her wi-fi and is put through to the TARDIS in Cumbria, 1207, where the Doctor is living a monastic existence in a cave. ("The bells of Saint John are ringing!" shout his fellow monks, as the police box phone trills incongruously.)

That's enough to bring the Time Lord to Clara's front door, plunging her into a madcap adventure that's part contemporary thriller, part screwball comedy. One sequence, in which the Intelligence tries to kill our heroes by turning the house lights of London into a landing strip, is as exhilarating as it is preposterous, especially when Clara is dragged into the Doctor's "snog box", only to emerge seconds later aboard the crashing plane, coffee cup still in hand.

Mixing these big action scenes with a barrage of quotable one-liners ("I can't tell the future, I just work there"), *The Bells of Saint John* is a supremely confident opener, brilliantly played by Matt Smith and Jenna-Louise Coleman.

The critics were generally positive: In *The Guardian*, Euan Ferguson said the episode was "complex, cutting edge and rather silly – but most of all it was splendid", while *Radio Times*' Patrick Mulkern hailed a "hugely entertaining" episode that showcased "Steven Moffat at his playful, confident best", and predicted great things for Coleman's "warm, sympathetic, gutsy" Clara. The *Daily Mirror*'s Jon Cooper described the story as the "TV equivalent of comfort food – apple crumble, onion gravy... a nice hunk of tangy, crumbling cheddar", which may or may not be a compliment, while the *Daily Mail* dispensed with anything as bothersome as hiring a TV critic and just nicked comments from Twitter.

The episode's overnight rating of 6.2 million saw it beaten by old rivals Ant and Dec but, predictably, by the time the final figures were revealed, *The Bells of Saint John*'s audience had climbed to an impressive 8.44 million, out-ranking everything else that week except *Coronation Street* and one episode of *EastEnders*. Which would absolutely, *definitely* put an end to all those stories about it not being as popular as it used to be. Right?

On April 1st, the BBC released evidence that this 50th anniversary shit was real (not their actual words) with the release of a photo of Matt Smith and David Tennant clutching a) their scripts and b) each other at the read-through for the episode. Word is the squees could heard as far away as Jupiter. And Tennant and Billie Piper weren't the only old faces returning, as a certain hideous orange creature from the Doctor's past was spotted filming on location in Neath. (Whoever just shouted "Bonnie Langford", shame on you. I'm talking about the Zygons, of course.)

Filming on the special had got under way on the TARDIS set a few days earlier, before which Marcus Wilson had announced: "Ladies and gentlemen. Fiftieth anniversary. Thank you for being here. Good luck." And no pressure, obviously.

David Tennant joined the shoot in early April, sporting his original 2005 suit. The actor admitted he'd struggled to recapture the tenth Doctor's voice while practising his lines at home, but a viewing of *The Stolen Earth / Journey's End* had done the trick.

John Hurt's appearance on set wearing what appeared to be the eighth Doctor's waistcoat and the ninth Doctor's leather jacket also set the internet ablaze with speculation. Could Hurt be playing some sort of amalgamation of two of his former selves? Were we about to have to start re-ordering our books and DVDs to make way for this interlocutor? Or was his character just really into cosplay?

Whatever the reason, the appearance of *that* jacket inevitably fuelled conjecture about whether Christopher Eccleston might be persuaded to turn up to the party. But a BBC statement on April 5th was quick to throw a jug of water over the idea: "Chris met with Steven Moffat a couple of times to talk about Steven's plans for the *Doctor Who* 50th anniversary episode," it said. "After careful thought, Chris decided not to be in the episode. He wishes the team all the best."[XIX]

The fact there were two meetings suggests Eccleston may at least have been tempted by the idea. Unless, of course, they went something like this:

First meeting:

SM: "Would you like to be in the *Doctor Who* 50th anniversary special?"

CE: "No."

Second meeting:

SM: "Are you *sure* you wouldn't you like to be in the *Doctor Who* 50th anniversary special?"

CE: "Yes."

Ice Warrior agrees to remove his armour (but only if it's integral to the script)

Neil Cross' *Doctor Who* debut brings a whole new meaning to the term space opera, as not only is it set in space, great chunks of it are accompanied by soaring arias.

Actually, it's more of a rock opera, as the Doctor whisks Clara off to the eponymous Rings of Akhaten – an inhabited cluster of planetoids, asteroids and other big space oids forming a rocky belt around a large, sun-like planet.

This is *Doctor Who* hoiking itself out of living rooms and shops and graveyards and attempting to demonstrate its big, sci-fi chops – and, to be fair, the visuals are largely impressive, complete with a bustling alien marketplace that stands up reasonably well against *Star Wars'* cantina (still the gold standard of alien menageries).

Separated from the Doctor, Clara runs into Merry Gejelh, the Queen of Years – a child who's hiding because she's due to sing at a ritual ceremony, and is terrified her performance will awaken an angry god, who will then consume the universe. And you thought *American Idol* was tough. (Although, given that Merry is played by Amelia Jones, daughter of Aled, maybe she's right to be worried.)

This is the cue for a lot of hokum, frankly, involving some rather dull quasi-religious sacraments, a soul-eating mummy in a glass box and a truly rubbish flying space moped (don't expect a Lego set), all accompanied by the Crouch End Festival Chorus.

The big reveal is that the angry god everyone's trying to soothe with lullabies is actually Akhaten itself, the planet turning out to be a

colossal parasitic creature that feeds on memories, stories and feelings (yes, another one). A sentient planet we can just about swallow – but did it really need eyes and a mouth and a nose, like a child's drawing of the moon? Or a pumpkin? (I mean, what would a planet even *do* with a nose? To say nothing of the size of the hankie it would need.)

The rousing (it says here) climax involves the Doctor literally trying to talk this bad boy to death with a grandstanding speech ("I've watched universes freeze and creations burn. I've seen things you wouldn't believe. I have lost things you will never understand. And I know things. Secrets that must never be told. Knowledge that must never be spoken. Knowledge that will make parasite gods blaze") that Matt Smith does a decent number on, up to the point he's called upon to shout "take it all, baby!" like an intergalactic Austin Powers, before Clara takes over and saves the day with an autumn leaf. (Don't ask.)

At this point, Akhaten shrivels up and dies, plunging everything into darkness. Quite where this leaves the people on the rings orbiting the thing is never explained – though it would probably be a good idea to get to work on developing oxygen, gravity, heat and the electric light pretty sharpish.

It is, despite the germ of some good ideas, all just too silly for words. "I've walked in universes where the laws of physics were devised by a madman," says the Doctor at one point. Well quite.

A few days later, London sightseers got more than they bargained for when filming for the anniversary special saw the TARDIS being hoisted high above Trafalgar Square, with Clara leaning out of the door and the Doctor hanging off the bottom. Either this was one of the show's most daring stunts yet, or the guy with the crane had arrived *way* too early. Director Nick Hurran and his team were also in action at the Tower of London, with Coleman joined by Jemma Redgrave – reprising her role as Kate Lethbridge-Stewart – and comedy actress Ingrid Oliver, who was seen sporting a *very* familiar stripey scarf.

The team then returned to Cardiff, where recording was briefly interrupted when a fire alarm went off at Roath Lock studios, resulting in the memorable sight of two Time Lords, several UNIT troops, three ETs from *Wizards vs Aliens* and a dozen or so doctors and nurses from *Casualty* standing cooling their heels in the car park. ("How many times have I told you?" grumbled the health and safety officer. "You can't open a space-time rift that close to a smoke detector.")

On April 19th, the world awoke to the acrid smell of the internet gently smoking as the title of the season finale was unveiled as *The Name of the Doctor*, along with a poster promising "His secret is revealed". Popular opinion was split between those speculating what the Doctor's name might turn out to be, and those outraged that that upstart Moffat should have the gall to slaughter such a sacred cow in the first place. Moffat, for his part, insisted the title wasn't a tease or a cheat – he really would be revealing the show's greatest secret. Everyone agreed that, if he *was* telling the truth, he'd better have a real doozy up his sleeve because, after a 50-year build-up, "Graeme" wasn't going to cut it.

In *Cold War*, Mark Gatiss delivers a *Doctor Who* base-under-siege story so shamelessly old-skool, you half expect it to be followed by Bruce Forsyth presiding over a potter's wheel. But what it might lack in subtext, emotional clout and all the other grown-up stuff that usually comes fitted as standard these days, it more than makes up for with a rip-roaring, solidly built adventure straight out of a 70s Target novelisation.

The main sell, obviously, is the return of the Ice Warriors – an idea that Steven Moffat was initially resistant to: "Mark Gatiss does go on," wrote Moffat in the *Radio Times*. "He's been on at me about the Ice Warriors since I took over the show. And, frankly, I kept disappointing him. I just wasn't that thrilled about unearthing yet another old monster. I felt slightly we'd done all the good ones." Then Gatiss pitched the story, and one idea in particular made Moffat's "hair stand on end".[38]

You can fill in your own gag about Moffat's hair here, but the idea he's referring to is probably the moment when our favourite Martian shucks off its chitinous carapace and disappears into the bowels of the stricken Soviet submarine in which the action unfolds. The reveal that the classic Ice Warrior silhouette – beautifully updated in a way that's faithful to the original, while wisely taking a few inches off the hips – is actually just armour (or, as Clara quips, a shell suit) is inspired, as a slimy, slithering alien stalking the crew of the sub is a lot scarier than a hulking great giant clomping about the place. Basically, this is *Alien* meets *The Hunt for Red October* – except neither of those featured David Warner singing the praises of Ultravox. (The title may be a pun, but it's also genuinely set during the Cold War, hence the frequent namechecks for Midge Ure's New Wave synthpop combo.)

Gatiss takes his cue from the better Ice Warrior stories of the 60s and 70s by portraying the Martians as a proud martial race with a strong code of honour. There's also more than a hint of 2005's classic *Dalek* in the clear and present danger presented by a lone warrior (in this case Grand Marshal Skaldak, sovereign of the Tharseesian Caste and vanquisher of the Phobos Heresy), while Clara's conversation with the chained prisoner can't help but recall Rose going eyeball-to-eyestalk in the earlier adventure. And Skaldak's first appearance, being thawed out of a big block of ice, is no less effective for being a direct lift from the creatures' debut 47 years earlier.

Douglas Mackinnon's direction is terrific – from the opening shot, in which his camera races through the ice floes of the North Pole, to its prowl down the hissing, steaming corridors of the sub's interior, Mackinnon finds the perfect blend of pacy action and clammy tension. He gets great performances from his cast, too: Liam Cunningham – the man who was so very nearly the eighth Doctor – brings a world-weary authority to Captain Zhukov, while his *Game of Thrones* colleague Tobias Menzies sneers menacingly as his Mother Russia-loving Lieutenant, Stepashin, a man who literally takes no prisoners. And David Warner – another nearly Doctor – is magnificent by dint of being David Warner.

You might question if it wouldn't have been better to keep the Martian creature in the shadows, rather than giving it its big close-up at the end. But then, very little about this episode serves as an advert for subtlety and suggestion. With *Cold War*, what you see is what you get. And we like what we see.

Journey Up and Down Some Corridors of the TARDIS

Doctor Who has flirted with ghost stories before – but *Hide* finds the series embracing the genre in all its door-slamming, candle-guttering, chain-clanking glory.

Specifically, it's a haunted house story, as the Doctor and Clara arrive at a large Gothic pile one storm-lashed night in 1974. There they find the present lord of the manor, Professor Alec Palmer, engaged in a series of experiments to find evidence of the house's resident spook, the Caliburn Ghost. "She's mentioned in local Saxon poetry and parish folk tales," explains Palmer. "The Wraith of the Lady, the Maiden in the Dark, the Witch of the Well."

Palmer is being assisted by Emma Grayling, an empath whose psychic ability appears to be able to summon the ghost. When the Doctor convinces Palmer he's a "man from the ministry", his host reluctantly agrees to let him join the ghost hunt – though Emma warns Clara that her fellow traveller has "a sliver of ice in his heart". Eeek.

This is the set-up for a truly spine-shivering excursion into the paranormal, as the Doctor and Clara venture into the black heart of the house. *Doctor Who* has rarely plunged headlong into such pulse-quickening territory, the brush of something in the dark, the snatched glimpses of a figure in the window and a truly terrifying apparition screaming out of the shadows making no concessions to the young or faint of heart.

Sadly, the story reveals its hand a little too soon. Yes, we know in *Doctor Who* we ultimately demand a rational explanation, but here the sci-fi bafflegab – wouldn'tcha know, it's not really a ghost, but a time traveller trapped in a pocket dimension – feels premature, and the episode is never as compelling again. In the final reel, the story even takes a sudden lurch into creature feature, as the Doctor is pursued through a forest by a snarling beastie.

Director Jamie Payne shoots these dark fairytale scenes beautifully – the creature itself is a barely-seen blur, appearing to slip between realities – and Matt Smith sells the idea of an unusually terrified Time Lord with conviction. But it's never really made clear *why* the Doctor

is so scared – surely, this is just another day at the office for the man who fights the monsters? And the less said about the resolution – in which the TARDIS flies in and scoops up the Doctor like Superman disguised as a wooden box – the better.

Apparently, Neil Cross (who largely atones for *The Rings of Akhaten* here) had originally wanted to keep the story as more of a confined chamber piece. It's a pity he didn't get his way, as *Hide* ends up being very much a game of two halves, with the time-travelling monster mash of the latter serving to slightly devalue the expertly constructed shivers of the opening act. It's still a fabulous piece of television, though – one of the most thrillingly atmospheric *Doctor Who* stories of the decade – and is well-served by its small cast. Alec and Emma's sweet, stumbling courtship is beautifully played by Dougray Scott and, in particular, Jessica Raine, and the regulars are on great form, despite Smith causing a minor tremor on the fan forums by mispronouncing Metebelis 3. (To be fair to Smith, he wasn't actually born when Jon Pertwee visited the blue planet in 1973. And the error was actually spotted by ever-vigilant fanboy Moffat, and the scene re-shot, but somehow the wrong version ended up in the final edit.)

As well as being *Doctor Who's* best-ever ghost story, *Hide* also serves as a love letter to the pioneering sci-fi dramatist Nigel Kneale. Cross has acknowledged the story's debt to Kneale's early 70s BBC chiller *The Stone Tape*, while Alec Palmer's character was originally supposed to be Bernard Quatermass himself, but the fan-pleasing crossover had to be abandoned when they were unable to unpick the rights issues. That's a shame, but the result is still something that even Kneale – who once airily dismissed *Doctor Who* as the sort of idea you might have in the bath, then forget about – would have to admit is a fitting tribute, and a fine slice of British sci-fi horror, to boot.

As tarty titles go, *Journey to the Centre of the TARDIS* certainly comes on strong – especially after six series in which the Doctor's time machine has kept herself firmly under wraps, only coquettishly revealing a well-turned corridor or two in *The Doctor's Wife*.

It wasn't like that in the old days, of course. Early 80s stories, in particular, featured numerous bedroom scenes (no, not like *that*) – and who could forget 1978's *The Invasion of Time*, in which a combination of spiralling inflation and industrial action had seen the interior of the TARDIS represented by a disused mental hospital in Redhill? Not Steven Moffat, obviously, as this episode was at least partly designed to compensate fans for that particular weeping sore. "Steven said – and he was telling the designer as much as me – we were all duty bound to atone for that," explained writer Stephen Thompson. "There's a huge amount written about the TARDIS and all its rooms. We've got 45 minutes and a limited budget. Quite a lot of what we do, we simply have to hint: there are suggestions of what you almost see but don't. But clearly, at the same time, you've got to deliver."[39]

Sadly, deliver is exactly what *Journey to the Centre of the TARDIS* fails to do. Instead of a fantastic voyage to the heart of the Doctor's impossible time ship, we get a standard running up and down corridors story. And the corridors aren't even that interesting – just your standard flatpack sci-fi corridors from the nearest Space Ikea. They don't even have *roundels*, for Chrissakes.

The plot is simple, and a wee bit silly. When a salvage ship captures the TARDIS, the Doctor tricks its three-man crew into helping him find Clara, who has somehow been thrown deep into the time machine's interior (must have been a hell of a shunt). The damaged time ship is also "leaking the past", which sounds like the cue for it to offer up some of its thrilling and ancient secrets (or at least a nice VT clips package), but, again, just translates as Clara being chased up and down corridors by some monsters (albeit rather terrifying monsters, cleverly shot by director Mat King).

Along the way, there are tantalising glimpses of what might have been. The TARDIS library (complete with the *Encyclopaedia Gallifrey* stored in whispering bottles) is an impressively gothic affair that recalls the 90s TV movie, and there's a brief glimpse of a swimming pool under the stars. The architectural reconfiguration system, rendered as a dense forest of lights, is also effective, and the exploded heart of the TARDIS, held in stasis with mangled engine parts hanging in a white void, doesn't disappoint. But the much-mythologised Eye of

Harmony is a bit forgettable, and it all feels like too little too late by then, especially as the plot – which might have distracted from the underwhelming visuals – is such thin gruel.

As the salvage crew, Ashley Walters, Mark Oliver and Jahvel Hall are saddled with three of the least interesting guest leads ever – a situation not helped when the latter, as the android Tricky, is revealed not to be an android at all – it's just a little joke his brothers have been playing on him all these years. LOL! This is surely a contender for the dumbest idea in any *Doctor Who* story, and sends the inquiring mind down numerous avenues it might prefer not to explore. Chief among them: did Tricky never wonder why an android needed to eat and... you know, attend to the other end of things? What exactly did he think he was flushing away down there – ball bearings?

Thompson's script is also drably devoid of memorable lines; there's a funny bit where the Doctor describes his own people as "smart bunch, Time Lords – no dress sense, dreadful hats, but smart" but that's its sole entry into *The Quotable Who*. And the plot resolution involves the Doctor literally pressing the re-set button – it actually says "big friendly button" on the top – to rewrite time and effectively return the story to factory settings. If even the people who lived through it end up finding this story completely forgettable, then what hope for the rest of us?

Back on Earth, the announcement of *Doctor Who*'s new co-executive producer came as a surprise to few. Aberystwyth-born Brian Minchin had risen through the ranks of BBC Wales, collecting numerous *Doctor Who* credits along the way: as well as production duties on *Torchwood* and *The Sarah Jane Adventures*, he had been a script editor during the Tennant-Smith transition, and had even written a *Who* novel for BBC Books. Following stints as exec producer on Toby Whithouse's *Being Human* and BBC Four's excellent but short-lived series based on Douglas Adams' Dirk Gently novels, he had been returned to the mothership where, it's fair to say, he probably wouldn't need to bother typing "Doctor Who" into Wikipedia.

"I'm thrilled and excited to be joining Steven Moffat on a show that has meant so much to me over the years," said Minchin. "I've watched in awe as Steven has taken *Doctor Who* to wild and imaginative places and I can't wait to get started on many more adventures with the Doctor."

Presumably starting with *Doctor Who in an Exciting Adventure with Some Spreadsheets*.

The Crimson Horror and Nightmare in Silver (Mild Discomfort in Taupe and other paint colours available on request)

Marking 100 episodes since *Doctor Who's* return to television, *The Crimson Horror* is hewn from pure Mark Gatiss DNA. From *The League of Gentlemen's* comic grotesques to his trilogy of Lucifer Box novels, via his scholarly TV essays on British horror, Gatiss has demonstrated an unswerving passion for a particularly lurid strain of gothic melodrama. And here he is finally allowed to fully indulge his passion for the Grand Guignol in a story so steeped in the tradition of grisly Victoriana that even one of the characters is moved to describe it as "the stuff of Penny Dreadfuls".

It's also one of *Doctor Who's* rare forays to the north country, specifically Yorkshire, where's there's trouble at'Mill – or, in this case, Sweetville, a model village in the style provided by such enlightened Victorian industrialists as Titus Salt.

Run by Mrs Winifred Gillyflower and her silent partner, Mr Sweet, Sweetville's stated mission is to save "the chosen few" from the coming apocalypse. In reality, its towering silo houses a giant rocket which will be used to spread "the crimson horror" – the poison produced by a parasitic, prehistoric red leech – across the Earth. Mr Sweet, it transpires, is the last survivor of a race that was causing trouble for the Silurians as far back as the late Cretaceous Period, and has now taken up residence on Mrs G's décolletage.

As you might imagine, Gatiss is having a hoot here – and he's not the only one. Diana Rigg and Rachael Stirling eat up their roles as the wicked harpy and her blind, disfigured daughter Ada, who Gillyflower Snr treats with nothing but contempt. "Kindly do not claw and slobber at my crinolen," admonishes Mrs

G, memorably, while Ada, on learning of her mother's betrayal, launches at her with an impassioned cry of "you perfidious hag!"

Matt Smith also gets to join in the fun, spending his early scenes as a blister red, stiff-limbed mutation, the product of Sweetville's experiments rejecting his Time Lord DNA – a Frankenstein's monster role that suits his lantern jaw looks perfectly.

When we do get to see him in action as the Doctor – and we're kept waiting half the episode – it's in a wedge of info-dump backstory wittily rendered by director Saul Metzstein as a scratchy, stuttering sepia film reel, complete with whirling fairground organ.

Also cutting loose is Jenny, here shedding her maid's outfit to perform a kick-ass judo routine in a black leather catsuit clearly intended as a tribute to Diana Rigg's most iconic role. Madam Vastra and, in particular, Strax also continue to be great value, especially the latter's argument with a horse.

The story delights in bizarre imagery, including supersized gramophones, a couple frozen under a bell jar mid-afternoon tea, and a wonderfully steampunky rocket – though nothing sticks in the memory quite like Dame Diana Rigg feeding her significant other by chucking handfuls of salt down the inside of her blouse during dinner.

With dialogue that frequently wobbles over the line into outright parody ("I've pickled things in 'ere as fair turn yer 'air as snowy as t'top o' Buckden Pike," says the gleefully ghoulish coroner), *The Crimson Horror* is a contender for *Doctor Who's* campiest hour – and that's in a show that once made Kate O'Mara dress up as Bonnie Langford. In lesser hands, it might have collapsed under the weight of its own archness, but Metszstein pitches it just right, the result being a minor gem.

Which is not how many would describe what followed it seven days later. Where *The Doctor's Wife* had seen Neil Gaiman playing with *Doctor Who's* mythology – partly by way of a romcom – the fantasy author approached his second script with a more fundamental aim: "With *Nightmare in Silver*, I want to send the kids behind the sofa," he declared. "It's what *Doctor Who* is meant to do. I loved the idea of making the Cybermen scary again. I wanted to create an emotional reaction that was similar to how I felt when I saw the Cybermen on the Moonbase."[40]

Sadly, unless the reaction he felt when he first saw 1966's *The Moonbase* was a snort of derision, we have to report that, second time around, Gaiman fell somewhat short of his ambition. The script's major fault lines are all there at the outset – firstly, it's set on a "theme park world", which is surely one of the naffest sci-fi concepts ever. Worse, the story is holed below the water line from the get-go by the inclusion of Clara's young charges, Angie and Artie, as temporary TARDIS travellers. No-one likes kids on telly at the best of times, and these two are instantly hateful – they're whining brats whose default response to the wonders of a whole new world is snotty sarcasm. Angie's *very* first line is to complain that "your stupid box can't even get us to the right place," and that's her at her most winning.

As soon as they've landed on Hedgewick's World of Wonders, a derelict intergalactic amusement park – think Alton Towers after a holocaust, or at least a run on the burger van – the Doctor starts to suspect something is wrong, not least when he's greeted by a chess-playing automaton fashioned from a rusty Cyberman. At this point, Clara decides the kids are tired, even though they've only just arrived, and, instead of taking them home or back to the TARDIS for a nap, the Doctor decides it's a good idea for them to bed down in the creepy room full of statues which he suspects might be dangerous. So you might want to think twice before hiring him as a babysitter. Just sayin'.

From here, things spin off at the most random tangents – a half-formed jumble of ideas that suggests the script was assembled from fridge poetry during an earthquake. Tamzin Outhwaite guests as the captain of a platoon of soldiers which serves no obvious purpose other than to put Clara in charge during the world's least convincing military coup. Meanwhile, sci-fi staple Warwick Davis guests as Porridge, a galactic emperor in absentia that recalls his previous role as an Ewok, only more gimmicky.

If the story has a trump card, it's its army of re-booted Cybermen, now sleeker than ever and finally freed from their clumpy, agonis-ingly slow march by a new "bullet time" effect that allows them to attack at impossible speed. Unfortunately, this innovation is barely used – perhaps it drains their batteries, like when you leave the backlight on your phone – while a genuinely breathtaking shot of them emerging from their Cyber tombs is so fleeting as to be virtually subliminal. Instead, they're reduced to staging a glacially slow attack on The Comical Castle – I'm not taking the piss, that's its actual name – and kidnapping Angie, who screams "Put me down, I hate you!" as if she's stumbled into a Kevin and Perry sketch. Has Neil Gaiman ever actually *met* any teenagers, one wonders, or has he just read about them in *The Beano*?

A major plot beat finds the Doctor being partially upgraded into a Cyberman – a potentially terrifying concept that ought to carry the same sense of dread as Jean-Luc Picard's conversion into Locutus of Borg in *Star Trek*. Instead, it just leads to endless scenes of the Doctor arguing with himself – literally spinning on his heel and shouting back at himself – which, despite Matt Smith's heroic efforts, is woefully undramatic. The fact the Cyber hive-mind is controlled by a "Cyber Planner" says it all. Not an emperor, not a marshal, not a commander, but a planner – the cyborg equivalent of Microsoft Outlook Calendar.

A confusing and desperately underpowered story, lacking any sense of jeopardy, Gaiman's sophomore script is a strong contender for New *Who*'s most clanging dud. Or, as Angie would say: *Nightmare in Silver*: I *hate* you!

Doctor Who fans complain over use of excessive Force

Doctor Who's place at the heart of the nation's cultural landscape saw it honoured at the 2013 BAFTA Television Awards – not with anything posh, like a Fellowship (that went to Michael Palin), but with a YouTube-style clips mash-up, followed by some brief comic business filmed on the TARDIS set with Matt Smith and Jenna Louise-Coleman. The Academy's chief executive, Amanda Berry, said: "There are only a handful of programmes that have the quality and longevity of *Doctor Who* and the ability to put the nation on their sofas – or indeed behind them – year after year. BAFTA raises a toast to *Doctor Who* on its 50th birthday this year." Which was nice. I guess.

As if to underline *Doctor Who*'s curiously fumbling, haphazard journey to greatness, the same day also brought the slightly embarrassing news that the show's best-kept secret – as revealed in the cliffhanger to *The Name of the Doctor* – had inadvertently been unveiled to 210 fans in the US when an American distributor accidentally sent out the Series Seven Part Two Blu-ray box sets a fortnight early. How Steven Moffat laughed. Again.

The show's brand manager, Edward Russell, was forced to appeal to fans' good nature and beg them to keep schtum until the episode's broadcast the following weekend. Moffat weighed in with a bit of bribery, promising to reward discretion with a special video of Matt Smith and David Tennant straight after the episode. (But presumably not *that* kind of special video.)

Meanwhile, most imaginative TV tie-in opp of the week went to DC Thomson, publishers of *The Beano*, who reprinted their entire 1981 summer special on the basis that the Doctor had briefly been seen reading it in *The Rings of Akhaten*. The Doctor and a Dalek also made an appearance on the cover of the latest issue, with Matt Smith's chin giving Desperate Dan a run for his money.

And it seemed we'd be seeing a lot more of the Chin, as both news and fan sites breathlessly reported that Smith had signed to appear in Series Eight. The source of the story was an interview with *The Sun*, in which Smith claimed that, when filming on the 50th special had wrapped, "We go on to the next series, which will either start filming at the end of this year or the start of 2014". So that was definitely that, then.

Meanwhile, in a university hall far, far away – Norfolk, to be precise – trouble flared when a sci-fi event organised by the Norwich *Star Wars* Club at the University of East Anglia was gatecrashed by *Doctor Who* fans from a rival local group. Things quickly escalated, and the police were called after reports a man had been assaulted.

"After a lengthy investigation," said a police spokesman – presumably while trying not to laugh – "talking to witnesses and reviewing good CCTV footage, it was confirmed that there was no assault. The two rival groups were spoken to and advised to keep out of each other's way."

Jim Poole, Norwich Sci-Fi Club's treasurer, told the BBC there was a history of rivalry and disputes between the two clubs – so it's probably handy he was dressed as Brigadier Lethbridge-Stewart, formerly of the United Nations, at the time. Mr Poole explained that he and a fellow fan, dressed as the fifth Doctor, had gone along to the event to get autographs of actors Graham Cole (aka *The Bill*'s PC Tony Stamp, and formerly a Cyberman, Marshman and the Melkur, among others) and Jeremy Bulloch (who was *The Time Warrior*'s Hal the Archer long before he donned Boba Fett's helmet) for a *Doctor Who* diary to be auctioned for charity. The tenth Doctor and Judge Dredd had waited outside.

"It's a bit sad and pathetic," said Mr Poole, who had ended the day in the back of a police car. "We're all in the same boat. We're not in competition. We'd like to extend the hand of friendship." (I'd be careful about that – remember what happened to Luke Skywalker.)

Dominic Warner, secretary of Norwich Star Wars Club, insisted it had all been blown out of proportion, and said the two clubs were having discussions about a meeting to resolve their differences. Ban Ki Moon – stay by your phone.

In happier news, it was revealed *Doctor Who* had once again topped the BBC's iPlayer charts for April, with some episodes clocking up more than two million requests. For gods' sake, nobody tell the *Star Wars* guys.

By the time May 18th rolled around, the secrets of the season finale were still very much under wraps, those 210 Americans in the know having done the decent thing. Or maybe they just hadn't got round to watching it yet.

The Name of the Doctor opens with what is undoubtedly *Doctor Who*'s most crowd-pleasing, crowd-*pleasuring*, even, pre-title sequence ever. It's Gallifrey. A very long time ago. Someone's broken into the TARDIS repair shop. It's William Hartnell! In colour(ish)! With Susan! He's stealing the TARDIS! Yes, it's *that* moment. *Doctor Who*'s year zero – the day our hero left his own people to save the universe and Saturday teatimes. But wait a minute, who's this? It's Clara Oswald! But surely that's impossible, even by her standards? And she's telling the Doctor he's about to make "a very big mistake".

Then Clara is lost. She doesn't know where she is. There's a flash of a familiar, migraine-inducing overcoat: it's Colin Baker, or someone who looks very much like he did 30 years ago, striding through the back of the shot. And then Tom – *actual* Tom, with Clara dropped into a scene from *The Invasion of Time*. And now she's in *Dragonfire*, bearing witness to the seventh Doctor's most controversial (and literal) cliffhanger. Then she's watching Jon Pertwee gunning Bessie down the road. And here she is chasing the second Doctor through... Palm Springs? San Diego? (Patrick Troughton has been digitally transplanted to an exotic locale from the Welsh drizzle of *The Five Doctors* – hence being somewhat overdressed in a fur coat.) A subliminal flash of the eighth Doctor, and a quick look at the fifth in *Arc of Infinity*. "I'm Clara Oswald," says the voiceover. "I'm the Impossible Girl. I was born to save the Doctor." Cue mass squeezing, outbreaks of fainting, and titles.

From this shamelessly, fabulously grand-standing opening, *The Name of the Doctor* continues to deliver thrill after giddy thrill. Not in the breathless, whizz-bang manner of a Russell T Davies season finale – the pace here is positively stately (Moffat claimed he was aiming for the same atmosphere of funereal foreboding as Tom Baker's swansong, *Logopolis*). But it's packed with the sort of ideas and images and iconography – not to mention dialogue – that feels epic without necessarily being large in scale.

At the heart of the piece, of course, is that cock-tease of a title. In a cell in Victorian London, a prisoner tells Madame Vastra: "The Doctor has a secret he will take to the grave. And it is discovered."

This is serious enough to warrant an emergency meeting of the Paternoster Gang and "the women" – Clara and River (or "the lady with the funny name and the space hair", as Clara calls her) – in a sort of astral, virtual reality conference call. But while everyone trades smarts, Vastra's home is invaded by the Whisper Men – terrifying, faceless beings with snarling fangs and an undertaker's wardrobe – leading Jenny to make a chilling confession:

"Someone's broken in... Someone's with us. Sorry, Ma'am, so sorry... I think I've been murdered."

Afterwards, Clara tells the Doctor about the prisoner's revelation, and his mention of a place River says the Doctor can never go to: Trenzalore. This draws that rarest of reactions – actual Time Lord tears – as the Doctor explains the prisoner's words have been misinterpreted. It's not his secret that is revealed, but his grave: "When you are a time traveller, there is one place you must never go. One place in all of space and time you must never, ever find yourself... Trenzalore is where I'm buried."

Trenzalore itself is a striking creation, a gothic boneyard of crumbling graves – including one with River's name carved on it. And, towering above them, rising into the night, the TARDIS – a shattered ruin, swollen to colossal proportions by a "size leak"; finally, after all these centuries, bigger on the outside. "It's a hell of a monument," says Clara. "What else would they bury me in?" asks the Doctor, grimly.

They're not on Trenzalore alone, obviously. The Great Intelligence and his whispering henchmen are also here – Richard E Grant's tombstone face looking never more at home. And, of course, the Doctor would never leave behind anything as boring as a body. In the console room – the decaying, ivy-choked heart of the dying TARDIS – is the scar tissue of the Doctor's many journeys through the time vortex; "the tracks of my tears". The Intelligence plans to enter this "open wound" and rewrite every living moment – "turn every one of your victories into defeats, poison every friendship, deliver pain to your every breath". Which is not very friendly, is it readers?

As the Doctor collapses, Clara realises what she must do: fulfil her destiny. Scatter herself through the Doctor's lives like confetti. A million echoes, a million Claras, all born to save the Doctor. It's a thrilling, wholly satisfying payoff to the Impossible Girl mystery.

And she's not the only impossible girl in the room, it turns out. The first time we met River Song, she died. Like Clara, she's an echo – and one, the Doctor admits, that should have long since faded. So this is the moment he has to let her go – a last kiss goodbye to the only woman who ever brought him to heel. Even if you've never really bought the idea of River Song as the Doctor's soulmate – and after all that impossible astronaut / robot wedding nonsense a couple of years back, who could blame you? – this is a sweet, touching farewell.

Leaping into his own time stream – preposterous, yes, but somehow Moffat convinces you to go with it – the Doctor finds Clara in a smouldering purgatory being jostled by numerous extras running past in his old costumes, like thieves fleeing a smash and grab at the *Doctor Who* Experience. (You probably wouldn't get far in the sixth Doctor's outfit.) But there's someone else – someone who's not running, but standing still and silent, his back to them. "What I did, I did without choice," he says in a familiar, husky rasp. "In the name of peace and sanity." "But not," cautions our hero, "in the name of the Doctor." At which point the figure turns around to reveal himself, and an on-screen caption announces: Introducing John Hurt as the Doctor.

Okay, so we knew it was going to be John Hurt. We've seen it in the papers. And, of course, Moffat's previous assertion that the episode's title wasn't a tease or a cheat turned out to be... well, a tease and a cheat. Because it was always going to be bunkum. (The unrepentant showrunner was firmly of the belief the ends justified the means. "It's a military campaign, working out how we get the tabloids talking about us, hopefully for good reasons," he told *Doctor Who Magazine*. "Media strategy, marketing and promotion – it sounds terribly dry, but what you're doing is trying to get people childishly excited about *Doctor Who*. That's what the marketing strategy is. It's not a cynical process."[40]) So forget the mischief and misdirection – that's just part of the game, a bit of fun – and focus instead on 45 minutes of electrifying, witty, scary, poignant television that sets *Doctor Who* up for its November anniversary in style.

After the broadcast, Moffat thanked the fans for keeping the plot revelations under wraps. "Well that was all a bit Keystone Cops, wasn't it?" he said in a message on the BBC's *Doctor Who* website. "Our biggest surprise, our most secret episode, a revelation about the Doctor that changes everything... and we'd have got away with it too, if we hadn't accidentally sent Blu-ray copies of *The Name of the Doctor* to 210

Doctor Who fans in America. Security-wise, that's not *good*, is it? I mean, it's not top-notch; it's hard to defend as professional-level, hardline secrecy.

"My favourite fact is that they're Blu-Rays. Listen, we don't just leak any old rubbish, we leak in high-def – 1080p or nothing, that's us. Every last pixel in beautifully rendered detail. It's like getting caught extra naked.

"But here's the thing. Never mind us blundering fools, check out the fans. Two hundred and ten of them, with the top-secret episode within their grasp – and because we asked nicely, they didn't breathe a word. Not one. Even *Doctor Who* websites have been closing their comments sections, just in case anyone blurts. I'm gobsmacked. I'm impressed. Actually, I'm humbled. And we are all very grateful.

"I wish I could send you all flowers, but I don't know where you live (and, given our record, you really shouldn't be sharing private information with us). So instead, here is a little video treat..."

Cue a minute-and-a-half of good-natured banter between an in-costume Matt Smith and David Tennant, discussing their shared experiences of life in the eye of the *Who* storm, and dropping teasing hints about their on-screen relationship in the upcoming special.

Flowers would have been nice as well, though.

The Daily Telegraph called *The Name of the Doctor* "momentous, moving, thrilling and very funny", while *Den of Geek* hailed the "most exciting, thrilling finale" of Moffat's tenure. *SFX* called the episode out as "a lot of middle, a stepping stone, a mere cog in a massive continuity machine" before asking: "To be honest, who cares when the cog is so gorgeously crafted it transcends mere function and dazzles in its own right?" *Digital Spy* cautioned that the story ran the risk of "alienating any viewer who doesn't know their Tom Baker from their Colin," but concluded: "In this 50th anniversary year, just this once, I think it's okay for *Doctor Who* to get its geek on". Only the *Daily Mirror* seemed in a grump, protesting, "There's not an awful lot of story here, and the big ideas don't get pulled off as interestingly or satisfyingly as the hyperbole surrounding them suggested".

With a robust 7.45 million viewers earning the finale a top ten place (and a million more watching via iPlayer), the series was clearly in rude health as it rolled headlong into its 50th anniversary campaign. And nothing, absolutely nothing, was going to spoil it. Right?

Apologies for the round robin...

"The BBC is today announcing that Matt Smith is to leave *Doctor Who* after four incredible years on the hit BBC One show," stated a press release issued by the Corporation on Saturday, June 1st. "Matt first stepped into the TARDIS in 2010 and will leave the role at the end of this year after starring in the unmissable 50th Anniversary in November and regenerating in the Christmas Special."

If a mere press release seemed a bit of a prosaic way of doing business after the previous handover – where both resignation and new appointment were announced on TV – it's because it wasn't entirely meant to be this way.

Yes, hard though it may be to believe, the announcement that the eleventh Doctor's tenure was coming to an end was yet another example of the BBC being bounced into action after being caught with its pants round its ankles due to another administrative cock-up. This time, the culprits were BBC Worldwide, who accidentally sent an internal email to hundreds of staff and a number of external licensees. In a discussion of scheduling issues surrounding the next series, the email said: "Editorially this will give the new Doctor a chance to really develop with the audience," before adding: "Apologies for this spoiler if you didn't know, but please treat this as confidential." (And definitely, definitely don't forward this to anyone outside the BBC, or press Reply All or... *oh shit*.)

"*Doctor Who* has been the most brilliant experience for me as an actor and a bloke, and that is largely is down to the cast, crew and fans of the show," said Smith in a statement. "Having Steven Moffat as showrunner write such varied, funny, mind-bending and brilliant scripts has been one of the greatest and most rewarding challenges of my career. It's been a privilege and a treat to work with Steven, he's a good friend and will continue to shape a brilliant world for the Doctor.

"The fans of *Doctor Who* around the world are unlike any other; they dress up, shout louder, know more about the history of the show (and speculate more about the future of the show) in a way that I've never seen before, your dedication is truly remarkable. Thank you so very much for supporting my incarnation of the Time Lord, number Eleven... It's been an honour to play this part, to follow the legacy of brilliant actors, and helm the TARDIS for a spell with 'the ginger, the nose and the impossible one'. But when ya gotta go, ya gotta go and Trenzalore calls. Thank you guys."

Steven Moffat said: "Every day, on every episode, in every set of rushes, Matt Smith surprised me: the way he'd turn a line, or spin on his heels, or make something funny, or out of nowhere make me cry, I just never knew what was coming next. The Doctor can be clown and hero, often at the same time, and Matt rose to both challenges magnificently.

"And even better than that, given the pressures of this extraordinary show, he is one of the nicest and hardest-working people I have ever had the privilege of knowing. Whatever we threw at him – sometimes literally – his behaviour was always worthy of the Doctor."

While the tributes flowed, press attention was already turning to Smith's replacement. At the bookies, early favourites Russell Tovey, Rupert Grint and Martin Freeman soon gave way to a two-way race between *Law & Order: UK* star Ben Daniels and Bond actor Rory Kinnear. David Beckham, Simon Cowell, Tom Cruise and Michael Jackson's daughter Paris also figured, because British tabloids are officially hil-aaaar-ious.

For Moffat, though, this was a time for a more personal reflection; in his *Doctor Who Magazine* column published a few weeks later, the showrunner wrote movingly of his friendship with Smith, noting how the actor would phone him up to offer moral support if he knew he was wrestling with a particularly tricksy script. "That is not, by any means, typical behaviour on the part of a television star," wrote Moffat. "But it is, I'm delighted to tell you, utterly typical of Matt Smith. These have been the maddest few years of my writing career – so many ridiculous adventures, so many things I thought I'd never do – and I could not have shared them with a kinder, more considerate, more entirely supportive friend than the man I completely refuse to call Smithers."[41]

Prince Charles "entitled by birthright to be the new Doctor Who," says BBC toady

Mid-June proved to be a purple patch for David Tennant. As well as being overwhelmingly voted Britain's favourite Time Lord in a nationwide YouGov survey (with 43% of the vote, the tenth Doctor polled almost as many of the rest of the Doctors combined), he was also awarded an Emmy for his work on (wait for it) *Star Wars*.

The actor scooped the gong for Outstanding Performer in an Animated Program for voicing Huyang, a droid who trains Jedi on how to build lightsabers in *The Clone Wars*. The Emmy would look fabulous on Tennant's mantelpiece and, best of all, he'd now have no trouble getting into *Star Wars* events in Norwich.

In fact, *Doctor Who* fans were rather too busy arguing with each other right now, as internet rumours that a haul of missing episodes from the 1960s had been rediscovered in Africa began to build a head of steam, with claim, counter-claim, innuendo, nudges, winks and outright bullshit feeding into so many online discussion threads, leading forum Gallifrey Base had to consolidate them into one giant Omnirumour.

The chatter got so loud, in fact, that the BBC felt obliged to issue a statement: "There are always rumours and speculation about *Doctor Who* missing episodes being discovered. However, we cannot confirm any new finds."

At the centre of the rumours was a company called Television International Enterprises Archive (TIEA). Founded by Phillip Morris, TIEA styled itself as "the world's foremost archive recovery company", with a mission to liberate vintage TV shows from whichever murderous, corrupt or simply disorganised states they had fallen into. In that sense, Morris was something of an Indiana Jones figure – except instead of hunting down powerful Biblical artefacts, he spent his time looking for old episodes of *Dr Finlay's Casebook* and the

like. (Not that he hadn't known real danger. In 2006, Morris had been one of eight oil workers kidnapped from a rig in the Niger Delta and held captive by gunmen for four days. He later told the *Daily Telegraph* that "acting like Tom Baker saved my life", though it's not clear exactly how. Maybe he'd disarmed them with a jelly baby?)

Morris followed up the BBC's statement with his own clarification: "TIEA does not hold any missing episodes of the long-running Dr Who series. The original videotapes were wiped [and] subsequent film copies were either returned to the BBC [or] sent to landfill. Odd fragments have surfaced – two episodes on 16mm film – but that's it. The programmes in question, like many others, were destroyed as they had no further commercial value. They are not missing but destroyed. The end. I am sorry if this upsets some people but these are the facts. I will be making no more statements on this subject." Well, that was us told.

Meanwhile, on the streets of Detroit, where he was filming *How to Catch a Monster*, Matt Smith – his luxuriant coiff replaced by a striking buzz cut – took time out to record a special thank you message to fans and colleagues in the form of Bob Dylan-style cue-cards. To "the crazy ginger one," "the one with the nose", "the impossible girl with the short red dress" and "the pen, the scribe, my mate Moff", Smith declared "you da best". "But most of all," he wrote, "without further ado, to the Fans, to You, the biggest Thank You." Oh stop it, you'll set us off again.

Smith returned to Cardiff in time for *Doctor Who*'s 50th birthday celebrations to receive the royal seal of approval, when the Prince of Wales and the Duchess of Cornwall (that's Charles and Camilla to the rest of you) visited the studio set at Roath Lock. Smith and the newly Louise-less Jenna Coleman gave the royal couple a lesson in how to fly the TARDIS, during which the Prince recalled watching the show as a teenager. History doesn't recall if he also asked for tips on how to make the current reigning monarch regenerate into a younger body, but after having a go at doing his own Dalek voice using Nicholas Briggs' ring modulator, he managed to resist the temptation to wheel around to the Palace and shout "Abdicate! Abdicate!" Director of Television

Danny Cohen, meanwhile, suggested Charles' Dalek impression had been so good, HRH might be in line to be the new Doctor. Suck-up.

Meanwhile, the BBC issued the first picture of David Bradley in costume as the first Doctor (or in costume as William Hartnell in costume as the first Doctor, if you want to be picky, and why wouldn't you?). Showing the actor, with an Astrakhan hat, standing in front of a faithful recreation of the original TARDIS prop in what was clearly the Totters Lane junkyard from *An Unearthly Child*, it sent an almost ghostly shiver of anticipation throughout fandom.

William Hartnell was also recreated in a more unusual way, when he and Matt Smith's likenesses were rendered in rows of corn as part of the annual York Maize Maze. The attraction – which also boasted a maize Dalek – was opened by Colin Baker, who hadn't encountered this much corn since (altogether now) he last wrestled with a Pip and Jane script. In total, the maze contained six miles of paths – at least five-and-a-half of them around Matt Smith's chin.

At the Royal Albert Hall, *Doctor Who* was once again a key fixture of the BBC's Proms, with two concerts combining Murray Gold's scores with classical pieces that had featured in the programme. To celebrate the 50th anniversary, alumni of the BBC Radiophonic Workshop performed a special suite of music from the "classic" series, while Gold himself premiered his own anniversary tribute in the form of "Song for Fifty," described by the composer as "a love song for *Doctor Who*" – though lines like "reconcile divergent creeds without succumbing to the lure of weapons" suggest he might be more of a Bacharach than a David.

Matt Smith and Jenna Coleman both appeared live – transported into the Albert Hall via a bit of comic business involving magic tickets and misplaced clothing – while Madame Vastra and Strax were joined in presenting duties by Peter Davison and, in a lovely nod to the occasion, an impossibly young-looking Carole Ann Ford. Once again, the concerts were a runaway success, the fastest-selling of the whole Proms series. Which just goes to prove the point they could liven up Rachmaninov's "Rhapsody on a Theme of Paganini" no end if they stuck a few space rhinos in it.

Doctor Who's importance to the BBC was underlined in the annual report from BBC Worldwide, which said the reduced episode count in 2012/13 had been a significant contributor to the company's fall in headline sales. In other words, the message to Steven Moffat was: type faster.

The show's annual pilgrimage to San Diego Comic-Con saw Moffat, Matt Smith, Jenna Coleman, Marcus Wilson, Mark Gatiss and David Bradley given a heroes' welcome, for which the crowd was rewarded with exclusive trailers for both the anniversary spesh and *An Adventure in Space and Time* (cue much grumbling back home when said trailers failed to appear for the benefit of licence payers).

Karen Gillan also caused a stir at the convention when she whipped off her wig to reveal her bald head, having shaved off her red locks for her role as villain Nebula in upcoming Marvel blockbuster *Guardians of the Galaxy*. With Matt Smith also sporting a shaved head from his recent Hollywood adventure, it was only a matter of time before Arthur Darvill received a call from his agent telling him she'd booked him a haircut. (In fact, Darvill was also doing rather well, having followed up his *Broadchurch* role with the lead in the Broadway production of the hit musical *Once*. It was safe to say that, for the Who Class of 2010, there would be no appearances in panto in Clacton-on-Sea this year.)

In late July, news of the latest *Doctor Who* spin-off emerged when the BBC invited fans to come along in costume to its Elstree studios for the recording of a new light entertainment pilot dedicated to the series. Details were scant, but there was speculation about what the new show might be called: *The Regeneration Game*? *Bokbusters*? *Hath I Got News For You*? *The Koquillian Pound Drop*?

The real big news, though, was that the 50th anniversary special was set to make history by being broadcast in more than 90 countries around the world *at the same time* – creating the biggest-ever global simulcast for a TV drama. "It's always been our ambition to work with our broadcast partners so that international *Doctor Who* fans can enjoy the 50th anniversary special at the same time as the

UK," said BBC Worldwide. "The time differences around the world mean that an evening transmission in the UK on the Saturday would see it being shown earlier the same day in North America and early on Sunday 24th November in Australia and New Zealand." Somehow, it seemed entirely fitting for *Doctor Who* that everyone was going to get to watch it at the same time – if not necessarily on the same day.

The special would also be shown in around 200 cinemas in the UK to give people who didn't own a 3D telly – which was everyone – the chance to experience it on the big screen in full sticky-out-o-vision. "The Doctor has always been a time traveller," said Steven Moffat. "On November 23rd, it won't be the bad guys conquering the Earth – everywhere, it will be the Day of the Doctor."

Readers of *Space Helmet* Volume I may wish to take a moment at this point to consider the BBC's treatment of the 25th anniversary special in 1988 – a small feature in the *Radio Times* and a TARDIS cake – and reflect on how far we've come. Unless you're Sylvester McCoy, in which case, probably best not to dwell on it.

By now, the guessing game surrounding the identity of the next Doctor had been through numerous twists and turns, some more plausible than others. At one point, betting on Rory Kinnear had been suspended by one bookmaker following newspaper reports he had been offered the role. "I don't know where it came from and how these things evolve," said a baffled Kinnear. "I haven't been, and I am totally certain that I will not be asked to be the next Doctor Who. If I was an actor who was really longing to play Doctor Who, then this would be torturous, but it's a programme I've never watched, so I don't even really know what it is." He was also keen to learn more about this beat combo he'd been told about called The Beatles.

Singer and fashion unusualist Paloma Faith created a ripple of interest when she tweeted that a friend who worked on *Doctor Who* had told her comedian Chris Addison had been cast in the role (prompting Addison to don a stripey scarf during a recording of panel show *Mock the Week*), while *The Wire* and *Luther* star Idris Elba ruled himself out of the running,

telling *Radio Times* he'd look "silly in a bow tie". Though not as silly as some *Luther* scripts.

The now-automatic clamour for a female Doctor gained the support of Dame Helen Mirren – just as long as it wasn't her. "I'm not going to be the first female Doctor, absolutely not – I wouldn't contemplate that," she told ITV's *Daybreak*. "But I do think it's time to have a female Doctor – I think a gay, black, female Doctor Who would be the best of all!" It would certainly make the audition process a lot shorter.

Then, on the last day of July, the bookies reported a sudden surge of interest in one Peter Capaldi. Readers of Volume I will recall the young Scot first making his presence felt bombarding the *Doctor Who* production office of the early 70s with endless letters, for which he received a signed copy of *The Mutants* script for his troubles, and writing to the *Radio Times* to lavish praise on their *Doctor Who 10th Anniversary Special*.

Since then, he'd dabbled in fanzine writing – his essay in praise of title sequence designer Bernard Lodge is full of earnest teenage ardour – and had been the singer in a punk band (Dreamboys, with Craig Ferguson on drums), before making his acting debut in Bill Forsyth's whimsical comedy classic *Local Hero*. As a writer-director, Capaldi had won an Academy Award for his 1995 short *Franz Kafka's It's a Wonderful Life*, and had also written and starred in the highly regarded British road movie *Soft Top, Hard Shoulder*.

Having appeared in more than 40 films and TV shows, from *The Crow Road* to *Midsomer Murders* – not to mention *Doctor Who* and *Torchwood: Children of Earth* – Capaldi was now best known for his BAFTA and British Comedy Award-winning role as spin doctor Malcolm Tucker in Armando Ianucci's scabrous political satire *The Thick of It* and its big screen spin-off *In the Loop*. As Number Ten's volcanic cabinet enforcer, Tucker had gifted the English language the word "omnishambles," and elevated swearing to a particularly sublime art form, including such memorable diatribes as "I will tear your fucking skin off, I will wear it to your mother's birthday party, and rub your nuts up and down her leg whilst whistling Bohemian fucking Rhapsody" and the cheery invitation to personal callers to "come the fuck in or fuck the fuck off". With Capaldi's name now being linked so closely with *Doctor Who*, the internet predictably exploded with blogs and video mash-ups in which the Doctor takes on his enemies with a sustained volley of potty-mouthed invective.

A few days later, the BBC came clean about that "entertainment pilot" – which would, in fact, see the twelfth Doctor unveiled live on BBC1 at 7pm the following Sunday.

As well as the big reveal, *Doctor Who Live: The Next Doctor* – which would also be simul-cast in America, Australia and Canada – prom-ised guest appearances from Matt Smith, Tom Baker and Peter Davison, alongside celebrity fans, Steven Moffat (described as "one of only ten people who knows the new Doctor's iden-tity") and a roll call of companions past and present.

"BBC One is the home of big live events and this special live show is the perfect way to reveal the identity of the next Doctor and share it with the nation," said the channel's Controller, Charlotte Moore. "The Doctor is a truly iconic role and I'm more than excited about the booking." (Love the use of the word "booking" there – like she's the entertainment secretary of a northern branch of the British Legion, not the head of Britain's flagship TV channel.)

By Sunday, most turf accountants had closed their books on the new *Doctor Who*, assuming it to be a done deal. A spokesman for William Hill said: "There is no point putting the market back out because as far as we and our punters are concerned, Peter Capaldi has almost cer-tainly bagged himself the *Doctor Who* gig, and we will already be paying out more than enough should that be the case."

With odds of 6/4, Capaldi's nearest rival was considered to be BAFTA-winning *Bring Me Sunshine* star Daniel Rigby (9/2), Ben Daniels (4/1) and Andrew Scott – psychotic Moriarty to Benedict Cumberbatch's Holmes – at 10/1. Certainly, it seemed a female Time Lord was out of the running when photographer Rankin told his Twitter followers he'd taken the official publicity picture of the new incumbent, add-ing: "He's going to be an ace Dr."

As Lizo Mzimba interviewed the queue of excitable fans snaking down the street outside, the new Doctor was driven into the BBC's

Elstree studios, laying on the back seat of a people carrier with a blanket over him. (At least he *hoped* he was being driven into the studios, and not being taken to a remote farm-house. Come to think of it, the driver's ski-mask *had* been a bit suspicious.)

Doctor Who knew?
(Answer: everyone)

At 7pm that evening, the moment *Doctor Who* fans all over the world had been waiting for... was still 20-odd minutes away, as Zoe Ball hosted the longest preamble to a major announcement since Winston Churchill added: "Oh, and by the way, we shall fight them on the beaches and never surrender. Cheers."

Highlights of *Doctor Who Live: The Bit Before the Next Doctor* included Peter Davison – shar-ing, for reasons that weren't entirely clear, the studio sofa with Liza Tarbuck and one of the kids from *Outnumbered* – tactfully avoiding the question when Zoe Ball asked if *Doctor Who* had been the best job he'd ever had, Stephen Hawking enthusing about William Hartnell and self-confessed "hardcore fan" Rufus Hound struggling with such basics as the name of the ninth Doctor ("Peter Eccleston," apparently).

A visibly emotional Matt Smith popped up to wish his successor luck, and told how, after *The Eleventh Hour* had gone out, the actor in question had come up to him in the street and told him he thought he was brilliant. "I really needed that – I needed a boost," said Smith, "and I never forgot it."

When the big moment came, Ball announced that "it's the end, but the moment has been prepared for" (surely the first time anyone had quoted from *Logopolis* on primetime TV). "It is finally time to put a new face to an old name," she continued. "He may be a thousand years old, but he's about to get a whole new lease of life. Here we go, the big reveal, joining us now, live in the studio exclusively on the BBC, please welcome, the twelfth Doctor, a hero for a whole new generation. It's..." – *X Factor*-style dramatic pause – "Peter Capaldi!"

At which point the new Doctor emerged from the time vortex set to rapturous applause, and immediately demonstrated his fan credentials with a bit of crowd-pleasing Hartnell lapel-fingering business.

"It's so wonderful not to keep this secret any longer," said Capaldi, taking his place on the sofa. "But it has been absolutely fantastic in its own way; so many wonderful things have happened. For instance, for a while I couldn't tell my daughter, who would be looking on the internet and discovering that people were saying so-and-so should be Doctor Who and so-and-so should be Doctor Who – and she was getting rather upset that they never mentioned me. And I said, 'Just rise above it darling, rise above it'."

Of the audition, he said: "It was quite hard because even though I'm a lifelong *Doctor Who* fan, I haven't really played Doctor Who since I was nine... So what I did was I downloaded some old scripts from the internet and practiced those in front of the mirror. But Steven had already written some scenes that referred to a Doctor of my ilk..."

The actor – at 55, the oldest incumbent since William Hartnell – recalled how he heard he'd got the gig: "I was actually filming in Prague, doing the BBC's adaptation of *The Three Musketeers* over there, playing Cardinal Richelieu, and I had my phone on silent, so I missed the call. And I looked at it and it said 'missed call ten minutes ago' and it was my dear agent, so I rang her up and said 'It's me' and she said 'Hello, Doctor,' and I just started to laugh – and I haven't stopped laughing since..."

"I'm surprised now to see Doctor Who looking back," he admitted. "You look in the mirror and suddenly, strangely, he's looking back and he's not me yet – but he's reaching out, and hopefully we'll get it together."

The interview concluded with Capaldi's heartfelt pean to the programme and its armies of followers.

"I think *Doctor Who* is an extraordinary show and the thing that strikes me about it is that it's still here after all this time. And the reason that I think that it's still here is because of the work of all the writers and the directors and the producers who've worked on the show, and the actors – and I don't just mean the fabulous actors who've played the Doctor, but all those actors who've sweated inside rubber monster costumes and those who wear

futuristic lurex catsuits. But the real reason, the big reason, that *Doctor Who* is still with us is because of every single viewer who ever turned on to watch this show – at any age, at any time in its history and in their history – and who took it into their heart, because *Doctor Who* belongs to all of us. Everyone made *Doctor Who*."

At which fans across the world wiped away a tear and thought: *You're gonna fit in here just fine, kid*.

The next morning, Rankin's portrait of the new Doctor striking a suitably enigmatic pose adorned the cover of every newspaper in Britain. "This was less a casting announcement than a global product launch, an exercise in brand-management equivalent to the unveiling of the latest iPhone," declared the *Telegraph*. *The Times* pointed to *Doctor Who's* status as one of the BBC's five "superbrands", alongside *Top Gear*, *Strictly Come Dancing*, BBC Earth and *Lonely Planet*. "Between them, the five superbrands account for 27% of BBC Worldwide's sales, contributing to annual profits of £156 million," said the paper, adding that "*Doctor Who* is the only one whose success centres on a single star, albeit it one who regenerates at regular intervals."

Its leader column, meanwhile, was flushed with patriotic pride, declaring: "If James Bond represents how Britain is seen by the world, perhaps *Doctor Who* represents how the country prefers to see itself. Wacky yet noble, chaotic yet fiercely intelligent, fearsome yet ultimately benign, the man from Gallifrey could not, really, be from anywhere else. Whoever he is, he's as British as his phone box."

The *Daily Mail*, naturally, couldn't resist an opportunity to put the boot into the auld enemy, asking on its front page "Was There a BBC Betting Coup on Dr Who?" and demanding: "After all the hype, Mr Potty Mouth had better be good."

Around seven million people tuned in for the announcement in the UK, joined by close to another million in the US and 0.4 million in Canada, with a further 40,000 Australians making the effort to get up at Stupid O'Clock (Eastern Standard Time) in the morning.

The announcement also owned Twitter: according to the BBC, there were a total of 542,000 tweets reacting to the news, peaking at 22,081 *a minute* as the new Doctor was revealed. At one point, seven of the UK's top ten trends were *Doctor Who*-related, with Steven Moffat taking the top spot during much of the Sunday build-up. Eat that, Justin Bieber.

Moffat expanded on Capaldi's casting in his *Doctor Who Magazine* column: "The first time I was involved in casting the Doctor, Peter did flick through my mind. But somehow it didn't feel right and, as I type, I'm struggling to explain why." The showrunner then struggled to explain why – claiming that David Tennant was too young to be followed by an older Doctor, but Matt Smith – who was even younger, but *seemed* older – had pushed the door open for an older Doctor. Or something like that. He revealed he had asked Mark Gatiss to make his own list, and Capaldi had been at the top of both. Though one of them could have copied, I suppose.

"We were being top secret, of course, so the audition was held at my house," the showrunner continued. "Oh, and did you enjoy our Top Secrecy, by the way? No-one knew it would be Peter. Except the betting shops, the newspapers and people."

The audition itself had taken place in Moffat's living room and was, he recalled, "one of those moments – the Doctor was in the room, and the search was over.... A phone call was made to the set of *The Musketeers* to inform the great man that a big blue box was about to close around his life forever."[42]

Interviewed in the same issue, Moffat said: "He's *always* looked like Doctor Who. The moment you say his name, you go, 'Of course!'. I actually don't mind the way it worked out, because the moment he was in the frame, people *wanted* it to be him.

"We'd already been talking about an older, trickier Doctor, I suppose. My vaguest sense was that we'd had – in a row – two fabulously successful, wonderful, youthful, adorable, accessible Doctors. But he's not *always* like that. So we were sort of thinking you can flip him. You know he's either the senior consultant who's secretly the undergraduate, or he's the undergraduate who's secretly the senior consultant. Those are the two poles of Doctorness."

The man himself – a longtime *DWM* reader[XX] – also made his own contribution in the form of a letter to the magazine, in which he revealed he'd been leafing through old back copies in a bid to "re-focus my inner Who", adding: "I can't wait to see this well worn face in comic form."

So there you had it: since his return to our screens eight years ago, the Doctor had been played by two fanboys with the show in their blood, and a third who'd grown into its biggest fan while in office. The other guy still didn't want to talk about it.

Christopher Eccleston signs for anniversary special (just not this one)

While one quinquagenarian was about to embark on an adventure in space and time, remarkable footage emerged of another whose flight into eternity had come crashing to a stop in the dressing room of a provincial theatre in Devon.

No footage of William Hartnell talking on camera was known to exist until Richard Bignell, a member of the *Doctor Who* Restoration Team employed to work on the DVD range, unearthed a three-minute interview conducted for the BBC's regional news show *Points West* while the actor was appearing as Buskin the Cobbler in an ill-starred production of *Puss in Boots*. Recorded less than three months after his last *Doctor Who* appearance, a T-shirted Hartnell – an arresting image in itself – is grilled in his dressing room by Roger Mills. But if the actor was bitter about having been wrenched away from *Doctor Who* to do panto in Taunton... then he was bloody well going to show it.

"No, I'm not brassed off," says Hartnell, clearly brassed off, when questioned about the Daleks' popularity. Mills asks if he thinks he'll ever shake the good Doctor off. "Oh yes, of course," says Hartnell tetchily. "How?" "By making a success of something else." "Do you see your future in pantomime?" asks Mills. "No," says Hartnell, firmly. "It's never appealed to me, to be in pantomime." It wasn't shaping up to be the *best* promotional interview ever. Mills appears to goad him by asking – twice – what qualities for pantomime he feels he lacks, to which Hartnell responds: "It's a different technique which lends itself only to what I call a variety type of actor. I'm not – I'm legitimate. I'm a legitimate character actor of the theatre and film."

"This pantomime ends this week," Mills concludes. "What does the future hold for you after this?" "Well, I don't quite know," he falters. "I've got a manager who looks after my affairs, you see, and er..." As ever with Hartnell, it's an exquisitely poignant mix of crabby, self-aggrandising braggadocio and punishing, paranoid self-doubt. Someone really ought to make a film about him.

The business of not being Doctor Who was also in focus as the BFI continued its year-long celebration of the series with a retrospective of the ninth Doctor's era (if that's not too strong a word). The panel featured Phil Collinson, director Joe Ahearne and Bruno Langley – surely Nine's definitive companion after Rose and Captain Jack and Mickey and Jackie and Lynda with a Y and that plastic arm he carried round for a bit in the first episode.

Eccleston being a no-show wasn't exactly a surprise, but he did send a message to the event, stating: "I love the BFI. I love the Doctor and hope you enjoy this presentation. Joe Ahearne directed five of the 13 episodes of the first series. He understood the tone the show needed completely – strong, bold, pacy visuals coupled with wit, warmth and a twinkle in the performance, missus.

"If Joe agrees to direct the 100th anniversary special, I will bring my sonic and a stair-lift and – providing the Daleks don't bring theirs – I, the ninth Doctor, vow to save the universe and all you apes in it."

So there you have it: he may have bailed on the 50th, but Christopher Eccleston had made a firm commitment to appear in the centenary celebrations. Though, it has to be said, there aren't many 99-year-olds who can carry off a leather jacket. (Also, memo to Eccleston: Dalek stair jokes – *really?* If you hadn't let your *DWM* subscription lapse, you'd know how passé that was.)

In Cardiff, cast and crew gathered in early September for the read-through on the Christmas special, with an extremely emotional Matt Smith struggling to get through his final lines, prompting Steven Moffat to leave his place at the other side of the room in order to give his mate a hug. "I'm not really a weepy guy," said Smith, "but suddenly it all got a bit... I don't know. I don't know what happened to me, to be honest with you."[43] When Smith and Jenna Coleman were photographed on location by a Welsh newspaper a few days later, fans were relieved to see the eleventh Doctor's trademark tonsorial splendour had been faithfully recreated by BBC Wales' best wigmakers in a manner that didn't look completely rubbish.

At the 2013 TV Choice Awards held in London's glittering West End, probably, *Doctor Who* was named Best Drama Series for the fourth year running. Peter Davison was on hand to present the trophy to Steven Moffat, who remarked: "I'm receiving an award about *Doctor Who* from Doctor Who while *Doctor Who* is busy filming in Cardiff!" In the Best Actor category, Matt Smith – aka Doctor Who – narrowly lost out to *Broadchurch's* David Tennant – aka Doctor Who, son-in-law of Doctor Who. ("Is there anyone in the house who *isn't* Doctor Who?")

In the second week of September, the title of the anniversary special was revealed as *The Day of the Doctor*. An "iconic image" (that's a poster, to you and me) was also released featuring David Tennant, Matt Smith, John Hurt and some explodey Dalek action. Behind the scenes, though, events were already moving beyond the anniversary towards a whole new era as, on the evening of Wednesday, October 2nd, director Jamie Payne snuck a guest on to the TARDIS set. Away from prying eyes, this was Peter Capaldi's first chance to get his hands on the time machine he'd be picking up the keys to the following day.

Capaldi reported for filming at 3.30 on Thursday afternoon, and spent around half-an-hour working alongside Matt Smith on the regeneration scene. "There's no ceremony about these things," Steven Moffat told *The Herald* newspaper. "Once they got to the end of Matt's bit, Peter came on and Matt had to give him his watch, his time machine and his girl, and go. They had a big hug and all that."

Principal filming wrapped on the Christmas special on Saturday, October 5th, bringing Matt Smith's days as the madman in a box to an end. "So it's goodnight from me," tweeted outgoing producer Marcus Wilson, "and it's goodnight from him. That's a wrap. Christmas 2013. Thank you all."

On set, Smith was trying – and failing – to put a brave face on it, while Jenna Coleman hung on like a shipwrecked sailor to a hunk of driftwood. "Literally, she will not take her arms off me," Smith faux protested. "I'm quite clingy today," admitted Coleman.[43]

Smith's golden wrap, as these things often are, was some finicky green screen business (specifically, the Doctor leaning out of the TARDIS grappling with the exterior phone) after which a teary Steven Moffat walked on to present the actor with his parting gift: the eleventh Doctor's sonic screwdriver in a presentation box.

"I'm glad I don't have two hearts, because they'd both be breaking at the moment," the showrunner told the assembled cast and crew. "I have a complaint against time travel: I would like today not to have arrived. Everybody, the biggest round of applause for the best and bravest Time Lord of them all: Matt Smith."

"It does feel like the end of an era," Moffat reflected. "And I don't just mean the fictional era of the show, I mean the real life, human era. Nearly five years ago, I was taking over from Russell, Matt was taking over from David, and the look on our faces was 'We can't win, nobody thinks we're going to, and this is going to be terrible'. So all these years later, it worked. My God, it worked."[43]

Trailer trashed

As Matt Smith joined the ranks of former Time Lords, his favourite predecessor was about to stage a comeback, of sorts. It began when Sunday tabloid The People ramped up the Omnirumour by claiming every missing episode of Doctor Who had been recovered from a TV station in Ethiopia. The Radio Times offered a more sober analysis, claiming that episodes from two Patrick Troughton stories had been returned to the archives, though BBC Worldwide's invitation to journalists to attend a press conference and screening later that week inevitably reignited much feverish speculation.

When the announcement finally came, it was both wonderful – and mildly anti-climactic. A total of nine lost episodes of the fifth season had been recovered from Nigeria – five from Who-does-Bond actioner The Enemy of the World, meaning that story was now complete, and four from revered Yetis in the Underground monster mash The Web of Fear, leaving only episode three of the six-parter still AWOL.

"The tapes had been gathering dust in a store room at a television station in Nigeria," said Philip Morris who, contrary to his previous "not missing but destroyed assertion", had discovered them in the city of Jos. "I remember wiping the dust off the masking tape on the canisters and my heart missed a beat as I saw the words 'Doctor Who'. When I read the story code, I realised I'd found something pretty special." Which just goes to show: committing Doctor Who production codes to memory is not a ridiculous waste of time.

Worldwide revealed that both stories, including a reconstructed version of the missing Web of Fear instalment[XXI], had been digitally remastered and would be available to download from iTunes from midnight – an idea that would have seemed as preposterous as Abominable Snowmen on the District line when the episodes had been recorded 45 years earlier.

Introducing the screening of The Web of Fear, Mark Gatiss, joined on stage by Frazer Hines and Deborah Watling, told the audience: "As long as I've been a Doctor Who fan – and that's a very long time – there's been one story that I hoped, prayed, begged would one day turn up from the 106 episodes that are tragically missing from the archives. This is perhaps the quintessential Doctor Who story. A fantastic monster, a claustrophobic, iconic setting and, best of all, one of the very greatest Doctors at the height of his powers."

The Web of Fear immediately went to number one on iTunes' UK TV series chart, with The Enemy of the World at number two; in the US, The Enemy of the World was at number two, with The Web of Fear at four, and both stories also made the top five in Australia and Canada – that's a black and white TV show made in a creaky studio on a shoestring budget 45 years ago outgunning the likes of Game of Thrones, Breaking Bad and Homeland. Yes, I know.

Naturally, rumours persist that this isn't the whole story. Some of the statements from the parties involved in episode recovery seem almost deliberately opaque, and many fans claim to have it on good authority this is just the start of a flood of recovered treasures. Ian Levine – who can claim to have done more than most to safeguard *Doctor Who*'s past – appears to exist in a near-permanent froth of indignant frustration about the lack of new announcements, if his Twitter account is anything to go by. But, at time of publication, the tally of missing *Doctor Who* episodes is holding steady at 97.

Frothing indignation was also in long supply when BBC One debuted a special trailer celebrating 50 years of *Doctor Who*. Rather than sling together a few old clips, this was a bespoke creation using a combination of stills, props, purpose-built sets and stand-in actors to create a giddy whirl through five decades of time travel, every frame lovingly filled with objects as iconic as Bessie and as obscure as the stuffed owl Sarah Jane takes home at the end of *The Hand of Fear*. (Let's call it Eric. Eric the owl.)

Matt Smith's voiceover, meanwhile, told viewers that "I've been running all my lives, through time and space, every second of every minute of every day for over 900 years." Which isn't technically true, as he lived on that cloud for ages, and spent much of the black and white era either lying down or on holiday. But that's not what upset some fans: what upset some fans was that the Doctors in the trailer didn't all get a fair crack of the whip, with the second only seen in silhouette, the eighth barely in shot and the poor old, much-abused sixth with his back to the camera. And you may want to adopt your best Comic Book Guy voice when protesting they didn't even get them In. The. Right. Order, Tom Baker leapfrogging Jon Pertwee and Paul McGann appearing after Christopher Eccleston. After all the time and love that had obviously been poured into the clip, the criticism seemed a bit mealy-mouthed. Though, on the other hand, if you're going to make a promo celebrating 50 years of *Doctor Who*, you wouldn't have thought it was *that* much of a stretch to include all the... you know, Doctor Whos.

At least Doctors Four through Eight were all present and correct for Big Finish's anniversary story, *The Light at the End*, which the company

unexpectedly released earlier than advertised in late October. Though it almost didn't happen at all, writer-director Nick Briggs claiming no-one at Big Finish had wanted "a whole story where they all stand round in a room together going 'I'm you!' 'And I'm you!' 'And I'm *you!*'"

"That's not drama," said Briggs. "It's a poisoned chalice, because it's all about expectation and wish-fulfilment. You can't write if you think there are thousands of people looking over your shoulder at what you're writing."

Two things changed their minds. One was a storyline proposed by John Dorney and the other – irony of ironies – was Tom Baker. "I have to say, Tom Baker was instrumental in this, because he'd come to me and said he felt for the 50th that all the Big Finish Doctors should get together and do a big story," explained producer David Richardson. "He added lots of weight to the idea"

"It just occurred to me that it might be good to have all the Doctors in, somehow or other," said Baker, nonchalantly.[44] Presumably no-one reminded him that, if he'd taken this attitude in 1983, Terrance Dicks wouldn't have had to flog himself half to death rewriting the entire *Five Doctors*.

Given all the goodwill and talent involved, it's a pity *The Light at the End* feels so scrappy. The main narrative is confusing and repetitive, not helped by reams of bafflegab about energy streams, time rams, dimensional stabilisation fields, temporal folding and the like, and chunks of pyrotechnic sound design apparently trying to approximate 500 wardrobes full of pans falling off a cliff.

Still, the story does give the public what they want in terms of plenty of fan-pleasing Doctor-on-Doctor action, with Tom Baker and Paul McGann – the Scouse wing of the operation – making for a particularly pleasing combo. There are cameos, too, for the first three incarnations, with William Russell and Frazer Hines taking over the duties of their respective leading men, and Big Finish regular Tim Treloar making a respectable job of the third Doctor.

In the US, BBC America announced a week-long "*Doctor Who* Takeover" for the end of November, with a deluge of documentaries and archive marathons grouped around the showpiece global premiere of *The Day of the Doctor*. And viewers got their first glimpse of the anniversary special when a trailer aired on both sides of the Atlantic; this time, fans of Sarah Jane's stuffed owl had to console themselves with shots of Matt Smith, David Tennant and John Hurt in action. Smith began popping up between programmes on BBC One, apparently interrupting transmissions to warn that "it's nearly time", while a model of the TARDIS began popping up on everything from The Queen Vic bar to Graham Norton's desk throughout November.

At the BFI, a preview screening of *An Adventure in Space and Time* was met with a standing ovation by the audience, with early reviews hailing Mark Gatiss' drama as "a masterpiece". As well as cast and crew, guests at the screening included Waris Hussein, Carole Ann Ford and Anneke Wills – all portrayed on screen, as is Jessica Carney, William Hartnell's granddaughter, who was clearly deeply moved by the film.

But for many, the biggest smack-me-round-the-kisser-and-call-me-Flavia moment of the anniversary build-up arrived unexpectedly on an unassuming Tuesday lunchtime when the BBC, in an apparent bid to maintain some element of surprise in a story that was starting to leak like a cardboard drainpipe, released a special mini-episode onto its Red Button service and the internet. Which promptly melted.

Here's the Eight who's going to regenerate

Night of the Doctor opens with a young woman at the controls of a crashing spaceship being offered medical attention by the onboard computer. "I'm trying to send a distress signal," she complains. "Stop talking about doctors." "I'm a doctor," says a familiar voice. "But probably not the one you're expecting." Which is something of an understatement – because it's only Paul bleedin' McGann!

Yes, the eighth Doctor is back, sporting a natty new costume and a less conspicuous hairdo, riding the plummeting ship all the way to its messy end in the twisted steel graveyard of the planet Karn. Oh yes, did we mention it's also a sequel to *The Brain of Morbius*? Obvs.

Killed on impact, the Doctor is brought back to life by the Sisterhood of Karn – but only for four minutes. "Four minutes?" he says brightly – "That's ages. What if I get bored, or need a television, couple of books? Anyone for chess? Bring me knitting."

Disgusted by his people's role in the endless Time War, the Doctor declares: "I don't suppose there's a need for a doctor any more. Make me a warrior now." Then, drinking from a chalice prepared by the Sisterhood, the eighth Doctor takes his last stand, his face engulfed in ribbons of regeneration energy before resolving into the features of a young John Hurt.

And that's that. After a 17-year wait, McGann's reprise is over in slightly shy of seven minutes. But *what* a seven minutes. Much like the Doctor himself, there's an awful lot Steven Moffat can pack into seven minutes (though he'd probably pass on the knitting) and, as a result, *Night of the Doctor* is a small but perfectly formed treat, filling in one of the series' biggest blanks – the end of the eighth Doctor – while sketching in more detail about the Time War, and providing a rollicking adventure, to boot. And Paul McGann simply shines, clearly relishing the chance for a victory lap and finally laying the ghost of his oft-quoted fear of being the George Lazenby of *Doctor Who*. (Incidentally, the argument about whether the TV Movie is canon may have long been put to bed, but here Moffat casually pops the lid on a whole new can of worms by having the eighth Doctor namecheck many of his Big Finish audio companions, too. I think we're gonna need a bigger spreadsheet.)

McGann admitted he'd hesitated before signing up to the project, before being persuaded by Nick Briggs that only good could possibly come of it. Once on board, he found his years in the booth at Big Finish allowed him to find the character quickly again. "I was warmed up, having done all the audios and played him for years anyway," McGann told *Doctor Who Magazine*. "All I had to do was put on the coat, get back on set and do it. It was no trouble at all. I thought, 'What's the catch? I'm doing a day's work here. This is brilliant.' It was exciting. I'm guessing, but had I not had the benefit of the audios, I'd have probably spent the first two or three hours in Cardiff slightly adrift, thinking 'Oh Jeez, how did this go? What am I? Who is this guy?'"[45]

According to McGann, the significance of the piece – its deft resolution of the eighth Doctor's fate – only occurred to him after filming, when he realised what a fitting send-off Steven Moffat had provided for the character.

"Because *Doctor Who* is character-based, it will always be more than the sum of any special effects, any of the appurtenances, which need to belong there. First and foremost, it's a character – a character that people have come to associate with, to trust. One character, many faces. At its soul, and in its best spirit, that's when it works. That's when you know you're in safe hands with the likes of Steven and Mark, and Russell T Davies before them, because these people understand that. And Peter Capaldi will realise that, because he's super-smart. What will have attracted him to it is what attracted me to it: the depth of the mythology and the character, which is actually perpetual. There's no end to these stories."[45]

"I have to say, all those years since 96 where perhaps I thought, as I did at one time, that the eighth Doctor... though liked in some quarters, perhaps wasn't so liked in others, and was only tolerated in the scheme of things... There's no doubt now, in my mind, that the eighth Doctor is part of it, that he's right there in the heart of it. He has earned his place, and that's really gratifying."[45]

Group hug, everyone?

McGann's renewed heat came too late to give him a boost in *Radio Times'* 50th anniversary poll to find the most popular Doctor and companion. While the eighth Doctor's 1.3% was enough to push him ahead of William Hartnell and last-placed Colin Baker, in truth there weren't many points to go round at the business end of the table after David Tennant secured a whopping 56% of the vote – which you don't need to be a Logopolitan to work out is more than all the other Doctors combined. Matt Smith came a distant second with 16%, while Tom Baker took bronze with 10%. And it was a double victory for the *Who* Class of '06 as Billie Piper took the honours for best companion, followed by Elisabeth Sladen and Catherine Tate. Kamelion was sadly unrated.

In a separate poll of *Doctor Who* Appreciation Society members, Tom Baker came out on top, taking almost double the number of votes of second-placed David Tennant. Baker also took gold in *Doctor Who Magazine's* 50th anniversary poll, with Matt Smith second and David Tennant third. Thus we can conclude, without any hesitation, that the most popular Doctor of all time is... um, can we get back to you on that?

On the other side of the world, *Doctor Who's* links with Australia were the subject of a Parliamentary motion by MP George Christiensen that also served to highlight the important role Australians had played in the history of the programme, including 60s staff writer C.E. "Bunny" Webber; Anthony Coburn, the writer of the very first story; theme composer Ron Grainer; incidental music composer Dudley Simpson; Tegan actress Janet Fielding and Kylie Minogue. Mr Christiensen also received cross-party support for a motion to invite *Doctor Who* to film an upcoming episode in. It's good to know the country's lawmakers were across all the big issues.

Back home, *Doctor Who* was honoured with a royal reception at Buckingham Palace to mark the series' 50th anniversary. Guests at the shindig included Tom Baker, Peter Davison, Matt Smith, John Hurt, Jenna Coleman, Catherine Tate, Steven Moffat and two Daleks, the latter presumably invited to provide some company for Prince Philip. (Actually, Her Maj was otherwise engaged, so hostess duties were performed by her daughter-in-law, Sophie, Countess of Wessex, on account of her being a self-confessed *Doctor Who* fan – or possibly just the best royal available at short notice.)

With the cork out of the bottle, the festivities began in earnest as Britain was battered by a Whonami of hype in the biggest national celebration since the Olympics. TV, radio, newspapers, magazines (including no fewer than 13 collectible *Radio Times* covers) and the worldwide web all willingly surrendered to the publicity onslaught, with even Google replacing its logo with avatars of the eleven Doctors and a Dalek game doodle.

Across the BBC, schedules were wiped in favour of more than 50 hours of *Who*-related programming. From Big Finish dramas on Radio 4 Extra to BBC Three's "Greatest Monsters and Villains" weekend, no corner of the Beeb's broadcasting empire was left untouched. For even the most dedicated fan, keeping up with it all was exhausting and, frankly, a little stressful, requiring the use of several computer programmes and, ideally, a good diary secretary.

Tentpole productions throughout the week included Matt Smith sparring with Professor Brian Cox in *The Science of Doctor Who*, while Smith and Jenna Coleman filmed some comic business aboard the TARDIS for BBC Three's *Doctor Who: The Ultimate Guide*, in which the Time Lord accidentally wiped his memory and had it restored via a patience-testing two-hour info-dump clips extravaganza in which the vacuous witterings of various celebrity talking heads ("There's like a dog that's electric...") were punctuated by the occasional genuine insight from the *Who* literati (Paul McGann was on particularly good form).

Matthew Sweet took a more rarefied approach in "You, Me and Doctor Who," a *Culture Show* special in which the writer, broadcaster and cultural relativist eschewed the usual jokes about stairs and sink plungers in favour of an impassioned argument for *Doctor Who*'s place at the heart of the British cultural dialogue. "*Doctor Who* is one of the most important things in our culture," said Sweet. "It's one of the most rich and interesting things that's ever been made in this country." In short order, Sweet's film also made the case for Delia Derbyshire being as important to the story of contemporary music as Phil Spector and The Beatles, while Caitlin Moran claimed that, without Russell T Davies, there would have been no civil partnerships or gay marriages in Britain. As a celebration of "a fable that has become part of everyone's lives," it could scarcely have been more impassioned.

William, it was really something

For many fans of a certain stripe, the most anticipated event of the birthday celebrations – perhaps even more so than the anniversary special itself – was the broadcast of *An Adventure in Space and Time*. A drama based on *Doctor Who*'s origins had been a long-cherished dream of more people than just Mark Gatiss, so the emotional investment – and the risk of disappointment – was high. But few could

have dared to hope it would turn out to be quite so extraordinary as what unfolded on television screens on the evening of November 21st, 2013.

Simply, the film is a masterpiece: a triumph of nuanced, multi-layered scripting that perfectly balances fan-pleasing detail with the need to provide a human drama with universal appeal. What's particularly clever is the way Gatiss doesn't just sprinkle the knowing nods and winks on top as a sugar-coating. He makes them serve the wider story of how an ageing actor found professional and personal redemption through a magical, fairytale character – and was then forced by his rapidly deteriorating health to give it up.

Take the photo calls in the Television Centre car park that punctuate the film with every change of cast. It's not just a box-ticking exercise to make sure Dodo, Ben, Polly et al get their moment on-screen; every time those flashbulbs pop, a little bit of William Hartnell – an emotionally fragile, highly-stung individual who can't bear goodbyes – dies. Or take William Russell's cameo (one of several from Hartnell era companions) as a fussy BBC commissionaire. He's not just there to give the man who was Ian Chesterton something to do – cherishable though that is – it's also an elegant shorthand to contrast the fusty, hidebound BBC with Sydney Newman's brash, impatient new broom. And when Hartnell snaps, "I'm a legitimate character actor of the stage and film!", it's not just a cheeky steal from the recently discovered *BBC Points West* interview, it's a pithy summation of how he viewed himself and the substandard work that, until *Doctor Who*, he was forced to grub around in.

The opening scene is a delightful tip of the hat to the alternative origin story provided by David Whitaker in the first *Doctor Who* novel, in which two teachers stumble across the TARDIS not in a junkyard but on Barnes Common. This time, though, it's Hartnell who stops in front of a police box on a lonely heath, clearly lost in a fog of his own confusion. He is on his way to his final *Doctor Who* recording ("I'm not ready, I need more time!" he snaps from his dressing room, and he's clearly not talking about his cufflinks). Then we see him striding down the corridor, cloak swishing dramatically, before taking his place on a beautifully faithful recreation of the original TARDIS console. The chronometer dials back from 1966 to 1963 – and our story begins.

Gatiss makes a virtue of parsing the many people and events that informed *Doctor Who's* creation into a more streamlined, TV-friendly narrative. He gets his excuses in early: "So many people have been at the birth of this thing, we'd be here all day," says Verity Lambert (Jessica Raine). So, sensibly, Gatiss pares it back to the story of Newman (Brian Cox in full showman mode), Lambert and Sacha Dhawan's Waris Hussein ("the pushy wog and the Jewish bird" as they style themselves) and, above all, Hartnell, the man for whom *Doctor Who* meant everything.

The love Gatiss has poured into his screenplay is matched by the "servicing departments" – in stark contrast to Verity Lambert's shoddy treatment at the time, wittily referenced here by designer Peter Brachacki arrogantly throwing the console together with a cotton reel, a couple of washers and some perforated cardboard. The recreations of classic early *Who* sets – from the court of Kublai Khan to the South Pole (complete with Cyberman having a crafty fag) are stunning. There is something about seeing behind the flats of that iconic Skaro corridor where the Doctor first met the Daleks, or the Totters Lane junkyard in the semi-darkness of a deserted studio, that makes you feel like you've genuinely travelled in time.

Director Terry McDonough delights with other visual touches, too, such as the lovely moon hanging over Television Centre on the night Soviet cosmonaut Valentina Tereshkova became the first woman in space (the sub-text being: this is less seismic than a woman producer at the BBC). And it's made all the more poignant knowing that, more by accident than design, *An Adventure in Space and Time* would be the last drama ever recorded at TVC.

At the heart of the piece is David Bradley's compelling performance as William Hartnell. Initially crabby and irritable, Bradley gradually begins to sand down Hartnell's more abrasive edges as, after a lifetime spent playing hard bastards, he delights in his newfound role of cosmic Pied Piper. (He likes the money, too, memorably telling his co-stars "our arses are in butter!") And then, as the arteriosclerosis that would eventually kill him tightens its ever-more cruel grip on his mind, Bradley portrays the actor's decline through a mixture of child-like bewilderment and steely, short-tempered rage. But when Sidney Newman summons him into his office to tell him that, while *Doctor Who* will continue, he will not, Hartnell summons all his dignity to offer gracious words about Patrick Troughton, followed by a moving passage from Lear's "Fortune goodnight" speech.

The most poignant moment of all, though, comes near the end when, back where we came in at that final studio session, Hartnell grips the TARDIS console for support, looks up and sees... Matt Smith, the eleventh Doctor himself, smiling back at him with such compassion, acknowledging a debt of gratitude for all the days still to come. Again, what makes it truly special is that it's so much more than just a crowd-pleasing cameo – it's the future reflecting back at Hartnell to say, "I know this feels like the end, but it isn't. This thing you've created will live on, and in 50 years' time they'll still be talking about you and everything you achieved. You will be the stuff of legend – the old man and his police box and his adventures in space and time."

The last word, fittingly, goes to William Hartnell himself, as the Doctor's farewell to Susan plays away on a monitor in a darkened studio gallery: "One day, I shall come back. Yes, I shall come back. Until then, there must be no regrets, no tears, no anxieties. Just go forward in all your beliefs, and prove to me that I am not mistaken in mine."

Extraordinary.

"I always knew I'd start the film with William Hartnell's last day, but then spin back to the very beginning," Mark Gatiss told *Doctor Who Magazine*. "The big challenge was finding a way to focus the story on, essentially, just four people. Bill Hartnell, of course, and then Sydney Newman, Verity Lambert and Waris Hussein."[46]

Gatiss said he'd already been asked by a friend who was playing series co-creator Donald Wilson, and had to gently inform him Wilson wasn't in it. "I realised I was going to spend the rest of my life having that conversation," said Gatiss. "The thing is, you just can't include everyone. It's not that I don't understand or appreciate the scale of Donald Wilson's contribution to *Doctor Who* as Head of Serials, or David Whitaker as script editor, or Bunny Webber's contribution to the format. But in the end I had to pack away my inner anorak and think 'This is a drama'."[46]

For the first Doctor's companions given cameo roles in the film, the mix of past and present, fact and fiction proved to be an emotional experience. "To hear those lines from the first episode again – yes, it was very strange," said William Russell. "We all got to know those lines very well, of course, because we had to do that episode twice. David does it very well indeed. He's such a talented actor, and very precise and particular, I think – which is just like Bill was himself."[47]

"It's astonishing, it really is," added Anneke Wills. "When I walked onto the set this morning and saw the TARDIS – *my* TARDIS – again, my heart was going boom-titty-boom-titty-boom. It's exactly how I remember it. I felt so *drawn* to it. And then, the next minute, there's David Bradley, putting his hands to his lapels... I gasped! I couldn't help it. David is playing it with such sensitivity. He's absolutely *inhabiting* the part. It's very moving.

"It's weird to be so old that you're suddenly seeing yourself as part of history – that you're someone in period dress from a historical time."[47]

Gatiss revealed that the original ending to *An Adventure in Space and Time* was going to be Super-8-style footage of Hartnell, Troughton and Pertwee – with Gatiss himself as the latter – taking part in the photo-shoot for *The Three Doctors* in 1972. Budget constraints put paid to that – but Gatiss wasn't about to miss his chance: "What I *could* afford," he told the BFI screening, "was to hire my own costume and, on the most stressful day of filming, get dressed up as Jon Pertwee and walk on to the set." Which is why, if you Google it, you'll find pictures of the third Doctor merrily gatecrashing the original regeneration scene.

William Hartnell's departure was also the subject of a timely restoration when *The Tenth Planet* appeared on DVD that week, recreating his missing final episode with a new animation, while his very first story, *An Unearthly Child*, was shown in full on BBC Four. A full 47 years after the role slipped from his grasp, it seemed the first Doctor was still firmly in the myth-making business. Would Hartnell have been surprised?

"He wouldn't be at all surprised – not one bit," insisted William Russell. "Bill really did think *Doctor Who* was going to go on forever. So he'd be very pleased by this. Very pleased indeed."[47]

A Day to remember

As the Day of the Doctor – or the Day of *The Day of the Doctor*, technically – dawned, Matt Smith and David Tennant could be found discussing the etiquette of multiple TARDIS occupancy in *The Sun*.

"Our Doctors sort of get on, then they don't and then they do again," said Smith. "It's like two brothers who are evenly matched, fencing a lot." "It's been really good fun," said Tennant. "I did think, 'Surely I'm too old to be doing this now?' and there were lots of things you become nervous about. 'What if Matt thinks I'm stepping on his toes? Or what if I can't remember how to do it?' And people almost expected me and Matt to be at loggerheads, but we've really enjoyed it."

"It's been interesting talking to him and comparing notes, going 'What about this? How did you deal with that?'" Smith told *Sci-fi Now* magazine. "It's a very singular, particular journey that not many people really understand. It's like a term of office, because you are a public figure, to some degree, it's something the public are very involved in. There are so many things you can't really share with anyone because it sounds like you're bragging or moaning. But actually you're just trying to find a context of how to deal with it and enjoy it. It's such a dominant thing in your life, I suppose, and that's quite hard to communicate to other people. Someone who knows that, you go 'Wow, it's a lot, isn't it?' The pluses outweigh the minuses tenfold."[48]

At London's cavernous ExCel, the official Celebration party was in full swing with one of the largest line-ups of guests from in-front and behind the cameras ever assembled. Tom Baker, in particular, was in typically impish form, refusing to face his fellow Time Lords in mock indignation at being made to share the stage with them. (At least we assume it was mock indignation – you can never quite tell

with Tom.[XXII]) Baker, Peter Davison, Colin
Baker and Sylvester McCoy also posed for pictures with Matt Smith – thus achieving what
The Five Doctors had failed to do by bringing
together five, er, Doctors.

With a *Doctor Who* guest seemingly obligatory for every TV sofa and radio studio in the
country (Matt Smith and David Tennant's
appearance on *The Graham Norton Show* was
particularly memorable for Tennant scribbling
his name on a fan who was on the process of
having all the surviving Doctors' autographs
turned into tattoos), local BBC stations got in
on the act with some delightful curios from the
highways and byways of *Who* history. Anyone
taking a road trip through the country on that
Saturday might, for example, have heard 60s
writers Victor Pemberton and Donald Tosh as
guests of BBC Radio Essex, Graham Cole discussing the art of Cyber acting on BBC Radio
Norfolk, John Leeson telling shaggy K-9 stories on BBC Leicester and Sylvester McCoy
talking to BBC Radio Scotland.

Inevitably, certain of the BBC's enemies
thought this was all a bit much, and there were
faint stirrings of discontent that perhaps it had
all got out of hand; this was, after all, just a TV
show. The issue was taken up on an edition of
the BBC's self-flagellating *Newswatch*, which
discussed the "endless plugging of a big BBC
franchise". But on the whole the national
mood seemed one of celebration and, even
among those who didn't watch the show, a
fond indulgence for a very British institution.

Not that it was just a UK party, of course –
this was a truly international celebration, with
fans in 94 countries all counting down to the
same moment when *Doctor Who* would make
broadcasting history with the world's largest
every global drama simulcast. With an expected worldwide television audience of tens of
millions – plus hundreds of thousands more
watching in 834 cinemas from Russia to
Ethiopia – there was some justification for calling *The Day of the Doctor* the most anticipated
TV event of all time. No pressure, then.

You can't blame Steven Moffat – who had
the pleasure, if that's the right word, of watching his work surrounded by hundreds of fans
at the BFI – for feeling a little daunted by the
task of doing justice to 50 years of *Doctor Who*
in 75 minutes. But he never allows his nerves

to show on the screen, striking the perfect balance between weighty tribute and fizzy adventure story to ensure *The Day of the Doctor* is
never overwhelmed by its sense of occasion.

Opening with a version of the original title
sequence and theme arrangement, and a recreation of the policeman passing by IM
Foreman's junkyard that was the programme's
very first shot, is a lovely way of bridging the
decades that only seems obvious in retrospect.
As is finding Clara is now a teacher at Coal Hill
School, just like Ian and Barbara – except,
where they made their entrance into the
TARDIS in a cramped Studio D at Lime Grove
while stagehands groped haplessly to keep the
doors from flapping open, Clara rides straight
into the police box on a motorbike. Why?
Because she can.

This sets the scene for a light, screwball
opening in which Kate Stewart's UNIT accidentally airlifts the TARDIS into London with
its occupants still inside (or, in the Doctor's
case, hanging off the outside), providing plenty of hero shots of the capital to reiterate
Doctor Who's Britishness to all those audiences
watching in Biloxi, Bulaweyo and Borisoglebsk.

Inside the National Gallery, Kate unveils a
living picture showing the fall of Arcadia,
Gallifrey's second city, during the Time War.
"Time Lord art," explains the Doctor. "Bigger
on the inside. A slice of real time, frozen."
Inside the painting, we find John Hurt's Doctor
with no name – so let's call him the War
Doctor, because everyone else does – preparing to unleash a drastic final solution to end
the conflict.

Putting the Time War on screen was always
going to disappoint, of course. It's an idea that
works better as mythology: the Doctor once
spoke of the "hell" of "the Skaro Degradations,
the Horde of Travesties, the Nightmare Child,
the Could-Have-Been King with his army of
Meanwhiles and Never-Weres". So it's a bit of
let-down to find it's really just an old-fashioned
scrap with laser guns and spaceships and stuff
blowing up.

Fortunately, the Doctor's weapon of choice is
more interesting. The Moment is so dangerous,
it comes with its own conscience. And because
it's the Doctor who's planning to use it to commit genocide against his own people, that
conscience comes with the familiar face of

Rose Tyler – or, more accurately, her sexy Bad Wolf alter ego.

The Moment is a great concept, and an excellent way to use Billie Piper without cheapening the memory of the Doctor and Rose's tragic separation. Again. Piper plays her quite flirty, as superweapons go, and her scenes with Hurt in a remote desert landscape are a treat – though it's hard not to wistfully speculate how they might have played with Christopher Eccleston, as originally intended.

Hurt gets to carry the weight of much of the serious stuff, as he contemplates burning the children of Gallifrey while his successors caper about trading smarts. David Tennant, in particular, makes his long-awaited return to *Doctor Who* in a busy, comic fashion, courting Queen Elizabeth I in scenes that showcase the tenth Doctor at his larkiest. Maybe that's entirely appropriate, but there's something about the relentless gag rate and Joanna Page's rather large reading of the Virgin Queen that give these scenes the feel of an extended Comic Relief skit. But hey, it's *Doctor Who*, not *2001: A Space Odyssey*, so what the heck.

It's fun to see the Zygons finally getting another shot at the Doctor after nearly 40 years, too, even if their invasion of Earth via old paintings is something of a sideshow to the main business of whether the Doctor can save himself from destroying Gallifrey. Moffat treats the Zygons' talent for body-swapping like a fun parlour game – which it is – and the transformation process is suitably icky, even if the costume design isn't quite as impressive as James Acheson and John Friedlander's original.

The interplay between Tennant and Smith – no small part of why many cinema-goers will have bought their popcorn – is as winning as you'd expect, Ten and Eleven striking up a friendly, almost affectionate rivalry. Hurt's Doctor, meanwhile, stands largely appalled by their giddy, timey-wimey frippery, which may or may not be Moffat's grudging nod to certain entrenched quarters of *Doctor Who* fandom.

At the midway point, Moffat slows things down by locking the three Doctors in the Tower of London to work through some guilt issues. At times, the moral dilemma at the heart of the story – to destroy or not to destroy – seems a bit overcooked, especially as the idea of a man weighed down by remorse doesn't fit

naturally with Smith and Tennant's enjoyable goofing. But it's worth it for the pay-off in which the Doctors use their combined intellect to figure out a complicated escape plan, only for Clara to arrive and point out to the Oncoming Storm that the cell door wasn't actually locked. (Jenna Coleman more than holds her own in such exalted company, and there's a lovely role for comedy actress Ingrid Oliver as Osgood, a Doctor-obsessed fangirl in a Tom Baker scarf.)

Moffat scatters rewards for the faithful viewer throughout the piece with an admirable lightness of touch. There are charming nods to everything from reversing the neutron flow to the joy of roundels ("What *are* the round things?"), while UNIT's classified Black Archive contains a pinboard full of old BBC publicity shots (few would have put money on Kamelion making an appearance in the special), some of which – like the picture of former UNIT staffer Mike Yates with Hartnell era sidekick Sara Kingdom – appear to have been specially photoshopped simply to cause continuity spasms. Or at least inspire a series of Big Finish spin-offs. Even better, Moffat takes two of Terrance Dicks' most familiar, well-loved idioms – "wheezing, groaning sound" and "never cruel or cowardly" and recasts them as heroic mission statements.

Having escaped the Tower, the Doctors return to this Black Archive in heroic fashion, striding shoulder-to-shoulder out of a painting surrounded by flying bits of recently dispatched Dalek, only to have Clara admonish them for showing off. Because this is *Doctor Who*, and that's not how we do things.

Moffat also gifts Ms Oswald perhaps the key passage of the script, as the Doctors resolve they have no choice but to go through with murdering the children of Gallifrey. "The three of you: the warrior, the hero, and you," she says, addressing Eleven. "We've got enough warriors. Any old idiot can be a hero." "Then what do I do?" he asks. "Do what you've always done," she tells him. "Be a Doctor."

And so he does. He finds another way. And, if we're honest, it's a bit of a dumb way: "freezing" Gallifrey in a moment in time so that it disappears, and the Daleks firing on it suddenly find themselves blasting at each other through the space left behind. It's the sort of stunt Roadrunner might pull on Wile E Coyote – the equivalent of suddenly noticing you've run over the edge of a cliff, even though your legs are still moving. But it's to Moffat and director Nick Hurran's credit that you don't really notice at the time, because what's actually happening on screen is so thrilling, so punch-the-air exhilarating, the maguffin could have been an actual fizzing Acme bomb and you'd hardly care.

"The calculations alone would take hundreds of years," says the High Council's General when the Doctors outline their plan. "Oh, hundreds and hundreds," agrees the Doctor. "But don't worry, I started a very long time ago..."

And there, hurtling towards the screen, is the first Doctor.[XXIII] And then the second, and then Doctors Three through Nine, cleverly chosen archive footage bringing every Time Lord to the party in a kaleidoscope of spinning police boxes, rushing together to save not just Gallifrey, but his own soul.

"All twelve of them," laments the General. "No, sir," says another Time Lord. "All *thirteen!*" And there they are – Peter Capaldi's attack eyebrows filling the screen as he crashes his own reunion before he's even got started. It's a brilliant, bold touch from Moffat, who never lets a boring thing like mere chronology get in the way of good television.

Job done, the War Doctor takes his leave – and immediately begins to regenerate, culminating in an almost subliminal shot of Christopher Eccleston.[XXIV] Ten departs, too, Moffat helpfully ensuring *Doctor Who* reference books don't need to be reprinted by keeping his final line ("I don't want to go") intact.

But the best is still to come. Alone in a room of the National Gallery – a room with curiously familiar round bits – the eleventh Doctor contemplates retiring and becoming a curator. "You know, I really think you might," says a voice. Well, not a voice so much as *the* voice – that velvety baritone that boomed out of every self-respecting TV set in the land during 1970s teatimes. And there he is – older, whiter, frailer, but with a twinkle undimmed by the passing decades: Tom bloody Baker.

"I never forget a face," says the Doctor. "In the years to come, you might find yourself revisiting a few," replies the curator. "But just the old favourites, eh?" (Is that the sound of Colin Baker choking on his champagne *Space Helmet* can hear?)

It's a goose-fleshing moment, to see the elder statesman of *Doctor Who* back for one final lap. And he has some important information to impart – when the Doctor asks why the Arcadia painting has two names, *No More* and *Gallifrey Falls*, the curator tells him it's all the same name: *Gallifrey Falls No More*.

So they did it. They rewrote the Time War, and saved their people. Gallifrey is out there, somewhere – lost in time, frozen in a heartbeat, but out there. And the Doctor is going to find it. A new mission to launch him into the next 50 years of adventures.

The Day of the Doctor ends with a perfect final shot of all 12 Doctors apparently standing on a cloud, dreaming of home and looking to the future. The message is clear: after 50 years, the trip of a lifetime has barely begun.

Five out of five(ish)

Tom Baker's contribution had been recorded in April, as part of Matt Smith's last filming day on the special. To help maintain secrecy, the 79-year-old had been spirited away from his Sussex home under cover of darkness, arriving in Cardiff at 4.30 in the morning. Not in the best of health that day, he initially felt unsettled by the adventure.

"My driver went off for an early breakfast and I was alone in freezing weather with only a gloomy caravan as shelter," Baker wrote on his blog. "I felt anxious as I walked about the dead BBC film sets and mulled over my mysterious little scene. Alone among dead sets and sad props and in cold weather my anxiety grew. I suddenly found the scene remote. I couldn't get a handle on it and I began to regret accepting the job. Too late, I was on site and soon to be on set. The time was now about 5.20 so there was plenty of time to become seriously miserable before the call for make-up. And I walked up and down in the semi darkness, nobody to talk to, nowhere to find a cup of hot Bovril: you get the picture."

Fortunately, Baker was saved by the presence of – who else? – the Doctor.

"My gloom was lifted by the arrival of Matt Smith," he wrote on his website, "who welcomed me so enthusiastically that I began to think life was worthwhile."

Having submitted himself to all that cloak and dagger subterfuge, Baker went and inadvertently blabbed about his contribution to *The Day of the Doctor* in an interview with the *Huffington Post* four days before broadcast. "I am in the special – I'm not supposed to tell you that," he said, less than cryptically. Fortunately, either no-one picked up on it or, being Tom Baker, they probably just assumed he was making it up. (Six months after Baker's return to the *Doctor Who* studio, Peter Capaldi had stepped on to the TARDIS set under a similar veil of secrecy, so that his eyebrows could recorded their debut scene for the anniversary special. And in this instance, the eyebrows managed to keep schtum.)

Almost snatching defeat from the jaws of victory, *Doctor Who Live: The Afterparty* was an attempt to keep the celebrations alive that came perilously close to derailing completely on live TV. "Highlights" included a doomed attempt to find the "ultimate *Doctor Who* companion" that saw hosts Zoe Ball and Rick Edwards haranguing a record-breaking line-up of former TARDIS travellers through a confused parlour game ("Sit down, Ace!"), insightful interviews (Rick Edwards: "Why do you think *Doctor Who* has endured for so long?"; Sarah Sutton: "Oh my goodness, I've no idea") and a preview of a *Doctor Who*-themed wedding with possibly the world's least thrilled bride. Most memorable of all, though, was an attempt to hook up with pop moppets One Direction in LA, which was beset by a glacial time lag that saw every one of Zoe Ball's questions ricocheting back and forth across the Atlantic at least four times. As the item descended into a cacophony of noise, Steven Moffat provided the defining image of the show, holding his head in his hands and muttering "in the name of God..."

That said, no amount of unprofessionalism – not even Rick Edwards declaring he would "drink any of K-9's fluids" – could detract from the sheer joy of seeing so many well-loved faces (from Carole Ann Ford and William Russell all the way through to Jenna Coleman, via Peter Davison, Colin Baker, Sylvester McCoy and Matt Smith) assembled under one roof. It remains a warm and fuzzy tribute to

Doctor Who's gloriously extended family, if not necessarily to the art of live broadcasting.

Most of that extended family also popped up in *The Five(Ish) Doctors Reboot*, the surprise cherry on the anniversary cake that was all the sweeter for having been kept under wraps until relatively late in the day.

Premiering on iPlayer and the BBC's Red Button service, it's a deliriously funny comic farce chronicling three ex-Time Lords' increasingly desperate attempts to bag a part in *The Day of the Doctor*. In the central roles, Peter Davison, Colin Baker and Sylvester McCoy send themselves up mercilessly – Baker is seen forcing his family to watch the extras on the *Vengeance on Varos* DVD ("I've locked all the doors"), while McCoy continually reminds his predecessors that he's busy "filming a big blockbuster movie directed by Oscar-winner Peter Jackson". Davison, meanwhile, reprises the needy, egoist version of himself from various convention videos, including a hilarious dream sequence in which Matt Smith, Jenna Coleman and Steven Moffat worship at the feet of their favourite Doctor.

In one scene, backstage at a convention, the trio fix Paul McGann with jealous stares while bitching about how much work he has, until the eighth Doctor tells them: "Whatever it is you're planning, I'm in... work permitting, obviously." Later, they stage a picket outside BBC Television Centre, before hitching a lift to Cardiff with John Barrowman, having uncovered the shocking truth about his secret wife and children. (The picket scene led some passers-by into believing Davison, Baker and McCoy were staging a *real* protest – which is a testament to their acting, if nothing else.)

Davison's "plan" involves the trio stealing their original costumes from the *Doctor Who* Experience and sneaking on the set of the 50th anniversary special when no-one's looking. For all the self-mockery, there's a genuine thrill to seeing the three Time Lords on the current TARDIS, while their wheeze of hiding under the sheets covering the Zygons in the National Gallery set holds out the tantalising possibility that it really is them lurking under there during *The Day of the Doctor*. (Alas, it isn't.)

Alongside Smith, Coleman, Moffat, David Tennant, Georgia Moffett, John Barrowman and around a dozen classic series companions

– the latter seen swirling around Moffat's head in a fan-pleasing riff on the fifth Doctor's regeneration – the production features cameos from the likes of Sean Pertwee, David Troughton, Frank Skinner and Olivia Colman, and even Peter Jackson and Sir Ian McKellen gamely play along from the set of *The Hobbit*. The undisputed star turn, though, comes from Russell T Davies, who tries to hustle his way into Davison's film, suggesting he could become the Doctor himself, complete with his own tenth Doctor-style catchphrase, "quelle dommage!".

A warm and witty tribute to *Doctor Who* and its extended family of actors, execs and fans, *The Five(Ish) Doctors Reboot* is a small but perfect diamond among the wealth of 50th anniversary treasures. Davison had originally embarked on the project as a bit of fun – a tongue-in-cheek protest about his lack of involvement in the anniversary special. But, during a visit to see her husband on the set of said special, Georgia Moffett[XXV] – now working as producer on her father's film – had shown the script to Faith Penhale, who passed it on to Steven Moffat. The showrunner was so impressed, he agreed to make some modest budget available, and also give Davison the use of BBC Wales facilities.

Of course, there's one figure whose absence from *The Five(Ish) Doctors Reboot* is as notable as it was from the original. Back in March, Peter Davison had sent Tom Baker a copy of the script for consideration, and later made several unsuccessful attempts to discuss the project with his predecessor. It was only when he saw *The Day of the Doctor* that the reason for Baker's actions – in so much as Tom Baker's actions can ever be reasonably be explained by *anything* – became clear. He couldn't be involved in a satirical film about trying to be in *The Day of the Doctor* because he was actually, you know, *in The Day of the Doctor*.

With no preview copies having been made available, Monday's papers saw the press passing first judgment on the anniversary special – with the *Telegraph*'s headline "a moving, triumphant labour of love" summing up the prevailing mood perfectly.

"This wasn't just a glorious adventure in its own right, but demonstrated everything we love about dear old *Doctor Who* – a combination of humour and darkness, knowing gags for the grown-ups and pratfalls for the kids," wrote the paper's Michael Hogan. "It crammed more ideas into 75 minutes than lesser shows do in several series. This was a labour of love of which Moffat, the BBC and all of us can be proud."

In his five-star review for *The Times*, Andrew Billen declared: "Steven Moffat, when he hits form – as I suppose he was obliged to do for this episode – writes the cleverest scripts on television. The playfulness with which, on Saturday, he engaged with the biggest issues might justly be called Stoppardian. Moffat's birthday gift to all us boys and girls is to have ensured there will be many more anniversaries."

In the *Daily Mail*, Jim Shelley described the story as "a clever, chaotic, infuriating combination of nifty, knowing detail and big, hollow, pompous bluster" – possibly the nicest thing the *Daily Mail*'s said about anything, ever.

As the final ratings for the worldwide broadcast emerged, the results read like a PR man's wet dream. With 12.8 million viewers, *The Day of the Doctor* was the No. 1 show for the week, and the highest-rated UK drama for three years. In cinemas, meanwhile, the film was the third-biggest box office hit of the weekend, behind *The Hunger Games: Catching Fire* and *Gravity*. In America, *The Day of the Doctor* went one better, its $4.8 million haul making it the second highest-grossing film of the day in cinemas, while the 2.4 million who watched it live on BBC America amounted to another new record for the channel.

The episode's global simulcast was rewarded with a certificate from Guinness World Records, whose editor-in-chief said: "Who else but the time-twisting Doctor could appear in 94 countries at once?! This outstanding achievement is testament to the fact that the longest-running sci-fi TV show in history is not just a well-loved UK institution, but a truly global success adored by millions of people."

Accepting the award, Steven Moffat said: "For years, the Doctor has been stopping everyone else from conquering the world. Now, just to show off, he's gone and done it himself!"

But apart from that, it had all been a bit of a flop, really.

"So Matt's the 13th Doctor, and he'll be followed by Peter, who's the 12th. Everybody clear on that? Good."

With the dust barely settled on the anniversary, the BBC aired the first teaser for the upcoming Christmas special, showing Matt Smith along with a Dalek, a Cyberman, a Silent and a Weeping Angel, and declaring: "This Christmas, Silence Will Fall."

In the House of Lords, meanwhile, *Doctor Who* figured prominently in a debate on the contribution of broadcast media to the British economy, with former BBC Director General Lord Birt among those praising the success of the global simulcast. Baroness Bonham-Carter of Yarnbury also attempted to visit maximum discomfort on one Baron Grade of Yarmouth, asking whether he'd still have axed the show if he'd known Sylvester McCoy would one day be replaced by John Hurt. Lord Grade nodded in the affirmative; he was nothing if not consistent.

That was all very well, of course, but the *real* debate was taking place elsewhere – namely, the grenade Steven Moffat had casually tossed under the thorny problem of Doctor numbering. "I've been really, really quite careful about the numbering of the Doctors," the showrunner insisted. "He's very specific, the John Hurt Doctor, that he doesn't take the name of the Doctor. So the eleventh Doctor is still the eleventh Doctor, and the tenth is still the tenth."[47]

In the same interview, Moffat admitted Christopher Eccleston had been his first choice for the anniversary special's third star: "But I was pretty certain Chris wouldn't do it, although he did agree to a couple of meetings. So instead we had the challenge and excitement of introducing a BBC audience to a brand new Doctor."[47]

And it wouldn't necessarily have made sense, Moffat argued, for the ninth Doctor to have been the one who fought in the Time War. "I was always nervous of that one, because it doesn't fit with *Rose* at all. He's a brand new Doctor in *Rose*, he's absolutely, definitely new[XXVI]. It couldn't have been Chris who pushed the button in the Time War, 'cos that's a new man, very explicitly, in that episode. I also had trouble, I have to be honest,

imagining it being Paul McGann's Doctor. So all this led me to the idea that, if you're going to sell to the Not-We audience a Doctor who essentially they haven't seen before, then you have a freer hand than saying it has to be one of the ones you've already had. And it was predicated on getting an enormous star to be able to do it. We got John Hurt, so that was cool!"[49]

In early December, Matt Smith entered rehearsals for his latest role as Patrick Bateman – the serial killer who hides a secret double life as an investment banker (or is it the other way round?) – in a stage musical adaptation of Bret Easton Ellis' *American Psycho*.

"I could have done it for another three years and been very happy," Smith told the *Sunday Times* of his decision to quit *Doctor Who*. "But... It's a monk's life, a chaste and staid existence." Meanwhile, Steven Moffat was talking up his young star's exit, promising: "Matt's performance in [the Christmas special] is mind-blowingly good. It's the best one he's ever done, and a contender for the best performance ever by anyone as the Doctor. Absolutely sensational."[47]

By 7.30pm on Christmas Day, the talking was over, as the eleventh Doctor arrived to take his heroic last bow. Watching *The Time of the Doctor*, though, it's hard to avoid a niggling feeling that Steven Moffat's main priority is housekeeping. He goes to great lengths to tidy up this Doctor's various dangling threads – we even find out what was behind the Doctor's Door of Nightmares in *The God Complex* – but, rather than tie these loose ends up in a neat bow, Moffat gifts us a very raggedy Christmas box indeed. You suspect it all makes very elegant sense in the showrunner's head and even, given a slide rule and enough time, on paper. But as a slice of post-turkey family entertainment, it feels garbled, confusing and not a little chaotic.

As we've come to expect, the pre-titles set up is a doozy: a kinetic bit of planet-hopping in which the Doctor blunders onto a Dalek spaceship brandishing a trophy kill eyestalk, then strolls into the midst of a Cyber army while carrying the severed head of one of their number like a handbag. This latter unfortunate fellow turns out to be the Time Lord's current travelling companion – given the nickname

Handles, he sits on the TARDIS console offering flight data and casual chit-chat in equal measure. As voiced by Kayvan Novack, he's rather adorable.

When the TARDIS phone rings, the Doctor has to answer from the outside, despite being in space surrounded by enemy ships of every stripe. It's Clara, inviting him to Christmas dinner. "I'm being shot at by Cybermen!" he protests. "Well, can't we do both?" asks Clara. And there's *Doctor Who* in a brazil-nutshell.

Later, there's some comic business in which the Doctor arrives at Clara's family lunch entirely naked. Press-ganged into pretending to be her boyfriend, he gives her a playful slap on the arse – surely the first example of Doctor-companion buttock contact since Colin Baker misguidedly bit Nicola Bryant on the bum during rehearsals for *The Twin Dilemma*.

So far, so delightful. It all starts to unravel when our heroes (now both technically naked to everyone but the viewer and the BBC Compliance Unit) travel to something called the Church of the Papal Mainframe – a militarised religious order in a giant spaceship that, like thousands of other vested interests, has been drawn to the orbit of the planet Trenzalore: the source of a mysterious message that is spreading fear throughout the universe. Here, the Doctor indulges in some heavy flirting with the "Mother Superious", Tasha Lem (Orla Brady), in what appears to be a few pages of leftover River Song script, while the Silence, Daleks, Weeping Angels et al are reduced to walk-on parts. (Not literally, of course, in the case of the last two.)

In a church bell tower in the Trenzalorian town of Christmas, the Doctor makes a startling discovery: the crack in time – that familiar, sinister broken smile in the fabric of reality – that launched this incarnation on his adventures four years ago. It's a lovely, iconic moment, so it's doubly unfortunate when this becomes the focus for the story's major fault line: a woolly idea about the Time Lords being trapped behind the wall (metaphysically, that is; the Time War didn't end with them being bricked up in a church) and only being able to return to the universe if the Doctor reveals his name to them... which will, in turn, trigger an all-out assault by the assembled armies of serious whoop-ass. And this, apparently, is why

the Silence were sworn to keep the Doctor's name under wraps by putting River Song in that lake and... um, anyway. You get the idea. Or maybe you don't. It's all a bit baffling, to be honest, and the rather brilliant notion that the Doctor's actions here create the entire "crack in time" crisis – Eleven's last stand setting up his very first adventure, effectively – is so buried in the mix, it's easy to miss altogether.

As an exercise in world-building – or town-building, anyway – Christmas never really convinces. Nor does the idea of the Doctor abandoning his restless wandering to stay there and protect its people – Matt Smith gradually disappearing under layers of latex in a centuries-long Mexican stand-off against the enemy hordes. (Though the wooden, yes wooden, Cybermen are *very* cool, and a Silent with a Dalek eyestalk is quite an arresting image). Clara, meanwhile, pinballs back and forth between Christmas town and Christmas dinner, desperately searching for a way into the story. She does eventually get to save the day, though – by whispering nice things about the Doctor into a crack in the wall. True story.

By now, the Doctor is so old he's about to cark it of natural causes. And this time, there's no hope of regenerating, because he's used up all his lives.

Hang on a minute, rewind that. He's used up all his *what* already? That's right: by adding the War Doctor and – wait for it – the "biological metacrisis" version of David Tennant from *Journey's End* into the mix, Moffat is now arguing that the eleventh Doctor is actually the thirteenth, so this really is It. Full stop. No more Doctor. End of.

Or it *would* be, if Clara's whispered sweet nothings hadn't convinced the Time Lords – the ones behind the wall, keep up – to give the Doctor a whole new life cycle, which he uses to blast the Daleks out of the sky in a pyrotechnic display of regeneration energy, (while leaving the population of Christmas strangely un-singed).

Here, Moffat's motivation feels less like housekeeping than full-blown obsessive compulsive cleaning. Sure, a certain breed of fan has worried away for years at what might happen when the Doctor runs out of all his regenerations – the fear being that the BBC will simply sacrifice one of its biggest cash cows so as not to upset narrative continuity. Maybe that's what inspired Moffat to put the idea to bed, but you can't help thinking the idea of the Doctor's final death might have made for something a bit more substantial and dramatic – a season arc, if you like that sort of thing – rather than being tacked on as an afterthought to Matt Smith's already overcrowded exit story.

Thankfully, just when it seems this most deserving of Doctors might be denied a fitting adieu, Moffat pulls something extraordinary out of the fire. After half an hour of being buried under rubber wrinkles, Matt Smith is once again the unconventionally handsome, lantern-jawed space boffin we've fallen in love with. But it's just an echo – a system "reset" – while he says his goodbyes.

And *what* goodbyes. "We're all different people all through our lives," he tells Clara. "And that's okay, that's good, you've got to keep moving, so long as you remember all the people that you used to be. I will not forget one line of this. Not one day. I swear. I will always remember when the Doctor was me." It's obviously a scene written as much for Smith, and his fans, as the eleventh Doctor himself, and you'd need a stony heart indeed not to forgive such a beautiful, heart-piercing indulgence.

And then, from nowhere, the TARDIS is covered in a child's drawings: young Amelia Pond's cartoon scrawls of her many adventures to come. And there she is, little Amelia, running around the console room before descending the stairs, all grown up now – Karen Gillan a perfect portrait of porcelain beauty – and placing a hand on the Doctor's cheek. Because who else, really, could usher him into the next life but her, the first face these eyes saw? "Raggedy man," says Amy soothingly. "Goodnight."

And then she's gone. The Doctor is alone with Clara, and there's the briefest, whipcrack flash of energy – he did all the fireworks on that bell tower – and suddenly a new man is in the room, fixing Clara with a bulging, mad-eyed stare the like of which we haven't seen on this ship for more than 30 years.

The new Doctor doesn't like the colour of his new kidneys. And he doesn't remember how to fly the TARDIS. Disaster looms, as it always must. Onwards.

Matt finish

"To the Whoniverse, thanks a million. You're the best. I'll miss you. And I'll miss the madness." That was the message tweeted by the BBC on behalf of Matt Smith after the closing credits of *The Time of the Doctor*. Some celebs use Twitter; real stars get corporations to tweet on their behalf.

In *DWM*, Steven Moffat explained the rationale behind the episode. "When I started writing Matt's Doctor, I thought: 'What if everything he was involved in was in some way a consequence of the battle he was fighting in his last episode?' So there's a battle out there in his last episode and, as a result of that battle he hasn't got involved in yet, things are coming back in time and getting at him. And he won't know what they are, or understand what they are, until he gets there. That was the plan. And that's what we've done!"[50]

Despite mixed reviews for the piece as a whole, most critics reserved praise for *The Time of the Doctor*'s outgoing star. "Smith has been so good as the ageless, sinister, childlike, loveable alien that it was almost a shame to see that expressive Easter Island head caked in make-up for the middle section of this episode," wrote Tim Martin in the *Telegraph*, "while the swelling strings and Shakespearian speechifying of the final quarter-hour seemed comically at odds with the intricate lunacy that animates his best performances." "Easily the highlight of this year's Christmas viewing, *The Time of the Doctor* not only gave Matt Smith a great send-off but also gave viewers a careful, concise and emotional hour of top-quality entertainment," said Jon Cooper in the *Mirror*. "And as is typical for *Who*, renewal and regeneration are only the start of a brand new adventure, and from his brief introduction ('Kidneys!') Peter Capaldi looks like a fine successor to take the world's favourite TV hero in a different and equally exciting direction."

With 11.4 million viewers tuning in to pay their last respects (that's a million-and-a-half more than *Coronation Street* on the other side – not that we fans have long memories or anything), and the episode unseating the 50th anniversary special as BBC America's most watched broadcast ever, *The Time of the Doctor* consolidated Team Smith-Moffat's work in holding the ratings line in the post Tennant-Davies era – a task many might once have considered an impossible ask.

If, as the journalist Andrew Harrison incisively pointed out, the tenth Doctor represented *Doctor Who's* "rock star years," then outgunning his predecessor was never a realistic possibility for the young Matt Smith. Four years earlier, simply taking the ball and not dropping it would have been considered an achievement: that Smith managed to do that while building the series' international profile – and becoming the first Time Lord to be nominated for a BAFTA for his troubles – is testament to the actors' extraordinarily nuanced performance. To play the Doctor, you have to be many things: commanding, playful, clever, silly, naïve, heroic, selfish, calculating, old, young, romantic, sexy, geeky, reckless... you must have the gravitas and authority to walk into the middle of a war zone and command instant respect... probably before tripping over and breaking something on the way out. You need the sort of easy grace that can charm the birds from the trees, while also being bumbling and awkward and a little bit daft. Matt Smith embodies all these qualities perhaps more effortlessly than any of his predecessors, turning on a sixpence from powerful demi-god to a flailing fool barely in control of his own limbs. He's the smartest guy in the room, and an endearingly clueless naïf – especially where matters of the heart are concerned. Smith's Doctor is both action hero and bookish nerd – Indiana Jones meets Mr Bean. Which is exactly what the Doctor should be.

Championing the eleventh Doctor as the ultimate Time Lord in a piece for *The Times*, the journalist Dominic Maxwell captured the essence of Matt Smith's performance perfectly: "As Steven Moffat pointed out, the different Doctors aren't all *that* different as they are written. They're all the outsider who knows best, the weirdo you want to be with. Yet Smith inhabits that outsider more fully than anyone since Tom Baker. Smith plays in a universe in which real human emotions have to be tackled; Baker excelled in the wooden-rackets era where the Doctor sidestepped all that, end of story. Smith is of the world as well as out of it."

A month after his on-screen departure, and with the cameras already rolling on the Peter Capaldi era of *Doctor Who*, Matt Smith sealed his time as the Doctor by winning Best Drama Performance at that year's National Television Awards, where *Doctor Who* was also named Best Drama. In an acceptance speech filmed backstage at the theatre where he was performing in *American Psycho*, Smith thanked everyone who had voted for making his time on *Doctor Who* "the best, most audacious part of my career to date" and claimed he would remain "forever grateful" to have played the role.

Talking to *The Big Issue* a couple of months earlier, Smith had reflected on his first cautious baby steps in the role, when he'd found himself thrown into the biggest job in television without a clue what he was supposed to do. "Let me tell you, just before my first episode was aired, I was really nervous," he recalled. "I just tried to remain true to my instincts. It is up to everyone else to decide how I've fared. I was never going to be everyone's favourite Doctor. But hopefully I am some people's."[51]

For his part, Steven Moffat admitted facing up to life after the eleventh Doctor was a daunting prospect – for personal as much as professional reasons. "One day I'm sure I'll work with Matt again, and we'll laugh about old times," he wrote in *Doctor Who Magazine* in the summer of 2013. "But I don't want to think about that right now. I want to think about the best of days. About the impossibility of replacing Russell T Davies and David Tennant in the two most brilliant jobs in television and the fact we didn't entirely screw it up. About all those episodes, all those monsters, and all those stories we're never going to tell you.

"I will never forget a moment of it – me and my mate Matt, making *Doctor Who*. Those were the days."[52]

Afterword: Eyebrow Culture

At time of publication, the twelfth Doctor and his attack eyebrows are still very much at large, his story still being written. For that reason, it's a story to be told in full in a future volume of Space Helmet, should any of us live long enough to see such a thing. (Indeed, the very idea may actively discourage many of you from doing so.)

Putting the show into hiatus during 2016 does, however, provide us with a useful opportunity to take a quick tour of the previous two years' edited highlights, and consider where it leaves Doctor Who as it celebrates its 53rd anniversary.

Also, they turned the Brigadier into a flying Cyberman, and we couldn't not mention it.

Doctor Who gets re-booted up the arse

You might have thought the energy expended during Doctor Who's golden jubilee year would have left the production team exhausted. But any thoughts of a lie down in a darkened room – or at least the occasional lunch hour – would have to wait until after the small business of re-launching the show. Again. Because 2014 was set to be a landmark year in the history of Doctor Who. Yes, another one.

Filming on Peter Capaldi's debut season got under way in the first few days of January, with the twelfth Doctor's costume unveiled a week later. Capaldi described his rather fetching dark blue Crombie coat, dark trousers and black boots combo as "simple, stark and back to basics" and "the only thing that made me feel like Doctor Who". "That was the key thing," the actor told the Sunday Times. "In my mind, the original Doctors had all dressed in dark colours, although I knew that was because it was in black and white." It probably also explained why they'd looked a little pale. There was one livid slash of colour, though, courtesy of the coat's red velvet lining, which recalled Jon Pertwee at the height of his peacock pomp. (Maybe if he asked really nicely, Capaldi could get his own space car, too?)

In a Doctor Who Magazine interview, Steven Moffat a promised a "radical change" in the form of a more "dangerous" Time Lord. "The last two Doctors have been your 'good boyfriend' Doctors," he explained. "But the Doctor isn't always like that.

"I think it was time to flip the show around a bit. The new version of the show is quite old now. It's very old. We need the kick-up-the-arse Doctor in a way, to frighten you and make you think, 'Oh, it's a different show again'."[1]

In March, though, the new Doctor proved himself anything but dangerous, as footage emerged of Capaldi reassuring a young fan with autism about the change her hero had undergone. Kneeling down on-set, Capaldi scrolls through his phone until he finds a picture of himself, Matt Smith and Jenna Coleman together. "Matt said to me to look after Doctor Who, and he gave me his watch that he wears, and he said that, in his own way, he was happy that it was me that was coming in," he tells the girl. "So I will do my very best to be as much fun and as friendly as he is."

Over the coming months and years, such interactions with fans would become a Capaldi trademark (on one occasion, he even wandered into the Doctor Who Experience, on his day off, just to say hello), in the same way Tom Baker had relished playing the Pied Piper of Gallifrey in the 70s. It is entirely heartwarming (though, on the downside, that promise to be as fun and friendly as his puppydog predecessor must have had Steven Moffat frantically leafing through scripts, deleting scenes like that one where the new Doctor bludgeons a kitten to death with a snooker ball in a sock).

"One thing the show does so well," Capaldi told the Sunday Times in July, "is balance the epic and the domestic. You can go from the edge of the universe to a pedestrian precinct. This Doctor loves watching stars being born in Andromeda; he's also thrilled to see litter blowing across a supermarket car park." (Which would prove extremely useful when further

BBC cost-cutting resulted in Doctor Who versus the Crisp Packet of Doom.)

In July – as the Monty Python team emerged from a TARDIS at the start of their sell-out reunion shows at The O2 in London – rough cuts of five Series Eight episodes were leaked online from the BBC's Latin American headquarters. The security breach prompted the Corporation to issue its now-standard request for fans not to reveal plot details, for the benefit of all those people over 40 who still waited for it to come on actual telly.

In late summer, Capaldi, Coleman and Moffat emerged blinking from the Roath Lock studios and immediately embarked on The Doctor Who World Tour – a promotional juggernaut that took in seven cities across five continents over 12 days. Highlights of the trip included the trio being mobbed in a South Korean airport, people sleeping on the sidewalk in New York to get a ticket to the screening, fangirls revealing surprisingly intimate tattoos in elaborate Gallifreyan script and a Mariachi band in Mexico City singing a heartfelt tribute to "Doctor Misterio." As launches go, it was a long way from the final season of *Doctor Who*'s original run in 1989, when the BBC couldn't even be bothered to cut a trailer, and the entire publicity effort had amounted to a half-page article in the *Radio Times* (which Sophie Aldred had to write herself). Backdrops like Sydney Opera House and Rio's Christ the Redeemer statue, meanwhile, proved somewhat more glamorous than the rainy quarry where Sylvester McCoy had the photo call for his first season. (Unless you're from Sydney or Rio, of course, in which case a gravel pit in Somerset might seem impossibly exotic.)

Film footage showed Capaldi receiving a rock star reception on stage in Sydney. (Seriously, go find it on YouTube – it makes that bit in *Iron Man* where Tony Stark flies into an expo to the strains of AC/DC look like the opening of a new mobile library exhibition.)

In Mexico, though, it was Moffat who proved the headline act. "It was like Sting or Bono," said Capaldi. "Steven is more popular here [than us]," agreed Coleman. "I went outside the hotel yesterday to sign autographs, and they were like 'Where's Moffat? Where's Moffat?'"[2] He was probably inside, signing off on the new Moff action figure. (Actually, the

man himself wasn't convinced by his sudden elevation to the new Justin Bieber, claiming standing with his stars always makes him "look like the fat roadie who thinks he's in the band".[3] Isn't that the drummer's job?)

After the last stop in Rio, the team headed home in time for the start of the new series. (Though the Doctor himself had a more pressing engagement: Peter Capaldi needed to be back in London by Thursday to take his car for its MOT.) Asked how they could possibly top this global publicity coup the following year, BBC Worldwide's Chris Allen joked they were going to "fire Peter into space". At least, Capaldi *assumed* they were joking.

Talking up the new series, Mark Gatiss promised a "tonal shift". "Since it came back in 2005, the default story, as a template, is *City of Death*," the writer of episode nine told *DWM*. "But as of this year it's a bit more like *Horror of Fang Rock*.... *Horror of Fang Rock* is more frightening. It's more serious. Okay, it has a great big ball of green snot in it, but it's fundamentally more creepy. That's how it feels it's going this year."[4]

Steven Moffat also revealed the new scripts had been written to incorporate longer scenes – possibly as a nod to the phenomenal success of HBO's *Game of Thrones*, which had eschewed the trend for rapid cutting in favour of a slower, more measured pace that compelled the actors to learn pages of dialogue per scene.

Another departure would be an increased focus on Clara's life between TARDIS hops. "In the same way we had Victorian Clara leading a double life," Jenna Coleman told *SciFi Now*, "this Clara has a life of home, school, domestic bliss, her flat in Shoreditch. And then the Doctor will bring the TARDIS and land in the bedroom or land in the stationary cupboard at school, and she'll go off and have adventures. In a way, she's kind of having her cake and eating it."[5] Fair enough – but if a bloke suddenly appears in your bedroom, don't go off and have adventures with him, call the police.

A new Doctor meant a new title sequence. Step forward Billy Hanshaw, a graphic designer and *Who* fan from Leeds who had uploaded his own sequence to YouTube, which caught the eye of Steven Moffat. "I happened across it, and it was the only new title idea I'd seen since

1963," said Moffat. "We got in touch with him, and said, 'Okay, we're going to do that one.'"

The finished sequence – a collaboration between Hanshaw and BBC Wales, in which the camera tumbles through the inner workings of a timepiece – is certainly impressive (which is less than can be said for the reedy new theme tune variant, which Murray Gold realised using a theremin – or possibly a paper and comb). But hopefully the show will stop short of a complete takeover by YouTubers, otherwise future seasons might just consist of endless hours of the Doctor sitting in his bedroom playing *Minecraft*.

Which came first, the chicken or the moon?

Debuting on BBC One, BBC America and in cinemas around the world, feature-length eighth series opener *Deep Breath* lands the new Doctor and Clara in Victorian London for a gothic and times creepy slice of Saturday night steampunk involving clockwork droids; a body-snatching, organ-harvesting restaurant; and a giant T-Rex stomping up the Thames.

The latter is really only there to provide the opening sequence with a money shot, and is hastily written out once said money's run out. Elsewhere, Steven Moffat's script is a veritable grab-bag of Victoriana: there are explicit references to "Sweeney Todd without the pies" and "Burke and Hare from space", while the Half-Face Man stalks the streets on the hunt for victims like a tick-tocking Jack the Ripper.

Despite informing the story's title, the idea of the clockwork villains not being able to detect you if you hold your breath – Moffat's latest riff on the patented "don't blink" wheeze – is as half-hearted (and casually discarded) as the dinosaur subplot, adding to the sense of rather too many ideas fighting for space. Hiring movie hotshot Ben Wheatley – whose credits include the acclaimed feature films *Kill List*, *A Field in England* and, more recently, *High-Rise* – as a special guest director also feels like something of a missed opportunity, as he's clearly been briefed to stick to the house style.

And the man himself? Compared to *The Eleventh Hour*'s frantic race against the clock, this is a positively stately introduction to the new Doctor that holds back from the full-on

charm offensive of Matt Smith's debut. Consequently, by the end, we're still not entirely sure who this unpredictable, volatile figure with the furious reflection and attack eyebrows is. It's a deliberate – and risky – gambit not attempted since Colin Baker played hard to get in his first story. And I'm sure I don't need to remind you how *that* ended.

Critics gave the episode a cautious welcome, though Capaldi himself fared better. "A blend of Doctor Doolittle and Sherlock Holmes, he crackled with fierce intelligence and nervous energy," wrote Michael Hogan in the *Daily Telegraph*, while *SFX* hailed a "compelling, surprising, wonderfully dangerous" reading of the role. In the *Radio Times*, Patrick Mulkern summed up the general consensus by declaring himself "nonplussed" by *Deep Breath* itself, but an instant fan of Capaldi's "fiercely intelligent, acerbic, bonkers, haunted, vulnerable" Doctor.

Many also noted that the surprise appearance of Matt Smith, calling from the past in the final reel to reassure Clara that this strange, unknowable alien was still the same man, was clearly aimed as much at the nervous viewing public as his companion.

With a hearty 9.17m said viewers turning in, *Doctor Who* was the second-most watched show of the week, behind ratings behemoth *The Great British Bake Off*. (Note to non-UK readers: yes, a baking contest really is the biggest British TV show of the decade. If *Doctor Who* really wants to compete at the top table, it should have taken the Daleks out of *Asylum of the Daleks* and just concentrated on Oswin's soufflé recipe.)

Capaldi's second outing, *Into the Dalek*, started life as a brainstorming session for possible *Doctor Who* computer games – and it shows. In Phil Ford and Steven Moffat's story, the Doctor and Clara are shrunk down to the size of action figures and sent into battle inside... well, the clue's in the title. Ford described the episode as "*Die Hard* in a Dalek", but the rather thin results don't quite merit that marquee description. It's diverting enough for two-thirds of its running time, but let down by a flabby, showboating final confrontation between the Doctor and his reluctant host – who he dubs "Rusty" – and several credulity-stretching leaps of logic by Clara that suggest she's either an absolute genius, or has snuck a look at helpimtrappedinadalek.com.

It's slightly unfortunate, then, it was this episode that AA Gill – the *Sunday Times'* flamboyantly vituperative TV critic – chose as the basis for one of his occasional *Doctor Who* demolition jobs. Of the new Time Lord, Gill wrote: "Peter Capaldi stumbled and gurned, then mimed and posed and postured and gasped and pranced and lolled and gaped and sighed and shrugged his way into the role... It wasn't an audition for a new part, rather a postmortem for a venerable career."

Better put him down as undecided.

If he thought *that* was stumbling, gurning, posturing and prancing, we can only wonder what Gill would have made of the following week's offering, *Robot of Sherwood*. Steven Moffat asked Mark Gatiss to write the story like "a buddy movie" – and the idea of Doctor Who and Robin Hood teaming up for a medieval version of *48 Hours* certainly has legs. Unfortunately, the result is as crashingly unfunny as its title, and the plotting so slapdash you can only assume there wasn't a fag-packet available to scribble it down on.

Casting Clara as the smart, long-suffering brains of the outfit is a nice idea in theory, but comes at the expense of turning both Doctor Who and Robin Hood – two of the great heroes of English folklore – into a pair of preening, bickering imbeciles. And it turns out its *way* too early into Capaldi's exploration of a new, more troublesome Doctor to drop him into a light comedy and expect him to pull off the dotty uncle act.

Steven Moffat admitted that the fourth story, *Listen*, was borne of "an entirely selfish desire". "I remember the first thing I said about this year's run is, 'I'm doing a chamber piece, with no money, in the middle, because I haven't done one in ages and I'd like to prove I can actually write',"[6] he told *DWM*.

To which we can only respond: Moffat should try being more selfish more often. Though not quite reaching the skyscraping heights of *Blink*, *Listen* nevertheless shares many of that story's acclaimed qualities – not least the fact it's absolutely *terrifying*, with a simple red blanket providing one of the series' all-time great scares. The fact we never find out what's *under* that blanket – Is it a monster? Or just a child mucking about? – only adds to the story's intriguing puzzle box of a premise, neatly summarised by the Doctor as: "What if no-one is ever really alone? What if every single living being has a companion, a silent passenger, a shadow?"

The episode also develops the rather sweet, stumbling romance between Clara and fellow teacher Danny Pink (the likeable Samuel Anderson), who have the hottest chemistry Coal Hill School has seen since Ian Chesterton last made eyes at Barbara Wright over a conical flask. Some fans, though, preferred to ignore such riches in favour of getting themselves in a tizz over a scene in which Clara goes back in time and hides under the Doctor's bed when he's a child. But that's some fans for you.

After a wobbly start, *Listen* signalled an upswing in quality for the latest run. The next episode, *Time Heist*, saw the Doctor assembling a gang for a bank job which, as the title suggests, involves knocking through time instead of just a wall (though there are plenty of those, too). It's a slick, funny, exciting caper that sees Capaldi asserting himself as the boss after half a season of letting Clara do all the heavy lifting. The Teller – a telepathic alien in an orange prison jumpsuit who sucks people's brains clean out of their heads (similar to the effect you get when one of the Kardashians opens their mouths) – is a proper *Doctor Who* monster, and guest star Keeley Hawes is good value, treading just the right side of camp as baddie-of-the-week Ms Delphox.

Coming three weeks after *Robot of Sherwood*, Gareth Roberts' *The Caretaker* is a lesson in how to do *Doctor Who* comedies (bottom line: write some good jokes). The elevator pitch – the Doctor goes undercover as Coal Hill School's new janitor in order to foil an alien invasion – is irresistible, and one that particularly suited to Capaldi's crabby, un-child-friendly incarnation.

Watching Capaldi and Jenna Coleman deftly knocking zingers back and forth is a joy, Coleman in particular demonstrating perfect comic timing as Clara's two worlds – which she has tried so hard to keep apart – collide with hair-frizzing results. Samuel Anderson also continues to impress, especially when he rumbles what's going on, and leaps to the conclusion that Clara is an alien and the Doctor her "space dad". The only sour note – apart from slightly comical, sub-CBBC monster the Skovox Blitzer – is the Doctor's continued aggression towards Danny on account of his soldiering past, a character trait that's as prejudiced and inconsistent as it is childishly petulant. Though, in fairness, the scripts don't shy from pointing this out.

Forced to move down the school bus to make room for *Strictly Come Dancing*, *The Caretaker* went out in *Doctor Who*'s new 8.30pm slot – the joint latest (with the TV movie) time the show had even been broadcast. But despite grumbles from parents that it was now on too late for children to watch – and the added complication of going mano-a-mano with *The X Factor* – the ratings (6.82m) barely registered a flicker.

Scripted by Peter Harness, the award-winning writer of the BBC's *Wallander* adaptations, *Kill the Moon* had seen the Doctor Who team returning to Lanzarote for the first time since 1984's *Planet of Fire*. And this time, no-one got into a tussle with a German nudist. (Or not one they were willing to talk about, anyway.)

Harness' premise – the moon has gained so much weight, it's playing merry hell with the Earth's tides, so a suicide bomb squad has been sent to blow it up – certainly has chutzpah, and proves the basis for a taut, gripping sci-fi thriller. An attack on the moonbase by giant, red-eyed spiders, meanwhile, makes for a nerve-shredding take on the classic base-under-siege formula – a mix of *Alien* and *Who*'s own *The Ark in Space* that takes maximum advantage of the new, NSF kids timeslot. (Peter Capaldi was particularly delighted to find that, even in the CGI era, being attacked by one of these creatures still involved rolling around wrestling a rubber prop, just like they did in the days when Jon Pertwee went beak-to-bouffant with a plastic pterodactyl.)

Most of the pre-match hype focused on how far the episode would push the new Doctor into darker territory, and how far it would stretch his relationship with Clara. Quite far, is the answer, resulting in a thrilling final confrontation in which, literally crying with rage, she threatens to "smack you so hard you'll regenerate". But the *real* contention was reserved for episode's science – if that's the right world, which it isn't – and, specifically,

the revelation that the moon is... that the moon is... Look, there's no easy way to do this, so I'll just come out with it. Specifically, the revelation that the moon is an egg.

There, I said it. The moon is an egg. An egg that hatches and gives birth to a sort of enormous bird thing (Shall we call it a space chicken? Let's), which promptly lays a *new* moon – one that's actually bigger than the space chicken it emerged from, which must have brought a tear to its eye. And to think, on a previous moon visit all we had to worry about was someone plugging a breach in the dome of the lunar base with a tea-tray. We can only assume Harness had engaged the services of same scientific consultant they used on *Button Moon*.

Many also read the story as an abortion parable – and a rabidly (so-called) pro-life one at that – but a slightly horrified Harness was at pains to stress this wasn't his intention. If we take him at his word on that, *Kill the Moon* is, for the most part, a terrific story, so it's unfortunate the Moon Egg left so many viewers' brains scrambled. But you can't help but sympathise with the likes of the *Radio Times*' Patrick Mulkern, who could barely keep a straight face as he shared details of the BBC's embargo to journalists stating, in plain type: "Please do not reveal that the moon is an egg."

At the end of Matt Smith's first series, the Doctor had received a warning about "an Egyptian goddess loose on the Orient Express – in space!" Replace the Egyptian goddess with a decaying corpse in rotting bandages, and you've pretty much got the plot of Jamie Mathieson's *Doctor Who* debut.

And a corker it is, too – a fizzy mash-up of Agatha Christie and Hammer Horror, *Mummy on the Orient Express* combines laugh-out-loud gags with a monster designed to give any kids still up (or perhaps just getting back from the pub) the heebie and, indeed, jeebies. The real-time countdown clock adds pace and energy, and there's a lovely, twinkly guest turn from comedian and *Who* superfan Frank Skinner.

Skinner is such a *DWM*-subscribing fanboy, in fact, that he was watching episode three of *The Sensorites* on the back of his tour bus when he received the call asking him to read for the part. (I wonder if Led Zeppelin also enjoyed binge-watching Hartnell classics on the bus, in between licking vodka off groupie's breasts?)

Mathieson scored a double-whammy by following up *Mummy* with another well-received offering just seven days later. *Flatline* is a "Doctor-lite" bottle episode (though you wouldn't necessarily notice on first viewing) that largely confines Peter Capaldi to barracks in a comically shrunk-down-to-size TARDIS that Clara carries around in her handbag. Which actually says quite a lot about their relationship these days.

With the Time Lord out of action, Ms Oswald assumes full Doctor duties, complete with sonic screwdriver, for a face-off with the Boneless: creatures from a 2D universe who reduce their victims to human graffiti. They're a great *Doctor Who* concept, and their transformation into marauding paint monsters is brilliantly realised by boutique effects company axisVFX. It's hard to imagine how a two-dimensional menace could be done better, short of bringing back Adric.

Once again, the ease with which Clara comes up with a brilliant solution stretches credibility to snapping point, but at least the Doctor is allowed to make a heroic entrance into his own show to reaffirm his status as "the man that stops the monsters".

In the Forest of the Night welcomes bestselling screenwriter and novelist Frank Cotterell Boyce into the *Who* family. Having won numerous major awards for his children's books, it's no surprise to find his script foregrounding a bunch of under-tens, in a fairytale in which the Doctor literally finds a little girl lost in the woods.

The wheeze here is that the entire Earth has been overrun by trees (for... reasons) – a really quite magical idea that, sadly, proves beyond the BBC's limited resources. While the CGI-rendered wide shots of Nelson's Column rising out of a green-carpeted capital are impressive, for most of the runtime it's painfully obvious they've just planted a few London bus stops and Underground signs in the middle of a Welsh wood.

The story also suffers from the affliction that dogs so much of this run: a hasty, pat and unsatisfactory ending. In this case, one in which the Doctor actually says – out loud – "We are going to call everyone on Earth and tell them to leave the trees alone". Good luck with finding a tariff that covers *that*.

In 2012, *Isles of Wonder* – Frank Cotterell Boyce's script for Danny Boyle's Olympic Opening Ceremony – was watched by a global audience of 900 million people, at least 899.9 million of whom agreed it was a triumph. It's fair to say *In the Forest of the Night* received a considerably more mixed response. Which is a shame, as there are plenty of moments of wonder here, too, it's just they don't really serve the wider story – almost as if Cotterell Boyce couldn't quite see the wood for the... well, you get the idea. Plus, for parents with kids of a certain age, it's hard to ignore the fact one of the child actors is also the voice of Peppa Pig, and might at any moment invite the Doctor to start jumping in muddy puddles.

Talk of muddy puddles brings us to *Dark Water* (no? suit yourselves), the opening gambit in Steven Moffat's two-part series finale, in which *Doctor Who* journeys Beyond! The! Grave! for a fearless adventure in the afterlife.

Oh, did I say fearless? I meant tasteless. Really quite shockingly tasteless. It starts with Danny Pink dying in a road accident. Not being sucked into a black hole or eaten by a giant squid, but run over in the street. Splat. "It wasn't terrible," observes Clara. "It was boring. It was ordinary."

Consumed by grief, she forces the Doctor to follow her late lover into the great beyond, the Promised Land. Heaven. Okay, so it's actually a virtual reality "Matrix data slice" – which sounds like something from the new Mr Kipling range – operated by Missy, the mad Mary Poppins lookalike who's been uploading souls to her iPad throughout this whole series.

But it's still full of actual dead people – including Danny – while front organisation The 3W Institute is named in honour of three words often spoken by the dearly departed. The words in question? "Fluffy Pink Ponies." Not really, they're "don't cremate me" – the implication being that the dead can still feel pain. "If you've had a recent loss," says one of the Institute's lackeys, "this might... this *will* be disturbing." *You think*?

Steven Moffat made his excuses early in a *DWM* preview, stating: "So long as we stay inside sci-fi territory, it doesn't bother me. Everything in *Doctor Who* tends to be accounted for scientifically – and I say 'scientifically' in the most enormous, flashing inverted commas that have ever been invented."[7] (Thankfully, such a thing *had* recently been invented – for the moon being a bloody egg.)

Anyway, it turns out Mary Poppins' plan is to download all the souls on her hard-drive into Cybermen who, in final episode *Death in Heaven*, fly out of the dome of St Paul's Cathedral[I] on a mission to scatter cyber-pollen all over the world, resulting in the dead rising from their graves. As Cybermen. (What? It could totally happen!)

And if you think that's off-the-chain, you'll need to work on a whole new series of facial expressions for the bit where Kate Lethbridge-Stewart is pushed out of an aeroplane and caught by a flying Cyber-Brigadier. Yes, that's right – it's the reanimated corpse of her dear old dad, who's now an airborne Cyberman. It's just a crying shame the budget wouldn't stretch to a stick-on moustache as well.

In keeping with the general tone, the ending is relentlessly bleak, as the Doctor and Clara part company – based on nothing more than a simple misunderstanding – and trudge their separate ways back to lonely, grief-stricken, miserable lives. Cue titles.

If there's a saving grace in all this, it's Michelle Gomez as Missy, who is actually revealed to be the latest incarnation of... well, I can't possibly imagine, can you readers?

Giving the Master a sex-change is a brilliant, audacious move by Moffat, and Gomez's performance is a masterclass in vaudeville villainy (in a good way). She's witty, flirty, petulant – but also lethal and utterly demented. (Just watch the way she toys with Osgood – Ingrid Oliver's likeable UNIT fangirl from *The Day of the Doctor* – like a mouse, before killing her in cold blood.) It's just as large a reading as John Simm's take, but Gomez is a much more natural fit for such theatrics. ("It's just because of the way I look, I suppose," the actress mused. "I'm easily castable as witches and bitches."[8])

The finale's rating of 7.6m saw the series finishing on a high, with the run having averaged 7.26m – barely a heartbeat below the average for the previous seven series, save for a small spike during David Tennant's final year. *Doctor Who* was the 16th most watched TV show of 2014 – some way below the top dog

(which was, sssshhh, daddy's other show) but still outperforming the likes of *EastEnders*, the hugely acclaimed drama *Happy Valley* and that other global superbrand, *Top Gear*.

Despite a shaky start and a misjudged finish, the middle half of the series had delivered a run of six great stories on the bounce, albeit often let down by hurried or just plain silly denouements (what was that the Doctor once said about not liking endings?). It also suffers from an over-reliance on Superclara saving the day with implausible feats of mental gymnastics – though, on the flipside, Jenna Coleman gives what is a contender for the strongest performance by any companion to date; her talent for quickfire, rat-a-tat comedy would have made her a knockout star in the golden age of the Hollywood screwball comedy, but she's equally at home with the big, emotional scenes. Given the inevitable straitjacket confines of the role, *Doctor Who* companions have always stood or fallen more on the performance than the writing, which is why, for all the character's maddening quirks and tics, Clara deserves her place at the top table of all-time greats.

And Peter Capaldi? When he's good, he knocks it out of the park, but there's a definite sense of him finding his feet this year. He admitted as much in an interview for *Radio Times*, stating: "I don't know if it's quite fallen into place yet. I think it's a mistake to get into a click, to get into a groove. I've tried to avoid finding a way to do it and then just repeating that. I'm trying all the time to see what works and what doesn't work."[9]

Others were more effusive in their praise, though, the critical consensus being it was good to have an older actor back in the part (though it's worth mentioning that many of these critics were gentlemen of a certain age themselves). Even Tom Baker offered his own glowing end-of-term report card. "Instantly one felt: this fellow comes from far, far away, he's strange," the fourth Doctor told *Radio Times*. "An instant frisson. And what's the word? Yes, got it! Alien, he's an alien. I salute him."[10] I bet he never actually watched it, though.

Capaldi's debut run also benefited from a welcome postscript in the form of 2014's Christmas special. Despite airing less than seven weeks after *Death in Heaven*, *Last Christmas* presents evidence of both Capaldi and Steven Moffat suddenly having worked out what needs to be done with this Doctor (including letting him take the reins of Santa's sleigh, giggling and whooping with boyish excitement).

A scary, funny mix of *Alien* (yes, again – but this time the homage is so explicit, they even joke about it), *The Thing* and *Miracle on 34th Street*, and featuring a winning turn from Nick Frost as a slightly blokeish Father Christmas, it's one of the best seasonal specials to date.

Thankfully, it also brings Clara back for a proper goodbye. Or at least, we're led to assume it's a goodbye, right up to the last minute, when her latest departure – as an old woman, this time – turns out to be one of the episode's many dreams within dreams, and she decides she's up for another round of adventures after all.

This wasn't just a feint on Moffat's part: Jenna Coleman really did hand in and then withdraw her notice. Twice. "I originally wrote her out in *Death in Heaven*," Moffat explained. "That was her last episode. And then she asked if she could be in Christmas. She came to the read-through and did the 'write out' version – and again changed her mind. But the truth is I never wanted her to go."[11]

Last Christmas was the 7th most watched show of the holidays, its audience of 8.2m reflecting a general ratings slide across the board. Even the top-rated show of the week, *Mrs Brown's Boys*, only managed 9.69m – though, admittedly, that's still 9.69m more than it deserved.

No More No More Mr Nice Guy

Speaking to *Doctor Who Magazine* in early 2015, Steven Moffat signalled a recalibration of the twelfth Doctor's character. "In terms of the journey we're all learning about at the moment – from 'script to mouth' as it were – if you give a very, very mildly acerbic line to Peter, it comes out like a gale force," he said.

"We're not bringing him back the same as we left him, at all. I think that was already evident at Christmas. He's left some of the burden of being the superhero of the universe behind. Also, Peter magnifies anything that is *dark*, so I'm pushing him the other way – I'm writing him quite funny this year. I think it was great fun to do for a year. But that's not how we're going to play the rest of him."[11]

Doctor Who scored a big publicity coup with the announcement that *Game of Thrones* actress Maisie Williams was to appear in the upcoming series. In a way, the fuss was a further demonstration of how HBO's all-conquering fantasy saga was now packing the sort of heat that *Who* had enjoyed five or ten years earlier. But then, no show can expect to rule forever – it's just the natural order of things. Like some sort of contest of... monarchs, or something.

In May, possibly realising it was fighting a losing battle trying to get young people to put their phones down and watch actual telly, the BBC decided to take the fight to them by launching *Doctor Who: The Fan Show*, in which a hyperactive YouTuber called Christel Dee ("well known for her tenth Doctor cosplay", it says here) wears wacky costumes, performs wacky sketches and does wacky interviews and wacky monologues while sporting a wacky haircut.

Meanwhile, Jenna Coleman was all over creaky old dead-tree media in June when *The Sun* splashed with "Dr Woo: Flirty Prince Harry Caught With Hand on Knee of TV Time Lord's Assistant". The "story" revealed how Clara Oswald and the fifth in line to the throne had hooked up at a charity polo match in a manner described by "onlookers" (i.e. someone else in *The Sun* newsroom) as "flirty and tactile".

Coleman, who was wearing a sultry off-the-shoulder dress (I'm still quoting, so don't write in) was sitting very close to the prince, and they were "laughing lots and touching each other". Apparently. Cue much fevered speculation about what this could mean for Coleman's relationship with Richard Madden – aka *Game of Thrones*' Robb Stark, who, on the plus side, had gone five better than Harry by actually being crowned king but who, on the downside, was dead.

When asked – as he often was – Steven Moffat described Series Nine as the Doctor and Clara's "glory years". "They surf along on all these terrible events, properly morally engaged, but still enjoying the living hell out of them,"[12] the showrunner told *SciFi Now*.

It was also revealed that Michelle Gomez would be making a fast return as Missy, with Moffat revealing he wanted to return to the days of the Master being a semi-regular character who "should turn up quite often, causing trouble".[12] And then, presumably, be forced into a face-saving team-up with the Doctor on account of her latest plan being entirely rubbish.

Also back with a vengeance would be cliffhangers and multi-part stories. "The 45-minute format served us incredibly well for ten years, but you almost had a muscle memory of where those 45 minutes would go," explained Moffat. "You'd think, 'Ah, it's time for the hero music, time for the Doctor to have his epiphany, time for the running to start'. Aside from having a lot more two-parters this time, we blur the lines between what's a two-parter and what's not. So you don't quite know that everything is going to wrap up when you hit 43 minutes.

"The only thing I ever missed in the 45-minute version of *Doctor Who* was that first episode feeling from the old series, where it's slow and ominous, like the first episode of *The Ark in Space*, where the Doctor wanders around and nothing really happens. It's utterly creepy, utterly involving, yet the story doesn't start for the full 25 minutes."[12]

The new run would open with a two-parter, for the first time in five years. "Why not start with a blockbuster?" mused Moffat. "It's like starting with a finale, and having a big, grand, movie-sized story.

"I liked it when we did that before [in 2011]," he added. "In fact, I'm slightly bemused why we didn't do it again."[13] No idea – maybe take it up with the guy in charge?

The morning before the series' late September launch, Jenna Coleman was a guest on Nick Grimshaw's *Radio 1 Breakfast Show*, during which she revealed – to gasps of surprise from precisely no-one – that this would be her last series of *Doctor Who*. No, seriously this time – she'd handed in her BBC canteen card and everything.

"I have left the TARDIS – it's happened," she told Grimmy. "I've filmed my last scenes."

Claiming she was still "in denial" about her decision, the actress added: "I see Peter all the time and I still see Matt all the time, so I kind of believe I still have the keys to the TARDIS." Which was all very sweet – but it would take a *lot* of explaining if Clara casually popped her head round the door in the middle of the space-time vortex, asking if anyone fancies a coffee.

Meanwhile, it was announced Coleman would star as a young Queen Victoria in a major new ITV drama charting the early years of the monarch's 63-year-reign. We can only imagine Prince Harry's face when he found out he'd been getting flirty and tactile with his great-great-great-great-grandmother.

Specs and hugs and rock and roll

Having pre-sold the series opener as a Doctor-Missy rematch, Steven Moffat whipped a rug from under the audience before the opening credits had even kicked in by having our hero attempt to rescue a small boy from the middle of a battlefield. "Introduce yourself," the Doctor tells the frightened child. "Tell me the name of the boy who isn't going to die today." "Davros," says the kid. "My name is Davros."

Ooops. His bad. This, of course, is a plot development some 40 years in the making, predicated on the line in *Genesis of the Daleks* where the Doctor asks Davros, "If someone pointed out a child that would grow up to be totally evil, a ruthless dictator who would destroy millions of lives, could you then kill that child?"

In *The Magician's Apprentice/The Witch's Familiar*, the Doctor gets the chance to answer his own question – and in some style, too, Moffat's script positively fizzing with an energy and invention that's remarkable in a 52-year-old TV property.

Following last year's slightly hesitant start, this time Peter Capaldi gets a rock star entrance – literally – wielding an electric guitar on top of a tank, sporting a pair of sonic shades. That's right, forget the boring old screwdriver: this year, the Doctor's all about wearable tech.

"I was watching Peter on the World Tour with his shades on, waving to the crowds, being such a rocker," Moffat explained. "I wanted to see that in his Doctor. My big note this year was, 'You're the raddled old rocker. If you want to play electric guitar on top of a tank, you damn well do it.'"[14]

The showrunner's confidence is also on display in his loving recreation of Skaro circa 1965. Admitting he'd "slightly wimped out" with *Asylum of the Daleks*, this time Moffat does the Dalek reunion for real. "What happens if you put the Hartnell ones next to the Russell T Davies ones?" he asked *DWM*. "Nothing! They look fine together. It doesn't matter. So this time around, we go all out."[15]

The Dalek control room, meanwhile, is described in the script as "a split-level riot of 60s *TV21* glory". Peter Capaldi, eternal fanboy that he is, likened it to the set of the Peter Cushing movies, while adding to the mid-60s vibe himself with a pair of checked trousers worn in tribute to William Hartnell. ("Are they too much?" he asked *DWM*, anxiously.)

In every other sense, though, Capaldi's retooled Doctor feels less like the spiky Hartnell than a heartfelt love letter to Tom Baker. With the previous season's abrasive edges sanded down ("We're doing hugging now?" asks a confused Clara. "I can't keep up") the new twelfth Doctor is a strange, funny, mercurial, unknowable pop-eyed alien who can't help but transport viewers of a certain age back to teatimes in the 1970s.

Even his hair appears to be trying to be Tom Baker, 2014's severe crop replaced by a tangle of grey curls. "I always wanted it to be longer, but everyone felt it was important to make a decisive change," Capaldi explained. "But my hair, it just grows. Some people think I'm going for the full Jon Pertwee bouffant!"[16]

The heart and soul of the piece are the electrically-charged confrontations between Capaldi's Doctor and Julian Bleach's Davros – now rivalling the great Michael Wisher for the definitive take on the character – which Moffat deliberately drew out in recognition that the scenes of Tom Baker and Wisher going eyeball-to-eye... thing in *Genesis* are, for all their brilliance, frustratingly brief. This time around, the pair are given the proper room and space to debate such weighty subjects as morality, philosophy and who's got the wrinkliest face.

One moment, in particular, is among *Who*'s all-time greats: on the brink of death, Davros asks to see Skaro's sun one last time with his own eyes. (Yes, he actually *does* have eyes – who knew?) As the sun rises, though, he is too weak to open them, prompting the Doctor – moved by his old enemy's deathbed remourse – to revive him with a little regeneration energy. It's a ruse, of course ("always your compassion is your downfall" hisses the old bastard), just one of many switchback reversals of fortune and sleights of hand in a beautifully constructed game of cat-and-mouse.

No stranger to a big entrance herself, Missy makes an attention-grabbing return by stopping all the world's planes dead in the sky. Michelle Gomez's playful psychosis routine is so watchable, you slightly feel for her being put in the shade by the Doctor-Davros title bout. But she earned a BAFTA nomination (*Who*'s first performance nod since Matt Smith five years earlier) for her troubles, so her contribution clearly wasn't entirely lost in the mix.

Despite being one of *Doctor Who*'s strongest-ever openers, *The Magician's Apprentice* was watched by a disappointing – but surely not disappointed – 6.5 million people. That's a drop of almost three million on the previous year's first episode, and less than the lowest-rated story of 2014. And with the initial overnights – still the figure most widely quoted in the media – showing just 4.5 million tuning in to watch it on the night, it was cause for concern, if still a little too soon for outright panic.

Having started the series evoking the aesthetic spirit of William Hartnell's *Doctor Who*, it's fitting that what came next was a twenty-first century spin on that classic Troughton era staple: the base under siege. And an underwater base at that, as the crew of subterranean mining facility The Drum find themselves under attack by the undead.

The pitch that Steven Moffat and writer Toby Whithouse had kicked around was "ghosts plus time travel", and the Doctor comes as close to believing in actual ghouls here as he's ever likely to.

Opening half *Under the Lake* delivers some effectively claustrophobic chills, climaxing with a genuinely horrific cliffhanger in which the ghost of the Doctor appears as an eyeless cadaver drifting silently through the inky depths. Re-booting the story at the midway point, concluding chapter *Before the Flood* opens with a to-camera lecture by a guitar-wielding Doctor about the Bootstrap Paradox (Google it), after which he launches into a muscular rock rendition of the *Doctor Who* theme over the opening titles. (The Time Lord might have had a little help in post-production, admitted a sheepish Peter Capaldi, who'd learned his craft during the punk era, when an understanding of actual chords was low on the agenda.)

Travelling back in time to a simulation of a Soviet village in 1980s Scotland, the Doctor meets the Fisher King – a towering, old-school vision in rotting skin and bleached bone who looks fabulous when lurking in the shadows, slightly less so when wobbling about in the Welsh mud in the middle of the afternoon. The creature was performed by three people: Neil Fingleton – at 7'7.56", the tallest man in Europe – took time out from playing giant Mag the Mighty in *Game of Thrones* to give us his best clomping, while the quietly menacing vocal (complete with delightfully retro "Time! Lord!") was provided by Peter Serafinowicz, the actor, comedian and writer whose voice credits range from *Star Wars'* Driver Dan to Cbeebies' Darth Maul. (Or is it the other way round?) Finally, the beast's guttural roar was provided by longtime *Who* fan Corey Taylor, lead singer of frightmask-wearing US heavy metal veterans Slipknot, whose songs include "Eyeless," "New Abortion," "Butcher's Hook," "Be Prepared for Hell" and "People=Shit". None of which are quite as bleak and nihilistic as *Dark Water/Death in Heaven*.

The Girl Who Died is an odd fish, even by *Doctor Who's* standards. For most of its running time, it's a larky comic caper in which the Doctor has to teach a Viking village full of fishermen and farmers to defend themselves against alien cyborgs the Mire (an impressively hulking addition to the show's monster canon). A playful mix of *The Magnificent Seven* and *Dad's Army*, it's so jaunty that at one point they actually play the Benny Hill theme (yes, really), while the use of electric eels as a weapon strays perilously close to the-moon-is-an-egg territory.

Then, in the last act, it suddenly takes a lurch into the dark, as the Doctor decides it's in his gift to bring a teenage Viking girl (a surprisingly underused Maisie Williams) back from the dead. In doing so, writers Steven

Moffat and Jamie Mathieson also offer a hand-waving explanation for why the Doctor looks like that Roman guy who David Tennant met. He chose this face, apparently, to remind him to always save at least someone, as Donna had entreated the tenth Doctor to do in Pompeii. (Though both of them being played by the same actor is probably also a factor.)

It turns out the side effects of resurrecting humans using alien technology, however, include a lot more than nausea and drowsiness – young Ashildr is now immortal, and destined to walk the Earth alone while watching everyone she loves wither and die. On the plus side, though, her life insurance premiums must be through the floor.

All this plays into *The Woman Who Lived*, in which the Doctor is reacquainted with Ashildr, now living a double life in Merrie England as Lady Me ("All the other names I chose died with whoever knew me; Me is who I am now") and a dandy highwayman known as the Knightmare.

Catherine Tregenna's script is a delightful character piece, its lengthy scenes of wit and wordplay between Peter Capaldi and Maisie Williams being what persuaded the teenager – who turned 18 during the shoot – to sign on for the role. "She's a remarkable young actress, and I think she's amazing in this," said Steven Moffat. "She's such a contrast with Peter. He's like a grand old Victorian barnstormer, and she's like a YouTuber."[13]

Me's library is full of journals recording her adventures across the centuries. "You don't seem the nostalgic type," the Doctor observes. "It's not nostalgia," she replies. "It's curiosity. I can't remember most of it. That's the trouble with an infinite life in a normal-sized brain."

Like much of the best *Doctor Who*, it's crammed with elegant, almost offhand dialogue that illuminates the human condition with the lightest of touches. "People are mayflies," says Me. "Breeding and dying, repeating the same mistakes. It's boring. And I'm stuck here, abandoned by the one man who should know what eternity feels like."

Next to all this, the actual sci-fi plot of the week – some fluff about an invasion by space lions that's resolved by a bit of gallows humour (literally: it's knockabout comedy in a noose) – is small mead, and not a little silly. But ignore that and savour some fine writing and performances in an intelligent and lyrical character study that stands and delivers in style.

Despite what some windy academic texts would have you believe, *Doctor Who* hasn't expended a huge amount of effort these past 50-odd years reflecting contemporary, real-world events. But you don't need a degree in international politics to see that Peter Harness' ambitious two-parter *The Zygon Invasion / Inversion* – in which a splinter group of the big barnacled baby monsters rejects assimilation into human society – has been written with at least one an eye on the evening news.

With explicit talk of radicalisation, immigration and drone strikes, the script dares to rub up against some pretty inflammatory issues. "I think we have to be awfully careful here," cautioned Steven Moffat, "but I would say within the terms of *Doctor Who*, which involves blobby monsters and action adventure, this is as close to addressing the modern world as we get."[13]

Moffat had asked Harness to write "an urban, global conspiracy thriller" – picking up on a plot thread he'd deliberately left hanging in *The Day of the Doctor* – and that's pretty much what we get, the action shifting between London, New Mexico and "Turmezistan" (which doesn't actually exist, but you could probably still point to it on a map).

It's pacy stuff that makes good use of the Zygons' shape-shifting powers, not least in allowing the Doctor to hook up with the late Osgood, who may or may not be the original or her Zygon copy (apparently it's not the sort of question you ask a girl – or her big orange alien seahorse duplicate, come to that). Jenna Coleman, meanwhile, is terrific in the dual roles of Clara and chief Zygon antagonist Bonnie, subtly shifting her performance between the characters in a way that's so nuanced and clever, it takes a while to notice she's even doing it. (Also: a terrifying orange creature called Bonnie? Is Harness writing *Space Helmet*'s jokes for us now?)

For many, the defining moment of the story – possibly the defining moment of Capaldi's tenure so far – is the Doctor's impassioned plea to Bonnie not to start a war. "And when this war is over, when you have a homeland free from humans, what do you think it's going to

be like?" he challenges her. "Do you know? Have you thought about it? Have you given it any consideration? Because you're very close to getting what you want. What's it going to be like? Paint me a picture. Are you going to live in houses? Do you want people to go to work? Will there be holidays? Will there be music? Do you think people will be allowed to play violins? Who's going to make the violins? Well? Oh, you don't actually know, do you? Because, like every other tantrum-ing child in history, Bonnie, you don't actually know what you want."

At times, it strays perilously close to sixth-form speechifying ("You don't know whose children are going to scream and burn! How many hearts will be broken! How many lives shattered!"), with Capaldi strutting and fretting like he's on the apron at the RSC. It's material that would leave lesser men floundering, but Capaldi really proves his mettle. And, rather brilliantly, the idea of two "Osgood boxes" – one of which releases a gas that's lethal to Zygons, and one that detonates a nuclear warhead – proves to be a feint on the Doctor's part. Both boxes are, in fact, empty. Because an empty box is all you need when your real weapons are words.

Sleep No More opens with Reece Shearsmith staring down the camera lens and warning: "You must *not* watch this." Which, given that ratings for the season were still stubbornly bumping along around the six million mark, was possibly a risky opening gambit. Unless they were trying a bit of reverse psychology?

The story – written by Shearsmith's former League of Gentlemen colleague Mark Gatiss – is *Doctor Who*'s first stab at a "found footage" adventure, to the extent that it doesn't even feature the opening titles or theme music.

Shearsmith plays Rasmussen, the inventor of technology that can squeeze a month's worth of sleep into five minutes (any parents reading will know the feeling), freeing up citizens to toil day and night for their corporate paymasters. But the latest software upgrade has come with a bug – a bug which takes the sleep dust from the corner of your eye and turns it into a marauding, er, sleep dust monster. Gatiss said he hoped the episode would "tap into primal fears" – and, let's face it, who *hasn't* worried that the yellow gunk in the corner of their eye would one day climb out and attempt to eat them? It's right up there with darkness, monsters under the bed and dentists.

The ensuing bug hunt aboard a crippled space station riffs heavily on *Alien* (yes, *again*) with the use of CCTV, helmet-cams and frequent bursts of hissing static and signal interference adding a kinetic energy to an otherwise slightly undercooked pass at the survival horror genre. Shearsmith, meanwhile, feels slightly wasted as a forgettable villain, complete with those Trevor Horn-style specs that are sci-fi shorthand for "futuristic corporate twat."

That reverse psychology didn't work, incidentally: the episode's audience of 5.61m was *Doctor Who*'s lowest rating since Sylvester McCoy's day. Its Appreciation Index (yes, that's still a thing) score was also the lowest since 2006's *Love & Monsters* (aka *The One Without David Tennant*). Just an idea, but maybe next time they should try opening with: "You *must* watch this, otherwise we'll come round and pull the legs off your cat."

Tenth episode *Face the Raven* puts an unusually strong emphasis on the fantasy part of the science fantasy equation, at least by *Doctor Who* standards, being almost entirely set in a hidden London street that's sheltering a conglomerate of alien refugees and intergalactic war criminals. Think Mos Eisley – *Star Wars*' "wretched hive of scum and villainy" – crossed with *The Old Curiosity Shop*, via Diagon Alley. (Writer Sarah Dolland had started her career on *Neighbours*, so a street full of strange, unbelievable creatures was well within her comfort zone.)

It is, the Doctor explains, a "trap street" – one of those mysterious thoroughfares you sometimes find on maps, which don't really exist. (In reality, map-makers put them on there to trap forgers, but copyright violations among the cartography community probably wouldn't make for a very exciting story. Though it would possibly still be more exciting than *In The Forest of the Night*.)

He and Clara have been brought there by Rigsy – Clara's "companion" from last year's *Flatline* – who has managed to get himself branded with a tattoo that's counting down to his death. (Let's not judge, we've all done stupid things on a night out. And it's still prefer-

able to that massive one Cheryl Cole had done on her arse.)

The tattoo is a actually "chronolock" that, when it reaches zero, leads a Quantum Shade – which normally appears in the form of raven – to come and claim the victim. Clara, being Clara, is convinced she can outsmart this date with destiny, and takes on the tattoo for the team. But her over-confidence in herself – and her unshakeable faith in the Doctor – ultimately proves her undoing, as it was always going to. And so it is that the Impossible Girl is fated to suffer the worst encounter with a bird since Michael Parkinson last met Rod Hull and Emu.

Yes, you read that right: Clara Oswald is dead – the first companion to be properly killed off since Adric, and the first anyone actually cared about since a long time before that. (*Kidding*. But you surely can't begrudge a man squeezing in one last Adric gag in the dying minutes?)

And she died screaming, too: a silent howl of pain as the raven swooped into her soul in an explosion of inky death, leaving her in a broken, twisted heap on the cobbles. Despite a creeping sense of inevitably over Clara's fate in recent weeks, it's still one of the show's all-time great chokers.

It's a black day for Clara and the Doctor, then – and it's not a great day for Me, either. (And by Me, I mean Ashildr – though I did feel a bit sniffly, thanks for asking.) Revealed as the unwitting architect of Clara's downfall as part of a ruse to lure the Doctor into a trap, the immortal former Viking has just made herself a very powerful – and very, very pissed off – enemy.

That trap is where the Doctor finds himself in *Heaven Sent* – by any measure, one of the most extraordinary episodes of *Doctor Who* ever made. Imprisoned inside a mechanical, puzzle-box of a castle constructed from his own nightmares, our hero is forced to repeat the same cycle of death and resurrection over four-and-a-half billion years, while being stalked at every step by the Veil, a terrifying, shrouded figure drawn from his childhood night terrors.

It's dark, uncompromising stuff, in which the Doctor literally digs his own grave and drags his dying, horribly charred body up the same staircase night after night after endless night. His only hope of escape, meanwhile, is bashing at a solid diamond wall with his bloodied fists, chipping his way out of the nightmare piece by tiny piece over billions of years. (Actually, it's not even diamond, it's Azbantium – 400 times tougher than diamond. Let's not make this too easy for him, eh?)

Performed almost entirely as a single-hander (save for some shuffling from the Veil and a brief appearance from Clara inside whatever the Doctor's equivalent of Sherlock's mind palace is), it's an astonishing tour de force from Peter Capaldi, giving arguably the finest performance of anyone in the role (and one for which he was longlisted for an Emmy) Incredible work, too, from Steven Moffat, director Rachel Talalay and Murray Gold, whose music box score is a wonder all of its own.

"It was possibly, in my entire career, the most difficult script I've ever had to write," admitted Moffat. "It was shockingly hard – I nearly went to pieces doing it."[13]

It's the sort of high wire act he couldn't have pulled off, he added, with a lesser leading man. "It's nice to showcase Peter Capaldi and say, 'Look! Look what we can do! There are loads of actors in TV who couldn't come close to this."[17]

The episode was universally praised by critics (though the AI, oddly, was a rather stubborn 80 – a full five points less than *Victory of the Daleks* – perhaps suggesting there's a limit to how far a Saturday night audience is willing to be pushed). In *The Times*, Andrew Billen likened Moffat to Ingmar Bergman: "*Heaven Sent* was as near a work of expressionist cinema as primetime Saturday night BBC One is ever likely to get," he wrote, hailing Capaldi's "bravura performance, with a touch of *Hamlet*". While conceding it was "not family entertainment" – and not what the show's creators, or even Russell T Davies, would probably have envisioned for it – he concluded: "A critic cannot call for more risk-taking then not acknowledge that the risks taken here were brilliant and worth it."

So powerful is *Heaven Sent*, in fact, that its cliffhanger reveal – in which the Doctor is shown finally to have made it back to Gallifrey

– feels positively incidental, its significance only revealing itself in hindsight to viewers punch-drunk on the preceding 55 minutes.

It transpires the Doctor's private torture chamber was a Time Lord creation designed to force him to confess his knowledge of the Hybrid, the subject of an ancient Time Lord prophecy that may or may not have been the reason the Doctor fled Gallifrey in the first place. Spending four-and-a-half billion years punching your way out of a trap of your own people's making perhaps isn't *quite* the homecoming he'd once had in mind – where were the balloons, for a start? – so instead, the Doctor drifts back into town like Clint Eastwood, drawing a line in the dirt with the heel of his boot in readiness for the ultimate stand-off. When he does finally speak, it is to tell Rassilon (the daddy of all Time Lords, now wearing the face of Donald Sumpter – famous across the land for his appearances in *The Wheel in Space* and *The Sea Devils*, and also some fly-by-night series called *Game of Thrones*) to "Get off my planet".

Lord President successfully banished, the Doctor reveals his plan – to use Time Lord technology to extract Clara Oswald from the moment before her death, even if it risks unravelling the entire universe. (Don't judge him – a guy can go a bit nuts after a few billion years of wall-punching.)

So, once again, it seems reports of Clara's demise may have been exaggerated – a common criticism of Moffat's *Doctor Who*, in which everyone is only a temporal re-set away from resurrection. Except maybe this time, it isn't going to be so easy: the extraction chamber has left Clara frozen between heartbeats, and this time all the Doctor's best jiggery and, indeed, pokery seem powerless to alter that fact. In desperation, he plans to wipe her memory of him so he can hide her from the Time Lords, but she rejects this Donna-style fate. "Tomorrow is entitled to no-one," she tells him, beautifully. "But I insist on my past."

In the end, it's the Doctor who is forced to forget Clara, which is how he ends up sitting on a barstool in a diner in the Nevada desert, telling his story to a very familiar-looking waitress. Familiar to us, anyway, if not to him. He even plays her a few chords of "Clara's Theme" on his trusty Yamaha 800. (That's a guitar, by the way. I know it sounds like a keyboard, but that would just be as cheesy as all hell.)

This is lovely stuff – "an epic story on a small scale", as the *Metro* newspaper put it. It's unusually wordy for a season finale, but perhaps that's no bad thing, especially when it feels like every word counts.

Which is not to say there's a shortage of eye candy – for possibly the first time ever, this is an extended tour of Gallifrey that doesn't disappoint. From the burnt orange skies and domed cityscapes to the fabled Cloisters – guarded by the Cloister Wraiths, screaming apparitions of dead Time Lords that serve as the Matrix's rather terrifying firewall – the Doctor's home world finally matches up to the brochure. It's certainly a long way from the soft furnishings and Habitat sofas that were on-trend there back in the 1980s.

Best of all is the extensive use of a classic-era TARDIS console: a shiny, pristine, hi-def recreation of that sacred white space introduced in the very first story that's guaranteed to induce a Proustian headrush in anyone over the age of 35. Steven Moffat acknowledged as much in his stage directions, which stated: "The Doctor is flying around the classic console like a distinguished Scottish actor who's slightly too excited for his own good." Well who wouldn't be?

By the end of the episode, the Doctor has been restored to his own, more baroque time ship, and the 60s model is in the hands of Maisie Williams' Me and Clara Oswald, now transformed from the Impossible Girl into the Immortal Girl – or possibly still on the point of death (the script is deliberately muddy on the issue). With the exterior stuck as that of a 50s diner, it teases the possibility of a spin-off that could *literally* run forever. (There are no plans for such a spin-off – but it's probably worth checking your inbox for a message from Big Finish in about ten years' time.)

So yes, maybe Moffat tricked us with another dead character who just wouldn't lie down and stay dead. Or maybe he didn't. Either way, Clara and the Doctor have been ripped from each other's lives and, as Rigsy's graffiti portrait of Clara falls away from the Time Lord's departing blue box in a shower of paint confetti, it's hard not to feel a catch in your throat.

"*Doctor Who* does that form of bereavement

rather well," Moffat reflected in that week's *Radio Times*. "We have an emotionally engaged hero and those women he knows are not like Bond girls. They don't just disappear between movies.

"When the Doctor ends a friendship, it tears him apart."[14]

The stuff of legend

The way things had been going, few would have been surprised if the 2015 Christmas special had been 60 minutes of the Doctor sitting alone in the dark next to a dead Christmas tree, repeatedly punching a frozen turkey. In fact, arriving on screens a brisk 20 days after *Hell Bent*, *The Husbands of River Song* was a deliberately frothy confection designed as a palate-cleanser after recent traumatic events.

"As it's the Christmas special, we can't maintain that level of darkness," admitted Steven Moffat. "We got really quite dark, and we have to remind people what this show is like normally. Also, we need to cheer the Doctor up. He was in a right old state by *Hell Bent*, so you need someone proactive to come into his life, kick him up the arse and remind him he has a laugh sometimes."[18]

The arse-kicker in question, of course, is a certain space-haired archaeologist, whose return – two years after the latest of her many last goodbyes – sets the scene for a giddy screwball comedy involving a stolen diamond, a head in a bag and a big, crunchy red robot to keep the kids happy.

Peter Capaldi proves an excellent Tracy to Alex Kingston's Hepburn – all comic exasperation in the face of her weapons-grade sass – and the scene where he has to feign wonder at the TARDIS being bigger on the inside is a delight. ("My entire understanding of physical space has been transformed!" he mugs. "Three-dimensional Euclidean geometry has been torn up, thrown in the air and snogged to death! My grasp of the universal constants of physical reality has been changed forever!")

There's a sting in the tail, of course, there always is. At the end, the Doctor and River stand gazing upon the Singing Towers of Darillium – originally namechecked way back in *Forest of the Dead* as the location of their last night together. Except, on Darillium, a night lasts 24 years. I'm sure we've all been on dates like that.

The Husbands of River Song is a sweet little chaser to one of the most widely acclaimed series of *Doctor Who* in some time. By giving the formula a vigorous shake – from two-parters and one-handers to found footage and edgy political thrillers – it feels like more of a radical re-boot than the previous run.

Talking to *Doctor Who Magazine*, Steven Moffat said it was his job to fight against his "terribly conservative" instincts, and remind himself that the show had always thrived on audacious leaps forward: "If you aren't naughty and radical, then you're not honouring it properly. Temperamentally, I'm in the front row of the arse-clenched, diehards saying 'You're not allowed to change anything!'" he added, admitting he'd agonised over how John Hurt's War Doctor would impact on the numbering system, until a senior BBC exec had asked "Who cares?" (That's a senior BBC exec who's clearly never been on a *Doctor Who* internet forum.)

"But professionally, I've got to put some swagger on and say, 'We've got to surprise you with this story'," added Moffat. "Yeah, Davros can have eyes after all, the Master is now a woman, or whatever."[17]

The other revelation during Series Nine was Peter Capaldi. Given free reign to play the role more like the charismatic space wizard he is in public appearances – when barely a week goes by without him popping up and surprising fans, recording heartwarming video messages or generally doing something magical – his new, more loose-limbed interpretation of the Doctor is an absolute joy.

Capaldi was busy channelling the spirit of Tom Baker in more than just his performance, too – he'd started to talk like him. "All I've got to do is walk into a room of people who like *Doctor Who* and they sort of stop and smile," he beamed. "If I wasn't the Doctor, that wouldn't happen. It's very easy to surf this tide of affection. That's a very privileged position for anyone to be in. Can you imagine, people smile when they see you all the time and they shout at you across the street, 'Doctor Who!' and they wave at you. A little kid came up to me and threw her arms around my shoulders. They want so little from you. They just want you to be Doctor Who."[19]

It's difficult, also, to overstate Jenna Coleman's contribution to this period of *Doctor Who*. As a character, Clara was a difficult sell at times, but Coleman was never off her game for as much as a line, and it's to her credit that the impossible girl ended up carving out a place in the front rank of the Doctor's fellow travellers.

The elephant in the ointment and the fly on the room in all this, though, was the ratings. Across the series, Capaldi's sophomore run had averaged 6.3 million viewers, rising to 6.8m when you factored in iPlayer and people watching it on devices on the bus, and suchlike. That compares to 7.26m / 8.3m the previous year – a drop in the total "reach" of nearly 1.5 million over just 12 months. To add further context, in 2014 *Doctor Who* was the 16th most-watched show on British television. In 2015, it was the 30th.

Speaking to *The Guardian*, Capaldi suggested the show was being "slightly used as a pawn in a Saturday night warfare", being bumped to a later 8.25 timeslot in favour of *Strictly Come Dancing*. Perhaps scheduling was part of the problem (though the initial episodes had gone out slightly earlier at 7.40pm) – certainly, it doesn't make it any easier attracting a new generation of young fans as the children of the Tennant and Smith eras grow up, move on and get distracted by newer, shinier baubles in the entertainment landscape. There were also gripes about the underwhelming promotional campaign compared to previous years – maybe they should have followed through with that promise to fire Peter Capaldi into space after all?

But there are other factors at play. Casting an older, craggier, less-eager-to-please Doctor, however good, was always going to be a risk – and certainly there's a notable absence of slippers, pyjamas and pencil cases bearing Capaldi's furious scowl. In Toys "R" Us, the shelf space allocated to *Doctor Who* has shrunk to a shadow of its former self, as has the circulation of kiddie-friendly comic *Doctor Who Adventures*. And there's no denying the show has pushed at the envelope recently in terms of how dark and scary it's prepared to be; if Mary Whitehouse thought the early Tom Baker years were guilty of serving up "teatime brutality for tots", what would she have made of the living nightmare that was *Heaven Sent*?

But then, there's a strong argument that television, films and other old media are increasingly a lost cause for today's children, who spend their days welded to their phones and tablets, dreaming of growing up to be YouTubers. Think *Star Wars: The Force Awakens* was a big deal? It's nothing compared to the likes of Felix Kjellberg – aka PewDewPie – a Swedish gamer whose Let's Play YouTube videos receive in the order of 266 million views per month. Joseph Garrett – a university dropout from Portsmouth who gabbles nonsense over *Minecraft* videos – receives an average of 3,000 messages from young fans *every day*. Closing in on five billion views, he's now extending his brand into book publishing, personal appearances and, of course, TV. After half a century of battling monsters in front of successive generations of captivated children, could this prove to be the Doctor's greatest threat yet?

A certain amount of natural wastage is also to be expected in a TV property that, even in its latest incarnation, is now a decade old. If *Doctor Who* isn't quite the force it was five or ten years earlier, it's far from alone. Most of the big beasts – from *The X Factor* to *New Tricks* and even our old friend *Coronation Street* – have suffered similar slumps. (That said, decline is by no means a given – after 13 series, *Strictly Come Dancing* is in ruder health than ever.)

The awards well that kept *Doctor Who* in silverware for much of the previous decade also appears in danger of running dry. These days, when Steven Moffat puts on his best bib and tucker, it's normally to collect a gong for *Sherlock* – though *Doctor Who* was clearly part of the equation when he received the OBE for services to drama in 2015.

But let's not join the Doctor in digging his own grave quite yet. By any measure, in the current television terrain, six million viewers for a drama – especially a fantasy drama – is a solid result. Plus, *Doctor Who* remains a truly global player, and its rise in the States appears unstoppable, with the Series Nine curtain-raiser delivering double-digit growth on the previous year, and once again setting a new record for BBC America.

Given its superbrand status, it's perhaps not surprising that, in early 2016, the BBC took the unusual step of publicly committing to *Doctor Who*'s future, at least in the medium-term. Though there would be no new episodes that year (bar a Christmas special), the corporation announced that the show would return in 2017 with Peter Capaldi and, overseeing his final series, Steven Moffat. Then, in 2018, *Doctor Who* will undergo its latest reinvention under new showrunner Chris Chibnall.

The *Broadchurch* creator – who first entered our story as a freckle-faced teenager way back in 1986 – will become the third lifelong *Who* fan in a row to be handed the keys to the show. "It's a privilege and a joy to be the next curator of this funny, scary and emotional family drama," said Chibnall. "I've loved *Doctor Who* since I was four years old, and I'm relishing the thought of working with the exceptional team at BBC Wales to create new characters, creatures and worlds for the Doctor to explore."

Interviewed for *Doctor Who Magazine*'s 500th issue in May 2016, Moffat admitted his original plan had been to do three years on the show, but that "I didn't enjoy my third year as much – it was a bit miserable.

"The workload was just insane," he added. "I wasn't coping well... The 50th was approaching, and I didn't know if I could make it work. It was a tough, tough time. My darkest hour on *Doctor Who*. And Matt, who was a friend and an ally, was leaving – I couldn't get him to stay. I felt like everything was blowing up around me – I was staggering into the 50th, with no Doctors contracted to appear in it, battered with endless hate mail about how I hadn't got William Hartnell back – he wouldn't reply to my texts! – and *Sherlock* Series Three at the same time.

"I was pretty miserable by the end of it, and couldn't bear that to be the end."

With help from Brian Minchin, he enjoyed his fourth series enough to sign up for a fifth, and for a while the 2015 Christmas special was designed to be his swansong – he even took River and the Doctor's story to its conclusion at the Singing Towers of Darillium as a parting gift to himself.

Then he was tasked with sounding out Chibnall as a potential replacement. "He talked about doing the third series of *Broadchurch*," said Moffat, "so I thought, 'Okay, fine, if I do one more series of *Doctor Who*...'"[20]

In April, the BBC unveiled the Doctor's fellow traveller for 2017 in the form of Pearl Mackie, a 28-year-old Bristol Old Vic Theatre School graduate currently making a name for herself in the West End. Her character, Bill, was introduced in a specially-shot scene with Peter Capaldi and the Daleks, broadcast at half-time during the FA Cup semi-final between Everton and Manchester United. Sadly, there wasn't time for any of the assembled pundits to give their analysis of the scene – a shame, as Bill showed genuine pace, while the Daleks failed to finish despite acres of space and the Doctor falling into the offside trap. Or something.

In a further demonstration if its faith in the brand, the Corporation has also commissioned a new, teen-friendly spin-off series set in Coal Hill School. Created by award-winning YA novelist Patrick Ness, *Class* (which Steven Moffat promises will finally deliver the long-cherished "British *Buffy*") will focus on a group of sixth-formers "facing their own worst fears, navigating a life of friends, parents, school work, sex, sorrow – and possibly the end of existence".

With *Coronation Street* graduate Katherine Kelly leading the cast as a new member of the Coal Hill School teaching staff, there's a pleasing sense of our story coming full circle – back to that fateful night in November 1963 when an old man first emerged from the London fog, whisking two teachers away in his magical box on an adventure that would change their – and all our – lives.

It certainly changed the life of a young Scottish boy called Peter Capaldi. "There's a sort of haunting quality to *Doctor Who* which I can't really put my finger on," mused the twelfth Doctor in 2015. "There's a sort of melancholia about it, which I don't understand. There's a light and a dark. I don't even like to talk about it very much.

"Essentially there's something there that it's not good to examine too closely. You know it when it's there, when *Doctor Who*'s there. And when it's not. And when we do the show, you struggle sometimes to get him there. And then suddenly you hit it and you don't know why. There's a scale to it. It's beyond that wall. It's being able to see beyond the roof, to be able to see beyond the sky, to be able to see beyond this moment yet still inhabit this moment.

"That's all a lot of blather. But you know what I mean."[21]

We do, Peter. We do.

Tony Hall, the Director General of the BBC, is another fan. "It was the BBC that brought William Hartnell to that scrapyard in 1963," he reflected in 2013. "The BBC who nurtured and invented the miracle of regeneration to explain cast changes. And after the decision to cancel the show was reversed, it was the BBC who reinvented it with some of the best acting and writing on television, anywhere in the world.

"And now you can watch *Doctor Who* almost anywhere in the world – in 206 territories to be exact, including the USA, Australia, Germany, France and Italy. Each has fans tuning in and buying the merchandise. All that helps the BBC to generate income to spend on high-quality programmes at home, not to mention burnishing the British reputation for innovation and quality TV."[22]

Given the parlous state *Doctor Who* was in at the start of this book – and the savage antipathy towards the show within the Corporation's higher echelons – that has to be music to the ears of any fan. All we need now is for the Conservative government not to close down the BBC before the production team get back to their desks. Keep everything crossed, people.

On the occasion of *Doctor Who*'s 50th birthday, Steven Moffat paid his own tribute to the TV show that had changed the course of his life, and the lives – in ways big and small – of millions like him.

"When the grand return was announced, there was instant joy and a bonfire of publicity," said Moffat. "When the show hit the screens, it was like a long-awaited explosion. And now, it seems, the Doctor was never away – because, in fact, he wasn't.

"What William Hartnell, Verity Lambert and Sydney Newman began all those years ago is a very rare kind of miracle. Heroes hardly ever become legends. Stories hardly ever become myths. But now and then, when you fire an arrow in the air, if your aim is true and the wind is set exactly right, it will fly forever."[22]

Sourcing Notations

Previously, on Space Helmet for a Cow...

1 Endgame, BBC, 2007

8. Doctor No

1 DWM #337
2 The Wilderness Years
3 The Seven Year Hitch
4 DWM #201
5 DWM #204
6 DWM #251
7 Elisabeth Sladen: The Autobiography (Aurum, 2011)
8 DWM Summer Special 1994
9 DWM #325
10 DWM #229
11 SFX Collection: Doctor Who (2005)
12 DWM #215
13 Doctor Who: Regeneration – The Story Behind the Revival of a Television Legend by Philip Segal with Gary Russell (HarperCollins, 2000)
14 SFX magazine, June 1996
15 DWM #337
16 DWM #308
17 DWM #333
18 DWM #275
19 DWM #317
20 DWM #278
21 DWM #312

22 DWM #319
23 Doctor Who: The New Audio Adventures – The Inside Story by Benjamin Cook (Big Finish, 2003)
24 DWM #359
25 DWM #285
26 DWM #316
27 DWM #295
26 DWM #294
27 DWM #314
28 DWM #349
29 DWM #310
30 DWM #321
31 DWM #341
32 DWM #330
33 DWM #336
34 DWM #352
35 Radio Times, November 22nd, 2003

9. Gone in 35,000 Seconds

1 Project: WHO? (BBC Radio 2, March 2005
2 DWM #463
3 SFX #128
4 DWM #337
5 DWM #360
6 DWM #342
7 Radio Times, March 26th, 2005
8 DWM #359
9 DWM #443
10 SFX #128
11 DWM #402
12 SFCrowsNest, January 2005
13 DWM #279

14 DWM #367
15 DWM #416
16 DWM #357
17 DWM #397
18 SFX #130

10. The Power of Squee

1 Sunday Magazine, August 14th 2005
2 SFX, May 2006
3 SFX, June 2006
4 SFX, April 2006
5 TV Times, first ed. June 2006
6 DWM #364
7 Radio Times, July 1st, 2006
8 SFX, Dec 2005
9 Radio Times, April 29th, 2006
10 Elisabeth Sladen: The Autobiography, Aaurum, 2011
11 SFX, October 2005
12 DWM #375
13 Radio Times, April 15, 2006
14 DWM #370
15 Radio Times, July 1, 2006
16 Doctor Who Confidential, March 31st, 2007
17 SFX, May 2007
18 DWM #387
19 DWM #383
20 DWM #382
21 DWM #401
22 DWM #414
23 Radio Times, June 19, 2007
24 TV & Satellite

Week, March 31, 2007
25 Doctor Who Confidential, April 14th, 2007
26 Radio Times, April 21, 2007
27 Ariel, BBC staff magazine, April 27, 2007
28 The Writer's Tale by Russell T Davies and Benjamin Cook, BBC Books, 2008, rev. 2009
29 DWM #384
30 DWM #394
31 DWM #413
32 DWM #364
33 DWM #416
34 DWM #386
35 DWM #390
36 (Radio Times, December 8, 2007
37 DWM #400
38 TV & Satellite Week, April 5, 2008
39 DWM #396
40 Doctor Who Confidential, May 17, 2008
41 DWM #395
42 DWM #410
43 DWM #398
44 Radio Times, November 10, 2007
45 Doctor Who Confidential, April 26, 2008
46 Radio Times, April 26, 2008
47 Radio Times, April 5, 2008
48 Doctor Who

Confidential, June 21, 2008

49 *Radio Times*, May 10, 2008

50 *DWM #391*

51 *DWM #397*

52 *Radio Times*, June 28, 2008

53 *SFX*, April 2008

54 *DWM #405*

55 *Doctor Who Confidential*, May 31, 2008

56 *DWM #399*

57 *DWM #402*

58 *DWM #401*

59 *DWM #402*

60 *DWM #418*

61 *Radio Times*, December 6, 2008

62 *Doctor Who Confidential*, January 3, 2009

63 *SFX*, April 2009

64 *DWM #407*

65 *Time Out*, April 2

66 *DWM #408*

67 *DWM #417*

68 *Doctor Who Confidential*, January 1, 2010

69 *Reader's Digest*, May 2013

70 *SFX*, November 2009

71 *DWM #415*

11. Bow Selecta!

1 BBC Series Five Press Pack, March 2010

2 *Esquire*, April 2010

3 *DWM #424*

4 *SFX*, May 2010

5 *Doctor Who Confidential*, May 8, 2010

6 *DWM #417*

7 *Radio Times*, June 12, 2010

8 *DWM #420*

9 *SFX*, June 2010

10 radiotimes.com, April 17, 2010

11 *DWM #431*

12 *Radio Times*, December 10th, 2010

13 *Doctor Who Confidential*, May 1

14 *DWM #427*

15 *Radio Times*, June 5, 2010

16 *Doctor Who Confidential*, June 5, 2010

17 *Radio Times*, June 12, 2010

18 *DWM #433*

19 *Den of Geek*, July 30, 2010

20 *Doctor Who: The Brilliant Book 2011*, BBC Books, 2010

21 *Doctor Who Confidential*, September 17th, 2011

22 *SFX*, May 2011

23 *SFX*, October 2011

24 *Doctor Who Confidential*, Sept 3, 2011

25 *The Brilliant Book of Doctor Who 2012*

26 *Radio Times*, January 21st, 2012

27 *Radio Times*, September 1st, 2012

28 *DWM #447*

29 *Radio Times*, April 30th, 2013

30 *DWM #460*

31 *DWM #450*

32 *SFX*, February 2013

33 *Radio Times*, December 15th, 2012

34 *DWM #456*

35 *JN-T: The Life and Scandalous Times of John Nathan-Turner*, Miwk Publishing, 2013

36 *DWM #458*

37 *SFX #233*

38 *Radio Times*, March 26th, 2013

39 *DWM #459*

40 *DWM #460*

41 *DWM #462*

42 *DWM #464*

43 *Behind the Lens: The Time of the Doctor*, BBC

44 *DWM #465*

45 *DWM #472*

46 *DWM #466*

47 *DWM #467*

48 *Sci-Fi Now #86*

49 *DWM #468*

50 *DWM #469*

51 *The Big Issue*, December 2013

52 *DWM #462*

Afterword: Eyebrow Culture

1 *DWM #469*

2 *Doctor Who: Earth Invasion* (DVD documentary)

3 *DWM #484*

4 *DWM #477*

5 *SciFi Now #96*

6 *DWM #477*

7 *DWM #479*

8 *DWM #480*

9 *Radio Times*, August 23, 2014

10 *Radio Times*, November 8, 2014

11 *DWM #484*

12 *Sci Fi Now #110*

13 *DWM #490*

14 *Radio Times*, December 5, 2015

15 *DWM #491*

16 *SciFi Now #110*

17 *DWM #493*

18 *DWM #494*

19 *SciFi Now #110*

20 *Doctor Who Magazine #500*

21 *SFX #266*

22 *Radio Times*, November 23, 2013

End Notes

Chapter 8

I. *Crime Traveller* was a rare 90s BBC foray into sci-fi. It was utter rubbish, but strangely popular. Despite this, the BBC axed it after just one series, presumably for breaching its "no sci-fi" clause.

Chapter 9

I. The interview was arranged by Russell T Davies – who personally sourced the magazine's cover image of Eccleston in *The Second Coming*. A long-time *DWM* reader and friend of then-editor Clayton Hickman, Davies was instrumental in ensuring the magazine didn't fall victim to *Doctor Who's* stringent new licensing arrangements. The showrunner went to even further lengths to ensure Big Finish kept its licence: "Years later, Russell told me about a big meeting at BBC Worldwide," Big Finish co-founder Gary Russell said in 2013. "They were going through what few licensees *Doctor Who* had. Big Finish was mentioned and Russell could see immediately that Mal Young was about to say 'shut it down'. Russell apparently leaned across to Mal and said, 'Don't worry about Big Finish, I'll deal with them, it's fine'."[2]

II. Gold had first written *Electricity* as a 2001 radio drama, which had won the Michael Imison Award for best new play. That's the same Michael Imison who spent the night in a van with a baby elephant back in Part One.

III. Here's *Space Helmet's* best effort: The Game Station is run by the Bad Wolf Corporation. Using the power of the time vortex, Rose takes the words "Bad Wolf" from the wall and scatters them throughout space and time as a memo to her recent self that all times and places are connected and... um, she can probably get back to the future if she uses the... er, TARDIS. But she could probably have worked that out anyway, what with it being a time machine and everything. Anyway, it's basically cosmic voodoo powered by a corporate logo. I guess we should just be grateful she wasn't in McDonalds at the time.

IV. Perhaps there was no greater demonstration of *Doctor Who's* newfound cultural cache than the emergence of its first-ever porn parody. In *Abducted by the Daleks*, four scantily-clad "disco babes" are pursued around time and space, groped with plungers and made to perform acts of girl-on-girl action for the gratification of Skaro's dirty dustbins. Or, er, so *Space Helmet's* researchers are led to believe, anyway.

Naturally, the Terry Nation estate was quick off the mark in trying to close down the film, telling *The Sun*: "The reason the Daleks are still the most sinister thing in the universe is because they do not make things like porn. They weren't ever intended to be sexual creatures. It's simple, Daleks do not do porn."

Not to be outdone, the film's creators (one of them calling himself "Billy Hartnell", which would surely have thrilled his namesake to no end) simply changed the title to *Abducted by the Daloids* – which not only sounds exceedingly painful, but does nothing to alter the fact that the props on screen are actual, you know, Daleks. Not that anyone was looking at *them*, I guess. Still, at the end of the day, we should perhaps be thankful for anything that resulted in *The Register* being able to run a news story with the headline "BBC Pulls Plug on Dalek Lesbian Romp Flick" (the spoilsports).

V. Eccleston also has a family to provide for: his son Albert was born in 2012, and his daughter Esme the following year. He and his wife Mischka divorced in 2015.

Chapter 10

I. *Star Trek* fans prefer the term Trekker, which is why you should always use Trekkie.

II. The SS *Pentallian* was originally called the *Icarus*, until the producers heard that was the name of the ship in *Sunshine*, Danny Boyle's in-no-way similar film about the crew of a spaceship charged with reigniting a dying sun.

The film, released just a few weeks before *42* was broadcast, is quite good, but suffers from a notable paucity of pub trivia.

III. Yes, I know we've already covered his third Hugo under *Blink* – but that's typical wibbly-wobbly, timey-wimey Moffat for you.

IV. Although the Caecilius family *is* named after the one featured in 70s school textbooks published by Cambridge University Press.

V. If you want to be picky – and hey, you like *Doctor Who*, why wouldn't you? – the BBC's Wimbledon coverage of Andy Murray's semi-final match peaked *slightly* higher. But not the whole programme, so *Doctor Who* still wins. So there.

VI. Other intriguing revelations in *The Writer's Tale* include Davies being asked to meet with George Lucas to discuss writing for *Star Wars: The Clone Wars*; details of a speculative *Doctor Who/Star Trek* crossover (shelved after *Enterprise* was cancelled in 2004); Martha and Mickey being written out of *Torchwood: Children of Earth* – the latter only a week before the read-through – after Freema Agyeman and Noel Clarke became unavailable; and, best of all, the fact that Davies was invited to appear on ITV celebrity skating contest *Dancing on Ice*. Now *that* we would pay to see.

Chapter 11

I. The crack was inspired by a similar one along the bedroom wall of Moffat's younger son Louis, roughly in the shape of a crooked smile. He didn't point it out to the lad ("in case he never slept again"), but thought it would make a good basis for a *Doctor Who* scare.

II. The library card the Doctor accidentally brandishes at the vampires instead of his psychic paper shows a picture of William Hartnell from *The Celestial Toymaker*. It's the second of three blink-and-you'll-miss-him appearances for the first Doctor in the 2010 series.

III. Nick Hobbs, the man inside the furry Ugg boots as royal beast Aggedor in the 70s Peladon stories, plays one of the pensioners.

IV. "We went further and further into it, and Matt got more and more emotional the more we did it," Toby Haynes told *Doctor Who Magazine*. "Matt prepped for it – he was listening to a song by Johnny Cash, it's the one where he's looking back on his life [Hurt]. Matt

was listening to that to get into the right frame of mind. He nailed it on the first take."[3]

V. Steven Moffat specified the spaceship should look like the starship *Enterprise*, to give the audience a handy visual shorthand.

VI. The name *The Doctor's Wife* has a bit of history. In the early 80s, John Nathan-Turner was so paranoid about an insider leaking plot secrets, he wrote *The Doctor's Wife* on an office planner (in the space that should have been allocated to *The Caves of Androzani*, fact fans) in an attempt to smoke out the culprit. Sadly, no-one took the bait.

VII. The army the Doctor assembles was originally supposed to include Captain Jack, but filming clashed with John Barrowman's commitments on *Torchwood: Miracle Day*.

VIII. Although he'd been disappointed to have stories for both Series Three and Series Four canned at an advanced stage, MacRae had gone on to write for the likes of ITV 'tec staples *Marple and Lewis*, and penned an award-winning children's book, *The Opposite*.

IX. The BBC edited a stronger gay sex scene out of the show, which was shown uncut on Starz. Obviously.

X. According to Steven Moffat, the eye-patches were another tribute to Nicholas Courtney, in honour of his most legendary convention anecdote.

XI. That same month, George Osborne hosted a Christmas party at 11 Downing Street for 40 terminally ill children, at which Matt Smith – an ambassador for the Starlight Foundation – was one of the special guests. One mother recalled how Smith came running down Downing Street and told her son he'd come all the way from Gallifrey to meet him.

XII. Two of the harvesters, Billis and Ven-Garr, are named in honour of Beth Willis and Piers Wengar.

XIII. St Cadoc's Hospital in Gwent, where Darvill had recorded his first scenes for *Doctor Who* three years earlier.

XIV. The production order for this run was timey-wimey, even by *Doctor Who's* standards. They started with episode four, then moved on to three, six, the Christmas special, five, one, two, eight and then nine. Obvious, when you think about it.

XV. Okay, I made that last one up. Though, incidentally, Edie McCredie actress Juliet

Cadzow would go on to voice the "ice governess" in *Doctor Who's* 2012 Christmas special.

XVI. There is one brief cameo by a Silurian called Bleytal: an abbreviated anagram of Barry Letts, it's Chris Chibnall's third Eocene to be named in honour of a member of the early 70s production team, and the second to be played by Richard Hope.

XVII. In August 2011, Dan Starkey had written to *Doctor Who Magazine* stating: "Commander Strax would be best served by being Madame Vastra's grumpy butler in the spin-off series we all mooted." And it seems such a spin-off *was* considered, with the Controller of Drama Commissioning, Ben Stephenson, seriously interested in the idea – until Steven Moffat realised (or possibly his wife pointed out) that he was already quite busy, actually. Whether the grumpy butler was Starkey's or Moffat's idea isn't clear but, if you're looking to get the boss' attention, it seems you could do worse than dropping a line to *DWM*.

XVIII. Just to add insult to injury, the paper also printed a picture of Baker with Jimmy Savile from the *Jim'll Fix It* mini-episode "A Fix With the Sontarans."

XIX. Moffat claimed Eccleston had thought about it "quite seriously" before declining. "It's just not the sort of thing he does," he told *The Guardian.* "The ninth Doctor turns up for the battle but not the party. But Chris was perfectly sweet and kind about it. And contrary to what was written at the time, he *in no way* messed us around."

XX. There were a lot of them about these days. In August 2013, *Doctor Who Magazine* recorded a 17% rise in circulation, to an average of 31,692 per issue. *Doctor Who Adventures*, by contrast, continued its freefall of recent years with a 23.3% drop – possibly suggesting all those young fans were now growing up and starting to take things much more seriously. Or possibly they just preferred *Ben 10.*

XXI. Philip Morris later revealed that episode three *had* been among the episodes discovered, but mysteriously disappeared before the films were returned to the BBC. Morris believes that, after word of the find got out, a private collector made an offer for the episode to a member of staff at the Nigerian TV station. So don't give up hope of seeing it one day...

XXII. Baker wrote how much he'd enjoyed the event: "It was tumult: the fans cheered as if I had come back from the dead and the cheering did the trick and for a few hours I was my old self. I travelled back in time: it was wonderful. I was too tired to stay for the evening screening of *The Day of the Doctor*, and the After Party, but I enjoyed it all. And I suspect the other old Doctors did too. It was very sweet to meet Colin Baker and Sylvester McCoy and Peter Davison and they were very kind and cheerful." [tombakerofficial.com]

XXIII. Actor John Guilor provided a (spot on) William Hartnell impression for the first Doctor – the first time, incidentally, we've ever heard that incarnation mention Gallifrey. (Guilor also voiced the first Doctor in animated scenes on the *Planet of Giants* DVD.)

XXIV. The shot stopped short of fully revealing Eccleston's features because Moffat thought it would be disrespectful in light of the actor's decision not to appear in the special.

XXV. The scene in which Georgia Moffett appears heavily pregnant, eating ice cream with a stick of celery, was actually filmed after she had given birth to her and David Tennant's second child, Wilfred. In the show, Wilfred is played by a cushion.

XXVI. Russell T Davies himself takes a different view. "No, I don't think he'd just regenerated," he told *Doctor Who Magazine* in 2015. "If you have certain physical features like big ears, or buck teeth, you look at them and sigh every time you look in the mirror. And I think, if you'd had eight different faces, even if you'd been in the current form for a hundred years, you'd still mutter at them. So it was meant as a nod to the fact he'd once had other faces. But I wrote the *Titanic* stuff and Krakatoa assuming that the ninth Doctor had been around for a while. He doesn't act very post-regeneration, does he? He appears in command, waving a bomb. This is a man who knows himself, and has known himself for a while." (*DWM #485*)

Afterword

I. The scenes of the Cybes walking out of St Paul's are an obvious, and rather nice, homage to the iconic sequence in 1968's *The Invasion.*

Acknowledgments

As with the previous volume, it should be noted that most of the raw data on these pages is drawn from secondary sources. (Though I did end up interviewing one Doctor Who myself, more by accident than design. See if you can spot which one.)

To this end, I am grateful to all those *Who* scholars who, over the years, have done the real hard work, putting in hours of research for numerous books, documentaries and magazine articles. I remain, of course, especially indebted to the good offices of *Doctor Who Magazine* which – particularly under the recent editorship of Gary Gillatt, Clayton Hickman and Tom Spilsbury – has managed to combine being the programme's official journal of record with being endlessly inventive and laugh-out-loud funny. (And let the record show that I also said this last time out, before they started paying me to write for them. It's important to know which kind of toadying you're guilty of.)

Thanks beyond measure are due to *Doctor Who*'s pre-eminent historian – and that's not too grand a word – Andrew Pixley, whose forensic attention to detail is the reason we know so much of what we know about this show. Thanks, too, to all the talented documentary makers who have contributed to the *Doctor Who* DVD range, and to Benjamin Cook, for his astute work in wrangling 30 years of *Doctor Who Magazine* interviews into the fabulous *In Their Own Words* series. Gary Russell and Philip Segal's book *Doctor Who: Regeneration* (Harper Collins, 2000) was hugely helpful in researching the TV movie. And the wonderful people at *Doctor Who News* (doctorwhonews.net) have built up an astonishingly comprehensive archive of daily news reports that are invaluable to any *Who* scholars who frequently forget to write things down.

I still thought of all the jokes myself, though.

Thanks also to the many good friends who continue to share my enduring love of this daft programme – you know who you are – and who helped this book by answering numerous ridiculous questions on Facebook.

But, once again, my biggest thanks must go to two people without whom none of this would have been possible in the first place. Firstly, to the great Lars Pearson – still a brilliant, insightful and sympathetic editor, and a diamond geezer (as they don't say in Iowa) to boot. And, finally, to my wonderful wife Rachel, who is giddy with joy at the prospect that this might finally be over (the book, I mean, not the marriage) so I can get back to helping with the kids' lunches. (Do you want to tell her about Volume III, or shall I?)

About the Author

Paul Kirkley is an award-winning journalist and former newspaper editor who writes regularly about *Doctor Who* for publications including *Doctor Who Magazine*, *RadioTimes.com*, *Doctor Who Figurine Collection* and *SFX*. He also writes features and celebrity interviews, and is the resident TV critic, for *Waitrose Weekend* (you'll find him by the tills). He lives in Cambridge with his wife Rachel and sons George and Thomas. He runs Interesting Media (interestingmedia.co.uk) and is also on Twitter (@prkirkley), but not as often as some people he could mention.

Dedication

Space Helmet for a Cow is dedicated to my mum and dad, Wendy and Adrian Kirkley, who gave me the sort of childhood where I felt safe enough to be scared by *Doctor Who*; to my sons George and Thomas, the next generation of *Who* fans (else there'll be trouble...); and to my wife Rachel, who has already given so much to the *Space Helmet* cause, I'm still not offended that she hasn't read it and, let's face it, probably never will.